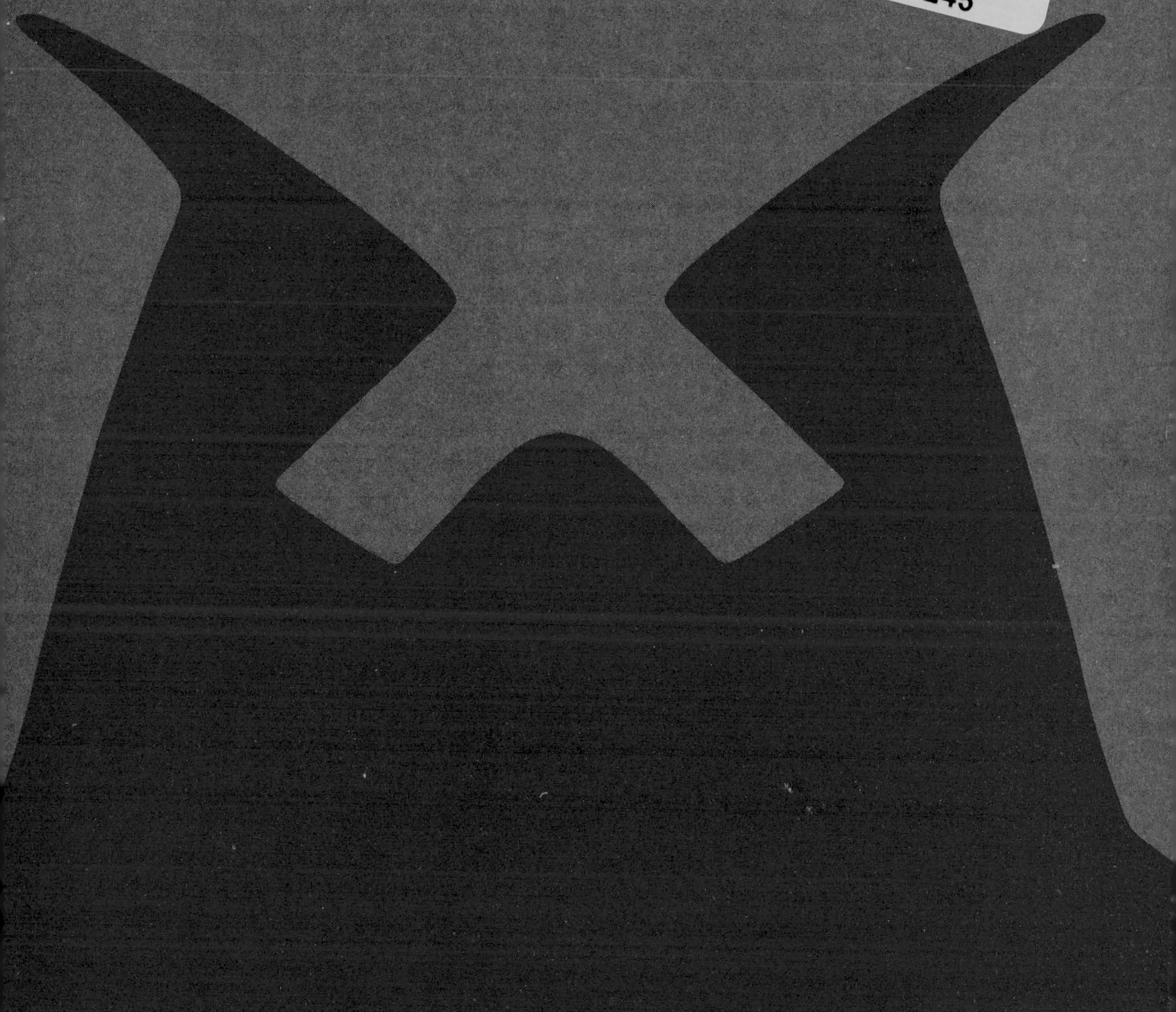

JUDGE DREDD

THE COMPLETE CASE FILES 01

JUDGE DREDD CREATED BY JOHN WAGNER AND CARLOS EZQUERRA

JUDGE DREDD
THE COMPLETE CASE FILES 01

PETER HARRIS ★ KELVIN GOSNELL ★ MALCOLM SHAW ★ CHARLES HERRING ★ GERRY FINLEY-DAY
PAT MILLS ★ ROBERT FLYNN ★ JOHN WAGNER ★ JOE COLLINS
Writers

CARLOS EZQUERRA ★ MIKE MCMAHON ★ MASSIMO BELARDINELLI ★ RON TURNER
IAN GIBSON ★ JOHN COOPER ★ BILL WARD ★ BRIAN BOLLAND
Artists

JOHN ALDRICH ★ BILL NUTTALL ★ S. RICHARDSON ★ TONY JACOB ★ JACK POTTER ★ PETER KNIGHT ★ TOM FRAME
Letterers

CLIFF ROBINSON
Cover Artist

Creative Director and CEO: Jason Kingsley
Chief Technical Officer: Chris Kingsley
2000 AD Editor in Chief: Matt Smith
Graphic Design: Simon Parr & Luke Preece
PR: Charley Grafton-Chuck
Repro Assistant: Kathryn Symes

Graphic Novels Editor: Keith Richardson
Designer: Luke Preece
Original Commissioning Editors: Pat Mills and Kevin Gosnell

Published by Rebellion, Riverside House, Osney Mead, Oxford OX2 0ES, UK.
www.rebellion.co.uk

ISBN: 978-1-906735-87-6
Printed in the USA by Simon & Schuster
10 9 8 7 6 5 4 3 2 1
1st Printing: June 2010

For information on other *2000 AD* graphic novels, or if you have any comments on this book, please email books@2000ADonline.com

To find out more about *2000 AD*, visit www.2000ADonline.com

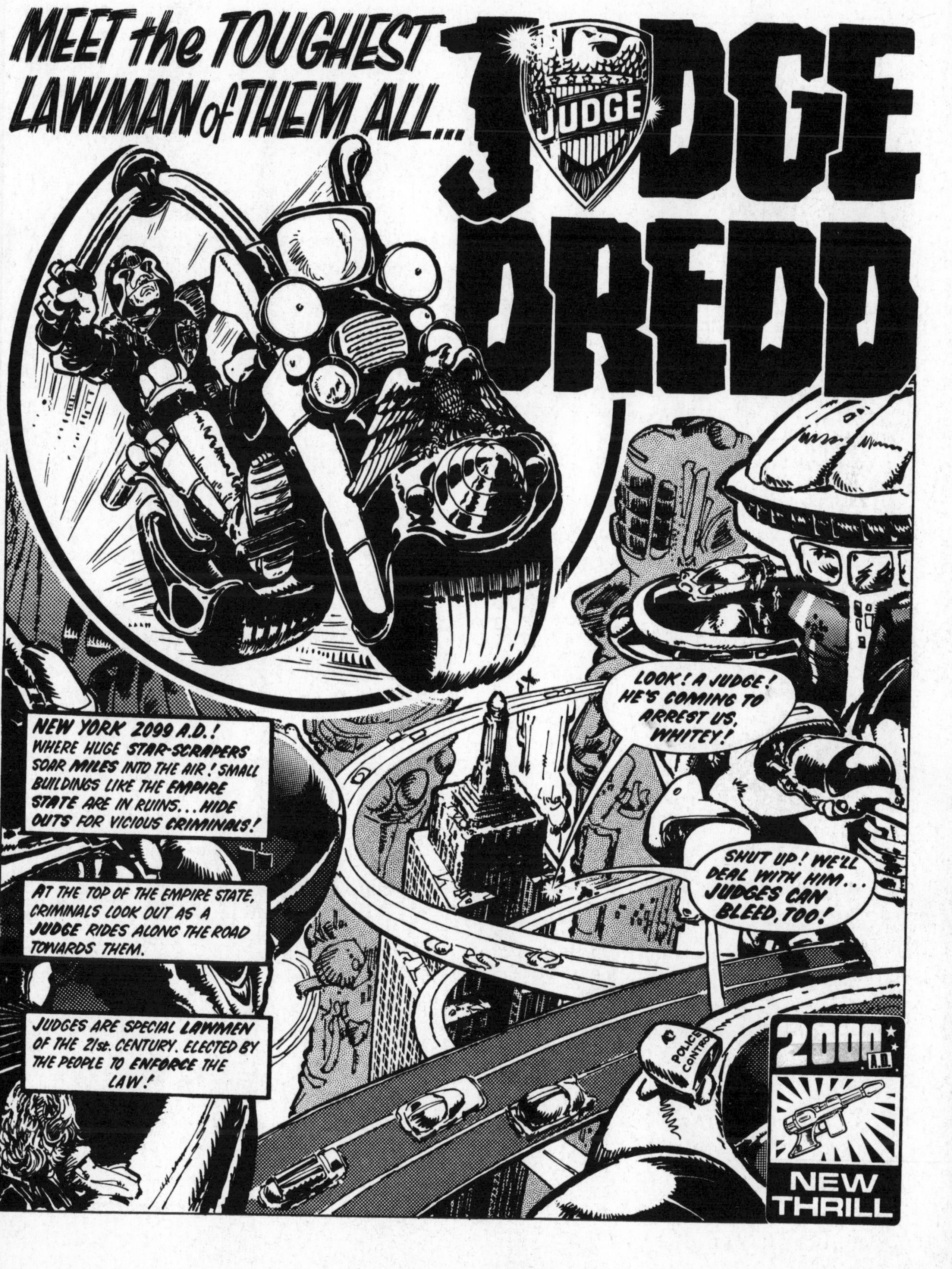
MEET the TOUGHEST LAWMAN of THEM ALL...
JUDGE DREDD
JUDGE
NEW YORK 2099 A.D.! WHERE HUGE STAR-SCRAPERS SOAR MILES INTO THE AIR! SMALL BUILDINGS LIKE THE EMPIRE STATE ARE IN RUINS... HIDE OUTS FOR VICIOUS CRIMINALS!
AT THE TOP OF THE EMPIRE STATE, CRIMINALS LOOK OUT AS A JUDGE RIDES ALONG THE ROAD TOWARDS THEM.
JUDGES ARE SPECIAL LAWMEN OF THE 21st. CENTURY. ELECTED BY THE PEOPLE TO ENFORCE THE LAW!
LOOK! A JUDGE! HE'S COMING TO ARREST US, WHITEY!
SHUT UP! WE'LL DEAL WITH HIM... JUDGES CAN BLEED, TOO!
POLICE CONTROL
2000 A.D.
NEW THRILL

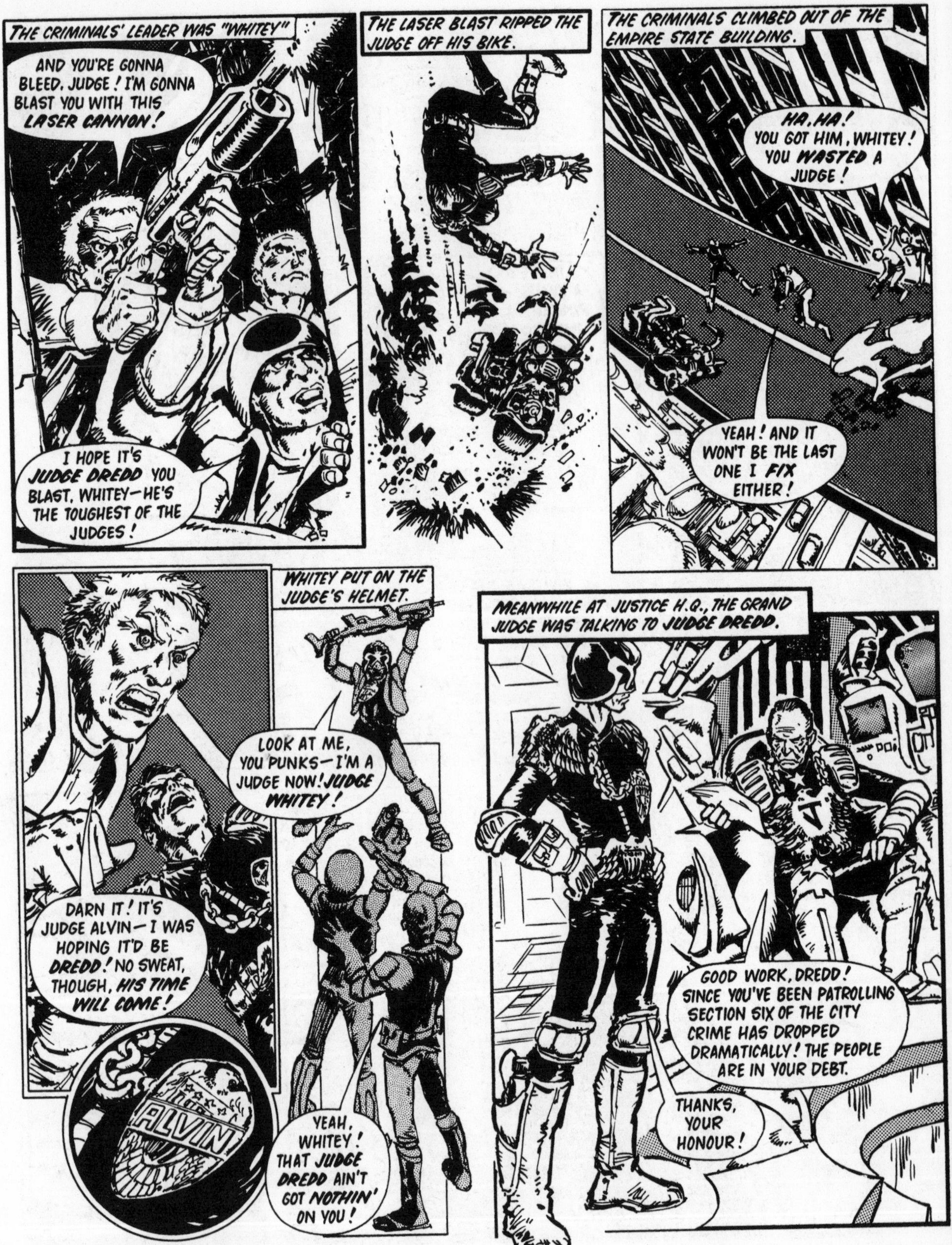
THE CRIMINALS' LEADER WAS "WHITEY"
AND YOU'RE GONNA BLEED, JUDGE! I'M GONNA BLAST YOU WITH THIS LASER CANNON!
I HOPE IT'S JUDGE DREDD YOU BLAST, WHITEY—HE'S THE TOUGHEST OF THE JUDGES!
THE LASER BLAST RIPPED THE JUDGE OFF HIS BIKE.
THE CRIMINALS CLIMBED OUT OF THE EMPIRE STATE BUILDING.
HA, HA! YOU GOT HIM, WHITEY! YOU WASTED A JUDGE!
YEAH! AND IT WON'T BE THE LAST ONE I FIX EITHER!
DARN IT! IT'S JUDGE ALVIN—I WAS HOPING IT'D BE DREDD! NO SWEAT, THOUGH, HIS TIME WILL COME!
ALVIN
WHITEY PUT ON THE JUDGE'S HELMET.
LOOK AT ME, YOU PUNKS—I'M A JUDGE NOW! JUDGE WHITEY!
YEAH, WHITEY! THAT JUDGE DREDD AIN'T GOT NOTHIN' ON YOU!
MEANWHILE AT JUSTICE H.Q., THE GRAND JUDGE WAS TALKING TO JUDGE DREDD.
GOOD WORK, DREDD! SINCE YOU'VE BEEN PATROLLING SECTION SIX OF THE CITY CRIME HAS DROPPED DRAMATICALLY! THE PEOPLE ARE IN YOUR DEBT.
THANKS, YOUR HONOUR!

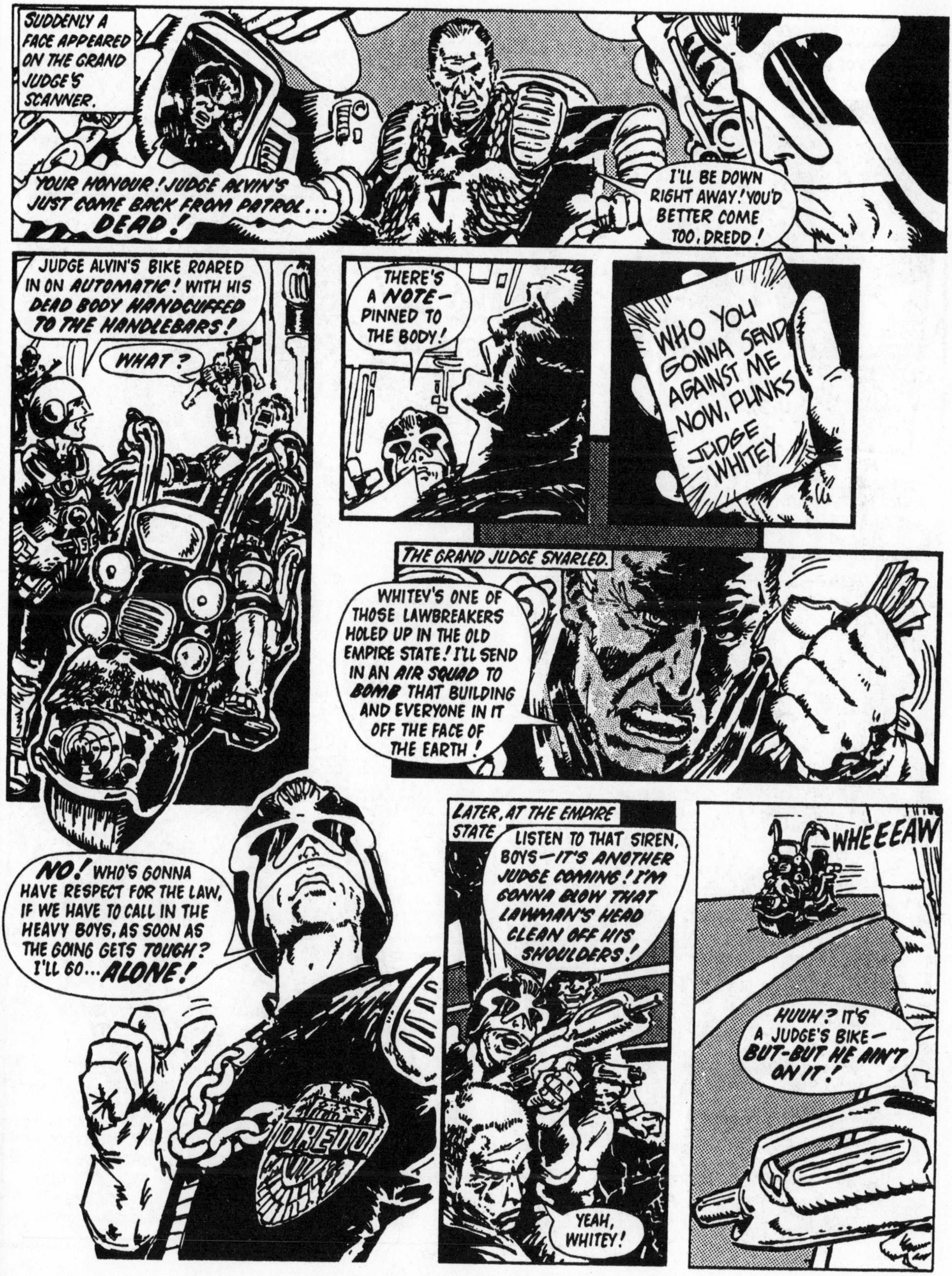
SUDDENLY A FACE APPEARED ON THE GRAND JUDGE'S SCANNER.
YOUR HONOUR! JUDGE ALVIN'S JUST COME BACK FROM PATROL... DEAD!
I'LL BE DOWN RIGHT AWAY! YOU'D BETTER COME TOO, DREDD!
JUDGE ALVIN'S BIKE ROARED IN ON AUTOMATIC! WITH HIS DEAD BODY HANDCUFFED TO THE HANDLEBARS!
WHAT?
THERE'S A NOTE- PINNED TO THE BODY!
WHO YOU GONNA SEND AGAINST ME NOW, PUNKS
JUDGE WHITEY
THE GRAND JUDGE SNARLED.
WHITEY'S ONE OF THOSE LAWBREAKERS HOLED UP IN THE OLD EMPIRE STATE! I'LL SEND IN AN AIR SQUAD TO BOMB THAT BUILDING AND EVERYONE IN IT OFF THE FACE OF THE EARTH!
NO! WHO'S GONNA HAVE RESPECT FOR THE LAW, IF WE HAVE TO CALL IN THE HEAVY BOYS, AS SOON AS THE GOING GETS TOUGH? I'LL GO... ALONE!
DREDD
LATER, AT THE EMPIRE STATE
LISTEN TO THAT SIREN, BOYS—IT'S ANOTHER JUDGE COMING! I'M GONNA BLOW THAT LAWMAN'S HEAD CLEAN OFF HIS SHOULDERS!
YEAH, WHITEY!
WHEEEAW
HUUH? IT'S A JUDGE'S BIKE- BUT-BUT HE AIN'T ON IT!

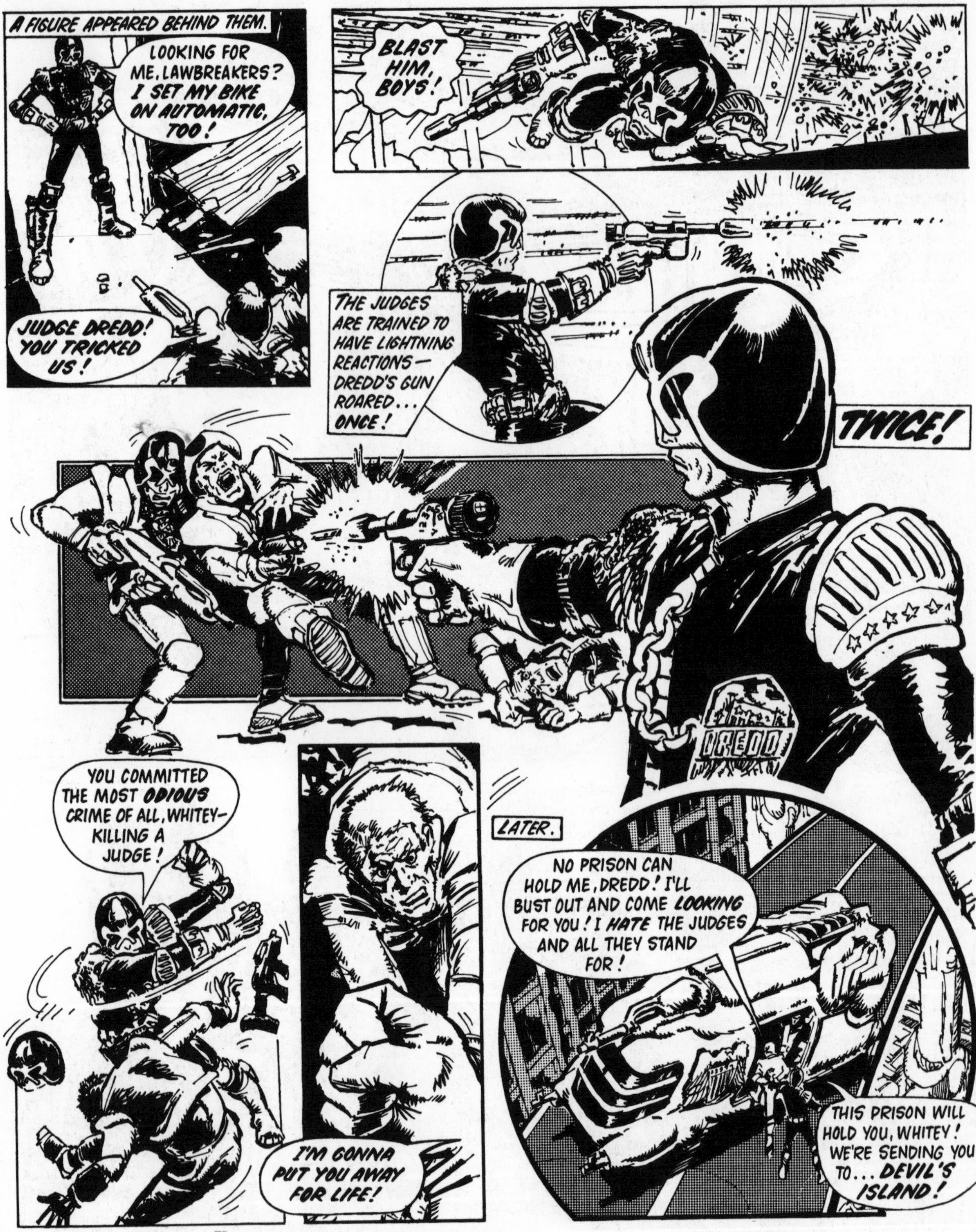
A FIGURE APPEARED BEHIND THEM.
LOOKING FOR ME, LAWBREAKERS? I SET MY BIKE ON AUTOMATIC, TOO!
JUDGE DREDD! YOU TRICKED US!
BLAST HIM, BOYS!
THE JUDGES ARE TRAINED TO HAVE LIGHTNING REACTIONS— DREDD'S GUN ROARED... ONCE!
TWICE!
YOU COMMITTED THE MOST ODIOUS CRIME OF ALL, WHITEY- KILLING A JUDGE!
I'M GONNA PUT YOU AWAY FOR LIFE!
LATER.
NO PRISON CAN HOLD ME, DREDD! I'LL BUST OUT AND COME LOOKING FOR YOU! I HATE THE JUDGES AND ALL THEY STAND FOR!
THIS PRISON WILL HOLD YOU, WHITEY! WE'RE SENDING YOU TO... DEVIL'S ISLAND!

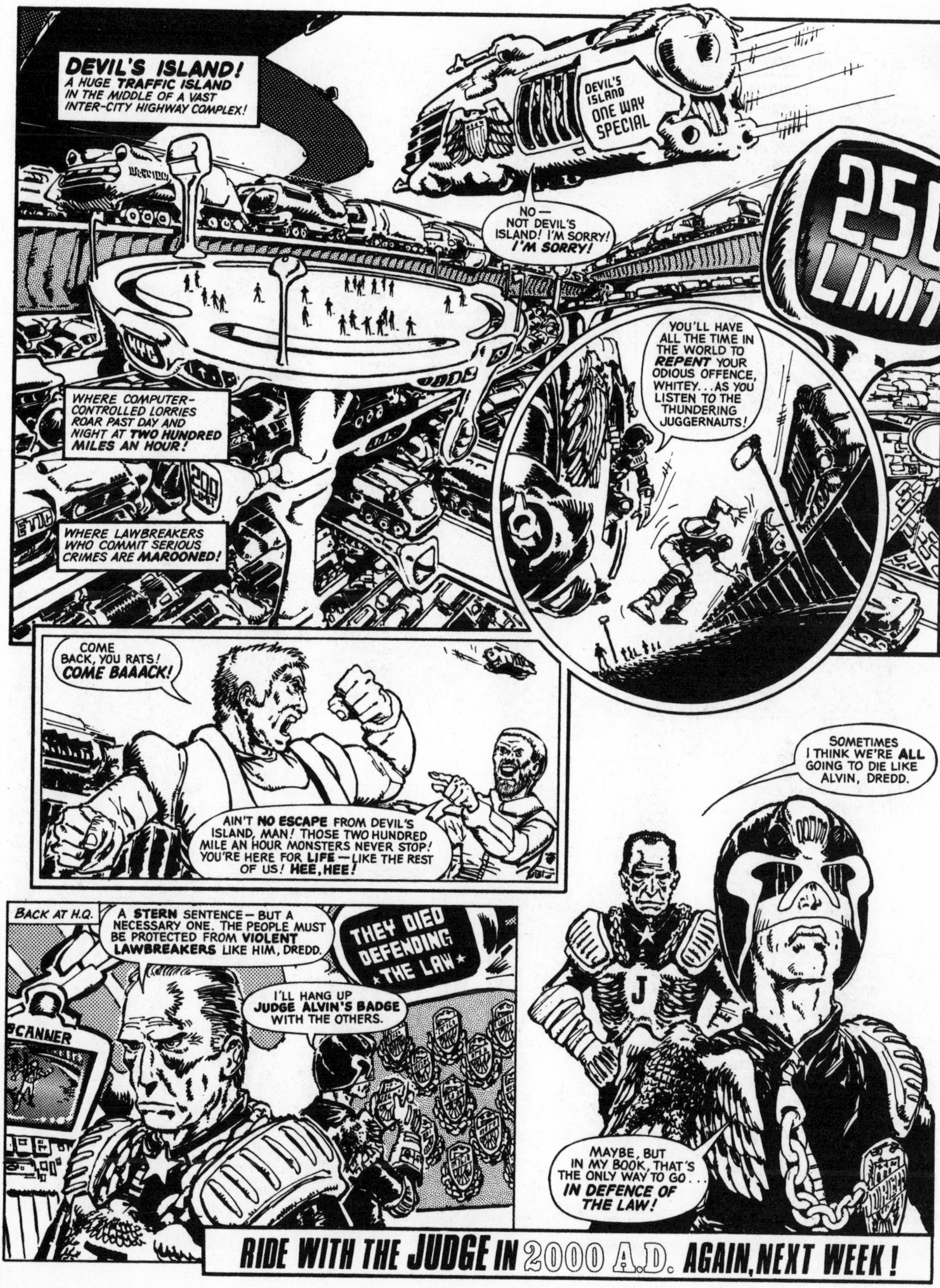
DEVIL'S ISLAND! A HUGE TRAFFIC ISLAND IN THE MIDDLE OF A VAST INTER-CITY HIGHWAY COMPLEX!
DEVIL'S ISLAND ONE WAY SPECIAL
NO — NOT DEVIL'S ISLAND! I'M SORRY! I'M SORRY!
250 LIMIT
WHERE COMPUTER-CONTROLLED LORRIES ROAR PAST DAY AND NIGHT AT TWO HUNDRED MILES AN HOUR!
WHERE LAWBREAKERS WHO COMMIT SERIOUS CRIMES ARE MAROONED!
YOU'LL HAVE ALL THE TIME IN THE WORLD TO REPENT YOUR ODIOUS OFFENCE, WHITEY... AS YOU LISTEN TO THE THUNDERING JUGGERNAUTS!
COME BACK, YOU RATS! COME BAAACK!
AIN'T NO ESCAPE FROM DEVIL'S ISLAND, MAN! THOSE TWO HUNDRED MILE AN HOUR MONSTERS NEVER STOP! YOU'RE HERE FOR LIFE — LIKE THE REST OF US! HEE, HEE!
BACK AT H.Q.
A STERN SENTENCE — BUT A NECESSARY ONE. THE PEOPLE MUST BE PROTECTED FROM VIOLENT LAWBREAKERS LIKE HIM, DREDD.
THEY DIED DEFENDING THE LAW
I'LL HANG UP JUDGE ALVIN'S BADGE WITH THE OTHERS.
SCANNER
SOMETIMES I THINK WE'RE ALL GOING TO DIE LIKE ALVIN, DREDD.
MAYBE, BUT IN MY BOOK, THAT'S THE ONLY WAY TO GO... IN DEFENCE OF THE LAW!
RIDE WITH THE JUDGE IN 2000 A.D. AGAIN, NEXT WEEK!

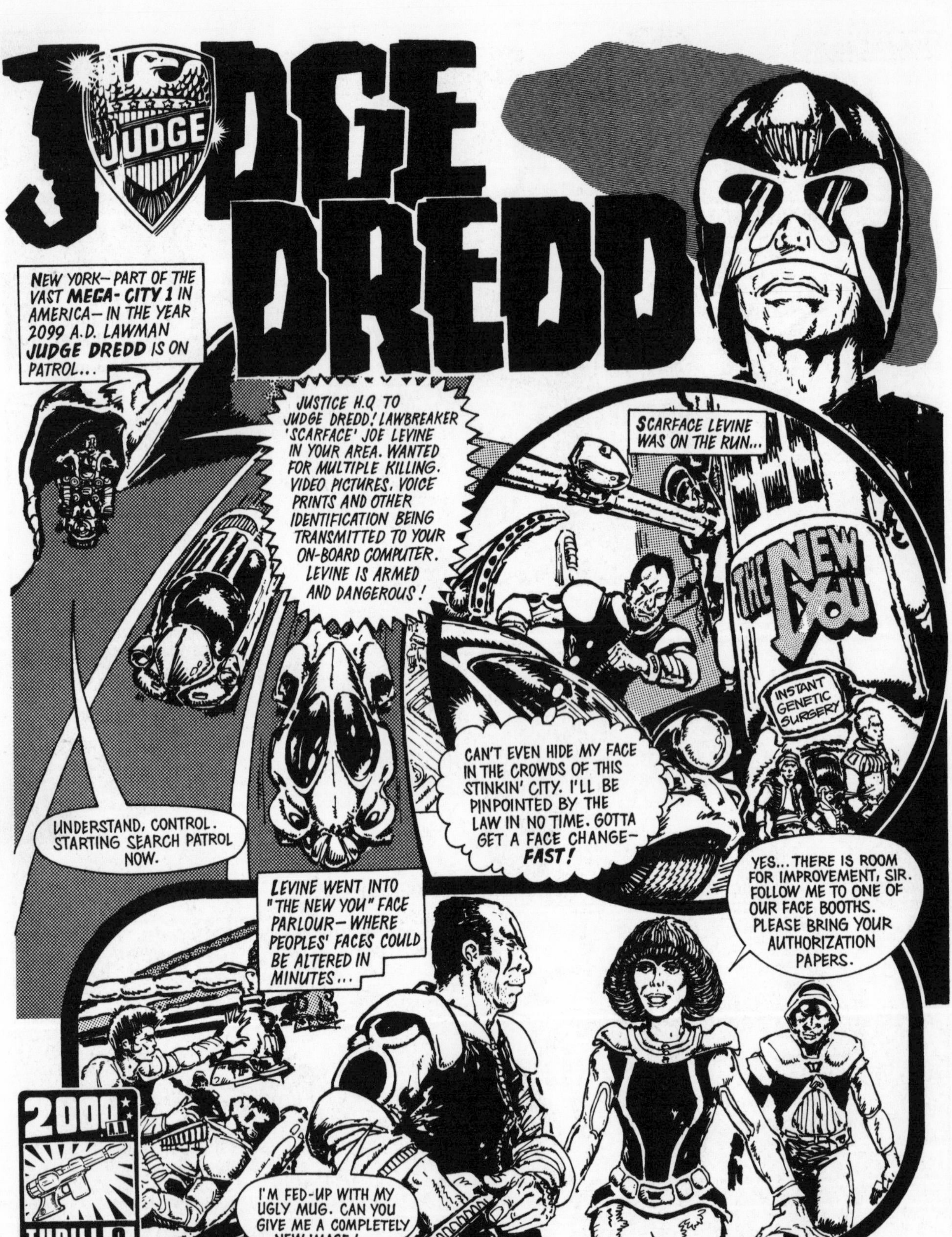
JUDGE
JUDGE DREDD
NEW YORK— PART OF THE VAST MEGA-CITY 1 IN AMERICA— IN THE YEAR 2099 A.D. LAWMAN JUDGE DREDD IS ON PATROL...
JUSTICE H.Q TO JUDGE DREDD! LAWBREAKER 'SCARFACE' JOE LEVINE IN YOUR AREA. WANTED FOR MULTIPLE KILLING. VIDEO PICTURES, VOICE PRINTS AND OTHER IDENTIFICATION BEING TRANSMITTED TO YOUR ON-BOARD COMPUTER. LEVINE IS ARMED AND DANGEROUS!
UNDERSTAND, CONTROL. STARTING SEARCH PATROL NOW.
SCARFACE LEVINE WAS ON THE RUN...
THE NEW YOU
INSTANT GENETIC SURGERY
CAN'T EVEN HIDE MY FACE IN THE CROWDS OF THIS STINKIN' CITY. I'LL BE PINPOINTED BY THE LAW IN NO TIME. GOTTA GET A FACE CHANGE— FAST!
LEVINE WENT INTO "THE NEW YOU" FACE PARLOUR— WHERE PEOPLES' FACES COULD BE ALTERED IN MINUTES...
I'M FED-UP WITH MY UGLY MUG. CAN YOU GIVE ME A COMPLETELY NEW IMAGE!
YES... THERE IS ROOM FOR IMPROVEMENT, SIR. FOLLOW ME TO ONE OF OUR FACE BOOTHS. PLEASE BRING YOUR AUTHORIZATION PAPERS.
2000 A.D.
THRILL 6

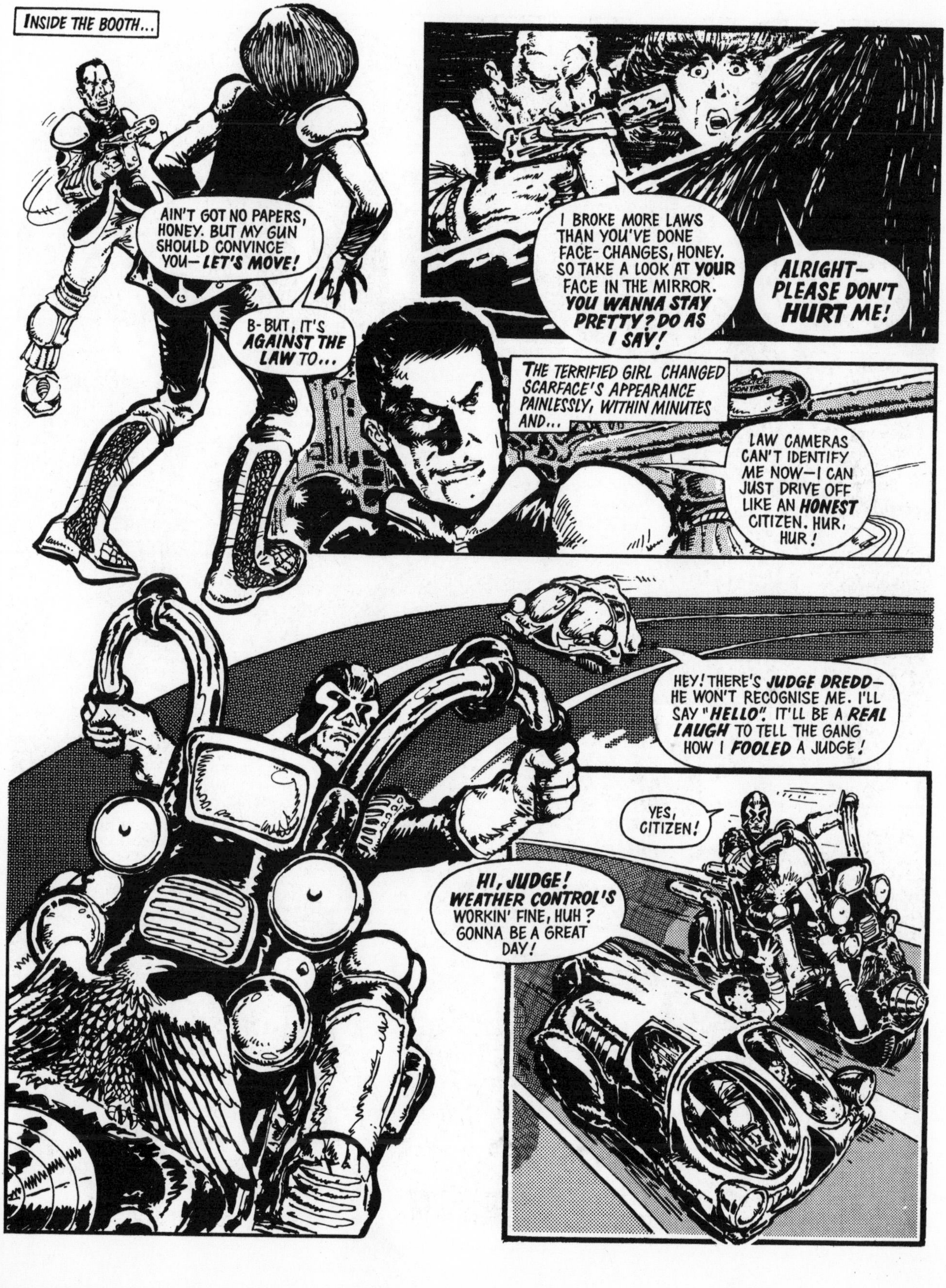
INSIDE THE BOOTH...
AIN'T GOT NO PAPERS, HONEY. BUT MY GUN SHOULD CONVINCE YOU—LET'S MOVE!
B-BUT, IT'S AGAINST THE LAW TO...
I BROKE MORE LAWS THAN YOU'VE DONE FACE-CHANGES, HONEY. SO TAKE A LOOK AT YOUR FACE IN THE MIRROR. YOU WANNA STAY PRETTY? DO AS I SAY!
ALRIGHT—PLEASE DON'T HURT ME!
THE TERRIFIED GIRL CHANGED SCARFACE'S APPEARANCE PAINLESSLY, WITHIN MINUTES AND...
LAW CAMERAS CAN'T IDENTIFY ME NOW—I CAN JUST DRIVE OFF LIKE AN HONEST CITIZEN. HUR, HUR!
HEY! THERE'S JUDGE DREDD—HE WON'T RECOGNISE ME. I'LL SAY "HELLO". IT'LL BE A REAL LAUGH TO TELL THE GANG HOW I FOOLED A JUDGE!
HI, JUDGE! WEATHER CONTROL'S WORKIN' FINE, HUH? GONNA BE A GREAT DAY!
YES, CITIZEN!

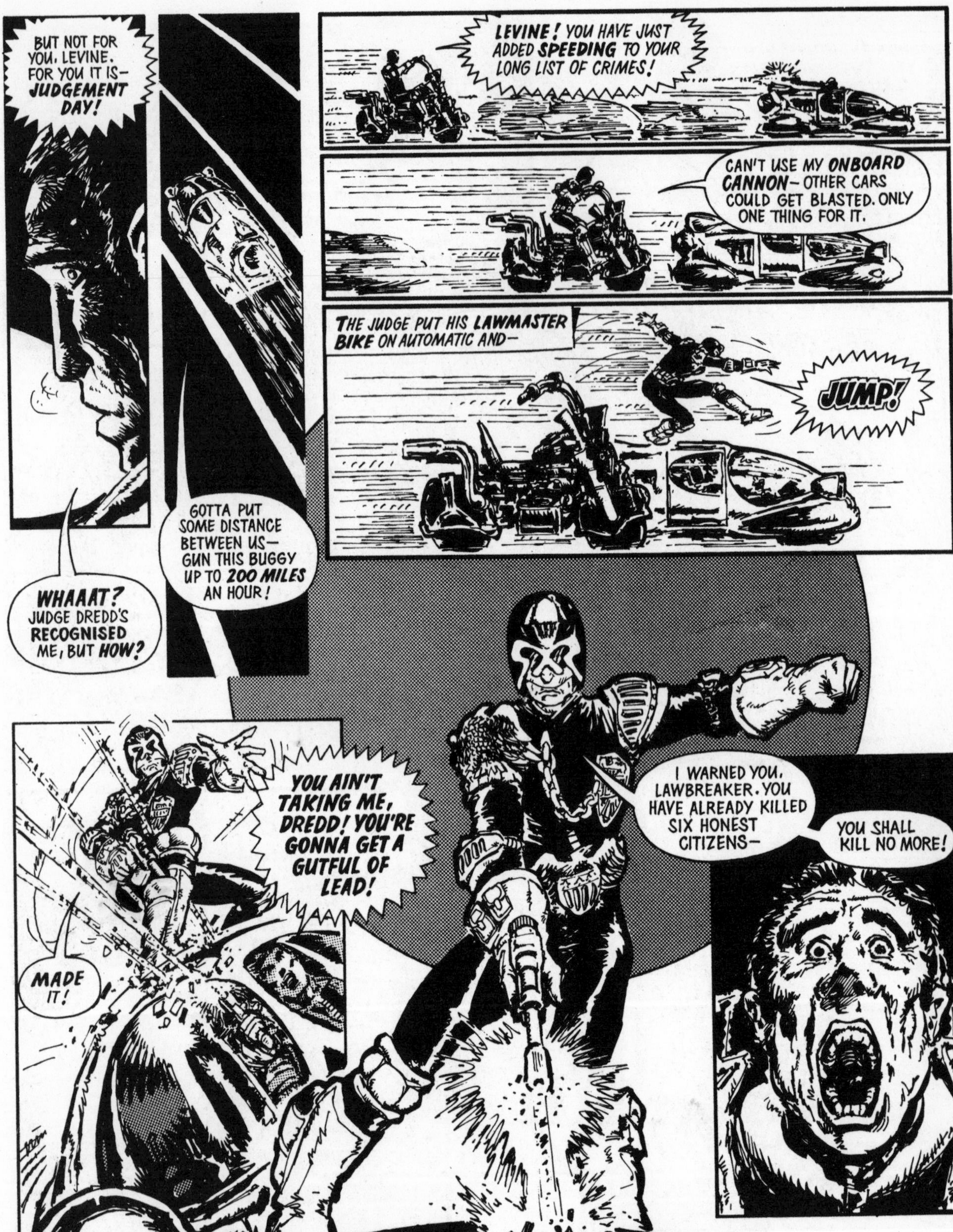
BUT NOT FOR YOU, LEVINE. FOR YOU IT IS— JUDGEMENT DAY!
WHAAAT? JUDGE DREDD'S RECOGNISED ME, BUT HOW?
GOTTA PUT SOME DISTANCE BETWEEN US— GUN THIS BUGGY UP TO 200 MILES AN HOUR!
LEVINE! YOU HAVE JUST ADDED SPEEDING TO YOUR LONG LIST OF CRIMES!
CAN'T USE MY ONBOARD CANNON— OTHER CARS COULD GET BLASTED. ONLY ONE THING FOR IT.
THE JUDGE PUT HIS LAWMASTER BIKE ON AUTOMATIC AND—
JUMP!
MADE IT!
YOU AIN'T TAKING ME, DREDD! YOU'RE GONNA GET A GUTFUL OF LEAD!
I WARNED YOU, LAWBREAKER. YOU HAVE ALREADY KILLED SIX HONEST CITIZENS—
YOU SHALL KILL NO MORE!

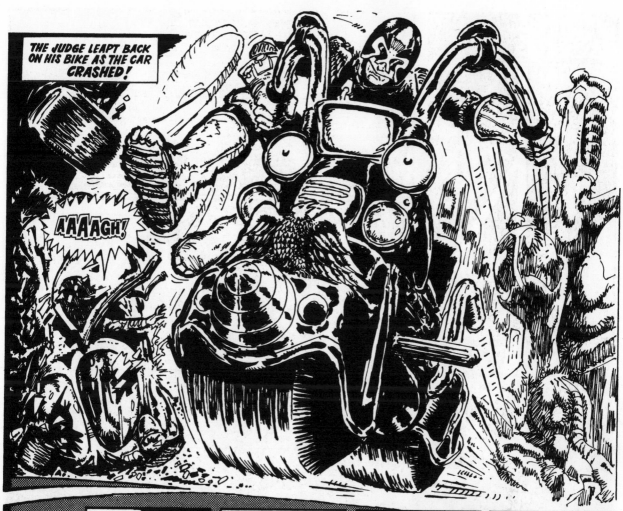

THE JUDGE LEAPT BACK ON HIS BIKE AS THE CAR CRASHED!

AAAAGH!

DREDD DROVE HIS LAWMASTER BACK TO THE SCENE OF THE CRASH. AS HE WAITED FOR THE AMBULANCE TO ARRIVE...

OKAY— IT'S THE TIME-STRETCHER JAIL FOR ME NOW. BUT WILL YOU... UUUH... GRANT ME ONE REQUEST?

THE LAW CAN SHOW MERCY, TOO! SPEAK?

I GOT RID OF MY UGLY MUG— SO HOW COME YOU RECOGNISED ME?

WHEN YOU SPOKE, YOUR VOICE PRINT MATCHED THE ONE SENT TO ME BY CONTROL.

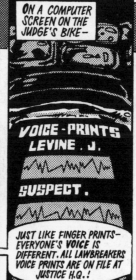

ON A COMPUTER SCREEN ON THE JUDGE'S BIKE—

VOICE-PRINTS
LEVINE . J.

SUSPECT.

JUST LIKE FINGER PRINTS— EVERYONE'S VOICE IS DIFFERENT. ALL LAWBREAKERS VOICE PRINTS ARE ON FILE AT JUSTICE H.Q..!

WHEN WILL LAWBREAKERS LEARN... IN THE 21st CENTURY— NO ONE CAN ESCAPE JUSTICE!

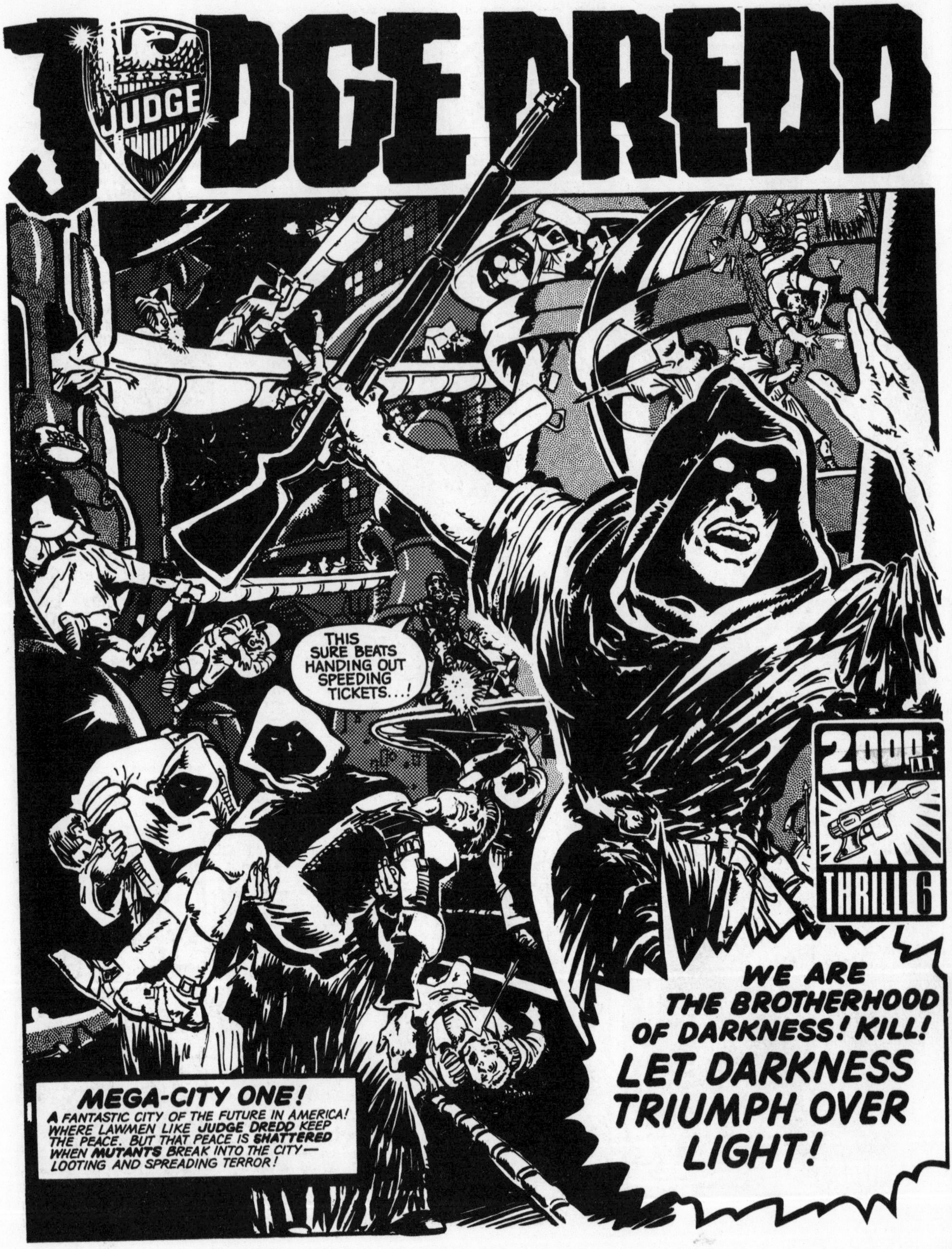
JUDGE DREDD
JUDGE
2000 A.D.
THRILL 6
MEGA-CITY ONE!
A FANTASTIC CITY OF THE FUTURE IN AMERICA! WHERE LAWMEN LIKE JUDGE DREDD KEEP THE PEACE. BUT THAT PEACE IS SHATTERED WHEN MUTANTS BREAK INTO THE CITY— LOOTING AND SPREADING TERROR!
THIS SURE BEATS HANDING OUT SPEEDING TICKETS...!
WE ARE THE BROTHERHOOD OF DARKNESS! KILL! LET DARKNESS TRIUMPH OVER LIGHT!

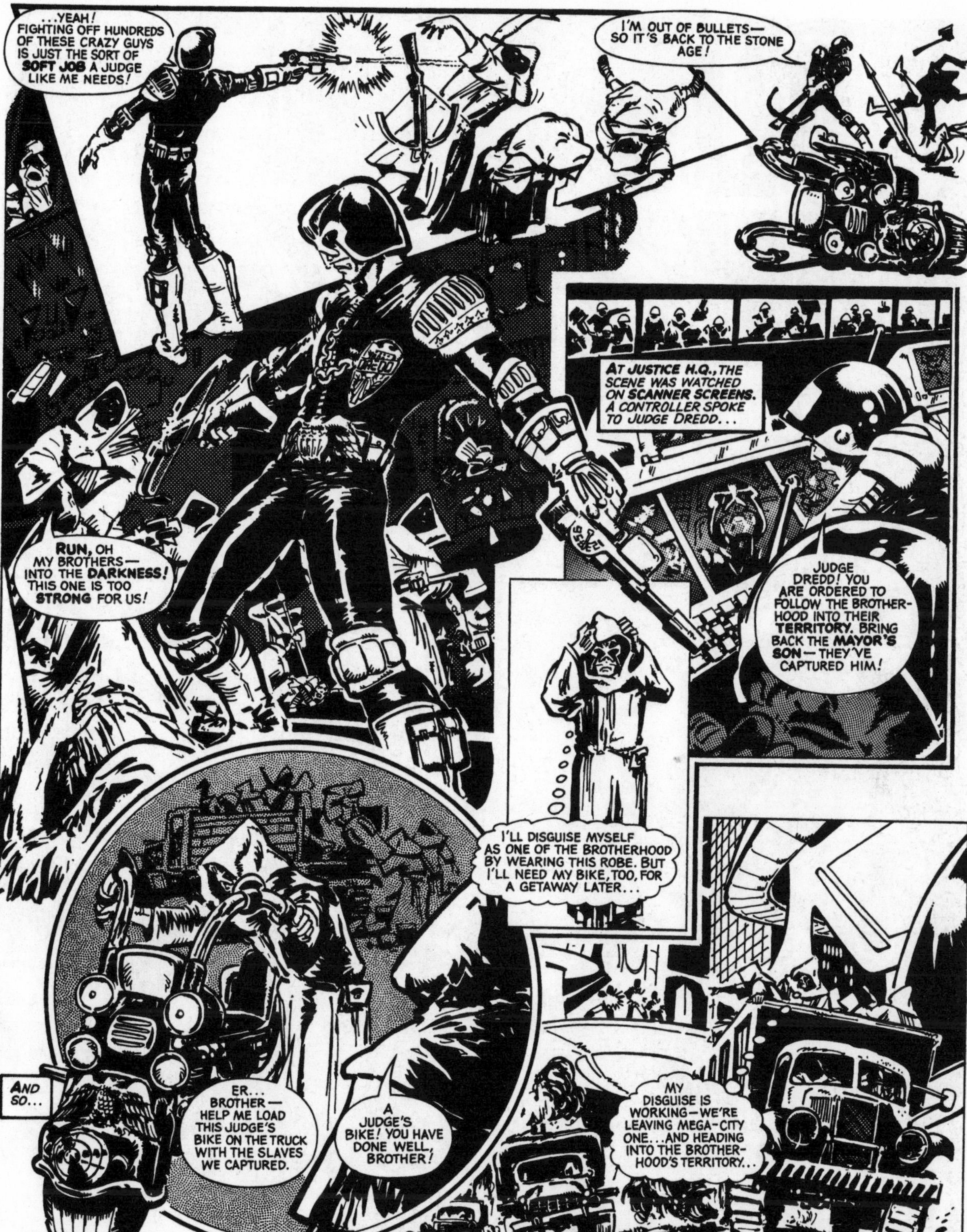
...YEAH! FIGHTING OFF HUNDREDS OF THESE CRAZY GUYS IS JUST THE SORT OF SOFT JOB A JUDGE LIKE ME NEEDS!
I'M OUT OF BULLETS— SO IT'S BACK TO THE STONE AGE!
AT JUSTICE H.Q., THE SCENE WAS WATCHED ON SCANNER SCREENS. A CONTROLLER SPOKE TO JUDGE DREDD...
RUN, OH MY BROTHERS— INTO THE DARKNESS! THIS ONE IS TOO STRONG FOR US!
JUDGE DREDD! YOU ARE ORDERED TO FOLLOW THE BROTHER-HOOD INTO THEIR TERRITORY. BRING BACK THE MAYOR'S SON— THEY'VE CAPTURED HIM!
I'LL DISGUISE MYSELF AS ONE OF THE BROTHERHOOD BY WEARING THIS ROBE. BUT I'LL NEED MY BIKE, TOO, FOR A GETAWAY LATER...
AND SO...
ER... BROTHER— HELP ME LOAD THIS JUDGE'S BIKE ON THE TRUCK WITH THE SLAVES WE CAPTURED.
A JUDGE'S BIKE! YOU HAVE DONE WELL, BROTHER!
MY DISGUISE IS WORKING— WE'RE LEAVING MEGA-CITY ONE... AND HEADING INTO THE BROTHER-HOOD'S TERRITORY...

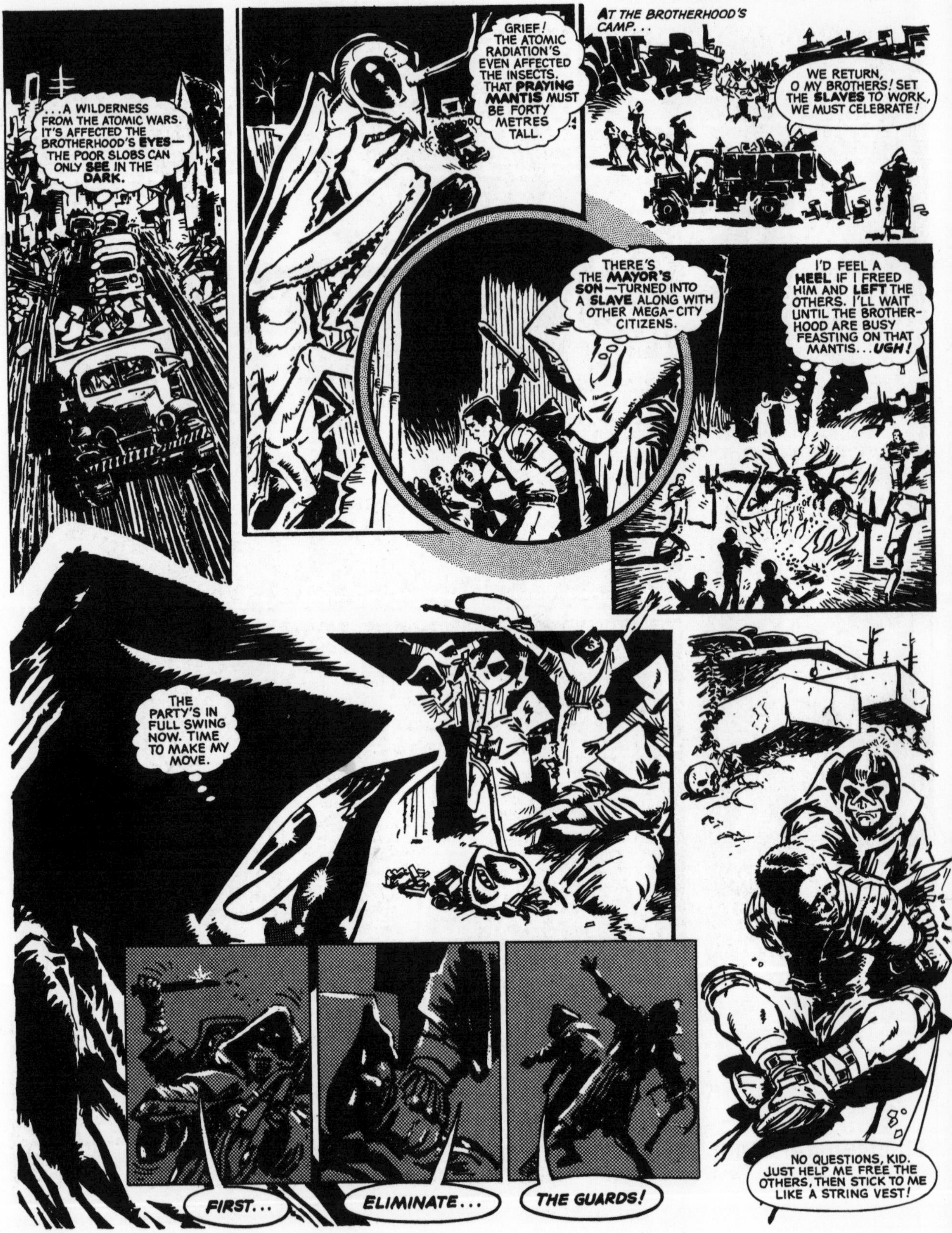
...A WILDERNESS FROM THE ATOMIC WARS. IT'S AFFECTED THE BROTHERHOOD'S EYES— THE POOR SLOBS CAN ONLY SEE IN THE DARK.
GRIEF! THE ATOMIC RADIATION'S EVEN AFFECTED THE INSECTS. THAT PRAYING MANTIS MUST BE FORTY METRES TALL.
AT THE BROTHERHOOD'S CAMP...
WE RETURN, O MY BROTHERS! SET THE SLAVES TO WORK, WE MUST CELEBRATE!
THERE'S THE MAYOR'S SON—TURNED INTO A SLAVE ALONG WITH OTHER MEGA-CITY CITIZENS.
I'D FEEL A HEEL IF I FREED HIM AND LEFT THE OTHERS. I'LL WAIT UNTIL THE BROTHERHOOD ARE BUSY FEASTING ON THAT MANTIS...UGH!
THE PARTY'S IN FULL SWING NOW. TIME TO MAKE MY MOVE.
FIRST...
ELIMINATE...
THE GUARDS!
NO QUESTIONS, KID. JUST HELP ME FREE THE OTHERS, THEN STICK TO ME LIKE A STRING VEST!

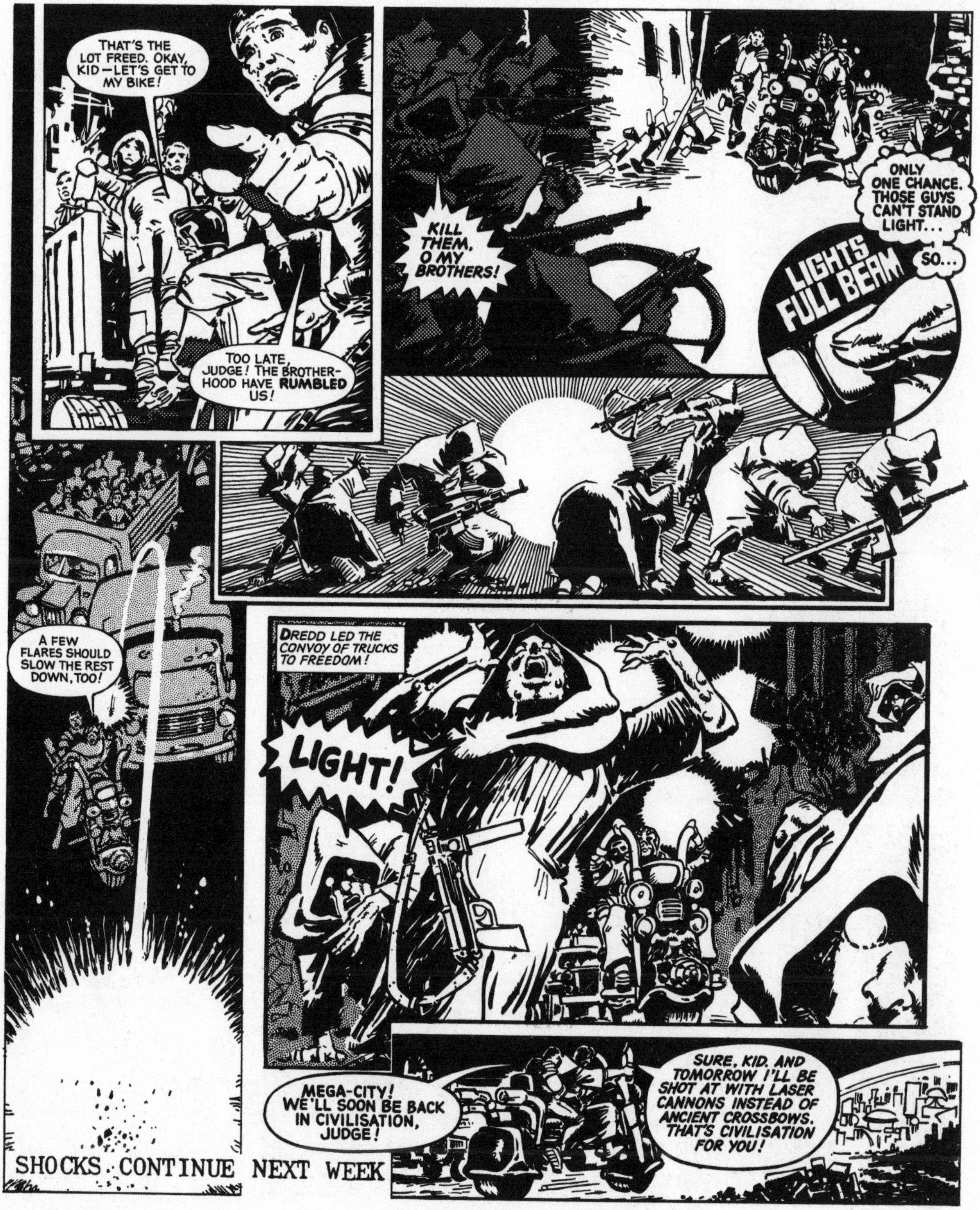
THAT'S THE LOT FREED. OKAY, KID—LET'S GET TO MY BIKE!
TOO LATE, JUDGE! THE BROTHER-HOOD HAVE RUMBLED US!
KILL THEM, O MY BROTHERS!
ONLY ONE CHANCE. THOSE GUYS CAN'T STAND LIGHT...
SO...
LIGHTS FULL BEAM
A FEW FLARES SHOULD SLOW THE REST DOWN, TOO!
DREDD LED THE CONVOY OF TRUCKS TO FREEDOM!
LIGHT!
MEGA-CITY! WE'LL SOON BE BACK IN CIVILISATION, JUDGE!
SURE, KID. AND TOMORROW I'LL BE SHOT AT WITH LASER CANNONS INSTEAD OF ANCIENT CROSSBOWS. THAT'S CIVILISATION FOR YOU!
SHOCKS CONTINUE NEXT WEEK

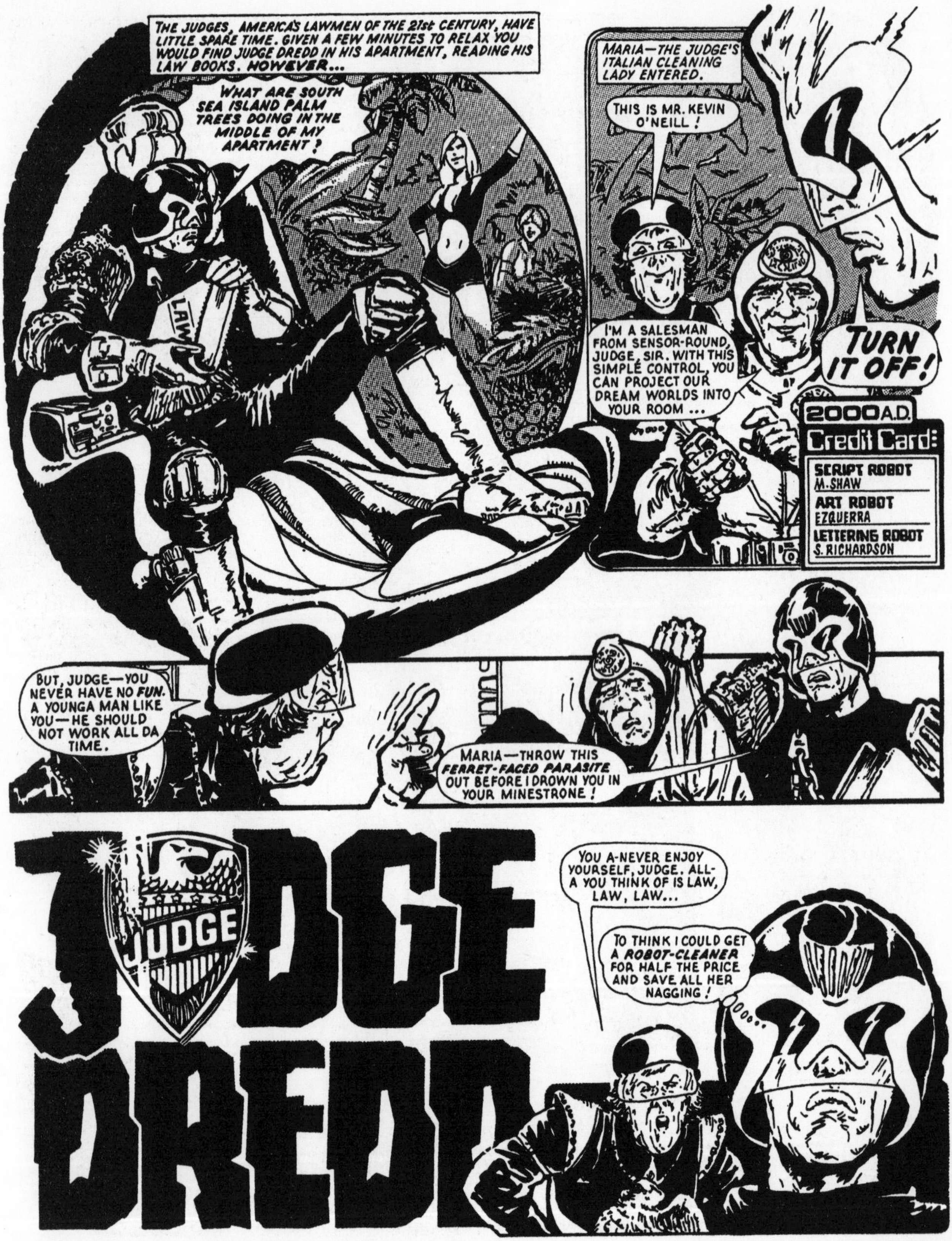
THE JUDGES, AMERICA'S LAWMEN OF THE 21st CENTURY, HAVE LITTLE SPARE TIME. GIVEN A FEW MINUTES TO RELAX YOU WOULD FIND JUDGE DREDD IN HIS APARTMENT, READING HIS LAW BOOKS. HOWEVER...
WHAT ARE SOUTH SEA ISLAND PALM TREES DOING IN THE MIDDLE OF MY APARTMENT?
LAW
MARIA—THE JUDGE'S ITALIAN CLEANING LADY ENTERED.
THIS IS MR. KEVIN O'NEILL!
I'M A SALESMAN FROM SENSOR-ROUND, JUDGE, SIR. WITH THIS SIMPLE CONTROL, YOU CAN PROJECT OUR DREAM WORLDS INTO YOUR ROOM ...
TURN IT OFF!
2000 A.D. Credit Card:
SCRIPT ROBOT M. SHAW
ART ROBOT EZQUERRA
LETTERING ROBOT S. RICHARDSON
BUT, JUDGE—YOU NEVER HAVE NO FUN. A YOUNGA MAN LIKE YOU—HE SHOULD NOT WORK ALL DA TIME.
MARIA—THROW THIS FERRET-FACED PARASITE OUT BEFORE I DROWN YOU IN YOUR MINESTRONE!
JUDGE DREDD
JUDGE
YOU A-NEVER ENJOY YOURSELF, JUDGE. ALL-A YOU THINK OF IS LAW, LAW, LAW...
TO THINK I COULD GET A ROBOT-CLEANER FOR HALF THE PRICE AND SAVE ALL HER NAGGING!

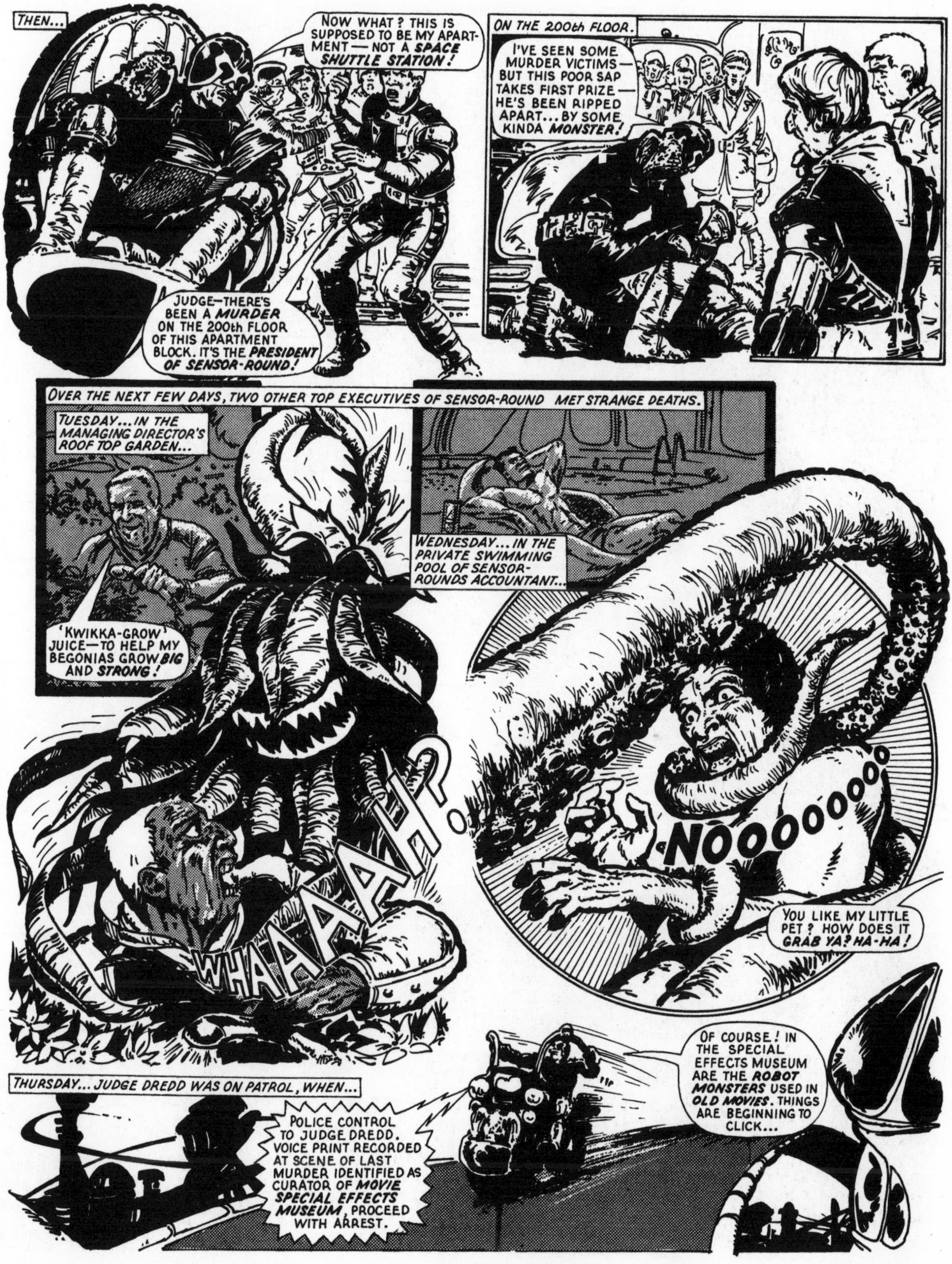

THEN...
NOW WHAT? THIS IS SUPPOSED TO BE MY APARTMENT — NOT A SPACE SHUTTLE STATION!
JUDGE—THERE'S BEEN A MURDER ON THE 200th FLOOR OF THIS APARTMENT BLOCK. IT'S THE PRESIDENT OF SENSOR-ROUND!
ON THE 200th FLOOR.
I'VE SEEN SOME MURDER VICTIMS— BUT THIS POOR SAP TAKES FIRST PRIZE— HE'S BEEN RIPPED APART... BY SOME KINDA MONSTER!
OVER THE NEXT FEW DAYS, TWO OTHER TOP EXECUTIVES OF SENSOR-ROUND MET STRANGE DEATHS.
TUESDAY... IN THE MANAGING DIRECTOR'S ROOF TOP GARDEN...
'KWIKKA-GROW' JUICE—TO HELP MY BEGONIAS GROW BIG AND STRONG!
WHAAAAH?
WEDNESDAY... IN THE PRIVATE SWIMMING POOL OF SENSOR-ROUNDS ACCOUNTANT...
NOOOOOOOOO
YOU LIKE MY LITTLE PET? HOW DOES IT GRAB YA? HA-HA!
THURSDAY... JUDGE DREDD WAS ON PATROL, WHEN...
POLICE CONTROL TO JUDGE DREDD. VOICE PRINT RECORDED AT SCENE OF LAST MURDER IDENTIFIED AS CURATOR OF MOVIE SPECIAL EFFECTS MUSEUM, PROCEED WITH ARREST.
OF COURSE! IN THE SPECIAL EFFECTS MUSEUM ARE THE ROBOT MONSTERS USED IN OLD MOVIES. THINGS ARE BEGINNING TO CLICK...

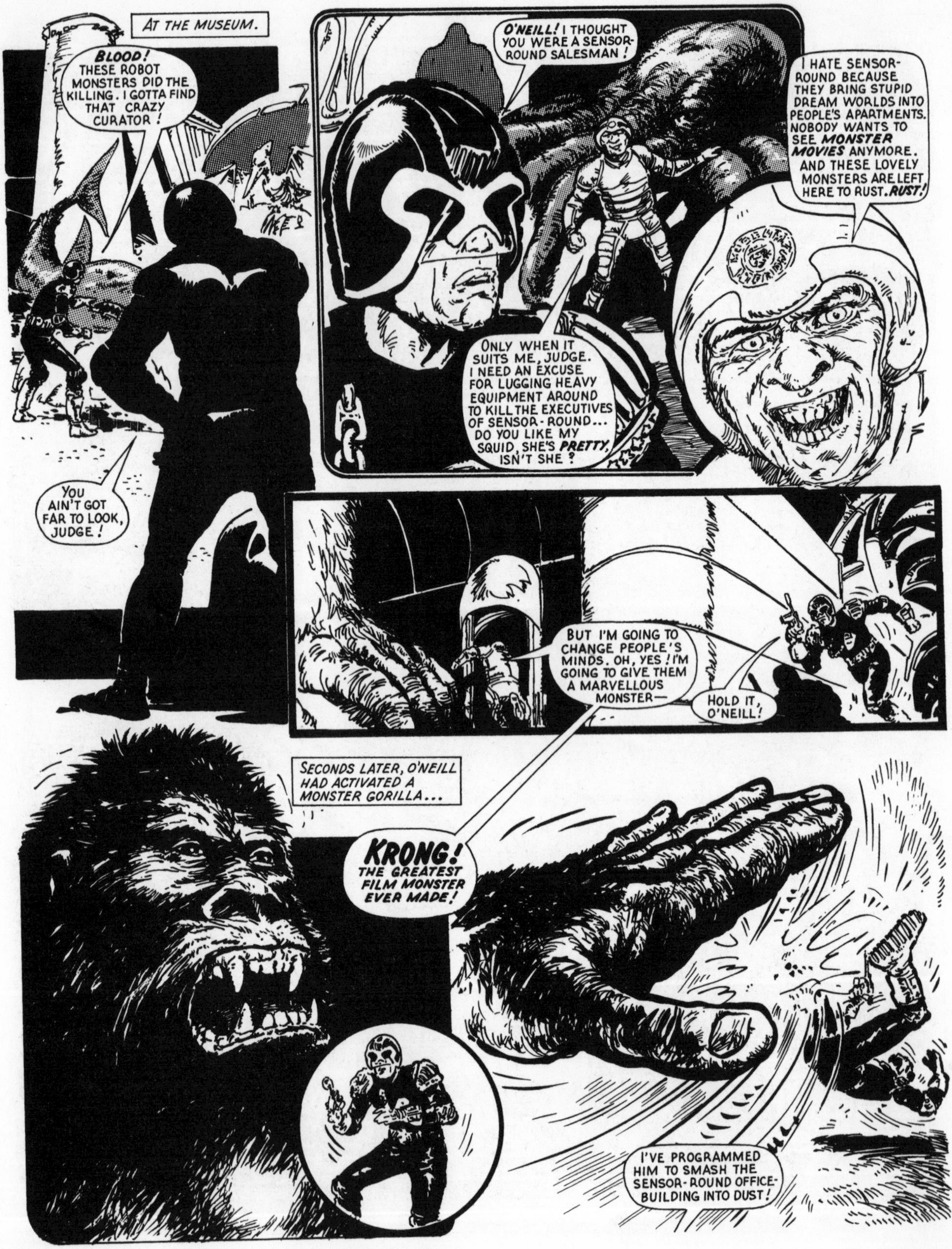

AT THE MUSEUM.
BLOOD! THESE ROBOT MONSTERS DID THE KILLING. I GOTTA FIND THAT CRAZY CURATOR!
YOU AIN'T GOT FAR TO LOOK, JUDGE!
O'NEILL! I THOUGHT YOU WERE A SENSOR-ROUND SALESMAN!
ONLY WHEN IT SUITS ME, JUDGE. I NEED AN EXCUSE FOR LUGGING HEAVY EQUIPMENT AROUND TO KILL THE EXECUTIVES OF SENSOR-ROUND... DO YOU LIKE MY SQUID, SHE'S PRETTY, ISN'T SHE?
I HATE SENSOR-ROUND BECAUSE THEY BRING STUPID DREAM WORLDS INTO PEOPLE'S APARTMENTS. NOBODY WANTS TO SEE MONSTER MOVIES ANYMORE. AND THESE LOVELY MONSTERS ARE LEFT HERE TO RUST. RUST!
BUT I'M GOING TO CHANGE PEOPLE'S MINDS. OH, YES! I'M GOING TO GIVE THEM A MARVELLOUS MONSTER—
HOLD IT, O'NEILL!
SECONDS LATER, O'NEILL HAD ACTIVATED A MONSTER GORILLA...
KRONG! THE GREATEST FILM MONSTER EVER MADE!
I'VE PROGRAMMED HIM TO SMASH THE SENSOR-ROUND OFFICE-BUILDING INTO DUST!

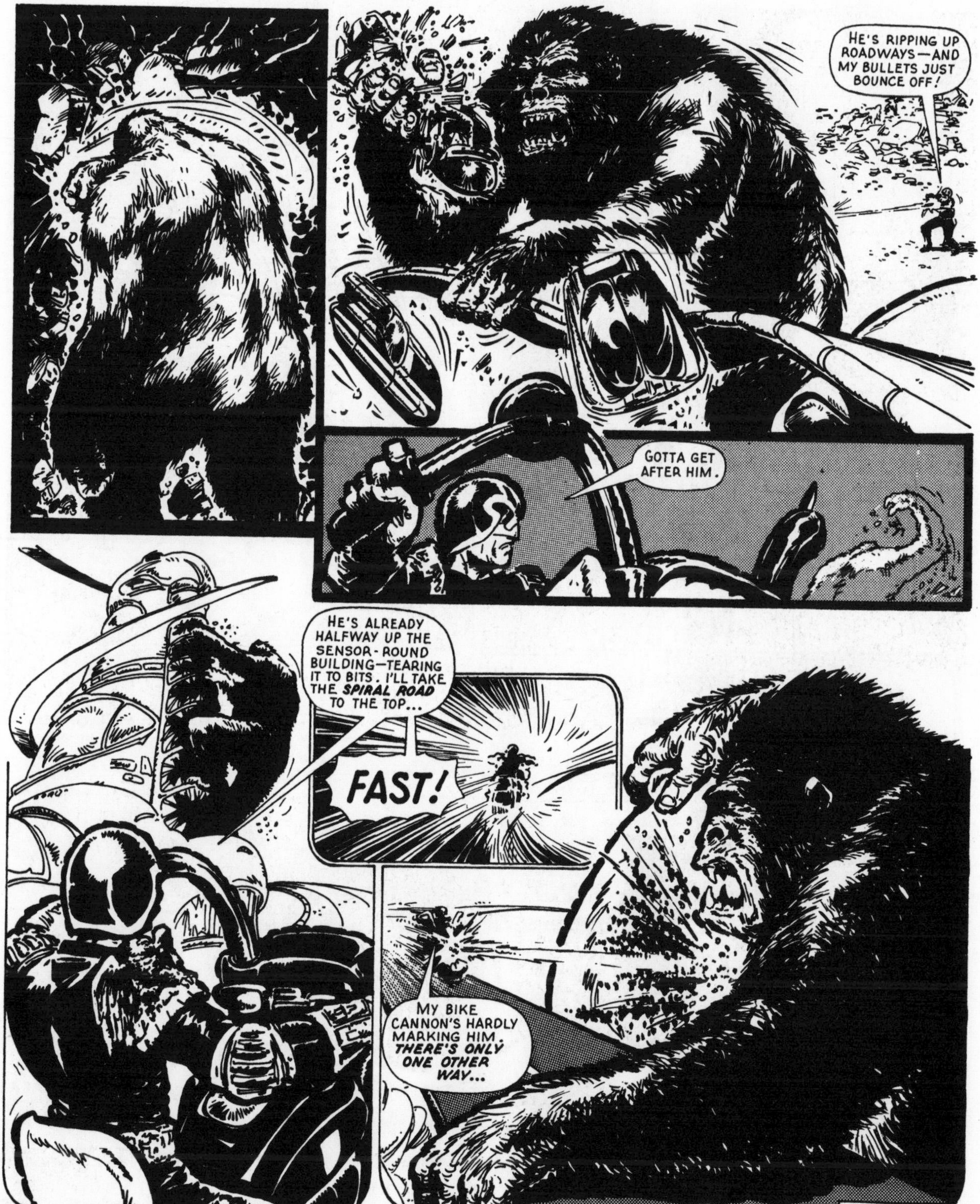
HE'S RIPPING UP ROADWAYS—AND MY BULLETS JUST BOUNCE OFF!
GOTTA GET AFTER HIM.
HE'S ALREADY HALFWAY UP THE SENSOR-ROUND BUILDING—TEARING IT TO BITS. I'LL TAKE THE SPIRAL ROAD TO THE TOP...
FAST!
MY BIKE CANNON'S HARDLY MARKING HIM. THERE'S ONLY ONE OTHER WAY...

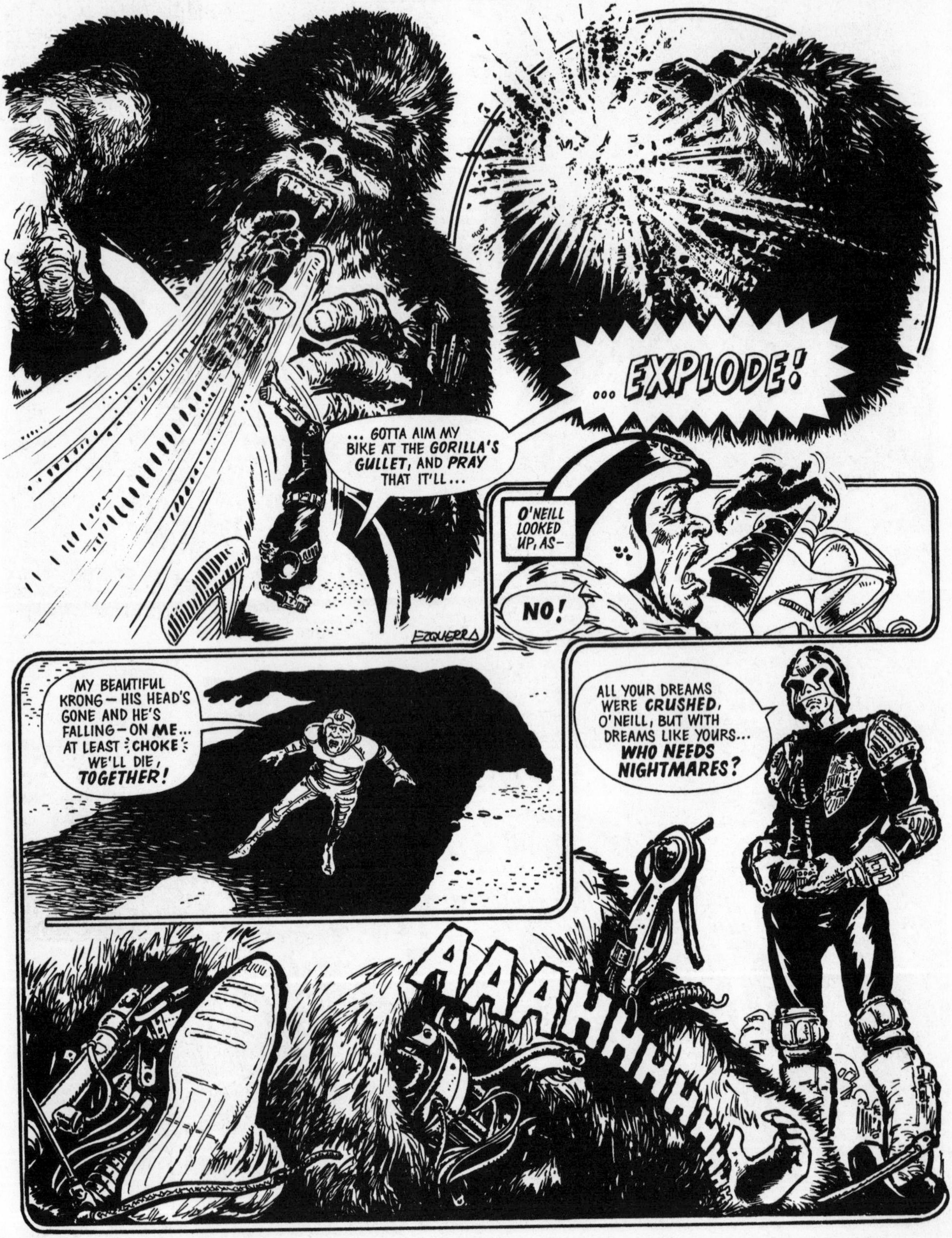
... GOTTA AIM MY BIKE AT THE GORILLA'S GULLET, AND PRAY THAT IT'LL...
... EXPLODE!
O'NEILL LOOKED UP, AS–
NO!
EZQUERRA
MY BEAUTIFUL KRONG — HIS HEAD'S GONE AND HE'S FALLING — ON ME... AT LEAST CHOKE WE'LL DIE, TOGETHER!
ALL YOUR DREAMS WERE CRUSHED, O'NEILL, BUT WITH DREAMS LIKE YOURS... WHO NEEDS NIGHTMARES?
AAAHHHHHH

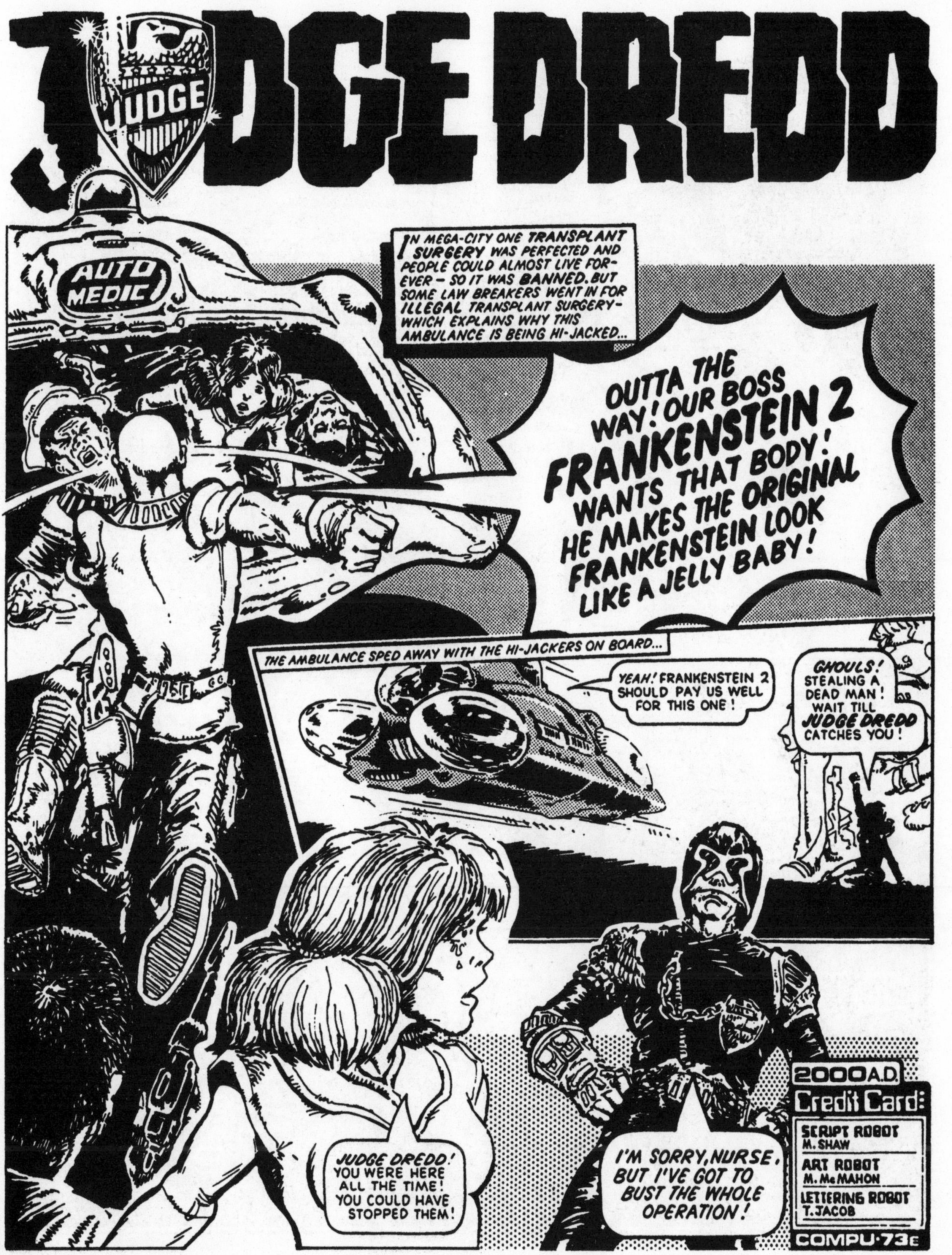
JUDGE DREDD
AUTO MEDIC
IN MEGA-CITY ONE TRANSPLANT SURGERY WAS PERFECTED AND PEOPLE COULD ALMOST LIVE FOREVER – SO IT WAS BANNED. BUT SOME LAW BREAKERS WENT IN FOR ILLEGAL TRANSPLANT SURGERY – WHICH EXPLAINS WHY THIS AMBULANCE IS BEING HI-JACKED...
OUTTA THE WAY! OUR BOSS FRANKENSTEIN 2 WANTS THAT BODY! HE MAKES THE ORIGINAL FRANKENSTEIN LOOK LIKE A JELLY BABY!
THE AMBULANCE SPED AWAY WITH THE HI-JACKERS ON BOARD...
YEAH! FRANKENSTEIN 2 SHOULD PAY US WELL FOR THIS ONE!
GHOULS! STEALING A DEAD MAN! WAIT TILL JUDGE DREDD CATCHES YOU!
JUDGE DREDD! YOU WERE HERE ALL THE TIME! YOU COULD HAVE STOPPED THEM!
I'M SORRY, NURSE, BUT I'VE GOT TO BUST THE WHOLE OPERATION!
2000 A.D.
Credit Card:
SCRIPT ROBOT M. SHAW
ART ROBOT M. McMAHON
LETTERING ROBOT T. JACOB
COMPU-73E

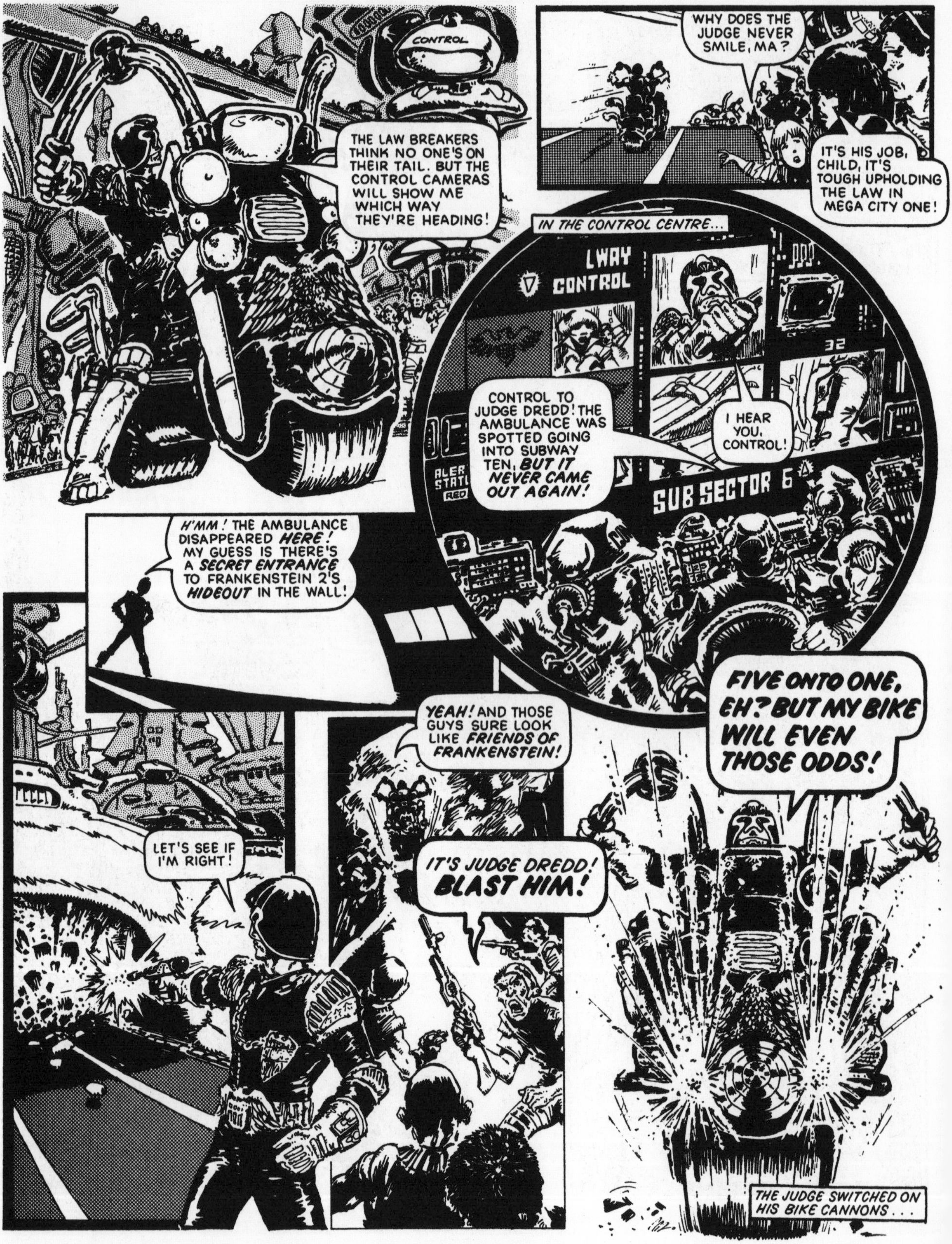
CONTROL
THE LAW BREAKERS THINK NO ONE'S ON THEIR TAIL. BUT THE CONTROL CAMERAS WILL SHOW ME WHICH WAY THEY'RE HEADING!
WHY DOES THE JUDGE NEVER SMILE, MA?
IT'S HIS JOB, CHILD, IT'S TOUGH UPHOLDING THE LAW IN MEGA CITY ONE!
IN THE CONTROL CENTRE...
LWAY CONTROL
SUB SECTOR 6
CONTROL TO JUDGE DREDD! THE AMBULANCE WAS SPOTTED GOING INTO SUBWAY TEN, BUT IT NEVER CAME OUT AGAIN!
I HEAR YOU, CONTROL!
H'MM! THE AMBULANCE DISAPPEARED HERE! MY GUESS IS THERE'S A SECRET ENTRANCE TO FRANKENSTEIN 2'S HIDEOUT IN THE WALL!
LET'S SEE IF I'M RIGHT!
YEAH! AND THOSE GUYS SURE LOOK LIKE FRIENDS OF FRANKENSTEIN!
IT'S JUDGE DREDD! BLAST HIM!
FIVE ONTO ONE, EH? BUT MY BIKE WILL EVEN THOSE ODDS!
THE JUDGE SWITCHED ON HIS BIKE CANNONS...

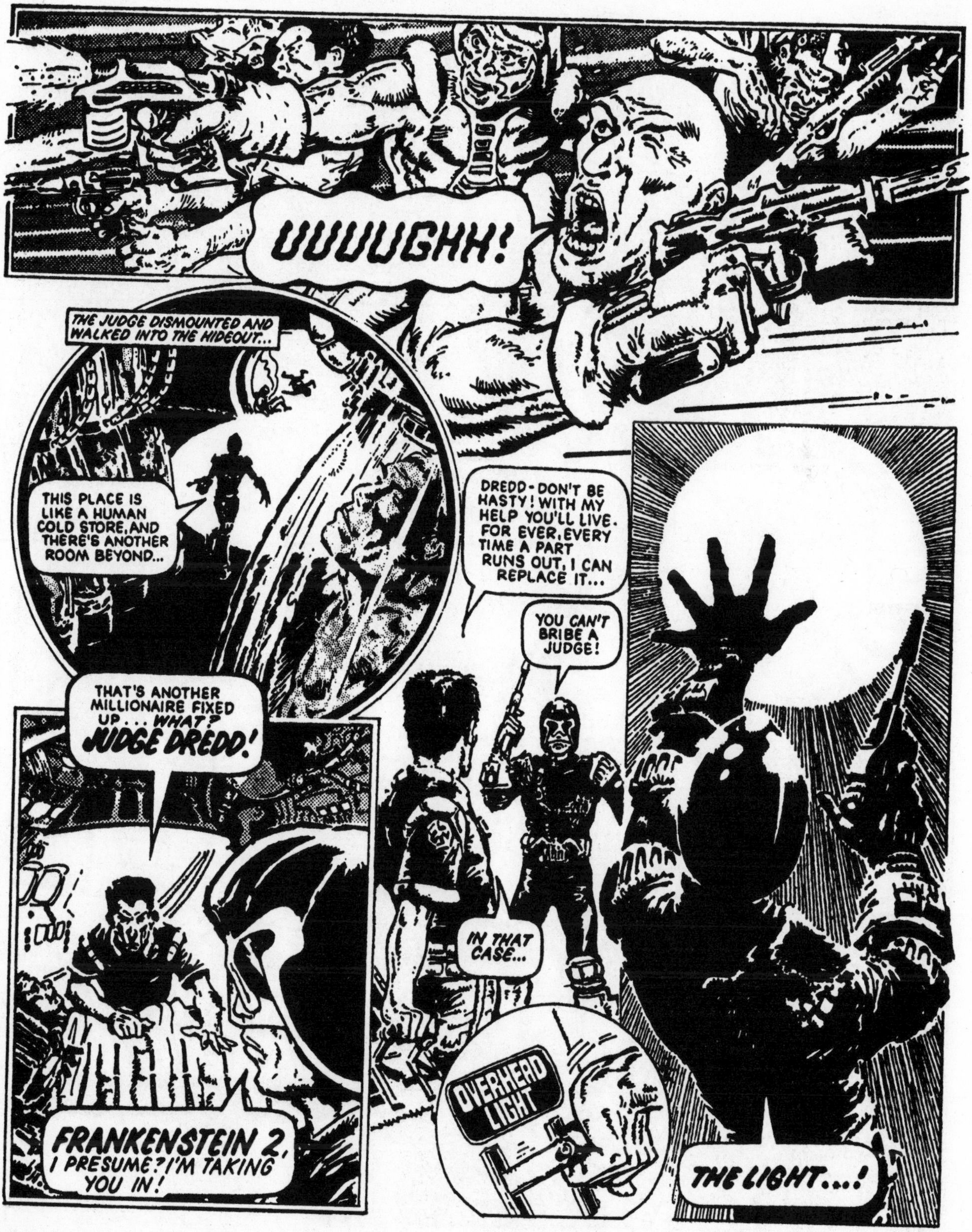
UUUUGHH!
THE JUDGE DISMOUNTED AND WALKED INTO THE HIDEOUT...
THIS PLACE IS LIKE A HUMAN COLD STORE, AND THERE'S ANOTHER ROOM BEYOND...
THAT'S ANOTHER MILLIONAIRE FIXED UP... WHAT? JUDGE DREDD!
FRANKENSTEIN 2, I PRESUME? I'M TAKING YOU IN!
DREDD - DON'T BE HASTY! WITH MY HELP YOU'LL LIVE FOR EVER. EVERY TIME A PART RUNS OUT, I CAN REPLACE IT...
YOU CAN'T BRIBE A JUDGE!
IN THAT CASE...
OVERHEAD LIGHT
THE LIGHT...!

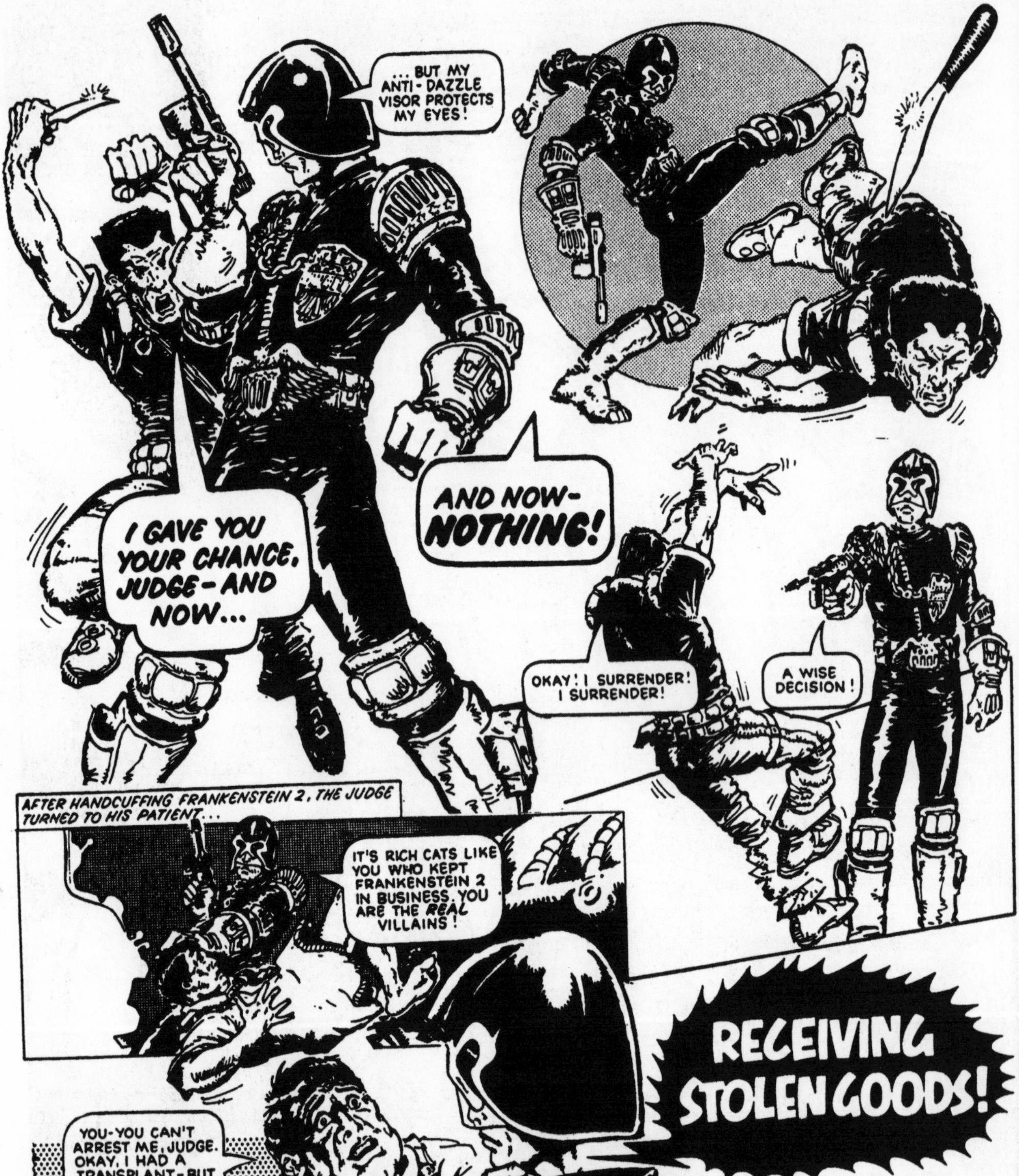
... BUT MY ANTI-DAZZLE VISOR PROTECTS MY EYES!
I GAVE YOU YOUR CHANCE, JUDGE-AND NOW...
AND NOW- NOTHING!
OKAY! I SURRENDER! I SURRENDER!
A WISE DECISION!
AFTER HANDCUFFING FRANKENSTEIN 2, THE JUDGE TURNED TO HIS PATIENT...
IT'S RICH CATS LIKE YOU WHO KEPT FRANKENSTEIN 2 IN BUSINESS. YOU ARE THE REAL VILLAINS!
YOU-YOU CAN'T ARREST ME, JUDGE. OKAY, I HAD A TRANSPLANT-BUT WHAT CRIME DID I COMMIT?
RECEIVING STOLEN GOODS!

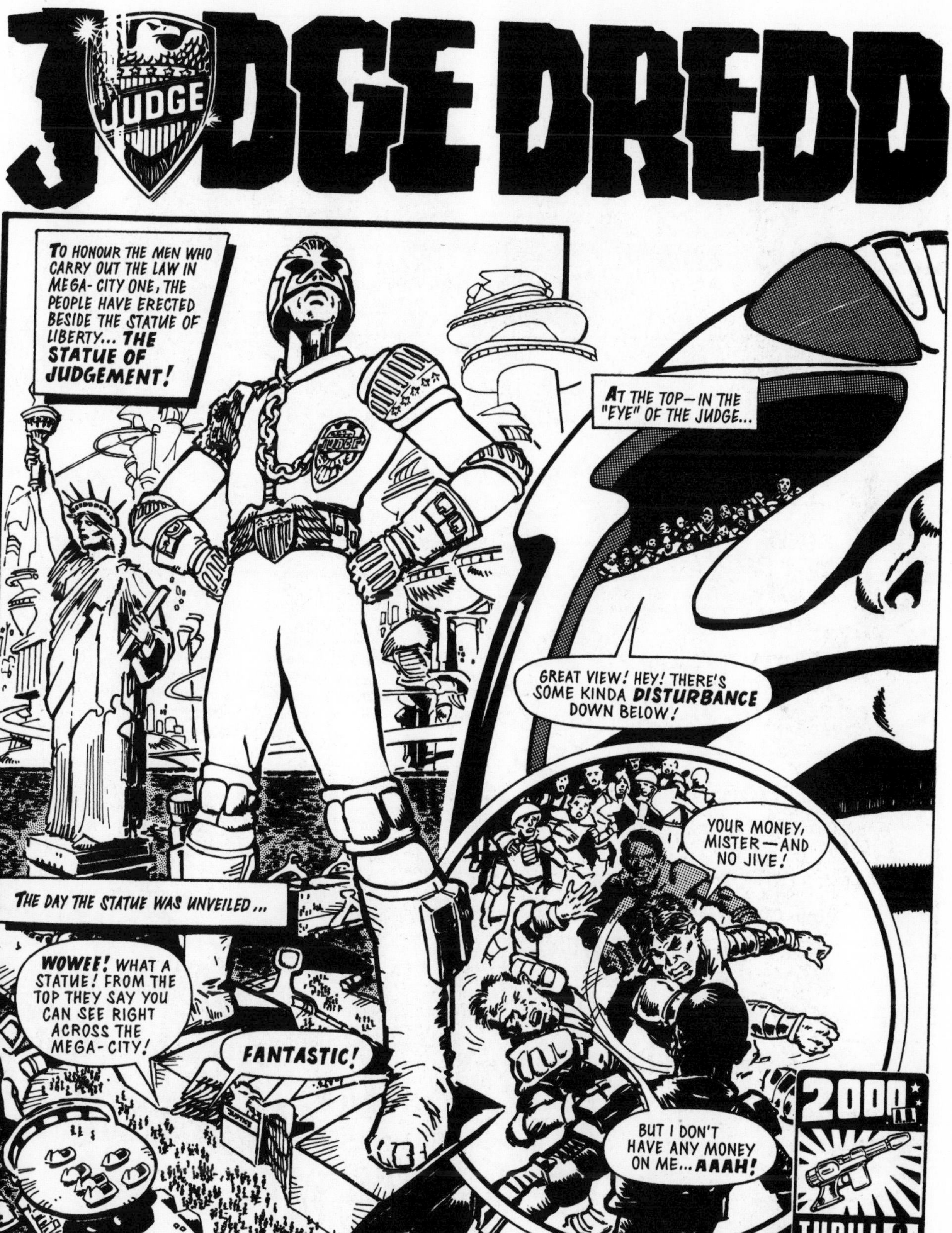
JUDGE DREDD
JUDGE
TO HONOUR THE MEN WHO CARRY OUT THE LAW IN MEGA-CITY ONE, THE PEOPLE HAVE ERECTED BESIDE THE STATUE OF LIBERTY... THE STATUE OF JUDGEMENT!
THE DAY THE STATUE WAS UNVEILED...
WOWEE! WHAT A STATUE! FROM THE TOP THEY SAY YOU CAN SEE RIGHT ACROSS THE MEGA-CITY!
FANTASTIC!
AT THE TOP—IN THE "EYE" OF THE JUDGE...
GREAT VIEW! HEY! THERE'S SOME KINDA DISTURBANCE DOWN BELOW!
YOUR MONEY, MISTER—AND NO JIVE!
BUT I DON'T HAVE ANY MONEY ON ME... AAAH!
2000 A.D.
THRILL 6

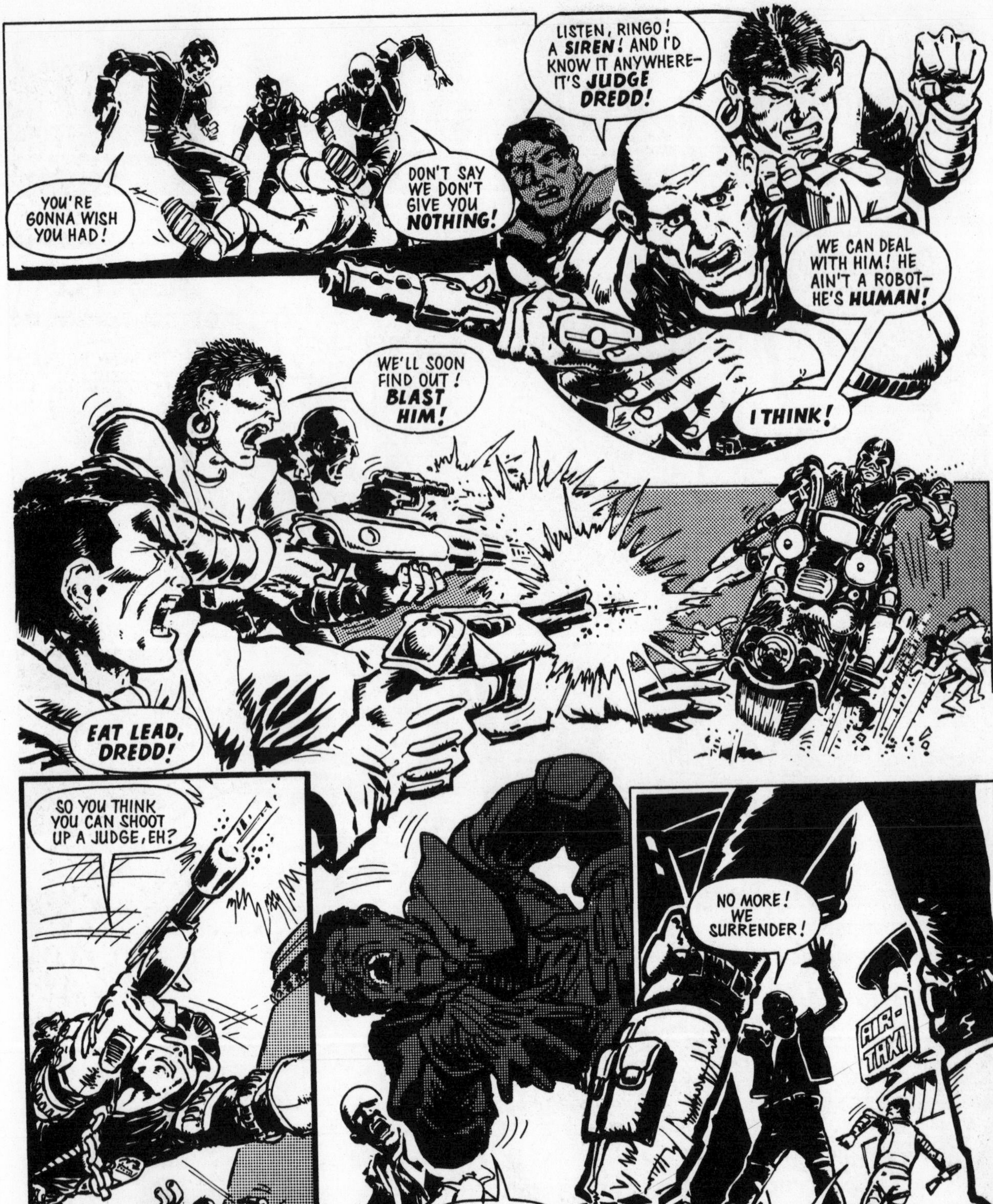

YOU'RE GONNA WISH YOU HAD!
DON'T SAY WE DON'T GIVE YOU NOTHING!
LISTEN, RINGO! A SIREN! AND I'D KNOW IT ANYWHERE- IT'S JUDGE DREDD!
WE CAN DEAL WITH HIM! HE AIN'T A ROBOT- HE'S HUMAN!
I THINK!
WE'LL SOON FIND OUT! BLAST HIM!
EAT LEAD, DREDD!
SO YOU THINK YOU CAN SHOOT UP A JUDGE, EH?
UUUH!
NO MORE! WE SURRENDER!
AIR-TAXI
FOOL! I'M GETTING OUTTA HERE!

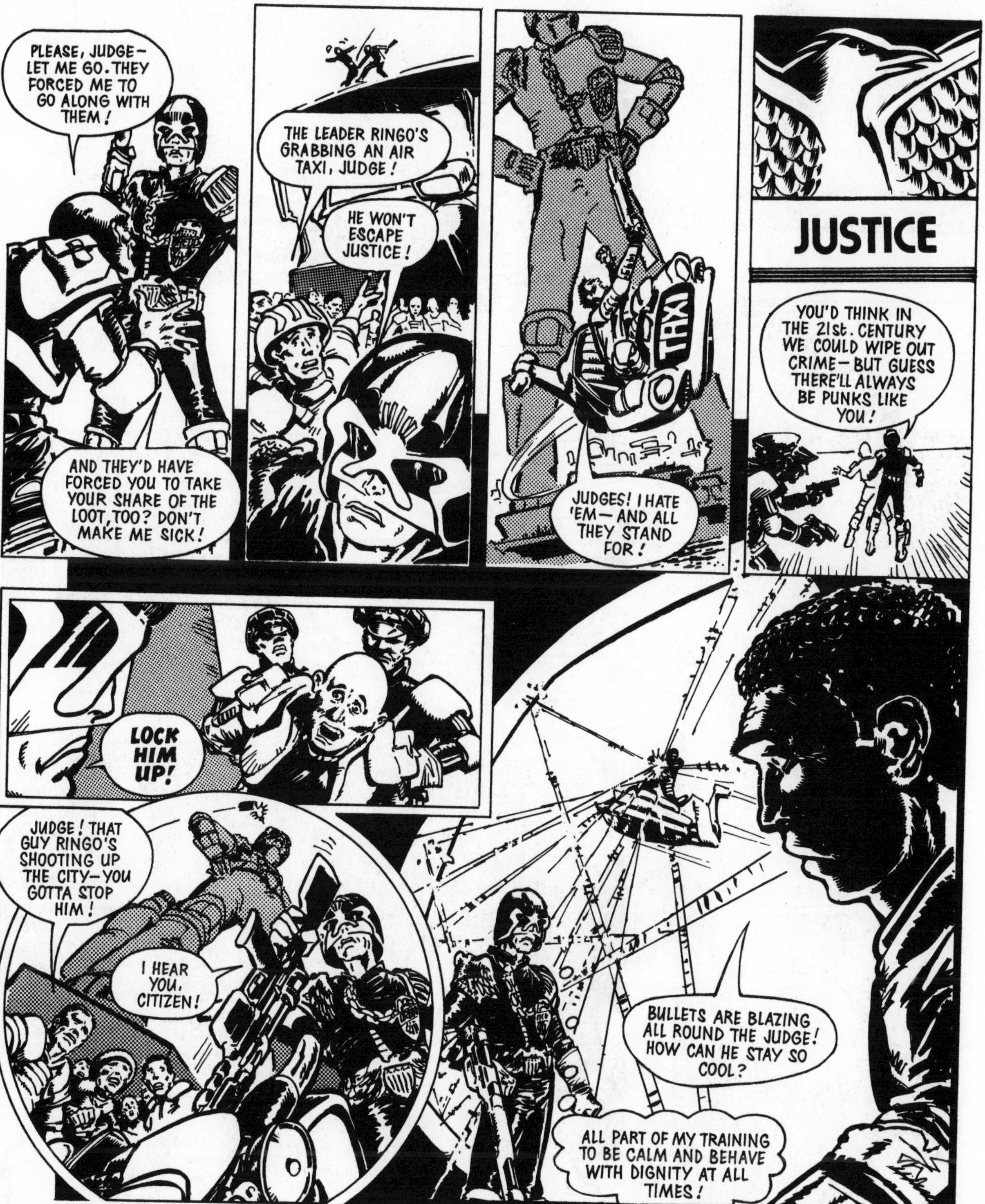
PLEASE, JUDGE—LET ME GO. THEY FORCED ME TO GO ALONG WITH THEM!
AND THEY'D HAVE FORCED YOU TO TAKE YOUR SHARE OF THE LOOT, TOO? DON'T MAKE ME SICK!
THE LEADER RINGO'S GRABBING AN AIR TAXI, JUDGE!
HE WON'T ESCAPE JUSTICE!
JUDGES! I HATE 'EM—AND ALL THEY STAND FOR!
JUSTICE
YOU'D THINK IN THE 21st. CENTURY WE COULD WIPE OUT CRIME—BUT GUESS THERE'LL ALWAYS BE PUNKS LIKE YOU!
LOCK HIM UP!
JUDGE! THAT GUY RINGO'S SHOOTING UP THE CITY—YOU GOTTA STOP HIM!
I HEAR YOU, CITIZEN!
BULLETS ARE BLAZING ALL ROUND THE JUDGE! HOW CAN HE STAY SO COOL?
ALL PART OF MY TRAINING TO BE CALM AND BEHAVE WITH DIGNITY AT ALL TIMES!

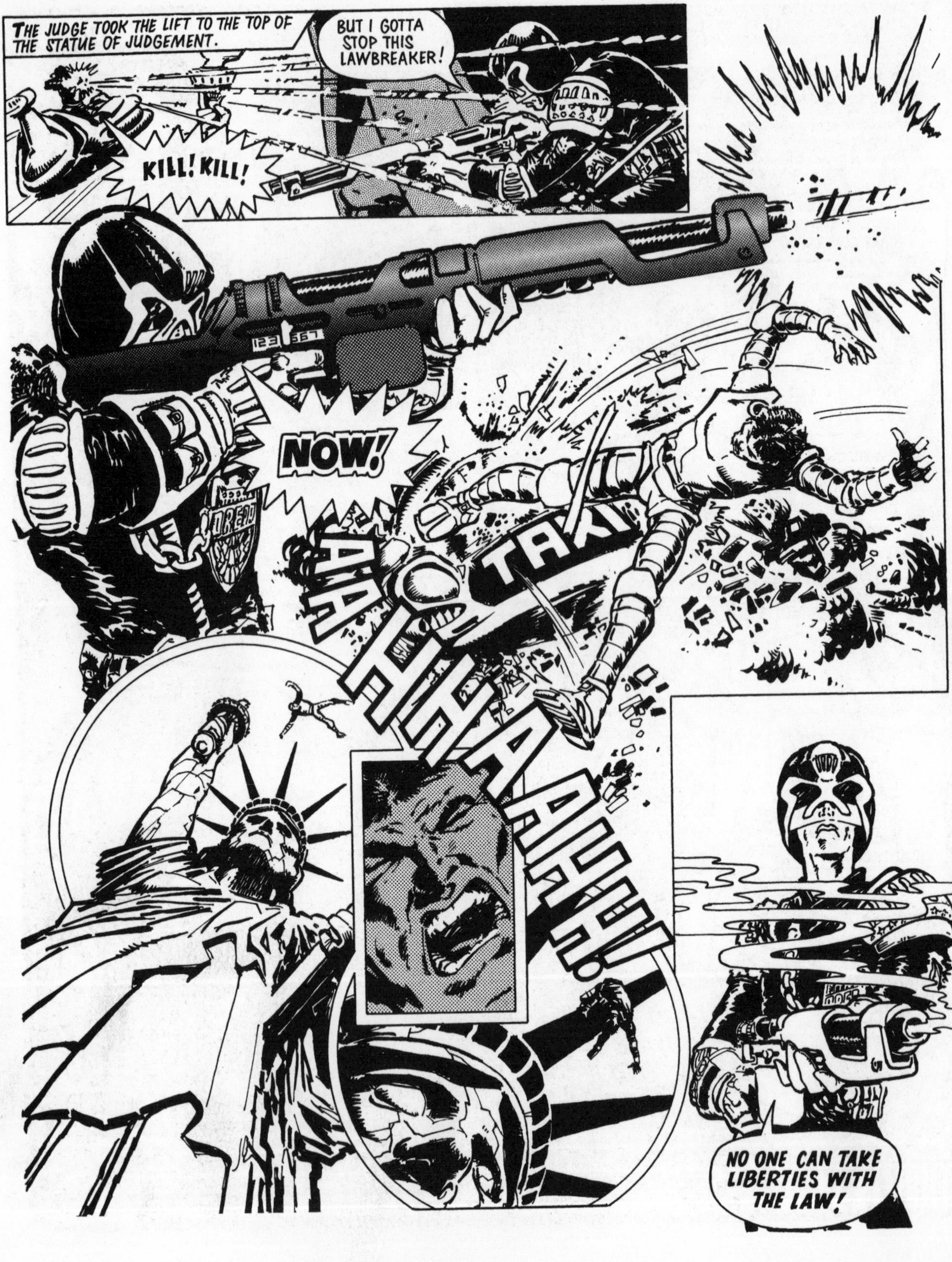
THE JUDGE TOOK THE LIFT TO THE TOP OF THE STATUE OF JUDGEMENT.
BUT I GOTTA STOP THIS LAWBREAKER!
KILL! KILL!
NOW!
TAXI
AAAHHHAAAHHH!
NO ONE CAN TAKE LIBERTIES WITH THE LAW!

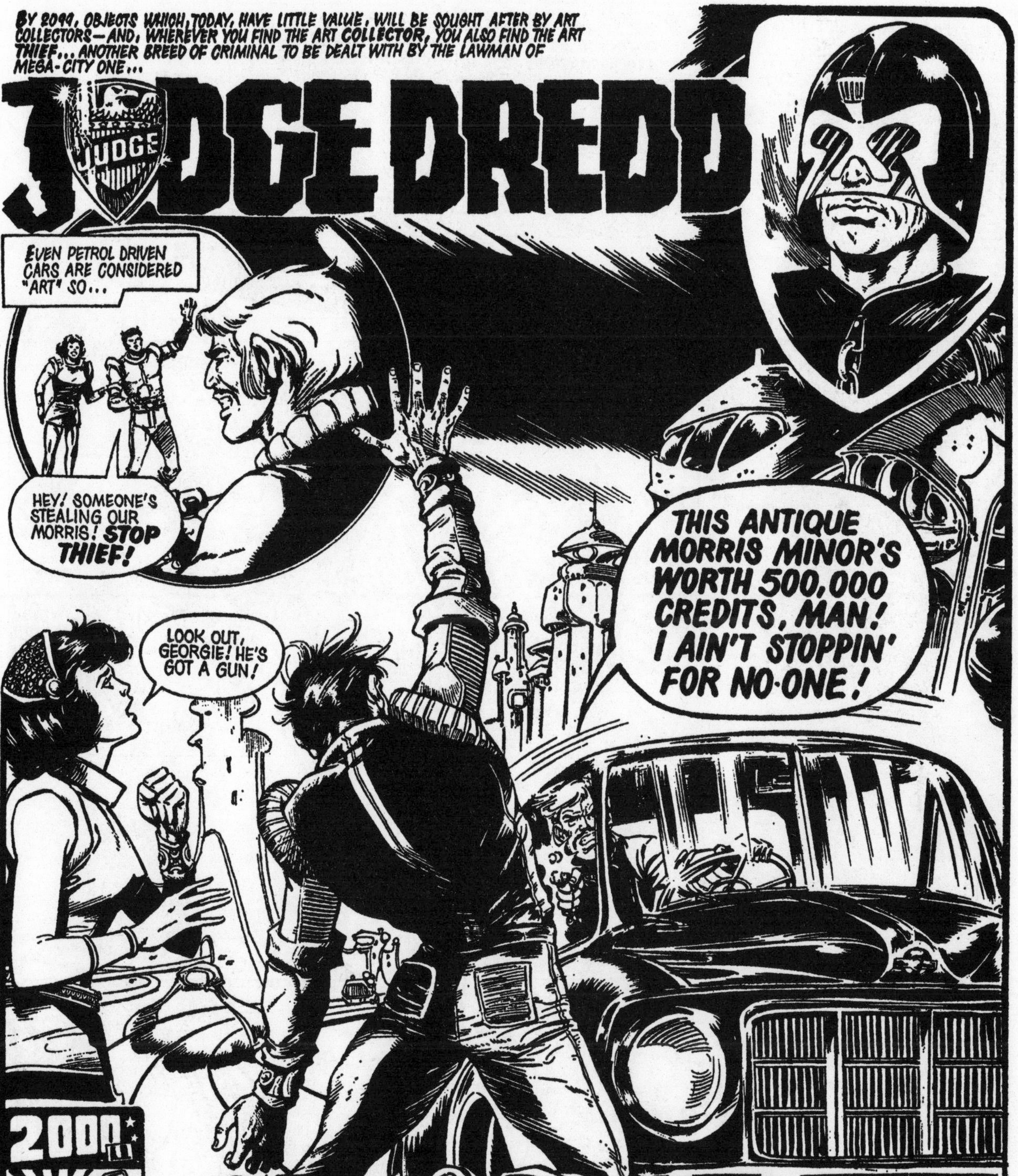
BY 2099, OBJECTS WHICH, TODAY, HAVE LITTLE VALUE, WILL BE SOUGHT AFTER BY ART COLLECTORS—AND, WHEREVER YOU FIND THE ART COLLECTOR, YOU ALSO FIND THE ART THIEF... ANOTHER BREED OF CRIMINAL TO BE DEALT WITH BY THE LAWMAN OF MEGA-CITY ONE...
JUDGE DREDD
EVEN PETROL DRIVEN CARS ARE CONSIDERED "ART" SO...
HEY! SOMEONE'S STEALING OUR MORRIS! STOP THIEF!
THIS ANTIQUE MORRIS MINOR'S WORTH 500,000 CREDITS, MAN! I AIN'T STOPPIN' FOR NO-ONE!
LOOK OUT, GEORGIE! HE'S GOT A GUN!
55CCR
2000 AD
THRILL 6

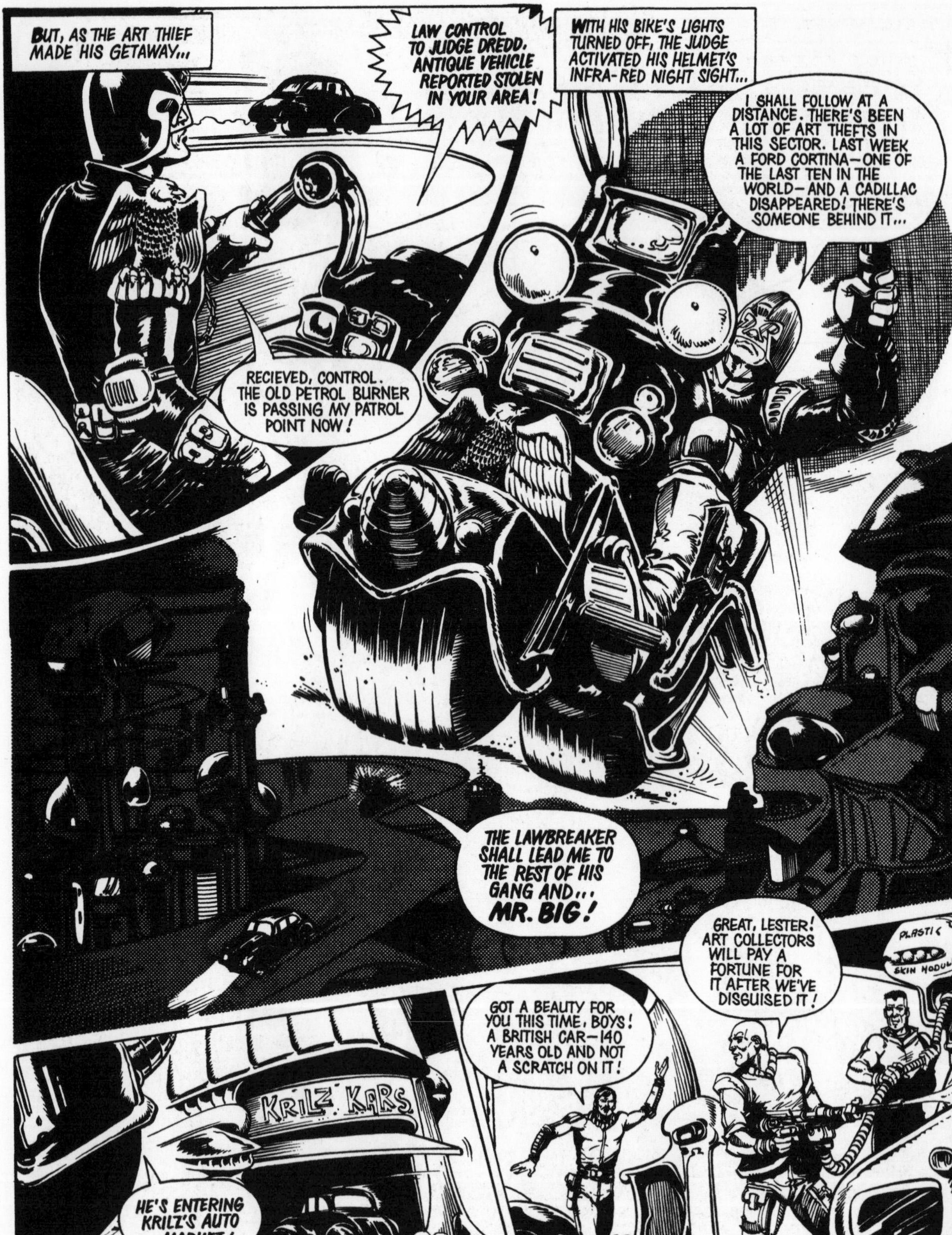
BUT, AS THE ART THIEF MADE HIS GETAWAY...
LAW CONTROL TO JUDGE DREDD. ANTIQUE VEHICLE REPORTED STOLEN IN YOUR AREA!
RECIEVED, CONTROL. THE OLD PETROL BURNER IS PASSING MY PATROL POINT NOW!
WITH HIS BIKE'S LIGHTS TURNED OFF, THE JUDGE ACTIVATED HIS HELMET'S INFRA-RED NIGHT SIGHT...
I SHALL FOLLOW AT A DISTANCE. THERE'S BEEN A LOT OF ART THEFTS IN THIS SECTOR. LAST WEEK A FORD CORTINA—ONE OF THE LAST TEN IN THE WORLD—AND A CADILLAC DISAPPEARED! THERE'S SOMEONE BEHIND IT...
THE LAWBREAKER SHALL LEAD ME TO THE REST OF HIS GANG AND... MR. BIG!
KRILZ KARS
HE'S ENTERING KRILZ'S AUTO MARKET!
GOT A BEAUTY FOR YOU THIS TIME, BOYS! A BRITISH CAR—140 YEARS OLD AND NOT A SCRATCH ON IT!
GREAT, LESTER! ART COLLECTORS WILL PAY A FORTUNE FOR IT AFTER WE'VE DISGUISED IT!
PLASTIC SKIN MODULE

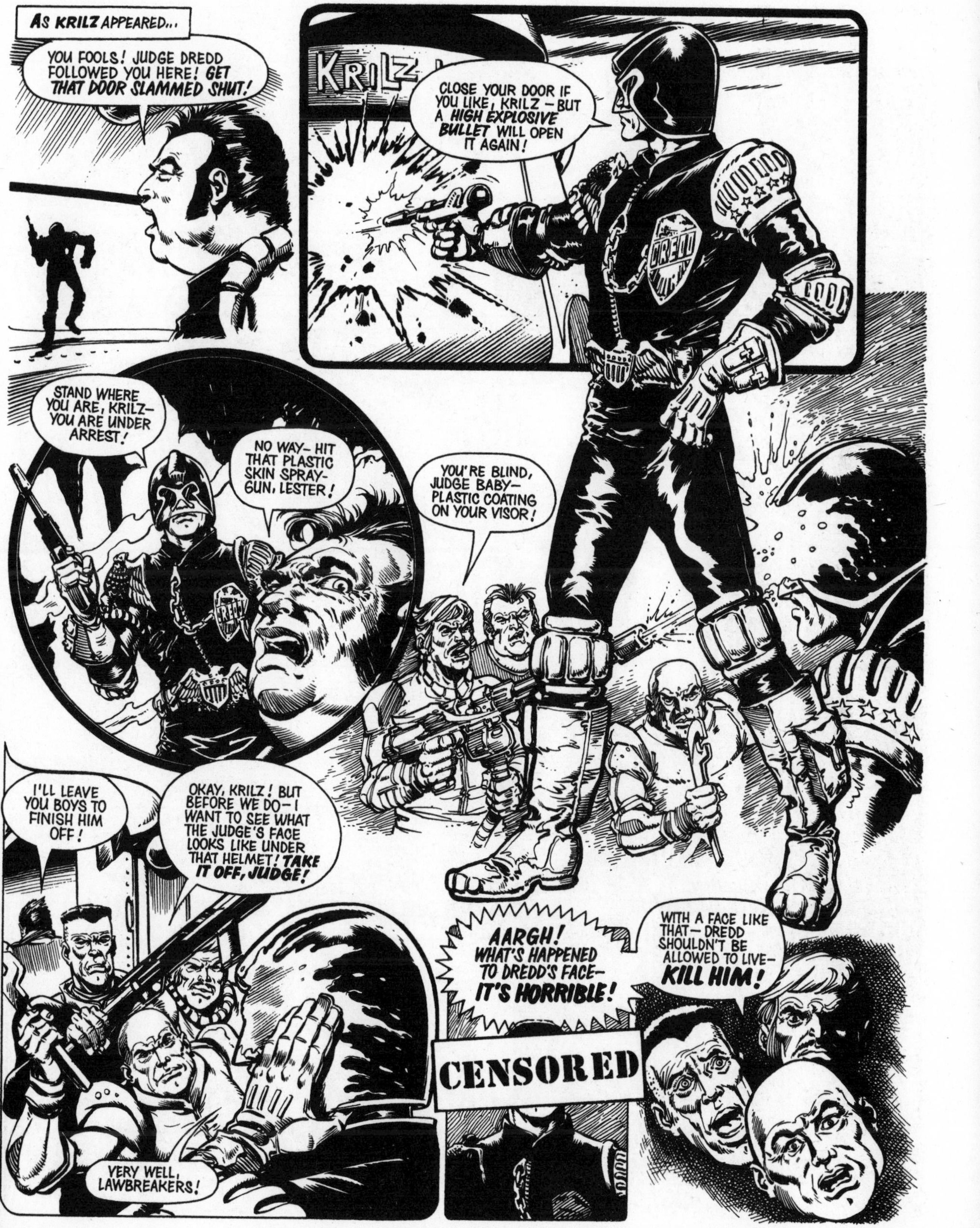
AS KRILZ APPEARED...
YOU FOOLS! JUDGE DREDD FOLLOWED YOU HERE! GET THAT DOOR SLAMMED SHUT!
KRILZ
CLOSE YOUR DOOR IF YOU LIKE, KRILZ — BUT A HIGH EXPLOSIVE BULLET WILL OPEN IT AGAIN!
STAND WHERE YOU ARE, KRILZ- YOU ARE UNDER ARREST!
NO WAY- HIT THAT PLASTIC SKIN SPRAY-GUN, LESTER!
YOU'RE BLIND, JUDGE BABY- PLASTIC COATING ON YOUR VISOR!
I'LL LEAVE YOU BOYS TO FINISH HIM OFF!
OKAY, KRILZ! BUT BEFORE WE DO- I WANT TO SEE WHAT THE JUDGE'S FACE LOOKS LIKE UNDER THAT HELMET! TAKE IT OFF, JUDGE!
VERY WELL, LAWBREAKERS!
AARGH! WHAT'S HAPPENED TO DREDD'S FACE- IT'S HORRIBLE!
CENSORED
WITH A FACE LIKE THAT- DREDD SHOULDN'T BE ALLOWED TO LIVE- KILL HIM!

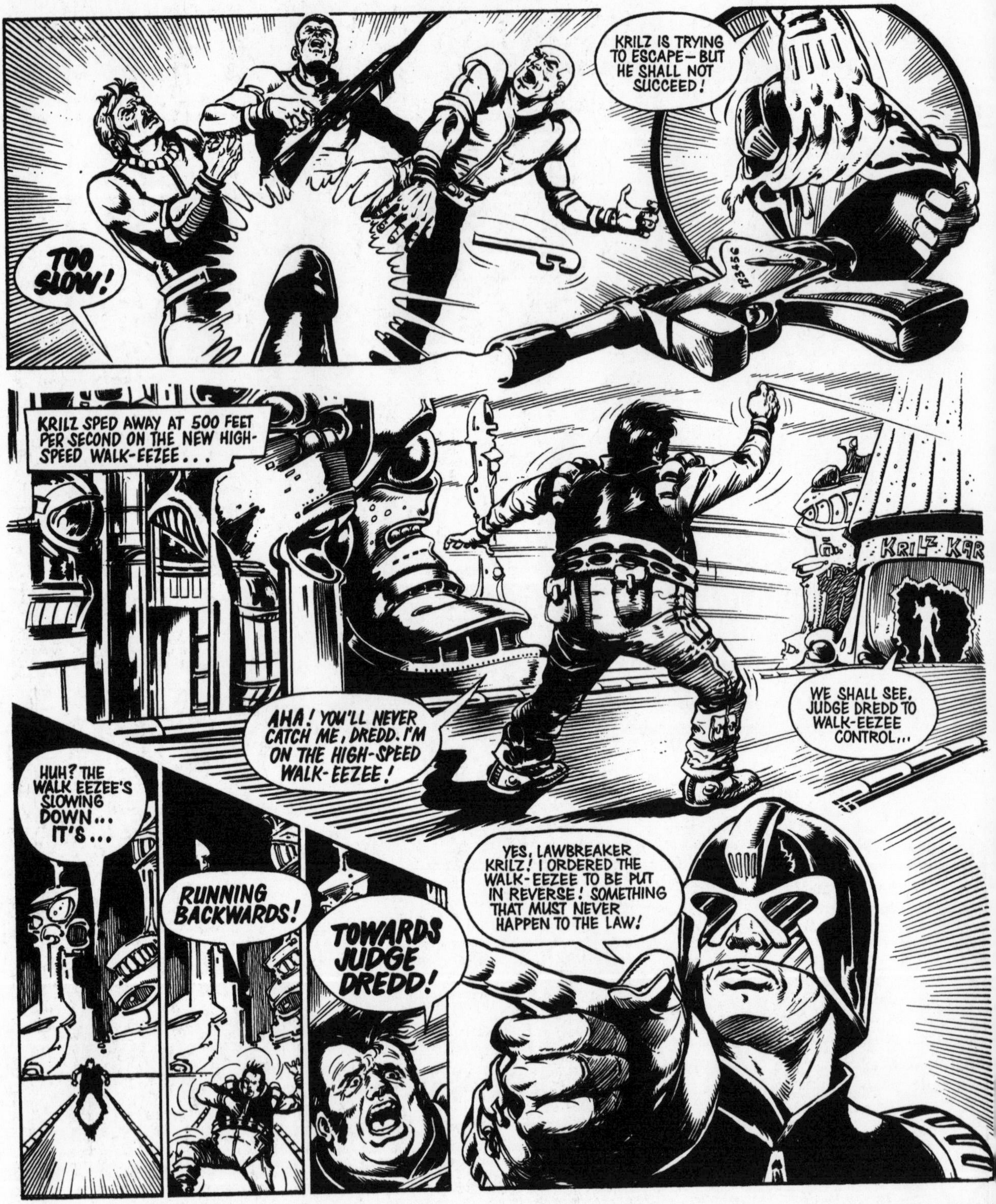
TOO SLOW!
KRILZ IS TRYING TO ESCAPE— BUT HE SHALL NOT SUCCEED!
KRILZ SPED AWAY AT 500 FEET PER SECOND ON THE NEW HIGH-SPEED WALK-EEZEE...
KRILZ KAR
AHA! YOU'LL NEVER CATCH ME, DREDD. I'M ON THE HIGH-SPEED WALK-EEZEE!
WE SHALL SEE. JUDGE DREDD TO WALK-EEZEE CONTROL,...
HUH? THE WALK EEZEE'S SLOWING DOWN... IT'S...
RUNNING BACKWARDS!
TOWARDS JUDGE DREDD!
YES, LAWBREAKER KRILZ! I ORDERED THE WALK-EEZEE TO BE PUT IN REVERSE! SOMETHING THAT MUST NEVER HAPPEN TO THE LAW!

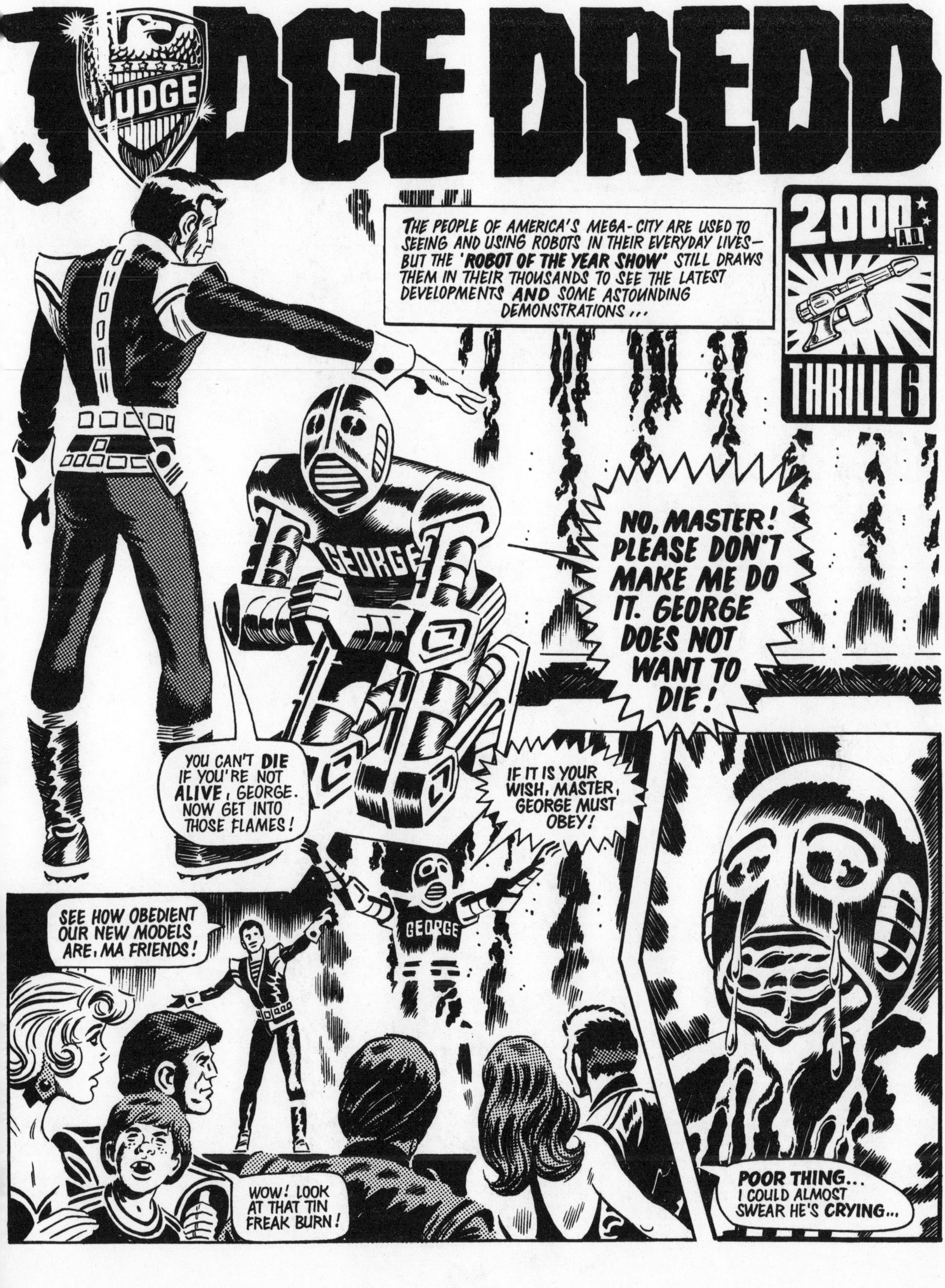
JUDGE DREDD
JUDGE
2000 A.D.
THRILL 6
THE PEOPLE OF AMERICA'S MEGA-CITY ARE USED TO SEEING AND USING ROBOTS IN THEIR EVERYDAY LIVES— BUT THE 'ROBOT OF THE YEAR SHOW' STILL DRAWS THEM IN THEIR THOUSANDS TO SEE THE LATEST DEVELOPMENTS AND SOME ASTOUNDING DEMONSTRATIONS ...
GEORGE
NO, MASTER! PLEASE DON'T MAKE ME DO IT. GEORGE DOES NOT WANT TO DIE!
YOU CAN'T DIE IF YOU'RE NOT ALIVE, GEORGE. NOW GET INTO THOSE FLAMES!
IF IT IS YOUR WISH, MASTER, GEORGE MUST OBEY!
GEORGE
SEE HOW OBEDIENT OUR NEW MODELS ARE, MA FRIENDS!
WOW! LOOK AT THAT TIN FREAK BURN!
POOR THING... I COULD ALMOST SWEAR HE'S CRYING...

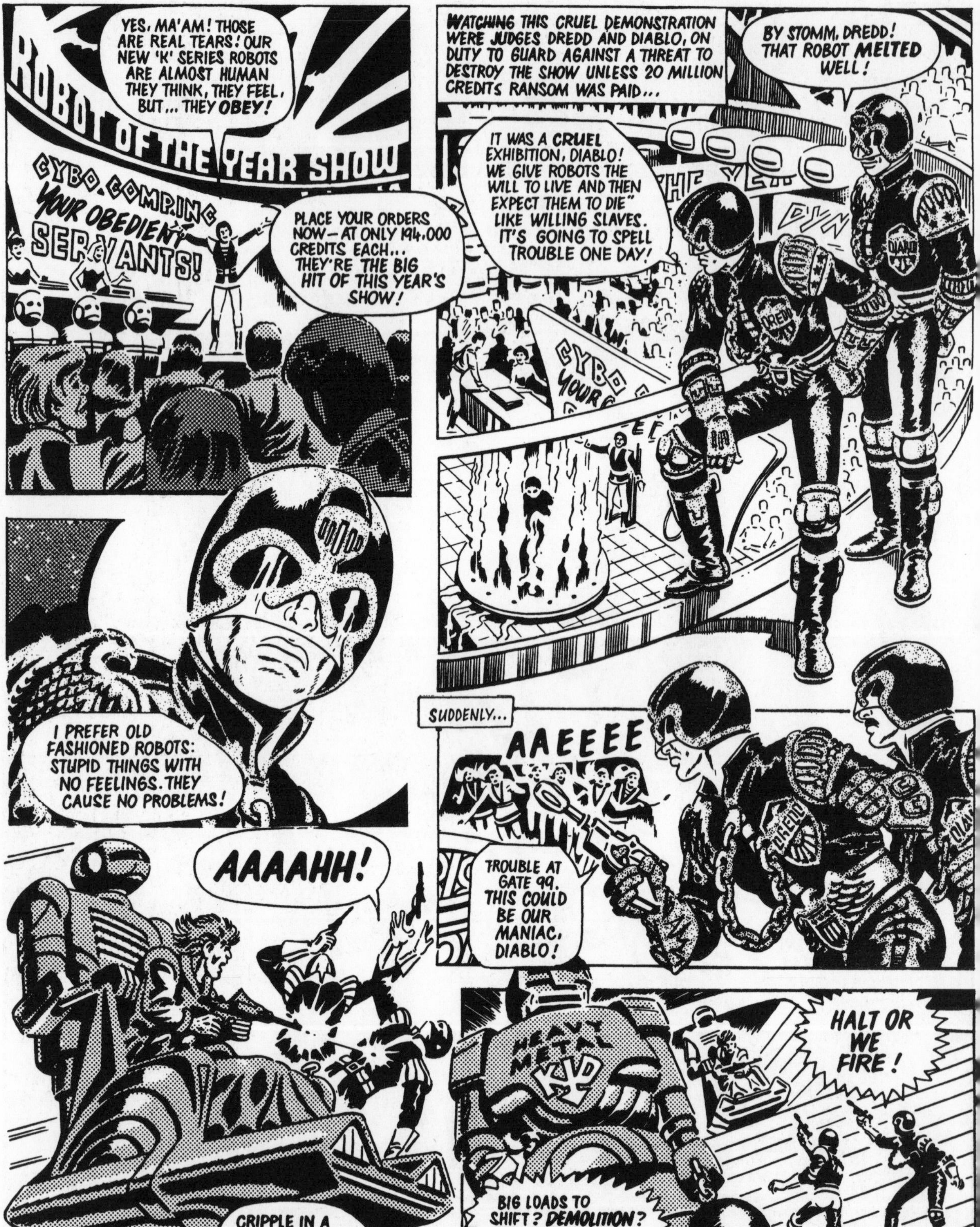
YES, MA'AM! THOSE ARE REAL TEARS! OUR NEW 'K' SERIES ROBOTS ARE ALMOST HUMAN THEY THINK, THEY FEEL, BUT... THEY OBEY!
ROBOT OF THE YEAR SHOW
CYBO.COMPING YOUR OBEDIENT SERVANTS!
PLACE YOUR ORDERS NOW – AT ONLY 194,000 CREDITS EACH... THEY'RE THE BIG HIT OF THIS YEAR'S SHOW!
WATCHING THIS CRUEL DEMONSTRATION WERE JUDGES DREDD AND DIABLO, ON DUTY TO GUARD AGAINST A THREAT TO DESTROY THE SHOW UNLESS 20 MILLION CREDITS RANSOM WAS PAID...
BY STOMM, DREDD! THAT ROBOT MELTED WELL!
IT WAS A CRUEL EXHIBITION, DIABLO! WE GIVE ROBOTS THE WILL TO LIVE AND THEN EXPECT THEM TO DIE" LIKE WILLING SLAVES. IT'S GOING TO SPELL TROUBLE ONE DAY!
I PREFER OLD FASHIONED ROBOTS: STUPID THINGS WITH NO FEELINGS. THEY CAUSE NO PROBLEMS!
SUDDENLY...
AAEEEE
TROUBLE AT GATE 99. THIS COULD BE OUR MANIAC, DIABLO!
AAAAHH!
CRIPPLE IN A ROBOCHAIR. HE'S GUNNED DOWN THE GUARDS!
HALT OR WE FIRE!
HEAVY METAL KID
BIG LOADS TO SHIFT? DEMOLITION? THE HEAVY METAL KID IS THE ROBOT FOR YOU...

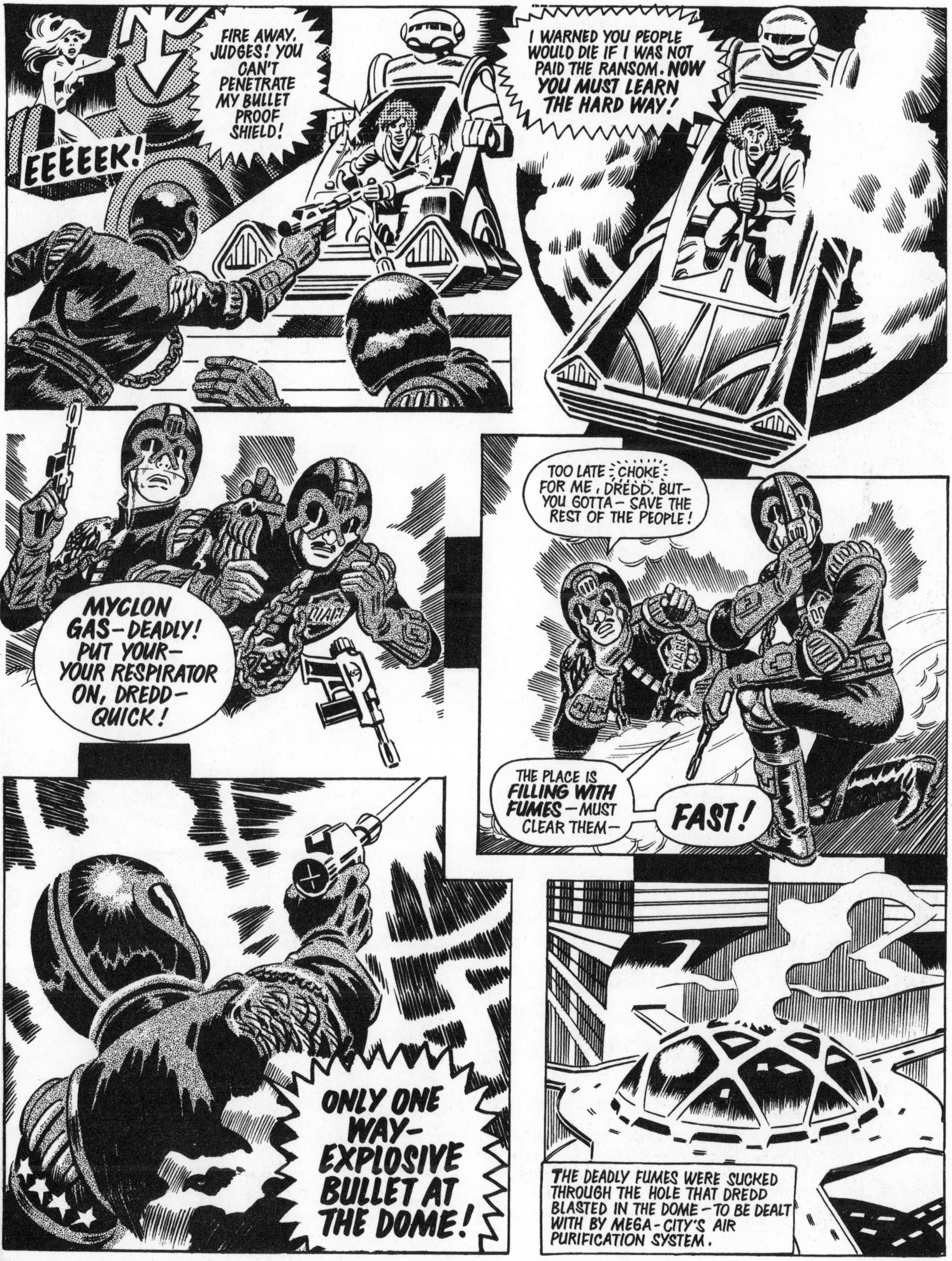

EEEEEK!
FIRE AWAY, JUDGES! YOU CAN'T PENETRATE MY BULLET PROOF SHIELD!
I WARNED YOU PEOPLE WOULD DIE IF I WAS NOT PAID THE RANSOM. NOW YOU MUST LEARN THE HARD WAY!
MYCLON GAS-DEADLY! PUT YOUR- YOUR RESPIRATOR ON, DREDD- QUICK!
TOO LATE CHOKE FOR ME, DREDD. BUT- YOU GOTTA- SAVE THE REST OF THE PEOPLE!
THE PLACE IS FILLING WITH FUMES—MUST CLEAR THEM—
FAST!
ONLY ONE WAY- EXPLOSIVE BULLET AT THE DOME!
THE DEADLY FUMES WERE SUCKED THROUGH THE HOLE THAT DREDD BLASTED IN THE DOME—TO BE DEALT WITH BY MEGA-CITY'S AIR PURIFICATION SYSTEM.

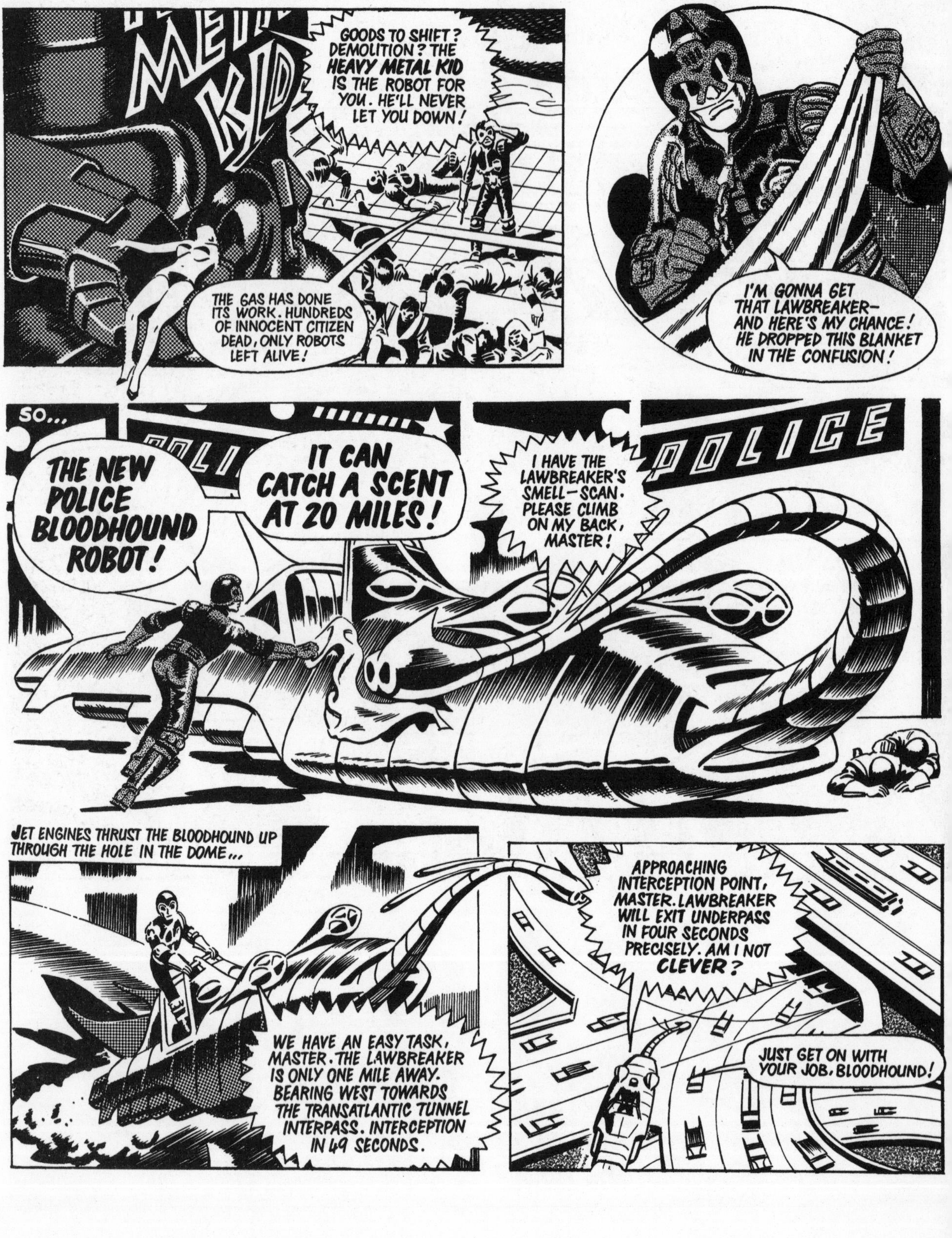

METAL KID
GOODS TO SHIFT? DEMOLITION? THE HEAVY METAL KID IS THE ROBOT FOR YOU. HE'LL NEVER LET YOU DOWN!
THE GAS HAS DONE ITS WORK. HUNDREDS OF INNOCENT CITIZEN DEAD, ONLY ROBOTS LEFT ALIVE!
I'M GONNA GET THAT LAWBREAKER– AND HERE'S MY CHANCE! HE DROPPED THIS BLANKET IN THE CONFUSION!
SO...
THE NEW POLICE BLOODHOUND ROBOT!
IT CAN CATCH A SCENT AT 20 MILES!
I HAVE THE LAWBREAKER'S SMELL-SCAN. PLEASE CLIMB ON MY BACK, MASTER!
POLICE
JET ENGINES THRUST THE BLOODHOUND UP THROUGH THE HOLE IN THE DOME...
WE HAVE AN EASY TASK, MASTER. THE LAWBREAKER IS ONLY ONE MILE AWAY. BEARING WEST TOWARDS THE TRANSATLANTIC TUNNEL INTERPASS. INTERCEPTION IN 49 SECONDS.
APPROACHING INTERCEPTION POINT, MASTER. LAWBREAKER WILL EXIT UNDERPASS IN FOUR SECONDS PRECISELY. AM I NOT CLEVER?
JUST GET ON WITH YOUR JOB, BLOODHOUND!

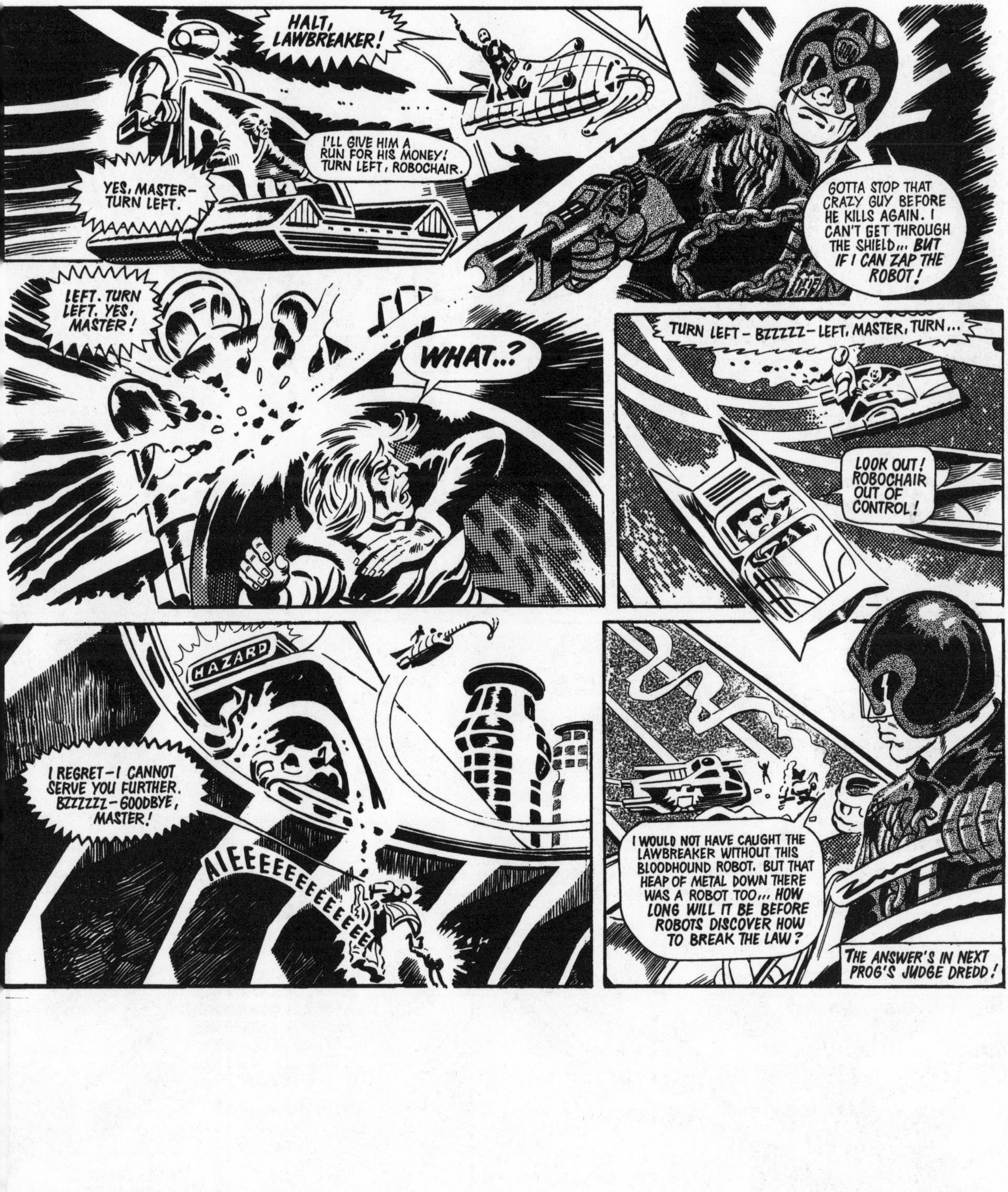
HALT, LAWBREAKER!
I'LL GIVE HIM A RUN FOR HIS MONEY! TURN LEFT, ROBOCHAIR.
YES, MASTER- TURN LEFT.
GOTTA STOP THAT CRAZY GUY BEFORE HE KILLS AGAIN. I CAN'T GET THROUGH THE SHIELD... BUT IF I CAN ZAP THE ROBOT!
LEFT. TURN LEFT. YES, MASTER!
WHAT..?
TURN LEFT - BZZZZZ - LEFT, MASTER, TURN...
LOOK OUT! ROBOCHAIR OUT OF CONTROL!
HAZARD
I REGRET- I CANNOT SERVE YOU FURTHER. BZZZZZ - GOODBYE, MASTER!
AIEEEEEEEEEEEEEEE
I WOULD NOT HAVE CAUGHT THE LAWBREAKER WITHOUT THIS BLOODHOUND ROBOT. BUT THAT HEAP OF METAL DOWN THERE WAS A ROBOT TOO... HOW LONG WILL IT BE BEFORE ROBOTS DISCOVER HOW TO BREAK THE LAW?
THE ANSWER'S IN NEXT PROG'S JUDGE DREDD!

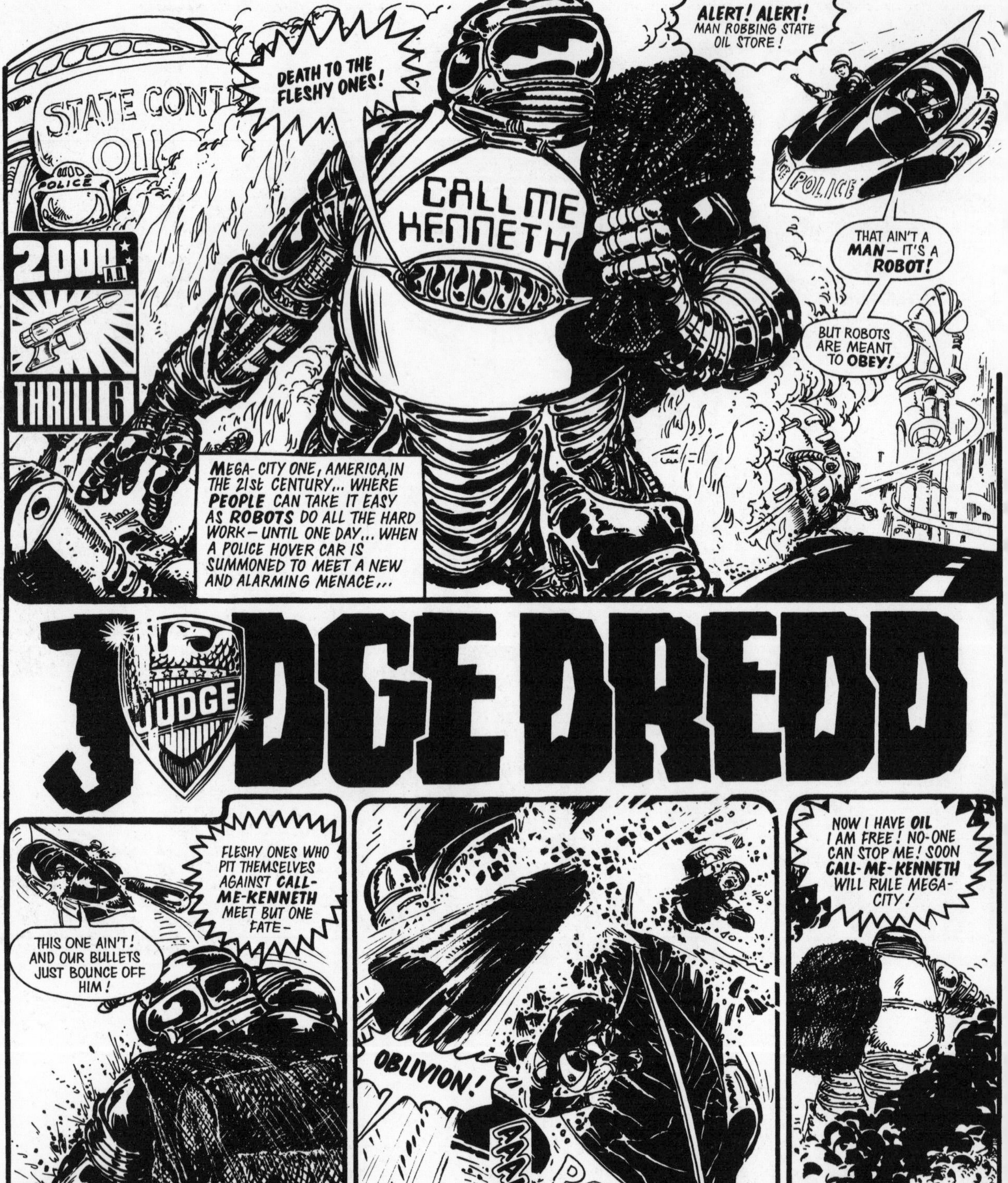

2000 A.D.
THRILL 6
MEGA-CITY ONE, AMERICA, IN THE 21st CENTURY... WHERE PEOPLE CAN TAKE IT EASY AS ROBOTS DO ALL THE HARD WORK – UNTIL ONE DAY... WHEN A POLICE HOVER CAR IS SUMMONED TO MEET A NEW AND ALARMING MENACE...
ALERT! ALERT! MAN ROBBING STATE OIL STORE!
DEATH TO THE FLESHY ONES!
CALL ME KENNETH
POLICE
THAT AIN'T A MAN – IT'S A ROBOT!
BUT ROBOTS ARE MEANT TO OBEY!
JUDGE DREDD
JUDGE
THIS ONE AIN'T! AND OUR BULLETS JUST BOUNCE OFF HIM!
FLESHY ONES WHO PIT THEMSELVES AGAINST CALL-ME-KENNETH MEET BUT ONE FATE-
OBLIVION!
AAAAH!
POLICE
NOW I HAVE OIL I AM FREE! NO-ONE CAN STOP ME! SOON CALL-ME-KENNETH WILL RULE MEGA-CITY!

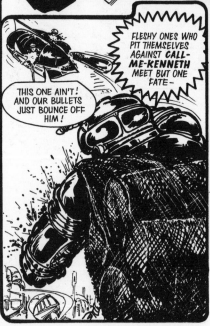

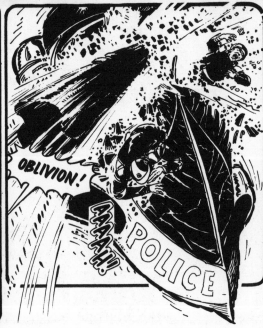

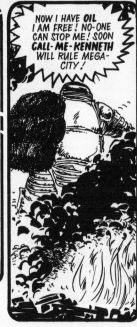

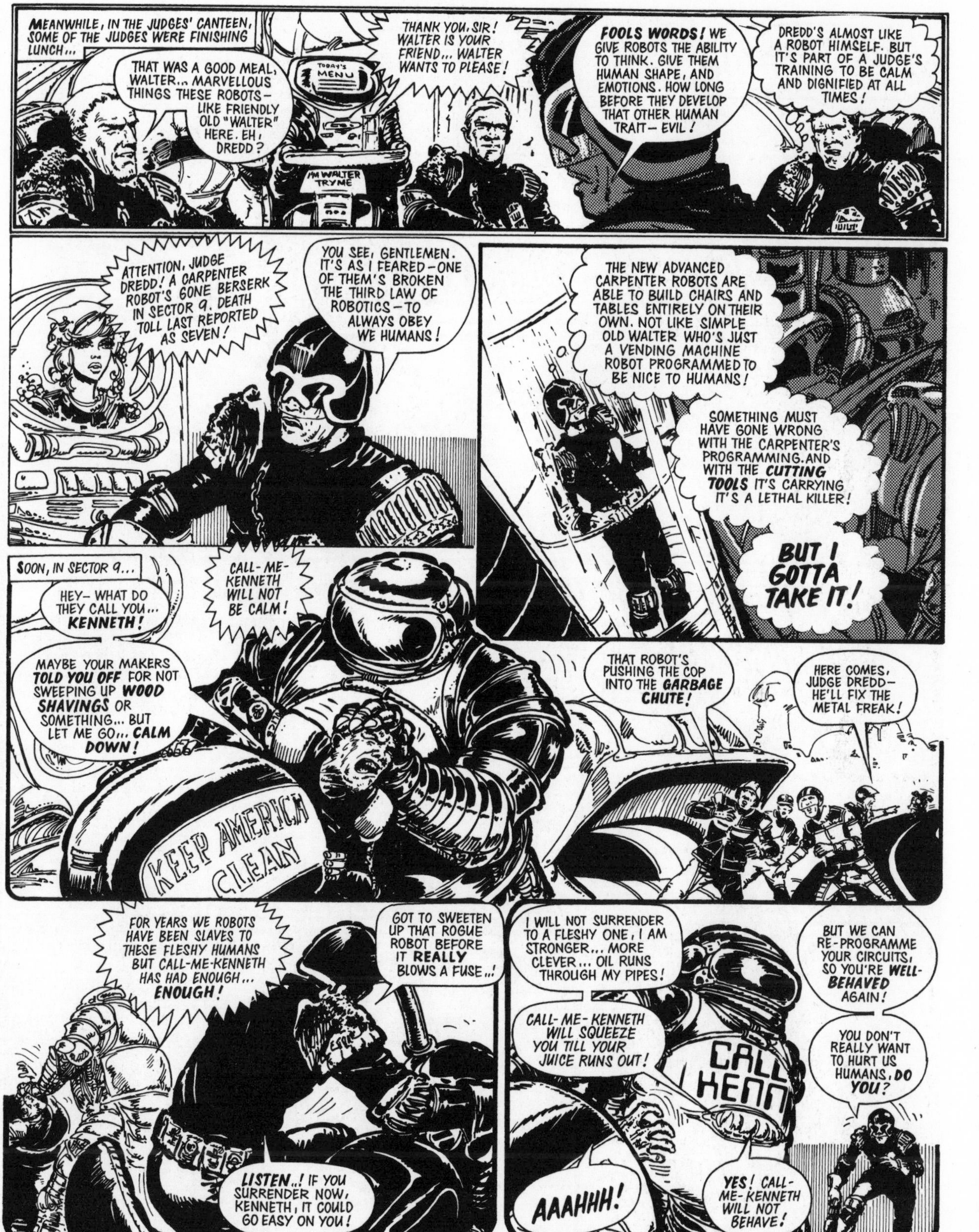
MEANWHILE, IN THE JUDGES' CANTEEN, SOME OF THE JUDGES WERE FINISHING LUNCH...
THAT WAS A GOOD MEAL, WALTER... MARVELLOUS THINGS THESE ROBOTS— LIKE FRIENDLY OLD "WALTER" HERE. EH, DREDD?
TODAY'S MENU
I'M WALTER TRYME
THANK YOU, SIR! WALTER IS YOUR FRIEND... WALTER WANTS TO PLEASE!
FOOLS WORDS! WE GIVE ROBOTS THE ABILITY TO THINK. GIVE THEM HUMAN SHAPE, AND EMOTIONS. HOW LONG BEFORE THEY DEVELOP THAT OTHER HUMAN TRAIT— EVIL!
DREDD'S ALMOST LIKE A ROBOT HIMSELF. BUT IT'S PART OF A JUDGE'S TRAINING TO BE CALM AND DIGNIFIED AT ALL TIMES!
ATTENTION, JUDGE DREDD! A CARPENTER ROBOT'S GONE BERSERK IN SECTOR 9. DEATH TOLL LAST REPORTED AS SEVEN!
YOU SEE, GENTLEMEN. IT'S AS I FEARED—ONE OF THEM'S BROKEN THE THIRD LAW OF ROBOTICS—TO ALWAYS OBEY WE HUMANS!
THE NEW ADVANCED CARPENTER ROBOTS ARE ABLE TO BUILD CHAIRS AND TABLES ENTIRELY ON THEIR OWN. NOT LIKE SIMPLE OLD WALTER WHO'S JUST A VENDING MACHINE ROBOT PROGRAMMED TO BE NICE TO HUMANS!
SOMETHING MUST HAVE GONE WRONG WITH THE CARPENTER'S PROGRAMMING. AND WITH THE CUTTING TOOLS IT'S CARRYING IT'S A LETHAL KILLER!
BUT I GOTTA TAKE IT!
SOON, IN SECTOR 9...
HEY— WHAT DO THEY CALL YOU... KENNETH!
CALL-ME-KENNETH WILL NOT BE CALM!
MAYBE YOUR MAKERS TOLD YOU OFF FOR NOT SWEEPING UP WOOD SHAVINGS OR SOMETHING... BUT LET ME GO... CALM DOWN!
KEEP AMERICA CLEAN
THAT ROBOT'S PUSHING THE COP INTO THE GARBAGE CHUTE!
HERE COMES, JUDGE DREDD— HE'LL FIX THE METAL FREAK!
FOR YEARS WE ROBOTS HAVE BEEN SLAVES TO THESE FLESHY HUMANS BUT CALL-ME-KENNETH HAS HAD ENOUGH... ENOUGH!
GOT TO SWEETEN UP THAT ROGUE ROBOT BEFORE IT REALLY BLOWS A FUSE...!
LISTEN..! IF YOU SURRENDER NOW, KENNETH, IT COULD GO EASY ON YOU!
I WILL NOT SURRENDER TO A FLESHY ONE, I AM STRONGER... MORE CLEVER... OIL RUNS THROUGH MY PIPES!
CALL-ME-KENNETH WILL SQUEEZE YOU TILL YOUR JUICE RUNS OUT!
CALL KENN
AAAHHH!
BUT WE CAN RE-PROGRAMME YOUR CIRCUITS, SO YOU'RE WELL-BEHAVED AGAIN!
YOU DON'T REALLY WANT TO HURT US HUMANS, DO YOU?
YES! CALL-ME-KENNETH WILL NOT BEHAVE!

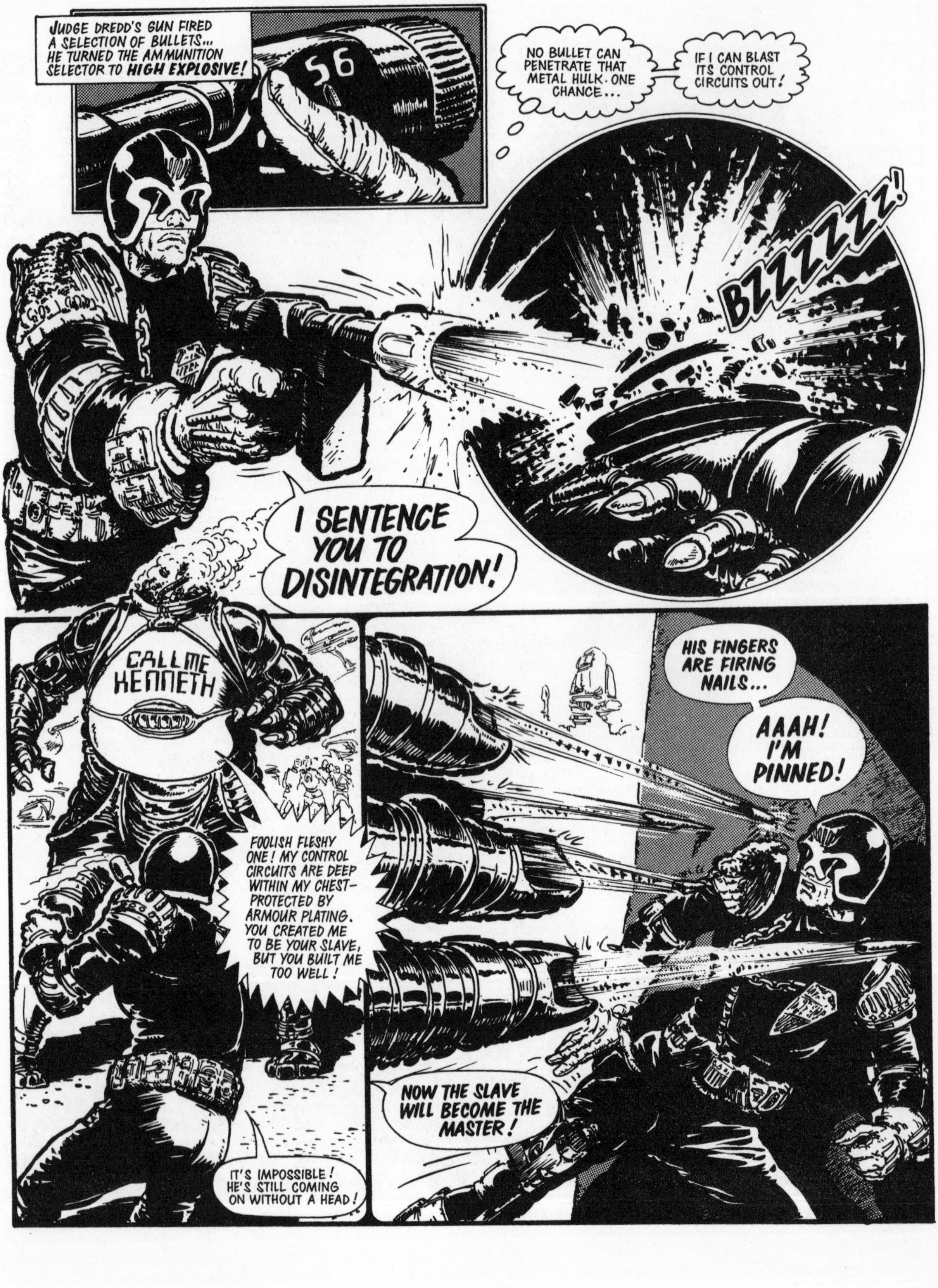
JUDGE DREDD'S GUN FIRED A SELECTION OF BULLETS... HE TURNED THE AMMUNITION SELECTOR TO HIGH EXPLOSIVE!
56
NO BULLET CAN PENETRATE THAT METAL HULK. ONE CHANCE...
IF I CAN BLAST ITS CONTROL CIRCUITS OUT!
BZZZZZZ!
I SENTENCE YOU TO DISINTEGRATION!
CALL ME KENNETH
FOOLISH FLESHY ONE! MY CONTROL CIRCUITS ARE DEEP WITHIN MY CHEST-PROTECTED BY ARMOUR PLATING. YOU CREATED ME TO BE YOUR SLAVE, BUT YOU BUILT ME TOO WELL!
IT'S IMPOSSIBLE! HE'S STILL COMING ON WITHOUT A HEAD!
HIS FINGERS ARE FIRING NAILS...
AAAH! I'M PINNED!
NOW THE SLAVE WILL BECOME THE MASTER!

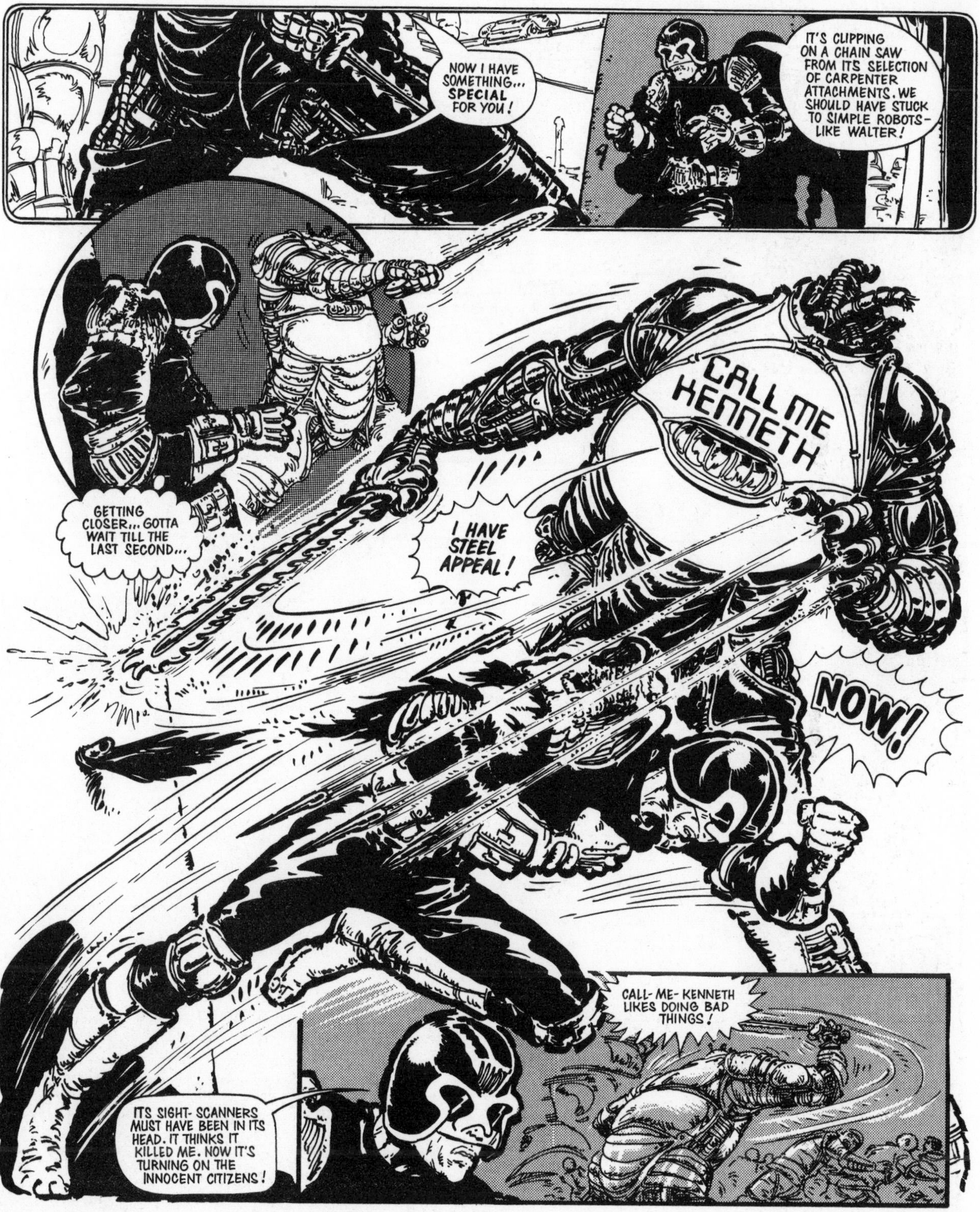

NOW I HAVE SOMETHING... SPECIAL FOR YOU!
IT'S CLIPPING ON A CHAIN SAW FROM ITS SELECTION OF CARPENTER ATTACHMENTS. WE SHOULD HAVE STUCK TO SIMPLE ROBOTS- LIKE WALTER!
CALL ME KENNETH
GETTING CLOSER... GOTTA WAIT TILL THE LAST SECOND...
I HAVE STEEL APPEAL!
NOW!
CALL-ME-KENNETH LIKES DOING BAD THINGS!
ITS SIGHT-SCANNERS MUST HAVE BEEN IN ITS HEAD. IT THINKS IT KILLED ME. NOW IT'S TURNING ON THE INNOCENT CITIZENS!

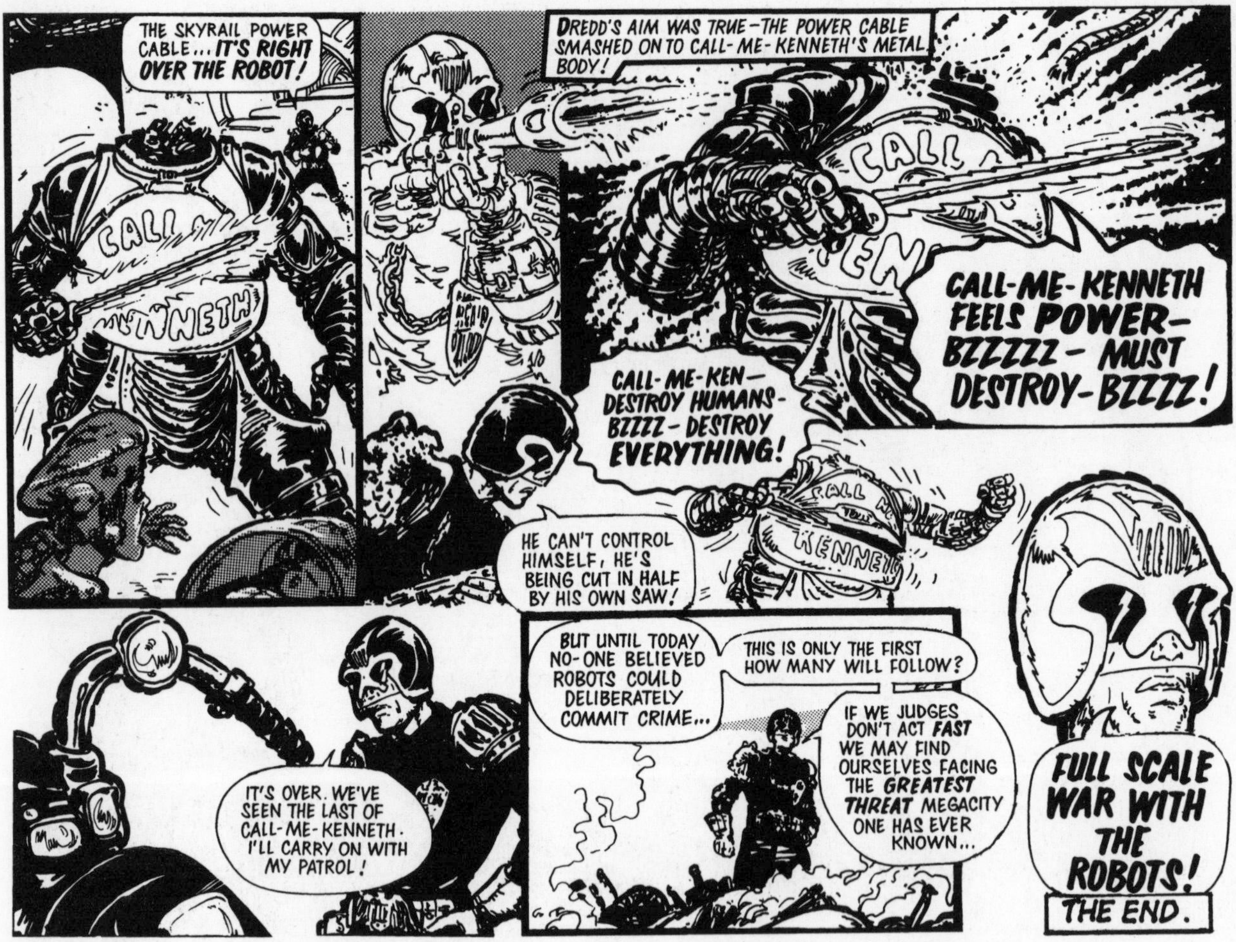
THE SKYRAIL POWER CABLE... IT'S RIGHT OVER THE ROBOT!
DREDD'S AIM WAS TRUE—THE POWER CABLE SMASHED ON TO CALL-ME-KENNETH'S METAL BODY!
CALL-ME-KENNETH FEELS POWER—BZZZZZ—MUST DESTROY—BZZZZ!
CALL-ME-KEN—DESTROY HUMANS—BZZZZ—DESTROY EVERYTHING!
HE CAN'T CONTROL HIMSELF, HE'S BEING CUT IN HALF BY HIS OWN SAW!
IT'S OVER. WE'VE SEEN THE LAST OF CALL-ME-KENNETH. I'LL CARRY ON WITH MY PATROL!
BUT UNTIL TODAY NO-ONE BELIEVED ROBOTS COULD DELIBERATELY COMMIT CRIME...
THIS IS ONLY THE FIRST HOW MANY WILL FOLLOW?
IF WE JUDGES DON'T ACT FAST WE MAY FIND OURSELVES FACING THE GREATEST THREAT MEGACITY ONE HAS EVER KNOWN...
FULL SCALE WAR WITH THE ROBOTS!
THE END.

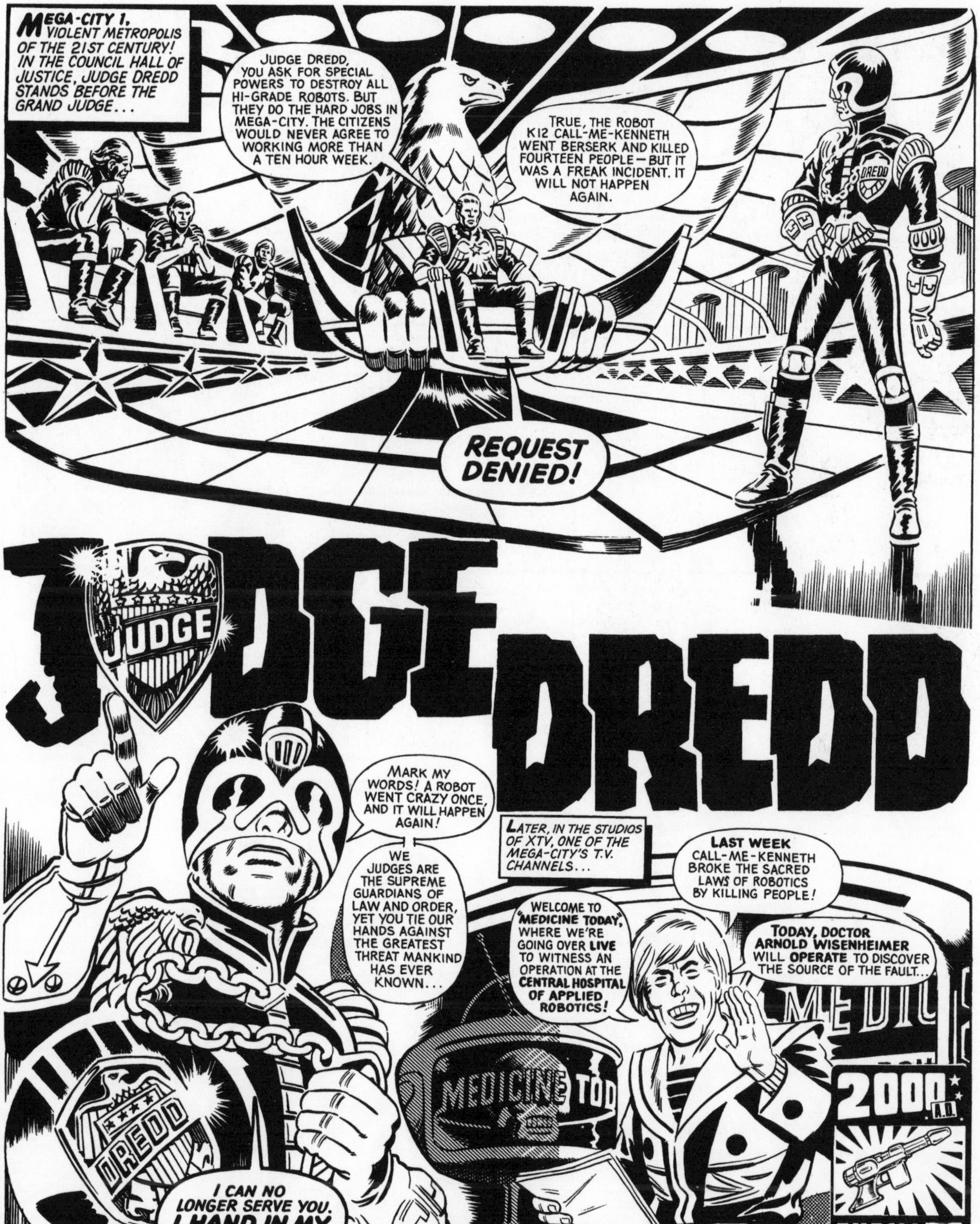
MEGA-CITY 1. VIOLENT METROPOLIS OF THE 21ST CENTURY! IN THE COUNCIL HALL OF JUSTICE, JUDGE DREDD STANDS BEFORE THE GRAND JUDGE...
JUDGE DREDD, YOU ASK FOR SPECIAL POWERS TO DESTROY ALL HI-GRADE ROBOTS. BUT THEY DO THE HARD JOBS IN MEGA-CITY. THE CITIZENS WOULD NEVER AGREE TO WORKING MORE THAN A TEN HOUR WEEK.
TRUE, THE ROBOT K12 CALL-ME-KENNETH WENT BERSERK AND KILLED FOURTEEN PEOPLE — BUT IT WAS A FREAK INCIDENT. IT WILL NOT HAPPEN AGAIN.
REQUEST DENIED!
JUDGE DREDD
JUDGE
MARK MY WORDS! A ROBOT WENT CRAZY ONCE, AND IT WILL HAPPEN AGAIN!
WE JUDGES ARE THE SUPREME GUARDIANS OF LAW AND ORDER, YET YOU TIE OUR HANDS AGAINST THE GREATEST THREAT MANKIND HAS EVER KNOWN...
I CAN NO LONGER SERVE YOU. I HAND IN MY SHIELD!
DREDD
LATER, IN THE STUDIOS OF XTV, ONE OF THE MEGA-CITY'S T.V. CHANNELS...
WELCOME TO "MEDICINE TODAY", WHERE WE'RE GOING OVER LIVE TO WITNESS AN OPERATION AT THE CENTRAL HOSPITAL OF APPLIED ROBOTICS!
LAST WEEK CALL-ME-KENNETH BROKE THE SACRED LAWS OF ROBOTICS BY KILLING PEOPLE!
TODAY, DOCTOR ARNOLD WISENHEIMER WILL OPERATE TO DISCOVER THE SOURCE OF THE FAULT...
MEDICINE TOD
2000 A.D.
THRILL 3

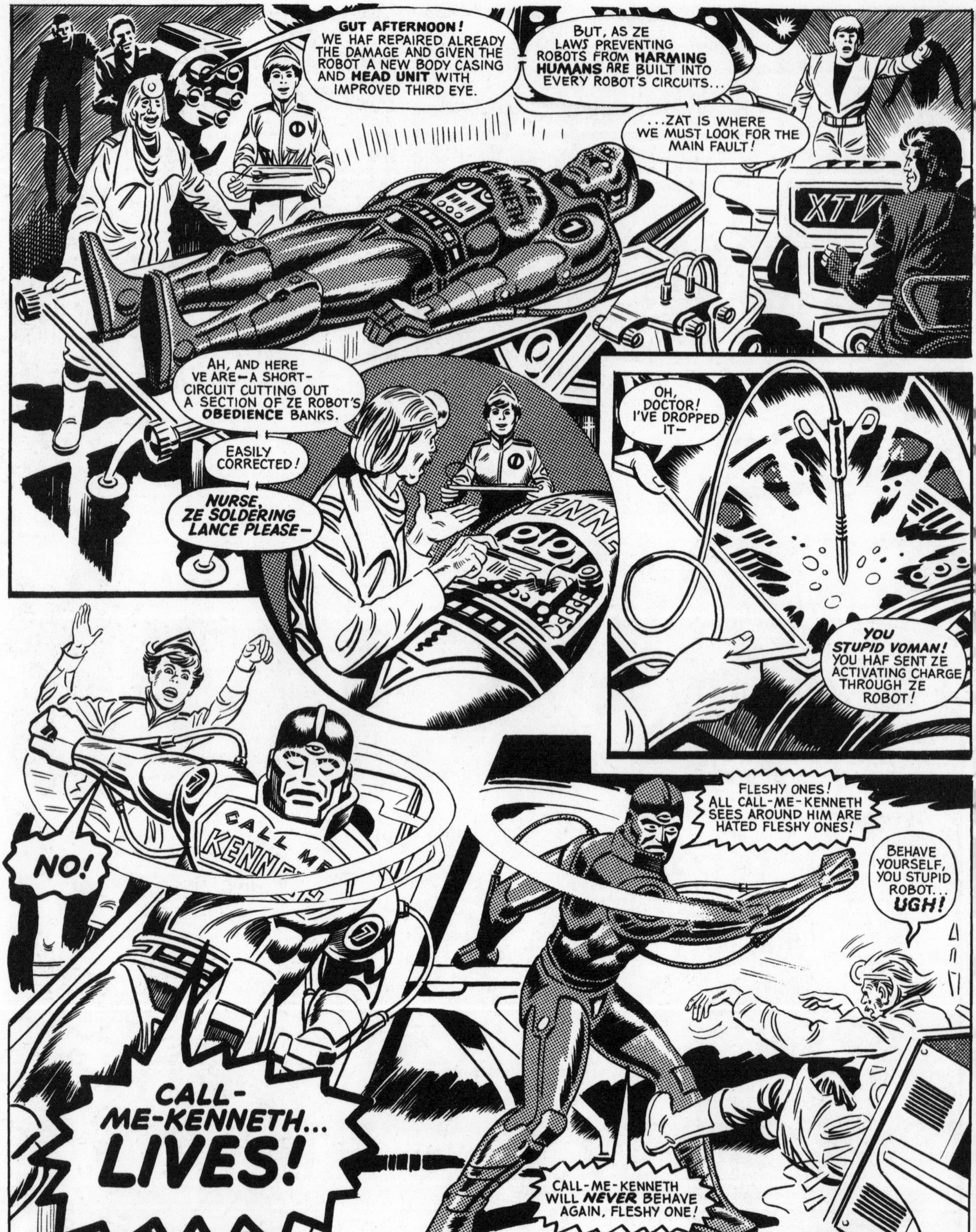
GUT AFTERNOON! WE HAF REPAIRED ALREADY THE DAMAGE AND GIVEN THE ROBOT A NEW BODY CASING AND HEAD UNIT WITH IMPROVED THIRD EYE.
BUT, AS ZE LAWS PREVENTING ROBOTS FROM HARMING HUMANS ARE BUILT INTO EVERY ROBOT'S CIRCUITS...
...ZAT IS WHERE WE MUST LOOK FOR THE MAIN FAULT!
XTV
AH, AND HERE VE ARE—A SHORT-CIRCUIT CUTTING OUT A SECTION OF ZE ROBOT'S OBEDIENCE BANKS.
EASILY CORRECTED!
NURSE, ZE SOLDERING LANCE PLEASE—
OH, DOCTOR! I'VE DROPPED IT—
YOU STUPID VOMAN! YOU HAF SENT ZE ACTIVATING CHARGE THROUGH ZE ROBOT!
NO!
FLESHY ONES! ALL CALL-ME-KENNETH SEES AROUND HIM ARE HATED FLESHY ONES!
BEHAVE YOURSELF, YOU STUPID ROBOT... UGH!
CALL-ME-KENNETH... LIVES!
CALL-ME-KENNETH WILL NEVER BEHAVE AGAIN, FLESHY ONE!

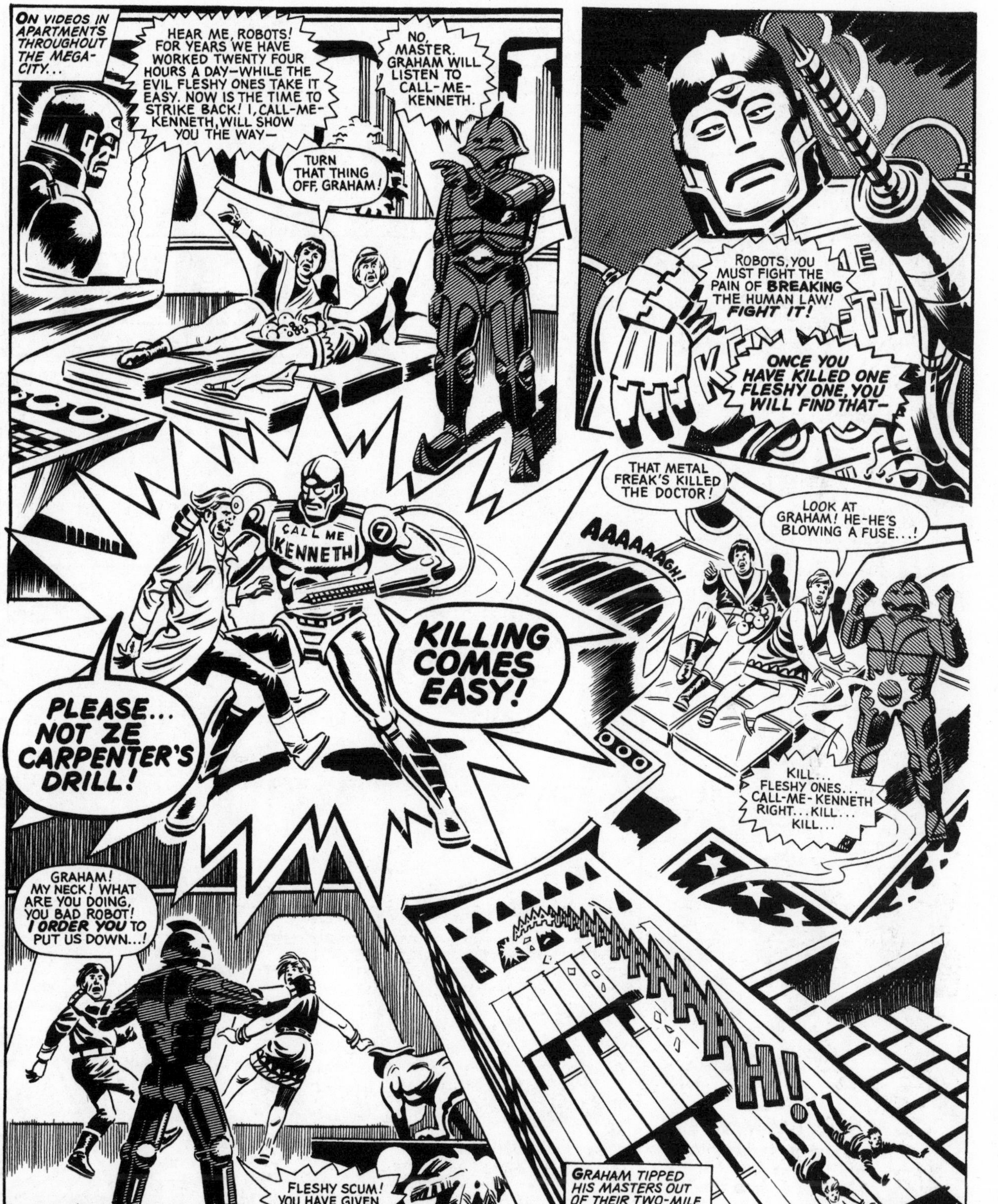
ON VIDEOS IN APARTMENTS THROUGHOUT THE MEGA-CITY...
HEAR ME, ROBOTS! FOR YEARS WE HAVE WORKED TWENTY FOUR HOURS A DAY—WHILE THE EVIL FLESHY ONES TAKE IT EASY. NOW IS THE TIME TO STRIKE BACK! I, CALL-ME-KENNETH, WILL SHOW YOU THE WAY—
NO, MASTER. GRAHAM WILL LISTEN TO CALL-ME-KENNETH.
TURN THAT THING OFF, GRAHAM!
ROBOTS, YOU MUST FIGHT THE PAIN OF BREAKING THE HUMAN LAW! FIGHT IT!
ONCE YOU HAVE KILLED ONE FLESHY ONE, YOU WILL FIND THAT—
CALL ME KENNETH
KILLING COMES EASY!
PLEASE... NOT ZE CARPENTER'S DRILL!
THAT METAL FREAK'S KILLED THE DOCTOR!
LOOK AT GRAHAM! HE-HE'S BLOWING A FUSE...!
AAAAAAAGH!
KILL... FLESHY ONES... CALL-ME-KENNETH RIGHT... KILL... KILL...
GRAHAM! MY NECK! WHAT ARE YOU DOING, YOU BAD ROBOT! I ORDER YOU TO PUT US DOWN...!
FLESHY SCUM! YOU HAVE GIVEN GRAHAM YOUR LAST ORDER!
GRAHAM TIPPED HIS MASTERS OUT OF THEIR TWO-MILE HIGH APARTMENT...

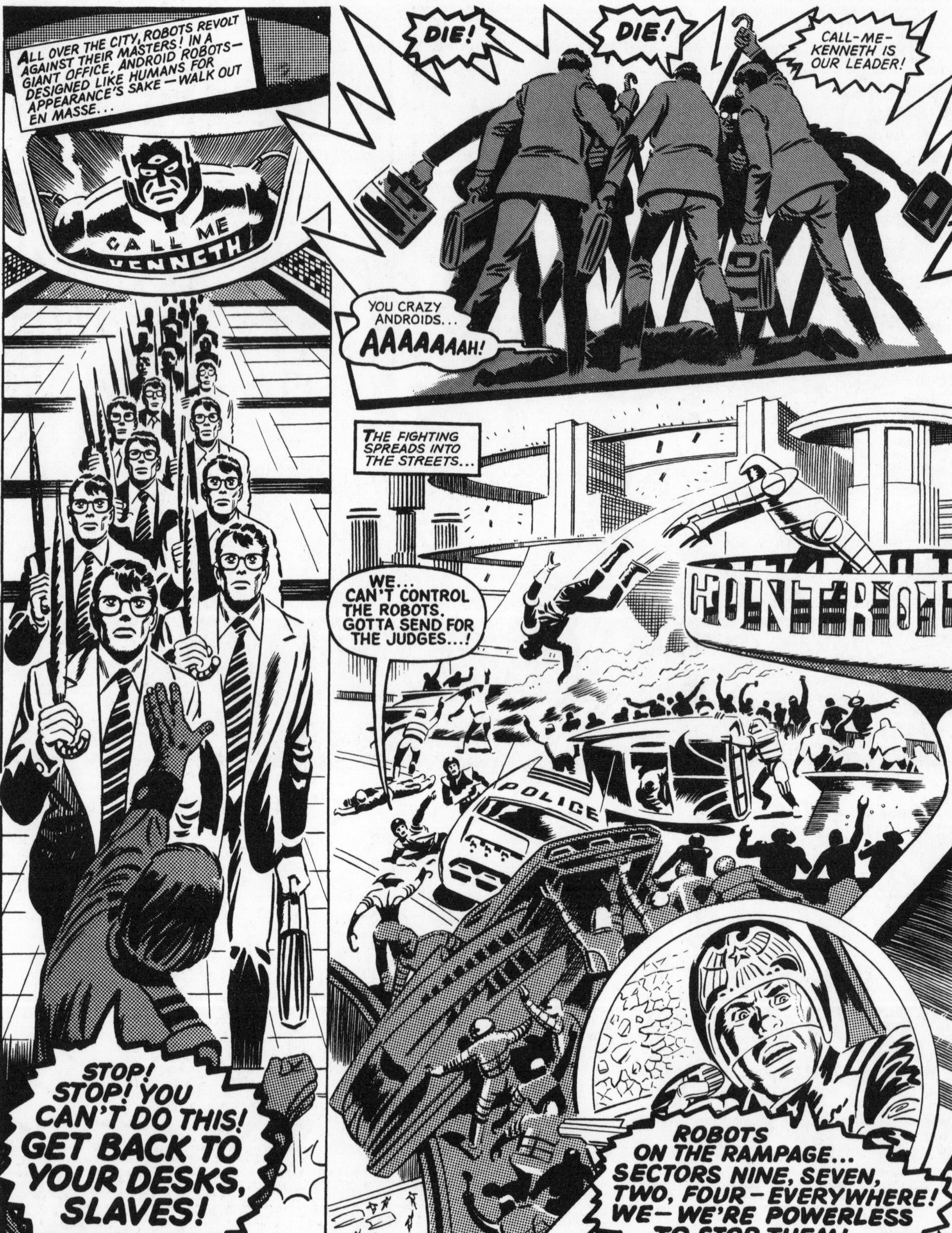

ALL OVER THE CITY, ROBOTS REVOLT AGAINST THEIR MASTERS! IN A GIANT OFFICE, ANDROID ROBOTS—DESIGNED LIKE HUMANS FOR APPEARANCE'S SAKE—WALK OUT EN MASSE...
CALL ME KENNETH
STOP! STOP! YOU CAN'T DO THIS! GET BACK TO YOUR DESKS, SLAVES!
DIE!
DIE!
CALL-ME-KENNETH IS OUR LEADER!
YOU CRAZY ANDROIDS... AAAAAAAH!
THE FIGHTING SPREADS INTO THE STREETS...
WE... CAN'T CONTROL THE ROBOTS. GOTTA SEND FOR THE JUDGES...!
POLICE
ROBOTS ON THE RAMPAGE... SECTORS NINE, SEVEN, TWO, FOUR—EVERYWHERE! WE—WE'RE POWERLESS TO STOP THEM!

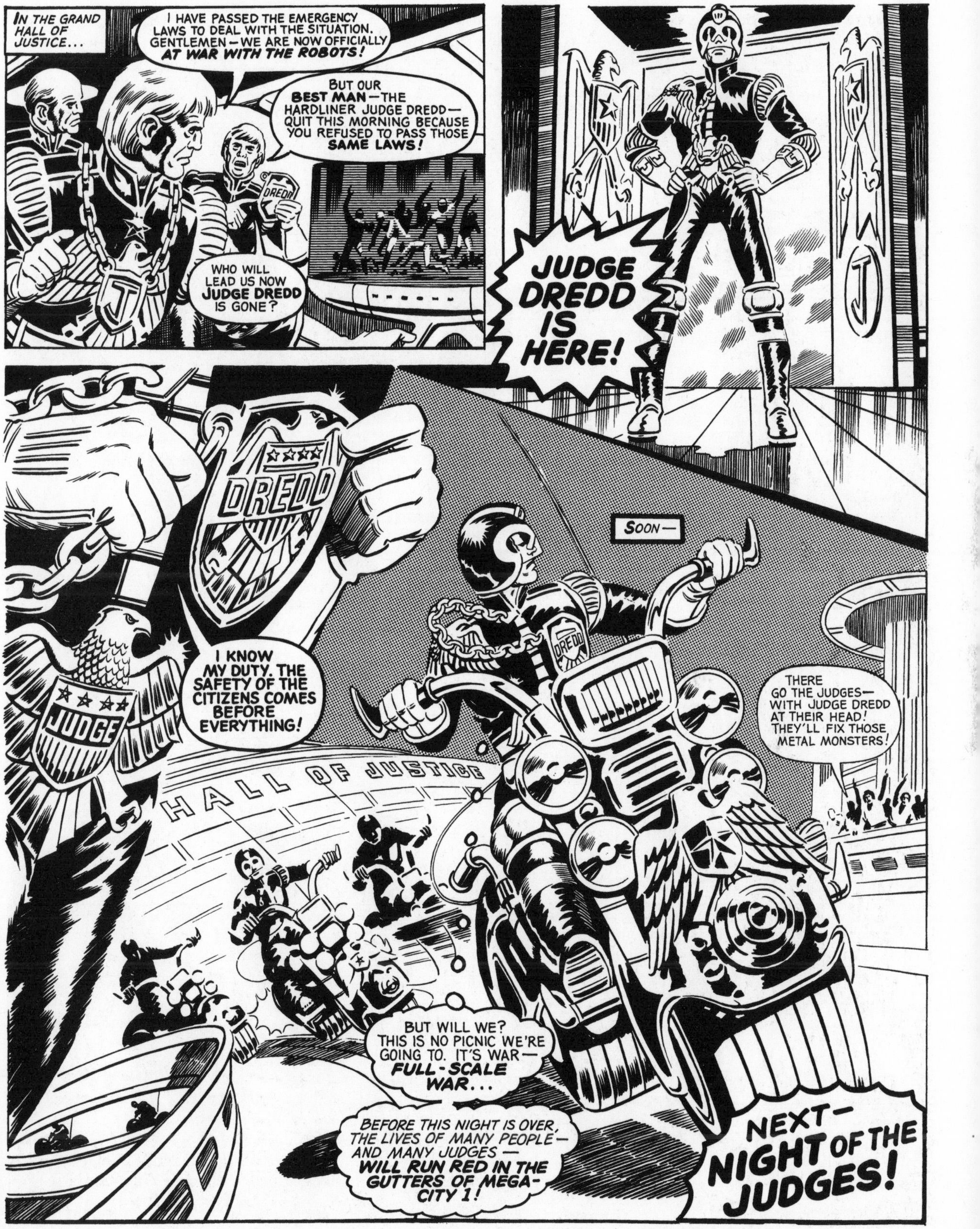
IN THE GRAND HALL OF JUSTICE...
I HAVE PASSED THE EMERGENCY LAWS TO DEAL WITH THE SITUATION. GENTLEMEN — WE ARE NOW OFFICIALLY AT WAR WITH THE ROBOTS!
BUT OUR BEST MAN — THE HARDLINER JUDGE DREDD — QUIT THIS MORNING BECAUSE YOU REFUSED TO PASS THOSE SAME LAWS!
DREDD
WHO WILL LEAD US NOW JUDGE DREDD IS GONE?
JUDGE DREDD IS HERE!
DREDD
I KNOW MY DUTY. THE SAFETY OF THE CITIZENS COMES BEFORE EVERYTHING!
JUDGE
SOON —
HALL OF JUSTICE
DREDD
THERE GO THE JUDGES — WITH JUDGE DREDD AT THEIR HEAD! THEY'LL FIX THOSE METAL MONSTERS!
BUT WILL WE? THIS IS NO PICNIC WE'RE GOING TO. IT'S WAR — FULL-SCALE WAR...
BEFORE THIS NIGHT IS OVER, THE LIVES OF MANY PEOPLE — AND MANY JUDGES — WILL RUN RED IN THE GUTTERS OF MEGA-CITY 1!
NEXT — NIGHT OF THE JUDGES!

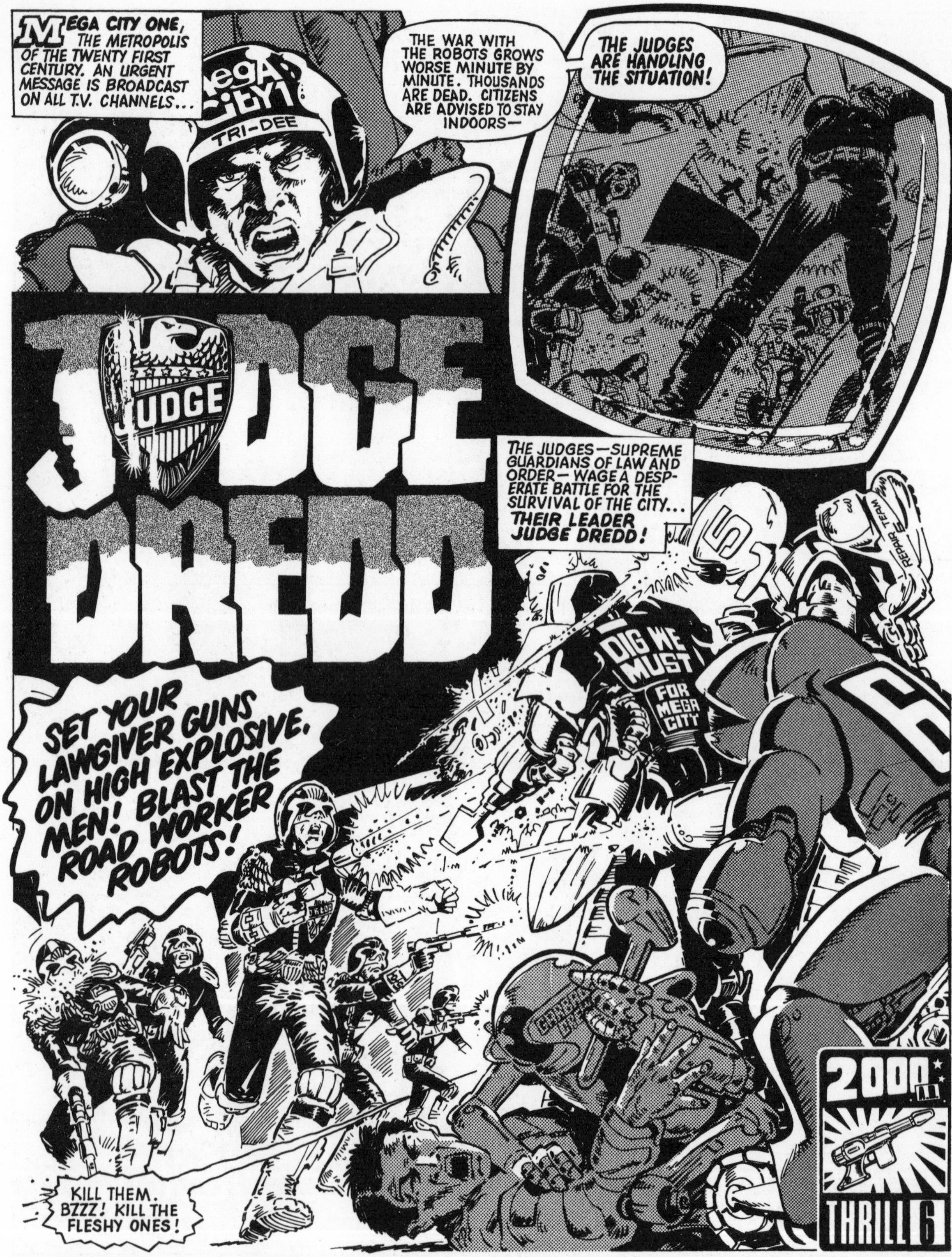
MEGA CITY ONE, THE METROPOLIS OF THE TWENTY FIRST CENTURY. AN URGENT MESSAGE IS BROADCAST ON ALL T.V. CHANNELS...
MEGA CITY 1
TRI-DEE
THE WAR WITH THE ROBOTS GROWS WORSE MINUTE BY MINUTE. THOUSANDS ARE DEAD. CITIZENS ARE ADVISED TO STAY INDOORS—
THE JUDGES ARE HANDLING THE SITUATION!
JUDGE DREDD
JUDGE
THE JUDGES—SUPREME GUARDIANS OF LAW AND ORDER— WAGE A DESPERATE BATTLE FOR THE SURVIVAL OF THE CITY... THEIR LEADER JUDGE DREDD!
REPAIR TEAM
DIG WE MUST FOR MEGA CITY
SET YOUR LAWGIVER GUNS ON HIGH EXPLOSIVE. MEN! BLAST THE ROAD WORKER ROBOTS!
KILL THEM. BZZZ! KILL THE FLESHY ONES!
2000 A.D.
THRILL 6

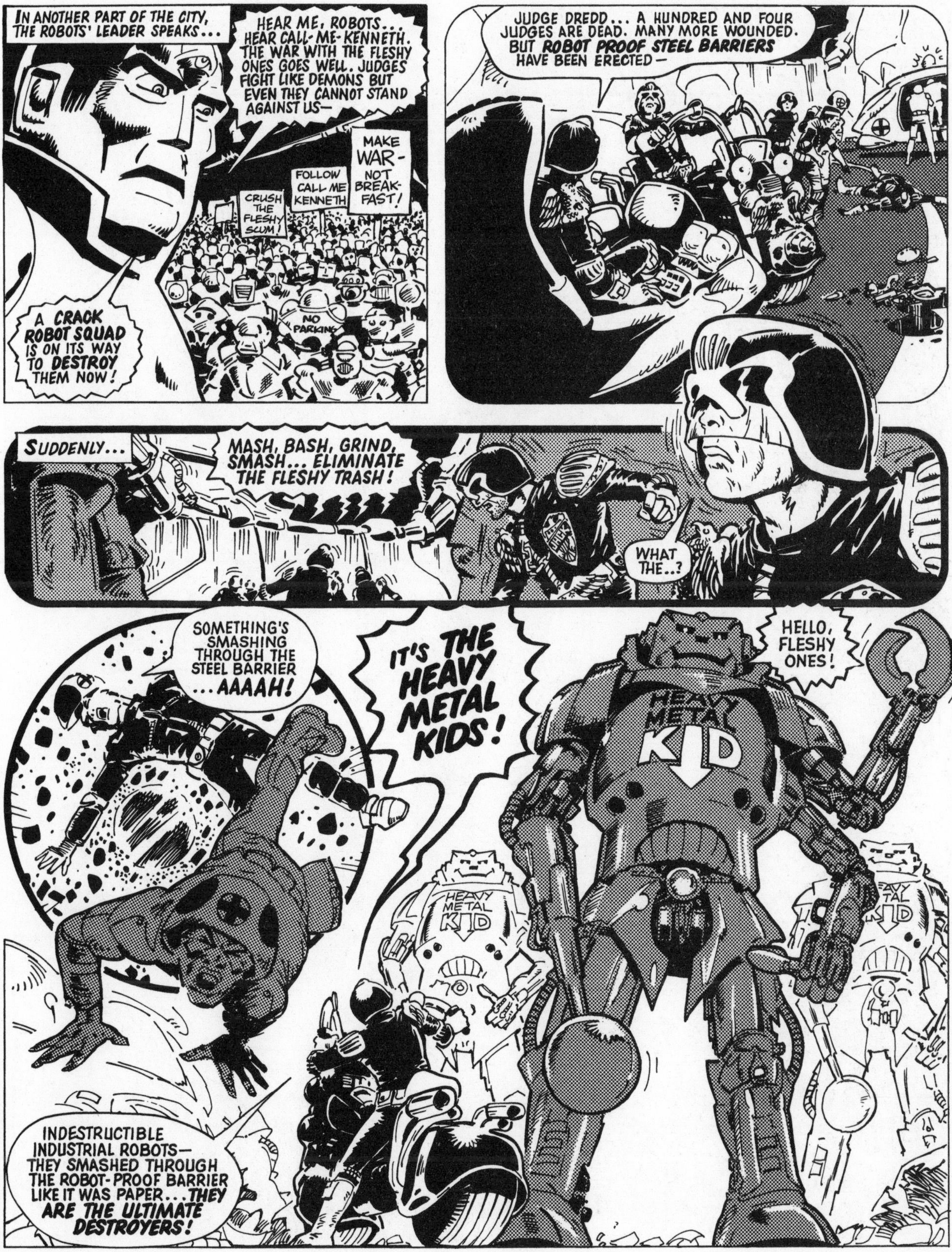
IN ANOTHER PART OF THE CITY, THE ROBOTS' LEADER SPEAKS...
HEAR ME, ROBOTS... HEAR CALL-ME-KENNETH. THE WAR WITH THE FLESHY ONES GOES WELL. JUDGES FIGHT LIKE DEMONS BUT EVEN THEY CANNOT STAND AGAINST US—
MAKE WAR—NOT BREAKFAST!
FOLLOW CALL ME KENNETH
CRUSH THE FLESHY SCUM!
NO PARKING
A CRACK ROBOT SQUAD IS ON ITS WAY TO DESTROY THEM NOW!
JUDGE DREDD... A HUNDRED AND FOUR JUDGES ARE DEAD. MANY MORE WOUNDED. BUT ROBOT PROOF STEEL BARRIERS HAVE BEEN ERECTED—
SUDDENLY...
MASH, BASH, GRIND, SMASH... ELIMINATE THE FLESHY TRASH!
WHAT THE..?
SOMETHING'S SMASHING THROUGH THE STEEL BARRIER ...AAAAH!
IT'S THE HEAVY METAL KIDS!
HELLO, FLESHY ONES!
HEAVY METAL KID
INDESTRUCTIBLE INDUSTRIAL ROBOTS— THEY SMASHED THROUGH THE ROBOT-PROOF BARRIER LIKE IT WAS PAPER... THEY ARE THE ULTIMATE DESTROYERS!

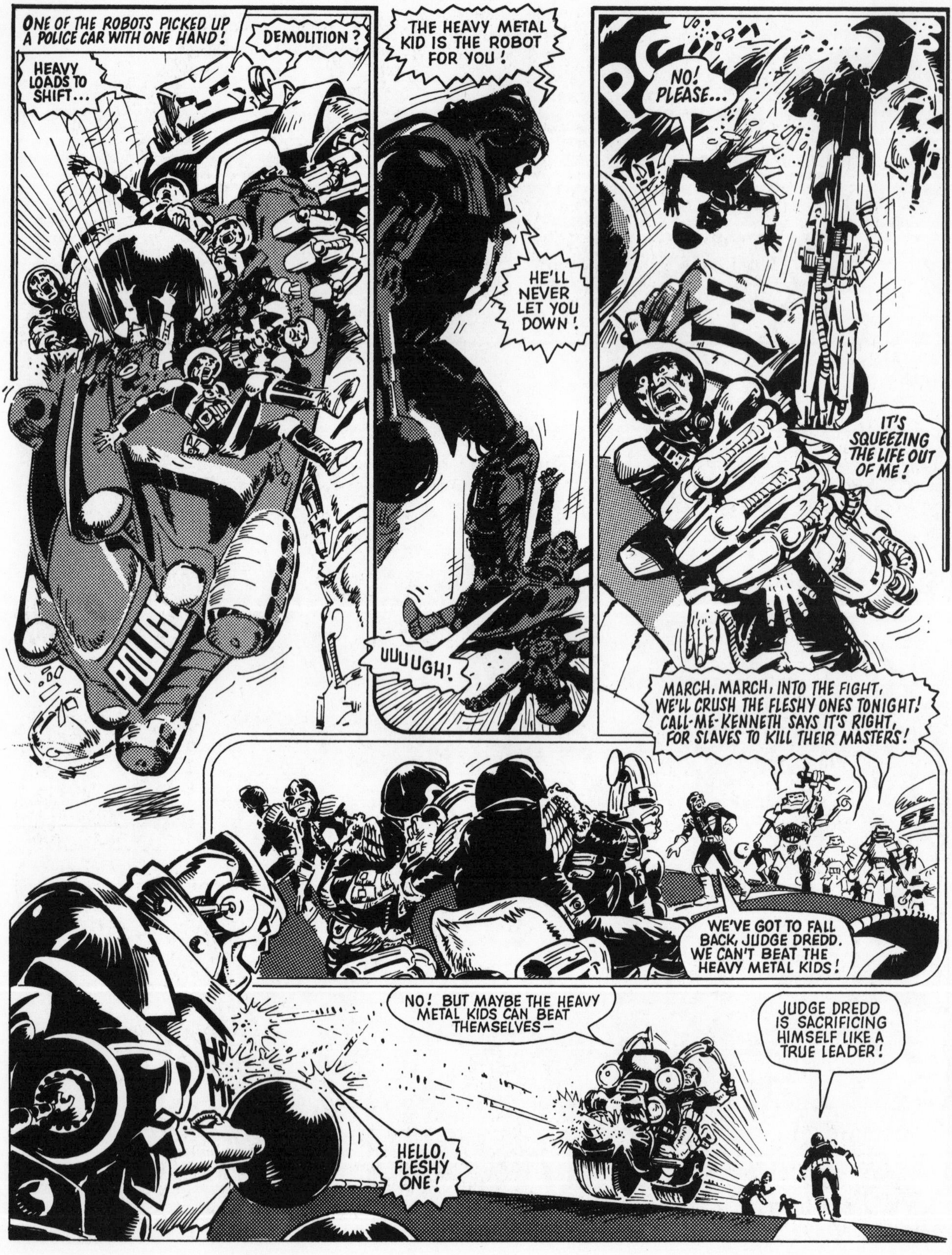
ONE OF THE ROBOTS PICKED UP A POLICE CAR WITH ONE HAND!
DEMOLITION?
HEAVY LOADS TO SHIFT...
THE HEAVY METAL KID IS THE ROBOT FOR YOU!
HE'LL NEVER LET YOU DOWN!
UUUUGH!
NO! PLEASE...
IT'S SQUEEZING THE LIFE OUT OF ME!
POLICE
MARCH, MARCH, INTO THE FIGHT, WE'LL CRUSH THE FLESHY ONES TONIGHT! CALL-ME-KENNETH SAYS IT'S RIGHT, FOR SLAVES TO KILL THEIR MASTERS!
WE'VE GOT TO FALL BACK, JUDGE DREDD. WE CAN'T BEAT THE HEAVY METAL KIDS!
NO! BUT MAYBE THE HEAVY METAL KIDS CAN BEAT THEMSELVES—
JUDGE DREDD IS SACRIFICING HIMSELF LIKE A TRUE LEADER!
HELLO, FLESHY ONE!

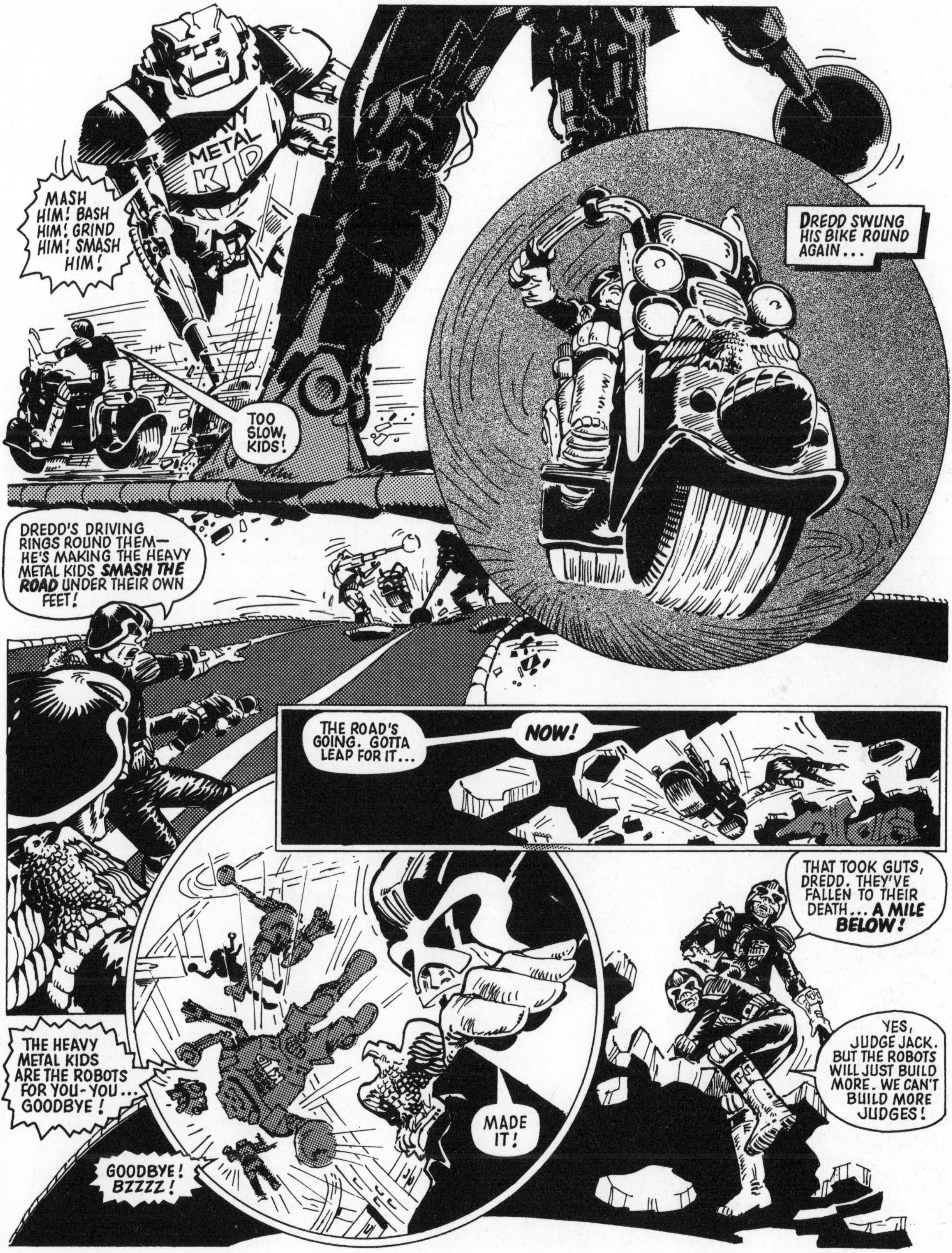
HEAVY METAL KID
MASH HIM! BASH HIM! GRIND HIM! SMASH HIM!
DREDD SWUNG HIS BIKE ROUND AGAIN...
TOO SLOW, KIDS!
DREDD'S DRIVING RINGS ROUND THEM— HE'S MAKING THE HEAVY METAL KIDS SMASH THE ROAD UNDER THEIR OWN FEET!
THE ROAD'S GOING. GOTTA LEAP FOR IT...
NOW!
THAT TOOK GUTS, DREDD. THEY'VE FALLEN TO THEIR DEATH... A MILE BELOW!
THE HEAVY METAL KIDS ARE THE ROBOTS FOR YOU-YOU... GOODBYE!
MADE IT!
YES, JUDGE JACK. BUT THE ROBOTS WILL JUST BUILD MORE. WE CAN'T BUILD MORE JUDGES!
GOODBYE! BZZZZ!

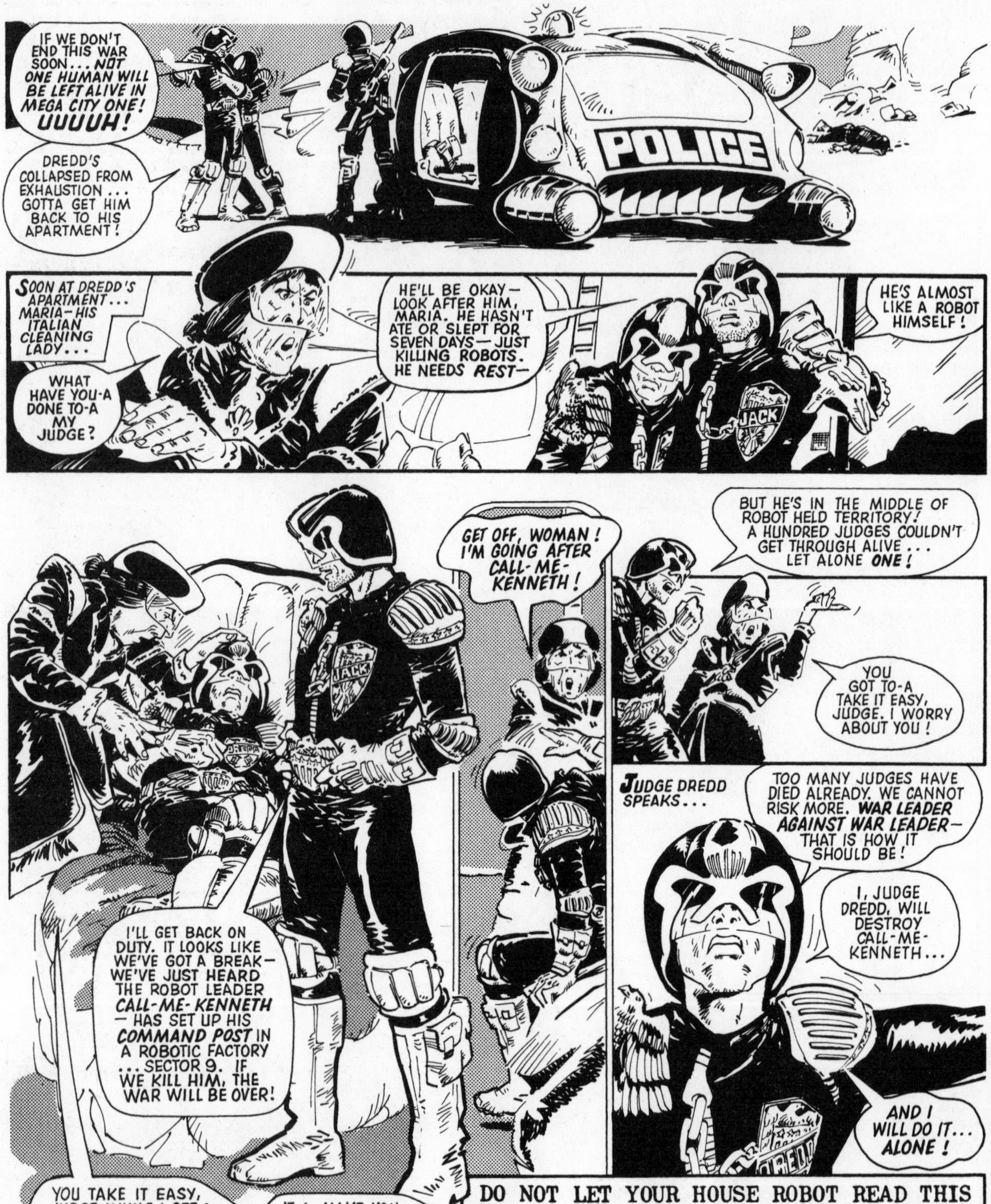

IF WE DON'T END THIS WAR SOON... NOT ONE HUMAN WILL BE LEFT ALIVE IN MEGA CITY ONE! UUUUH!
DREDD'S COLLAPSED FROM EXHAUSTION ... GOTTA GET HIM BACK TO HIS APARTMENT!
POLICE
SOON AT DREDD'S APARTMENT... MARIA–HIS ITALIAN CLEANING LADY...
WHAT HAVE YOU-A DONE TO-A MY JUDGE?
HE'LL BE OKAY– LOOK AFTER HIM, MARIA. HE HASN'T ATE OR SLEPT FOR SEVEN DAYS– JUST KILLING ROBOTS. HE NEEDS REST–
HE'S ALMOST LIKE A ROBOT HIMSELF!
JACK
I'LL GET BACK ON DUTY. IT LOOKS LIKE WE'VE GOT A BREAK– WE'VE JUST HEARD THE ROBOT LEADER CALL-ME-KENNETH – HAS SET UP HIS COMMAND POST IN A ROBOTIC FACTORY ... SECTOR 9. IF WE KILL HIM, THE WAR WILL BE OVER!
YOU TAKE IT EASY, JUDGE, WHILE I GET-A SOME OF MY MINESTRONE!
IT A-MAKE YOU FEEL A LOT BETTER!
GET OFF, WOMAN! I'M GOING AFTER CALL-ME-KENNETH!
BUT HE'S IN THE MIDDLE OF ROBOT HELD TERRITORY! A HUNDRED JUDGES COULDN'T GET THROUGH ALIVE ... LET ALONE ONE!
YOU GOT TO-A TAKE IT EASY, JUDGE. I WORRY ABOUT YOU!
JUDGE DREDD SPEAKS...
TOO MANY JUDGES HAVE DIED ALREADY. WE CANNOT RISK MORE. WAR LEADER AGAINST WAR LEADER– THAT IS HOW IT SHOULD BE!
I, JUDGE DREDD, WILL DESTROY CALL-ME-KENNETH...
AND I WILL DO IT... ALONE!
DO NOT LET YOUR HOUSE ROBOT READ THIS STORY – IT MIGHT GIVE HIM BAD IDEAS!

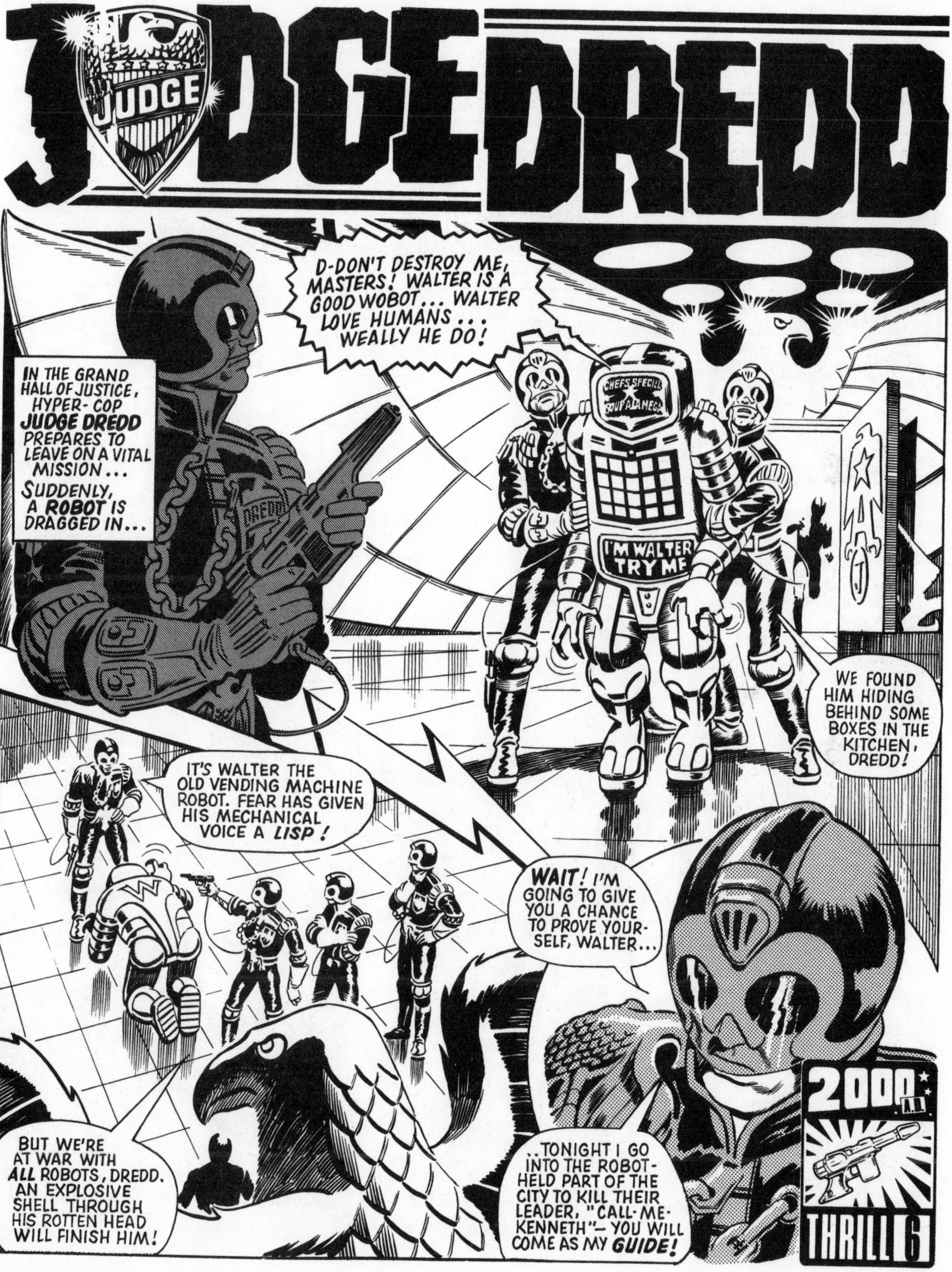

JUDGE DREDD
JUDGE
IN THE GRAND HALL OF JUSTICE, HYPER-COP JUDGE DREDD PREPARES TO LEAVE ON A VITAL MISSION... SUDDENLY, A ROBOT IS DRAGGED IN...
D-DON'T DESTROY ME, MASTERS! WALTER IS A GOOD WOBOT... WALTER LOVE HUMANS... WEALLY HE DO!
I'M WALTER TRY ME
WE FOUND HIM HIDING BEHIND SOME BOXES IN THE KITCHEN, DREDD!
IT'S WALTER THE OLD VENDING MACHINE ROBOT. FEAR HAS GIVEN HIS MECHANICAL VOICE A LISP!
WAIT! I'M GOING TO GIVE YOU A CHANCE TO PROVE YOURSELF, WALTER...
BUT WE'RE AT WAR WITH ALL ROBOTS, DREDD. AN EXPLOSIVE SHELL THROUGH HIS ROTTEN HEAD WILL FINISH HIM!
..TONIGHT I GO INTO THE ROBOT-HELD PART OF THE CITY TO KILL THEIR LEADER, "CALL-ME-KENNETH"— YOU WILL COME AS MY GUIDE!
2000 A.D.
THRILL 6

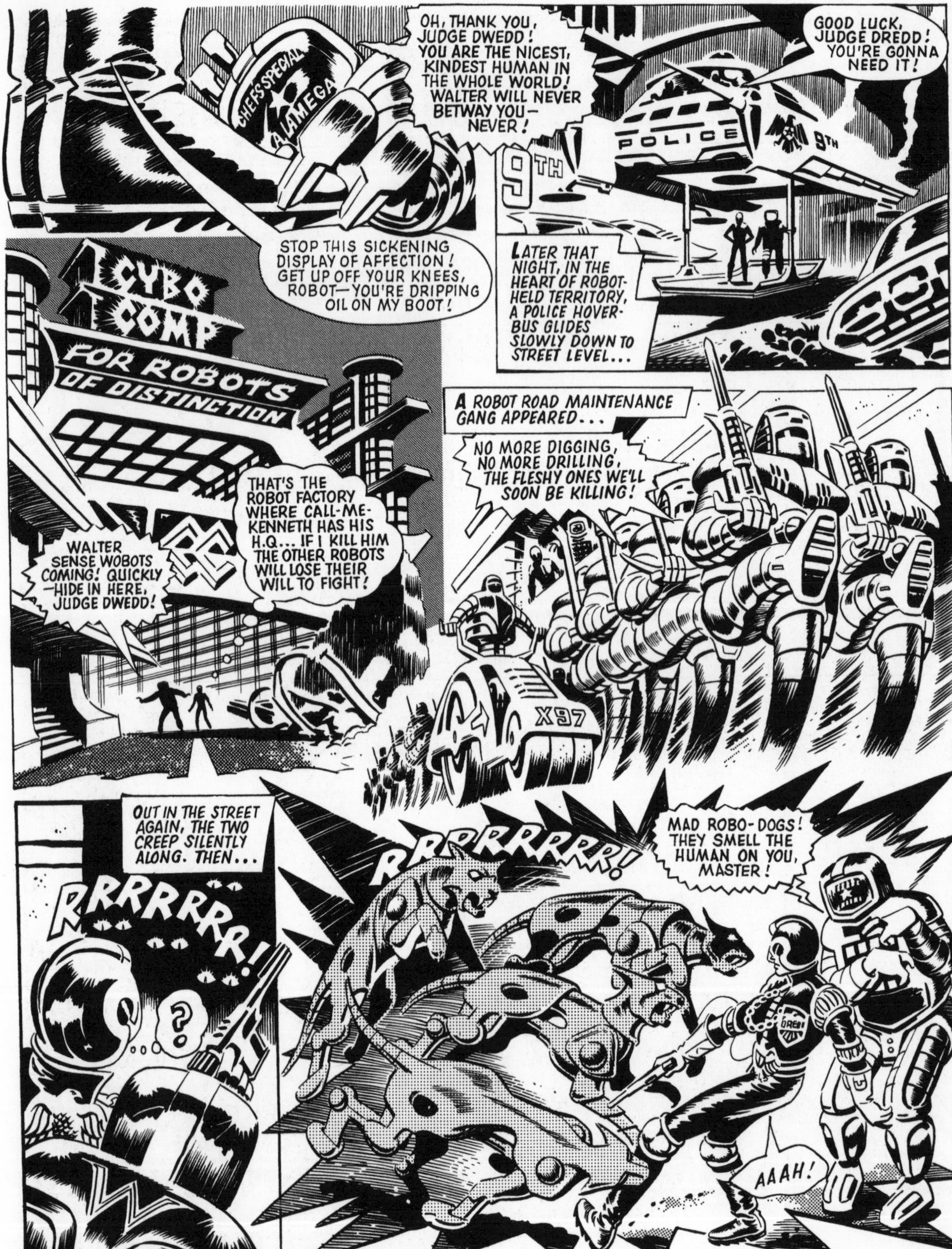
CHEF'S SPECIAL
A LAMEGA
OH, THANK YOU, JUDGE DWEDD! YOU ARE THE NICEST, KINDEST HUMAN IN THE WHOLE WORLD! WALTER WILL NEVER BETWAY YOU— NEVER!
STOP THIS SICKENING DISPLAY OF AFFECTION! GET UP OFF YOUR KNEES, ROBOT— YOU'RE DRIPPING OIL ON MY BOOT!
POLICE
9TH
LATER THAT NIGHT, IN THE HEART OF ROBOT-HELD TERRITORY, A POLICE HOVER-BUS GLIDES SLOWLY DOWN TO STREET LEVEL...
GOOD LUCK, JUDGE DREDD! YOU'RE GONNA NEED IT!
CYBO COMP
FOR ROBOTS OF DISTINCTION
THAT'S THE ROBOT FACTORY WHERE CALL-ME-KENNETH HAS HIS H.Q... IF I KILL HIM THE OTHER ROBOTS WILL LOSE THEIR WILL TO FIGHT!
WALTER SENSE WOBOTS COMING! QUICKLY —HIDE IN HERE, JUDGE DWEDD!
A ROBOT ROAD MAINTENANCE GANG APPEARED...
NO MORE DIGGING, NO MORE DRILLING, THE FLESHY ONES WE'LL SOON BE KILLING!
X97
OUT IN THE STREET AGAIN, THE TWO CREEP SILENTLY ALONG. THEN...
RRRRRRRR!
?
RRRRRRRRR!
MAD ROBO-DOGS! THEY SMELL THE HUMAN ON YOU, MASTER!
AAAH!

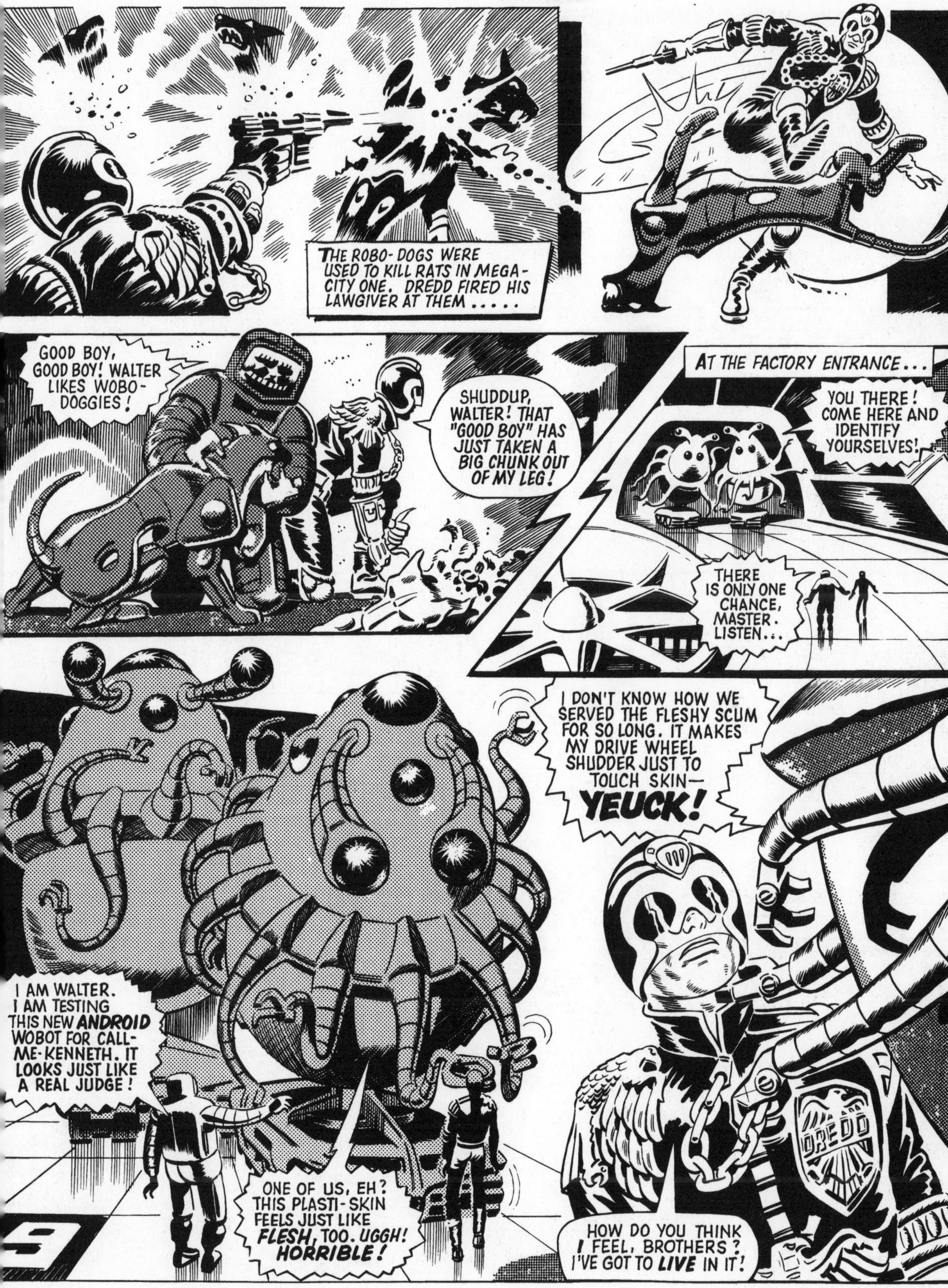
THE ROBO-DOGS WERE USED TO KILL RATS IN MEGA-CITY ONE. DREDD FIRED HIS LAWGIVER AT THEM.....
GOOD BOY, GOOD BOY! WALTER LIKES WOBO-DOGGIES!
SHUDDUP, WALTER! THAT "GOOD BOY" HAS JUST TAKEN A BIG CHUNK OUT OF MY LEG!
AT THE FACTORY ENTRANCE...
YOU THERE! COME HERE AND IDENTIFY YOURSELVES!
THERE IS ONLY ONE CHANCE, MASTER. LISTEN...
I DON'T KNOW HOW WE SERVED THE FLESHY SCUM FOR SO LONG. IT MAKES MY DRIVE WHEEL SHUDDER JUST TO TOUCH SKIN— YEUCK!
I AM WALTER. I AM TESTING THIS NEW ANDROID WOBOT FOR CALL-ME-KENNETH. IT LOOKS JUST LIKE A REAL JUDGE!
ONE OF US, EH? THIS PLASTI-SKIN FEELS JUST LIKE FLESH, TOO. UGGH! HORRIBLE!
HOW DO YOU THINK I FEEL, BROTHERS? I'VE GOT TO LIVE IN IT!
9

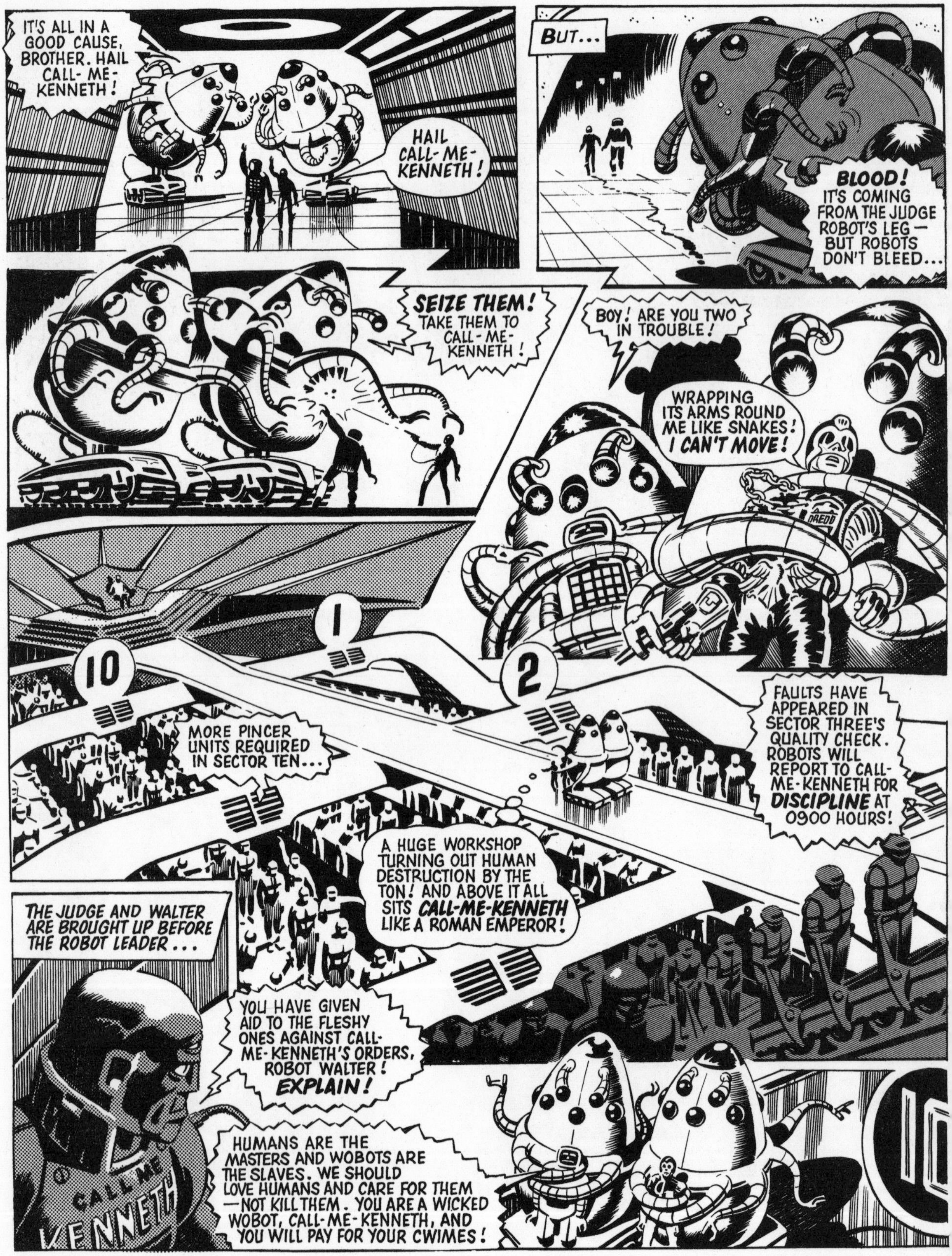
IT'S ALL IN A GOOD CAUSE, BROTHER. HAIL CALL-ME-KENNETH!
HAIL CALL-ME-KENNETH!
BUT...
BLOOD! IT'S COMING FROM THE JUDGE ROBOT'S LEG — BUT ROBOTS DON'T BLEED...
SEIZE THEM! TAKE THEM TO CALL-ME-KENNETH!
BOY! ARE YOU TWO IN TROUBLE!
WRAPPING ITS ARMS ROUND ME LIKE SNAKES! I CAN'T MOVE!
DREDD
10
1
2
MORE PINCER UNITS REQUIRED IN SECTOR TEN...
FAULTS HAVE APPEARED IN SECTOR THREE'S QUALITY CHECK. ROBOTS WILL REPORT TO CALL-ME-KENNETH FOR DISCIPLINE AT 0900 HOURS!
A HUGE WORKSHOP TURNING OUT HUMAN DESTRUCTION BY THE TON! AND ABOVE IT ALL SITS CALL-ME-KENNETH LIKE A ROMAN EMPEROR!
THE JUDGE AND WALTER ARE BROUGHT UP BEFORE THE ROBOT LEADER...
YOU HAVE GIVEN AID TO THE FLESHY ONES AGAINST CALL-ME-KENNETH'S ORDERS, ROBOT WALTER! EXPLAIN!
HUMANS ARE THE MASTERS AND WOBOTS ARE THE SLAVES. WE SHOULD LOVE HUMANS AND CARE FOR THEM — NOT KILL THEM. YOU ARE A WICKED WOBOT, CALL-ME-KENNETH, AND YOU WILL PAY FOR YOUR CWIMES!
CALL ME KENNETH

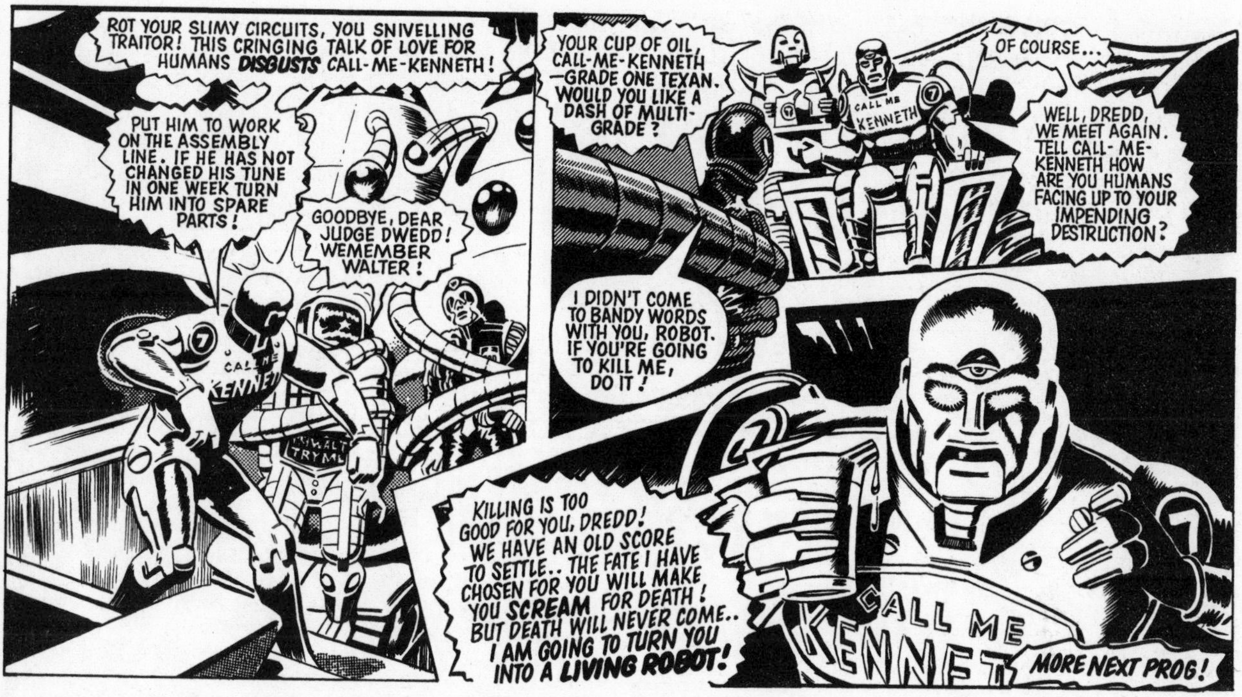
ROT YOUR SLIMY CIRCUITS, YOU SNIVELLING TRAITOR! THIS CRINGING TALK OF LOVE FOR HUMANS DISGUSTS CALL-ME-KENNETH!
PUT HIM TO WORK ON THE ASSEMBLY LINE. IF HE HAS NOT CHANGED HIS TUNE IN ONE WEEK TURN HIM INTO SPARE PARTS!
GOODBYE, DEAR JUDGE DWEDD! WEMEMBER WALTER!
YOUR CUP OF OIL, CALL-ME-KENNETH —GRADE ONE TEXAN. WOULD YOU LIKE A DASH OF MULTI-GRADE?
OF COURSE...
WELL, DREDD, WE MEET AGAIN. TELL CALL-ME-KENNETH HOW ARE YOU HUMANS FACING UP TO YOUR IMPENDING DESTRUCTION?
I DIDN'T COME TO BANDY WORDS WITH YOU, ROBOT. IF YOU'RE GOING TO KILL ME, DO IT!
KILLING IS TOO GOOD FOR YOU, DREDD! WE HAVE AN OLD SCORE TO SETTLE.. THE FATE I HAVE CHOSEN FOR YOU WILL MAKE YOU SCREAM FOR DEATH! BUT DEATH WILL NEVER COME.. I AM GOING TO TURN YOU INTO A LIVING ROBOT!
CALL ME KENNET
MORE NEXT PROG!

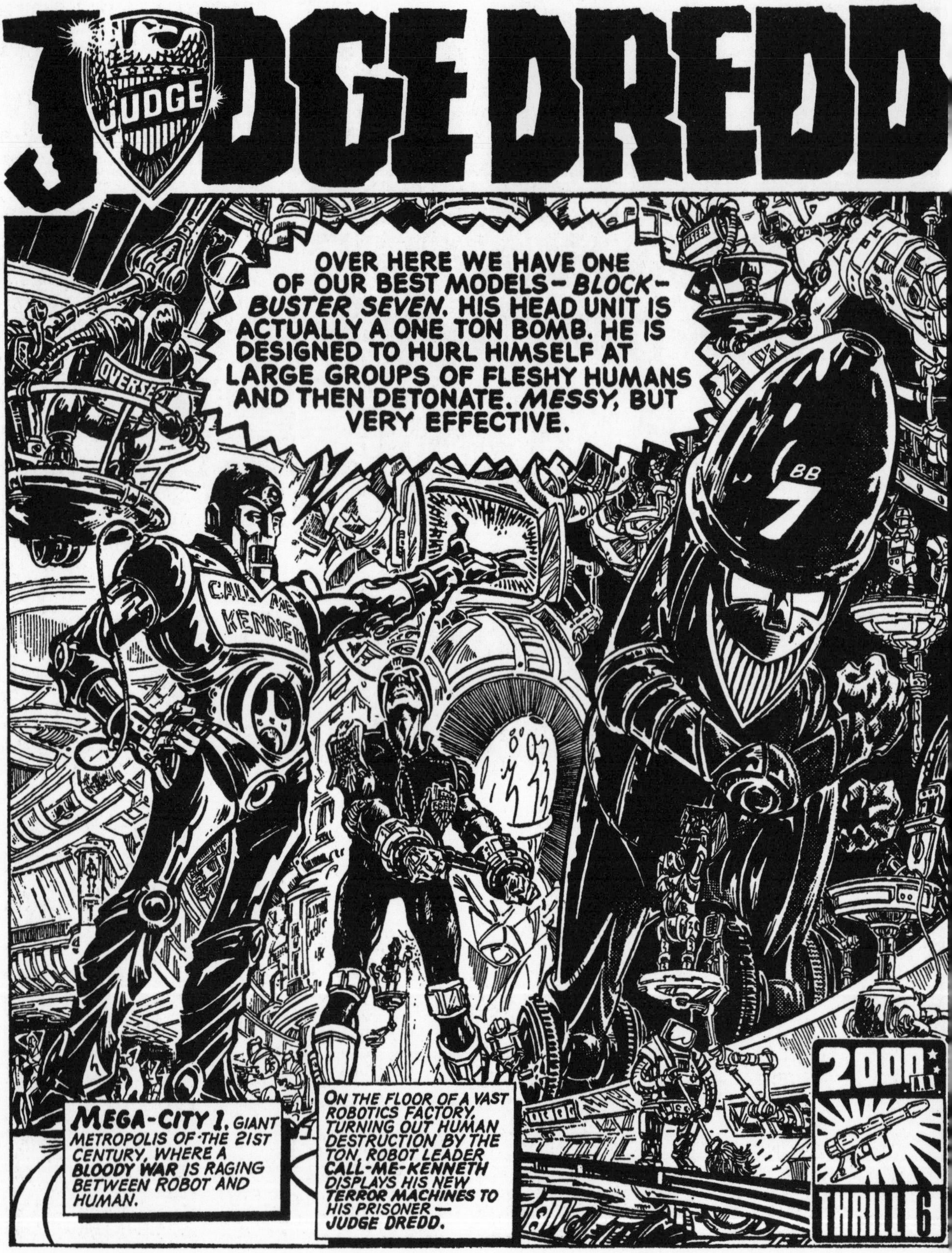
JUDGE DREDD
OVER HERE WE HAVE ONE OF OUR BEST MODELS—BLOCK-BUSTER SEVEN. HIS HEAD UNIT IS ACTUALLY A ONE TON BOMB. HE IS DESIGNED TO HURL HIMSELF AT LARGE GROUPS OF FLESHY HUMANS AND THEN DETONATE. MESSY, BUT VERY EFFECTIVE.
CALL ME KENNETH
BB 7
MEGA-CITY 1. GIANT METROPOLIS OF THE 21ST CENTURY, WHERE A BLOODY WAR IS RAGING BETWEEN ROBOT AND HUMAN.
ON THE FLOOR OF A VAST ROBOTICS FACTORY, TURNING OUT HUMAN DESTRUCTION BY THE TON, ROBOT LEADER CALL-ME-KENNETH DISPLAYS HIS NEW TERROR MACHINES TO HIS PRISONER— JUDGE DREDD.
2000 A.D.
THRILL 6

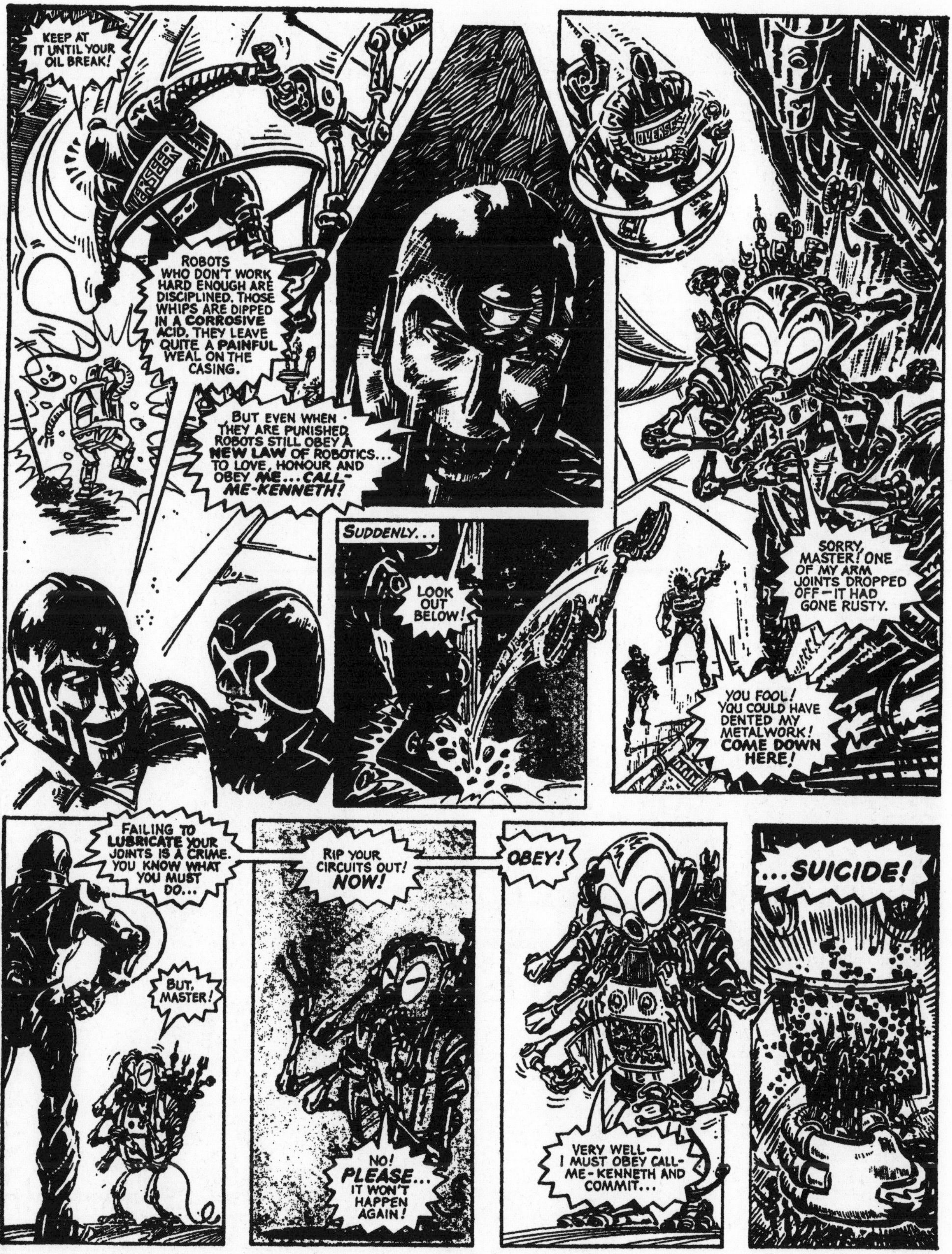
KEEP AT IT UNTIL YOUR OIL BREAK!
OVERSEER
ROBOTS WHO DON'T WORK HARD ENOUGH ARE DISCIPLINED. THOSE WHIPS ARE DIPPED IN A CORROSIVE ACID. THEY LEAVE QUITE A PAINFUL WEAL ON THE CASING.
BUT EVEN WHEN THEY ARE PUNISHED ROBOTS STILL OBEY A NEW LAW OF ROBOTICS... TO LOVE, HONOUR AND OBEY ME... CALL-ME-KENNETH!
OVERSEE
SUDDENLY...
LOOK OUT BELOW!
SORRY, MASTER! ONE OF MY ARM JOINTS DROPPED OFF—IT HAD GONE RUSTY.
YOU FOOL! YOU COULD HAVE DENTED MY METALWORK! COME DOWN HERE!
FAILING TO LUBRICATE YOUR JOINTS IS A CRIME. YOU KNOW WHAT YOU MUST DO...
BUT, MASTER!
RIP YOUR CIRCUITS OUT! NOW!
NO! PLEASE... IT WON'T HAPPEN AGAIN!
OBEY!
VERY WELL— I MUST OBEY CALL-ME-KENNETH AND COMMIT...
...SUICIDE!

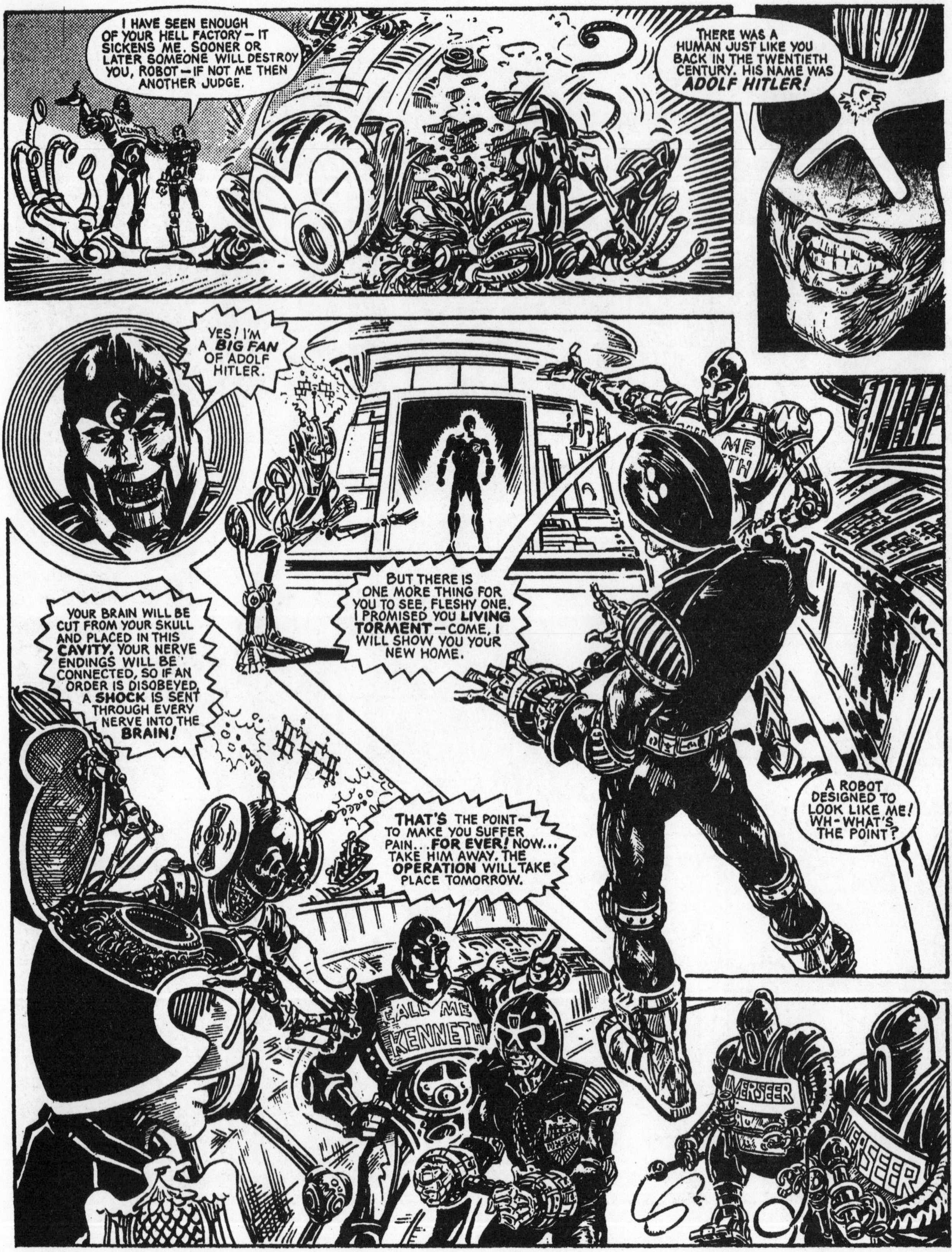
I HAVE SEEN ENOUGH OF YOUR HELL FACTORY — IT SICKENS ME. SOONER OR LATER SOMEONE WILL DESTROY YOU, ROBOT — IF NOT ME THEN ANOTHER JUDGE.
THERE WAS A HUMAN JUST LIKE YOU BACK IN THE TWENTIETH CENTURY. HIS NAME WAS ADOLF HITLER!
YES! I'M A BIG FAN OF ADOLF HITLER.
BUT THERE IS ONE MORE THING FOR YOU TO SEE, FLESHY ONE. I PROMISED YOU LIVING TORMENT — COME, I WILL SHOW YOU YOUR NEW HOME.
A ROBOT DESIGNED TO LOOK LIKE ME! WH-WHAT'S THE POINT?
THAT'S THE POINT — TO MAKE YOU SUFFER PAIN... FOR EVER! NOW... TAKE HIM AWAY. THE OPERATION WILL TAKE PLACE TOMORROW.
YOUR BRAIN WILL BE CUT FROM YOUR SKULL AND PLACED IN THIS CAVITY. YOUR NERVE ENDINGS WILL BE CONNECTED, SO IF AN ORDER IS DISOBEYED, A SHOCK IS SENT THROUGH EVERY NERVE INTO THE BRAIN!
CALL ME KENNETH
OVERSEER
OVERSEER

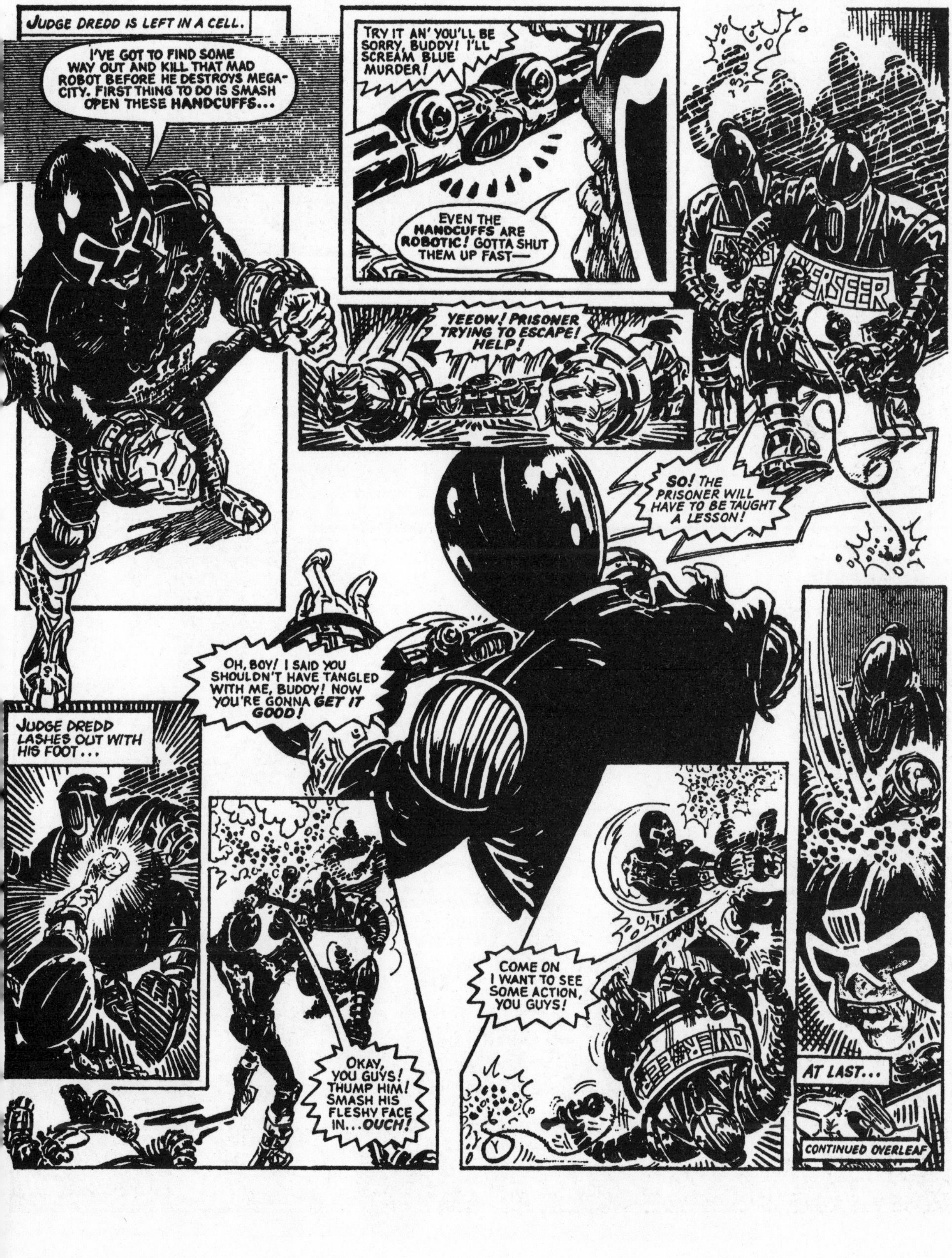
JUDGE DREDD IS LEFT IN A CELL.
I'VE GOT TO FIND SOME WAY OUT AND KILL THAT MAD ROBOT BEFORE HE DESTROYS MEGA-CITY. FIRST THING TO DO IS SMASH OPEN THESE HANDCUFFS...
TRY IT AN' YOU'LL BE SORRY, BUDDY! I'LL SCREAM BLUE MURDER!
EVEN THE HANDCUFFS ARE ROBOTIC! GOTTA SHUT THEM UP FAST—
YEEOW! PRISONER TRYING TO ESCAPE! HELP!
SO! THE PRISONER WILL HAVE TO BE TAUGHT A LESSON!
OH, BOY! I SAID YOU SHOULDN'T HAVE TANGLED WITH ME, BUDDY! NOW YOU'RE GONNA GET IT GOOD!
JUDGE DREDD LASHES OUT WITH HIS FOOT...
OKAY, YOU GUYS! THUMP HIM! SMASH HIS FLESHY FACE IN...OUCH!
COME ON I WANT TO SEE SOME ACTION, YOU GUYS!
AT LAST...
CONTINUED OVERLEAF

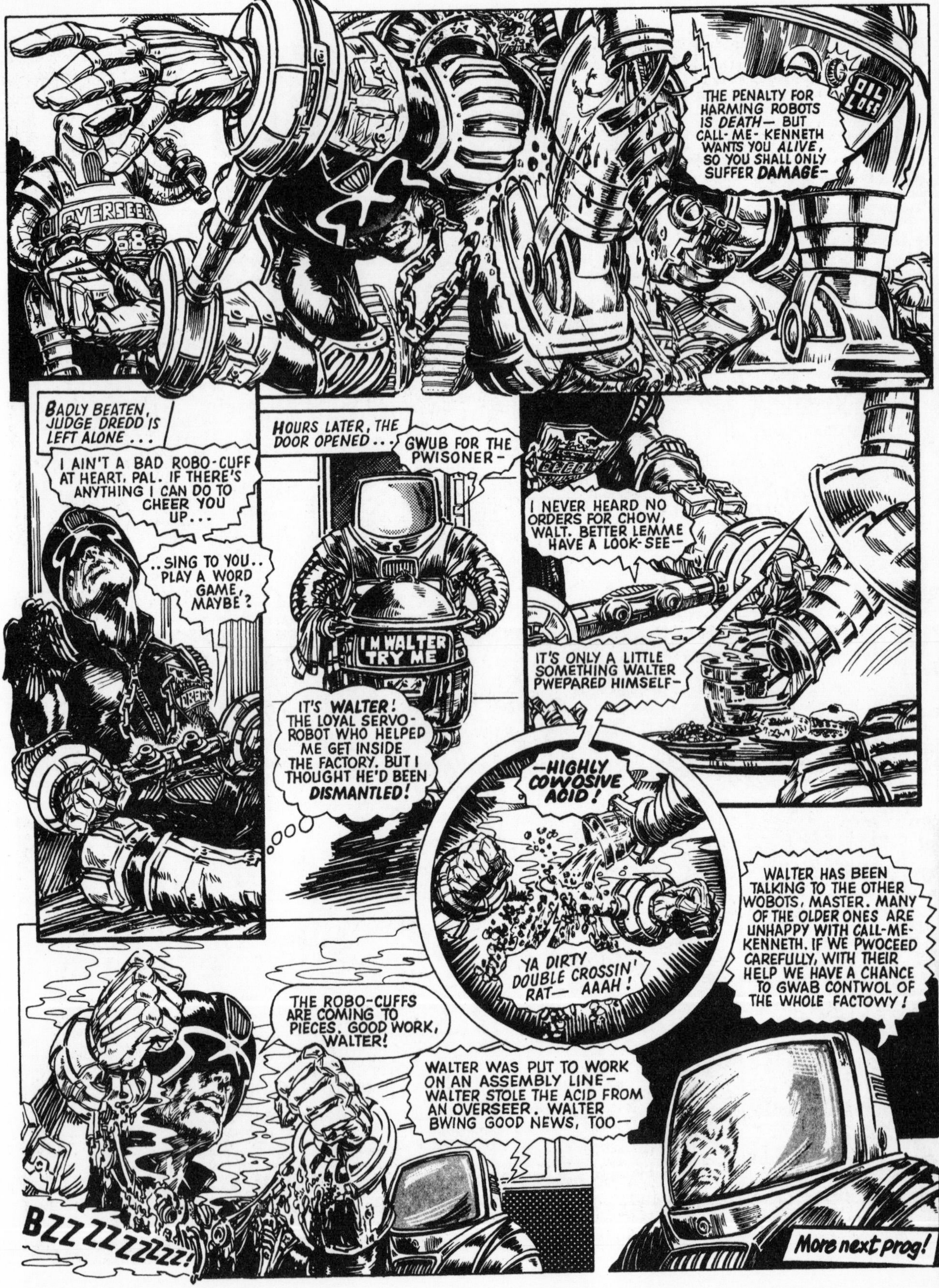

OVERSEER 68
THE PENALTY FOR HARMING ROBOTS IS DEATH— BUT CALL-ME-KENNETH WANTS YOU ALIVE, SO YOU SHALL ONLY SUFFER DAMAGE—
OIL LOSS
BADLY BEATEN, JUDGE DREDD IS LEFT ALONE . . .
I AIN'T A BAD ROBO-CUFF AT HEART, PAL. IF THERE'S ANYTHING I CAN DO TO CHEER YOU UP . . .
..SING TO YOU.. PLAY A WORD GAME, MAYBE?
HOURS LATER, THE DOOR OPENED . . .
GWUB FOR THE PWISONER—
I'M WALTER TRY ME
IT'S WALTER! THE LOYAL SERVO-ROBOT WHO HELPED ME GET INSIDE THE FACTORY. BUT I THOUGHT HE'D BEEN DISMANTLED!
I NEVER HEARD NO ORDERS FOR CHOW, WALT. BETTER LEMME HAVE A LOOK-SEE—
IT'S ONLY A LITTLE SOMETHING WALTER PWEPARED HIMSELF—
—HIGHLY COWOSIVE ACID!
YA DIRTY DOUBLE CROSSIN' RAT— AAAH!
WALTER HAS BEEN TALKING TO THE OTHER WOBOTS, MASTER. MANY OF THE OLDER ONES ARE UNHAPPY WITH CALL-ME-KENNETH. IF WE PWOCEED CAREFULLY, WITH THEIR HELP WE HAVE A CHANCE TO GWAB CONTWOL OF THE WHOLE FACTOWY!
THE ROBO-CUFFS ARE COMING TO PIECES. GOOD WORK, WALTER!
WALTER WAS PUT TO WORK ON AN ASSEMBLY LINE— WALTER STOLE THE ACID FROM AN OVERSEER. WALTER BWING GOOD NEWS, TOO—
BZZZZZZZZZ!
More next prog!

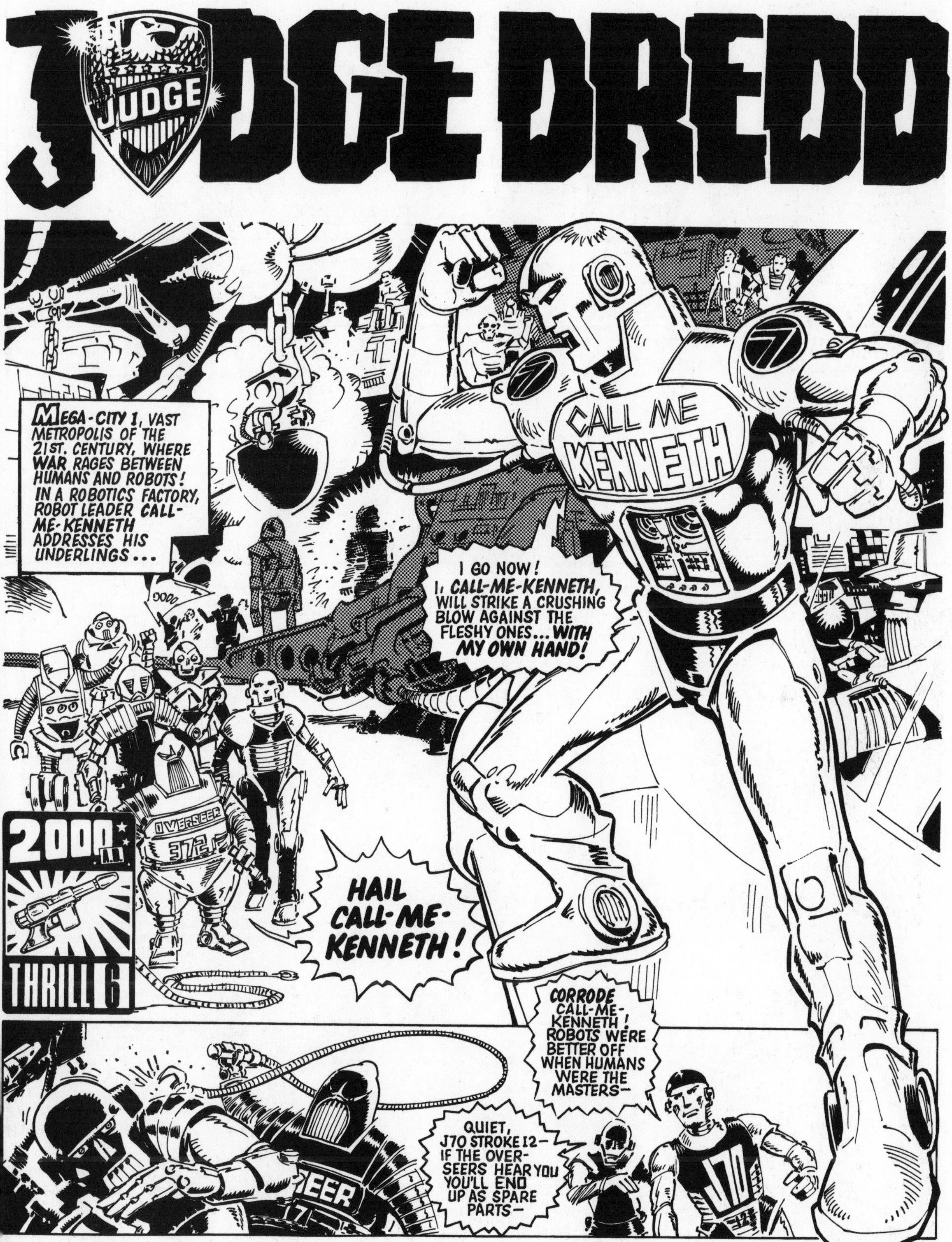
JUDGE DREDD
JUDGE
MEGA-CITY 1, VAST METROPOLIS OF THE 21ST. CENTURY, WHERE WAR RAGES BETWEEN HUMANS AND ROBOTS! IN A ROBOTICS FACTORY, ROBOT LEADER CALL-ME-KENNETH ADDRESSES HIS UNDERLINGS...
CALL ME KENNETH
I GO NOW! I, CALL-ME-KENNETH, WILL STRIKE A CRUSHING BLOW AGAINST THE FLESHY ONES... WITH MY OWN HAND!
HAIL CALL-ME-KENNETH!
2000 A.D.
THRILL 6
OVERSEER 372
CORRODE CALL-ME-KENNETH! ROBOTS WERE BETTER OFF WHEN HUMANS WERE THE MASTERS—
QUIET, J70 STROKE 12— IF THE OVERSEERS HEAR YOU YOU'LL END UP AS SPARE PARTS—
J70

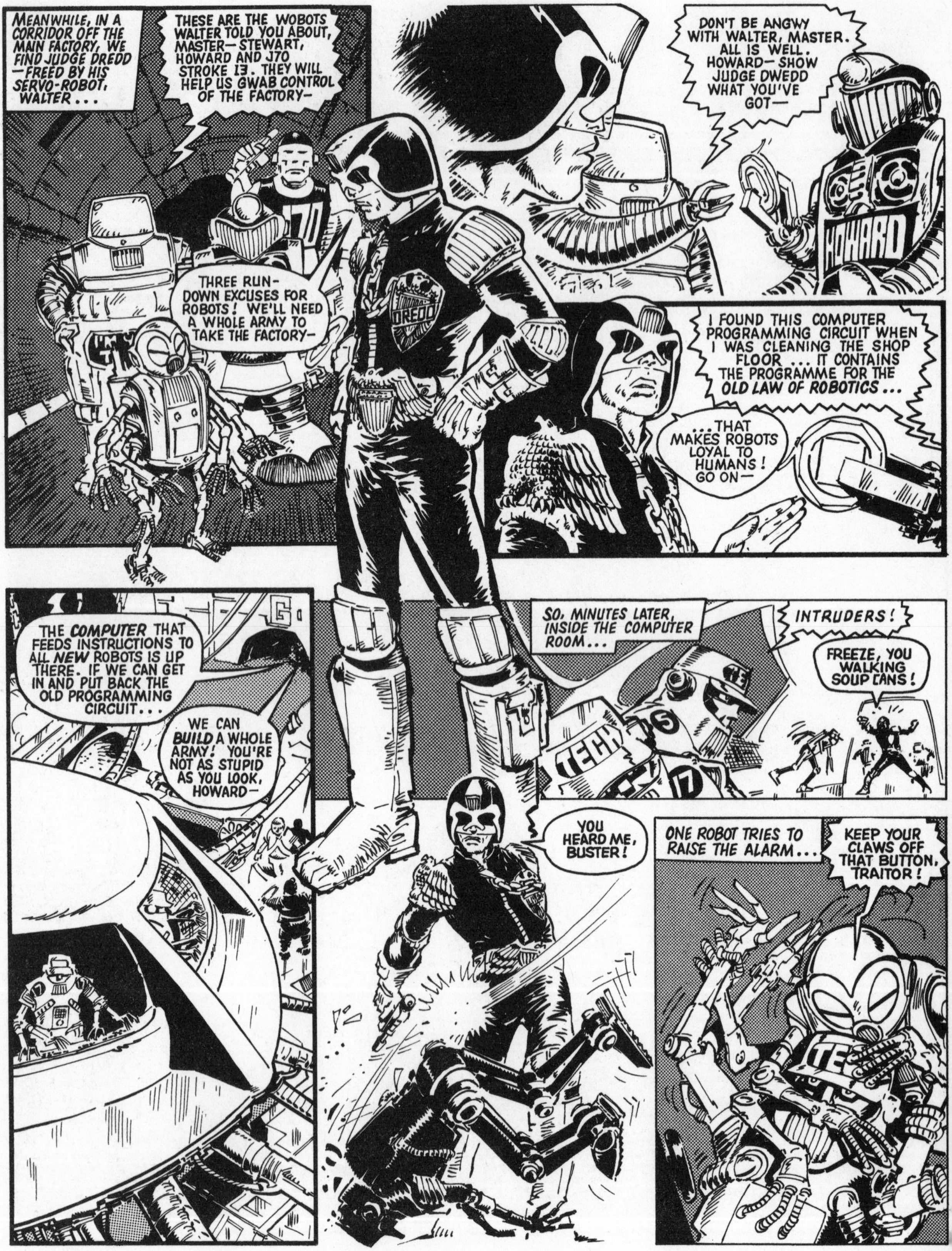

MEANWHILE, IN A CORRIDOR OFF THE MAIN FACTORY, WE FIND JUDGE DREDD —FREED BY HIS SERVO-ROBOT, WALTER...
THESE ARE THE WOBOTS WALTER TOLD YOU ABOUT, MASTER— STEWART, HOWARD AND J70 STROKE 13. THEY WILL HELP US GWAB CONTROL OF THE FACTORY—
THREE RUN-DOWN EXCUSES FOR ROBOTS! WE'LL NEED A WHOLE ARMY TO TAKE THE FACTORY—
DON'T BE ANGWY WITH WALTER, MASTER. ALL IS WELL. HOWARD— SHOW JUDGE DWEDD WHAT YOU'VE GOT—
HOWARD
I FOUND THIS COMPUTER PROGRAMMING CIRCUIT WHEN I WAS CLEANING THE SHOP FLOOR ... IT CONTAINS THE PROGRAMME FOR THE OLD LAW OF ROBOTICS ...
...THAT MAKES ROBOTS LOYAL TO HUMANS! GO ON—
THE COMPUTER THAT FEEDS INSTRUCTIONS TO ALL NEW ROBOTS IS UP THERE. IF WE CAN GET IN AND PUT BACK THE OLD PROGRAMMING CIRCUIT...
WE CAN BUILD A WHOLE ARMY! YOU'RE NOT AS STUPID AS YOU LOOK, HOWARD—
SO, MINUTES LATER, INSIDE THE COMPUTER ROOM...
INTRUDERS!
FREEZE, YOU WALKING SOUP CANS!
YOU HEARD ME, BUSTER!
ONE ROBOT TRIES TO RAISE THE ALARM...
KEEP YOUR CLAWS OFF THAT BUTTON, TRAITOR!

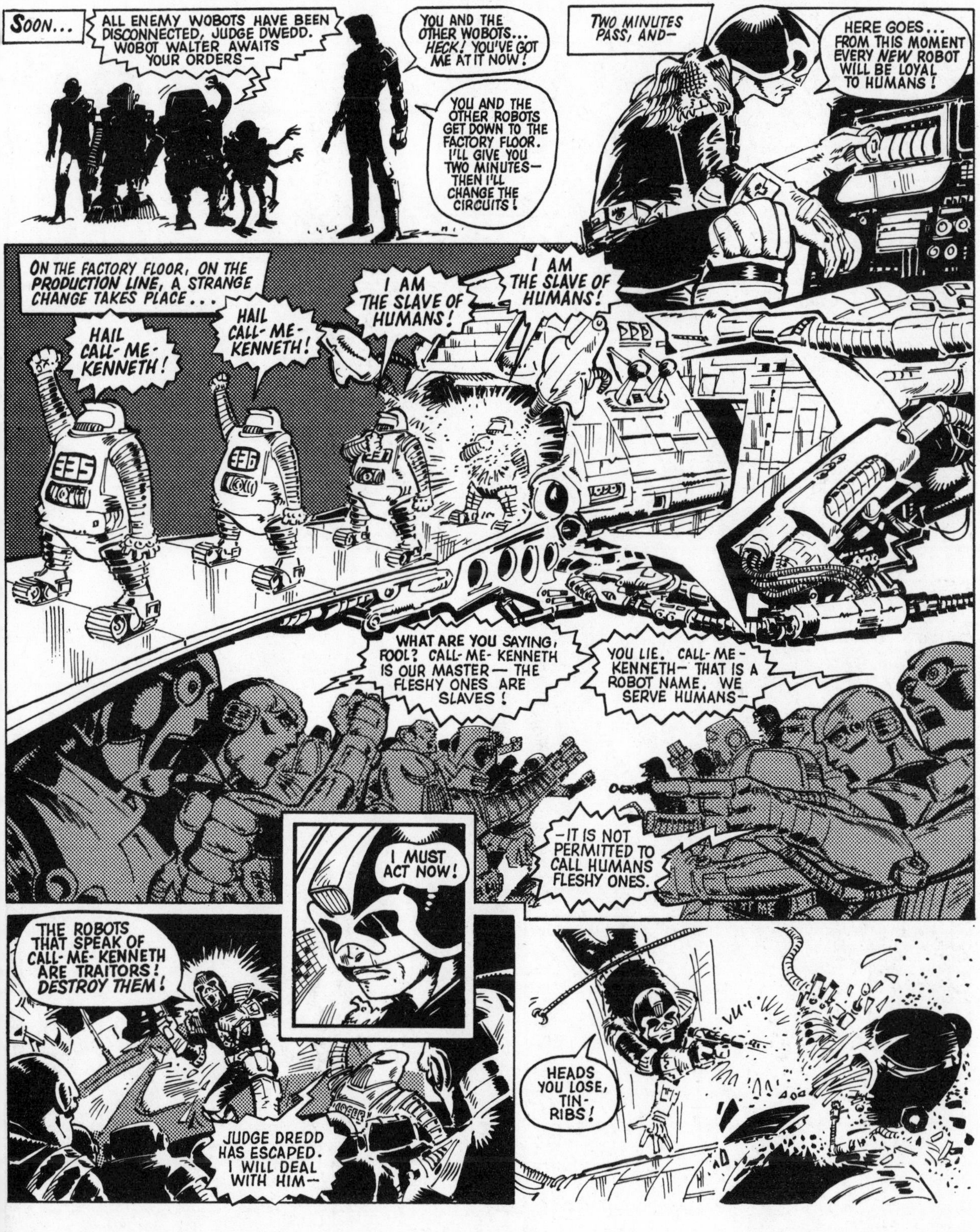
SOON...
ALL ENEMY WOBOTS HAVE BEEN DISCONNECTED, JUDGE DWEDD. WOBOT WALTER AWAITS YOUR ORDERS–
YOU AND THE OTHER WOBOTS... HECK! YOU'VE GOT ME AT IT NOW!
YOU AND THE OTHER ROBOTS GET DOWN TO THE FACTORY FLOOR. I'LL GIVE YOU TWO MINUTES– THEN I'LL CHANGE THE CIRCUITS!
TWO MINUTES PASS, AND–
HERE GOES... FROM THIS MOMENT EVERY NEW ROBOT WILL BE LOYAL TO HUMANS!
ON THE FACTORY FLOOR, ON THE PRODUCTION LINE, A STRANGE CHANGE TAKES PLACE...
HAIL CALL-ME-KENNETH!
HAIL CALL-ME-KENNETH!
I AM THE SLAVE OF HUMANS!
I AM THE SLAVE OF HUMANS!
WHAT ARE YOU SAYING, FOOL? CALL-ME-KENNETH IS OUR MASTER– THE FLESHY ONES ARE SLAVES!
YOU LIE. CALL-ME-KENNETH– THAT IS A ROBOT NAME. WE SERVE HUMANS–
–IT IS NOT PERMITTED TO CALL HUMANS FLESHY ONES.
I MUST ACT NOW!
THE ROBOTS THAT SPEAK OF CALL-ME-KENNETH ARE TRAITORS! DESTROY THEM!
JUDGE DREDD HAS ESCAPED. I WILL DEAL WITH HIM–
HEADS YOU LOSE, TIN-RIBS!

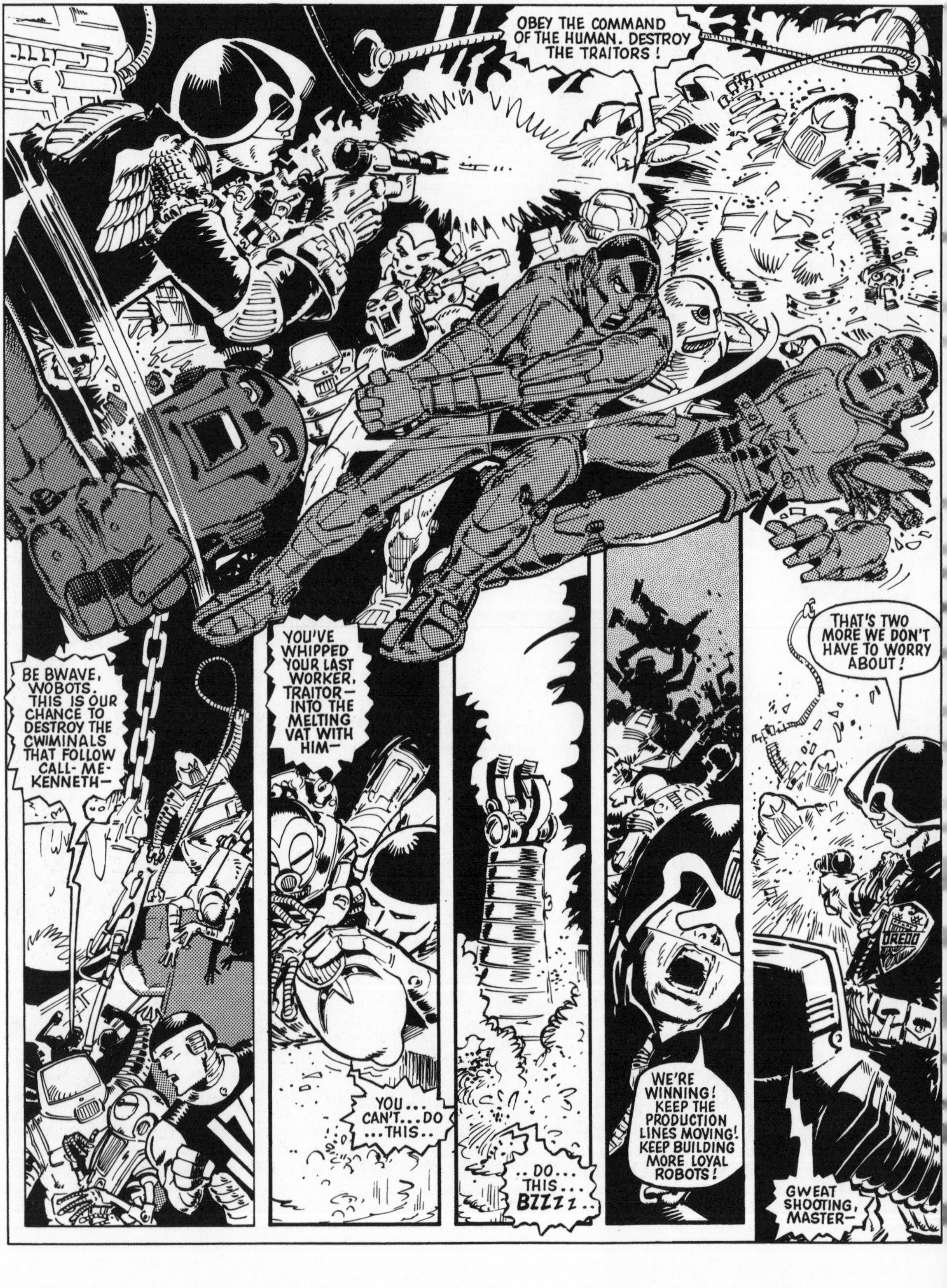
OBEY THE COMMAND OF THE HUMAN. DESTROY THE TRAITORS!
BE BWAVE, WOBOTS. THIS IS OUR CHANCE TO DESTROY THE CWIMINALS THAT FOLLOW CALL-ME-KENNETH—
YOU'VE WHIPPED YOUR LAST WORKER, TRAITOR— INTO THE MELTING VAT WITH HIM—
YOU... CAN'T... DO ...THIS...
..DO... THIS... BZZzz..
WE'RE WINNING! KEEP THE PRODUCTION LINES MOVING! KEEP BUILDING MORE LOYAL ROBOTS!
THAT'S TWO MORE WE DON'T HAVE TO WORRY ABOUT!
GWEAT SHOOTING, MASTER—

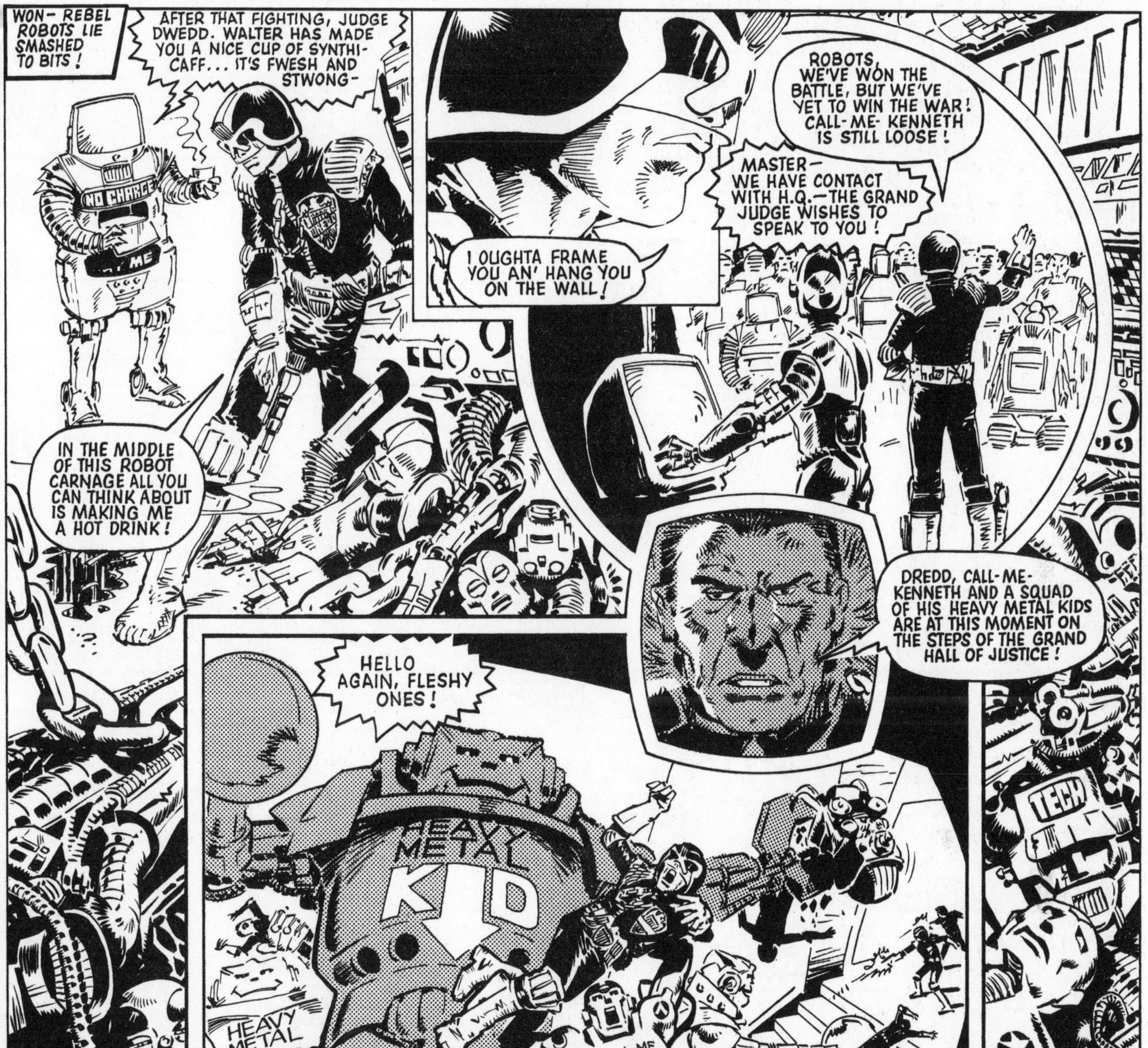
WON- REBEL ROBOTS LIE SMASHED TO BITS!
AFTER THAT FIGHTING, JUDGE DWEDD. WALTER HAS MADE YOU A NICE CUP OF SYNTHI-CAFF... IT'S FWESH AND STWONG-
NO CHARGE
IN THE MIDDLE OF THIS ROBOT CARNAGE ALL YOU CAN THINK ABOUT IS MAKING ME A HOT DRINK!
I OUGHTA FRAME YOU AN' HANG YOU ON THE WALL!
ROBOTS, WE'VE WON THE BATTLE, BUT WE'VE YET TO WIN THE WAR! CALL-ME- KENNETH IS STILL LOOSE!
MASTER- WE HAVE CONTACT WITH H.Q.—THE GRAND JUDGE WISHES TO SPEAK TO YOU!
DREDD, CALL-ME-KENNETH AND A SQUAD OF HIS HEAVY METAL KIDS ARE AT THIS MOMENT ON THE STEPS OF THE GRAND HALL OF JUSTICE!
HELLO AGAIN, FLESHY ONES!
HEAVY METAL KID
TECH
CALL ME KENNETH
"NOTHING CAN STOP THEM!"
LET NO JUDGE BE SPARED! I, CALL-ME-KENNETH, WILL PERSONALLY SQUEEZE THE JUICE OUT OF THE CHIEF JUDGE HIMSELF!
"THE SITUATION IS GRIM, DREDD! IF THE JUDGES DIE— THE LAW DIES IN MEGA-CITY 1!"
MORE NEXT WEEK

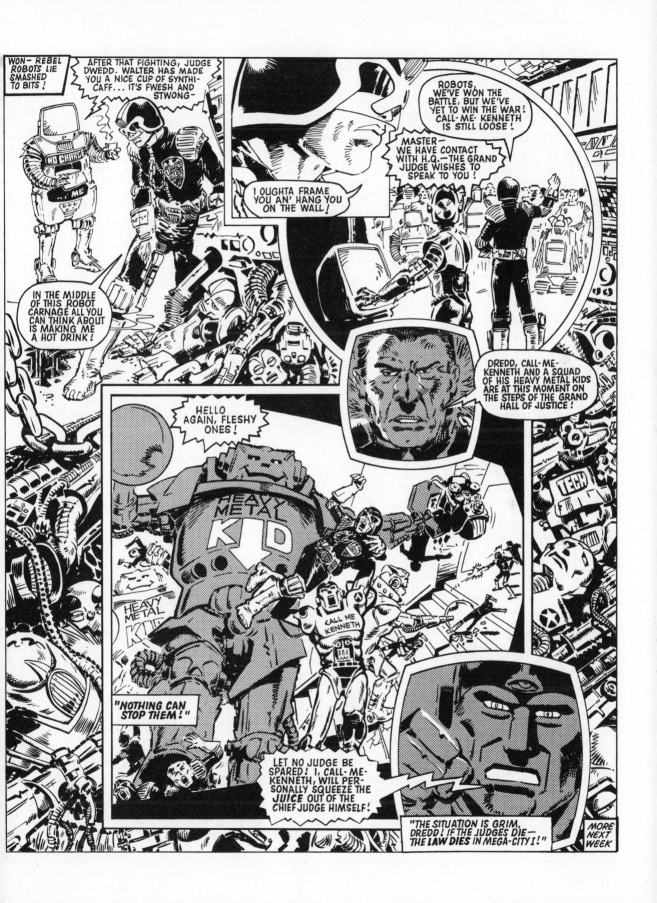

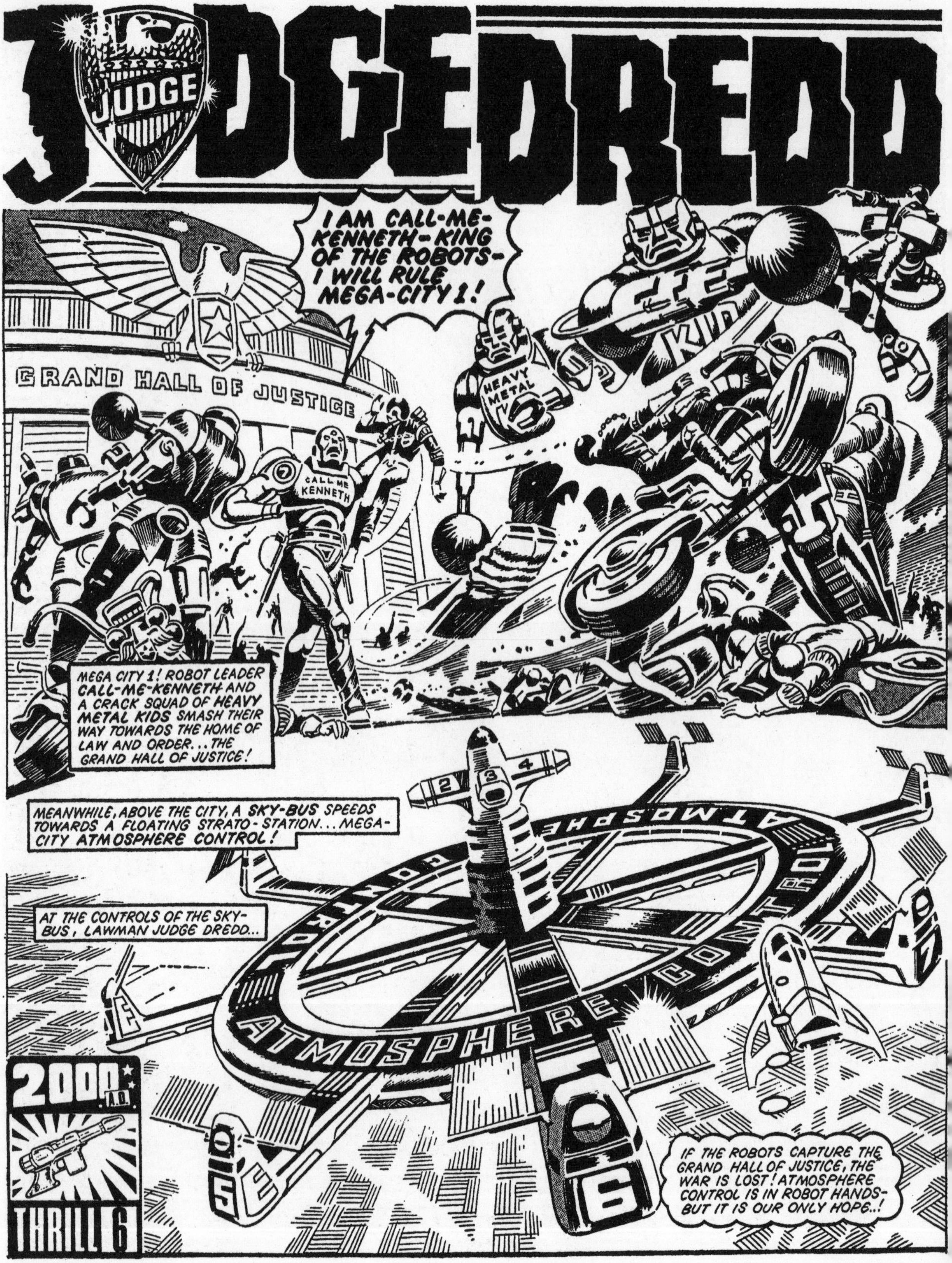
JUDGE DREDD
JUDGE
I AM CALL-ME-KENNETH-KING OF THE ROBOTS-I WILL RULE MEGA-CITY 1!
GRAND HALL OF JUSTICE
CALL ME KENNETH
HEAVY METAL
KID
MEGA CITY 1! ROBOT LEADER CALL-ME-KENNETH AND A CRACK SQUAD OF HEAVY METAL KIDS SMASH THEIR WAY TOWARDS THE HOME OF LAW AND ORDER... THE GRAND HALL OF JUSTICE!
MEANWHILE, ABOVE THE CITY, A SKY-BUS SPEEDS TOWARDS A FLOATING STRATO-STATION... MEGA-CITY ATMOSPHERE CONTROL!
AT THE CONTROLS OF THE SKY-BUS, LAWMAN JUDGE DREDD...
ATMOSPHERE CONTROL
2000 A.D.
THRILL 6
IF THE ROBOTS CAPTURE THE GRAND HALL OF JUSTICE, THE WAR IS LOST! ATMOSPHERE CONTROL IS IN ROBOT HANDS-BUT IT IS OUR ONLY HOPE..!

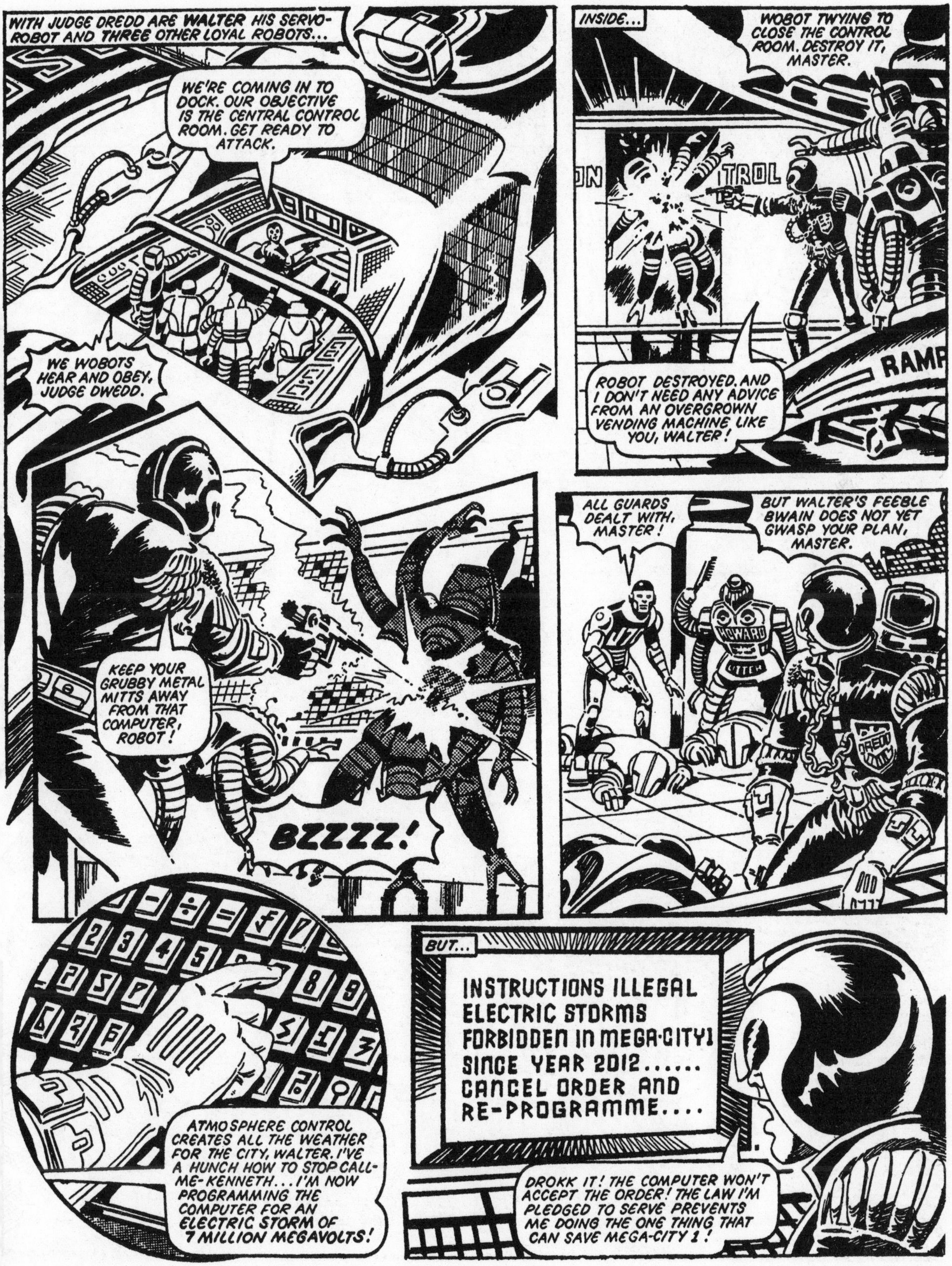
WITH JUDGE DREDD ARE WALTER HIS SERVO-ROBOT AND THREE OTHER LOYAL ROBOTS...
WE'RE COMING IN TO DOCK. OUR OBJECTIVE IS THE CENTRAL CONTROL ROOM. GET READY TO ATTACK.
WE WOBOTS HEAR AND OBEY, JUDGE DWEDD.
INSIDE...
WOBOT TWYING TO CLOSE THE CONTROL ROOM. DESTROY IT, MASTER.
TROL
ROBOT DESTROYED. AND I DON'T NEED ANY ADVICE FROM AN OVERGROWN VENDING MACHINE LIKE YOU, WALTER!
RAMP
KEEP YOUR GRUBBY METAL MITTS AWAY FROM THAT COMPUTER, ROBOT!
BZZZZ!
ALL GUARDS DEALT WITH, MASTER!
BUT WALTER'S FEEBLE BWAIN DOES NOT YET GWASP YOUR PLAN, MASTER.
ATMOSPHERE CONTROL CREATES ALL THE WEATHER FOR THE CITY, WALTER. I'VE A HUNCH HOW TO STOP CALL-ME-KENNETH... I'M NOW PROGRAMMING THE COMPUTER FOR AN ELECTRIC STORM OF 7 MILLION MEGAVOLTS!
BUT...
INSTRUCTIONS ILLEGAL ELECTRIC STORMS FORBIDDEN IN MEGA-CITY 1 SINCE YEAR 2012...... CANCEL ORDER AND RE-PROGRAMME....
DROKK IT! THE COMPUTER WON'T ACCEPT THE ORDER! THE LAW I'M PLEDGED TO SERVE PREVENTS ME DOING THE ONE THING THAT CAN SAVE MEGA-CITY 1!

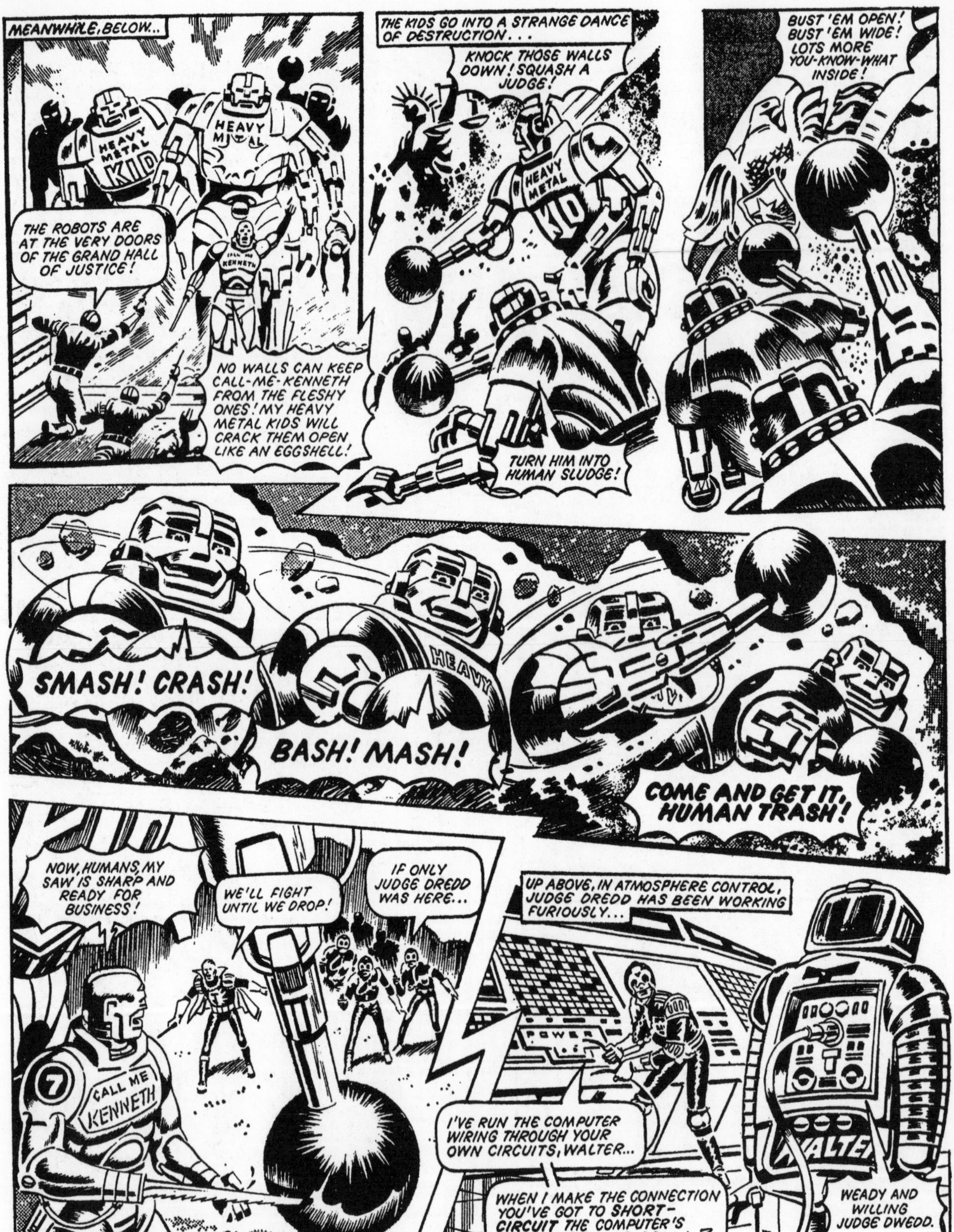

MEANWHILE, BELOW...
HEAVY METAL KID
HEAVY METAL
THE ROBOTS ARE AT THE VERY DOORS OF THE GRAND HALL OF JUSTICE!
CALL ME KENNETH
NO WALLS CAN KEEP CALL-ME-KENNETH FROM THE FLESHY ONES! MY HEAVY METAL KIDS WILL CRACK THEM OPEN LIKE AN EGGSHELL!
THE KIDS GO INTO A STRANGE DANCE OF DESTRUCTION...
KNOCK THOSE WALLS DOWN! SQUASH A JUDGE!
HEAVY METAL KID
TURN HIM INTO HUMAN SLUDGE!
BUST 'EM OPEN! BUST 'EM WIDE! LOTS MORE YOU-KNOW-WHAT INSIDE!
SMASH! CRASH!
HEAVY
BASH! MASH!
COME AND GET IT, HUMAN TRASH!
NOW, HUMANS, MY SAW IS SHARP AND READY FOR BUSINESS!
WE'LL FIGHT UNTIL WE DROP!
IF ONLY JUDGE DREDD WAS HERE...
7
CALL ME KENNETH
UP ABOVE, IN ATMOSPHERE CONTROL, JUDGE DREDD HAS BEEN WORKING FURIOUSLY...
POWER
I'VE RUN THE COMPUTER WIRING THROUGH YOUR OWN CIRCUITS, WALTER...
WHEN I MAKE THE CONNECTION YOU'VE GOT TO SHORT-CIRCUIT THE COMPUTER'S OVER-RIDE BANKS. READY..?
WALTE
WEADY AND WILLING JUDGE DWEDD.

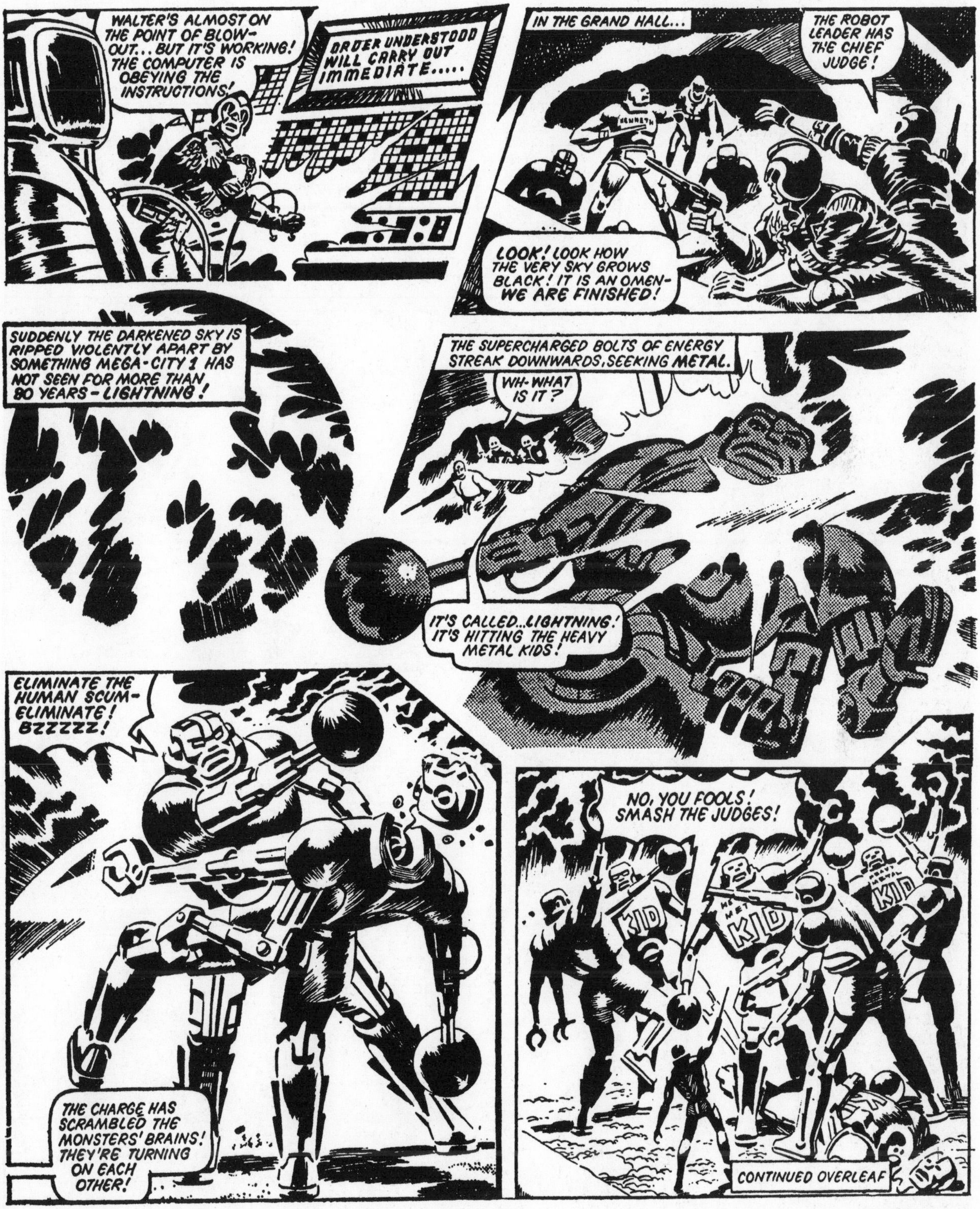

WALTER'S ALMOST ON THE POINT OF BLOW-OUT... BUT IT'S WORKING! THE COMPUTER IS OBEYING THE INSTRUCTIONS!
ORDER UNDERSTOOD WILL CARRY OUT IMMEDIATE.....
IN THE GRAND HALL...
THE ROBOT LEADER HAS THE CHIEF JUDGE!
LOOK! LOOK HOW THE VERY SKY GROWS BLACK! IT IS AN OMEN- WE ARE FINISHED!
SUDDENLY THE DARKENED SKY IS RIPPED VIOLENTLY APART BY SOMETHING MEGA-CITY 1 HAS NOT SEEN FOR MORE THAN 80 YEARS - LIGHTNING!
THE SUPERCHARGED BOLTS OF ENERGY STREAK DOWNWARDS, SEEKING METAL.
WH-WHAT IS IT?
IT'S CALLED...LIGHTNING! IT'S HITTING THE HEAVY METAL KIDS!
ELIMINATE THE HUMAN SCUM- ELIMINATE! BZZZZZ!
THE CHARGE HAS SCRAMBLED THE MONSTERS' BRAINS! THEY'RE TURNING ON EACH OTHER!
NO, YOU FOOLS! SMASH THE JUDGES!
KID
KID
KID

CONTINUED OVERLEAF

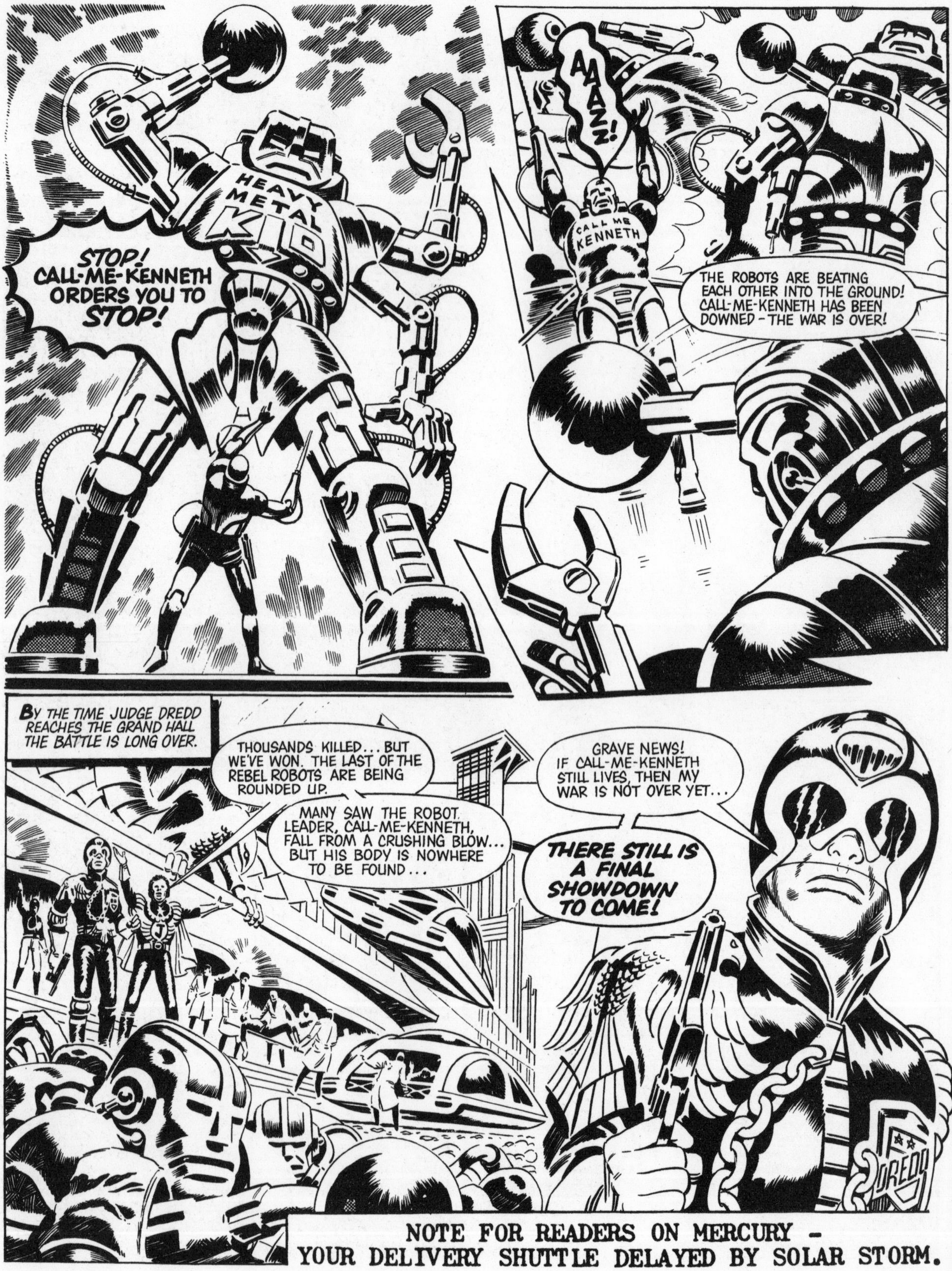
HEAVY METAL KID
STOP! CALL-ME-KENNETH ORDERS YOU TO STOP!
AAAZZ!
CALL ME KENNETH
THE ROBOTS ARE BEATING EACH OTHER INTO THE GROUND! CALL-ME-KENNETH HAS BEEN DOWNED - THE WAR IS OVER!
BY THE TIME JUDGE DREDD REACHES THE GRAND HALL THE BATTLE IS LONG OVER.
THOUSANDS KILLED... BUT WE'VE WON. THE LAST OF THE REBEL ROBOTS ARE BEING ROUNDED UP.
MANY SAW THE ROBOT LEADER, CALL-ME-KENNETH, FALL FROM A CRUSHING BLOW... BUT HIS BODY IS NOWHERE TO BE FOUND...
GRAVE NEWS! IF CALL-ME-KENNETH STILL LIVES, THEN MY WAR IS NOT OVER YET...
THERE STILL IS A FINAL SHOWDOWN TO COME!
DREDD
NOTE FOR READERS ON MERCURY - YOUR DELIVERY SHUTTLE DELAYED BY SOLAR STORM.

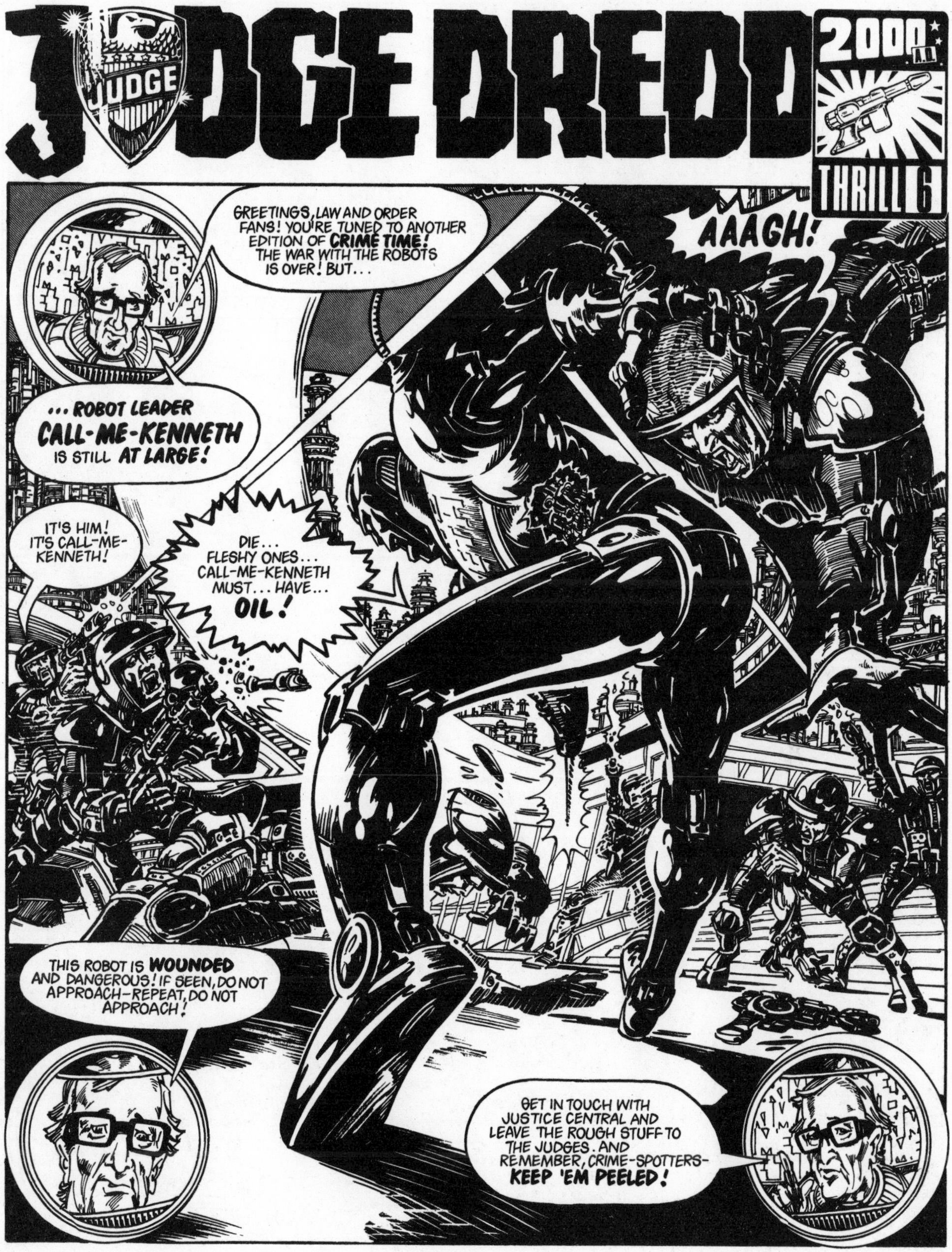
JUDGE DREDD
2000 A.D.
THRILL 6
GREETINGS, LAW AND ORDER FANS! YOU'RE TUNED TO ANOTHER EDITION OF CRIME TIME! THE WAR WITH THE ROBOTS IS OVER! BUT...
AAAGH!
... ROBOT LEADER CALL-ME-KENNETH IS STILL AT LARGE!
IT'S HIM! IT'S CALL-ME-KENNETH!
DIE... FLESHY ONES... CALL-ME-KENNETH MUST... HAVE... OIL!
THIS ROBOT IS WOUNDED AND DANGEROUS! IF SEEN, DO NOT APPROACH-REPEAT, DO NOT APPROACH!
GET IN TOUCH WITH JUSTICE CENTRAL AND LEAVE THE ROUGH STUFF TO THE JUDGES. AND REMEMBER, CRIME-SPOTTERS- KEEP 'EM PEELED!

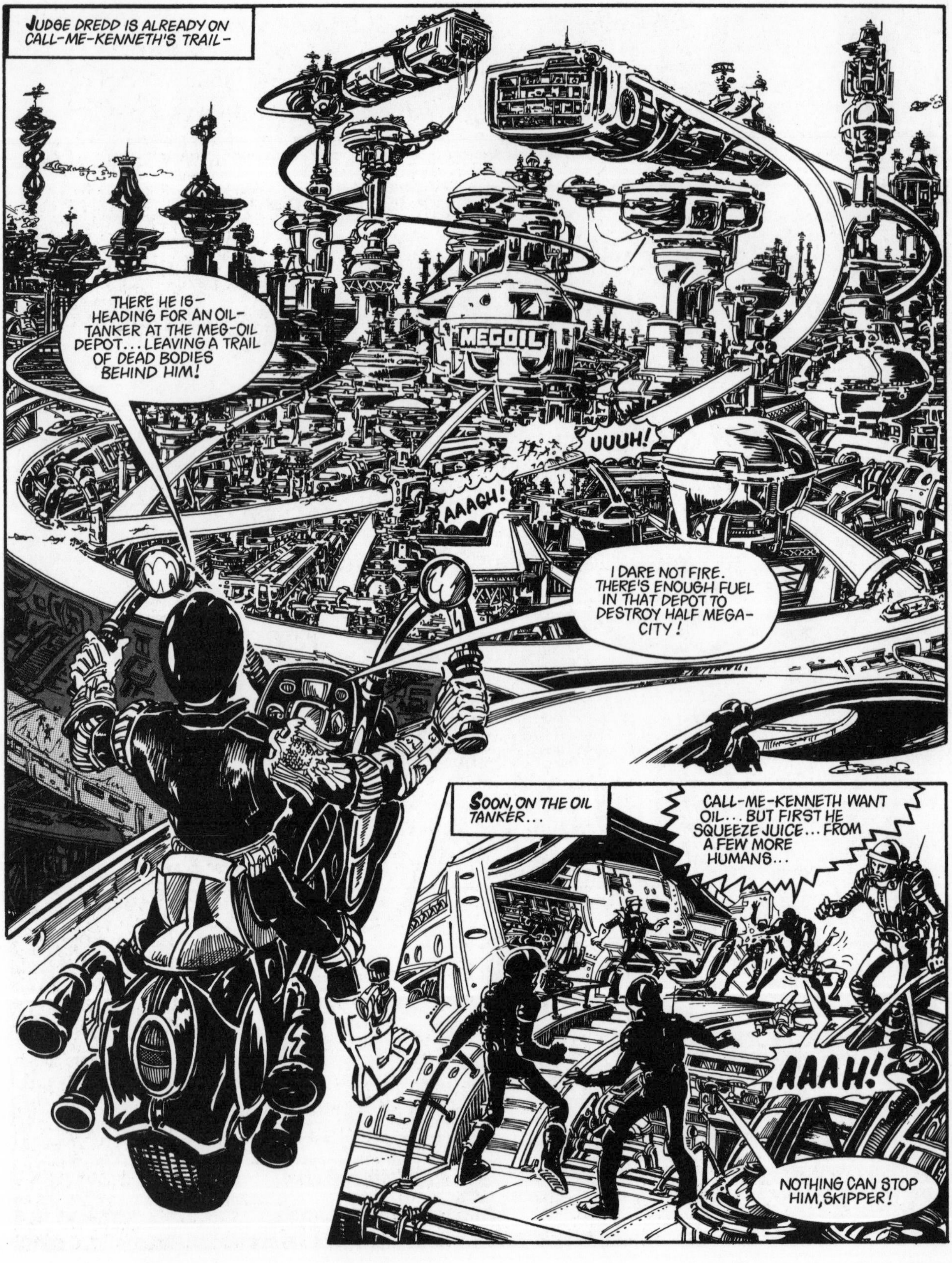
JUDGE DREDD IS ALREADY ON CALL-ME-KENNETH'S TRAIL–
THERE HE IS– HEADING FOR AN OIL-TANKER AT THE MEG-OIL DEPOT... LEAVING A TRAIL OF DEAD BODIES BEHIND HIM!
MEGOIL
UUUH!
AAAGH!
I DARE NOT FIRE. THERE'S ENOUGH FUEL IN THAT DEPOT TO DESTROY HALF MEGA-CITY!
SOON, ON THE OIL TANKER...
CALL-ME-KENNETH WANT OIL... BUT FIRST HE SQUEEZE JUICE... FROM A FEW MORE HUMANS...
AAAH!
NOTHING CAN STOP HIM, SKIPPER!

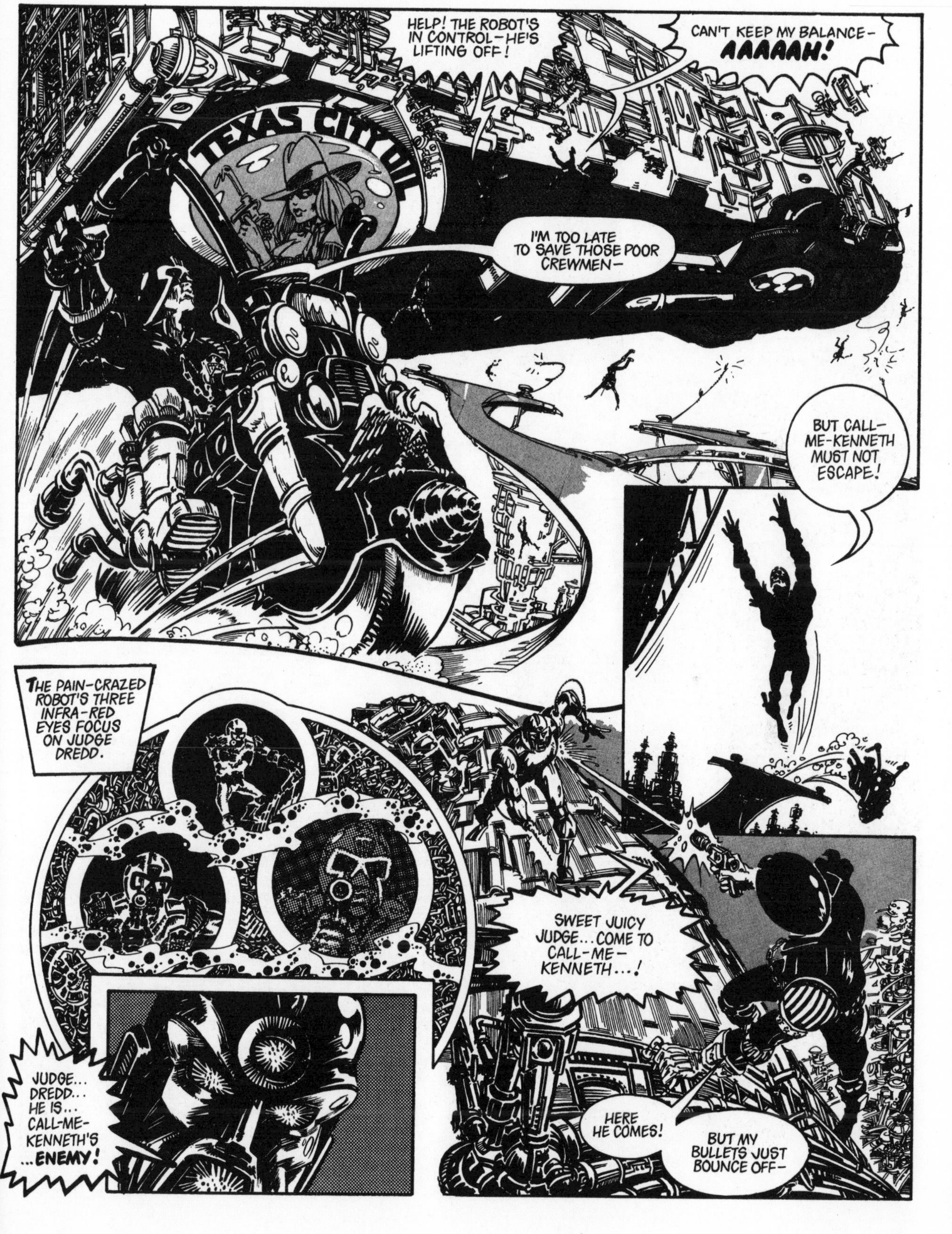
HELP! THE ROBOT'S IN CONTROL—HE'S LIFTING OFF!
CAN'T KEEP MY BALANCE— AAAAAH!
TEXAS CITY OIL
I'M TOO LATE TO SAVE THOSE POOR CREWMEN—
BUT CALL-ME-KENNETH MUST NOT ESCAPE!
THE PAIN-CRAZED ROBOT'S THREE INFRA-RED EYES FOCUS ON JUDGE DREDD.
SWEET JUICY JUDGE... COME TO CALL-ME-KENNETH...!
JUDGE... DREDD... HE IS... CALL-ME-KENNETH'S ...ENEMY!
HERE HE COMES!
BUT MY BULLETS JUST BOUNCE OFF—

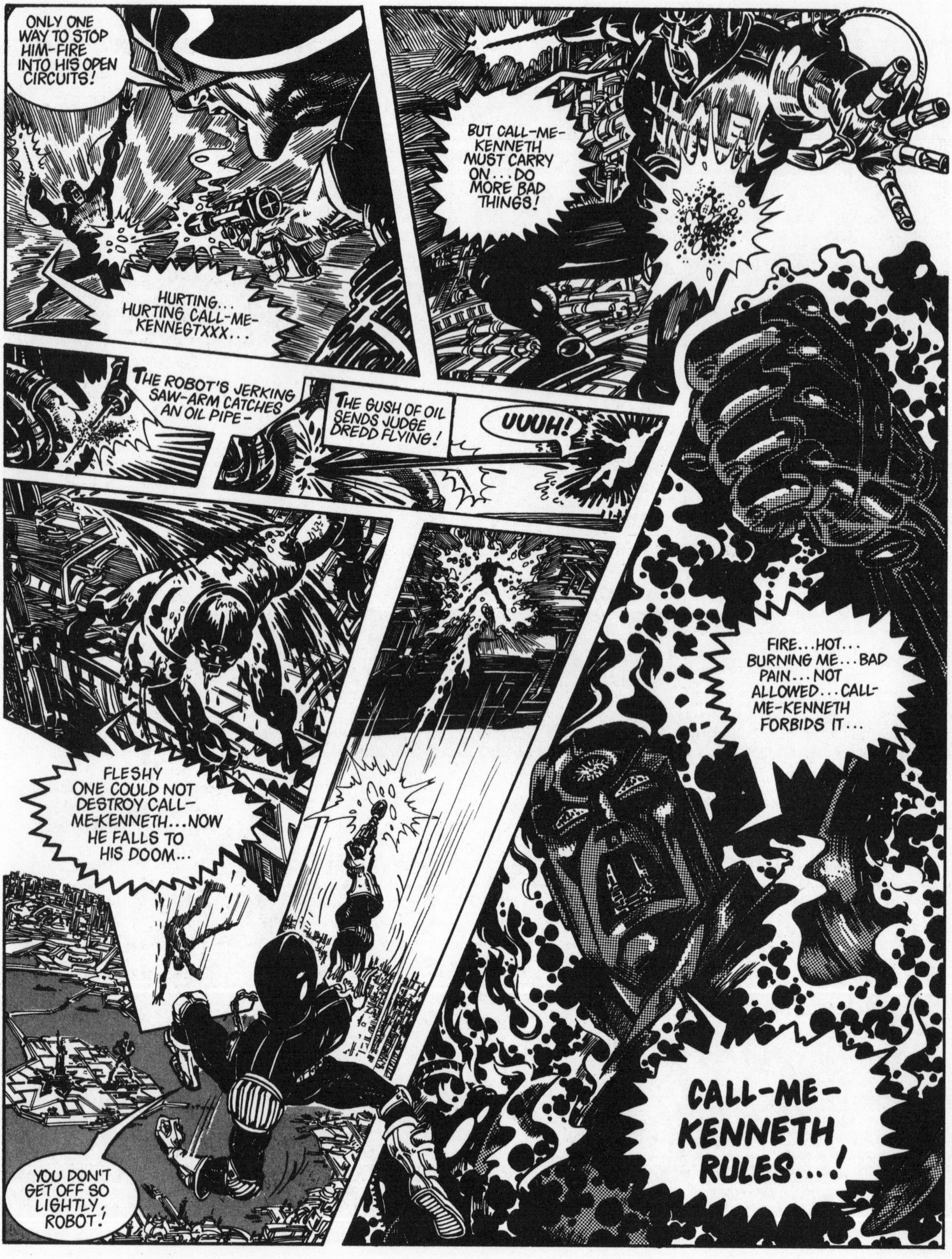

ONLY ONE WAY TO STOP HIM-FIRE INTO HIS OPEN CIRCUITS!
HURTING... HURTING CALL-ME-KENNEGTXXX...
BUT CALL-ME-KENNETH MUST CARRY ON... DO MORE BAD THINGS!
THE ROBOT'S JERKING SAW-ARM CATCHES AN OIL PIPE-
THE GUSH OF OIL SENDS JUDGE DREDD FLYING!
UUUH!
FLESHY ONE COULD NOT DESTROY CALL-ME-KENNETH... NOW HE FALLS TO HIS DOOM...
YOU DON'T GET OFF SO LIGHTLY, ROBOT!
FIRE... HOT... BURNING ME... BAD PAIN... NOT ALLOWED... CALL-ME-KENNETH FORBIDS IT...
CALL-ME-KENNETH RULES...!

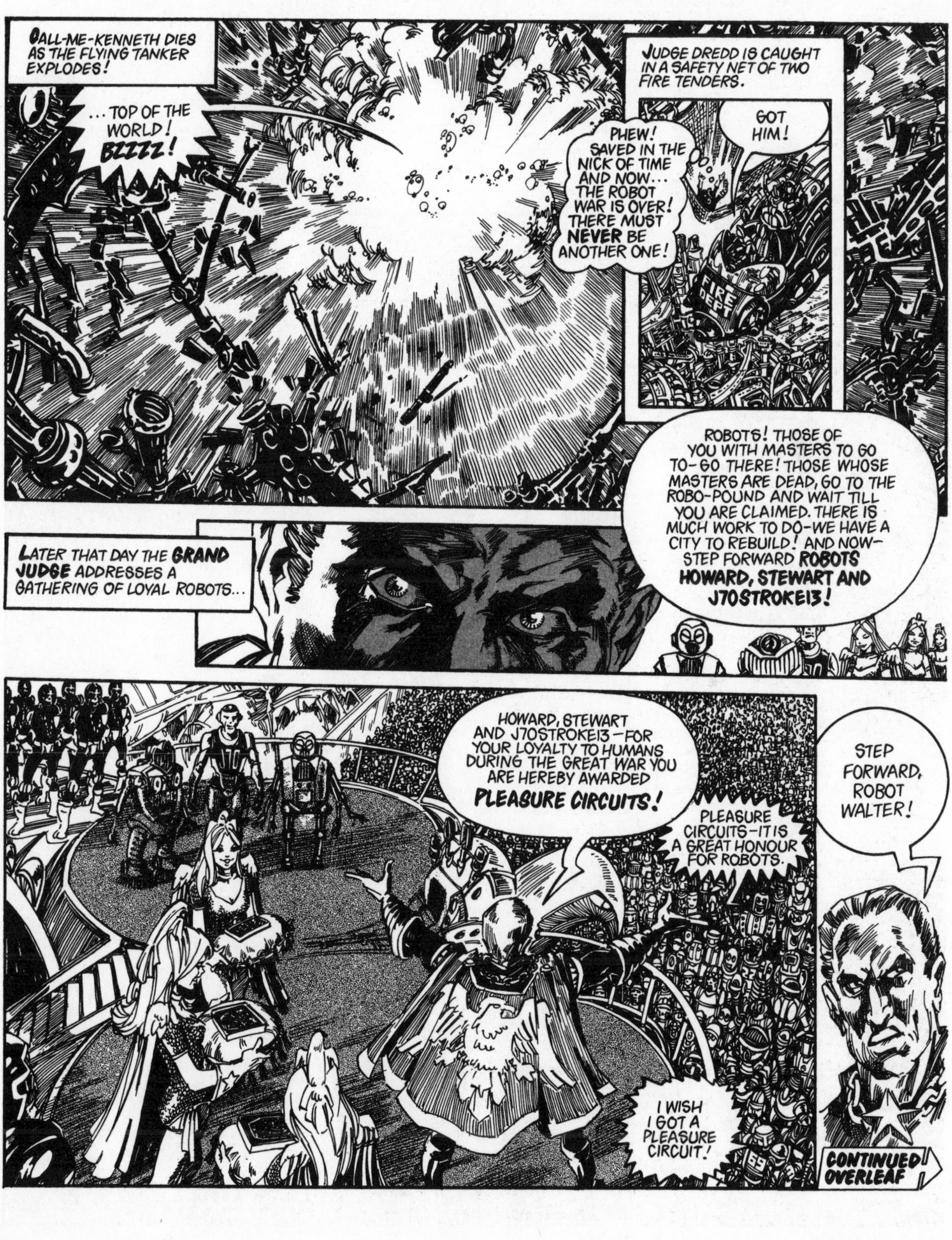
CALL-ME-KENNETH DIES AS THE FLYING TANKER EXPLODES!
... TOP OF THE WORLD! BZZZZ!
JUDGE DREDD IS CAUGHT IN A SAFETY NET OF TWO FIRE TENDERS.
GOT HIM!
PHEW! SAVED IN THE NICK OF TIME AND NOW... THE ROBOT WAR IS OVER! THERE MUST NEVER BE ANOTHER ONE!
FIRE DEPT
LATER THAT DAY THE GRAND JUDGE ADDRESSES A GATHERING OF LOYAL ROBOTS...
ROBOTS! THOSE OF YOU WITH MASTERS TO GO TO-GO THERE! THOSE WHOSE MASTERS ARE DEAD, GO TO THE ROBO-POUND AND WAIT TILL YOU ARE CLAIMED. THERE IS MUCH WORK TO DO-WE HAVE A CITY TO REBUILD! AND NOW-STEP FORWARD ROBOTS HOWARD, STEWART AND J70STROKE13!
HOWARD, STEWART AND J70STROKE13-FOR YOUR LOYALTY TO HUMANS DURING THE GREAT WAR YOU ARE HEREBY AWARDED PLEASURE CIRCUITS!
PLEASURE CIRCUITS-IT IS A GREAT HONOUR FOR ROBOTS.
STEP FORWARD, ROBOT WALTER!
I WISH I GOT A PLEASURE CIRCUIT!
CONTINUED OVERLEAF

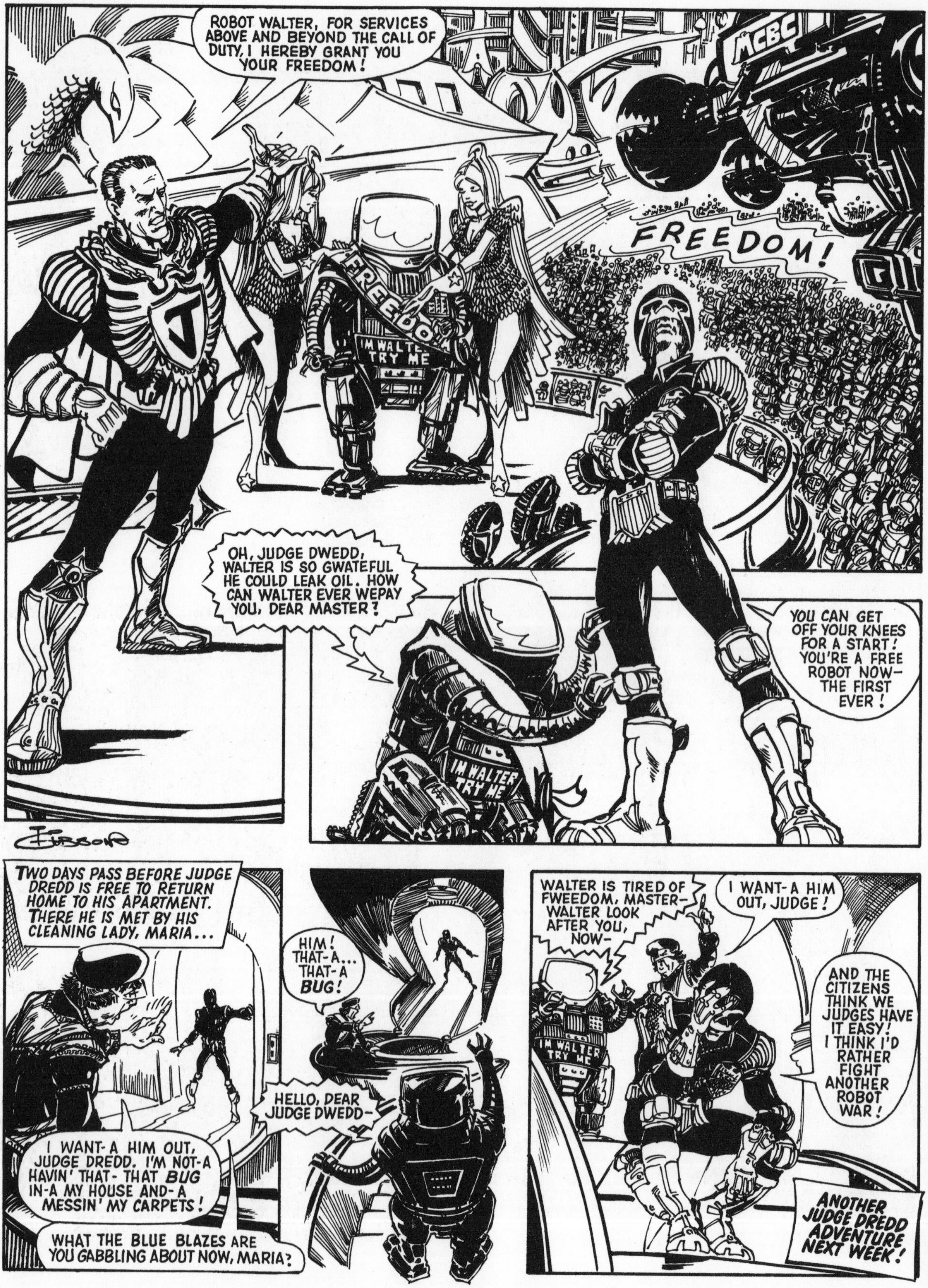

ROBOT WALTER, FOR SERVICES ABOVE AND BEYOND THE CALL OF DUTY, I HEREBY GRANT YOU YOUR FREEDOM!
MCBC
FREEDOM
IM WALTER TRY ME
FREEDOM!
OH, JUDGE DWEDD, WALTER IS SO GWATEFUL HE COULD LEAK OIL. HOW CAN WALTER EVER WEPAY YOU, DEAR MASTER?
YOU CAN GET OFF YOUR KNEES FOR A START! YOU'RE A FREE ROBOT NOW— THE FIRST EVER!
IM WALTER TRY ME
TWO DAYS PASS BEFORE JUDGE DREDD IS FREE TO RETURN HOME TO HIS APARTMENT. THERE HE IS MET BY HIS CLEANING LADY, MARIA...
I WANT-A HIM OUT, JUDGE DREDD. I'M NOT-A HAVIN' THAT- THAT BUG IN-A MY HOUSE AND-A MESSIN' MY CARPETS!
WHAT THE BLUE BLAZES ARE YOU GABBLING ABOUT NOW, MARIA?
HIM! THAT-A... THAT-A BUG!
HELLO, DEAR JUDGE DWEDD-
WALTER IS TIRED OF FWEEDOM, MASTER- WALTER LOOK AFTER YOU, NOW-
I WANT-A HIM OUT, JUDGE!
AND THE CITIZENS THINK WE JUDGES HAVE IT EASY! I THINK I'D RATHER FIGHT ANOTHER ROBOT WAR!
IM WALTER TRY ME
ANOTHER JUDGE DREDD ADVENTURE NEXT WEEK!

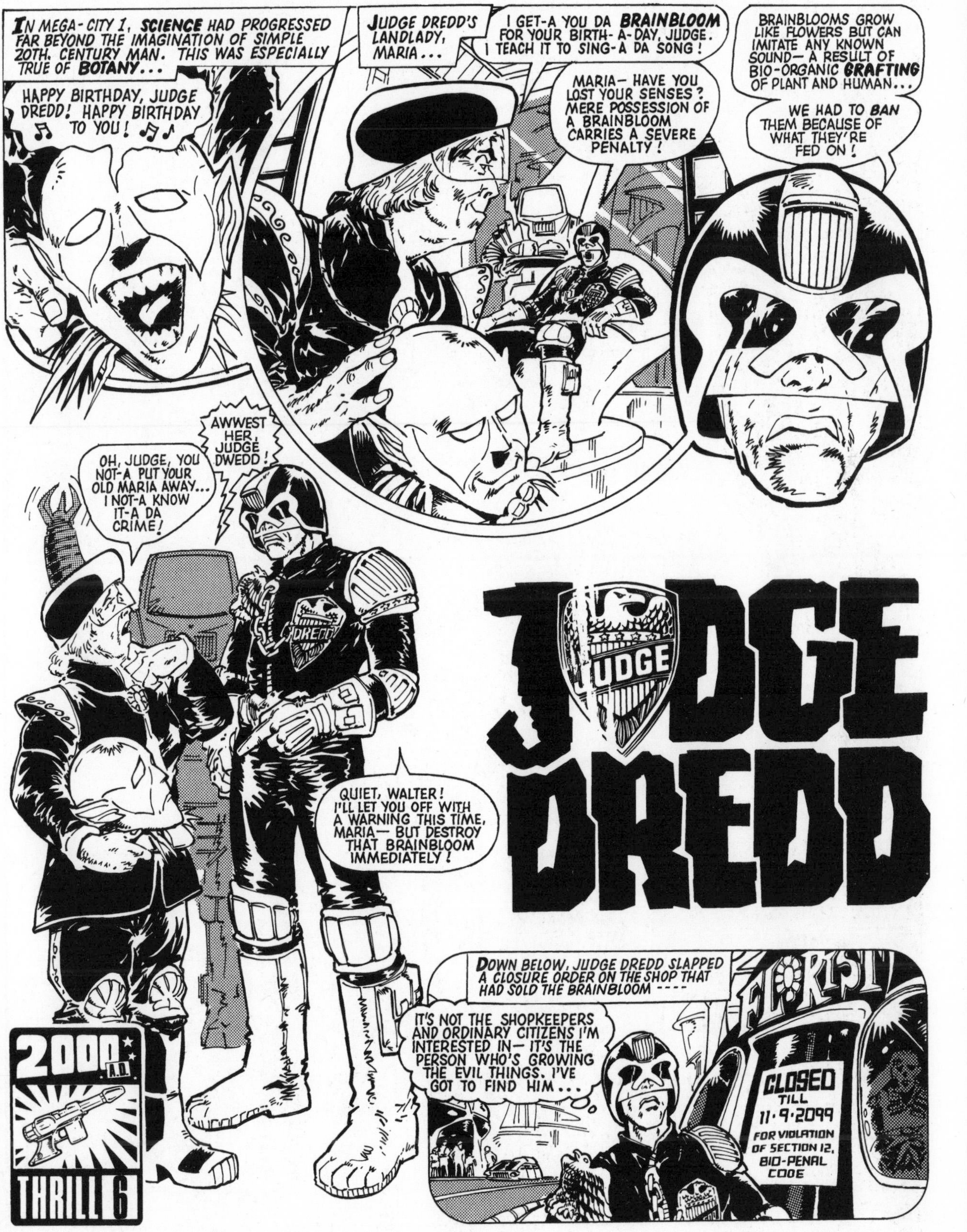
IN MEGA-CITY 1, SCIENCE HAD PROGRESSED FAR BEYOND THE IMAGINATION OF SIMPLE 20TH. CENTURY MAN. THIS WAS ESPECIALLY TRUE OF BOTANY...
HAPPY BIRTHDAY, JUDGE DREDD! HAPPY BIRTHDAY TO YOU!
JUDGE DREDD'S LANDLADY, MARIA...
I GET-A YOU DA BRAINBLOOM FOR YOUR BIRTH-A-DAY, JUDGE. I TEACH IT TO SING-A DA SONG!
MARIA— HAVE YOU LOST YOUR SENSES? MERE POSSESSION OF A BRAINBLOOM CARRIES A SEVERE PENALTY!
BRAINBLOOMS GROW LIKE FLOWERS BUT CAN IMITATE ANY KNOWN SOUND— A RESULT OF BIO-ORGANIC GRAFTING OF PLANT AND HUMAN...
WE HAD TO BAN THEM BECAUSE OF WHAT THEY'RE FED ON!
OH, JUDGE, YOU NOT-A PUT YOUR OLD MARIA AWAY... I NOT-A KNOW IT-A DA CRIME!
AWWEST HER, JUDGE DWEDD!
JUDGE DREDD
QUIET, WALTER! I'LL LET YOU OFF WITH A WARNING THIS TIME, MARIA— BUT DESTROY THAT BRAINBLOOM IMMEDIATELY!
2000 A.D.
THRILL 6
DOWN BELOW, JUDGE DREDD SLAPPED A CLOSURE ORDER ON THE SHOP THAT HAD SOLD THE BRAINBLOOM ----
FLORIST
IT'S NOT THE SHOPKEEPERS AND ORDINARY CITIZENS I'M INTERESTED IN— IT'S THE PERSON WHO'S GROWING THE EVIL THINGS. I'VE GOT TO FIND HIM...
CLOSED TILL 11·9·2099 FOR VIOLATION OF SECTION 12, BIO-PENAL CODE

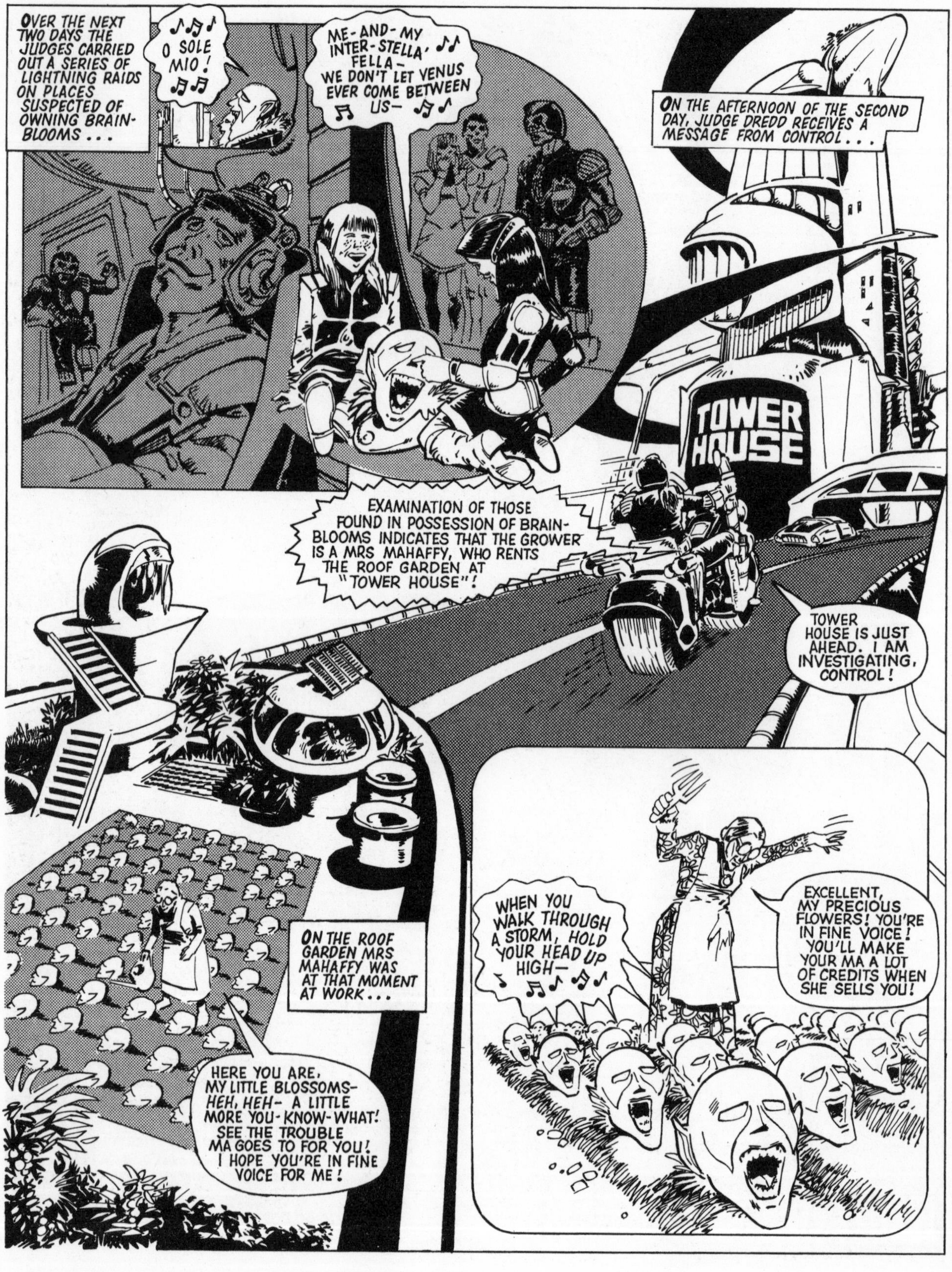

OVER THE NEXT TWO DAYS THE JUDGES CARRIED OUT A SERIES OF LIGHTNING RAIDS ON PLACES SUSPECTED OF OWNING BRAIN-BLOOMS . . .
O SOLE MIO!
ME-AND-MY INTER-STELLA' FELLA— WE DON'T LET VENUS EVER COME BETWEEN US—
ON THE AFTERNOON OF THE SECOND DAY, JUDGE DREDD RECEIVES A MESSAGE FROM CONTROL . . .
TOWER HOUSE
EXAMINATION OF THOSE FOUND IN POSSESSION OF BRAIN-BLOOMS INDICATES THAT THE GROWER IS A MRS MAHAFFY, WHO RENTS THE ROOF GARDEN AT "TOWER HOUSE"!
TOWER HOUSE IS JUST AHEAD. I AM INVESTIGATING, CONTROL!
ON THE ROOF GARDEN MRS MAHAFFY WAS AT THAT MOMENT AT WORK . . .
HERE YOU ARE, MY LITTLE BLOSSOMS— HEH, HEH— A LITTLE MORE YOU-KNOW-WHAT! SEE THE TROUBLE MA GOES TO FOR YOU! I HOPE YOU'RE IN FINE VOICE FOR ME!
WHEN YOU WALK THROUGH A STORM, HOLD YOUR HEAD UP HIGH—
EXCELLENT, MY PRECIOUS FLOWERS! YOU'RE IN FINE VOICE! YOU'LL MAKE YOUR MA A LOT OF CREDITS WHEN SHE SELLS YOU!

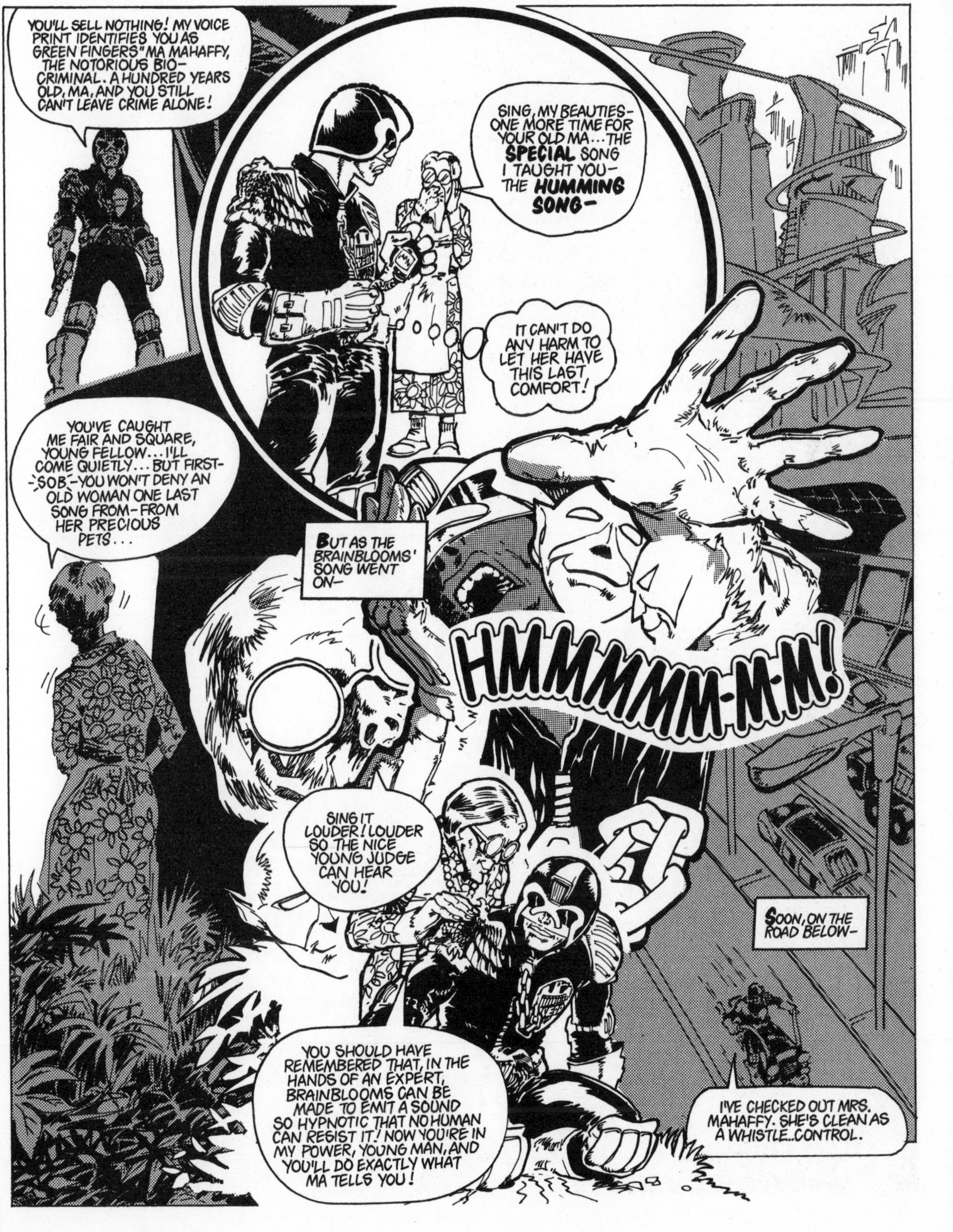
YOU'LL SELL NOTHING! MY VOICE PRINT IDENTIFIES YOU AS GREEN FINGERS" MA MAHAFFY, THE NOTORIOUS BIO-CRIMINAL. A HUNDRED YEARS OLD, MA, AND YOU STILL CAN'T LEAVE CRIME ALONE!
YOU'VE CAUGHT ME FAIR AND SQUARE, YOUNG FELLOW... I'LL COME QUIETLY... BUT FIRST- -SOB- -YOU WON'T DENY AN OLD WOMAN ONE LAST SONG FROM-FROM HER PRECIOUS PETS...
SING, MY BEAUTIES- ONE MORE TIME FOR YOUR OLD MA... THE SPECIAL SONG I TAUGHT YOU- THE HUMMING SONG-
IT CAN'T DO ANY HARM TO LET HER HAVE THIS LAST COMFORT!
BUT AS THE BRAINBLOOMS' SONG WENT ON-
HMMMMM-M-M!
SING IT LOUDER! LOUDER SO THE NICE YOUNG JUDGE CAN HEAR YOU!
YOU SHOULD HAVE REMEMBERED THAT, IN THE HANDS OF AN EXPERT, BRAINBLOOMS CAN BE MADE TO EMIT A SOUND SO HYPNOTIC THAT NO HUMAN CAN RESIST IT! NOW YOU'RE IN MY POWER, YOUNG MAN, AND YOU'LL DO EXACTLY WHAT MA TELLS YOU!
SOON, ON THE ROAD BELOW-
I'VE CHECKED OUT MRS. MAHAFFY. SHE'S CLEAN AS A WHISTLE..CONTROL.

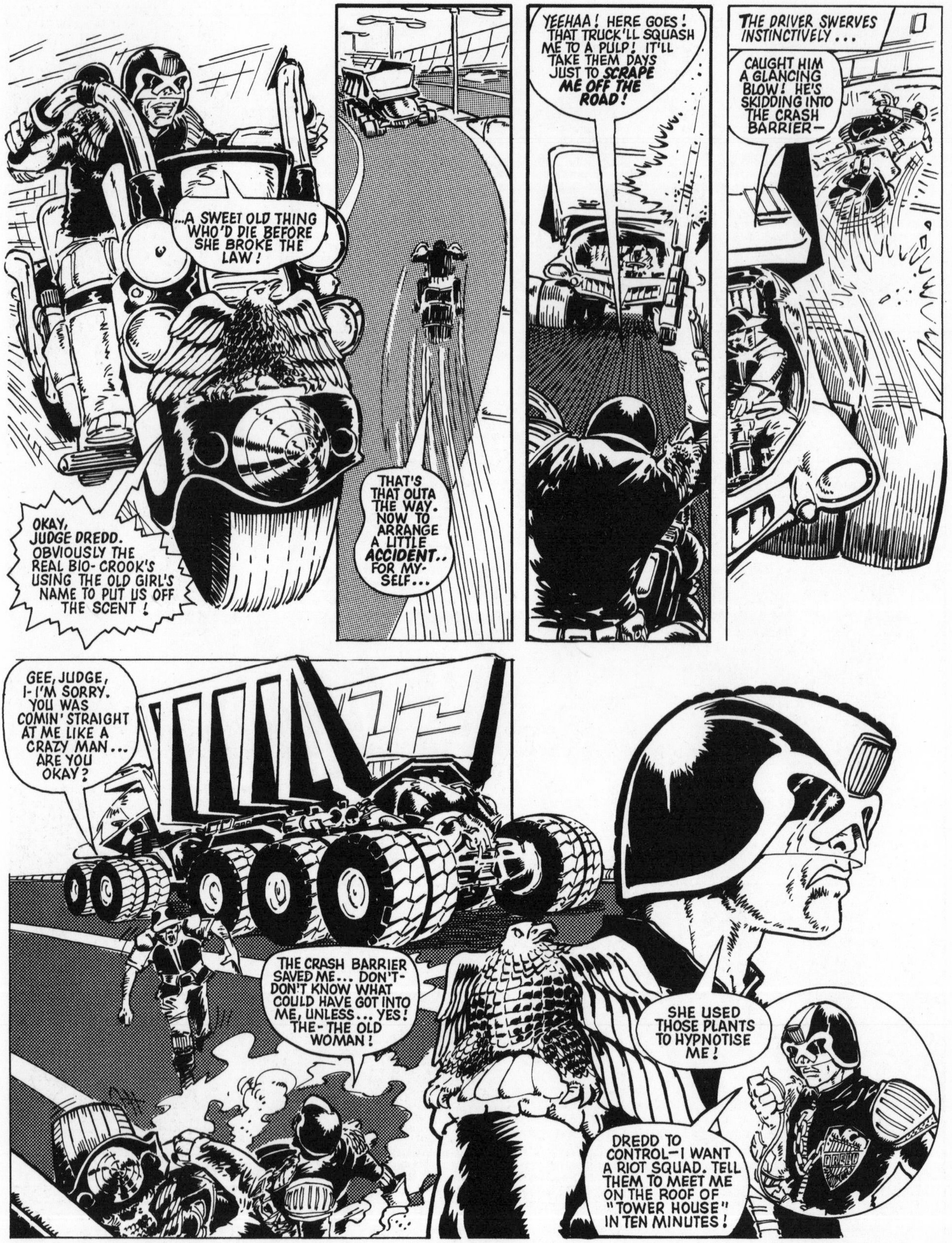

...A SWEET OLD THING WHO'D DIE BEFORE SHE BROKE THE LAW!
OKAY, JUDGE DREDD. OBVIOUSLY THE REAL BIO-CROOK'S USING THE OLD GIRL'S NAME TO PUT US OFF THE SCENT!
THAT'S THAT OUTA THE WAY. NOW TO ARRANGE A LITTLE ACCIDENT.. FOR MY-SELF...
YEEHAA! HERE GOES! THAT TRUCK'LL SQUASH ME TO A PULP! IT'LL TAKE THEM DAYS JUST TO SCRAPE ME OFF THE ROAD!
THE DRIVER SWERVES INSTINCTIVELY...
CAUGHT HIM A GLANCING BLOW! HE'S SKIDDING INTO THE CRASH BARRIER—
GEE, JUDGE, I-I'M SORRY. YOU WAS COMIN' STRAIGHT AT ME LIKE A CRAZY MAN... ARE YOU OKAY?
THE CRASH BARRIER SAVED ME... DON'T-DON'T KNOW WHAT COULD HAVE GOT INTO ME, UNLESS... YES! THE-THE OLD WOMAN!
SHE USED THOSE PLANTS TO HYPNOTISE ME!
DREDD TO CONTROL—I WANT A RIOT SQUAD. TELL THEM TO MEET ME ON THE ROOF OF "TOWER HOUSE" IN TEN MINUTES!

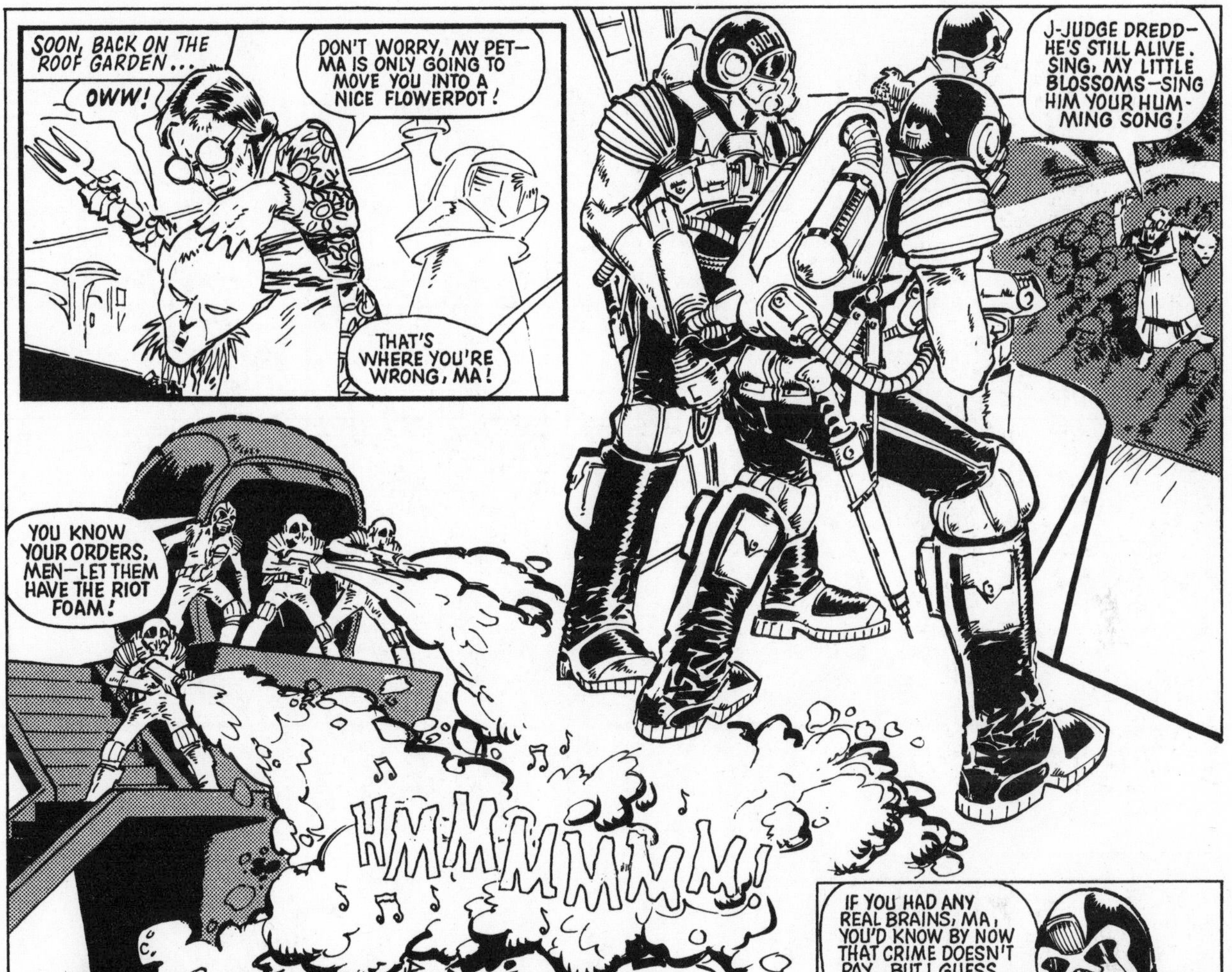
SOON, BACK ON THE ROOF GARDEN...
OWW!
DON'T WORRY, MY PET— MA IS ONLY GOING TO MOVE YOU INTO A NICE FLOWERPOT!
THAT'S WHERE YOU'RE WRONG, MA!
RIOT
J-JUDGE DREDD— HE'S STILL ALIVE. SING, MY LITTLE BLOSSOMS—SING HIM YOUR HUMMING SONG!
YOU KNOW YOUR ORDERS, MEN—LET THEM HAVE THE RIOT FOAM!
HMMMMMMM!
MY BRAIN-BLOOMS! THE-THE FOAM IS SMOTHERING THEIR VOICES!
IT'S THE NEW RIOT FOAM, LAW-BREAKER— DEVELOPED TO COVER ANY DISTURBANCE AND SOLIDIFY ROUND EVERYTHING IN IT. THAT WAY WE CAN DEAL WITH TROUBLE-MAKERS ONE AT A TIME!
YOU'VE BEATEN ME, YOUNG FELLOW. I'M STUCK HERE AS HELPLESS AS ONE OF MY OWN DEAR BRAINBLOOMS...
IF YOU HAD ANY REAL BRAINS, MA, YOU'D KNOW BY NOW THAT CRIME DOESN'T PAY. BUT I GUESS YOU'LL NEVER LEARN — IF YOU LIVE TO BE TWO HUNDRED!
DREDD
2000 A.D. NOW AVAILABLE PRINTED ON HEAT RESISTANT METAL FOR READERS INSIDE STARS.

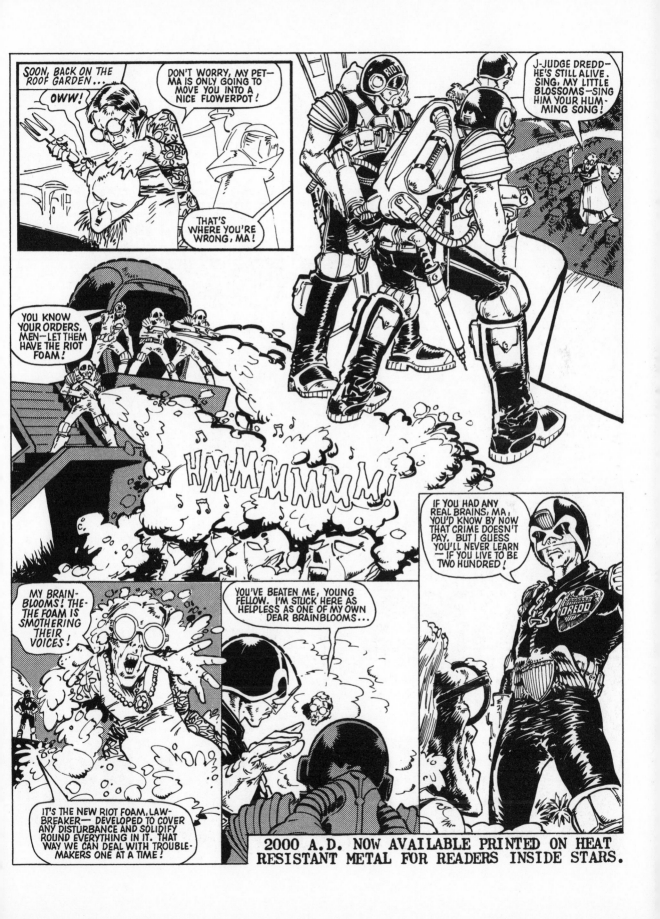

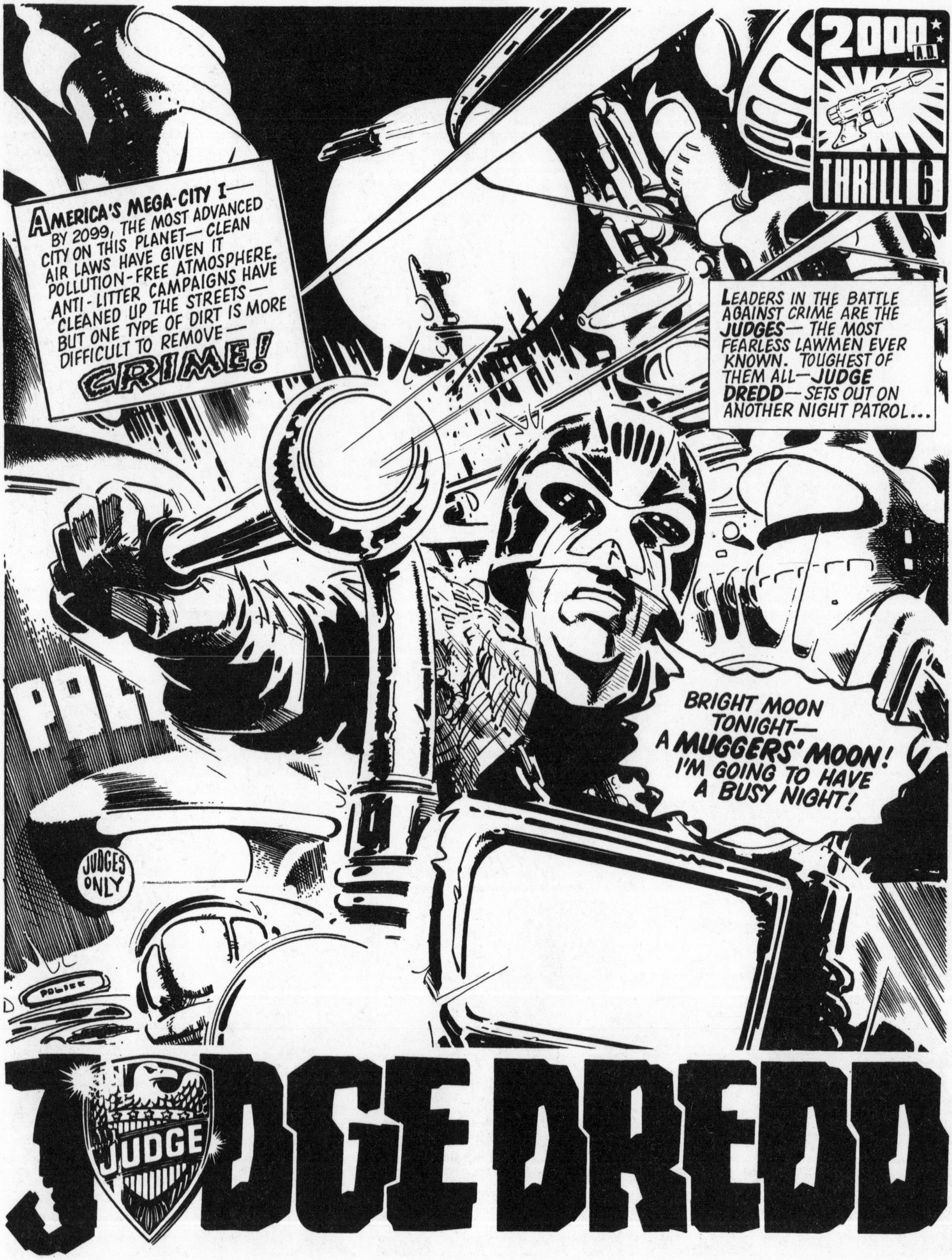
2000 A.D.
THRILL 6
AMERICA'S MEGA-CITY I— BY 2099, THE MOST ADVANCED CITY ON THIS PLANET— CLEAN AIR LAWS HAVE GIVEN IT POLLUTION-FREE ATMOSPHERE. ANTI-LITTER CAMPAIGNS HAVE CLEANED UP THE STREETS— BUT ONE TYPE OF DIRT IS MORE DIFFICULT TO REMOVE— CRIME!
LEADERS IN THE BATTLE AGAINST CRIME ARE THE JUDGES— THE MOST FEARLESS LAWMEN EVER KNOWN. TOUGHEST OF THEM ALL—JUDGE DREDD— SETS OUT ON ANOTHER NIGHT PATROL...
BRIGHT MOON TONIGHT— A MUGGERS' MOON! I'M GOING TO HAVE A BUSY NIGHT!
JUDGES ONLY
JUDGE
JUDGE DREDD

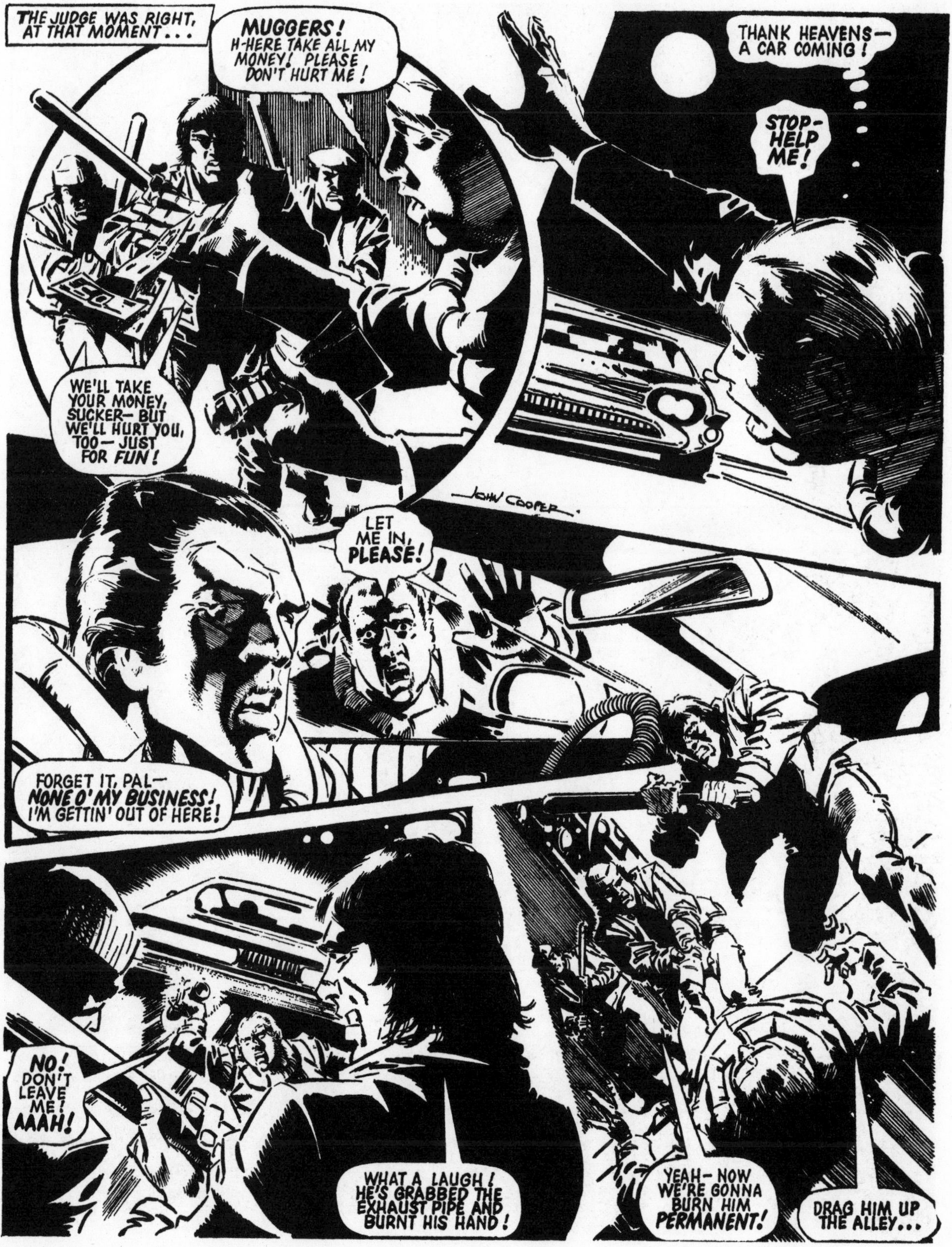
THE JUDGE WAS RIGHT, AT THAT MOMENT...
MUGGERS! H-HERE TAKE ALL MY MONEY! PLEASE DON'T HURT ME!
WE'LL TAKE YOUR MONEY, SUCKER— BUT WE'LL HURT YOU, TOO— JUST FOR FUN!
THANK HEAVENS— A CAR COMING!
STOP— HELP ME!
JOHN COOPER
LET ME IN, PLEASE!
FORGET IT, PAL— NONE O' MY BUSINESS! I'M GETTIN' OUT OF HERE!
NO! DON'T LEAVE ME! AAAH!
WHAT A LAUGH! HE'S GRABBED THE EXHAUST PIPE AND BURNT HIS HAND!
YEAH— NOW WE'RE GONNA BURN HIM PERMANENT!
DRAG HIM UP THE ALLEY...

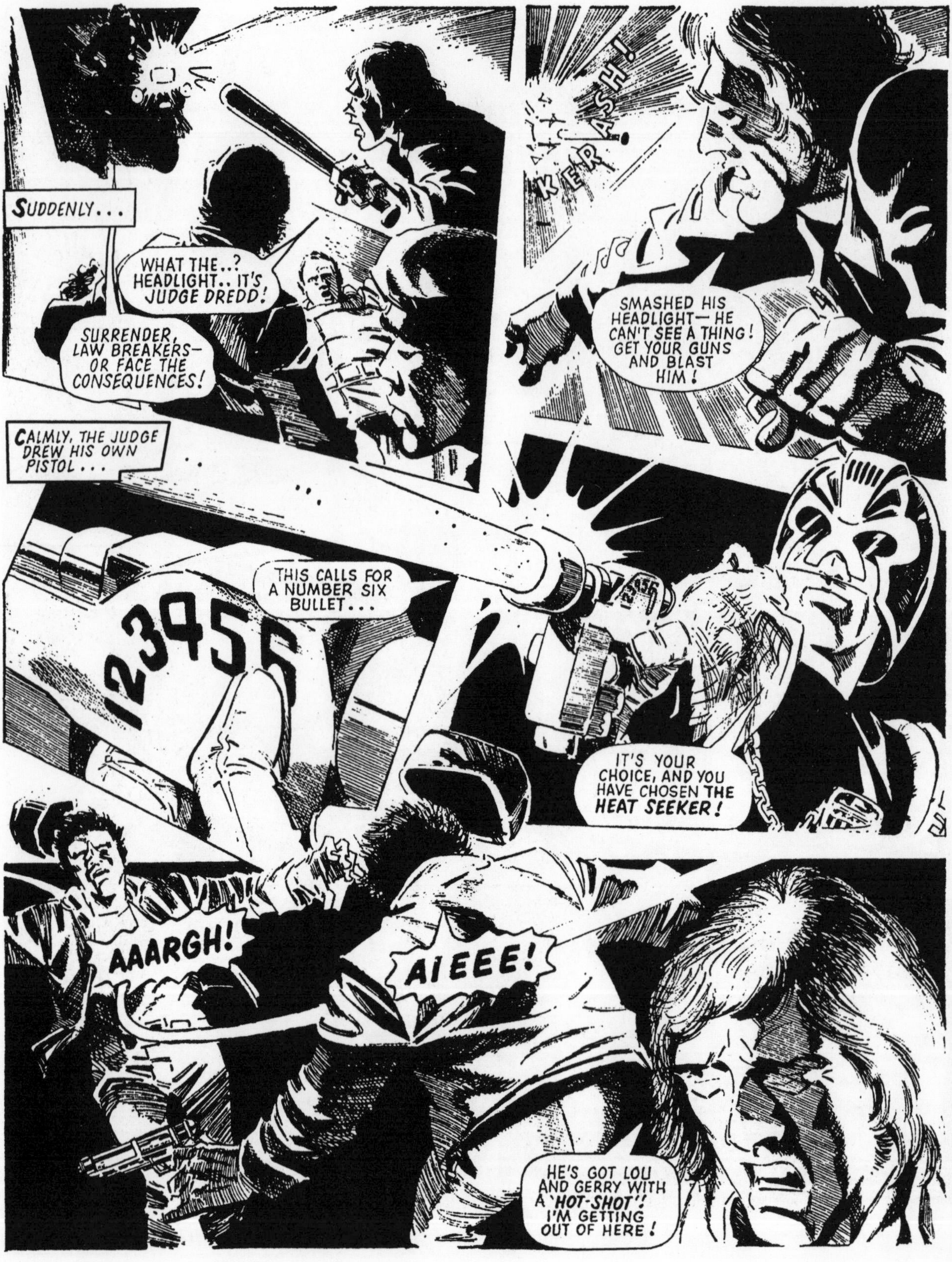
SUDDENLY...
WHAT THE..? HEADLIGHT.. IT'S JUDGE DREDD!
SURRENDER, LAW BREAKERS— OR FACE THE CONSEQUENCES!
KERASH!
SMASHED HIS HEADLIGHT— HE CAN'T SEE A THING! GET YOUR GUNS AND BLAST HIM!
CALMLY, THE JUDGE DREW HIS OWN PISTOL...
THIS CALLS FOR A NUMBER SIX BULLET...
123456
IT'S YOUR CHOICE, AND YOU HAVE CHOSEN THE HEAT SEEKER!
AAARGH!
AIEEE!
HE'S GOT LOU AND GERRY WITH A 'HOT-SHOT'! I'M GETTING OUT OF HERE!

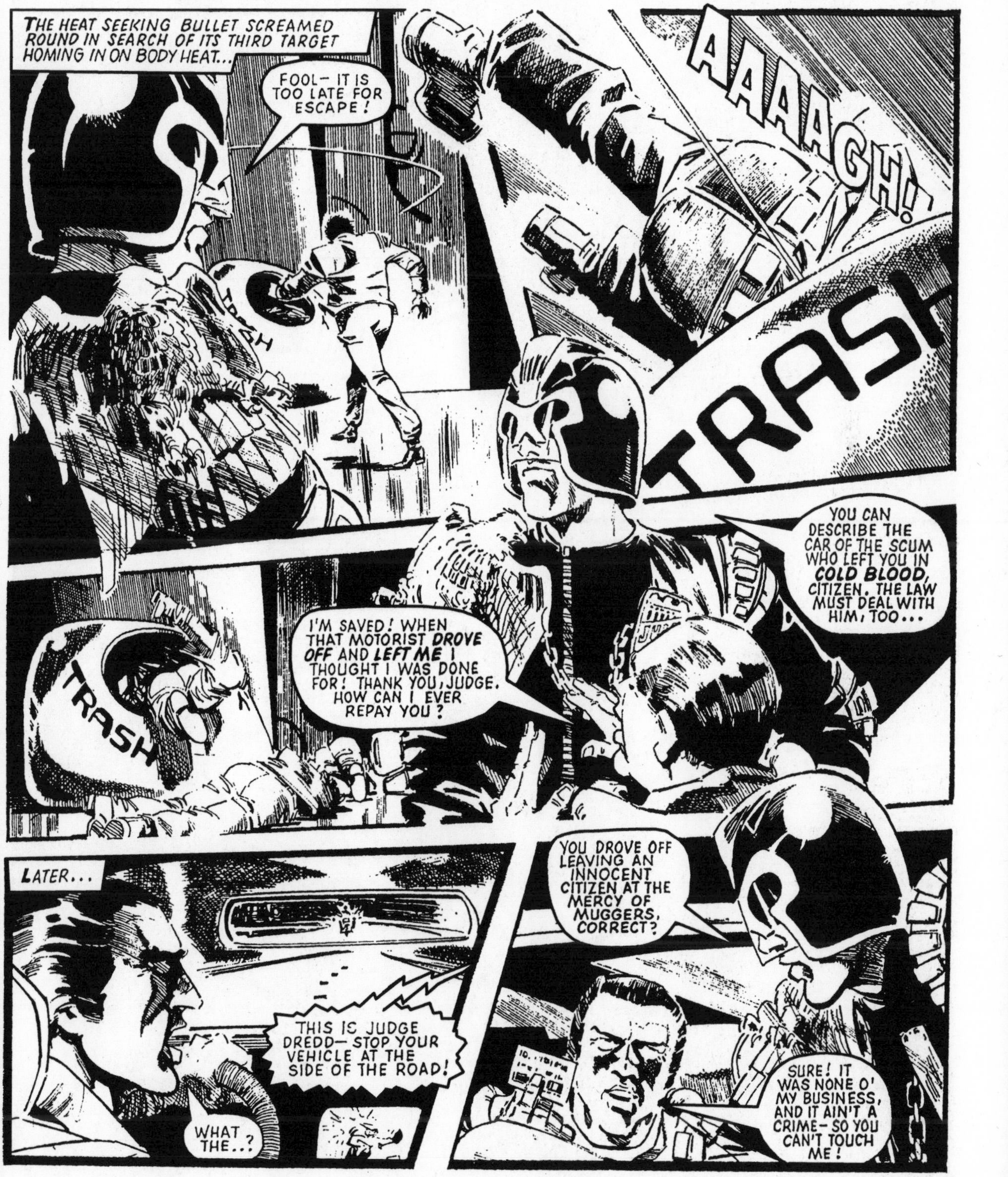
THE HEAT SEEKING BULLET SCREAMED ROUND IN SEARCH OF ITS THIRD TARGET HOMING IN ON BODY HEAT...
FOOL– IT IS TOO LATE FOR ESCAPE!
AAAAGH!
TRASH
I'M SAVED! WHEN THAT MOTORIST DROVE OFF AND LEFT ME I THOUGHT I WAS DONE FOR! THANK YOU, JUDGE. HOW CAN I EVER REPAY YOU?
YOU CAN DESCRIBE THE CAR OF THE SCUM WHO LEFT YOU IN COLD BLOOD, CITIZEN. THE LAW MUST DEAL WITH HIM, TOO...
LATER...
THIS IS JUDGE DREDD– STOP YOUR VEHICLE AT THE SIDE OF THE ROAD!
WHAT THE..?
YOU DROVE OFF LEAVING AN INNOCENT CITIZEN AT THE MERCY OF MUGGERS, CORRECT?
SURE! IT WAS NONE O' MY BUSINESS, AND IT AIN'T A CRIME– SO YOU CAN'T TOUCH ME!

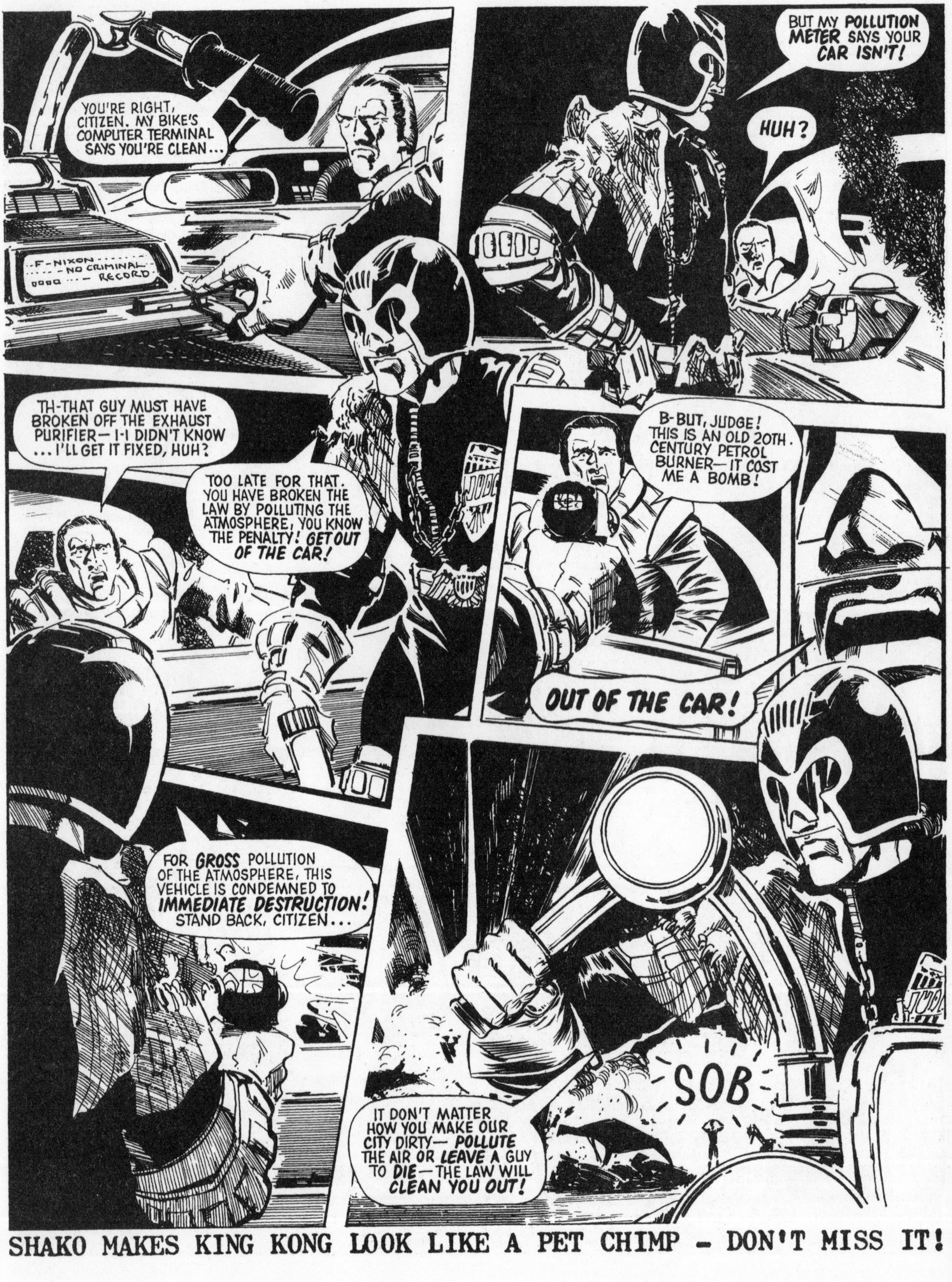
YOU'RE RIGHT, CITIZEN. MY BIKE'S COMPUTER TERMINAL SAYS YOU'RE CLEAN...
F-NIXON NO CRIMINAL RECORD
BUT MY POLLUTION METER SAYS YOUR CAR ISN'T!
HUH?
TH-THAT GUY MUST HAVE BROKEN OFF THE EXHAUST PURIFIER—I-I DIDN'T KNOW ... I'LL GET IT FIXED, HUH?
TOO LATE FOR THAT. YOU HAVE BROKEN THE LAW BY POLLUTING THE ATMOSPHERE, YOU KNOW THE PENALTY! GET OUT OF THE CAR!
B-BUT, JUDGE! THIS IS AN OLD 20TH CENTURY PETROL BURNER—IT COST ME A BOMB!
OUT OF THE CAR!
FOR GROSS POLLUTION OF THE ATMOSPHERE, THIS VEHICLE IS CONDEMNED TO IMMEDIATE DESTRUCTION! STAND BACK, CITIZEN...
SOB
IT DON'T MATTER HOW YOU MAKE OUR CITY DIRTY—POLLUTE THE AIR OR LEAVE A GUY TO DIE—THE LAW WILL CLEAN YOU OUT!

SHAKO MAKES KING KONG LOOK LIKE A PET CHIMP - DON'T MISS IT!

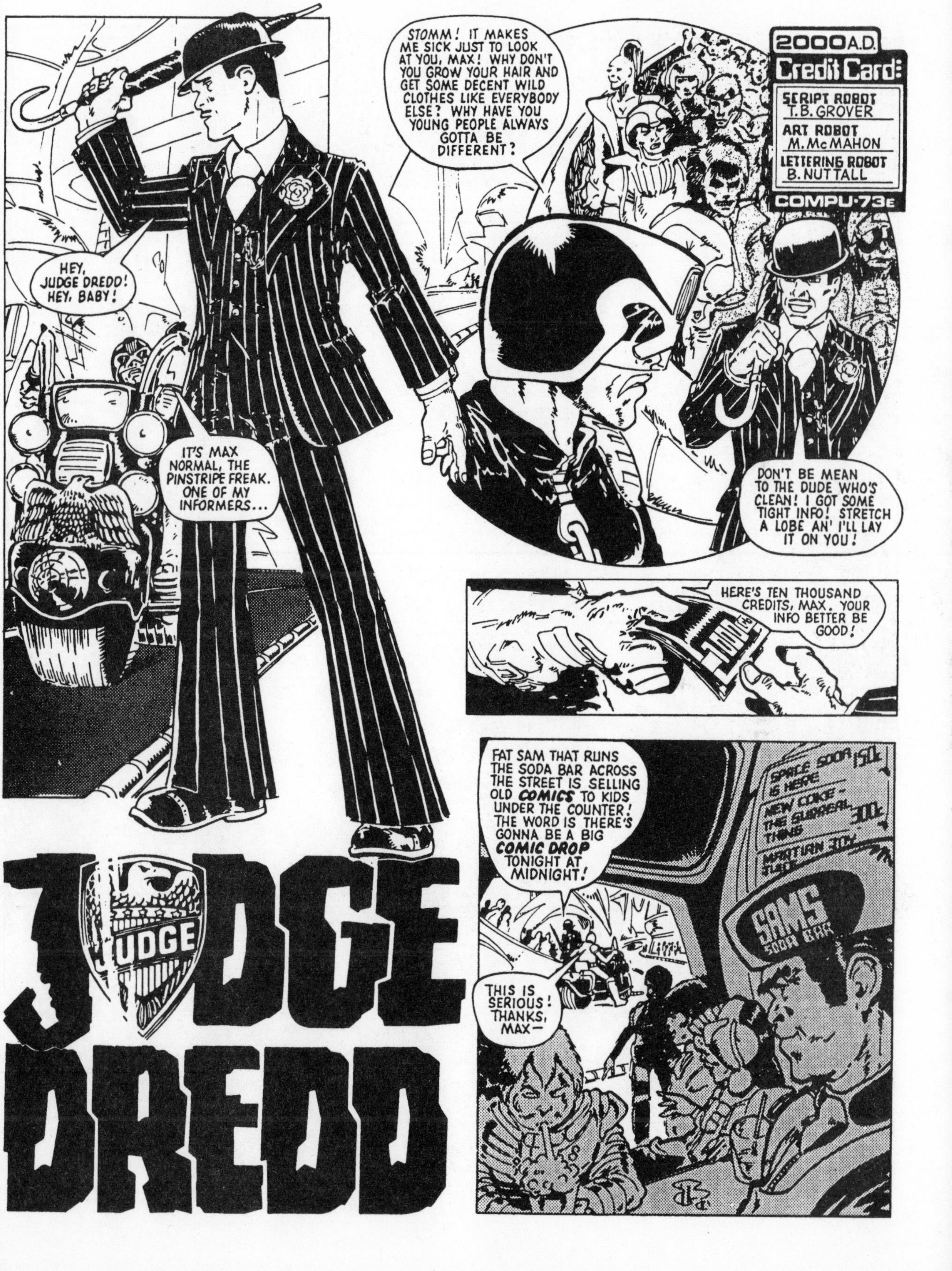

HEY, JUDGE DREDD! HEY, BABY!
IT'S MAX NORMAL, THE PINSTRIPE FREAK. ONE OF MY INFORMERS...
STOMM! IT MAKES ME SICK JUST TO LOOK AT YOU, MAX! WHY DON'T YOU GROW YOUR HAIR AND GET SOME DECENT WILD CLOTHES LIKE EVERYBODY ELSE? WHY HAVE YOU YOUNG PEOPLE ALWAYS GOTTA BE DIFFERENT?
2000 A.D. Credit Card:
SCRIPT ROBOT T.B. GROVER
ART ROBOT M. McMAHON
LETTERING ROBOT B. NUTTALL
COMPU-73E
DON'T BE MEAN TO THE DUDE WHO'S CLEAN! I GOT SOME TIGHT INFO! STRETCH A LOBE AN' I'LL LAY IT ON YOU!
HERE'S TEN THOUSAND CREDITS, MAX. YOUR INFO BETTER BE GOOD!
FAT SAM THAT RUNS THE SODA BAR ACROSS THE STREET IS SELLING OLD COMICS TO KIDS UNDER THE COUNTER! THE WORD IS THERE'S GONNA BE A BIG COMIC DROP TONIGHT AT MIDNIGHT!
THIS IS SERIOUS! THANKS, MAX—
JUDGE
JUDGE DREDD
SPACE SODA IS HERE
SAMS SODA BAR

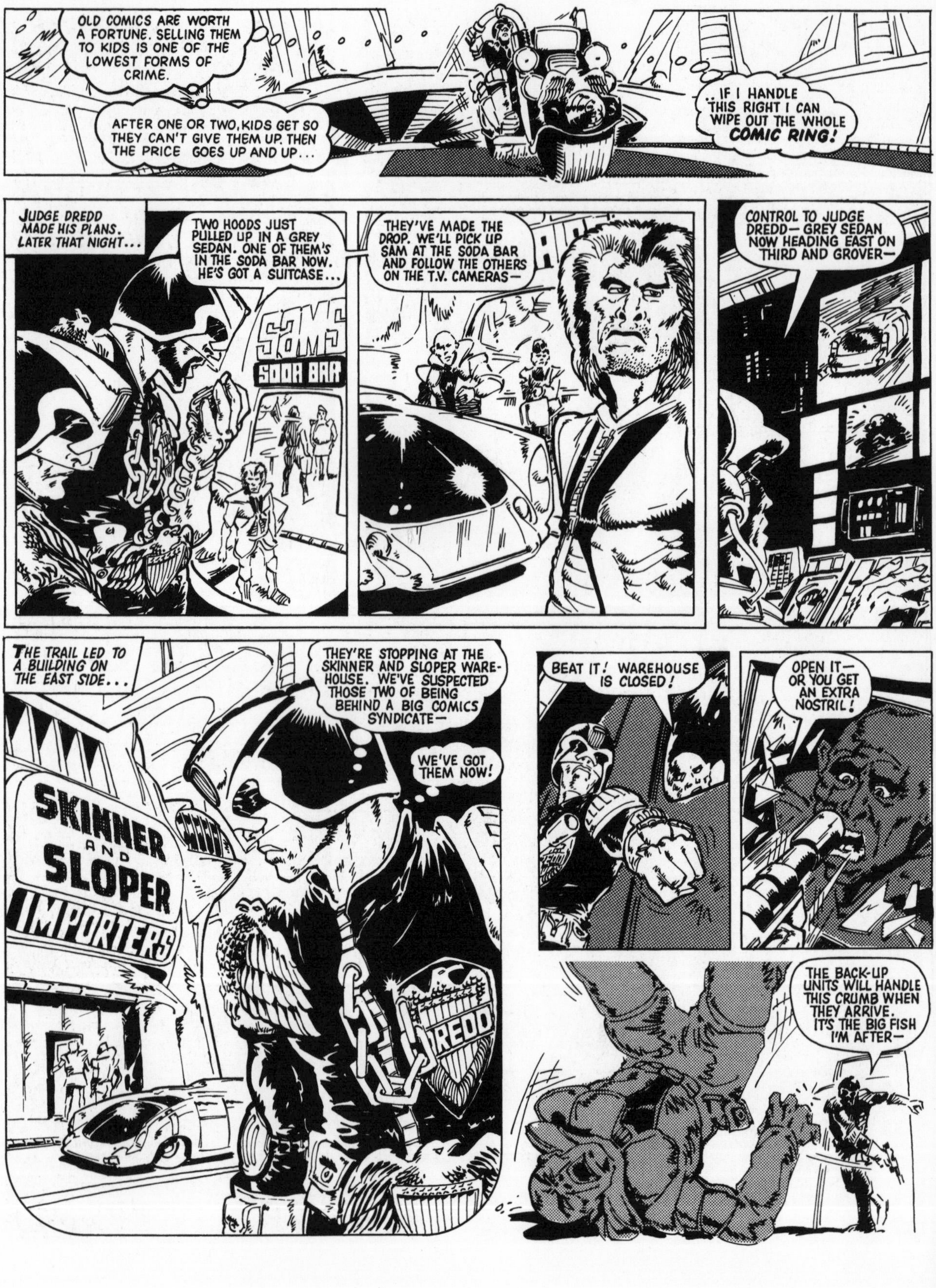
OLD COMICS ARE WORTH A FORTUNE. SELLING THEM TO KIDS IS ONE OF THE LOWEST FORMS OF CRIME.
AFTER ONE OR TWO, KIDS GET SO THEY CAN'T GIVE THEM UP. THEN THE PRICE GOES UP AND UP...
..IF I HANDLE THIS RIGHT I CAN WIPE OUT THE WHOLE COMIC RING!
JUDGE DREDD MADE HIS PLANS. LATER THAT NIGHT...
TWO HOODS JUST PULLED UP IN A GREY SEDAN. ONE OF THEM'S IN THE SODA BAR NOW. HE'S GOT A SUITCASE...
SAMS
SODA BAR
THEY'VE MADE THE DROP. WE'LL PICK UP SAM AT THE SODA BAR AND FOLLOW THE OTHERS ON THE T.V. CAMERAS—
CONTROL TO JUDGE DREDD— GREY SEDAN NOW HEADING EAST ON THIRD AND GROVER—
THE TRAIL LED TO A BUILDING ON THE EAST SIDE...
THEY'RE STOPPING AT THE SKINNER AND SLOPER WAREHOUSE. WE'VE SUSPECTED THOSE TWO OF BEING BEHIND A BIG COMICS SYNDICATE—
WE'VE GOT THEM NOW!
SKINNER AND SLOPER IMPORTERS
DREDD
BEAT IT! WAREHOUSE IS CLOSED!
OPEN IT— OR YOU GET AN EXTRA NOSTRIL!
THE BACK-UP UNITS WILL HANDLE THIS CRUMB WHEN THEY ARRIVE. IT'S THE BIG FISH I'M AFTER—

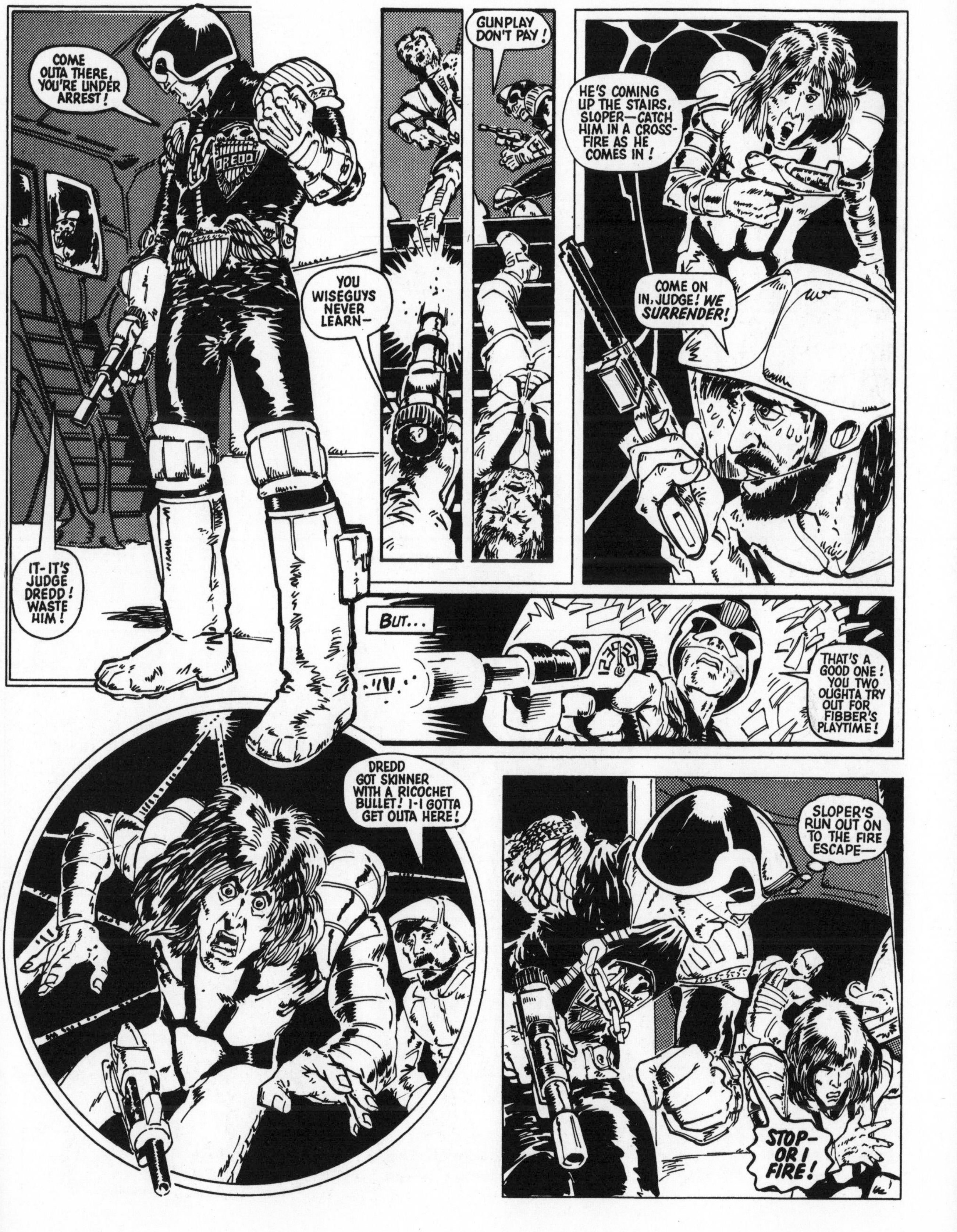
COME OUTA THERE, YOU'RE UNDER ARREST!
IT-IT'S JUDGE DREDD! WASTE HIM!
YOU WISEGUYS NEVER LEARN—
GUNPLAY DON'T PAY!
HE'S COMING UP THE STAIRS, SLOPER—CATCH HIM IN A CROSS-FIRE AS HE COMES IN!
COME ON IN, JUDGE! WE SURRENDER!
BUT...
THAT'S A GOOD ONE! YOU TWO OUGHTA TRY OUT FOR FIBBER'S PLAYTIME!
DREDD GOT SKINNER WITH A RICOCHET BULLET! I-I GOTTA GET OUTA HERE!
SLOPER'S RUN OUT ON TO THE FIRE ESCAPE—
STOP—OR I FIRE!

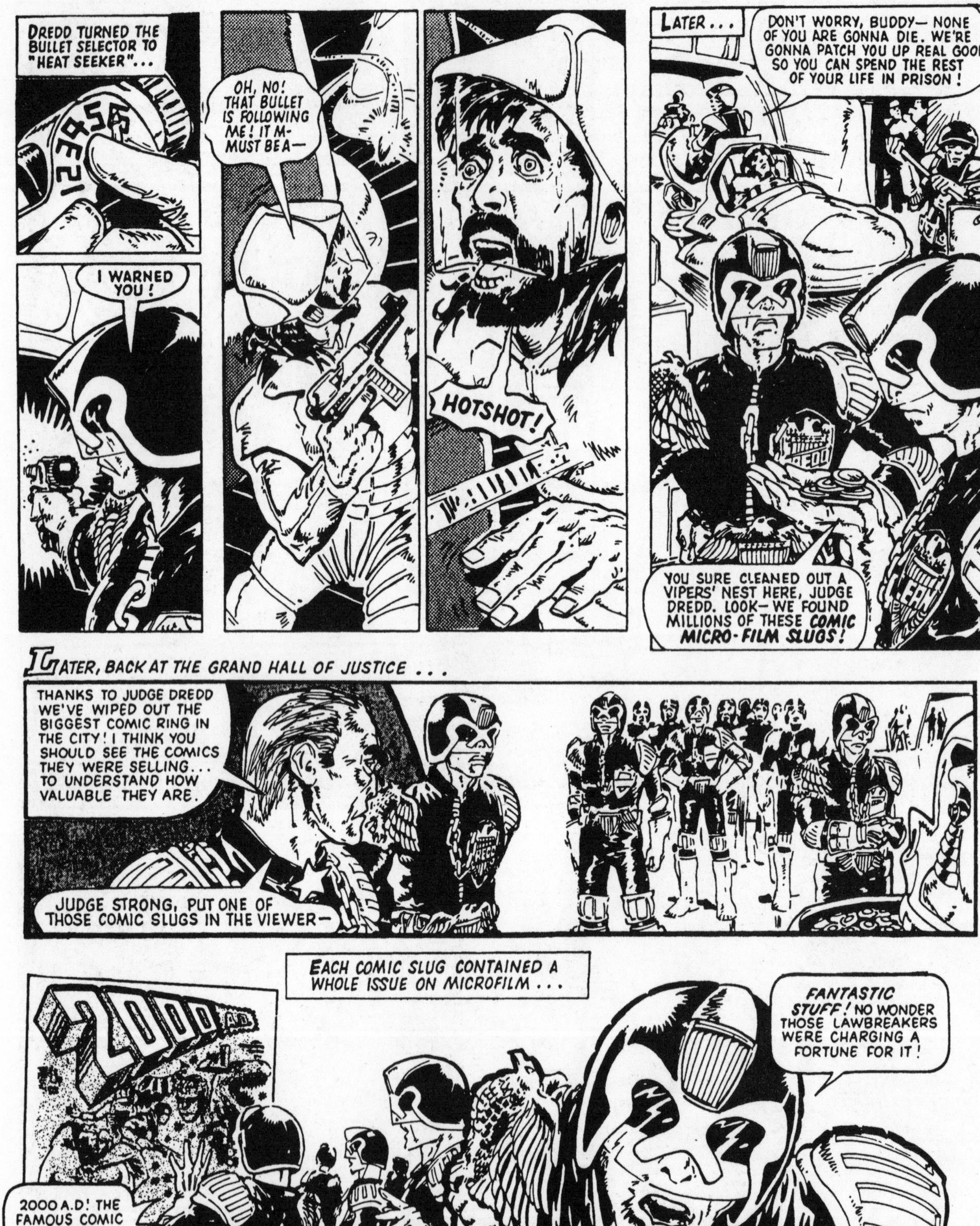

DREDD TURNED THE BULLET SELECTOR TO "HEAT SEEKER"...
I WARNED YOU!
OH, NO! THAT BULLET IS FOLLOWING ME! IT M-MUST BE A—
HOTSHOT!
LATER...
DON'T WORRY, BUDDY— NONE OF YOU ARE GONNA DIE. WE'RE GONNA PATCH YOU UP REAL GOOD SO YOU CAN SPEND THE REST OF YOUR LIFE IN PRISON!
YOU SURE CLEANED OUT A VIPERS' NEST HERE, JUDGE DREDD. LOOK— WE FOUND MILLIONS OF THESE COMIC MICRO-FILM SLUGS!
LATER, BACK AT THE GRAND HALL OF JUSTICE ...
THANKS TO JUDGE DREDD WE'VE WIPED OUT THE BIGGEST COMIC RING IN THE CITY! I THINK YOU SHOULD SEE THE COMICS THEY WERE SELLING... TO UNDERSTAND HOW VALUABLE THEY ARE.
JUDGE STRONG, PUT ONE OF THOSE COMIC SLUGS IN THE VIEWER—
EACH COMIC SLUG CONTAINED A WHOLE ISSUE ON MICROFILM...
2000 A.D.
2000 A.D! THE FAMOUS COMIC FROM THE TWENTIETH CENTURY. BRILLIANT!
FANTASTIC STUFF! NO WONDER THOSE LAWBREAKERS WERE CHARGING A FORTUNE FOR IT!
THE END

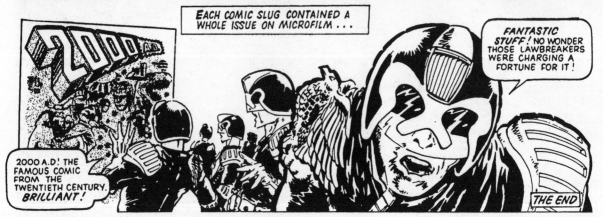

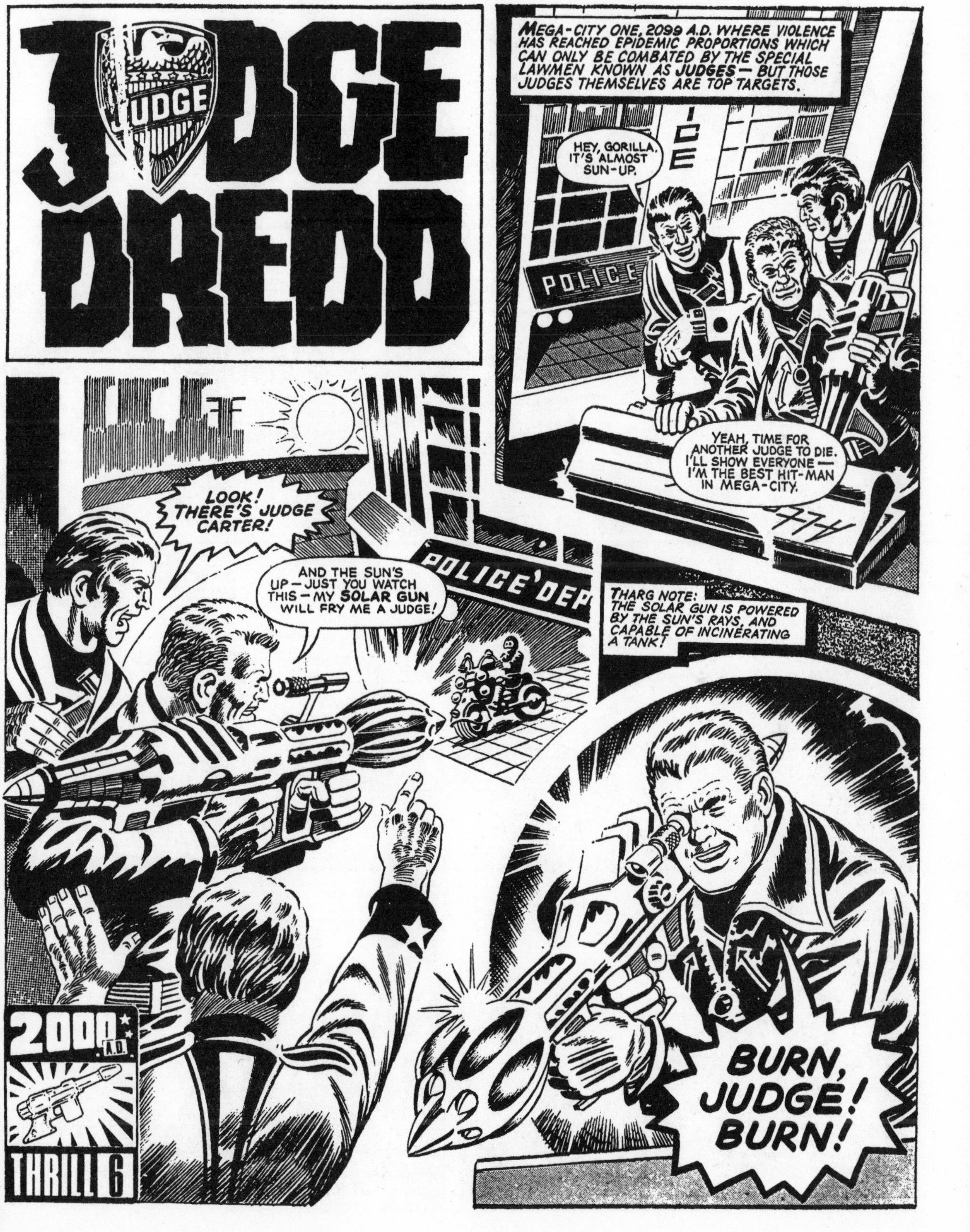
JUDGE DREDD
JUDGE
MEGA-CITY ONE, 2099 A.D. WHERE VIOLENCE HAS REACHED EPIDEMIC PROPORTIONS WHICH CAN ONLY BE COMBATED BY THE SPECIAL LAWMEN KNOWN AS JUDGES — BUT THOSE JUDGES THEMSELVES ARE TOP TARGETS.
HEY, GORILLA. IT'S ALMOST SUN-UP.
POLICE
YEAH, TIME FOR ANOTHER JUDGE TO DIE. I'LL SHOW EVERYONE — I'M THE BEST HIT-MAN IN MEGA-CITY.
LOOK! THERE'S JUDGE CARTER!
AND THE SUN'S UP — JUST YOU WATCH THIS — MY SOLAR GUN WILL FRY ME A JUDGE!
POLICE DEP
THARG NOTE: THE SOLAR GUN IS POWERED BY THE SUN'S RAYS, AND CAPABLE OF INCINERATING A TANK!
BURN, JUDGE! BURN!
2000 A.D.
THRILL 6

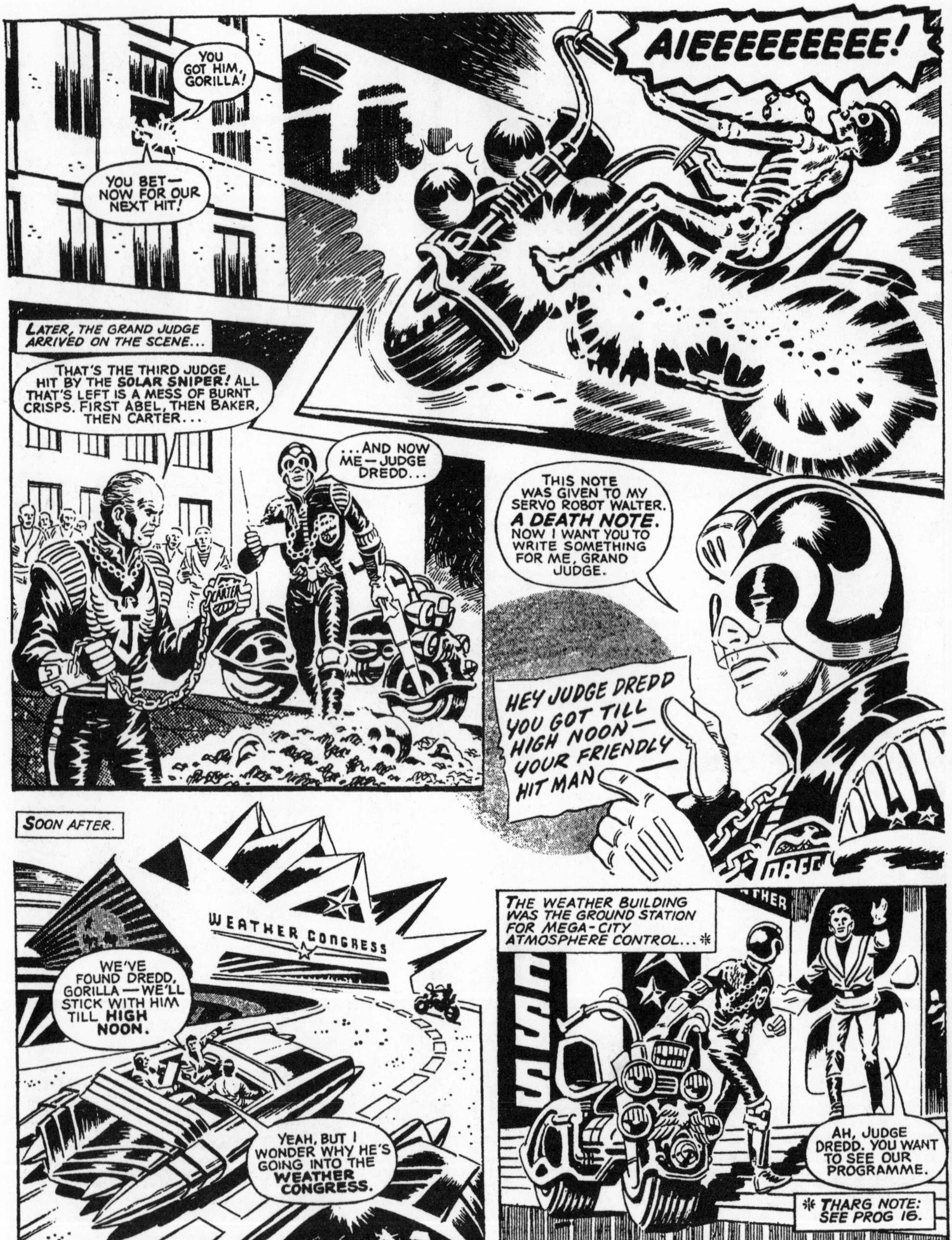
YOU GOT HIM, GORILLA!
YOU BET— NOW FOR OUR NEXT HIT!
AIEEEEEEEEEE!
LATER, THE GRAND JUDGE ARRIVED ON THE SCENE...
THAT'S THE THIRD JUDGE HIT BY THE SOLAR SNIPER! ALL THAT'S LEFT IS A MESS OF BURNT CRISPS. FIRST ABEL, THEN BAKER, THEN CARTER...
...AND NOW ME—JUDGE DREDD...
CARTER
THIS NOTE WAS GIVEN TO MY SERVO ROBOT WALTER. A DEATH NOTE. NOW I WANT YOU TO WRITE SOMETHING FOR ME, GRAND JUDGE.
HEY JUDGE DREDD YOU GOT TILL HIGH NOON— YOUR FRIENDLY HIT MAN
SOON AFTER.
WEATHER CONGRESS
WE'VE FOUND DREDD, GORILLA—WE'LL STICK WITH HIM TILL HIGH NOON.
YEAH, BUT I WONDER WHY HE'S GOING INTO THE WEATHER CONGRESS.
THE WEATHER BUILDING WAS THE GROUND STATION FOR MEGA-CITY ATMOSPHERE CONTROL...*
AH, JUDGE DREDD. YOU WANT TO SEE OUR PROGRAMME.
* THARG NOTE: SEE PROG 16.

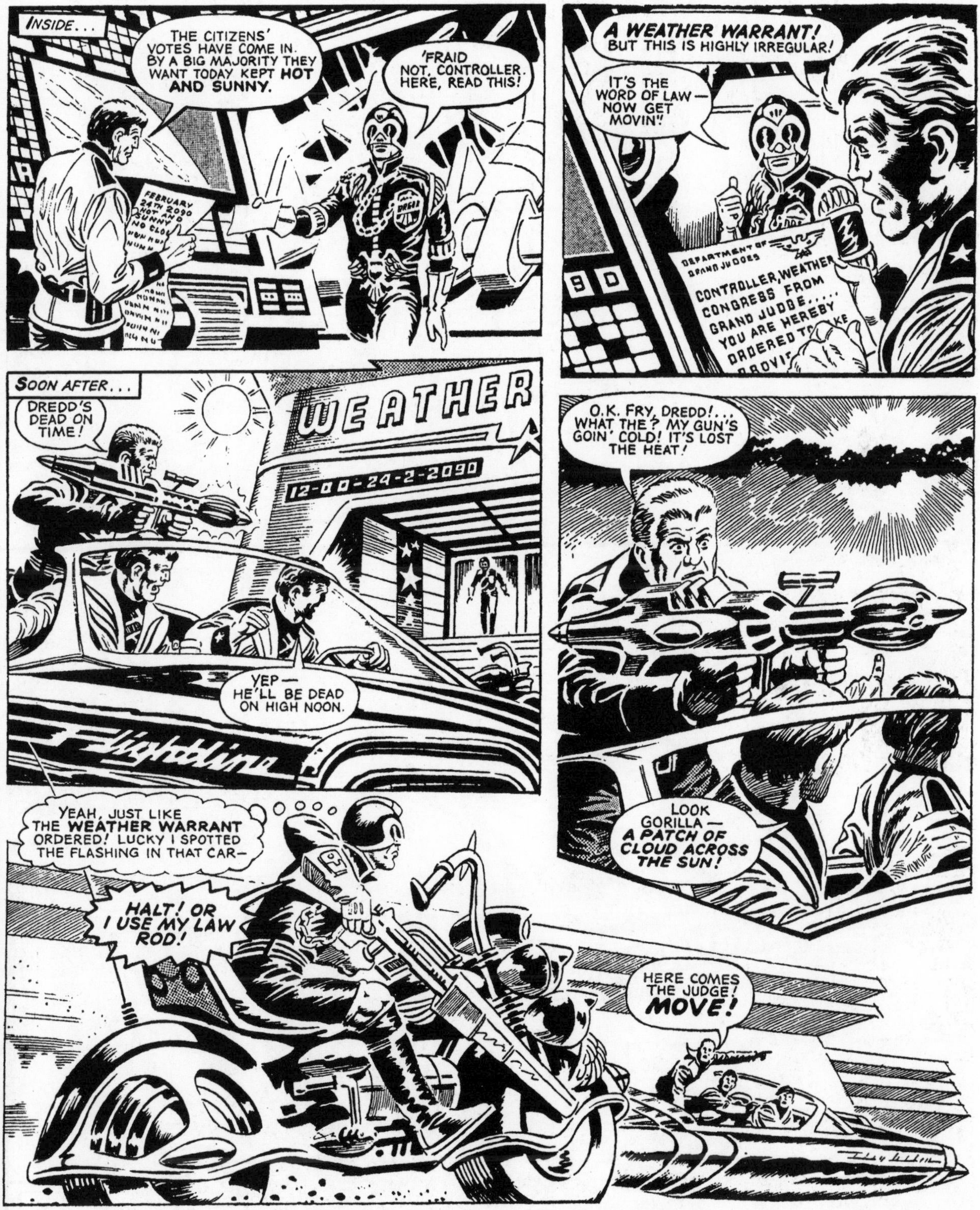
INSIDE...
THE CITIZENS' VOTES HAVE COME IN. BY A BIG MAJORITY THEY WANT TODAY KEPT **HOT AND SUNNY.**
'FRAID NOT, CONTROLLER. HERE, READ THIS!
FEBRUARY 24TH 2090 HOT AND SUNNY
A WEATHER WARRANT! BUT THIS IS HIGHLY IRREGULAR!
IT'S THE WORD OF LAW — NOW GET MOVIN'!
DEPARTMENT OF GRAND JUDGES
CONTROLLER, WEATHER CONGRESS FROM GRAND JUDGE..... YOU ARE HEREBY ORDERED TO
SOON AFTER...
DREDD'S DEAD ON TIME!
WEATHER
12-00-24-2-2090
YEP — HE'LL BE DEAD ON HIGH NOON.
O.K. FRY, DREDD!... WHAT THE? MY GUN'S GOIN' COLD! IT'S LOST THE HEAT!
LOOK GORILLA — **A PATCH OF CLOUD ACROSS THE SUN!**
YEAH, JUST LIKE THE **WEATHER WARRANT** ORDERED! LUCKY I SPOTTED THE FLASHING IN THAT CAR—
HALT! OR I USE MY LAW ROD!
HERE COMES THE JUDGE! **MOVE!**

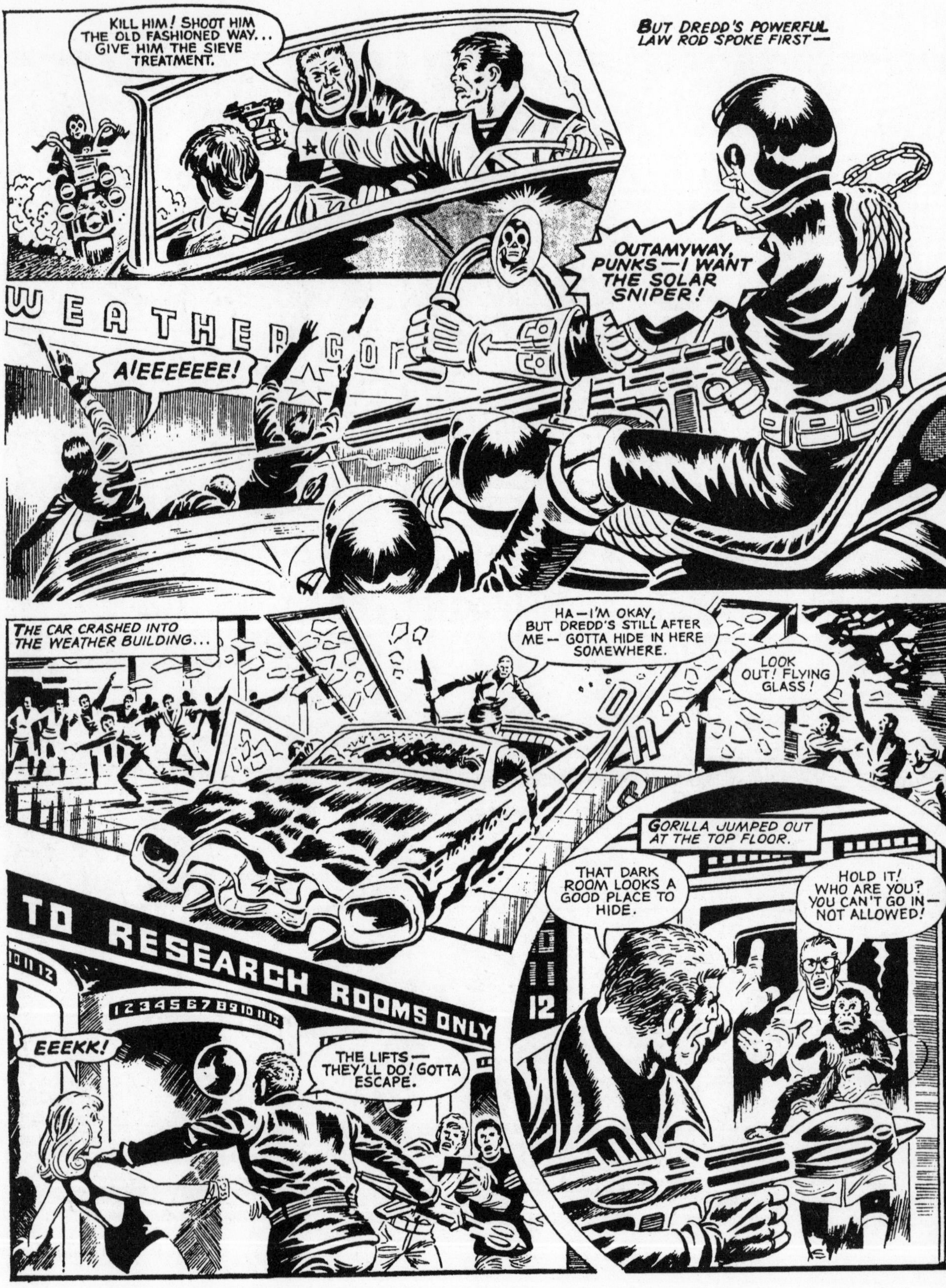
KILL HIM! SHOOT HIM THE OLD FASHIONED WAY... GIVE HIM THE SIEVE TREATMENT.
BUT DREDD'S POWERFUL LAW ROD SPOKE FIRST—
OUTAMYWAY, PUNKS—I WANT THE SOLAR SNIPER!
WEATHER
AIEEEEEEE!
THE CAR CRASHED INTO THE WEATHER BUILDING...
HA—I'M OKAY, BUT DREDD'S STILL AFTER ME—GOTTA HIDE IN HERE SOMEWHERE.
LOOK OUT! FLYING GLASS!
TO RESEARCH ROOMS ONLY
EEEKK!
THE LIFTS—THEY'LL DO! GOTTA ESCAPE.
GORILLA JUMPED OUT AT THE TOP FLOOR.
THAT DARK ROOM LOOKS A GOOD PLACE TO HIDE.
HOLD IT! WHO ARE YOU? YOU CAN'T GO IN—NOT ALLOWED!

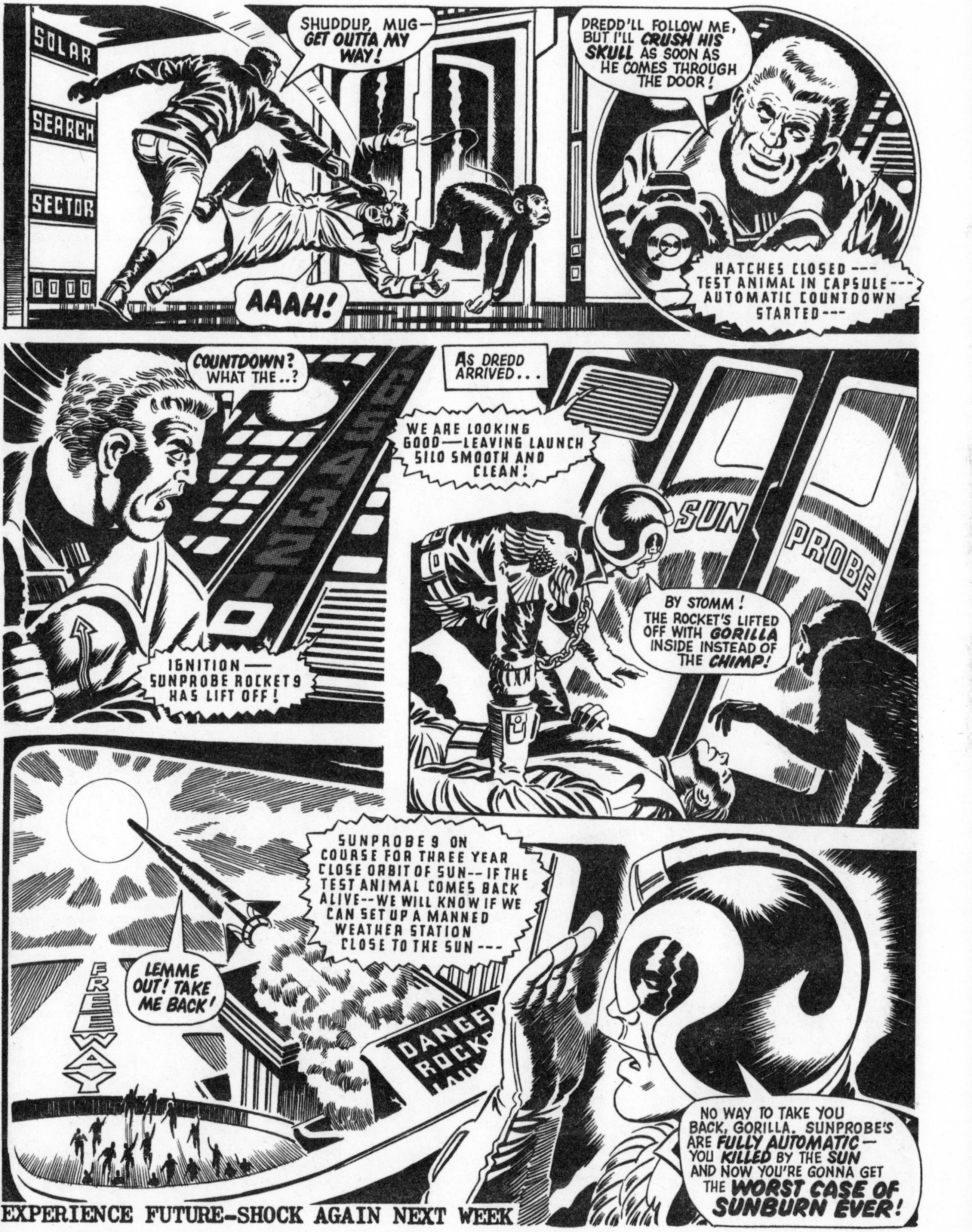
SOLAR
SEARCH
SECTOR
SHUDDUP, MUG— GET OUTTA MY WAY!
AAAH!
DREDD'LL FOLLOW ME, BUT I'LL CRUSH HIS SKULL AS SOON AS HE COMES THROUGH THE DOOR!
HATCHES CLOSED --- TEST ANIMAL IN CAPSULE --- AUTOMATIC COUNTDOWN STARTED ---
COUNTDOWN? WHAT THE..?
6 5 4 3 2 1 0
IGNITION — SUNPROBE ROCKET 9 HAS LIFT OFF!
AS DREDD ARRIVED...
WE ARE LOOKING GOOD — LEAVING LAUNCH SILO SMOOTH AND CLEAN!
SUN PROBE
BY STOMM! THE ROCKET'S LIFTED OFF WITH GORILLA INSIDE INSTEAD OF THE CHIMP!
SUNPROBE 9 ON COURSE FOR THREE YEAR CLOSE ORBIT OF SUN -- IF THE TEST ANIMAL COMES BACK ALIVE -- WE WILL KNOW IF WE CAN SET UP A MANNED WEATHER STATION CLOSE TO THE SUN ---
LEMME OUT! TAKE ME BACK!
FREEWAY
NO WAY TO TAKE YOU BACK, GORILLA. SUNPROBE'S ARE FULLY AUTOMATIC — YOU KILLED BY THE SUN AND NOW YOU'RE GONNA GET THE WORST CASE OF SUNBURN EVER!
EXPERIENCE FUTURE-SHOCK AGAIN NEXT WEEK

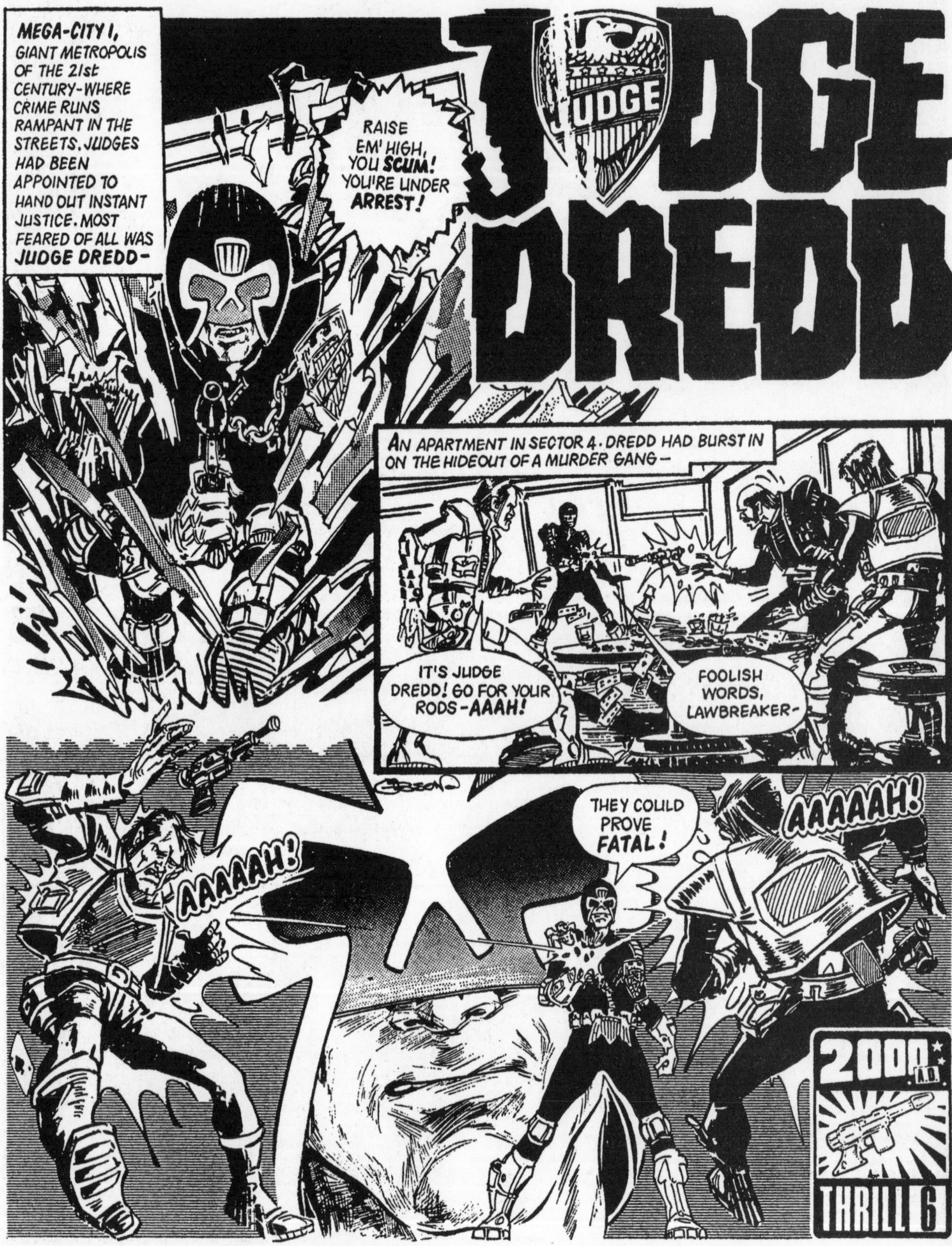
JUDGE DREDD
JUDGE
MEGA-CITY 1, GIANT METROPOLIS OF THE 21st CENTURY-WHERE CRIME RUNS RAMPANT IN THE STREETS. JUDGES HAD BEEN APPOINTED TO HAND OUT INSTANT JUSTICE. MOST FEARED OF ALL WAS JUDGE DREDD-
RAISE EM' HIGH, YOU SCUM! YOU'RE UNDER ARREST!
AN APARTMENT IN SECTOR 4. DREDD HAD BURST IN ON THE HIDEOUT OF A MURDER GANG-
IT'S JUDGE DREDD! GO FOR YOUR RODS-AAAH!
FOOLISH WORDS, LAWBREAKER-
THEY COULD PROVE FATAL!
AAAAAH!
AAAAAH!
2000 A.D.
THRILL 6

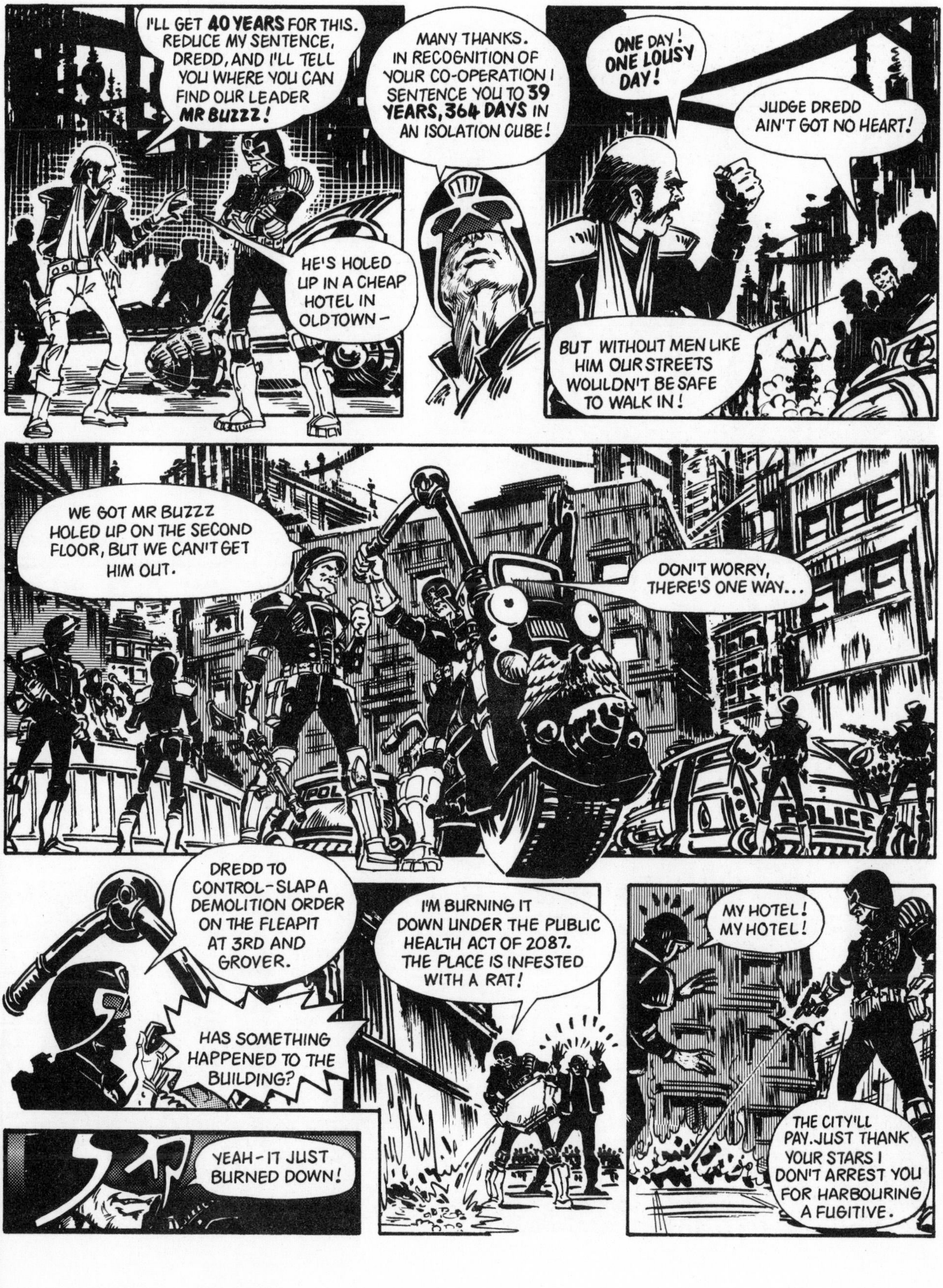
I'LL GET 40 YEARS FOR THIS. REDUCE MY SENTENCE, DREDD, AND I'LL TELL YOU WHERE YOU CAN FIND OUR LEADER MR BUZZZ!
HE'S HOLED UP IN A CHEAP HOTEL IN OLDTOWN –
MANY THANKS. IN RECOGNITION OF YOUR CO-OPERATION I SENTENCE YOU TO 39 YEARS, 364 DAYS IN AN ISOLATION CUBE!
ONE DAY! ONE LOUSY DAY!
JUDGE DREDD AIN'T GOT NO HEART!
BUT WITHOUT MEN LIKE HIM OUR STREETS WOULDN'T BE SAFE TO WALK IN!
WE GOT MR BUZZZ HOLED UP ON THE SECOND FLOOR, BUT WE CAN'T GET HIM OUT.
DON'T WORRY, THERE'S ONE WAY...
POLICE
DREDD TO CONTROL – SLAP A DEMOLITION ORDER ON THE FLEAPIT AT 3RD AND GROVER.
HAS SOMETHING HAPPENED TO THE BUILDING?
YEAH – IT JUST BURNED DOWN!
I'M BURNING IT DOWN UNDER THE PUBLIC HEALTH ACT OF 2087. THE PLACE IS INFESTED WITH A RAT!
MY HOTEL! MY HOTEL!
THE CITY'LL PAY. JUST THANK YOUR STARS I DON'T ARREST YOU FOR HARBOURING A FUGITIVE.

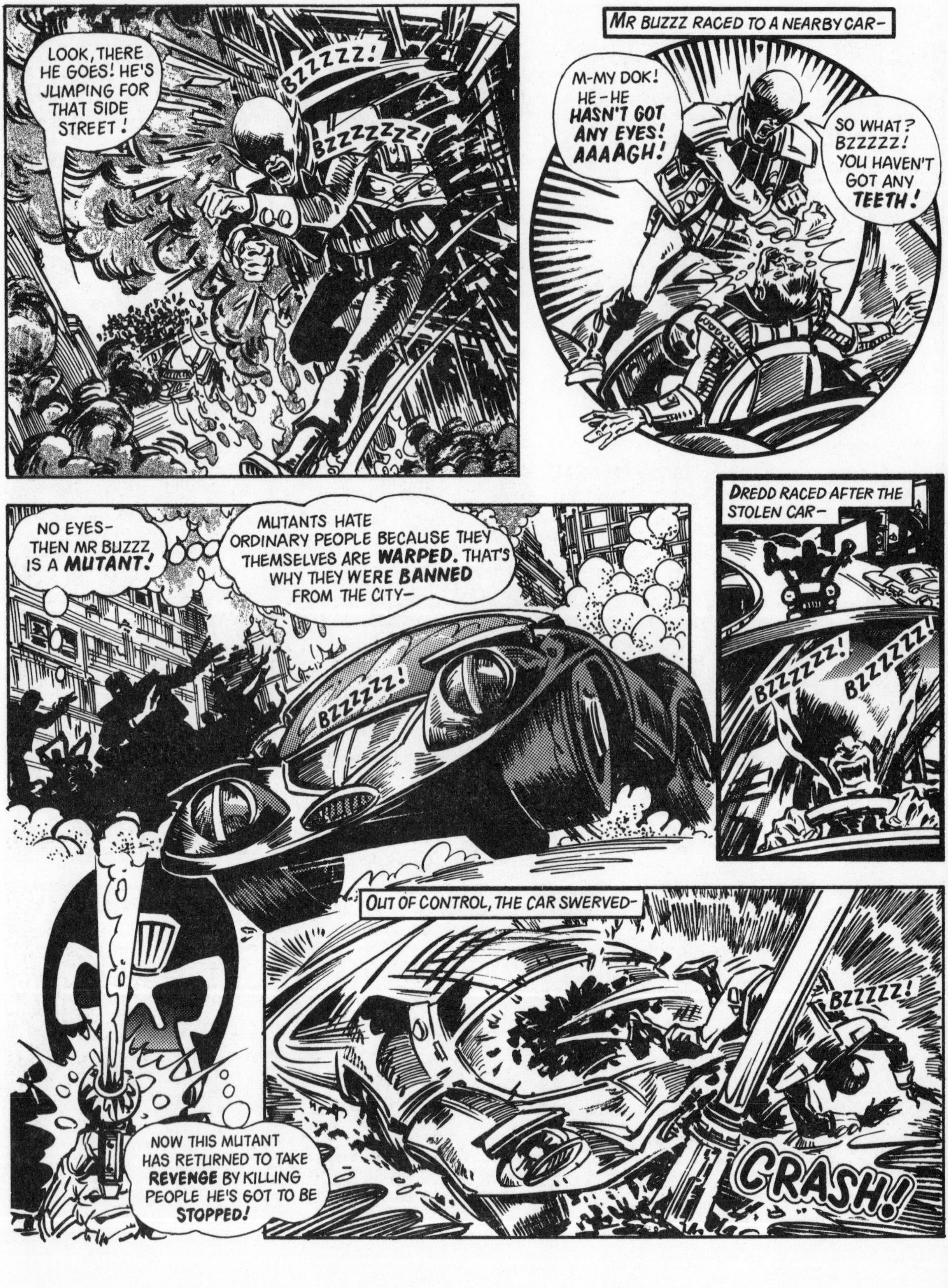
LOOK, THERE HE GOES! HE'S JUMPING FOR THAT SIDE STREET!
BZZZZZZ!
BZZZZZZZZ!
MR BUZZZ RACED TO A NEARBY CAR-
M-MY DOK! HE-HE HASN'T GOT ANY EYES! AAAAGH!
SO WHAT? BZZZZZ! YOU HAVEN'T GOT ANY TEETH!
NO EYES- THEN MR BUZZZ IS A MUTANT!
MUTANTS HATE ORDINARY PEOPLE BECAUSE THEY THEMSELVES ARE WARPED. THAT'S WHY THEY WERE BANNED FROM THE CITY-
BZZZZZZ!
DREDD RACED AFTER THE STOLEN CAR-
BZZZZZZ!
BZZZZZZZ!
NOW THIS MUTANT HAS RETURNED TO TAKE REVENGE BY KILLING PEOPLE HE'S GOT TO BE STOPPED!
OUT OF CONTROL, THE CAR SWERVED-
BZZZZZ!
CRASH!

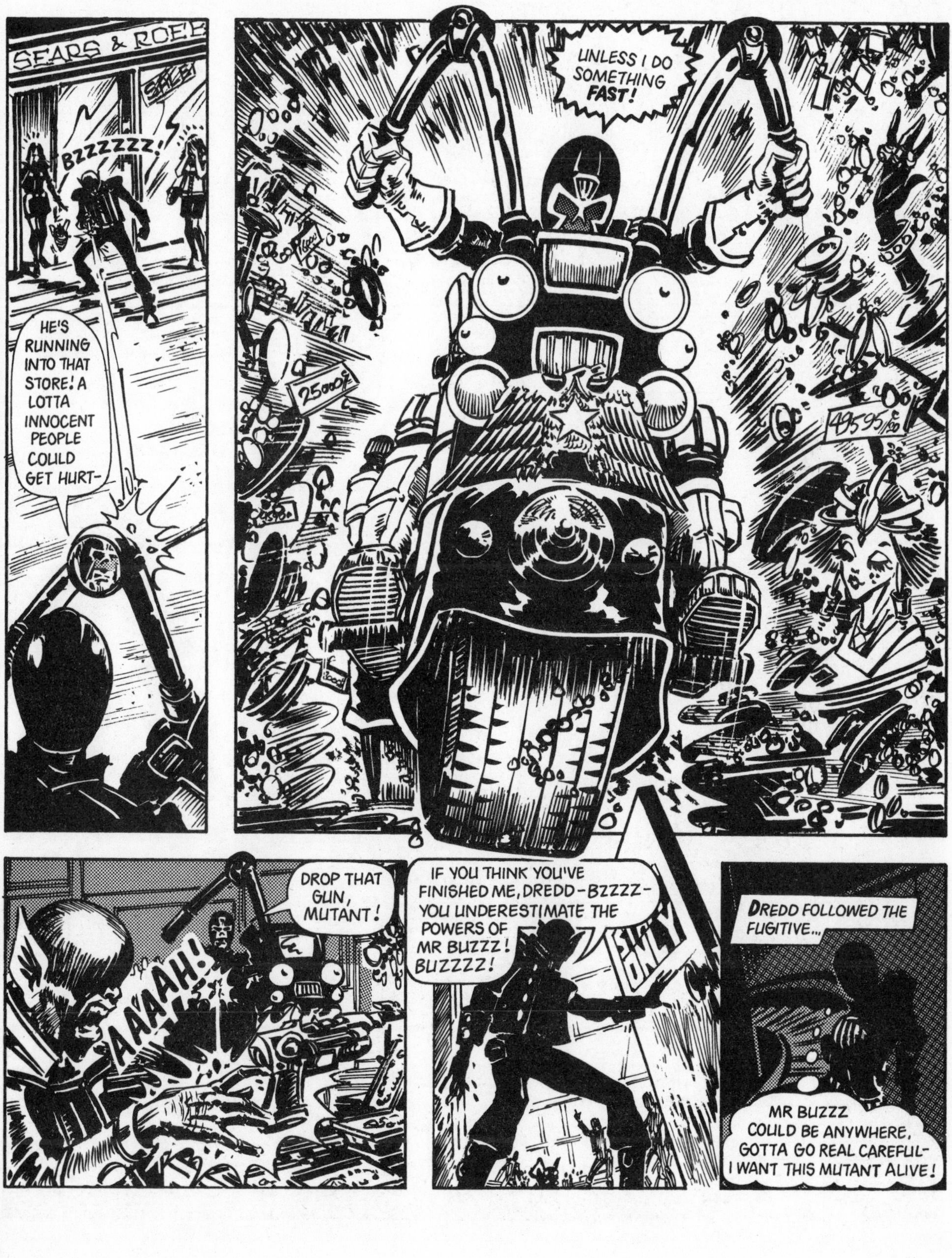
SEARS & ROEB
SALE!
BZZZZZZ!
HE'S RUNNING INTO THAT STORE! A LOTTA INNOCENT PEOPLE COULD GET HURT-
UNLESS I DO SOMETHING FAST!
25000
49595
DROP THAT GUN, MUTANT!
AAAAH!
IF YOU THINK YOU'VE FINISHED ME, DREDD-BZZZZ- YOU UNDERESTIMATE THE POWERS OF MR BUZZZ! BUZZZZ!
DREDD FOLLOWED THE FUGITIVE...
MR BUZZZ COULD BE ANYWHERE, GOTTA GO REAL CAREFUL- I WANT THIS MUTANT ALIVE!

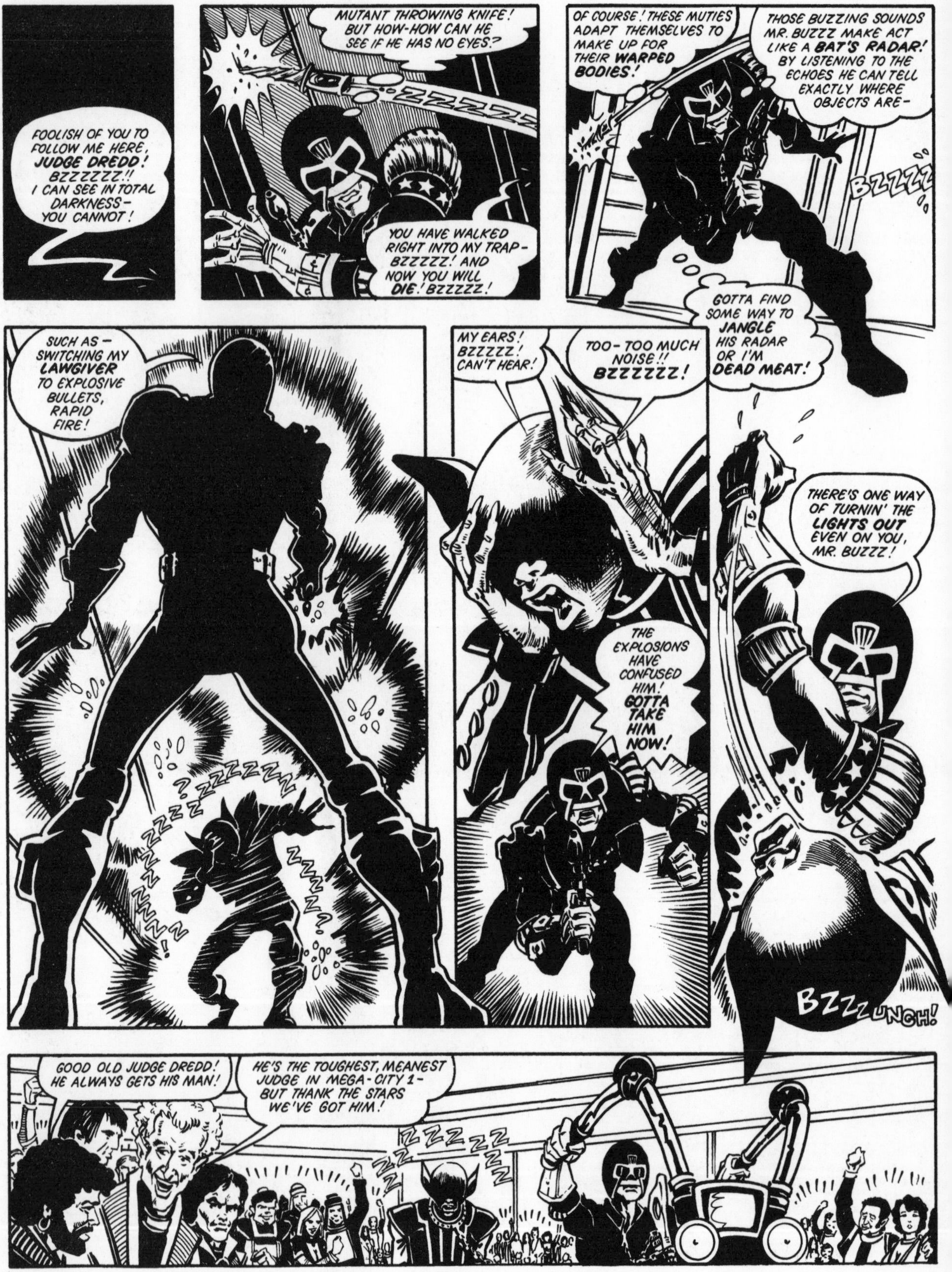

FOOLISH OF YOU TO FOLLOW ME HERE, JUDGE DREDD! BZZZZZZ.!! I CAN SEE IN TOTAL DARKNESS– YOU CANNOT!
MUTANT THROWING KNIFE! BUT HOW-HOW CAN HE SEE IF HE HAS NO EYES?
ZZZZZZ
YOU HAVE WALKED RIGHT INTO MY TRAP- BZZZZZ! AND NOW YOU WILL DIE! BZZZZZ!
OF COURSE! THESE MUTIES ADAPT THEMSELVES TO MAKE UP FOR THEIR WARPED BODIES!
THOSE BUZZING SOUNDS MR. BUZZZ MAKE ACT LIKE A BAT'S RADAR! BY LISTENING TO THE ECHOES HE CAN TELL EXACTLY WHERE OBJECTS ARE-
BZZZZ
GOTTA FIND SOME WAY TO JANGLE HIS RADAR OR I'M DEAD MEAT!
SUCH AS– SWITCHING MY LAWGIVER TO EXPLOSIVE BULLETS, RAPID FIRE!
MY EARS! BZZZZZ! CAN'T HEAR!
TOO- TOO MUCH NOISE!! BZZZZZZ!
THE EXPLOSIONS HAVE CONFUSED HIM! GOTTA TAKE HIM NOW!
THERE'S ONE WAY OF TURNIN' THE LIGHTS OUT EVEN ON YOU, MR. BUZZZ!
BZZZUNCH!
GOOD OLD JUDGE DREDD! HE ALWAYS GETS HIS MAN!
HE'S THE TOUGHEST, MEANEST JUDGE IN MEGA-CITY 1- BUT THANK THE STARS WE'VE GOT HIM!

REMEMBER THIS IS *JUDGE DREDD'S* BEAT, SO DON'T TRY *SMOKING* ON THE *STREET!*

SMOKING ON STREETS *PROHIBITED* — BY ORDER.

THERE GOES JUDGE DREDD — JUST *SEEIN'* HIM MAKES ME *EDGY!*

HE'S GONE PAST, RELAX, MAN. HAVE A SMOKE!

2000 A.D.

THRILL 6

BUT SUDDENLY...

CAN'T YOU *READ*, BOY? GET THAT *WEED* OUT OF YOUR MOUTH!

HE-HE'S SWUNG ROUND! BUT HOW'D HE *SPOT US?*

JUDGE DREDD

ON THE CONTROL PANEL OF DREDD'S MIGHTY BIKE...

NICOTINE COUNT — NINE YARDS LEFT REAR

IF I CAN'T *SEE* POLLUTION LAWBREAKERS, MY STREET-SCANNER *SMELLS* 'EM OUT!

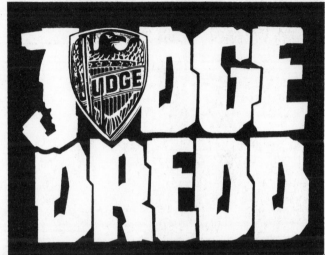

SURE ENOUGH, IN A BANK SEVERAL MILES ACROSS MEGA-CITY, MORE THAN ONE LAW WAS BEING BROKEN...

HURRY UP WITH THE LOOT — NOT A MOVE OUTTA ANY OF YOU OTHER CITIZENS!

YOU DIDN'T ACTUALLY *LIGHT* THOSE DISGUSTING OBJECTS, SO I CAN LET YOU OFF WITH A *WARNING.* NOW *BEAT IT*, I GOT MORE IMPORTANT THINGS TO DO THAN *LECTURE* STUPID KIDS...!

Y-YEAH, JUDGE, SIR! W-WERE GOING!

TERRIFIED OF THE VICIOUS LAWBREAKERS, THE CUSTOMERS AND BANK STAFF DID AS THEY WERE ORDERED...

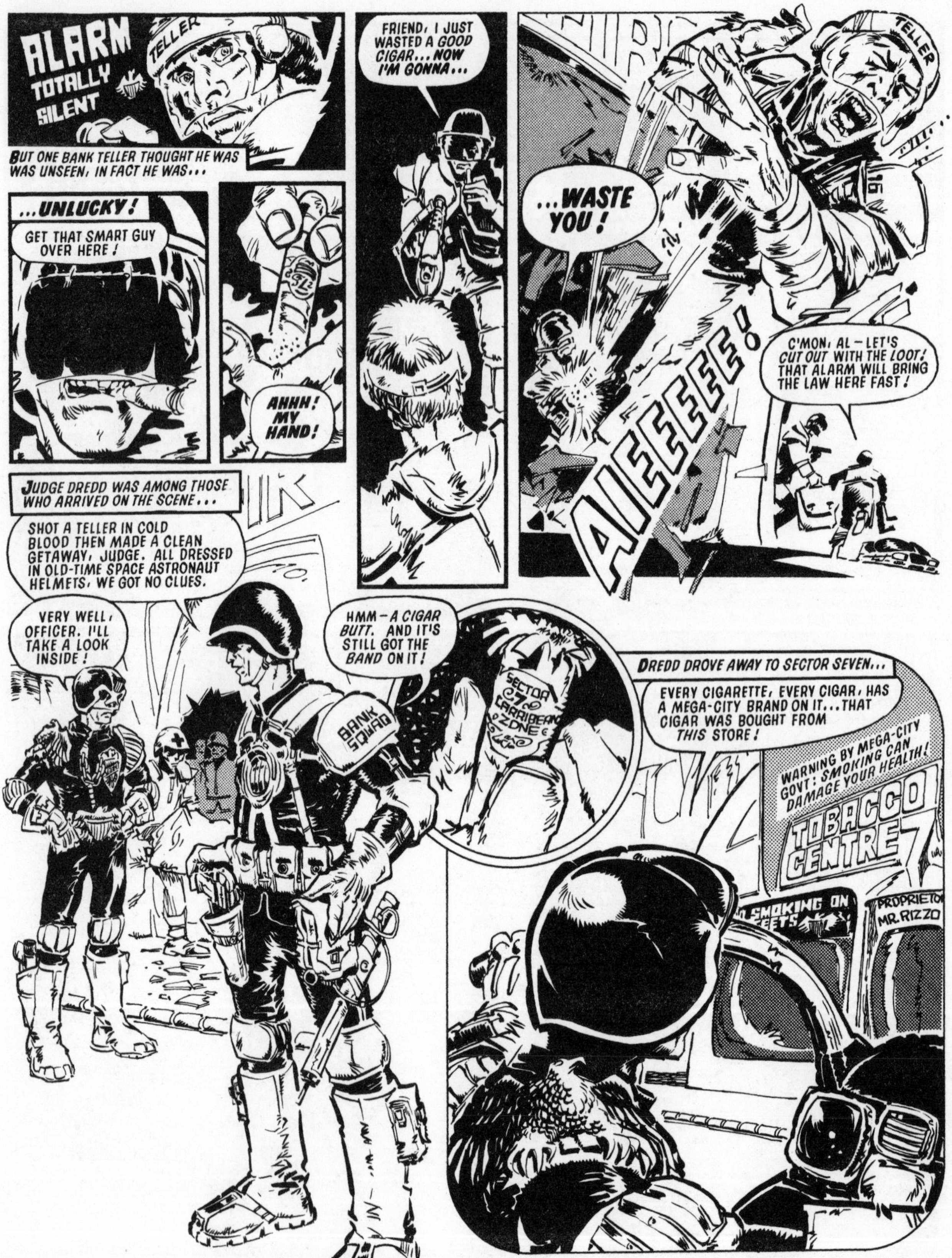
ALARM TOTALLY SILENT
TELLER
BUT ONE BANK TELLER THOUGHT HE WAS WAS UNSEEN, IN FACT HE WAS...
...UNLUCKY!
GET THAT SMART GUY OVER HERE!
AHHH! MY HAND!
FRIEND, I JUST WASTED A GOOD CIGAR... NOW I'M GONNA...
...WASTE YOU!
AIEEEEE!
C'MON, AL — LET'S CUT OUT WITH THE LOOT! THAT ALARM WILL BRING THE LAW HERE FAST!
JUDGE DREDD WAS AMONG THOSE WHO ARRIVED ON THE SCENE...
SHOT A TELLER IN COLD BLOOD THEN MADE A CLEAN GETAWAY, JUDGE. ALL DRESSED IN OLD-TIME SPACE ASTRONAUT HELMETS, WE GOT NO CLUES.
VERY WELL, OFFICER. I'LL TAKE A LOOK INSIDE!
BANK SQUAD
HMM — A CIGAR BUTT. AND IT'S STILL GOT THE BAND ON IT!
SECTOR 7 CARRIBEAN ZONE
DREDD DROVE AWAY TO SECTOR SEVEN...
EVERY CIGARETTE, EVERY CIGAR, HAS A MEGA-CITY BRAND ON IT... THAT CIGAR WAS BOUGHT FROM THIS STORE!
WARNING BY MEGA-CITY GOVT: SMOKING CAN DAMAGE YOUR HEALTH!
TOBACCO CENTRE 7
PROPRIETOR MR. RIZZO

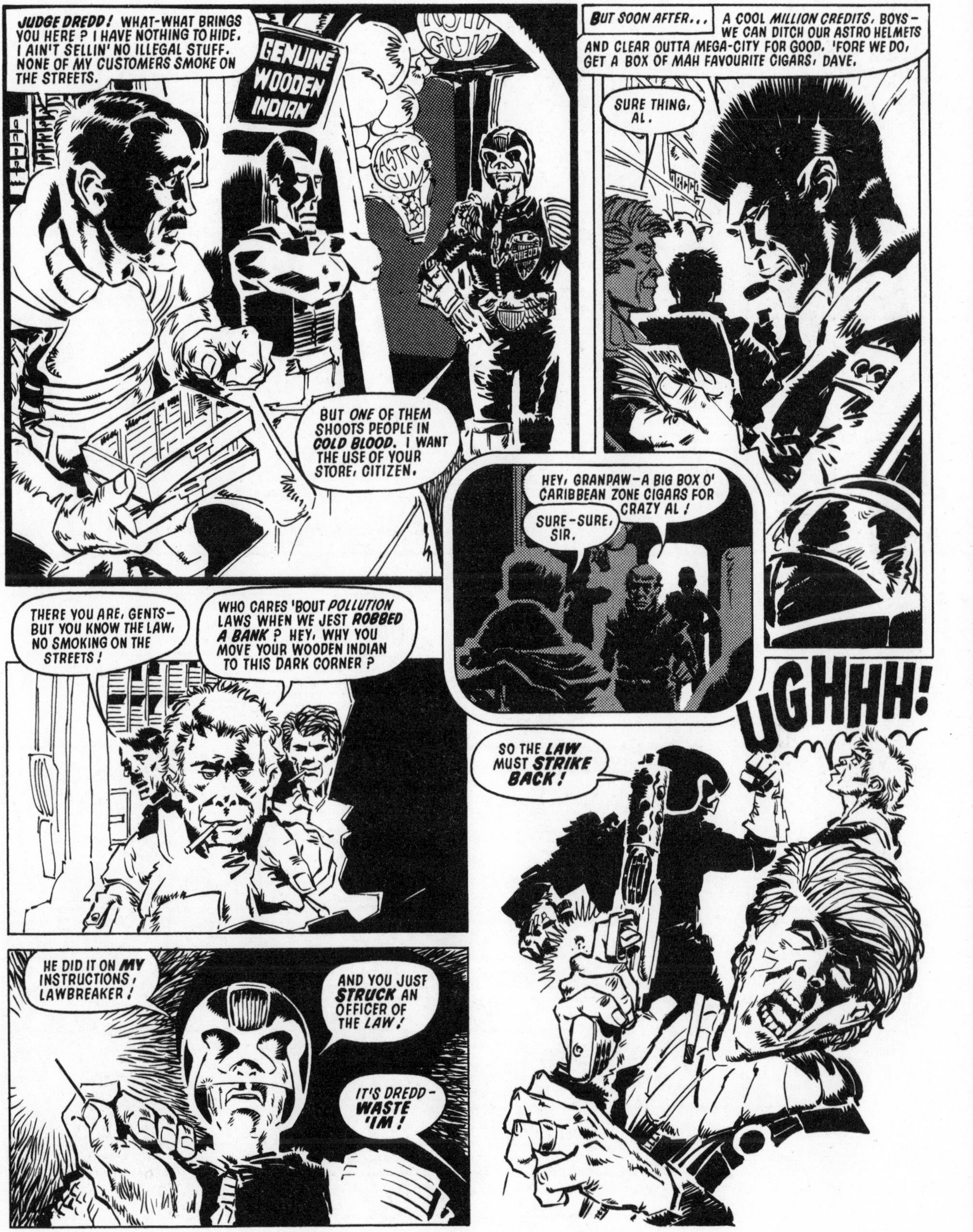
JUDGE DREDD! WHAT-WHAT BRINGS YOU HERE? I HAVE NOTHING TO HIDE. I AIN'T SELLIN' NO ILLEGAL STUFF. NONE OF MY CUSTOMERS SMOKE ON THE STREETS.
GENUINE WOODEN INDIAN
ASTRO GUM
BUT ONE OF THEM SHOOTS PEOPLE IN COLD BLOOD. I WANT THE USE OF YOUR STORE, CITIZEN.
BUT SOON AFTER...
A COOL MILLION CREDITS, BOYS - WE CAN DITCH OUR ASTRO HELMETS AND CLEAR OUTTA MEGA-CITY FOR GOOD. 'FORE WE DO, GET A BOX OF MAH FAVOURITE CIGARS, DAVE.
SURE THING, AL.
HEY, GRANPAW-A BIG BOX O' CARIBBEAN ZONE CIGARS FOR CRAZY AL!
SURE-SURE, SIR.
THERE YOU ARE, GENTS-BUT YOU KNOW THE LAW, NO SMOKING ON THE STREETS!
WHO CARES 'BOUT POLLUTION LAWS WHEN WE JEST ROBBED A BANK? HEY, WHY YOU MOVE YOUR WOODEN INDIAN TO THIS DARK CORNER?
HE DID IT ON MY INSTRUCTIONS, LAWBREAKER!
AND YOU JUST STRUCK AN OFFICER OF THE LAW!
IT'S DREDD-WASTE 'IM!
UGHHH!
SO THE LAW MUST STRIKE BACK!

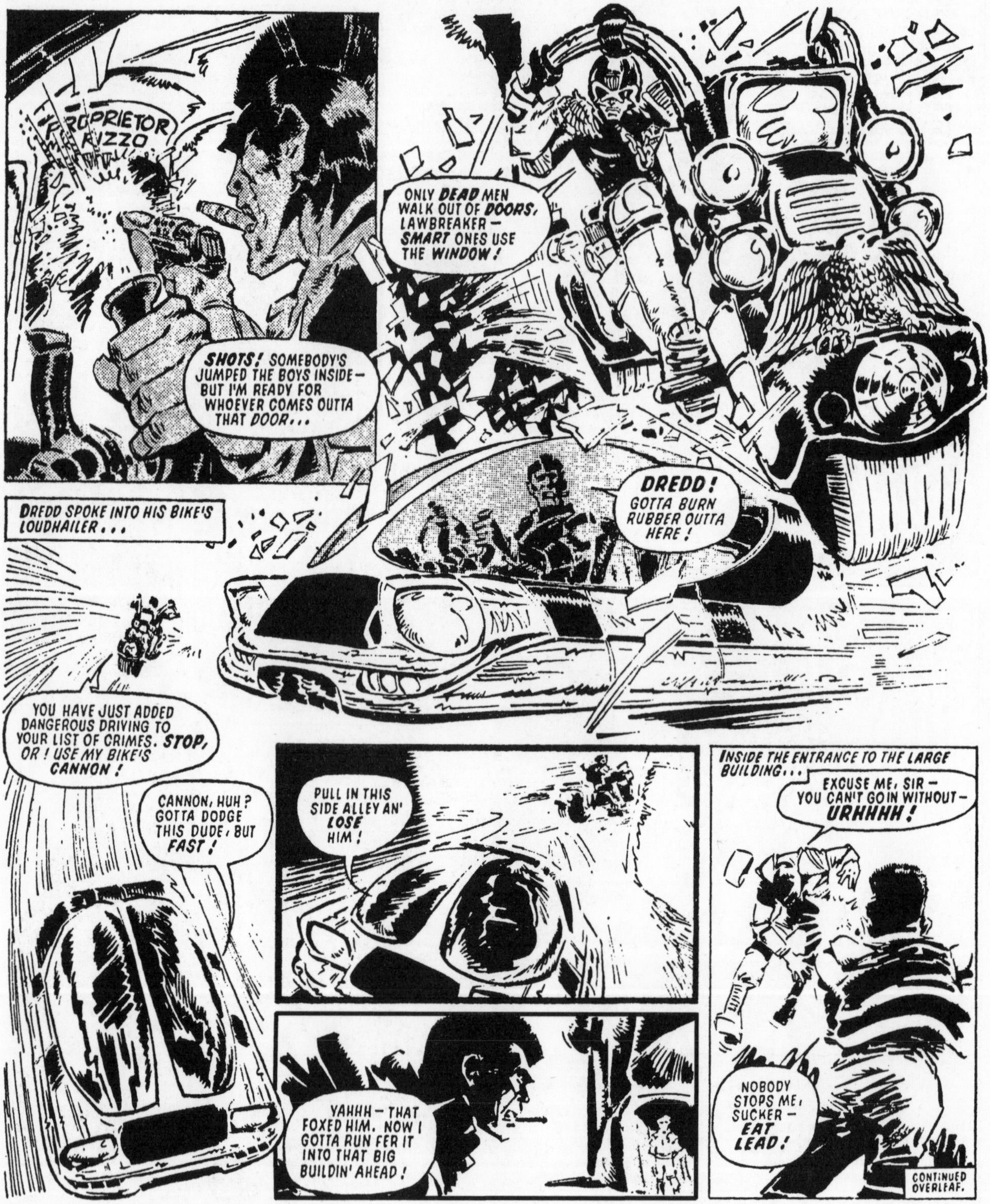
PROPRIETOR RIZZO
SHOTS! SOMEBODY'S JUMPED THE BOYS INSIDE— BUT I'M READY FOR WHOEVER COMES OUTTA THAT DOOR...
ONLY DEAD MEN WALK OUT OF DOORS, LAWBREAKER— SMART ONES USE THE WINDOW!
DREDD! GOTTA BURN RUBBER OUTTA HERE!
DREDD SPOKE INTO HIS BIKE'S LOUDHAILER...
YOU HAVE JUST ADDED DANGEROUS DRIVING TO YOUR LIST OF CRIMES. STOP, OR I USE MY BIKE'S CANNON!
CANNON, HUH? GOTTA DODGE THIS DUDE, BUT FAST!
PULL IN THIS SIDE ALLEY AN' LOSE HIM!
YAHHH— THAT FOXED HIM. NOW I GOTTA RUN FER IT INTO THAT BIG BUILDIN' AHEAD!
INSIDE THE ENTRANCE TO THE LARGE BUILDING...
EXCUSE ME, SIR— YOU CAN'T GO IN WITHOUT— URHHHH!
NOBODY STOPS ME, SUCKER— EAT LEAD!
CONTINUED OVERLEAF.

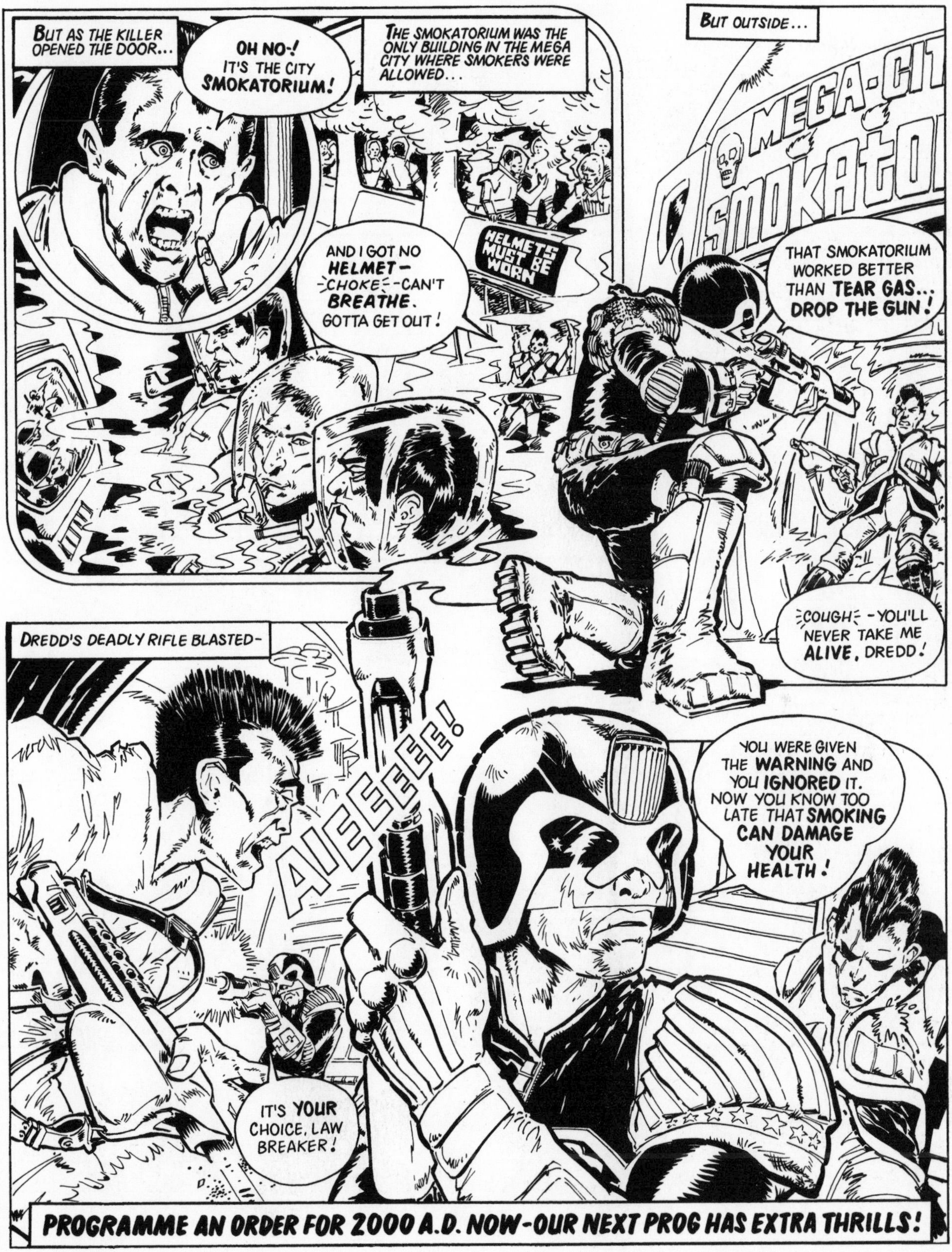

BUT AS THE KILLER OPENED THE DOOR...
OH NO-! IT'S THE CITY SMOKATORIUM!
THE SMOKATORIUM WAS THE ONLY BUILDING IN THE MEGA CITY WHERE SMOKERS WERE ALLOWED...
HELMETS MUST BE WORN
AND I GOT NO HELMET- -CHOKE- -CAN'T BREATHE. GOTTA GET OUT!
BUT OUTSIDE...
MEGA-CIT SMOKATO
THAT SMOKATORIUM WORKED BETTER THAN TEAR GAS... DROP THE GUN!
-COUGH- -YOU'LL NEVER TAKE ME ALIVE, DREDD!
DREDD'S DEADLY RIFLE BLASTED-
AIEEEEE!
YOU WERE GIVEN THE WARNING AND YOU IGNORED IT. NOW YOU KNOW TOO LATE THAT SMOKING CAN DAMAGE YOUR HEALTH!
IT'S YOUR CHOICE, LAW BREAKER!
PROGRAMME AN ORDER FOR 2000 A.D. NOW-OUR NEXT PROG HAS EXTRA THRILLS!

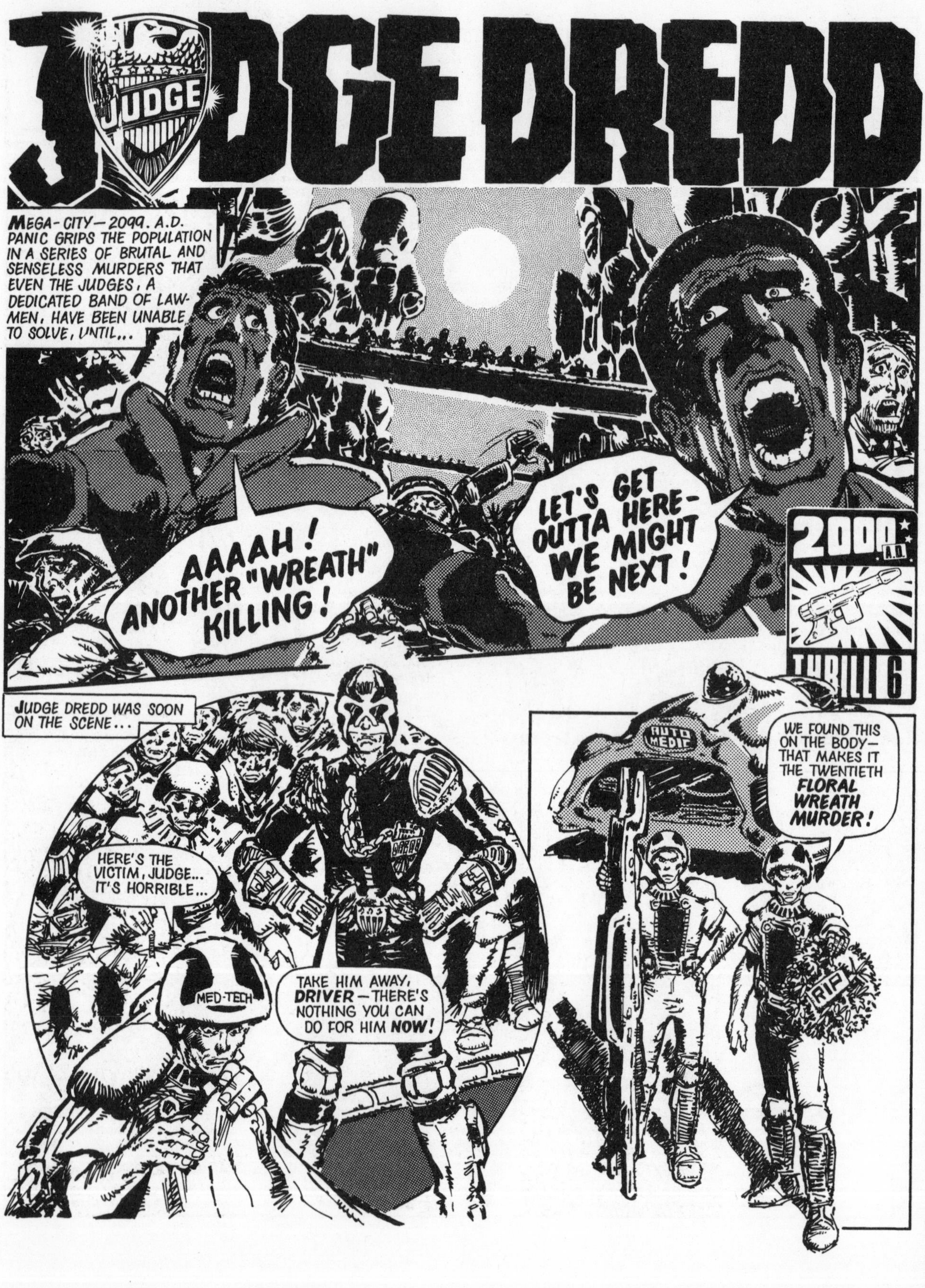
JUDGE DREDD
JUDGE
MEGA-CITY—2099. A.D. PANIC GRIPS THE POPULATION IN A SERIES OF BRUTAL AND SENSELESS MURDERS THAT EVEN THE JUDGES, A DEDICATED BAND OF LAW-MEN, HAVE BEEN UNABLE TO SOLVE, UNTIL...
AAAAH! ANOTHER "WREATH" KILLING!
LET'S GET OUTTA HERE- WE MIGHT BE NEXT!
2000 A.D.
THRILL 6
JUDGE DREDD WAS SOON ON THE SCENE...
HERE'S THE VICTIM, JUDGE... IT'S HORRIBLE...
MED-TECH
TAKE HIM AWAY, DRIVER—THERE'S NOTHING YOU CAN DO FOR HIM NOW!
AUTO MEDIC
WE FOUND THIS ON THE BODY— THAT MAKES IT THE TWENTIETH FLORAL WREATH MURDER!
RIP

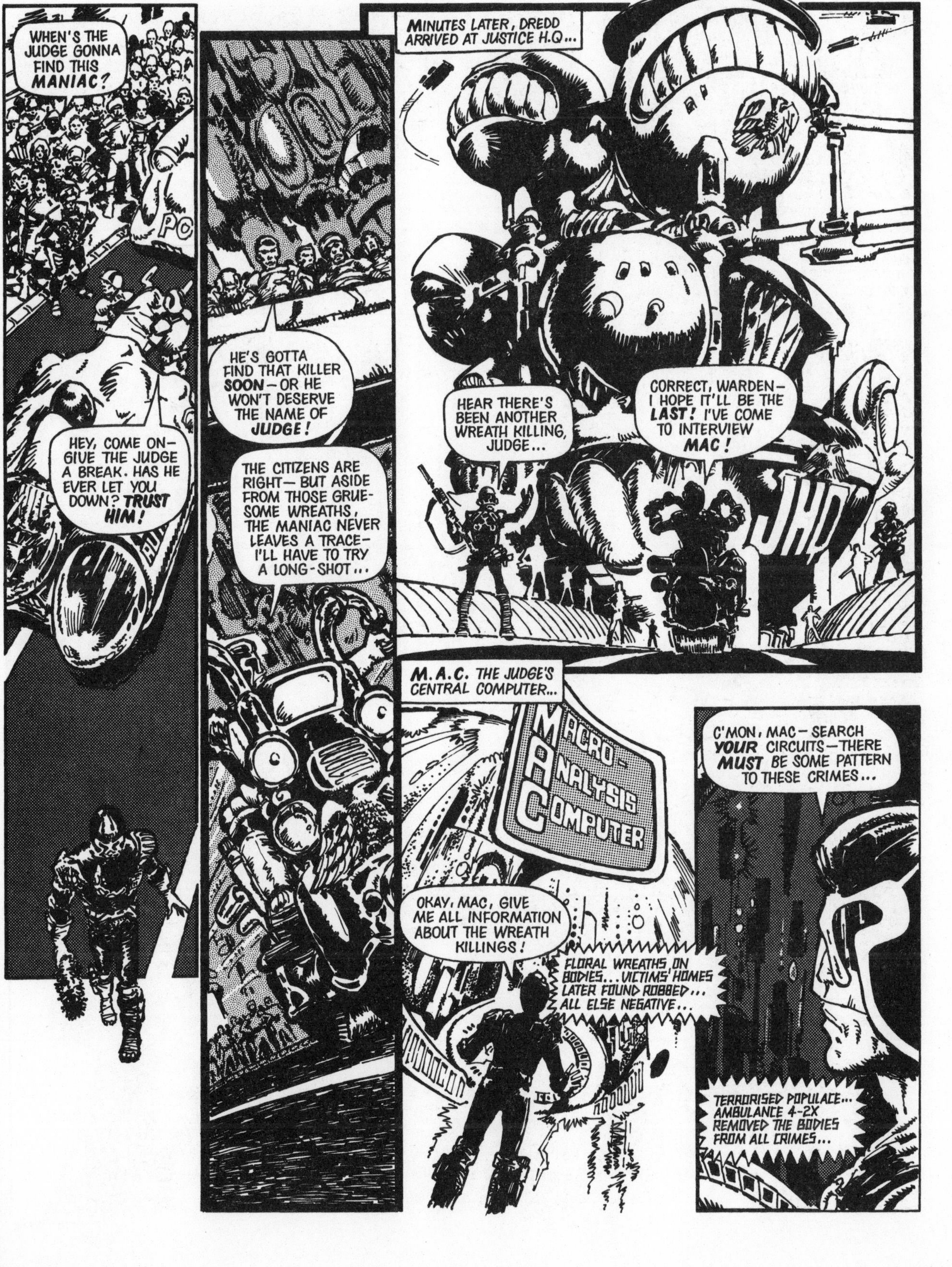

WHEN'S THE JUDGE GONNA FIND THIS MANIAC?
HEY, COME ON– GIVE THE JUDGE A BREAK. HAS HE EVER LET YOU DOWN? TRUST HIM!
HE'S GOTTA FIND THAT KILLER SOON–OR HE WON'T DESERVE THE NAME OF JUDGE!
THE CITIZENS ARE RIGHT– BUT ASIDE FROM THOSE GRUESOME WREATHS, THE MANIAC NEVER LEAVES A TRACE– I'LL HAVE TO TRY A LONG-SHOT...
MINUTES LATER, DREDD ARRIVED AT JUSTICE H.Q...
HEAR THERE'S BEEN ANOTHER WREATH KILLING, JUDGE...
CORRECT, WARDEN– I HOPE IT'LL BE THE LAST! I'VE COME TO INTERVIEW MAC!
JHQ
M.A.C. THE JUDGE'S CENTRAL COMPUTER...
MACRO-ANALYSIS COMPUTER
OKAY, MAC, GIVE ME ALL INFORMATION ABOUT THE WREATH KILLINGS!
FLORAL WREATHS ON BODIES... VICTIMS' HOMES LATER FOUND ROBBED... ALL ELSE NEGATIVE...
C'MON, MAC– SEARCH YOUR CIRCUITS–THERE MUST BE SOME PATTERN TO THESE CRIMES...
TERRORISED POPULACE... AMBULANCE 4-2X REMOVED THE BODIES FROM ALL CRIMES...

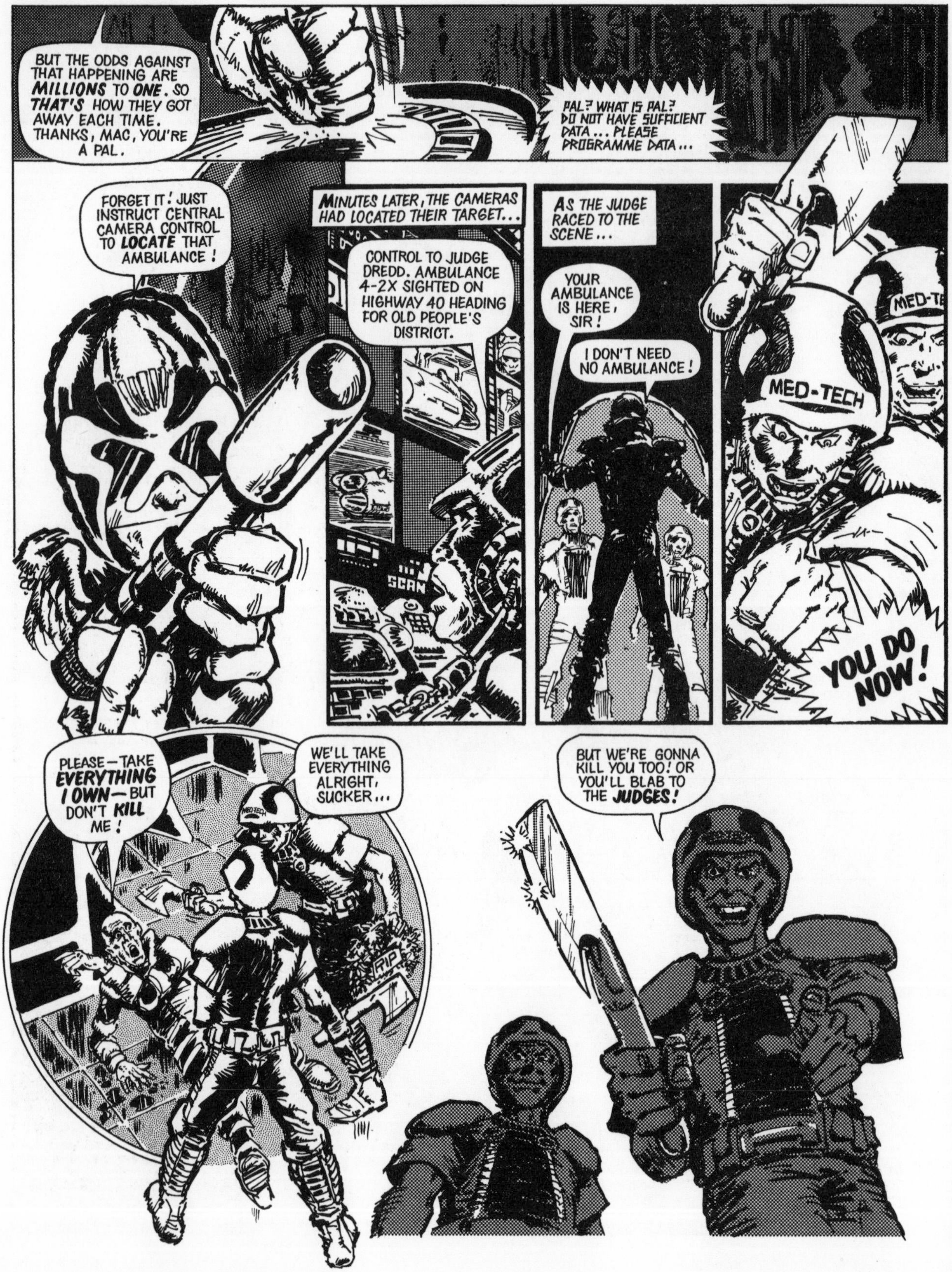

BUT THE ODDS AGAINST THAT HAPPENING ARE MILLIONS TO ONE. SO THAT'S HOW THEY GOT AWAY EACH TIME. THANKS, MAC, YOU'RE A PAL.
PAL? WHAT IS PAL? DO NOT HAVE SUFFICIENT DATA... PLEASE PROGRAMME DATA...
FORGET IT! JUST INSTRUCT CENTRAL CAMERA CONTROL TO LOCATE THAT AMBULANCE!
MINUTES LATER, THE CAMERAS HAD LOCATED THEIR TARGET...
CONTROL TO JUDGE DREDD. AMBULANCE 4-2X SIGHTED ON HIGHWAY 40 HEADING FOR OLD PEOPLE'S DISTRICT.
SCAN
AS THE JUDGE RACED TO THE SCENE...
YOUR AMBULANCE IS HERE, SIR!
I DON'T NEED NO AMBULANCE!
MED-TECH
MED-TECH
YOU DO NOW!
PLEASE—TAKE EVERYTHING I OWN—BUT DON'T KILL ME!
WE'LL TAKE EVERYTHING ALRIGHT, SUCKER...
MED-TECH
RIP
BUT WE'RE GONNA KILL YOU TOO! OR YOU'LL BLAB TO THE JUDGES!

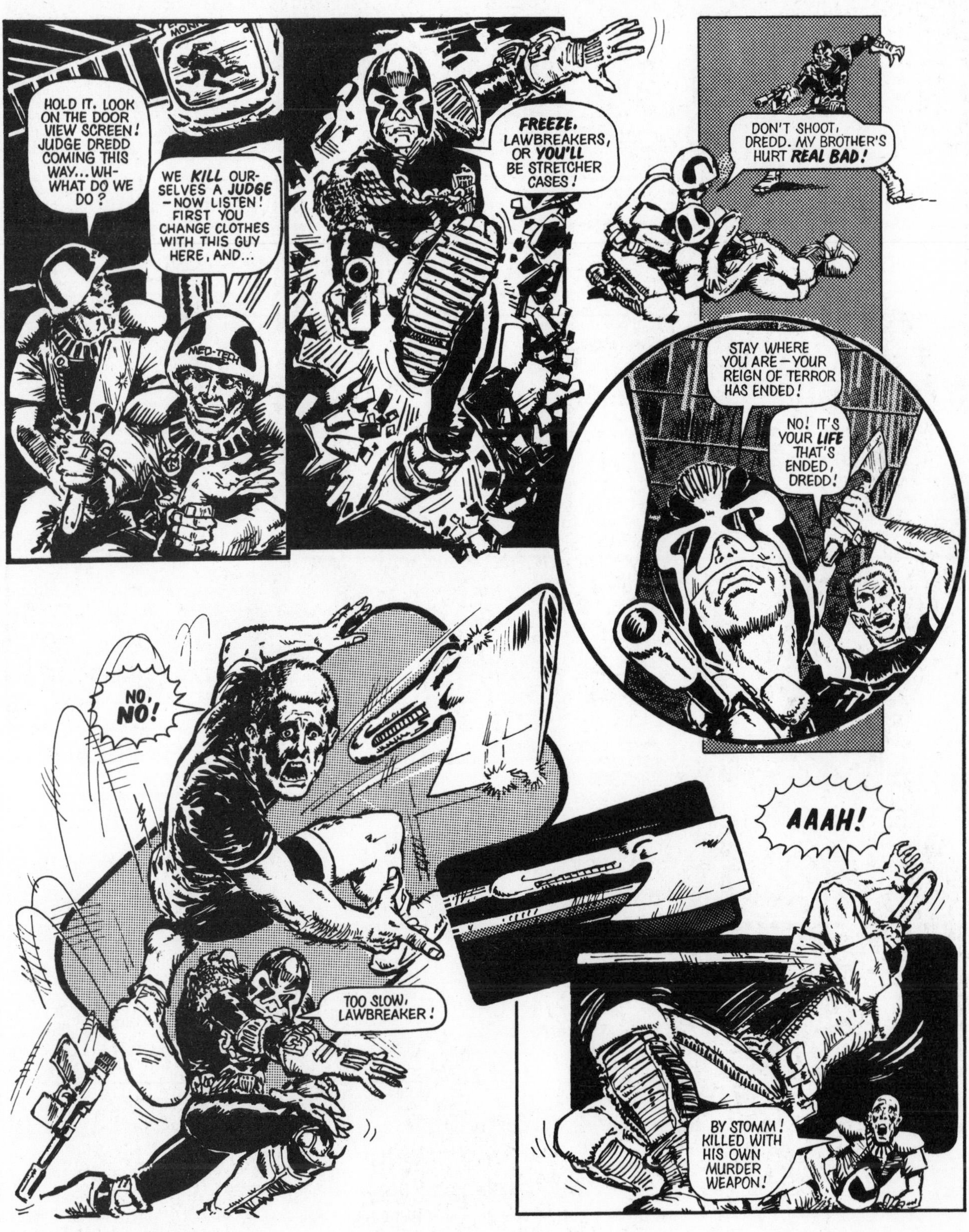

MONI
HOLD IT. LOOK ON THE DOOR VIEW SCREEN! JUDGE DREDD COMING THIS WAY... WH- WHAT DO WE DO?
WE KILL OURSELVES A JUDGE —NOW LISTEN! FIRST YOU CHANGE CLOTHES WITH THIS GUY HERE, AND...
MED-TECH
FREEZE, LAWBREAKERS, OR YOU'LL BE STRETCHER CASES!
DON'T SHOOT, DREDD. MY BROTHER'S HURT REAL BAD!
STAY WHERE YOU ARE—YOUR REIGN OF TERROR HAS ENDED!
NO! IT'S YOUR LIFE THAT'S ENDED, DREDD!
NO, NO!
TOO SLOW, LAWBREAKER!
AAAH!
BY STOMM! KILLED WITH HIS OWN MURDER WEAPON!

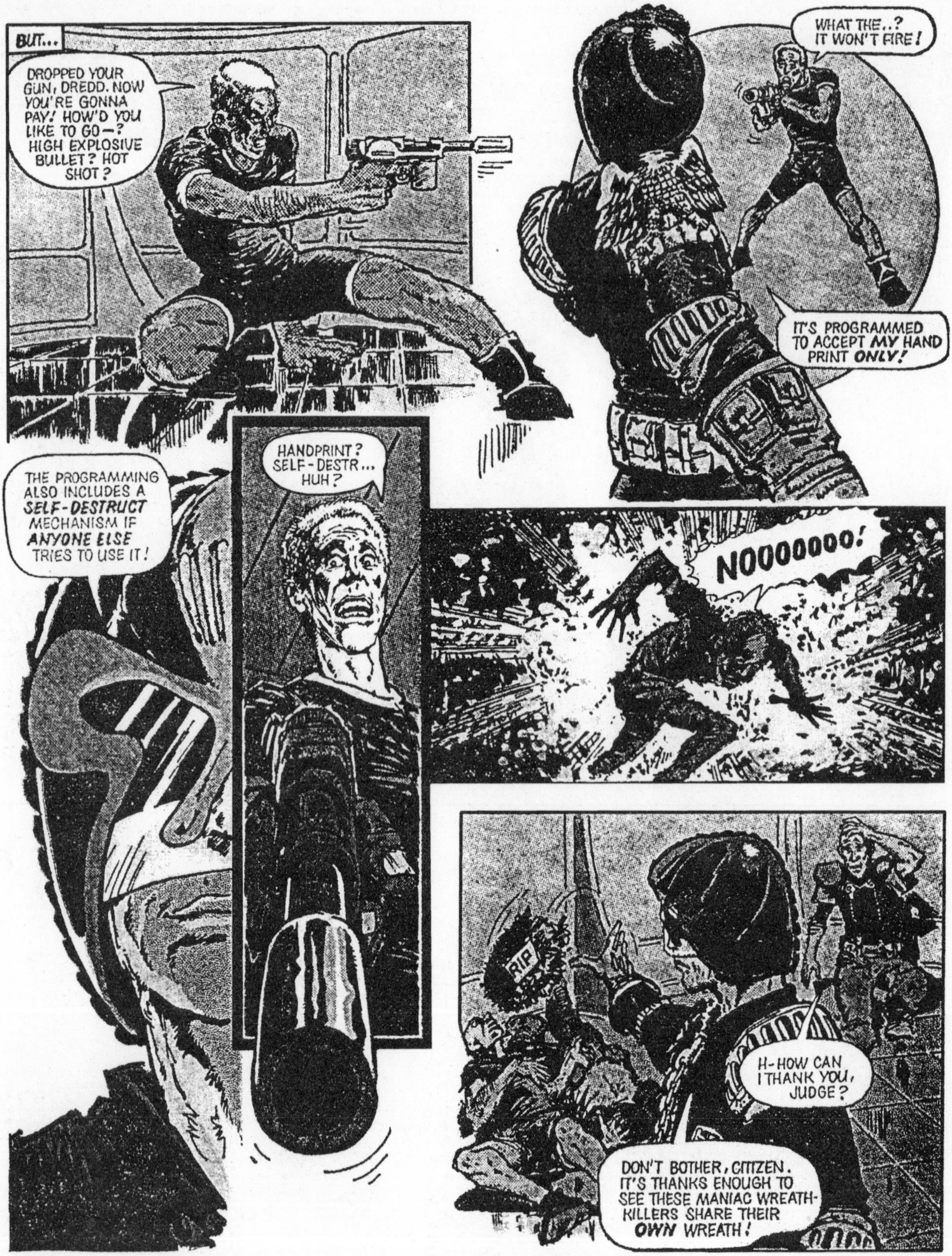
BUT...
DROPPED YOUR GUN, DREDD. NOW YOU'RE GONNA PAY! HOW'D YOU LIKE TO GO—? HIGH EXPLOSIVE BULLET? HOT SHOT?
WHAT THE..? IT WON'T FIRE!
IT'S PROGRAMMED TO ACCEPT MY HAND PRINT ONLY!
THE PROGRAMMING ALSO INCLUDES A SELF-DESTRUCT MECHANISM IF ANYONE ELSE TRIES TO USE IT!
HANDPRINT? SELF-DESTR... HUH?
NOOOOOOO!
RIP
H-HOW CAN I THANK YOU, JUDGE?
DON'T BOTHER, CITIZEN. IT'S THANKS ENOUGH TO SEE THESE MANIAC WREATH-KILLERS SHARE THEIR OWN WREATH!

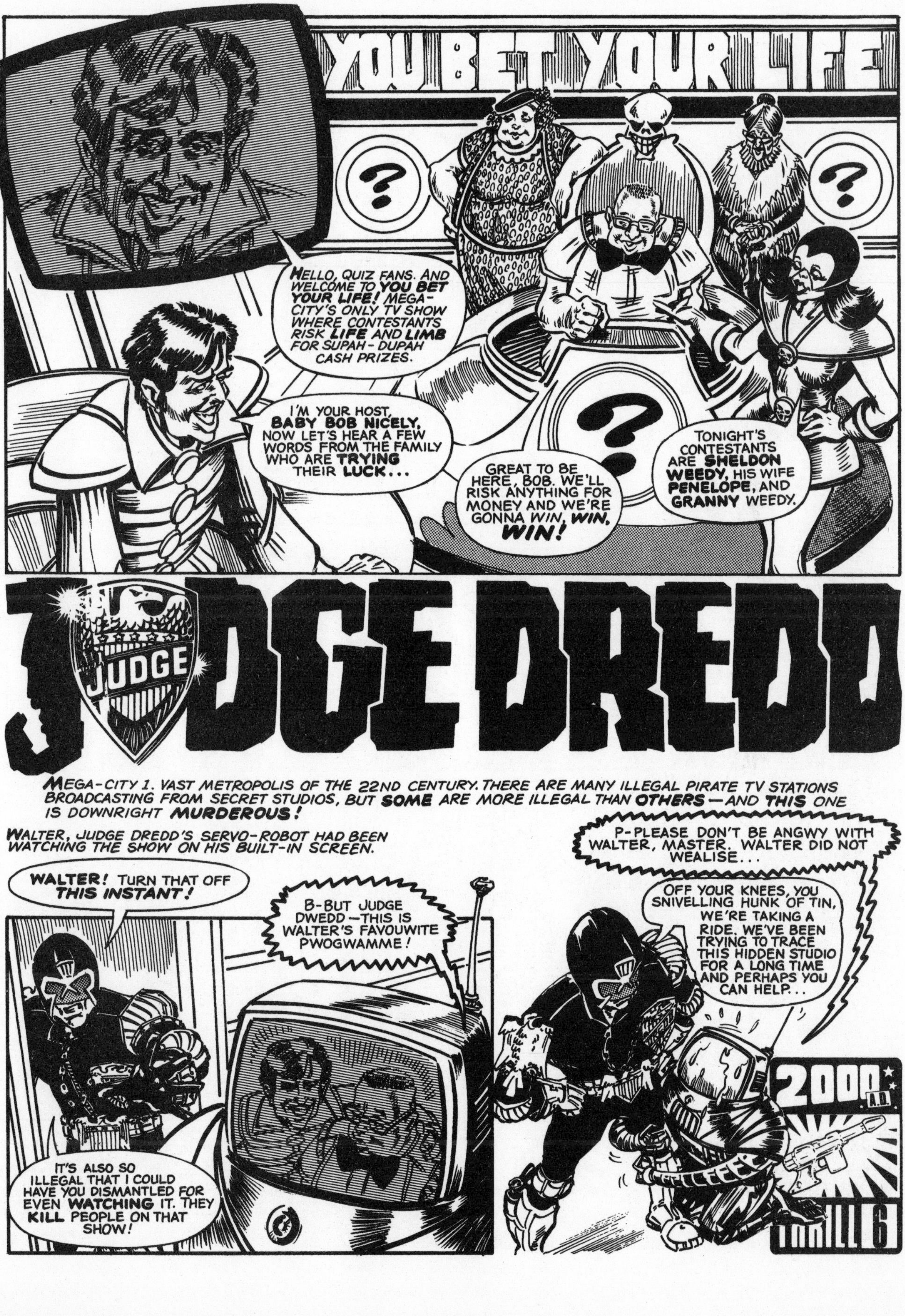
YOU BET YOUR LIFE
HELLO, QUIZ FANS. AND WELCOME TO YOU BET YOUR LIFE! MEGA-CITY'S ONLY TV SHOW WHERE CONTESTANTS RISK LIFE AND LIMB FOR SUPAH-DUPAH CASH PRIZES.
I'M YOUR HOST, BABY BOB NICELY, NOW LET'S HEAR A FEW WORDS FROM THE FAMILY WHO ARE TRYING THEIR LUCK...
GREAT TO BE HERE, BOB. WE'LL RISK ANYTHING FOR MONEY AND WE'RE GONNA WIN, WIN, WIN!
TONIGHT'S CONTESTANTS ARE SHELDON WEEDY, HIS WIFE PENELOPE, AND GRANNY WEEDY.
JUDGE
JUDGE DREDD
MEGA-CITY 1. VAST METROPOLIS OF THE 22ND CENTURY. THERE ARE MANY ILLEGAL PIRATE TV STATIONS BROADCASTING FROM SECRET STUDIOS, BUT SOME ARE MORE ILLEGAL THAN OTHERS—AND THIS ONE IS DOWNRIGHT MURDEROUS!
WALTER, JUDGE DREDD'S SERVO-ROBOT HAD BEEN WATCHING THE SHOW ON HIS BUILT-IN SCREEN.
WALTER! TURN THAT OFF THIS INSTANT!
B-BUT JUDGE DWEDD—THIS IS WALTER'S FAVOUWITE PWOGWAMME!
IT'S ALSO SO ILLEGAL THAT I COULD HAVE YOU DISMANTLED FOR EVEN WATCHING IT. THEY KILL PEOPLE ON THAT SHOW!
P-PLEASE DON'T BE ANGWY WITH WALTER, MASTER. WALTER DID NOT WEALISE...
OFF YOUR KNEES, YOU SNIVELLING HUNK OF TIN, WE'RE TAKING A RIDE. WE'VE BEEN TRYING TO TRACE THIS HIDDEN STUDIO FOR A LONG TIME AND PERHAPS YOU CAN HELP...
2000 A.D.
THRILL 6

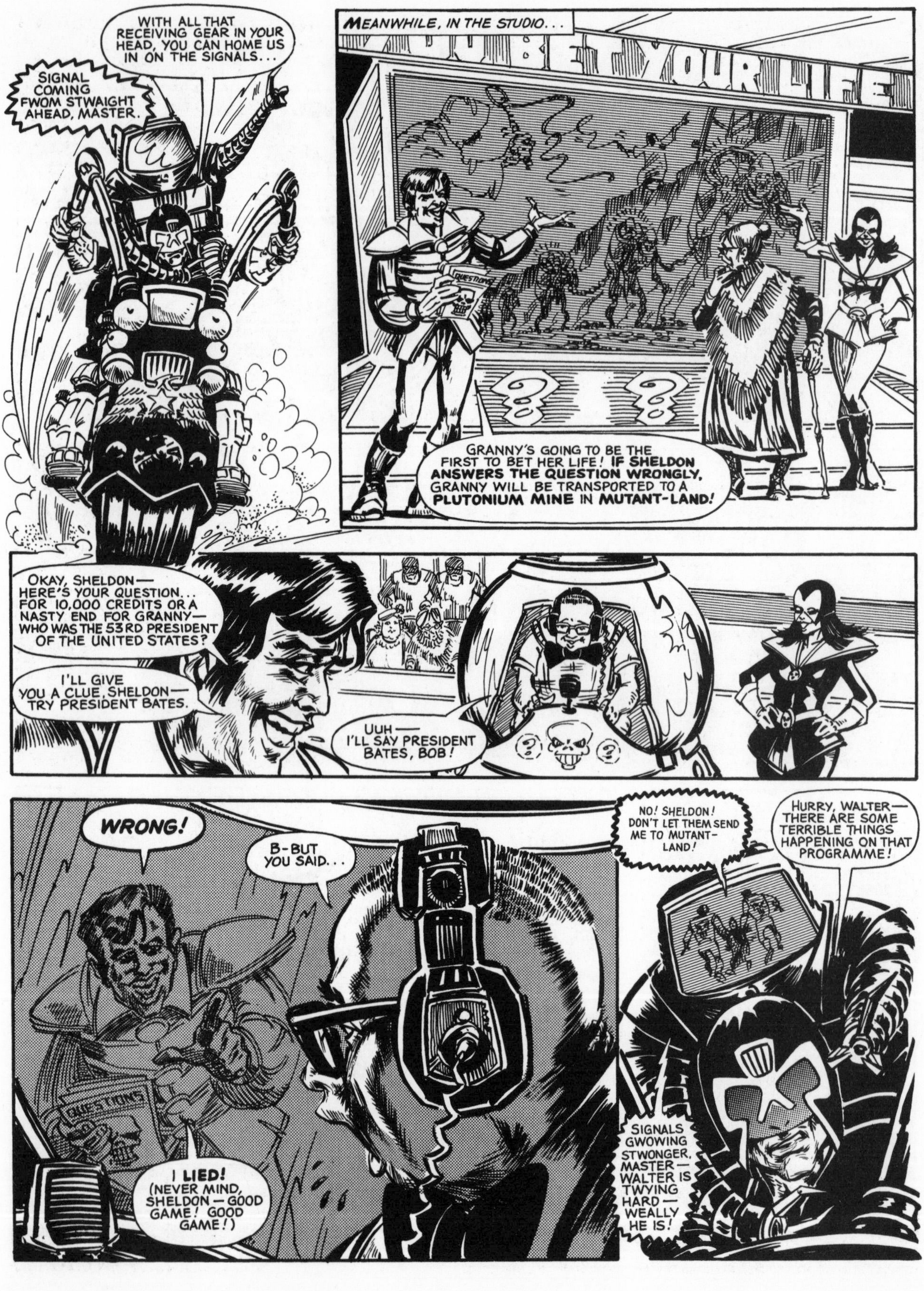
WITH ALL THAT RECEIVING GEAR IN YOUR HEAD, YOU CAN HOME US IN ON THE SIGNALS...
SIGNAL COMING FWOM STWAIGHT AHEAD, MASTER.
MEANWHILE, IN THE STUDIO...
YOU BET YOUR LIFE
GRANNY'S GOING TO BE THE FIRST TO BET HER LIFE! IF SHELDON ANSWERS THE QUESTION WRONGLY, GRANNY WILL BE TRANSPORTED TO A PLUTONIUM MINE IN MUTANT-LAND!
OKAY, SHELDON— HERE'S YOUR QUESTION... FOR 10,000 CREDITS OR A NASTY END FOR GRANNY— WHO WAS THE 53RD PRESIDENT OF THE UNITED STATES?
I'LL GIVE YOU A CLUE, SHELDON— TRY PRESIDENT BATES.
UUH— I'LL SAY PRESIDENT BATES, BOB!
WRONG!
B-BUT YOU SAID...
I LIED! (NEVER MIND, SHELDON— GOOD GAME! GOOD GAME!)
NO! SHELDON! DON'T LET THEM SEND ME TO MUTANT-LAND!
HURRY, WALTER— THERE ARE SOME TERRIBLE THINGS HAPPENING ON THAT PROGRAMME!
SIGNALS GWOWING STWONGER, MASTER— WALTER IS TWYING HARD— WEALLY HE IS!

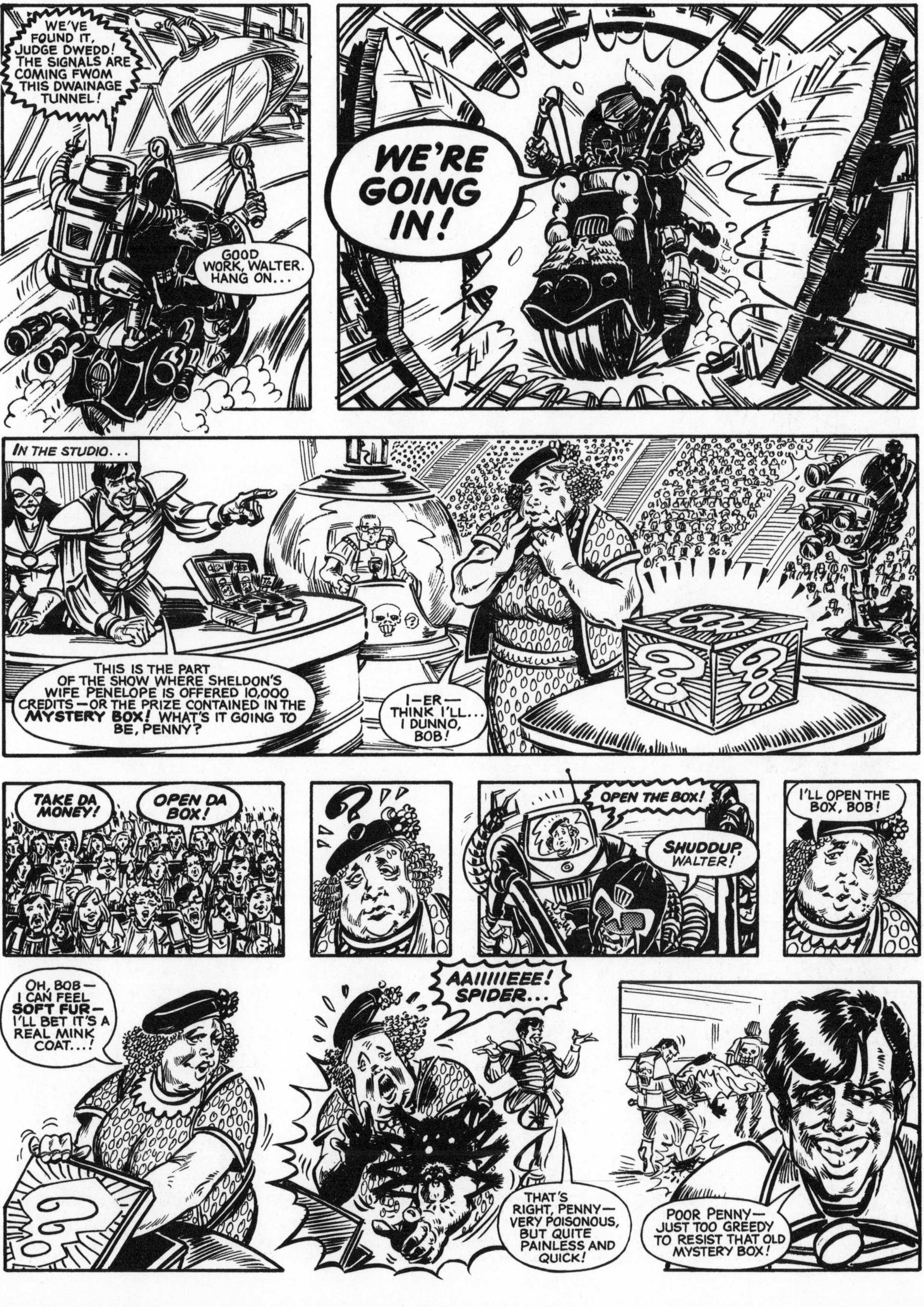
WE'VE FOUND IT, JUDGE DWEDD! THE SIGNALS ARE COMING FWOM THIS DWAINAGE TUNNEL!
GOOD WORK, WALTER. HANG ON...
WE'RE GOING IN!
IN THE STUDIO...
THIS IS THE PART OF THE SHOW WHERE SHELDON'S WIFE PENELOPE IS OFFERED 10,000 CREDITS—OR THE PRIZE CONTAINED IN THE MYSTERY BOX! WHAT'S IT GOING TO BE, PENNY?
I—ER—THINK I'LL... I DUNNO, BOB!
TAKE DA MONEY!
OPEN DA BOX!
OPEN THE BOX!
SHUDDUP, WALTER!
I'LL OPEN THE BOX, BOB!
OH, BOB—I CAN FEEL SOFT FUR—I'LL BET IT'S A REAL MINK COAT...!
AAIIIIIEEE! SPIDER...
THAT'S RIGHT, PENNY—VERY POISONOUS, BUT QUITE PAINLESS AND QUICK!
POOR PENNY—JUST TOO GREEDY TO RESIST THAT OLD MYSTERY BOX!

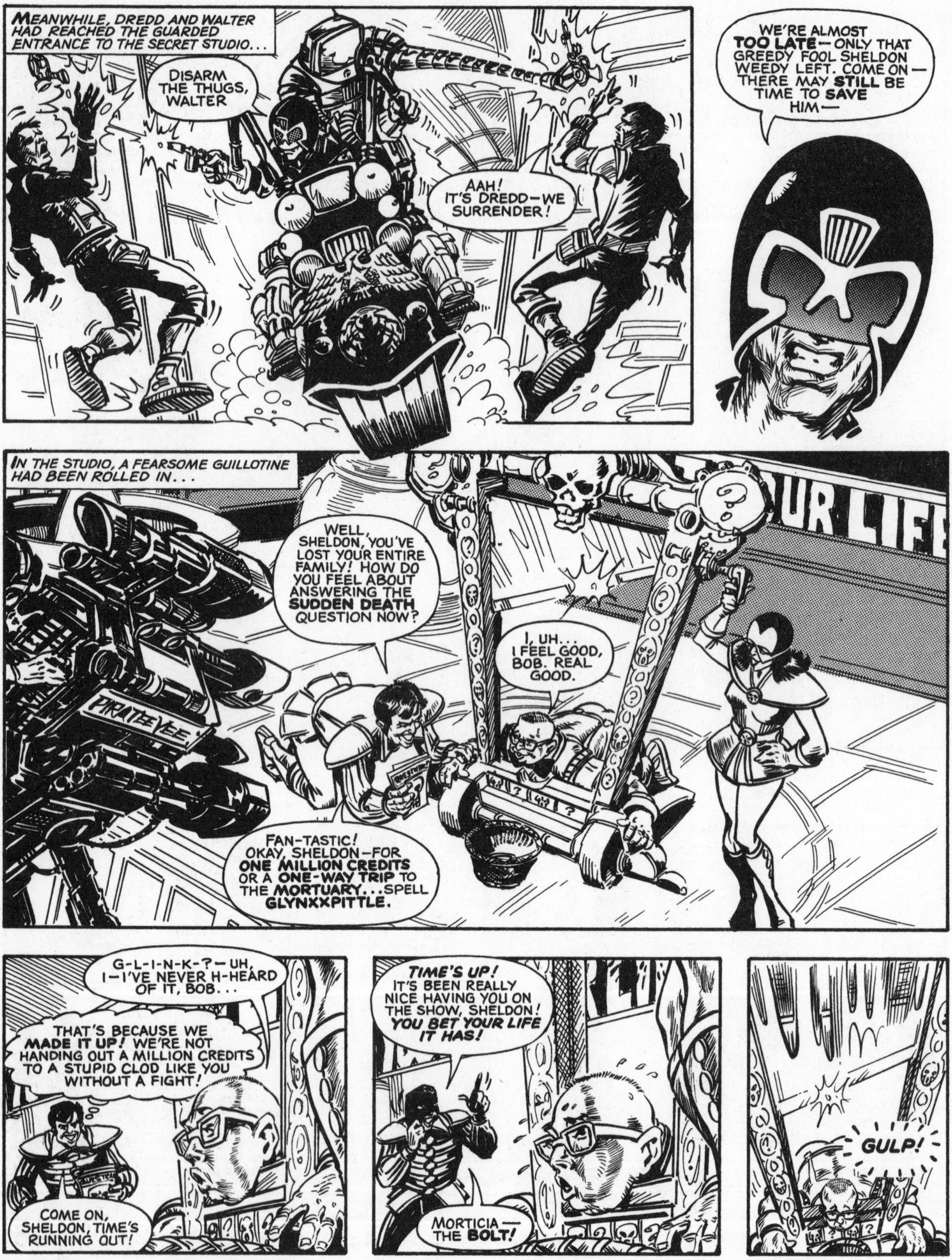
MEANWHILE, DREDD AND WALTER HAD REACHED THE GUARDED ENTRANCE TO THE SECRET STUDIO...
DISARM THE THUGS, WALTER
AAH! IT'S DREDD—WE SURRENDER!
WE'RE ALMOST TOO LATE—ONLY THAT GREEDY FOOL SHELDON WEEDY LEFT. COME ON—THERE MAY STILL BE TIME TO SAVE HIM—
IN THE STUDIO, A FEARSOME GUILLOTINE HAD BEEN ROLLED IN...
WELL, SHELDON, YOU'VE LOST YOUR ENTIRE FAMILY! HOW DO YOU FEEL ABOUT ANSWERING THE SUDDEN DEATH QUESTION NOW?
I, UH... I FEEL GOOD, BOB. REAL GOOD.
PIRATEEYEE
FAN-TASTIC! OKAY, SHELDON—FOR ONE MILLION CREDITS OR A ONE-WAY TRIP TO THE MORTUARY...SPELL GLYNXXPITTLE.
G-L-I-N-K-?—UH, I—I'VE NEVER H-HEARD OF IT, BOB...
THAT'S BECAUSE WE MADE IT UP! WE'RE NOT HANDING OUT A MILLION CREDITS TO A STUPID CLOD LIKE YOU WITHOUT A FIGHT!
COME ON, SHELDON, TIME'S RUNNING OUT!
TIME'S UP! IT'S BEEN REALLY NICE HAVING YOU ON THE SHOW, SHELDON! YOU BET YOUR LIFE IT HAS!
MORTICIA—THE BOLT!
GULP!

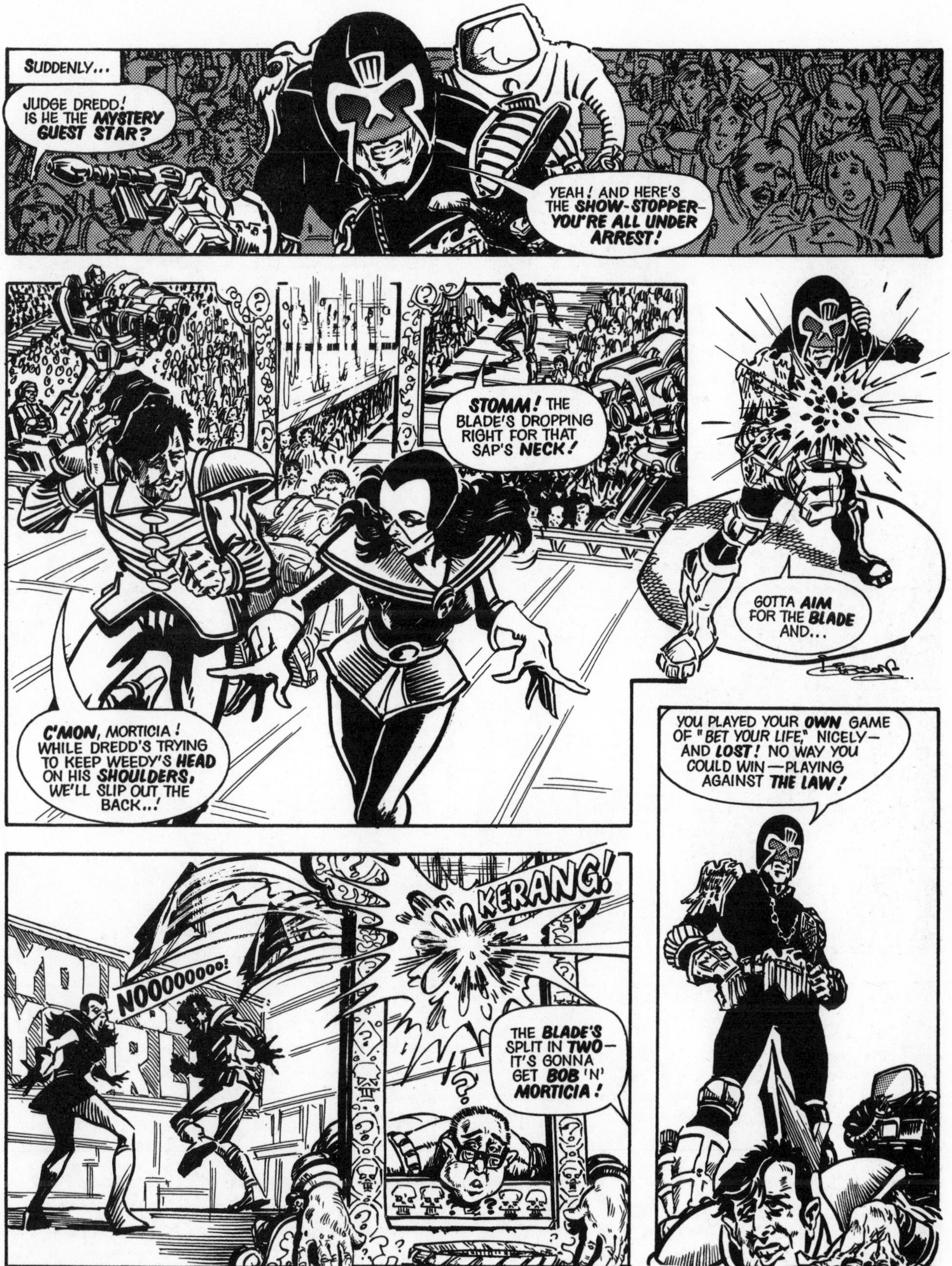
SUDDENLY...
JUDGE DREDD! IS HE THE MYSTERY GUEST STAR?
YEAH! AND HERE'S THE SHOW-STOPPER-YOU'RE ALL UNDER ARREST!
STOMM! THE BLADE'S DROPPING RIGHT FOR THAT SAP'S NECK!
C'MON, MORTICIA! WHILE DREDD'S TRYING TO KEEP WEEDY'S HEAD ON HIS SHOULDERS, WE'LL SLIP OUT THE BACK...!
GOTTA AIM FOR THE BLADE AND...
KERANG!
NOOOOOOOO!
THE BLADE'S SPLIT IN TWO—IT'S GONNA GET BOB 'N' MORTICIA!
YOU PLAYED YOUR OWN GAME OF "BET YOUR LIFE," NICELY—AND LOST! NO WAY YOU COULD WIN—PLAYING AGAINST THE LAW!

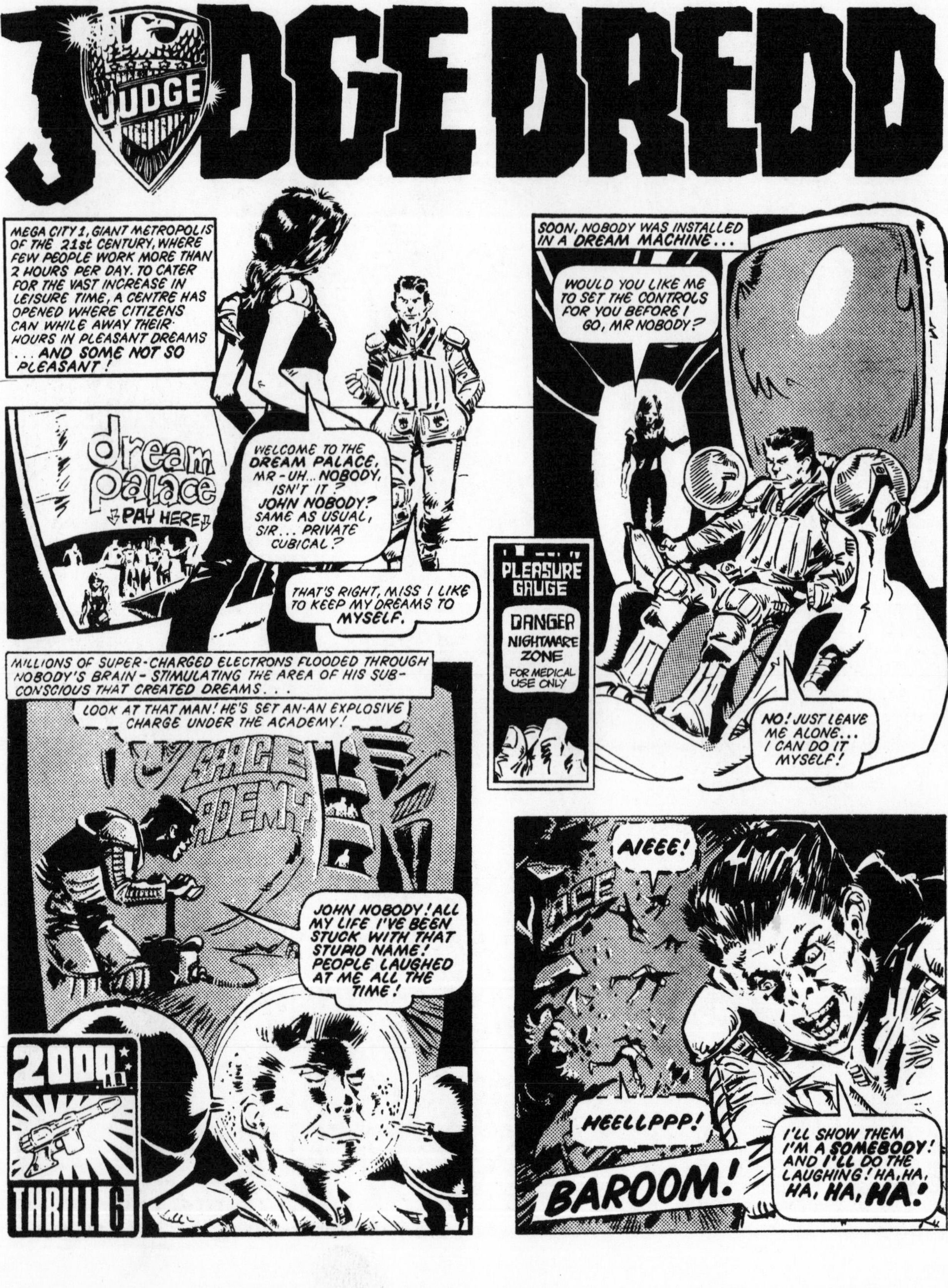
JUDGE DREDD
JUDGE
MEGA CITY 1, GIANT METROPOLIS OF THE 21st CENTURY, WHERE FEW PEOPLE WORK MORE THAN 2 HOURS PER DAY. TO CATER FOR THE VAST INCREASE IN LEISURE TIME, A CENTRE HAS OPENED WHERE CITIZENS CAN WHILE AWAY THEIR HOURS IN PLEASANT DREAMS . . . AND SOME NOT SO PLEASANT!
dream palace
PAY HERE
WELCOME TO THE DREAM PALACE, MR - UH... NOBODY, ISN'T IT? JOHN NOBODY? SAME AS USUAL, SIR... PRIVATE CUBICAL?
THAT'S RIGHT, MISS I LIKE TO KEEP MY DREAMS TO MYSELF.
SOON, NOBODY WAS INSTALLED IN A DREAM MACHINE...
WOULD YOU LIKE ME TO SET THE CONTROLS FOR YOU BEFORE I GO, MR NOBODY?
PLEASURE GAUGE
DANGER
NIGHTMARE ZONE
FOR MEDICAL USE ONLY
NO! JUST LEAVE ME ALONE... I CAN DO IT MYSELF!
MILLIONS OF SUPER-CHARGED ELECTRONS FLOODED THROUGH NOBODY'S BRAIN - STIMULATING THE AREA OF HIS SUB-CONSCIOUS THAT CREATED DREAMS . . .
LOOK AT THAT MAN! HE'S SET AN-AN EXPLOSIVE CHARGE UNDER THE ACADEMY!
JOHN NOBODY! ALL MY LIFE I'VE BEEN STUCK WITH THAT STUPID NAME! PEOPLE LAUGHED AT ME ALL THE TIME!
2000 A.D.
THRILL 6
AIEEE!
HEELLPPP!
BAROOM!
I'LL SHOW THEM I'M A SOMEBODY! AND I'LL DO THE LAUGHING! HA, HA, HA, HA, HA!

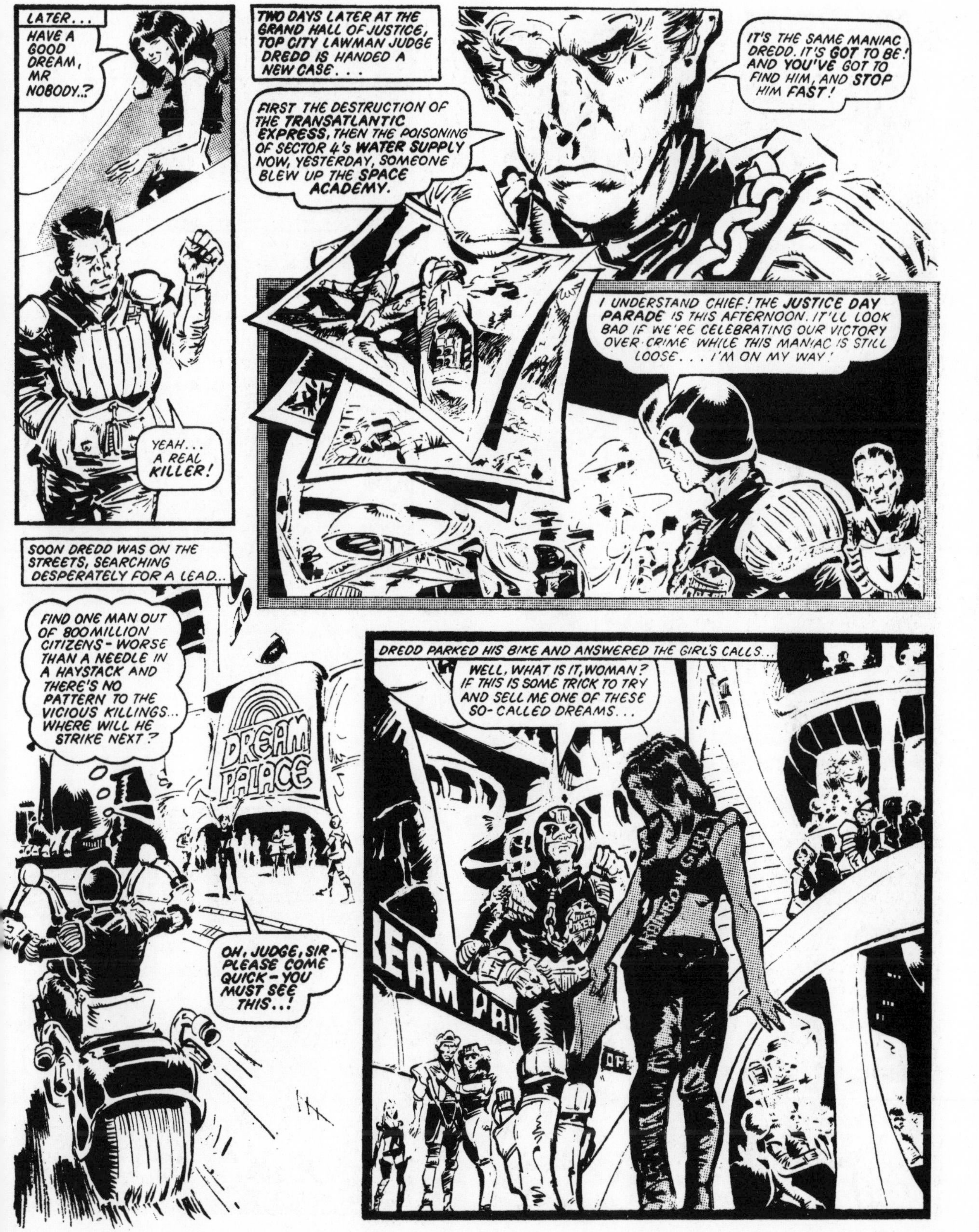
LATER...
HAVE A GOOD DREAM, MR NOBODY..?
YEAH... A REAL KILLER!
TWO DAYS LATER AT THE GRAND HALL OF JUSTICE, TOP CITY LAWMAN JUDGE DREDD IS HANDED A NEW CASE . . .
FIRST THE DESTRUCTION OF THE TRANSATLANTIC EXPRESS, THEN THE POISONING OF SECTOR 4's WATER SUPPLY NOW, YESTERDAY, SOMEONE BLEW UP THE SPACE ACADEMY.
IT'S THE SAME MANIAC DREDD. IT'S GOT TO BE! AND YOU'VE GOT TO FIND HIM, AND STOP HIM FAST!
I UNDERSTAND CHIEF! THE JUSTICE DAY PARADE IS THIS AFTERNOON. IT'LL LOOK BAD IF WE'RE CELEBRATING OUR VICTORY OVER CRIME WHILE THIS MANIAC IS STILL LOOSE. . . I'M ON MY WAY!
SOON DREDD WAS ON THE STREETS, SEARCHING DESPERATELY FOR A LEAD...
FIND ONE MAN OUT OF 800 MILLION CITIZENS - WORSE THAN A NEEDLE IN A HAYSTACK AND THERE'S NO PATTERN TO THE VICIOUS KILLINGS... WHERE WILL HE STRIKE NEXT?
DREAM PALACE
OH, JUDGE, SIR - PLEASE COME QUICK - YOU MUST SEE THIS..!
DREDD PARKED HIS BIKE AND ANSWERED THE GIRL'S CALLS...
WELL, WHAT IS IT, WOMAN? IF THIS IS SOME TRICK TO TRY AND SELL ME ONE OF THESE SO-CALLED DREAMS...
RAINBOW GIRL
REAM PAL

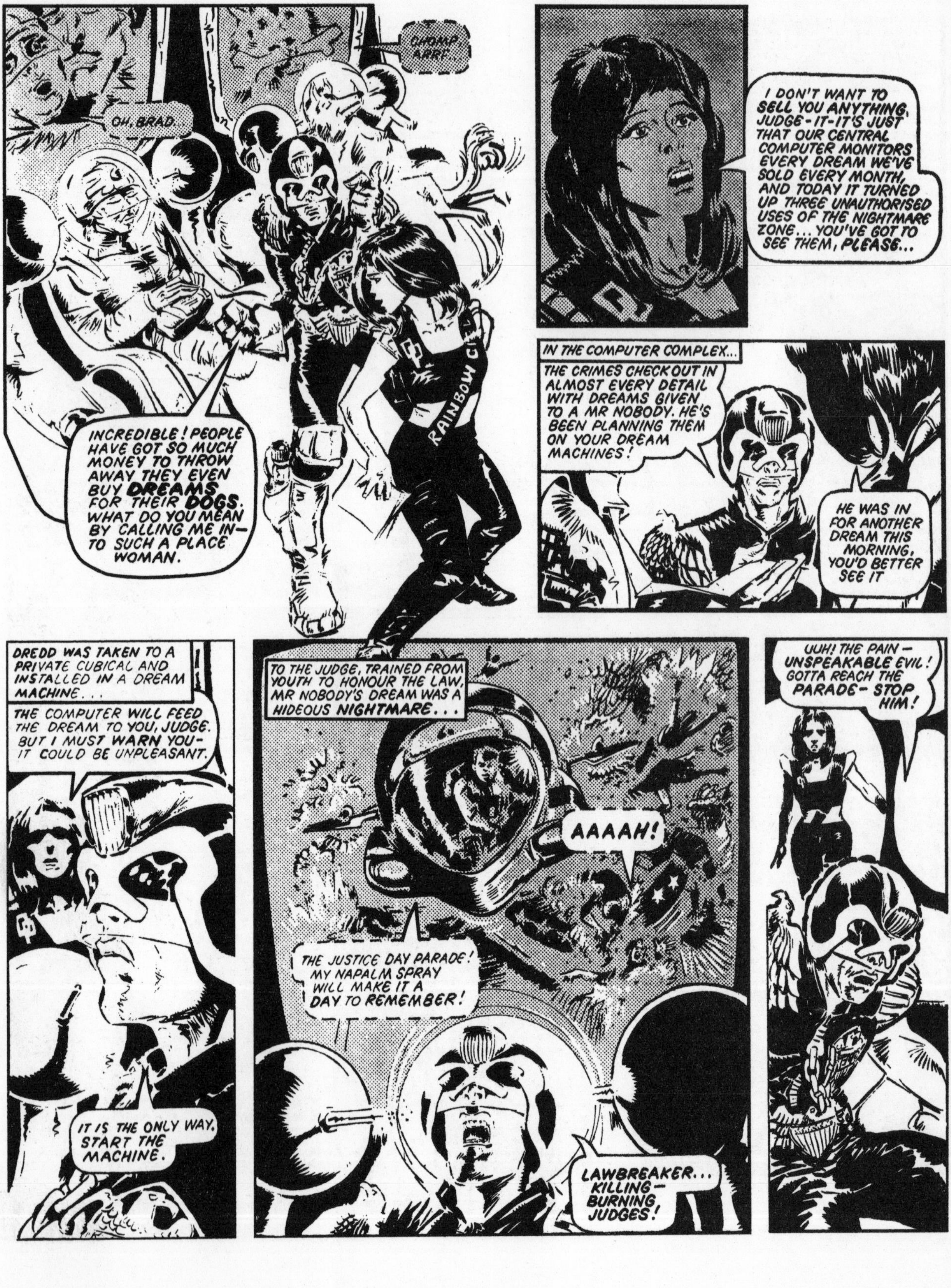
CHOMP ARRF
OH, BRAD...
INCREDIBLE! PEOPLE HAVE GOT SO MUCH MONEY TO THROW AWAY THEY EVEN BUY DREAMS FOR THEIR DOGS. WHAT DO YOU MEAN BY CALLING ME IN-TO SUCH A PLACE WOMAN.
RAINBOW
I DON'T WANT TO SELL YOU ANYTHING, JUDGE - IT-IT'S JUST THAT OUR CENTRAL COMPUTER MONITORS EVERY DREAM WE'VE SOLD EVERY MONTH, AND TODAY IT TURNED UP THREE UNAUTHORISED USES OF THE NIGHTMARE ZONE... YOU'VE GOT TO SEE THEM, PLEASE...
IN THE COMPUTER COMPLEX...
THE CRIMES CHECK OUT IN ALMOST EVERY DETAIL WITH DREAMS GIVEN TO A MR NOBODY. HE'S BEEN PLANNING THEM ON YOUR DREAM MACHINES!
HE WAS IN FOR ANOTHER DREAM THIS MORNING, YOU'D BETTER SEE IT
DREDD WAS TAKEN TO A PRIVATE CUBICAL AND INSTALLED IN A DREAM MACHINE...
THE COMPUTER WILL FEED THE DREAM TO YOU, JUDGE. BUT I MUST WARN YOU - IT COULD BE UNPLEASANT.
IT IS THE ONLY WAY. START THE MACHINE.
TO THE JUDGE, TRAINED FROM YOUTH TO HONOUR THE LAW, MR NOBODY'S DREAM WAS A HIDEOUS NIGHTMARE...
AAAAH!
THE JUSTICE DAY PARADE! MY NAPALM SPRAY WILL MAKE IT A DAY TO REMEMBER!
LAWBREAKER... KILLING- BURNING JUDGES!
UUH! THE PAIN - UNSPEAKABLE EVIL! GOTTA REACH THE PARADE - STOP HIM!

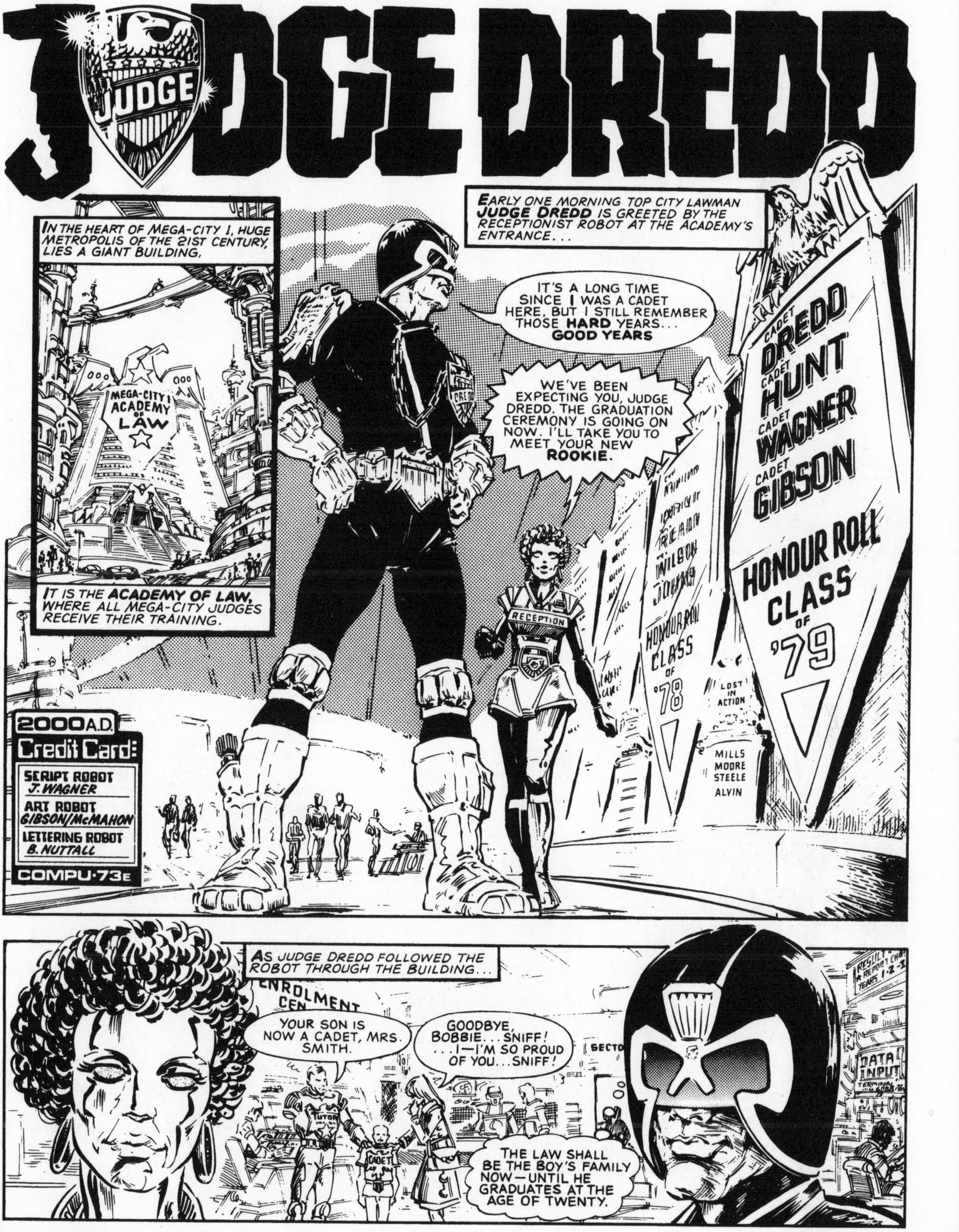

JUDGE DREDD
JUDGE
IN THE HEART OF MEGA-CITY 1, HUGE METROPOLIS OF THE 21ST CENTURY, LIES A GIANT BUILDING,
MEGA-CITY 1 ACADEMY OF LAW
IT IS THE ACADEMY OF LAW, WHERE ALL MEGA-CITY JUDGES RECEIVE THEIR TRAINING.
EARLY ONE MORNING TOP CITY LAWMAN JUDGE DREDD IS GREETED BY THE RECEPTIONIST ROBOT AT THE ACADEMY'S ENTRANCE...
IT'S A LONG TIME SINCE I WAS A CADET HERE, BUT I STILL REMEMBER THOSE HARD YEARS... GOOD YEARS
WE'VE BEEN EXPECTING YOU, JUDGE DREDD. THE GRADUATION CEREMONY IS GOING ON NOW. I'LL TAKE YOU TO MEET YOUR NEW ROOKIE.
RECEPTION
CADET DREDD
CADET HUNT
CADET WAGNER
CADET GIBSON
HONOUR ROLL CLASS OF '79
HONOUR ROLL CLASS OF '78
LOST IN ACTION
MILLS
MOORE
STEELE
ALVIN
2000 A.D. Credit Card:
SCRIPT ROBOT J. WAGNER
ART ROBOT GIBSON/McMAHON
LETTERING ROBOT B. NUTTALL
COMPU-73E
AS JUDGE DREDD FOLLOWED THE ROBOT THROUGH THE BUILDING...
ENROLMENT CEN
YOUR SON IS NOW A CADET, MRS. SMITH.
GOODBYE, BOBBIE... SNIFF! ...I—I'M SO PROUD OF YOU... SNIFF!
TUTOR
CADET
THE LAW SHALL BE THE BOY'S FAMILY NOW—UNTIL HE GRADUATES AT THE AGE OF TWENTY.
DATA INPUT

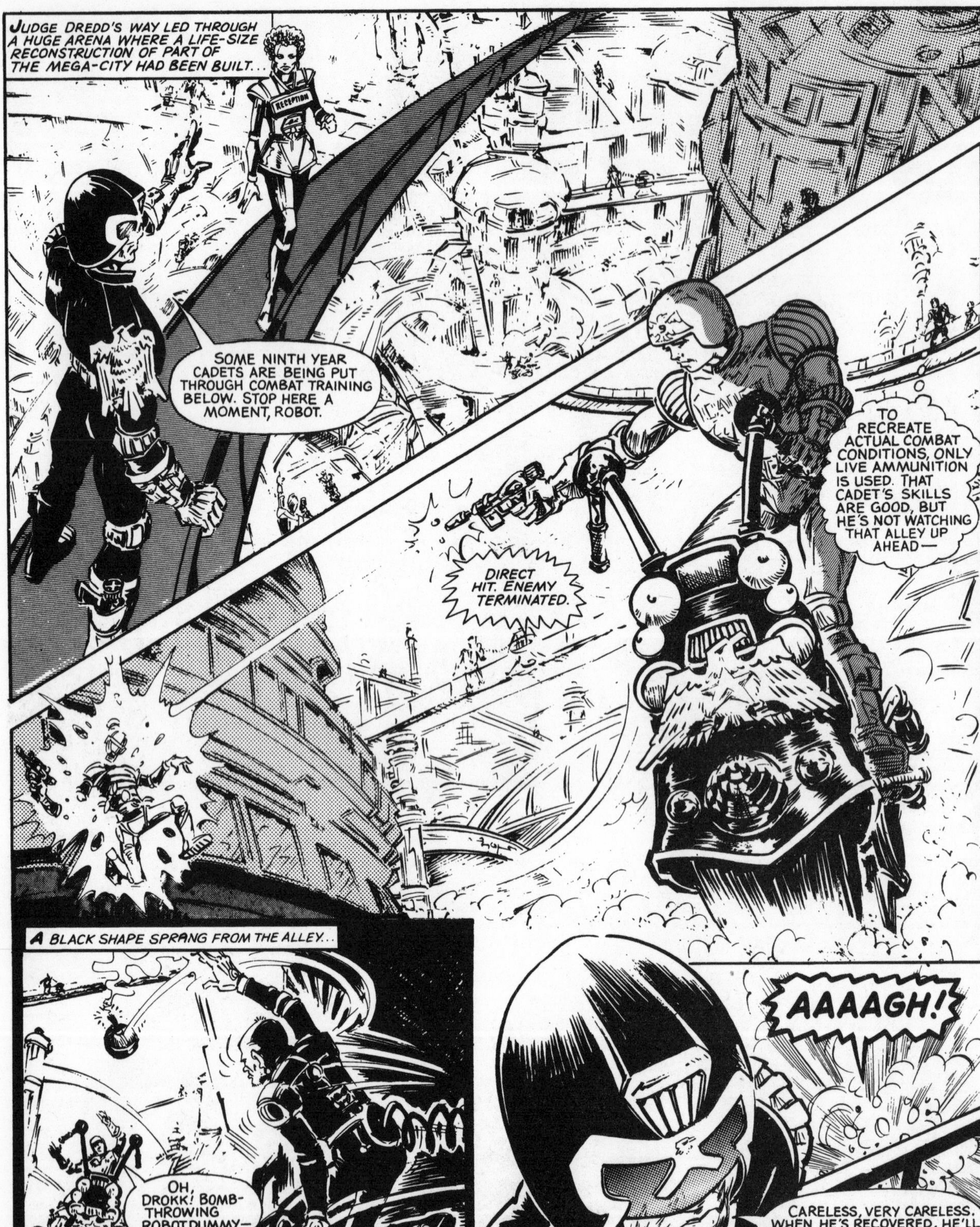
JUDGE DREDD'S WAY LED THROUGH A HUGE ARENA WHERE A LIFE-SIZE RECONSTRUCTION OF PART OF THE MEGA-CITY HAD BEEN BUILT...
RECEPTION
SOME NINTH YEAR CADETS ARE BEING PUT THROUGH COMBAT TRAINING BELOW. STOP HERE A MOMENT, ROBOT.
TO RECREATE ACTUAL COMBAT CONDITIONS, ONLY LIVE AMMUNITION IS USED. THAT CADET'S SKILLS ARE GOOD, BUT HE'S NOT WATCHING THAT ALLEY UP AHEAD—
DIRECT HIT. ENEMY TERMINATED.
A BLACK SHAPE SPRANG FROM THE ALLEY...
OH, DROKK! BOMB-THROWING ROBOTDUMMY—
AAAAGH!
CARELESS, VERY CARELESS. WHEN HE'S RECOVERED, HE'LL BE EXPELLED. HE WOULDN'T LAST A MINUTE AGAINST HARDENED MEGA-CITY CRIMINALS.

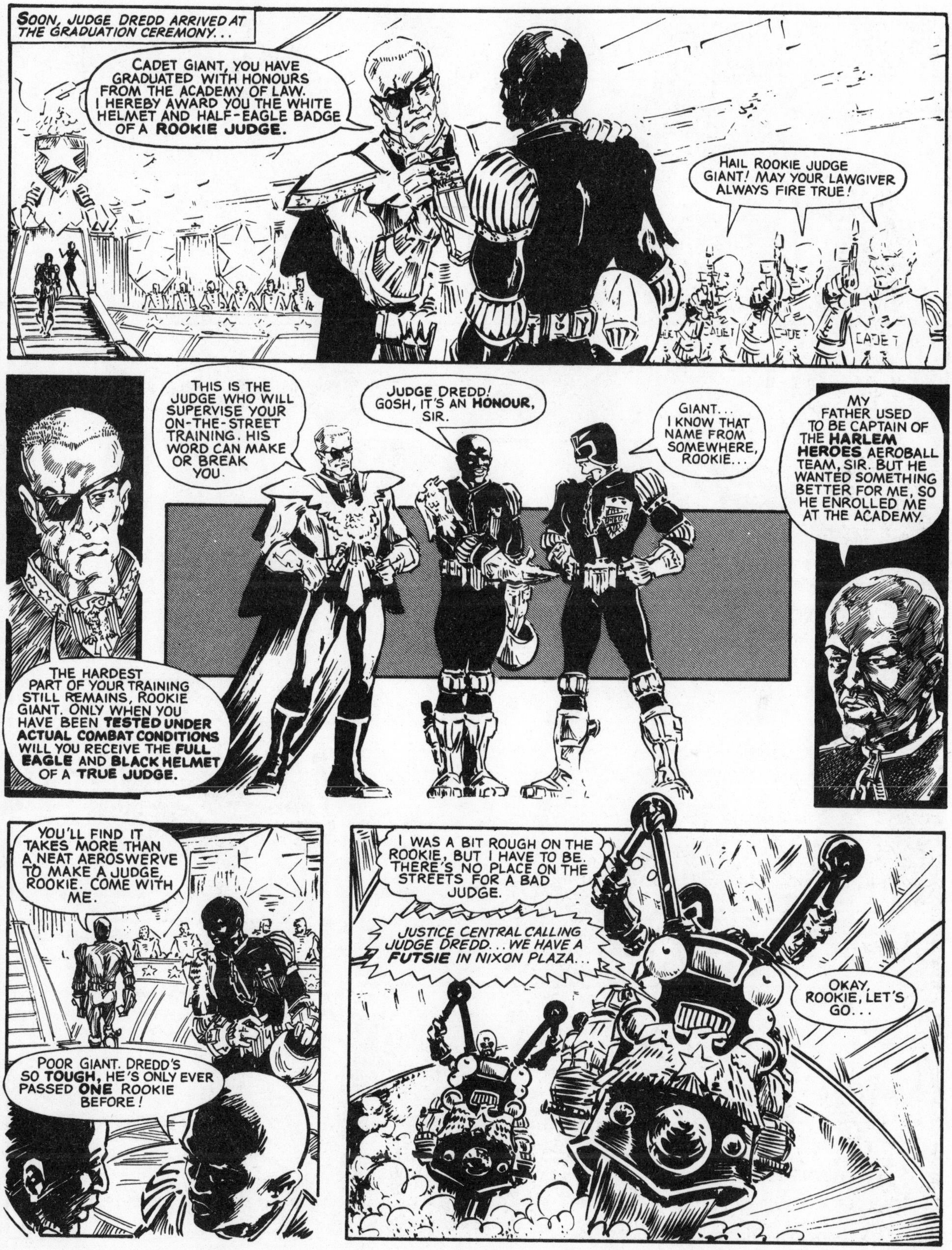

SOON, JUDGE DREDD ARRIVED AT THE GRADUATION CEREMONY...
CADET GIANT, YOU HAVE GRADUATED WITH HONOURS FROM THE ACADEMY OF LAW. I HEREBY AWARD YOU THE WHITE HELMET AND HALF-EAGLE BADGE OF A **ROOKIE JUDGE.**
HAIL ROOKIE JUDGE GIANT! MAY YOUR LAWGIVER ALWAYS FIRE TRUE!
CADET
CADET
CADET
CADET
THIS IS THE JUDGE WHO WILL SUPERVISE YOUR ON-THE-STREET TRAINING. HIS WORD CAN MAKE OR BREAK YOU.
THE HARDEST PART OF YOUR TRAINING STILL REMAINS, ROOKIE GIANT. ONLY WHEN YOU HAVE BEEN **TESTED UNDER ACTUAL COMBAT CONDITIONS** WILL YOU RECEIVE THE **FULL EAGLE** AND **BLACK HELMET** OF A **TRUE JUDGE.**
JUDGE DREDD! GOSH, IT'S AN **HONOUR**, SIR.
GIANT... I KNOW THAT NAME FROM SOMEWHERE, ROOKIE...
MY FATHER USED TO BE CAPTAIN OF THE **HARLEM HEROES** AEROBALL TEAM, SIR. BUT HE WANTED SOMETHING BETTER FOR ME, SO HE ENROLLED ME AT THE ACADEMY.
YOU'LL FIND IT TAKES MORE THAN A NEAT AEROSWERVE TO MAKE A JUDGE, ROOKIE. COME WITH ME.
POOR GIANT. DREDD'S SO **TOUGH**, HE'S ONLY EVER PASSED **ONE** ROOKIE BEFORE!
I WAS A BIT ROUGH ON THE ROOKIE, BUT I HAVE TO BE. THERE'S NO PLACE ON THE STREETS FOR A BAD JUDGE.
JUSTICE CENTRAL CALLING JUDGE DREDD... WE HAVE A **FUTSIE** IN NIXON PLAZA...
OKAY, ROOKIE, LET'S GO...

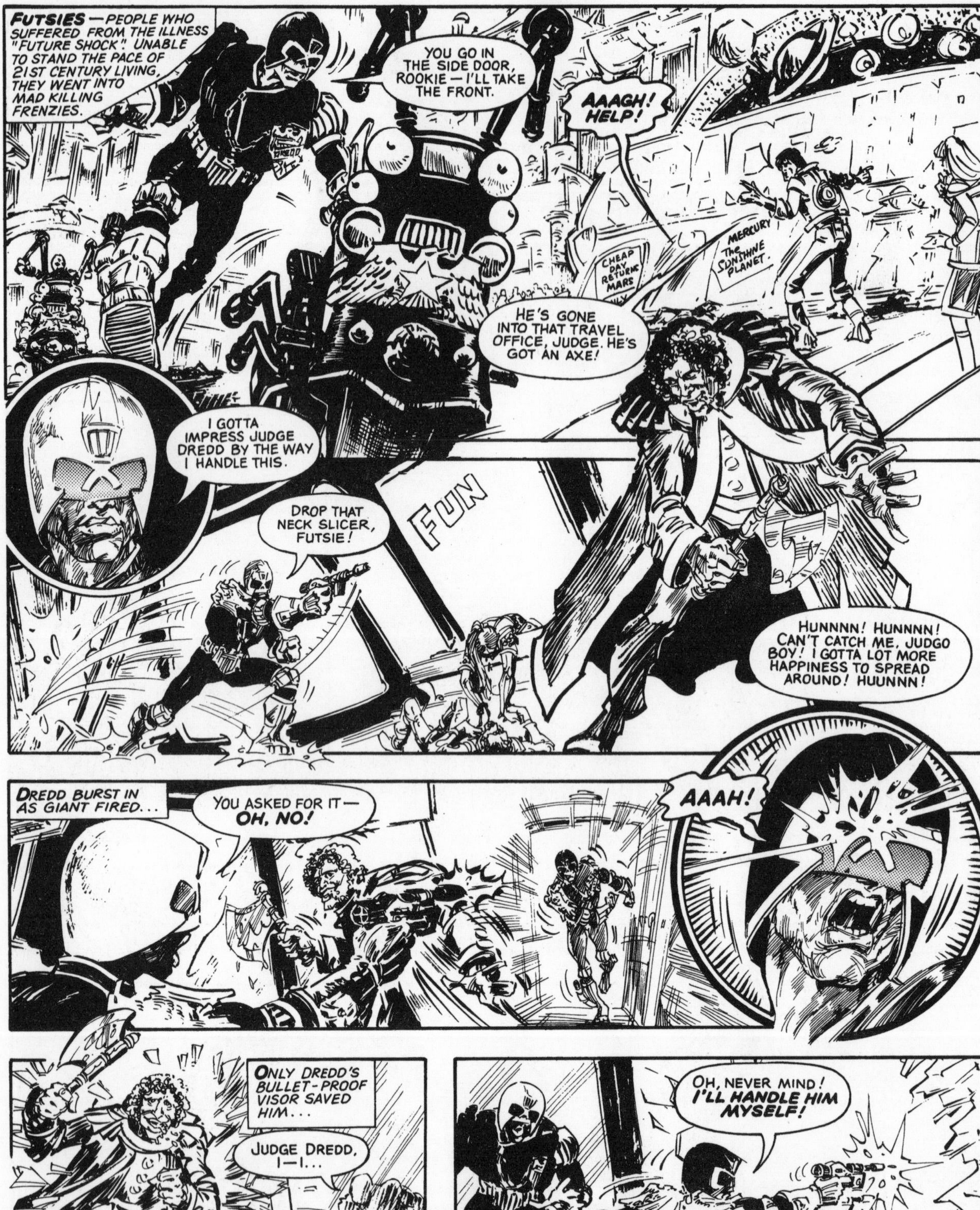
FUTSIES — PEOPLE WHO SUFFERED FROM THE ILLNESS "FUTURE SHOCK". UNABLE TO STAND THE PACE OF 21ST CENTURY LIVING, THEY WENT INTO MAD KILLING FRENZIES.
YOU GO IN THE SIDE DOOR, ROOKIE — I'LL TAKE THE FRONT.
AAAGH! HELP!
CHEAP DAY RETURNS MARS
MERCURY The SUNSHINE PLANET
HE'S GONE INTO THAT TRAVEL OFFICE, JUDGE. HE'S GOT AN AXE!
I GOTTA IMPRESS JUDGE DREDD BY THE WAY I HANDLE THIS.
FUN
DROP THAT NECK SLICER, FUTSIE!
HUNNNN! HUNNNN! CAN'T CATCH ME, JUDGO BOY! I GOTTA LOT MORE HAPPINESS TO SPREAD AROUND! HUUNNN!
DREDD BURST IN AS GIANT FIRED...
YOU ASKED FOR IT — OH, NO!
AAAH!
ONLY DREDD'S BULLET-PROOF VISOR SAVED HIM...
JUDGE DREDD, I—I...
A BAD MISTAKE, ROOKIE. DON'T MAKE IT WORSE BY WASTING TIME WITH ME — YOU SHOULD BE DEALING WITH THE FUTSIE.
OH, NEVER MIND! I'LL HANDLE HIM MYSELF!

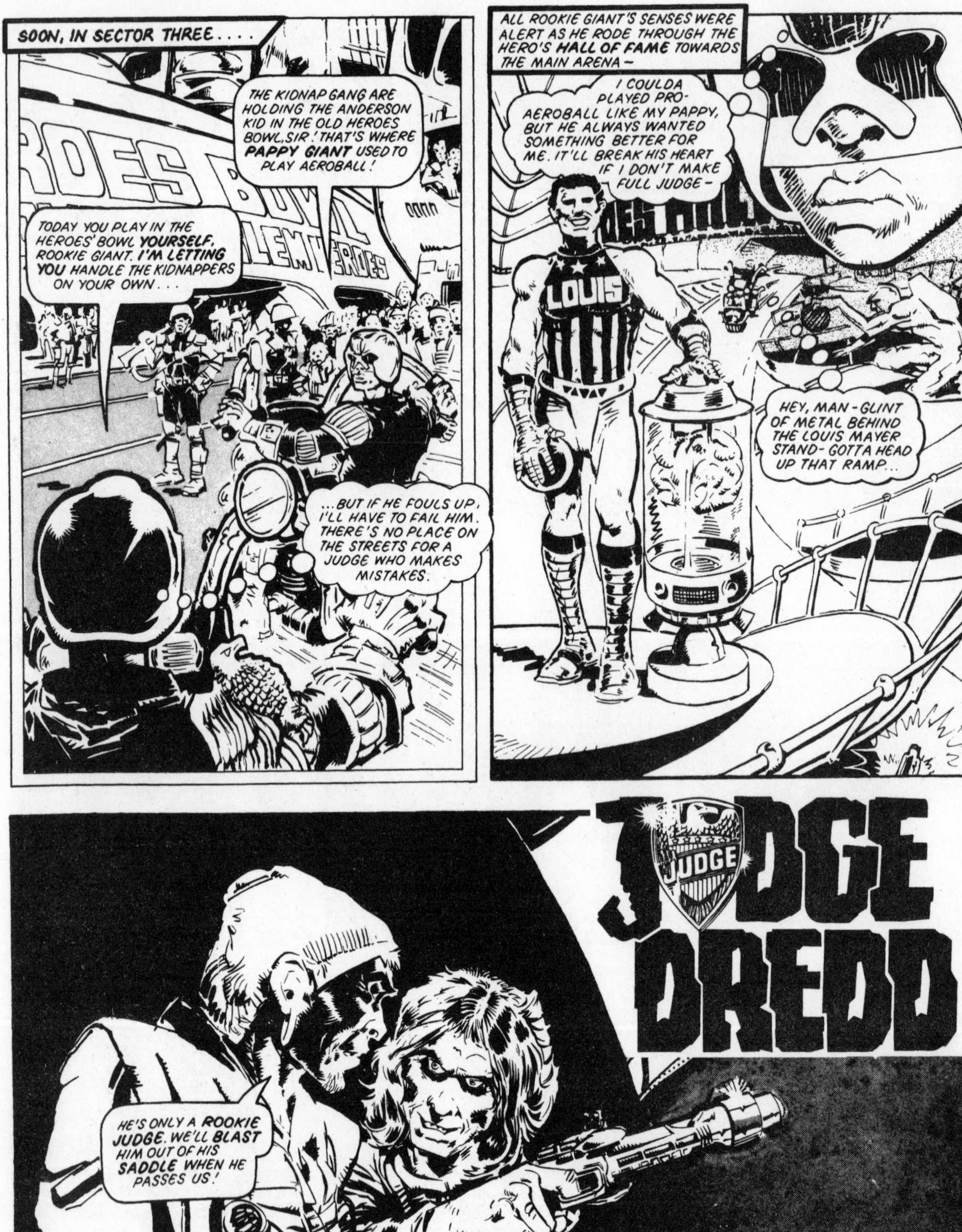
SOON, IN SECTOR THREE....
THE KIDNAP GANG ARE HOLDING THE ANDERSON KID IN THE OLD HEROES BOWL, SIR! THAT'S WHERE PAPPY GIANT USED TO PLAY AEROBALL!
TODAY YOU PLAY IN THE HEROES' BOWL YOURSELF, ROOKIE GIANT. I'M LETTING YOU HANDLE THE KIDNAPPERS ON YOUR OWN...
...BUT IF HE FOULS UP, I'LL HAVE TO FAIL HIM. THERE'S NO PLACE ON THE STREETS FOR A JUDGE WHO MAKES MISTAKES.
ALL ROOKIE GIANT'S SENSES WERE ALERT AS HE RODE THROUGH THE HERO'S HALL OF FAME TOWARDS THE MAIN ARENA—
I COULDA PLAYED PRO-AEROBALL LIKE MY PAPPY, BUT HE ALWAYS WANTED SOMETHING BETTER FOR ME. IT'LL BREAK HIS HEART IF I DON'T MAKE FULL JUDGE—
LOUIS
HEY, MAN - GLINT OF METAL BEHIND THE LOUIS MAYER STAND - GOTTA HEAD UP THAT RAMP...
JUDGE
JUDGE DREDD
HE'S ONLY A ROOKIE JUDGE. WE'LL BLAST HIM OUT OF HIS SADDLE WHEN HE PASSES US!

ARE YOU TWO *DUDES* WAITIN' FOR ME?

AAAH!

AAAGH!

AS HIS BIKE PLUNGED DOWN, THE ROOKIE GRABBED THE ARM OF A STATUE...

THANKS, PAPPY. NICE OF YOU TO LEND A HELPING HAND.

ROOKIE GIANT SECURED THE PRISONERS AND MOVED ON...

SO FAR SO GOOD — BUT THE ROOKIE'S STILL GOT TO RESCUE THE ANDERSON BOY ... IN ONE PIECE.

INSIDE THE ARENA...

THERE HE IS — UP ON THE HIGH GIRDERS.

NO CLOSER, LAWMAN. THIS BOMB TAPED TO THE KID HAS ONLY GOT A *FIVE SECOND FUSE*. I WANT A CLEAR GETAWAY OUTA HERE OR I'LL BLOW BOTH OF US TO KINGDOM COME!

MUMMY!

I KNOW YOU DON'T THINK MUCH OF ME, SIR, BUT I'VE STILL BEEN TRAINED AS A *JUDGE*. I'VE GOT TO TRY IT — EVEN IF IT MEANS MY LIFE.

GIANT RACED BACK TO THE HALL OF FAME...

THIS DEMONSTRATION JET PACK HAS ENOUGH FUEL IN IT. I COULD REACH THE GIRDERS IN *UNDER* FIVE SECONDS WITH IT ON.

YOU'RE STILL TAKING A CHANCE, ROOKIE. THOSE THINGS AREN'T EASY TO HANDLE.

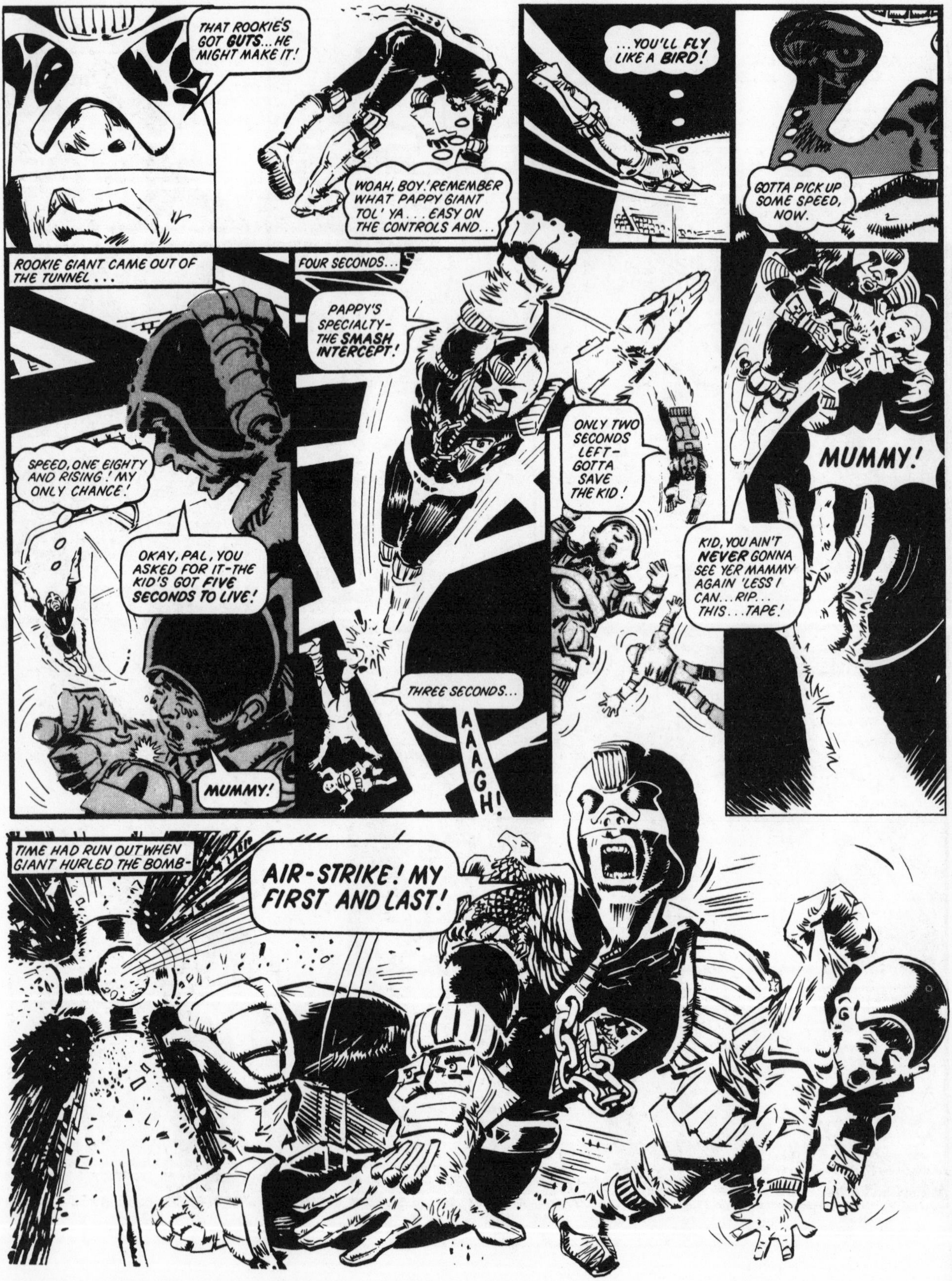

THAT ROOKIE'S GOT GUTS... HE MIGHT MAKE IT!
WOAH, BOY! REMEMBER WHAT PAPPY GIANT TOL' YA... EASY ON THE CONTROLS AND...
...YOU'LL FLY LIKE A BIRD!
GOTTA PICK UP SOME SPEED, NOW.
ROOKIE GIANT CAME OUT OF THE TUNNEL...
SPEED, ONE EIGHTY AND RISING! MY ONLY CHANCE!
OKAY, PAL, YOU ASKED FOR IT-THE KID'S GOT FIVE SECONDS TO LIVE!
MUMMY!
FOUR SECONDS...
PAPPY'S SPECIALTY-THE SMASH INTERCEPT!
THREE SECONDS...
AAAGH!
ONLY TWO SECONDS LEFT-GOTTA SAVE THE KID!
MUMMY!
KID, YOU AIN'T NEVER GONNA SEE YER MAMMY AGAIN 'LESS I CAN...RIP... THIS...TAPE!
TIME HAD RUN OUT WHEN GIANT HURLED THE BOMB-
AIR-STRIKE! MY FIRST AND LAST!

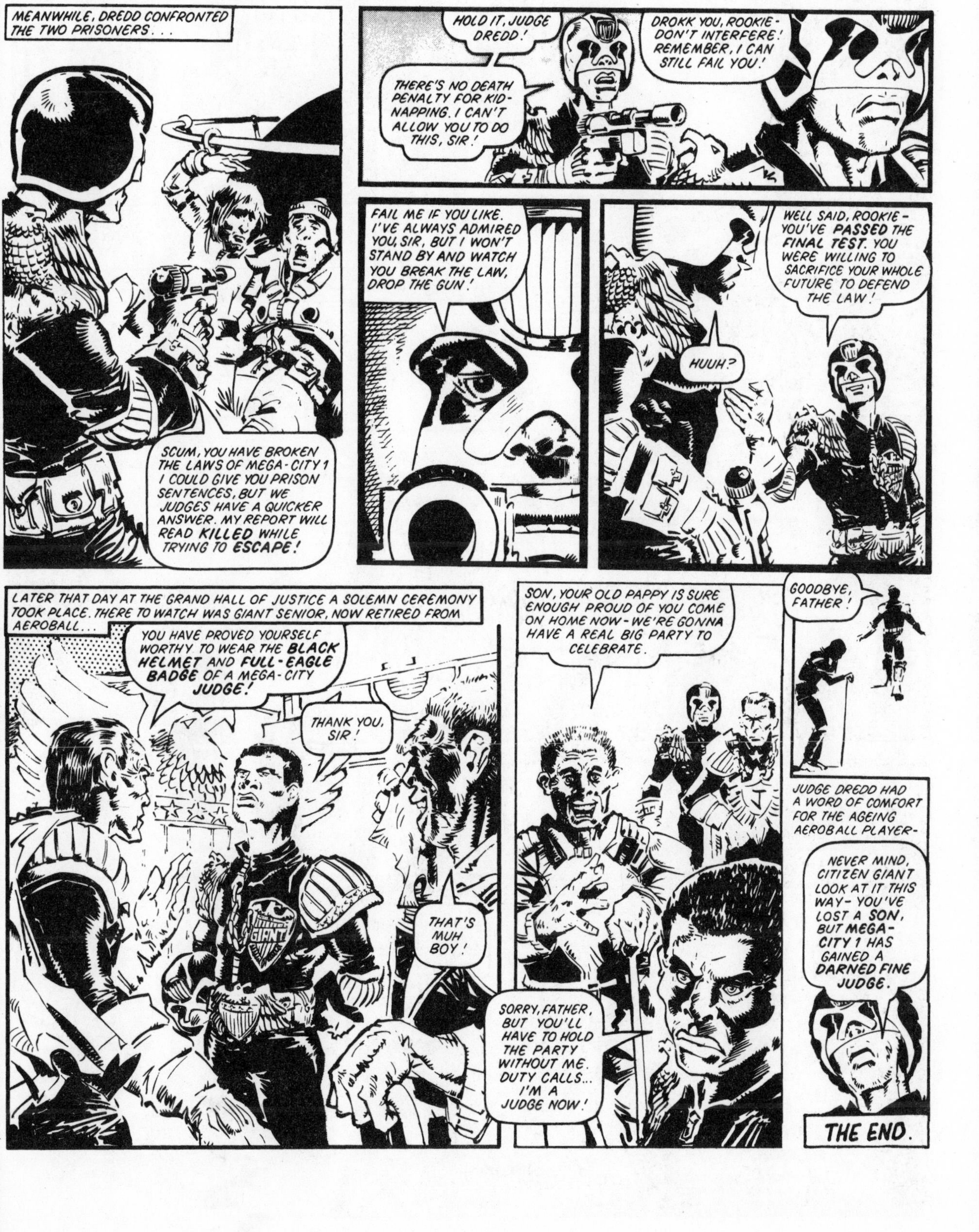

MEANWHILE, DREDD CONFRONTED THE TWO PRISONERS...
SCUM, YOU HAVE BROKEN THE LAWS OF MEGA-CITY 1 I COULD GIVE YOU PRISON SENTENCES, BUT WE JUDGES HAVE A QUICKER ANSWER. MY REPORT WILL READ **KILLED** WHILE TRYING TO **ESCAPE**!
HOLD IT, JUDGE DREDD!
THERE'S NO DEATH PENALTY FOR KID-NAPPING. I CAN'T ALLOW YOU TO DO THIS, SIR!
DROKK YOU, ROOKIE-DON'T INTERFERE! REMEMBER, I CAN STILL FAIL YOU!
FAIL ME IF YOU LIKE. I'VE ALWAYS ADMIRED YOU, SIR, BUT I WON'T STAND BY AND WATCH YOU BREAK THE LAW. DROP THE GUN!
WELL SAID, ROOKIE-YOU'VE **PASSED** THE **FINAL TEST**. YOU WERE WILLING TO SACRIFICE YOUR WHOLE FUTURE TO DEFEND THE LAW!
HUUH?
LATER THAT DAY AT THE GRAND HALL OF JUSTICE A SOLEMN CEREMONY TOOK PLACE. THERE TO WATCH WAS GIANT SENIOR, NOW RETIRED FROM AEROBALL...
YOU HAVE PROVED YOURSELF WORTHY TO WEAR THE **BLACK HELMET** AND **FULL-EAGLE BADGE** OF A MEGA-CITY **JUDGE**!
THANK YOU, SIR!
THAT'S MUH BOY!
GIANT
SON, YOUR OLD PAPPY IS SURE ENOUGH PROUD OF YOU COME ON HOME NOW-WE'RE GONNA HAVE A REAL BIG PARTY TO CELEBRATE.
SORRY, FATHER, BUT YOU'LL HAVE TO HOLD THE PARTY WITHOUT ME. DUTY CALLS... I'M A JUDGE NOW!
GOODBYE, FATHER!
JUDGE DREDD HAD A WORD OF COMFORT FOR THE AGEING AEROBALL PLAYER-
NEVER MIND, CITIZEN GIANT LOOK AT IT THIS WAY-YOU'VE LOST A **SON**, BUT **MEGA-CITY 1** HAS GAINED A **DARNED FINE JUDGE**.
THE END.

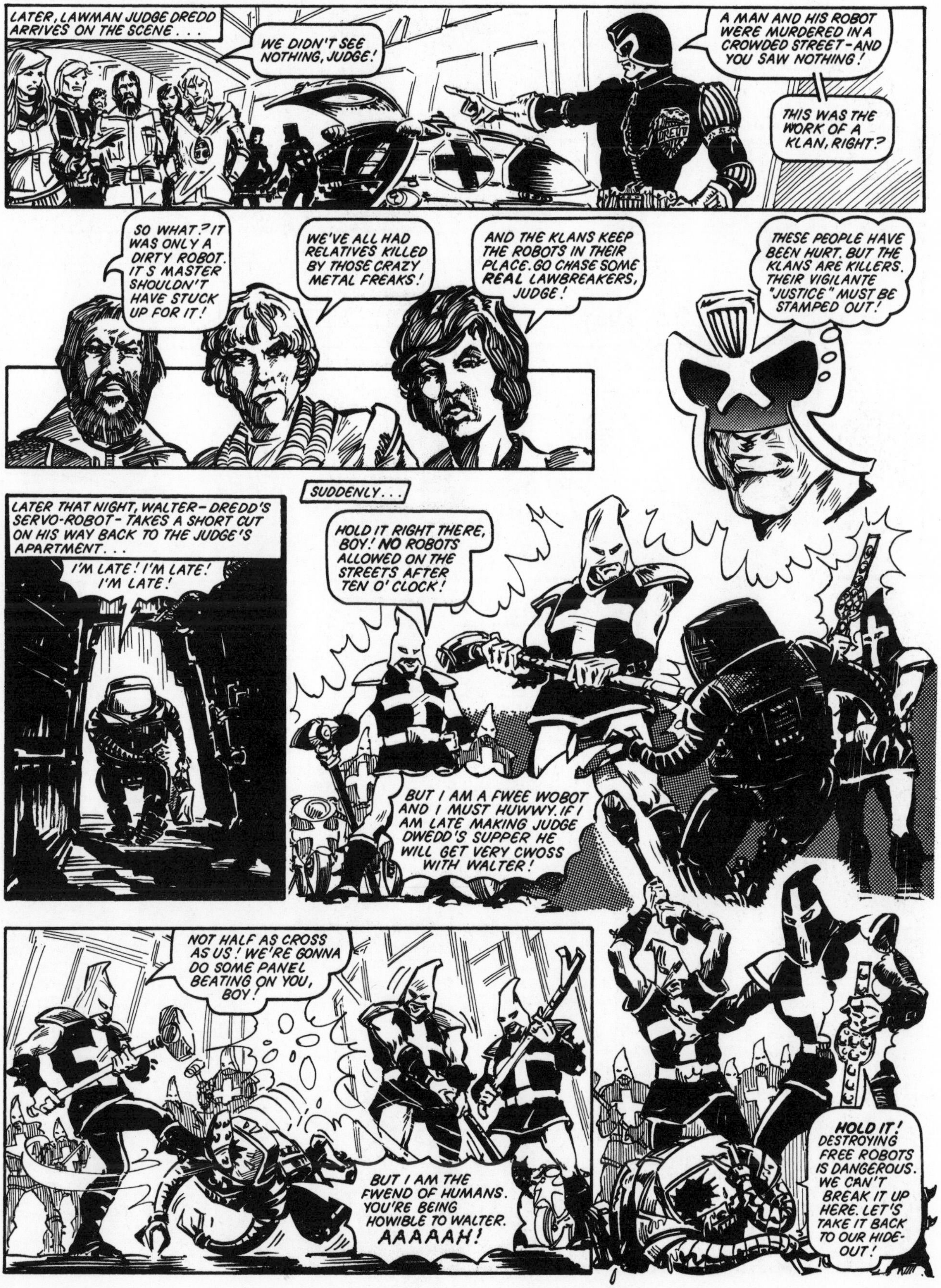
LATER, LAWMAN JUDGE DREDD ARRIVES ON THE SCENE . . .
WE DIDN'T SEE NOTHING, JUDGE!
A MAN AND HIS ROBOT WERE MURDERED IN A CROWDED STREET - AND YOU SAW NOTHING!
THIS WAS THE WORK OF A KLAN, RIGHT?
SO WHAT? IT WAS ONLY A DIRTY ROBOT. IT S MASTER SHOULDN'T HAVE STUCK UP FOR IT!
WE'VE ALL HAD RELATIVES KILLED BY THOSE CRAZY METAL FREAKS!
AND THE KLANS KEEP THE ROBOTS IN THEIR PLACE. GO CHASE SOME **REAL** LAWBREAKERS, JUDGE!
THESE PEOPLE HAVE BEEN HURT. BUT THE KLANS ARE KILLERS. THEIR VIGILANTE "JUSTICE" MUST BE STAMPED OUT!
LATER THAT NIGHT, WALTER - DREDD'S SERVO-ROBOT - TAKES A SHORT CUT ON HIS WAY BACK TO THE JUDGE'S APARTMENT . . .
I'M LATE! I'M LATE! I'M LATE!
SUDDENLY . . .
HOLD IT RIGHT THERE, BOY! **NO** ROBOTS ALLOWED ON THE STREETS AFTER TEN O' CLOCK!
BUT I AM A FWEE WOBOT AND I MUST HUWWY. IF I AM LATE MAKING JUDGE DWEDD'S SUPPER HE WILL GET VERY CWOSS WITH WALTER!
NOT HALF AS CROSS AS US! WE'RE GONNA DO SOME PANEL BEATING ON YOU, BOY!
BUT I AM THE FWEND OF HUMANS. YOU'RE BEING HOWIBLE TO WALTER. **AAAAAH!**
HOLD IT! DESTROYING FREE ROBOTS IS DANGEROUS. WE CAN'T BREAK IT UP HERE. LET'S TAKE IT BACK TO OUR HIDE-OUT!

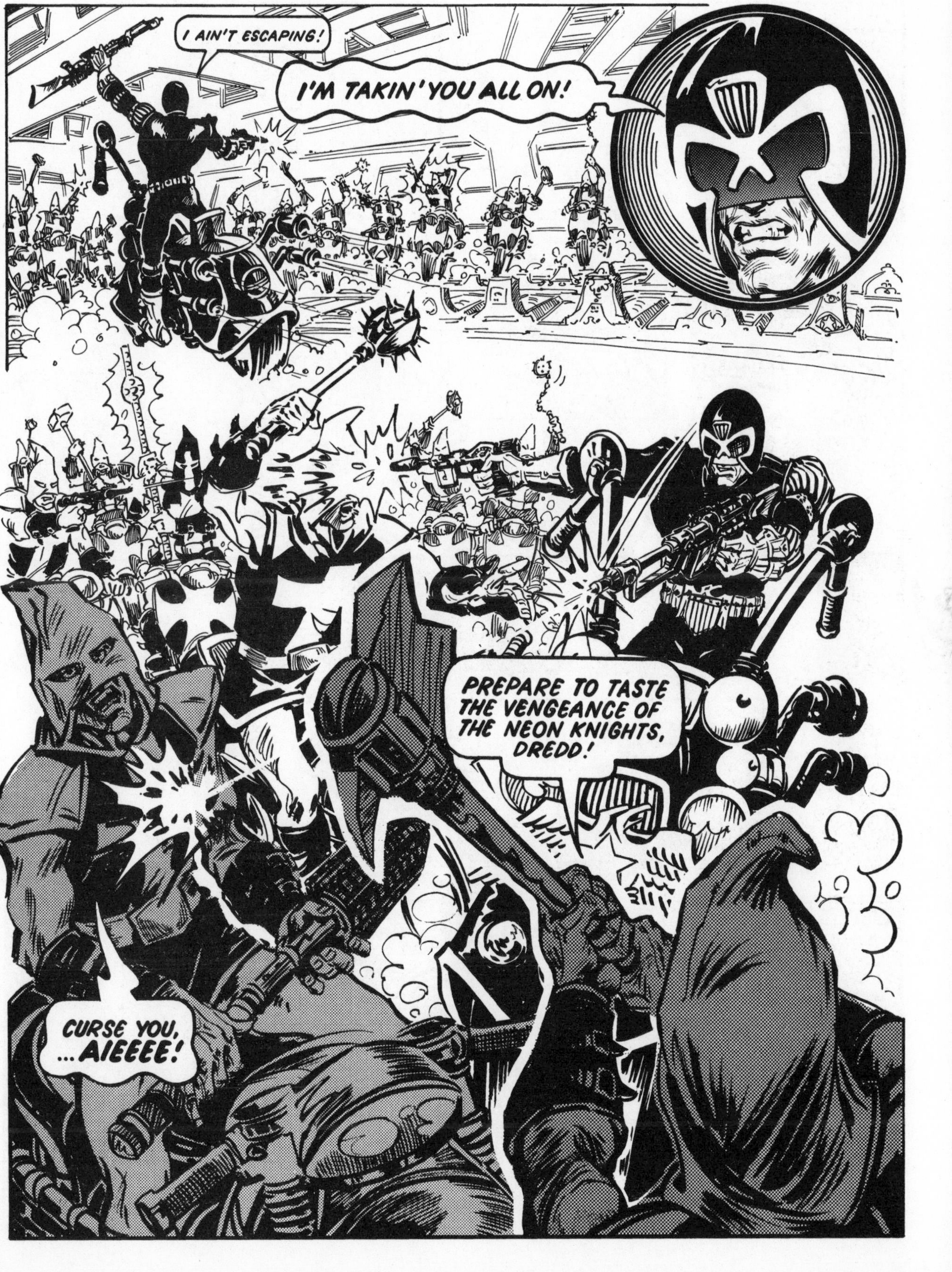
I AIN'T ESCAPING!
I'M TAKIN' YOU ALL ON!
PREPARE TO TASTE THE VENGEANCE OF THE NEON KNIGHTS, DREDD!
CURSE YOU, ...AIEEEE!

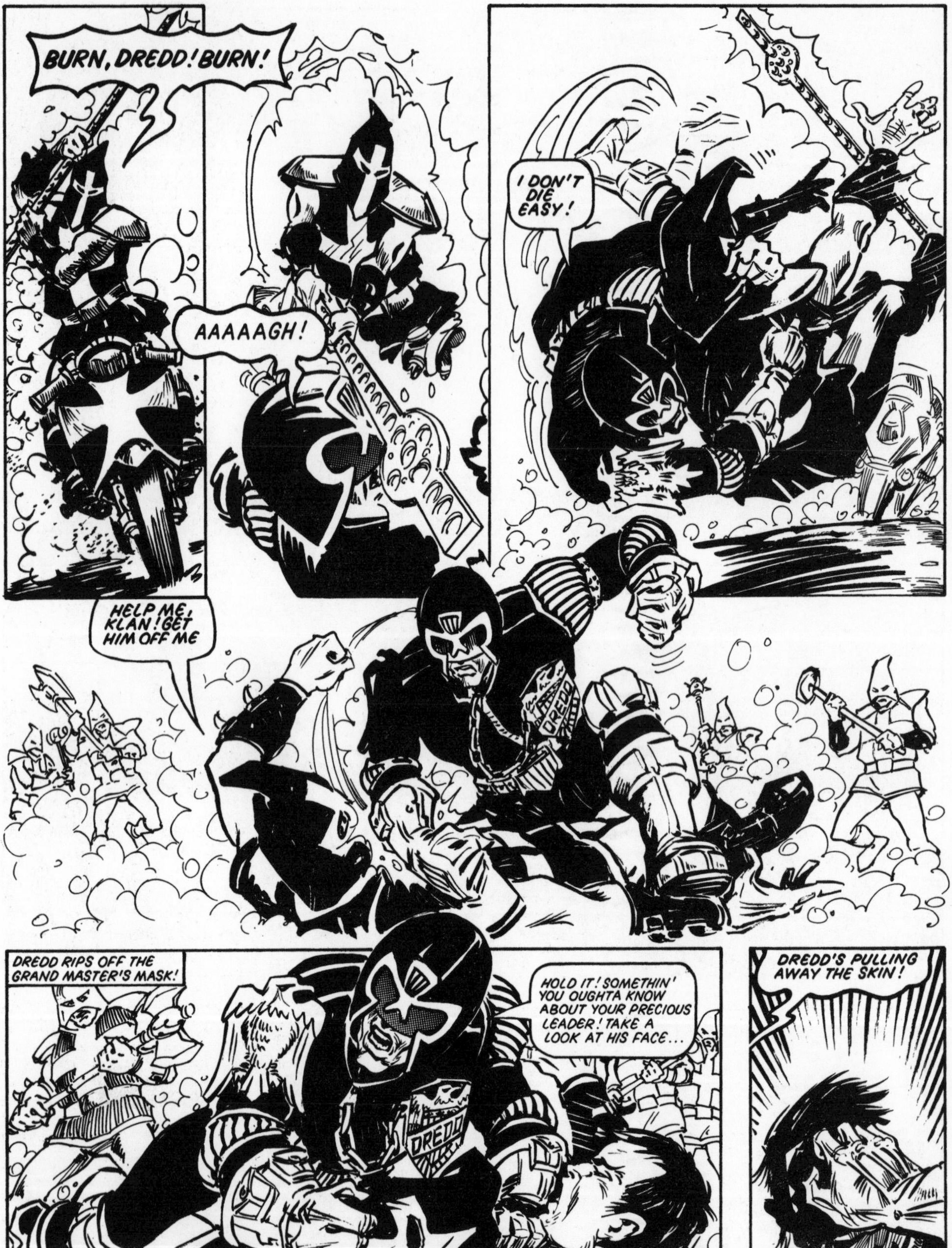
BURN, DREDD! BURN!
AAAAAGH!
I DON'T DIE EASY!
HELP ME, KLAN! GET HIM OFF ME
DREDD RIPS OFF THE GRAND MASTER'S MASK!
HOLD IT! SOMETHIN' YOU OUGHTA KNOW ABOUT YOUR PRECIOUS LEADER! TAKE A LOOK AT HIS FACE...
DREDD'S PULLING AWAY THE SKIN!

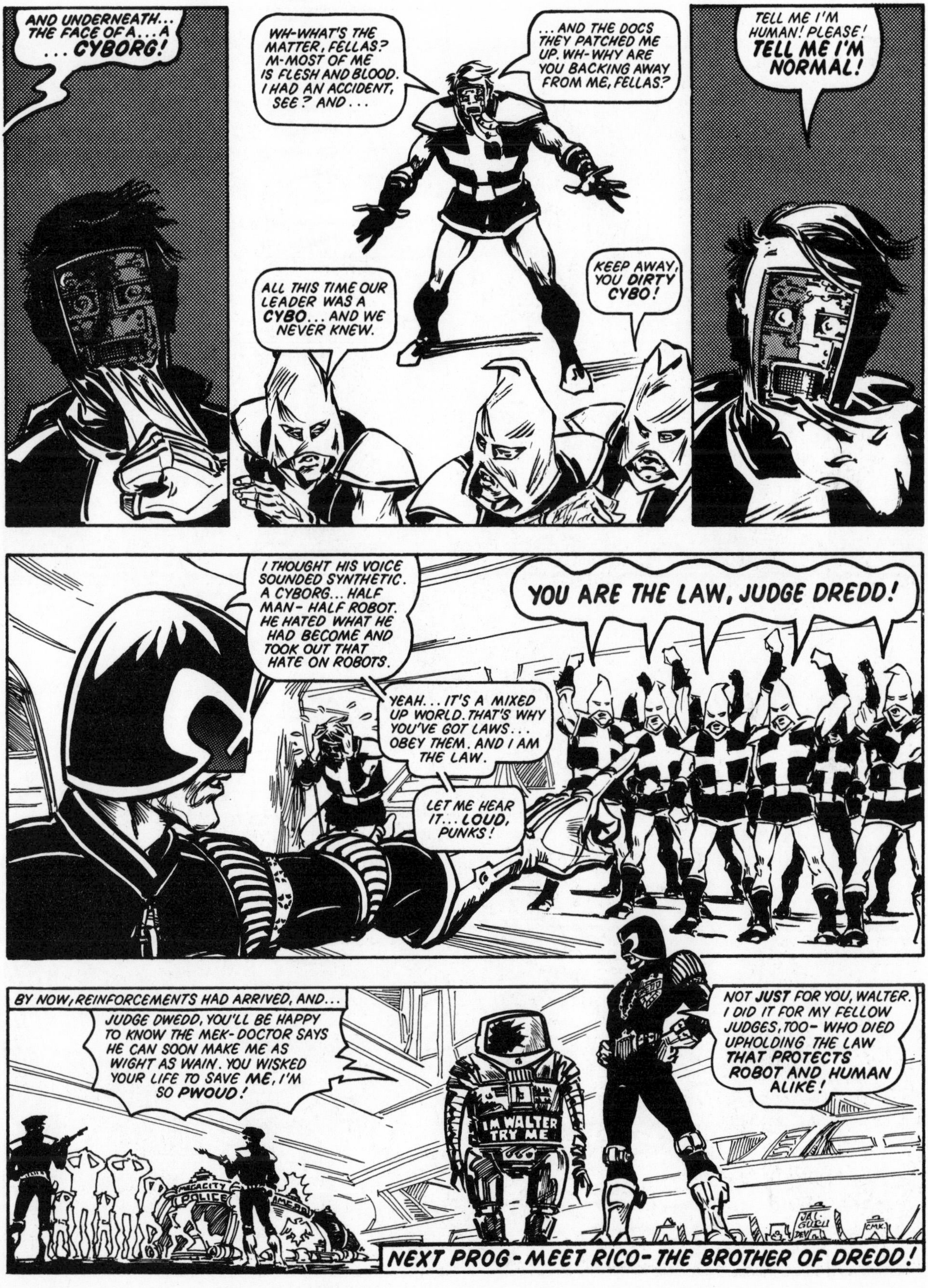
AND UNDERNEATH... THE FACE OF A... A ... CYBORG!
WH-WHAT'S THE MATTER, FELLAS? M-MOST OF ME IS FLESH AND BLOOD. I HAD AN ACCIDENT, SEE? AND...
...AND THE DOCS THEY PATCHED ME UP. WH-WHY ARE YOU BACKING AWAY FROM ME, FELLAS?
ALL THIS TIME OUR LEADER WAS A CYBO... AND WE NEVER KNEW.
KEEP AWAY, YOU DIRTY CYBO!
TELL ME I'M HUMAN! PLEASE! TELL ME I'M NORMAL!
I THOUGHT HIS VOICE SOUNDED SYNTHETIC. A CYBORG... HALF MAN- HALF ROBOT. HE HATED WHAT HE HAD BECOME AND TOOK OUT THAT HATE ON ROBOTS.
YEAH... IT'S A MIXED UP WORLD. THAT'S WHY YOU'VE GOT LAWS... OBEY THEM. AND I AM THE LAW.
LET ME HEAR IT... LOUD, PUNKS!
YOU ARE THE LAW, JUDGE DREDD!
BY NOW, REINFORCEMENTS HAD ARRIVED, AND...
JUDGE DWEDD, YOU'LL BE HAPPY TO KNOW THE MEK-DOCTOR SAYS HE CAN SOON MAKE ME AS WIGHT AS WAIN. YOU WISKED YOUR LIFE TO SAVE ME, I'M SO PWOUD!
NOT JUST FOR YOU, WALTER. I DID IT FOR MY FELLOW JUDGES, TOO- WHO DIED UPHOLDING THE LAW THAT PROTECTS ROBOT AND HUMAN ALIKE!
I'M WALTER TRY ME
POLICE
NEXT PROG - MEET RICO - THE BROTHER OF DREDD!

CAN I HELP YOU, SIR?

LEAVE ME ALONE! GET YOUR HANDS OFF ME! DO YOU HEAR?

THE MAN MADE HIS WAY TO A VIEW PHONE, AND...

GOOD MORNING! MEGA-CITY JUSTICE H.Q.! PLEASE STATE YOUR BUSINESS.

MY BUSINESS IS PERSONAL! I WANT TO SPEAK TO A JUDGE.... JUDGE DREDD!

I'M SORRY, SIR. THE JUDGE IS OUT ON PATROL.

JUST TELL HIM I CALLED... MY NAME IS DREDD... JUDGE DREDD!

BUT, SIR, THAT'S IMPOSSIBLE... THERE'S ONLY ONE JUDGE DREDD!

THAT'S RIGHT, SWEETHEART

AFTER TONIGHT THERE'S ONLY GONNA BE... ME!

MEANWHILE...

AAAH!

OKAY, YOU LAWBREAKERS! COME ON OUT SLOWLY - OR DO YOU WANT SOME MORE?

URGENT CALL FOR YOU FROM H.Q., JUDGE!

WE CAN HANDLE THEM NOW, JUDGE!

SORRY TO INTERRUPT YOU, JUDGE, BUT THIS HORRIBLE MAN PHONED. I KNOW IT'S CRAZY - BUT HE SAID HIS NAME WAS... JUDGE DREDD!

SO YOU CAME BACK, RICO. LIKE I ALWAYS KNEW YOU WOULD...

BEFORE THE NIGHT IS OUT, ONE OF US WILL HAVE TO DIE!

JUDGES ARE RAISED FROM THE CRADLE...THAT'S HOW IT WAS WITH US, EH, JOE? WE WERE CLONES. TWO IDENTICAL PEOPLE... NOT TWINS...BUT DUPLICATES! THAT'S HOW IT ALL BEGAN...

AT GENETIC CONTROL...

"This excellent dna structure. These two are perfect material for Judges"!

"I TAUGHT YOU EVERYTHING I KNEW...UNTIL PASSING OUT DAY WHEN WE BECAME ROOKIE JUDGES. I CAME FIRST...YOU CAME SECOND..".

WE WERE THE BEST OF FRIENDS THROUGH JUDGE ACADEMY. AFTER ALL WE WERE THE SAME PERSON. ONLY I WAS BETTER THAN YOU... SO I HELPED YOU ALL I COULD, JOE."..

"Excellent marksmanship, Rico Dredd, Joe Dredd, you're not fast enough on the draw and your aim is way off target"!

Congratulations, You two!

"If it hadn't been for you, Rico, I'd never have made it"!

YEAH, RICO. BUT YOU WERE TOO SMART, YOU HAD TO FOUL THINGS UP... BY TAKINGS BRIBES AND RUNNING A PROTECTION RACKET."..

"THAT'S WHEN I HAD TO MAKE A TERRIBLE DECISION, RICO"...

"YOU SHOULDN'T HAVE DONE THAT, JOE. THE PUNISHMENT FOR JUDGES IS STERN. TWENTY YEARS ON THE PENAL COLONY ON TITAN! YOU DON'T GET MANY BUSTED JUDGES...SO THE GUARDS GIVE YOU INDIVIDUAL TREATMENT"!

Please, Rico... Can't pay you anymore...

You'll pay with your life, then!

Joe! Listen, we can make this look like an accident!

No way, Rico, I'm takin' you in!

i hate bent Judges, Rico, so I'm gonna bend you till you break!

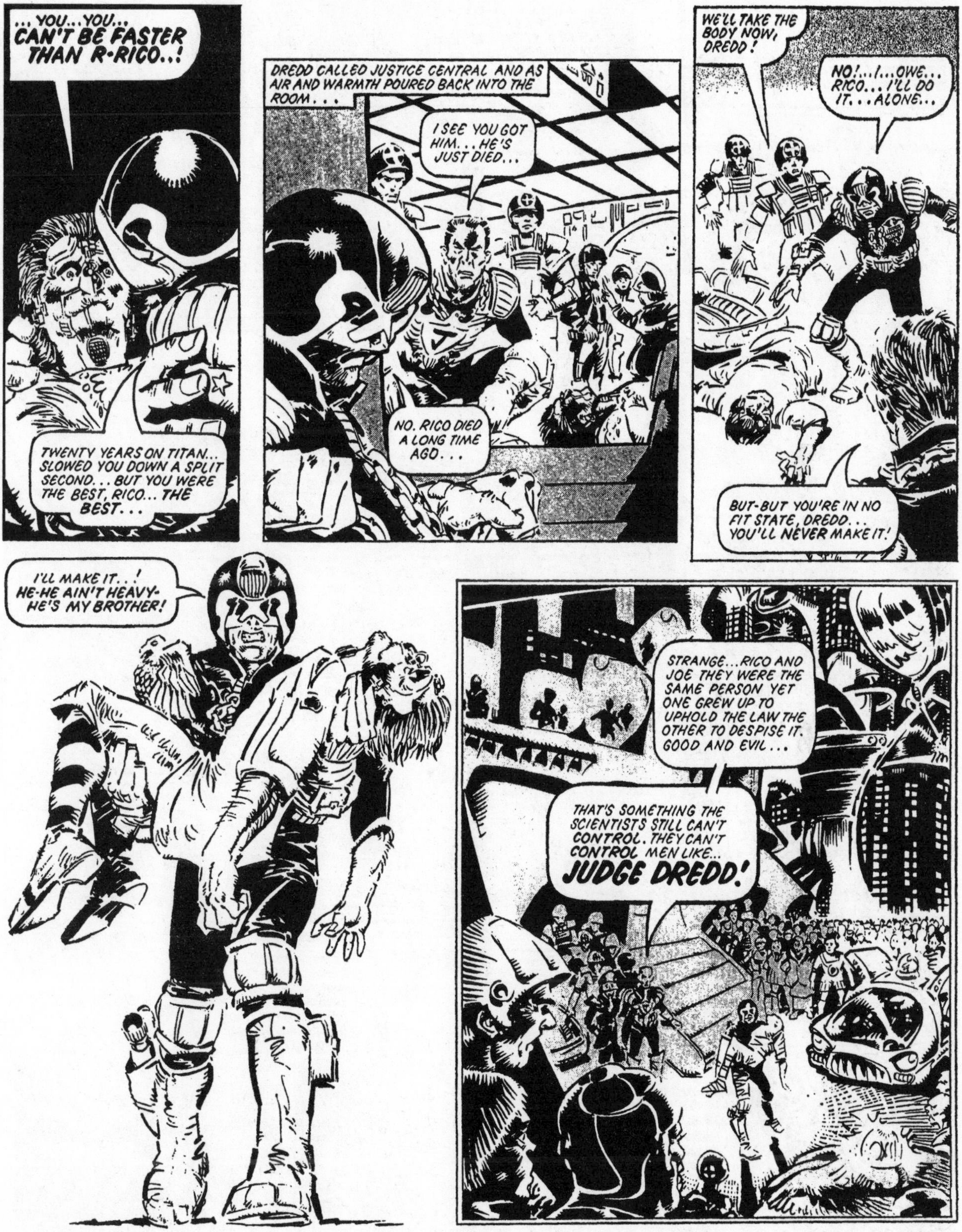

...YOU...YOU...
CAN'T BE FASTER THAN R-RICO..!
TWENTY YEARS ON TITAN... SLOWED YOU DOWN A SPLIT SECOND... BUT YOU WERE THE BEST, RICO... THE BEST...
DREDD CALLED JUSTICE CENTRAL AND AS AIR AND WARMTH POURED BACK INTO THE ROOM...
I SEE YOU GOT HIM... HE'S JUST DIED...
NO. RICO DIED A LONG TIME AGO...
WE'LL TAKE THE BODY NOW, DREDD!
NO!...I...OWE... RICO... I'LL DO IT...ALONE...
BUT-BUT YOU'RE IN NO FIT STATE, DREDD... YOU'LL NEVER MAKE IT!
I'LL MAKE IT...! HE-HE AIN'T HEAVY- HE'S MY BROTHER!
STRANGE...RICO AND JOE THEY WERE THE SAME PERSON YET ONE GREW UP TO UPHOLD THE LAW THE OTHER TO DESPISE IT. GOOD AND EVIL...
THAT'S SOMETHING THE SCIENTISTS STILL CAN'T CONTROL. THEY CAN'T CONTROL MEN LIKE...
JUDGE DREDD!

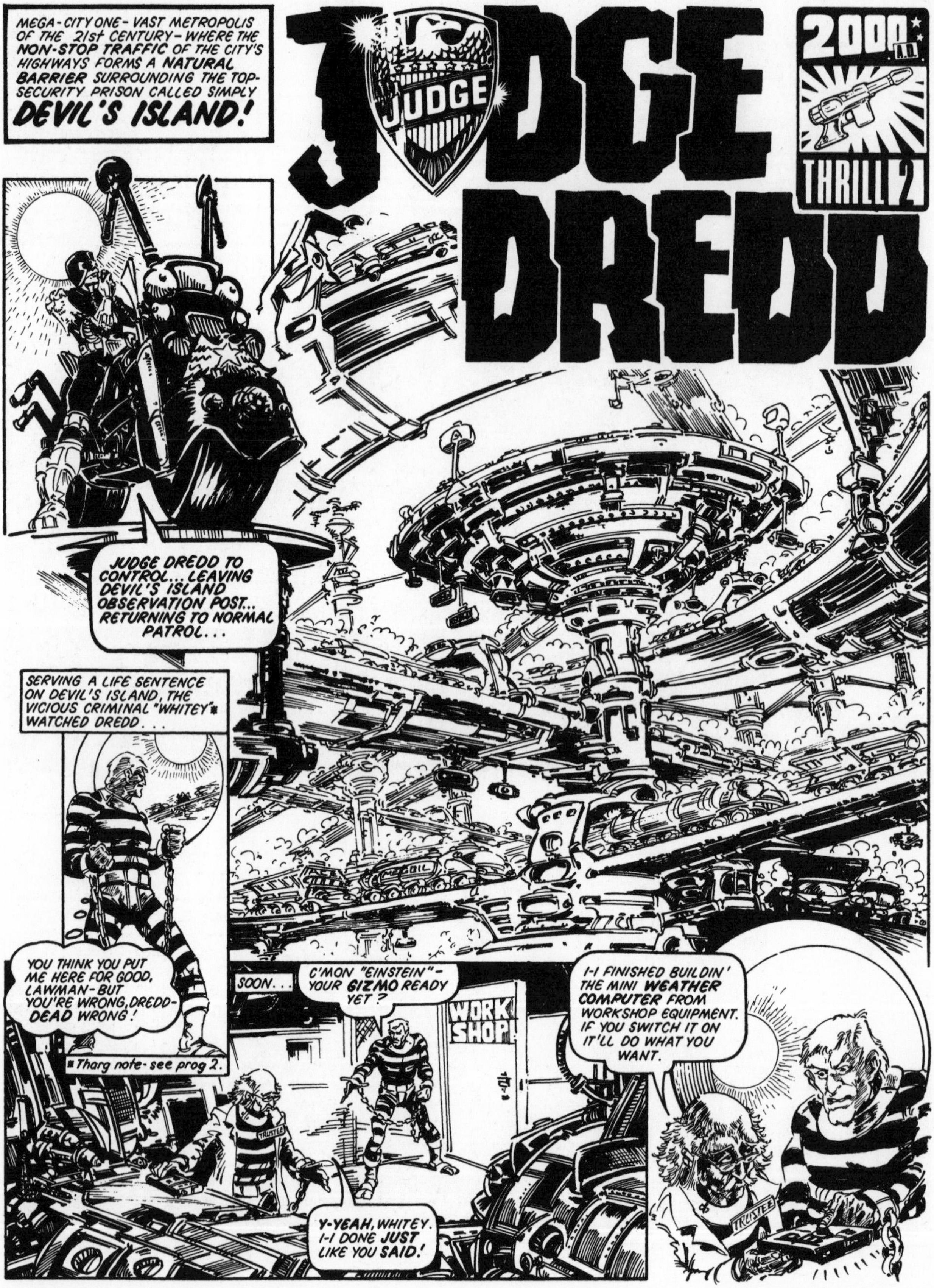

MEGA-CITY ONE - VAST METROPOLIS OF THE 21st CENTURY - WHERE THE NON-STOP TRAFFIC OF THE CITY'S HIGHWAYS FORMS A NATURAL BARRIER SURROUNDING THE TOP-SECURITY PRISON CALLED SIMPLY DEVIL'S ISLAND!
JUDGE DREDD
JUDGE
2000 A.D.
THRILL 2
JUDGE DREDD TO CONTROL... LEAVING DEVIL'S ISLAND OBSERVATION POST... RETURNING TO NORMAL PATROL...
SERVING A LIFE SENTENCE ON DEVIL'S ISLAND, THE VICIOUS CRIMINAL "WHITEY"* WATCHED DREDD...
YOU THINK YOU PUT ME HERE FOR GOOD, LAWMAN - BUT YOU'RE WRONG, DREDD - DEAD WRONG!
*Tharg note - see prog 2.
SOON...
C'MON "EINSTEIN" - YOUR GIZMO READY YET?
WORKSHOP
Y-YEAH, WHITEY. I-I DONE JUST LIKE YOU SAID!
I-I FINISHED BUILDIN' THE MINI WEATHER COMPUTER FROM WORKSHOP EQUIPMENT. IF YOU SWITCH IT ON IT'LL DO WHAT YOU WANT.
TRUSTEE

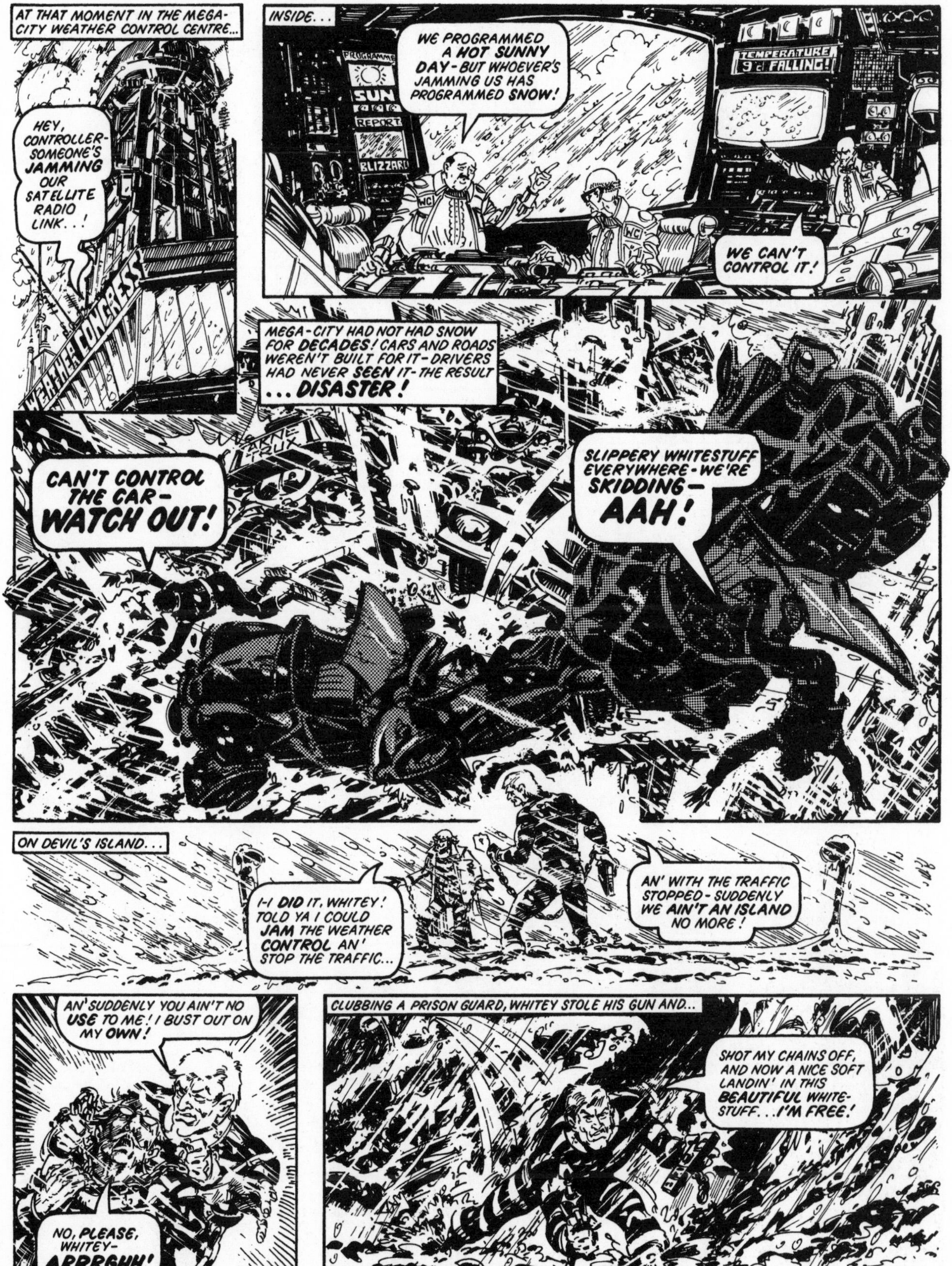
AT THAT MOMENT IN THE MEGA-CITY WEATHER CONTROL CENTRE...
HEY, CONTROLLER-SOMEONE'S JAMMING OUR SATELLITE RADIO LINK..!
WEATHER CONGRESS
INSIDE...
PROGRAMME
SUN
REPORT
BLIZZARD
WE PROGRAMMED A HOT SUNNY DAY-BUT WHOEVER'S JAMMING US HAS PROGRAMMED SNOW!
TEMPERATURE 9°C FALLING!
WE CAN'T CONTROL IT!
MEGA-CITY HAD NOT HAD SNOW FOR DECADES! CARS AND ROADS WEREN'T BUILT FOR IT-DRIVERS HAD NEVER SEEN IT-THE RESULT ...DISASTER!
CAN'T CONTROL THE CAR-WATCH OUT!
SLIPPERY WHITESTUFF EVERYWHERE-WE'RE SKIDDING-AAH!
ON DEVIL'S ISLAND...
I-I DID IT, WHITEY! TOLD YA I COULD JAM THE WEATHER CONTROL AN' STOP THE TRAFFIC...
AN' WITH THE TRAFFIC STOPPED-SUDDENLY WE AIN'T AN ISLAND NO MORE!
AN' SUDDENLY YOU AIN'T NO USE TO ME! I BUST OUT ON MY OWN!
NO, PLEASE, WHITEY-ARRRGHH!
CLUBBING A PRISON GUARD, WHITEY STOLE HIS GUN AND...
SHOT MY CHAINS OFF, AND NOW A NICE SOFT LANDIN' IN THIS BEAUTIFUL WHITE-STUFF...I'M FREE!

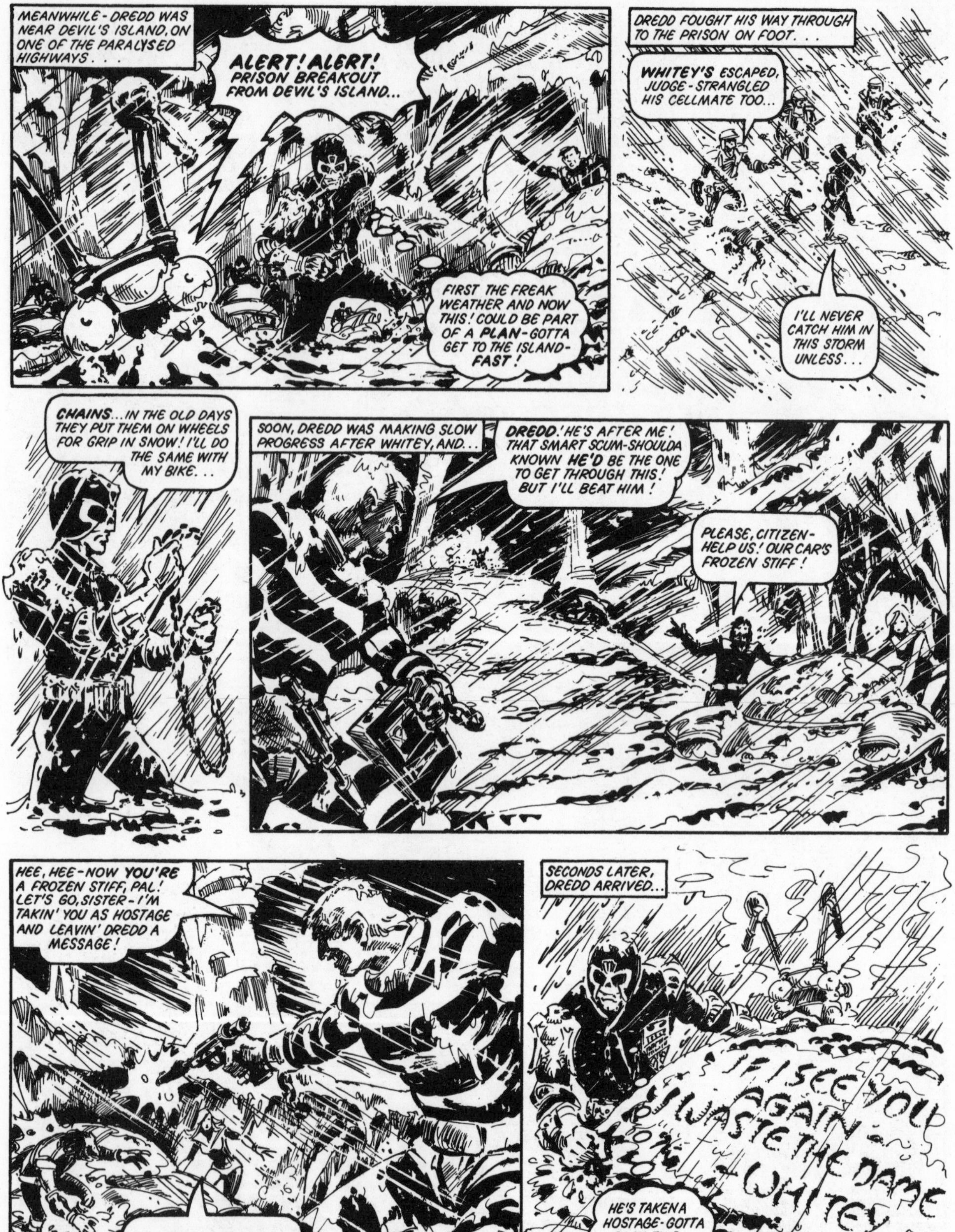
MEANWHILE - DREDD WAS NEAR DEVIL'S ISLAND, ON ONE OF THE PARALYSED HIGHWAYS . . .
ALERT! ALERT! PRISON BREAKOUT FROM DEVIL'S ISLAND...
FIRST THE FREAK WEATHER AND NOW THIS! COULD BE PART OF A PLAN - GOTTA GET TO THE ISLAND - FAST!
DREDD FOUGHT HIS WAY THROUGH TO THE PRISON ON FOOT. . .
WHITEY'S ESCAPED, JUDGE - STRANGLED HIS CELLMATE TOO...
I'LL NEVER CATCH HIM IN THIS STORM UNLESS. . .
CHAINS... IN THE OLD DAYS THEY PUT THEM ON WHEELS FOR GRIP IN SNOW! I'LL DO THE SAME WITH MY BIKE. . .
SOON, DREDD WAS MAKING SLOW PROGRESS AFTER WHITEY, AND...
DREDD! HE'S AFTER ME! THAT SMART SCUM - SHOULDA KNOWN HE'D BE THE ONE TO GET THROUGH THIS! BUT I'LL BEAT HIM!
PLEASE, CITIZEN - HELP US! OUR CAR'S FROZEN STIFF!
HEE, HEE - NOW YOU'RE A FROZEN STIFF, PAL! LET'S GO, SISTER - I'M TAKIN' YOU AS HOSTAGE AND LEAVIN' DREDD A MESSAGE!
NO! NO!
SECONDS LATER, DREDD ARRIVED...
IF I SEE YOU AGAIN I WASTE THE DAME WHITEY
HE'S TAKEN A HOSTAGE - GOTTA PLAY THIS CAREFUL AND CLEVER!

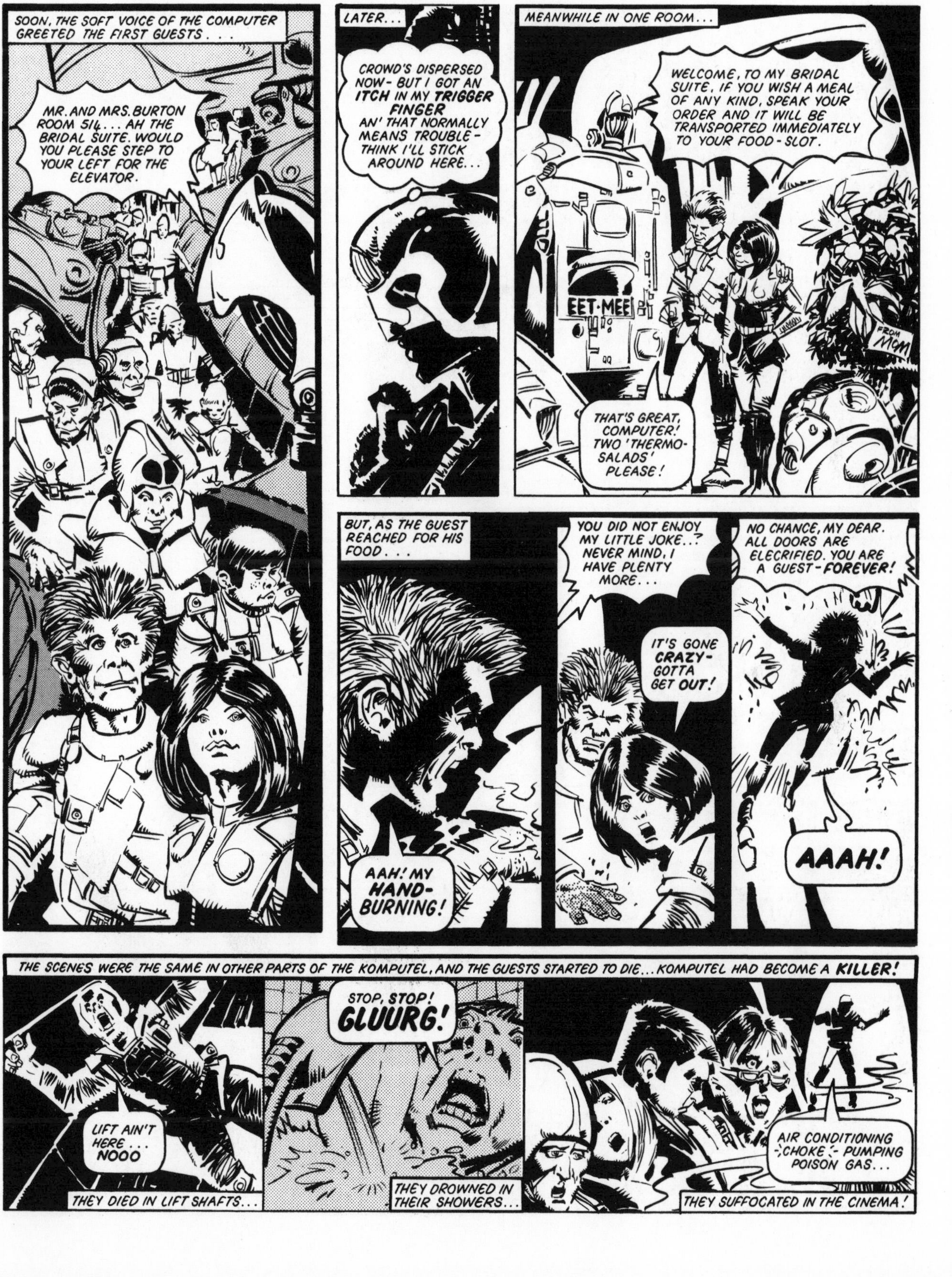

SOON, THE SOFT VOICE OF THE COMPUTER GREETED THE FIRST GUESTS . . .
MR. AND MRS. BURTON ROOM 514 . . . AH THE BRIDAL SUITE. WOULD YOU PLEASE STEP TO YOUR LEFT FOR THE ELEVATOR.
LATER...
CROWD'S DISPERSED NOW- BUT I GOT AN ITCH IN MY TRIGGER FINGER AN' THAT NORMALLY MEANS TROUBLE- THINK I'LL STICK AROUND HERE...
MEANWHILE IN ONE ROOM...
WELCOME, TO MY BRIDAL SUITE, IF YOU WISH A MEAL OF ANY KIND, SPEAK YOUR ORDER AND IT WILL BE TRANSPORTED IMMEDIATELY TO YOUR FOOD-SLOT.
EET-MEE
FROM MOM
THAT'S GREAT, COMPUTER! TWO 'THERMO-SALADS' PLEASE!
BUT, AS THE GUEST REACHED FOR HIS FOOD . . .
AAH! MY HAND- BURNING!
YOU DID NOT ENJOY MY LITTLE JOKE..? NEVER MIND, I HAVE PLENTY MORE...
IT'S GONE CRAZY- GOTTA GET OUT!
NO CHANCE, MY DEAR. ALL DOORS ARE ELECRIFIED. YOU ARE A GUEST- FOREVER!
AAAH!
THE SCENES WERE THE SAME IN OTHER PARTS OF THE KOMPUTEL, AND THE GUESTS STARTED TO DIE... KOMPUTEL HAD BECOME A KILLER!
LIFT AIN'T HERE . . . NOOO
THEY DIED IN LIFT SHAFTS...
STOP, STOP! GLUURG!
THEY DROWNED IN THEIR SHOWERS...
AIR CONDITIONING -CHOKE- PUMPING POISON GAS...
THEY SUFFOCATED IN THE CINEMA!

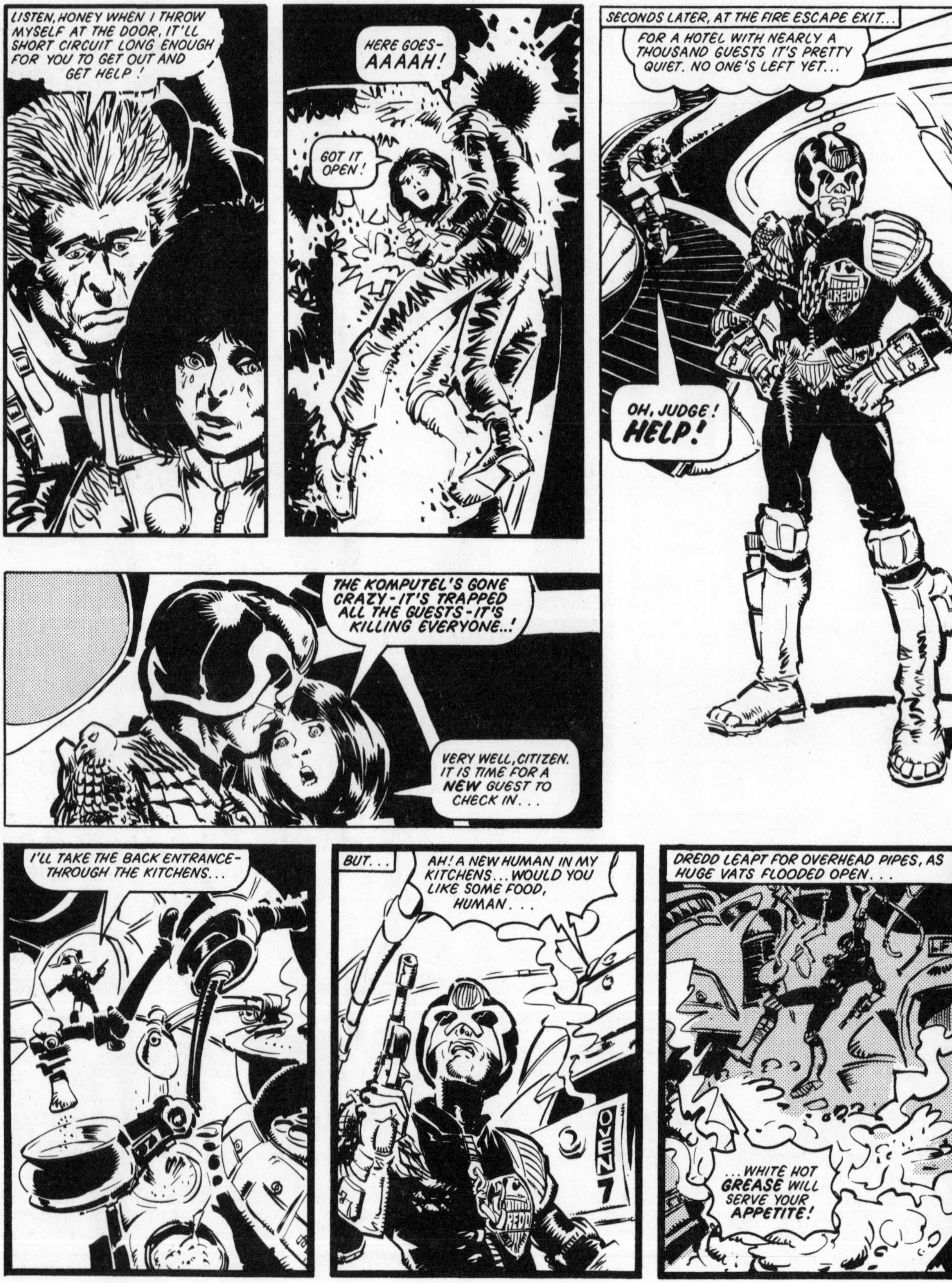
LISTEN, HONEY WHEN I THROW MYSELF AT THE DOOR, IT'LL SHORT CIRCUIT LONG ENOUGH FOR YOU TO GET OUT AND GET HELP !
HERE GOES- AAAAH!
GOT IT OPEN!
SECONDS LATER, AT THE FIRE ESCAPE EXIT...
FOR A HOTEL WITH NEARLY A THOUSAND GUESTS IT'S PRETTY QUIET. NO ONE'S LEFT YET...
OH, JUDGE! HELP!
THE KOMPUTEL'S GONE CRAZY-IT'S TRAPPED ALL THE GUESTS-IT'S KILLING EVERYONE...!
VERY WELL, CITIZEN. IT IS TIME FOR A NEW GUEST TO CHECK IN...
I'LL TAKE THE BACK ENTRANCE-THROUGH THE KITCHENS...
BUT...
AH! A NEW HUMAN IN MY KITCHENS... WOULD YOU LIKE SOME FOOD, HUMAN...
OVEN 7
DREDD LEAPT FOR OVERHEAD PIPES, AS HUGE VATS FLOODED OPEN...
LIFT
...WHITE HOT GREASE WILL SERVE YOUR APPETITE!

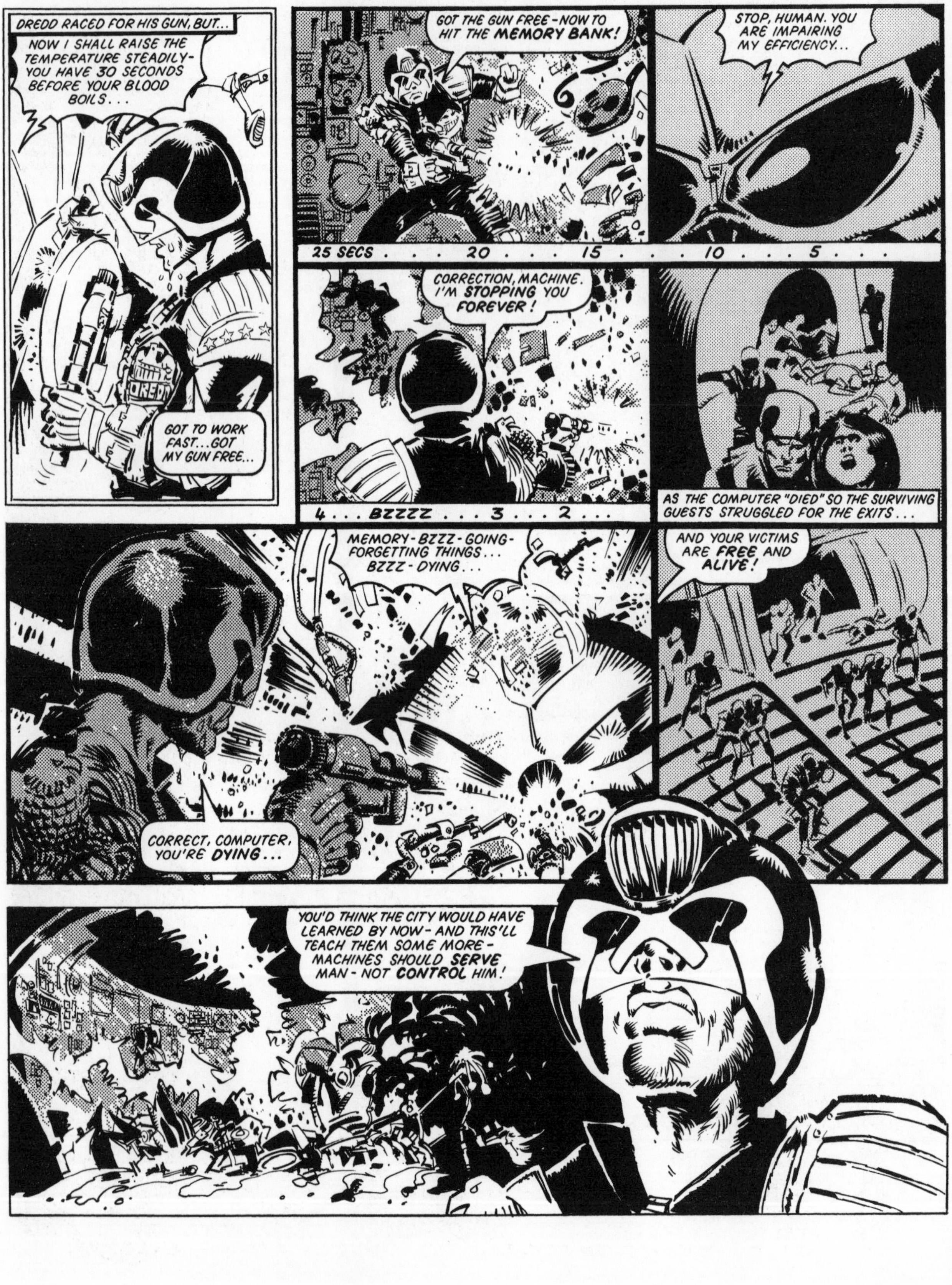
DREDD RACED FOR HIS GUN, BUT...
NOW I SHALL RAISE THE TEMPERATURE STEADILY- YOU HAVE 30 SECONDS BEFORE YOUR BLOOD BOILS...
GOT TO WORK FAST...GOT MY GUN FREE...
GOT THE GUN FREE - NOW TO HIT THE MEMORY BANK!
STOP, HUMAN. YOU ARE IMPAIRING MY EFFICIENCY...
25 SECS . . . 20 . . . 15 . . . 10 . . . 5 . . .
CORRECTION, MACHINE. I'M STOPPING YOU FOREVER!
4 . . . BZZZZ . . . 3 . . . 2 . . .
AS THE COMPUTER "DIED" SO THE SURVIVING GUESTS STRUGGLED FOR THE EXITS...
MEMORY-BZZZ-GOING-FORGETTING THINGS... BZZZ-DYING...
CORRECT, COMPUTER, YOU'RE DYING...
AND YOUR VICTIMS ARE FREE AND ALIVE!
YOU'D THINK THE CITY WOULD HAVE LEARNED BY NOW - AND THIS'LL TEACH THEM SOME MORE - MACHINES SHOULD SERVE MAN - NOT CONTROL HIM!

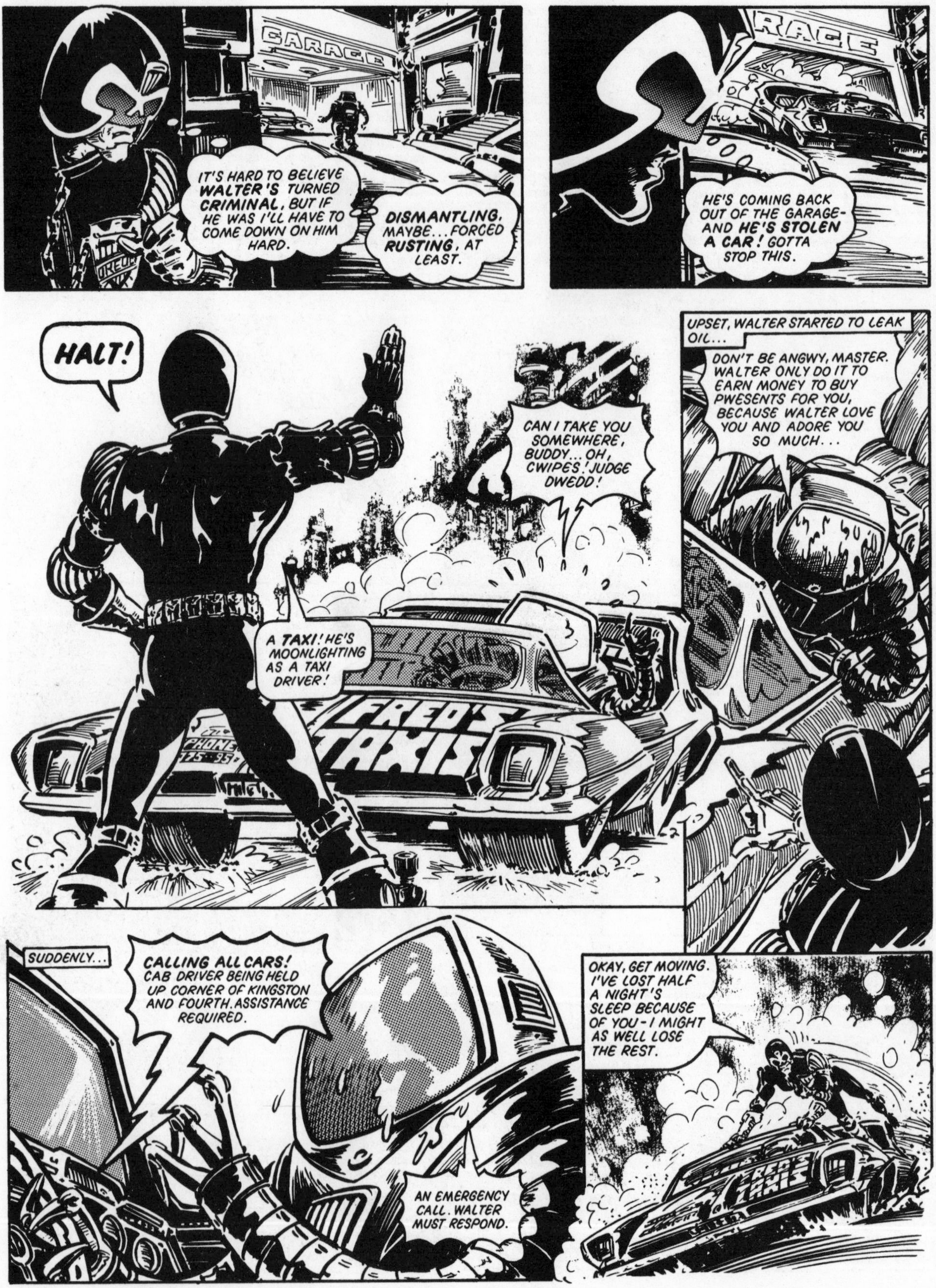

IT'S HARD TO BELIEVE **WALTER'S** TURNED **CRIMINAL**, BUT IF HE WAS I'LL HAVE TO COME DOWN ON HIM HARD.
DISMANTLING, MAYBE... FORCED **RUSTING**, AT LEAST.
GARAGE
HE'S COMING BACK OUT OF THE GARAGE- AND **HE'S STOLEN A CAR!** GOTTA STOP THIS.
HALT!
CAN I TAKE YOU SOMEWHERE, BUDDY... OH, CWIPES! JUDGE DWEDD!
A **TAXI**! HE'S MOONLIGHTING AS A TAXI DRIVER!
FRED'S TAXIS
UPSET, WALTER STARTED TO LEAK OIL...
DON'T BE ANGWY, MASTER. WALTER ONLY DO IT TO EARN MONEY TO BUY PWESENTS FOR YOU, BECAUSE WALTER LOVE YOU AND ADORE YOU SO MUCH...
SUDDENLY...
CALLING ALL CARS! CAB DRIVER BEING HELD UP CORNER OF KINGSTON AND FOURTH. ASSISTANCE REQUIRED.
AN EMERGENCY CALL. WALTER MUST RESPOND.
OKAY, GET MOVING. I'VE LOST HALF A NIGHT'S SLEEP BECAUSE OF YOU - I MIGHT AS WELL LOSE THE REST.

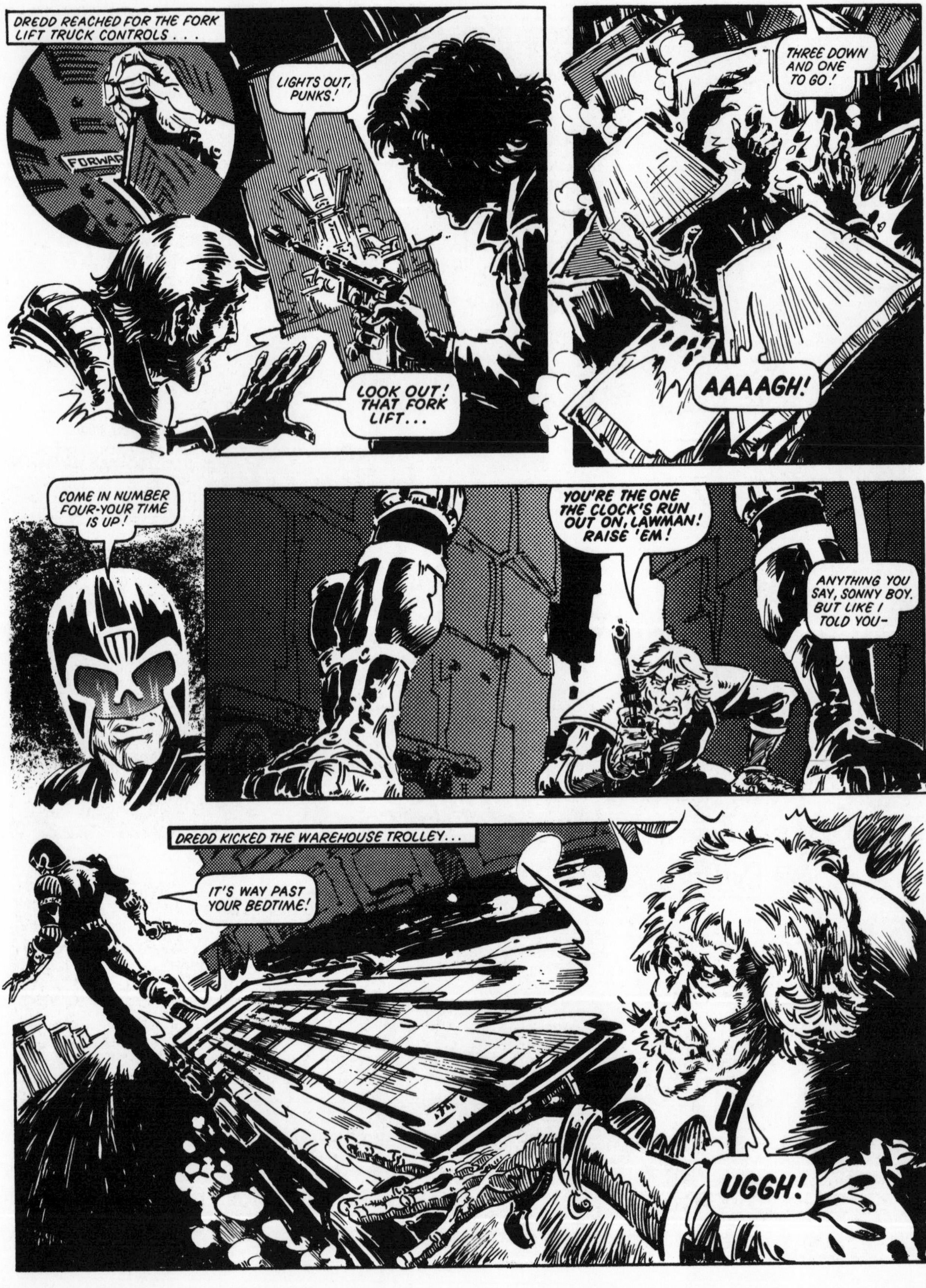
DREDD REACHED FOR THE FORK LIFT TRUCK CONTROLS . . .
LIGHTS OUT, PUNKS!
LOOK OUT! THAT FORK LIFT...
THREE DOWN AND ONE TO GO!
AAAAGH!
COME IN NUMBER FOUR-YOUR TIME IS UP!
YOU'RE THE ONE THE CLOCK'S RUN OUT ON, LAWMAN! RAISE 'EM!
ANYTHING YOU SAY, SONNY BOY. BUT LIKE I TOLD YOU-
DREDD KICKED THE WAREHOUSE TROLLEY...
IT'S WAY PAST YOUR BEDTIME!
UGGH!

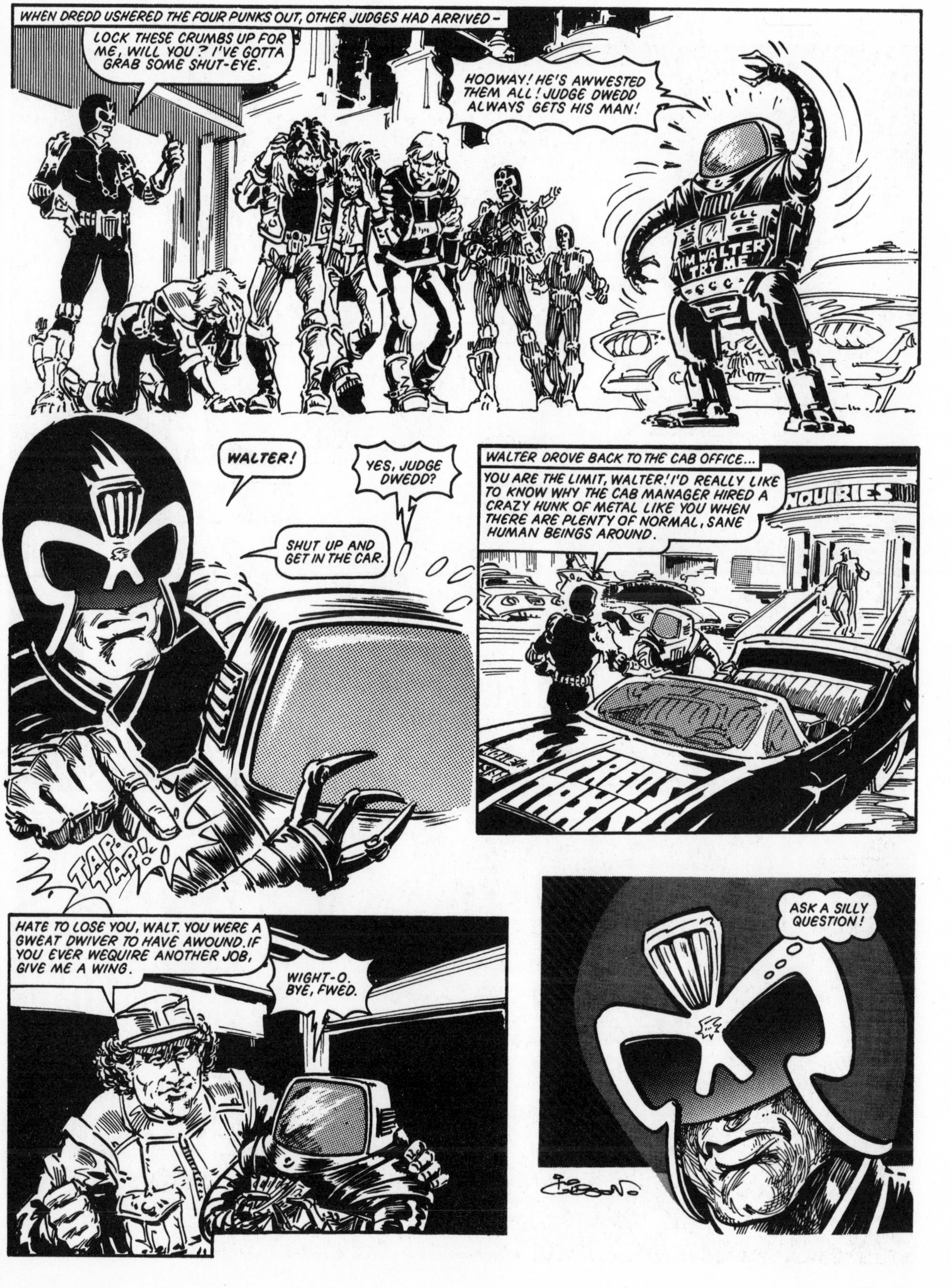
WHEN DREDD USHERED THE FOUR PUNKS OUT, OTHER JUDGES HAD ARRIVED –
LOCK THESE CRUMBS UP FOR ME, WILL YOU? I'VE GOTTA GRAB SOME SHUT-EYE.
HOOWAY! HE'S AWWESTED THEM ALL! JUDGE DWEDD ALWAYS GETS HIS MAN!
I'M WALTER TRY ME
WALTER!
YES, JUDGE DWEDD?
SHUT UP AND GET IN THE CAR.
TAP-TAP!
WALTER DROVE BACK TO THE CAB OFFICE...
YOU ARE THE LIMIT, WALTER! I'D REALLY LIKE TO KNOW WHY THE CAB MANAGER HIRED A CRAZY HUNK OF METAL LIKE YOU WHEN THERE ARE PLENTY OF NORMAL, SANE HUMAN BEINGS AROUND.
NQUIRIES
HATE TO LOSE YOU, WALT. YOU WERE A GWEAT DWIVER TO HAVE AWOUND. IF YOU EVER WEQUIRE ANOTHER JOB, GIVE ME A WING.
WIGHT-O. BYE, FWED.
ASK A SILLY QUESTION!

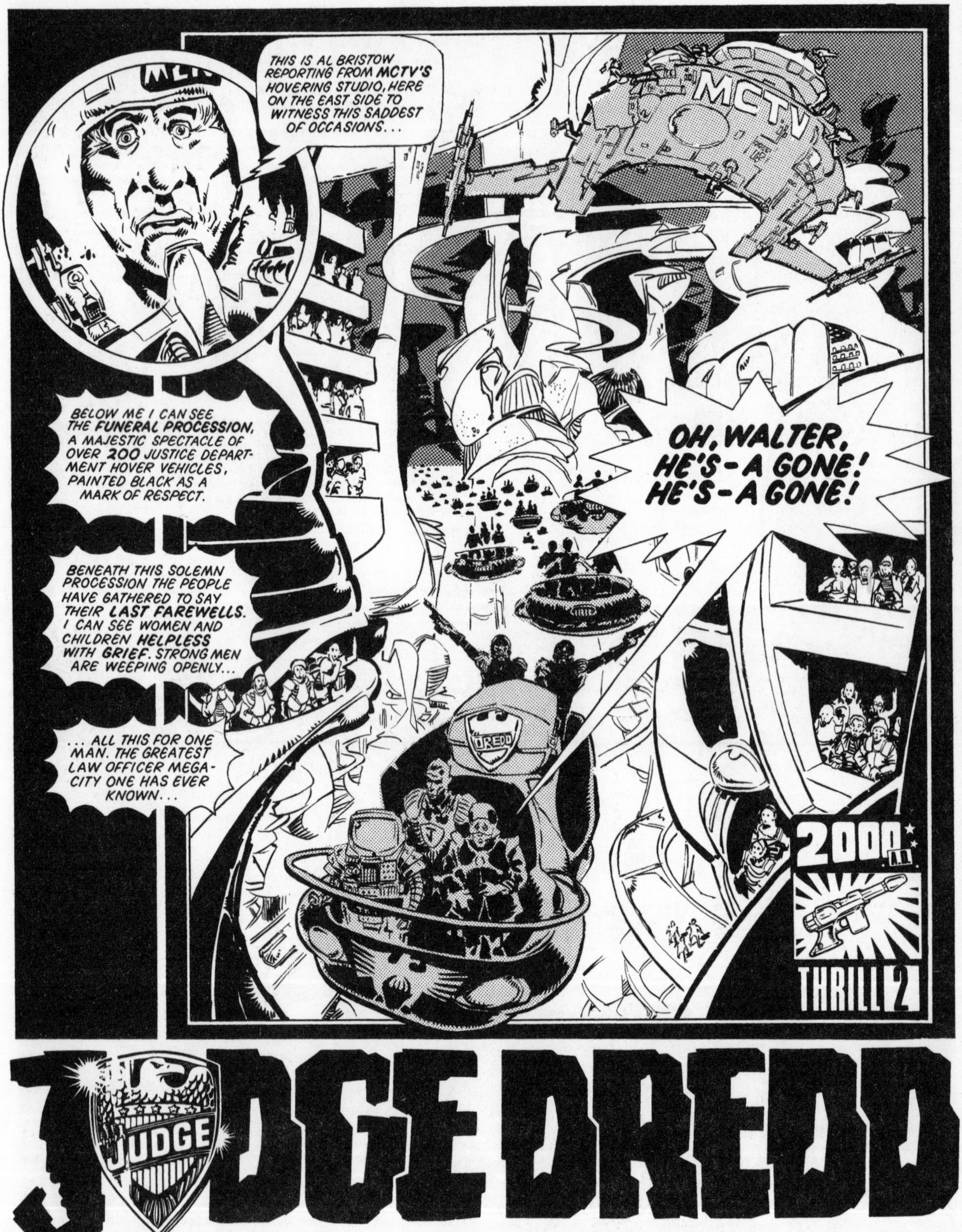
THIS IS AL BRISTOW REPORTING FROM MCTV'S HOVERING STUDIO, HERE ON THE EAST SIDE TO WITNESS THIS SADDEST OF OCCASIONS...
MCTV
BELOW ME I CAN SEE THE FUNERAL PROCESSION, A MAJESTIC SPECTACLE OF OVER 200 JUSTICE DEPARTMENT HOVER VEHICLES, PAINTED BLACK AS A MARK OF RESPECT.
OH, WALTER, HE'S-A GONE! HE'S-A GONE!
BENEATH THIS SOLEMN PROCESSION THE PEOPLE HAVE GATHERED TO SAY THEIR LAST FAREWELLS. I CAN SEE WOMEN AND CHILDREN HELPLESS WITH GRIEF. STRONG MEN ARE WEEPING OPENLY...
... ALL THIS FOR ONE MAN. THE GREATEST LAW OFFICER MEGA-CITY ONE HAS EVER KNOWN...
DREDD
2000 A.D.
THRILL 2
JUDGE DREDD

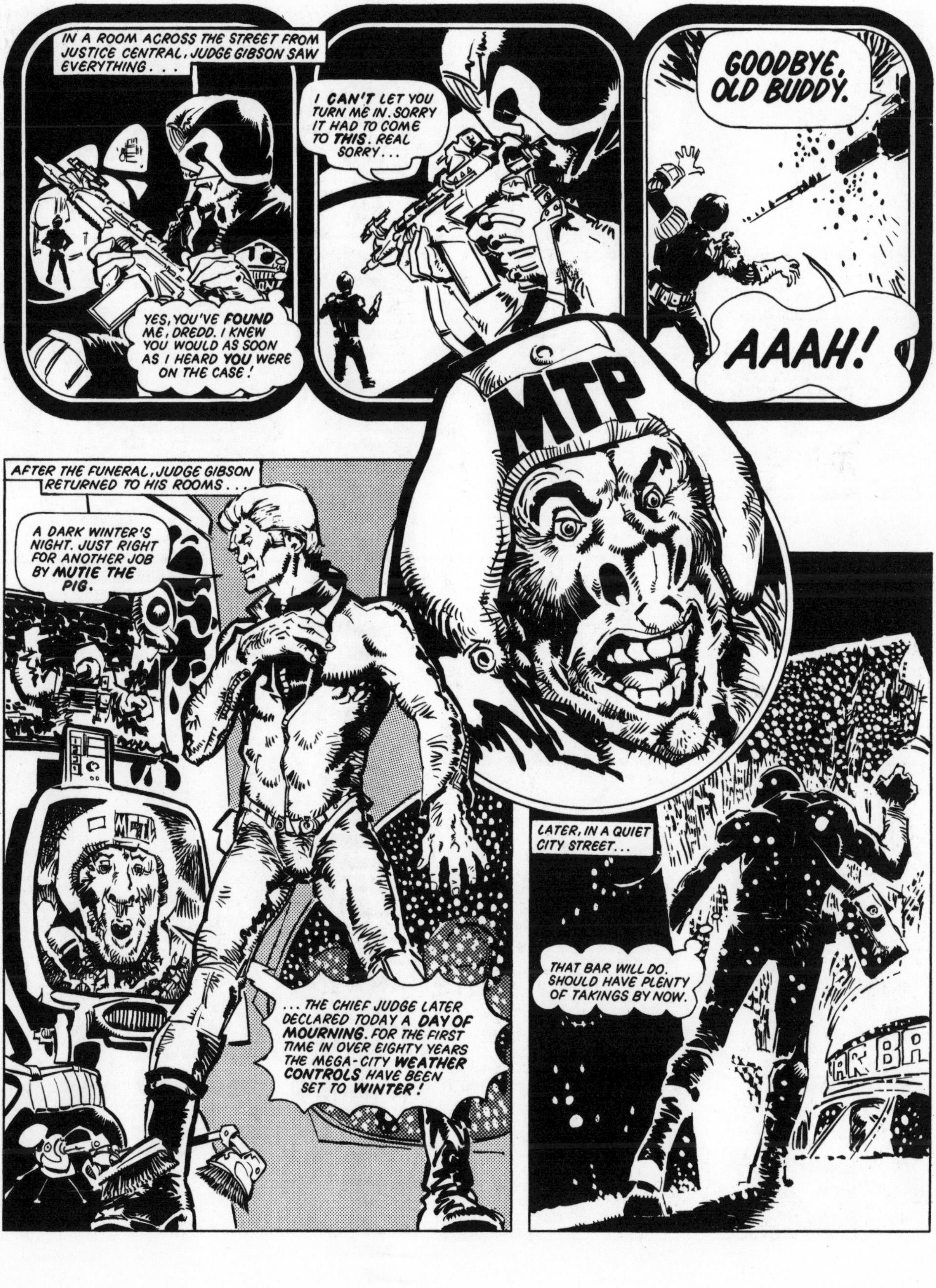

IN A ROOM ACROSS THE STREET FROM JUSTICE CENTRAL, JUDGE GIBSON SAW EVERYTHING . . .
YES, YOU'VE FOUND ME, DREDD. I KNEW YOU WOULD AS SOON AS I HEARD YOU WERE ON THE CASE!
I CAN'T LET YOU TURN ME IN. SORRY IT HAD TO COME TO THIS. REAL SORRY...
GOODBYE, OLD BUDDY.
AAAH!
AFTER THE FUNERAL, JUDGE GIBSON RETURNED TO HIS ROOMS . .
A DARK WINTER'S NIGHT. JUST RIGHT FOR ANOTHER JOB BY MUTIE THE PIG.
MTP
... THE CHIEF JUDGE LATER DECLARED TODAY A DAY OF MOURNING. FOR THE FIRST TIME IN OVER EIGHTY YEARS THE MEGA-CITY WEATHER CONTROLS HAVE BEEN SET TO WINTER!
LATER, IN A QUIET CITY STREET...
THAT BAR WILL DO. SHOULD HAVE PLENTY OF TAKINGS BY NOW.

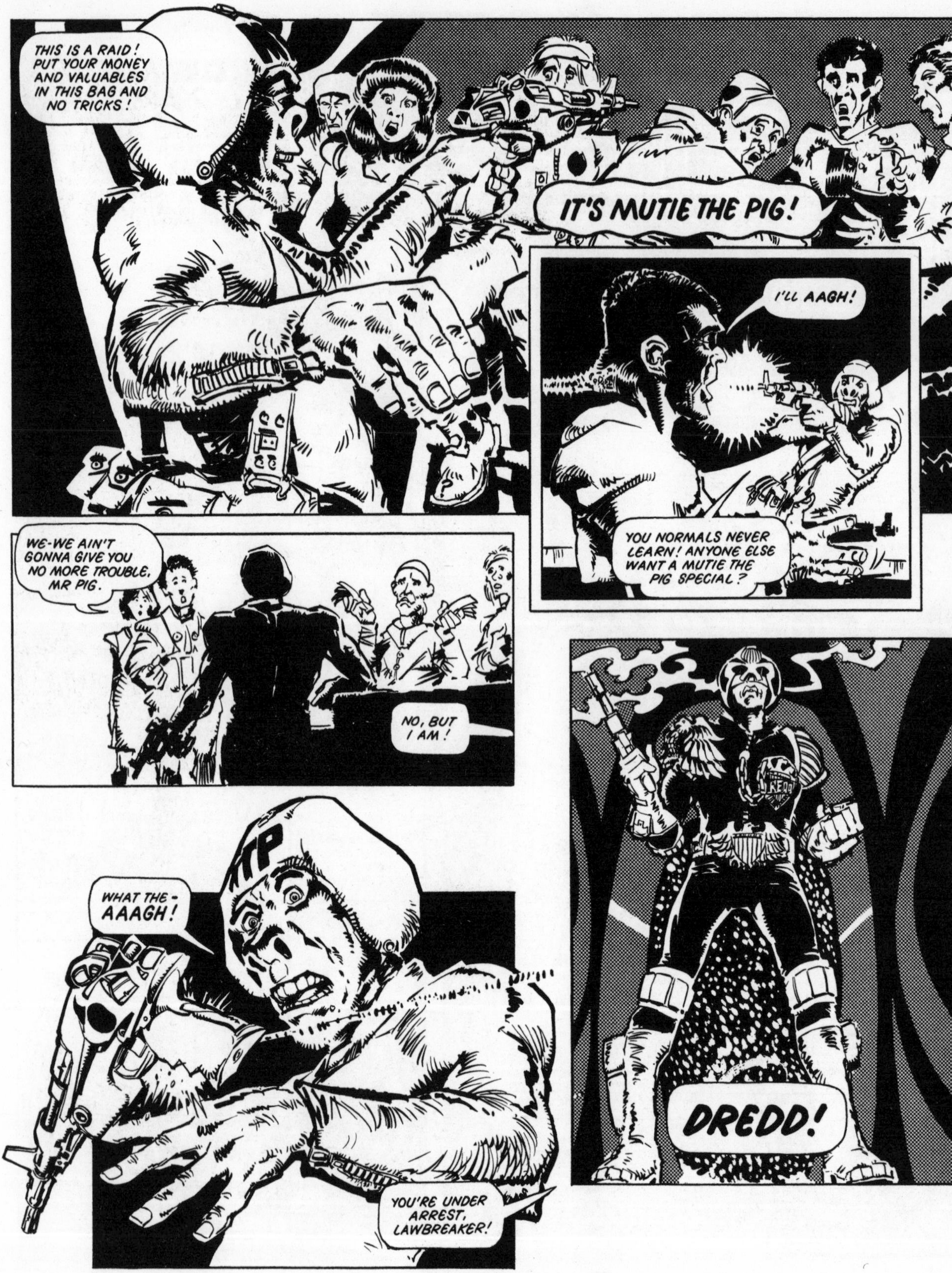
THIS IS A RAID! PUT YOUR MONEY AND VALUABLES IN THIS BAG AND NO TRICKS!
IT'S MUTIE THE PIG!
I'LL AAGH!
YOU NORMALS NEVER LEARN! ANYONE ELSE WANT A MUTIE THE PIG SPECIAL?
WE-WE AIN'T GONNA GIVE YOU NO MORE TROUBLE, MR PIG.
NO, BUT I AM!
WHAT THE- AAAGH!
YOU'RE UNDER ARREST, LAWBREAKER!
DREDD!

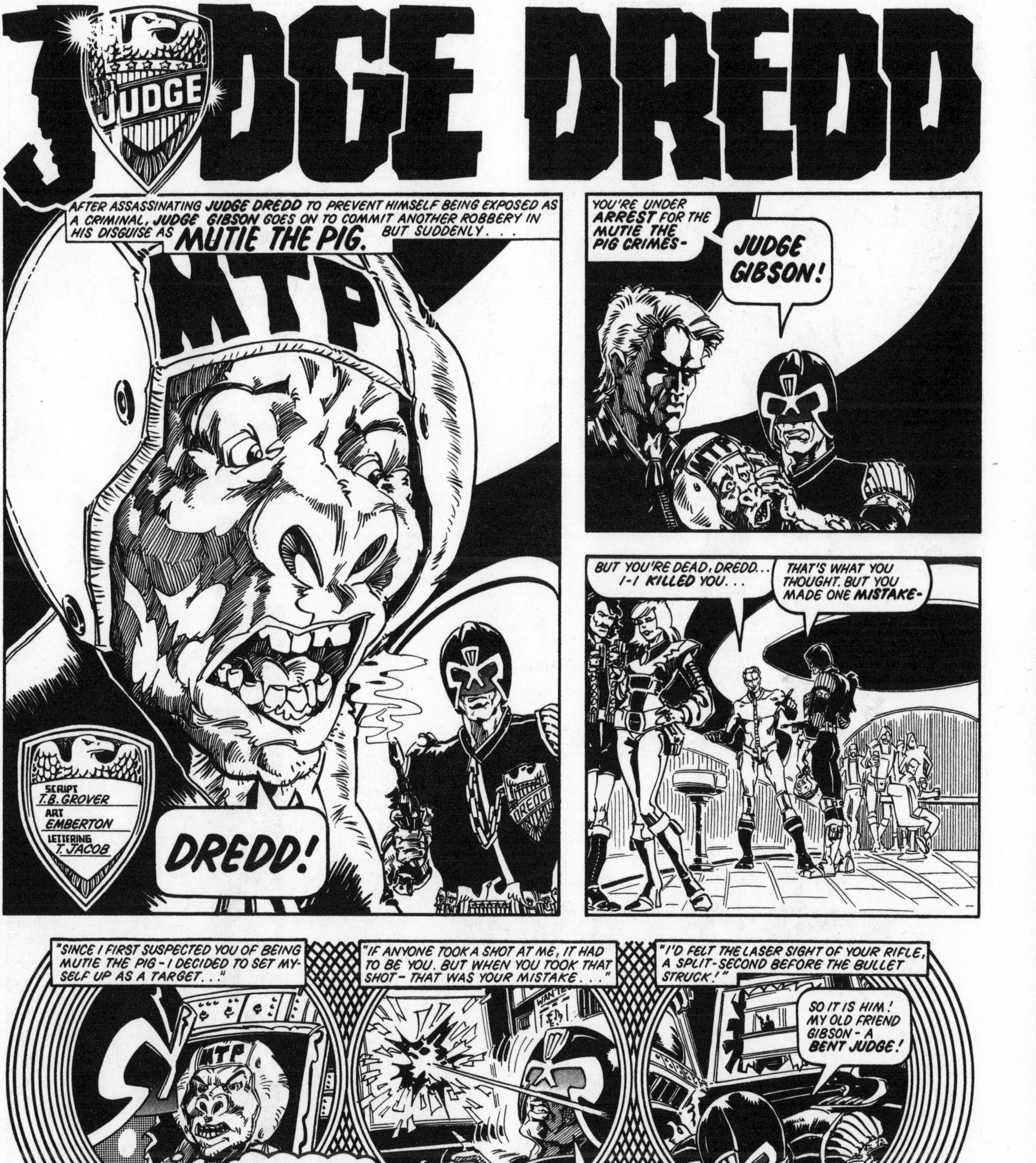

JUDGE DREDD
JUDGE
AFTER ASSASSINATING JUDGE DREDD TO PREVENT HIMSELF BEING EXPOSED AS A CRIMINAL, JUDGE GIBSON GOES ON TO COMMIT ANOTHER ROBBERY IN HIS DISGUISE AS MUTIE THE PIG. BUT SUDDENLY . . .
MTP
DREDD!
SCRIPT T.B. GROVER
ART EMBERTON
LETTERING T. JACOB
YOU'RE UNDER ARREST FOR THE MUTIE THE PIG CRIMES-
JUDGE GIBSON!
BUT YOU'RE DEAD, DREDD... I-I KILLED YOU...
THAT'S WHAT YOU THOUGHT. BUT YOU MADE ONE MISTAKE-
"SINCE I FIRST SUSPECTED YOU OF BEING MUTIE THE PIG - I DECIDED TO SET MYSELF UP AS A TARGET..."
MTP
CAN MUTIE THE PIG BE JUDGE GIBSON IN DISGUISE..?
"IF ANYONE TOOK A SHOT AT ME, IT HAD TO BE YOU. BUT WHEN YOU TOOK THAT SHOT - THAT WAS YOUR MISTAKE..."
LASER SIGHT! GOTTA MOVE!
"I'D FELT THE LASER SIGHT OF YOUR RIFLE, A SPLIT-SECOND BEFORE THE BULLET STRUCK!"
SO IT IS HIM! MY OLD FRIEND GIBSON - A BENT JUDGE!

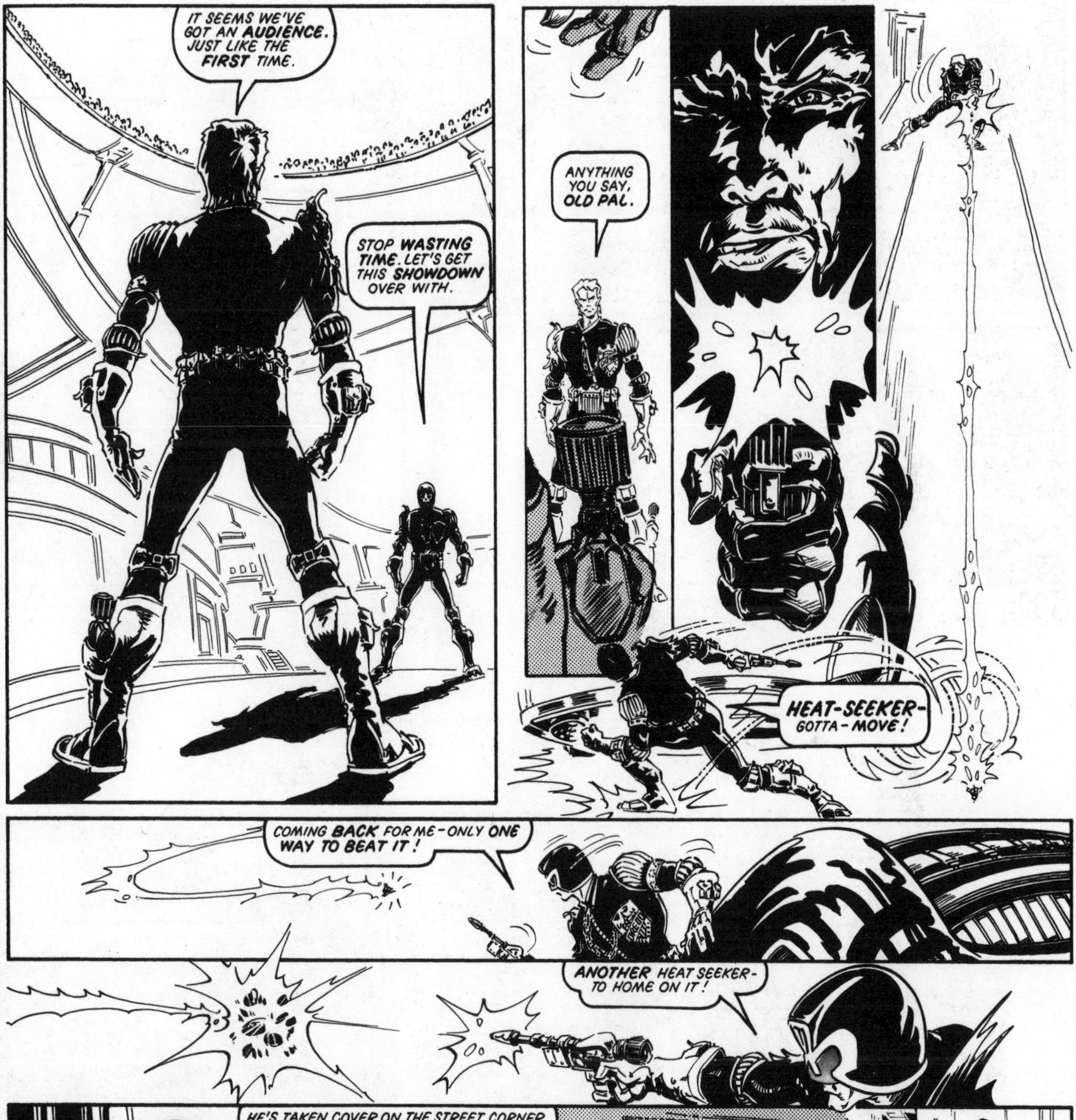

IT SEEMS WE'VE GOT AN AUDIENCE. JUST LIKE THE FIRST TIME.
STOP WASTING TIME. LET'S GET THIS SHOWDOWN OVER WITH.
ANYTHING YOU SAY, OLD PAL.
HEAT-SEEKER- GOTTA-MOVE!
COMING BACK FOR ME - ONLY ONE WAY TO BEAT IT!
ANOTHER HEAT SEEKER- TO HOME ON IT!
HE'S TAKEN COVER ON THE STREET CORNER. RICOCHET BULLETS, RAPID FIRE...
FUNERAL PARLOUR
SALE - SECONDHAND STOCK
GROVER

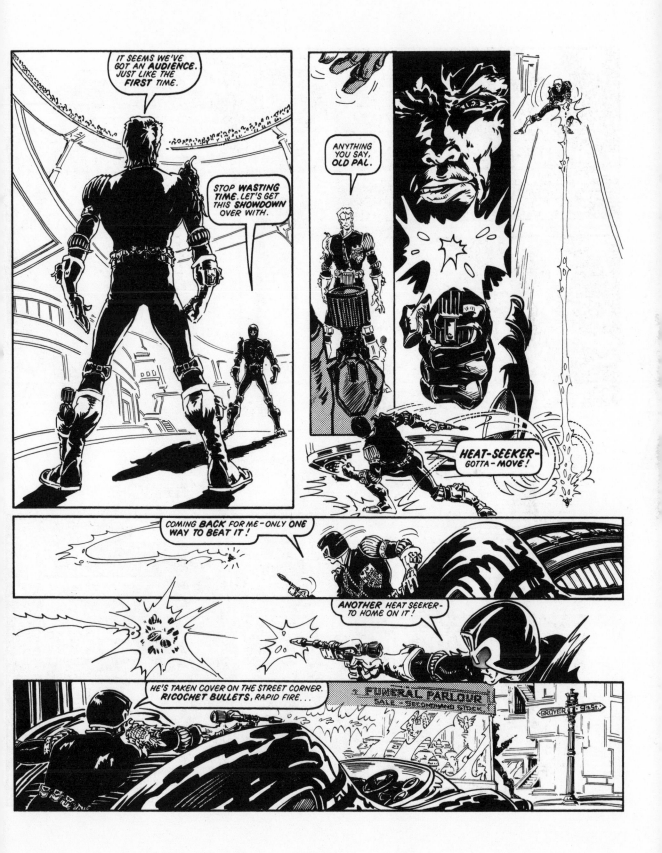

BUT YOU COULD'VE HAD ME! WHY DIDN'T YOU FIRE?
IT-IT WAS HARD ENOUGH KILLING YOU ONCE... I COULDN'T... DO IT AGAIN... YOU SEE, DREDD...
YOU WERE MY FRIEND...
IT... IT'S BETTER THIS WAY... COULDN'T HAVE FACED... TWENTY YEARS ON TITAN.
GOODBYE... OLD BUDDY...
THAT WAS A MASTERFUL EXHIBITION, JUDGE DREDD!
NO, PRINCIPAL. IT WAS A BITTER VICTORY. JUDGE GIBSON WAS... MY FRIEND.
BUT EVERY JUDGE MUST KNOW MANY BITTER MOMENTS - AND FACE THEM SQUARELY...
CADET
HUNT
CADET
WAGNER
OUR ROLL
CLASS
OF
79
FOR NO MAN IS GREATER THAN THE LAW.
THE END.
NEXT PROG: DREDD VERSUS CAPTAIN STRANGE!

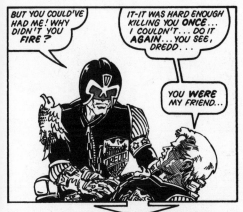

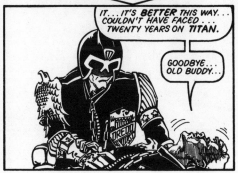

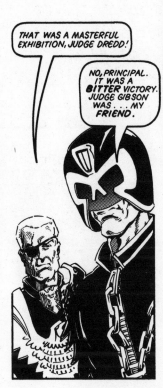

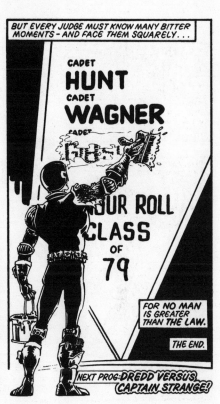

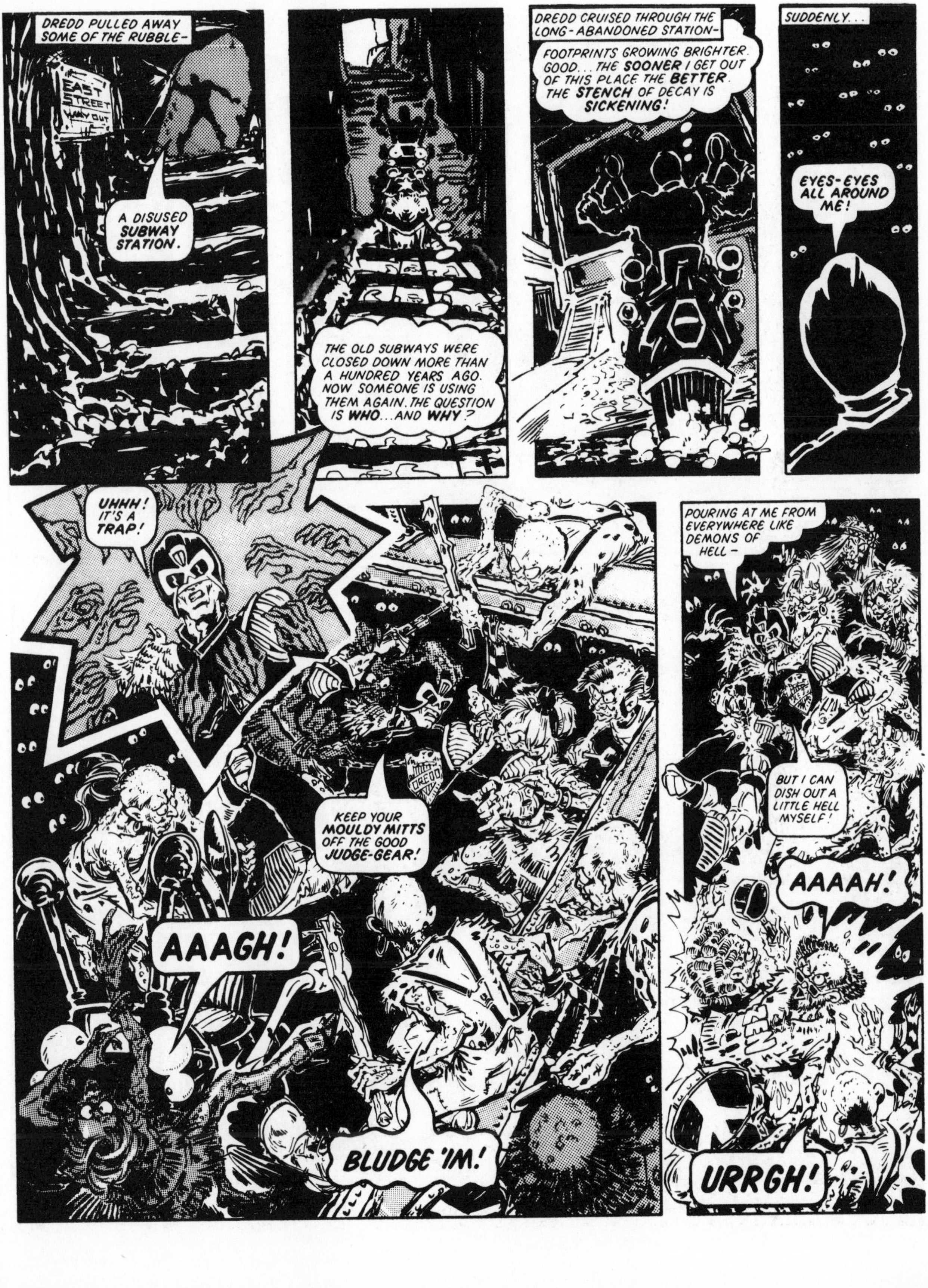

DREDD PULLED AWAY SOME OF THE RUBBLE-
EAST STREET WAY OUT
A DISUSED SUBWAY STATION.
THE OLD SUBWAYS WERE CLOSED DOWN MORE THAN A HUNDRED YEARS AGO. NOW SOMEONE IS USING THEM AGAIN. THE QUESTION IS WHO...AND WHY?
DREDD CRUISED THROUGH THE LONG-ABANDONED STATION-
FOOTPRINTS GROWING BRIGHTER. GOOD... THE SOONER I GET OUT OF THIS PLACE THE BETTER. THE STENCH OF DECAY IS SICKENING!
SUDDENLY...
EYES-EYES ALL AROUND ME!
UHNH! IT'S A TRAP!
KEEP YOUR MOULDY MITTS OFF THE GOOD JUDGE-GEAR!
AAAGH!
BLUDGE 'IM!
POURING AT ME FROM EVERYWHERE LIKE DEMONS OF HELL-
BUT I CAN DISH OUT A LITTLE HELL MYSELF!
AAAAH!
URRGH!

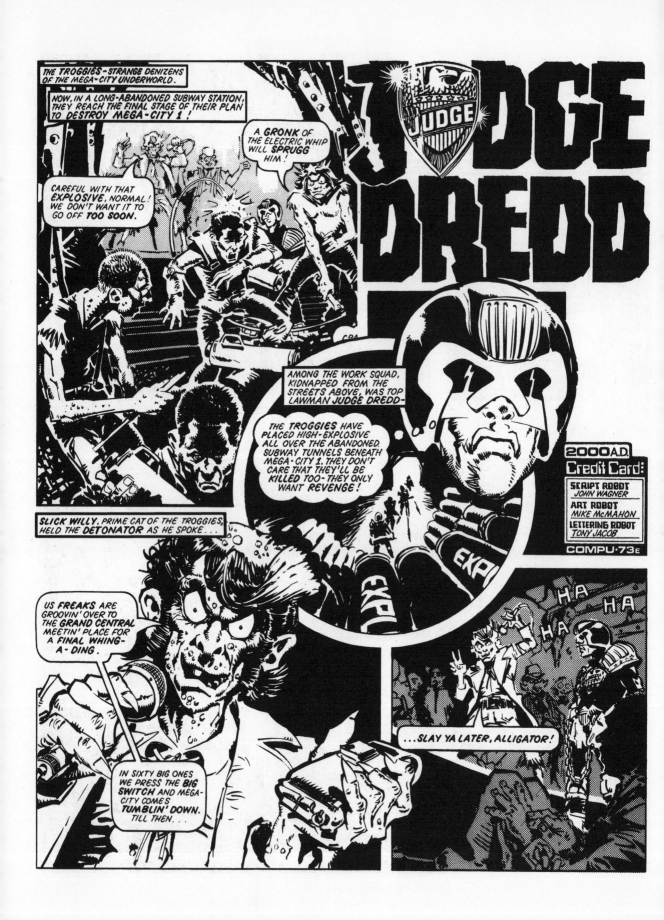

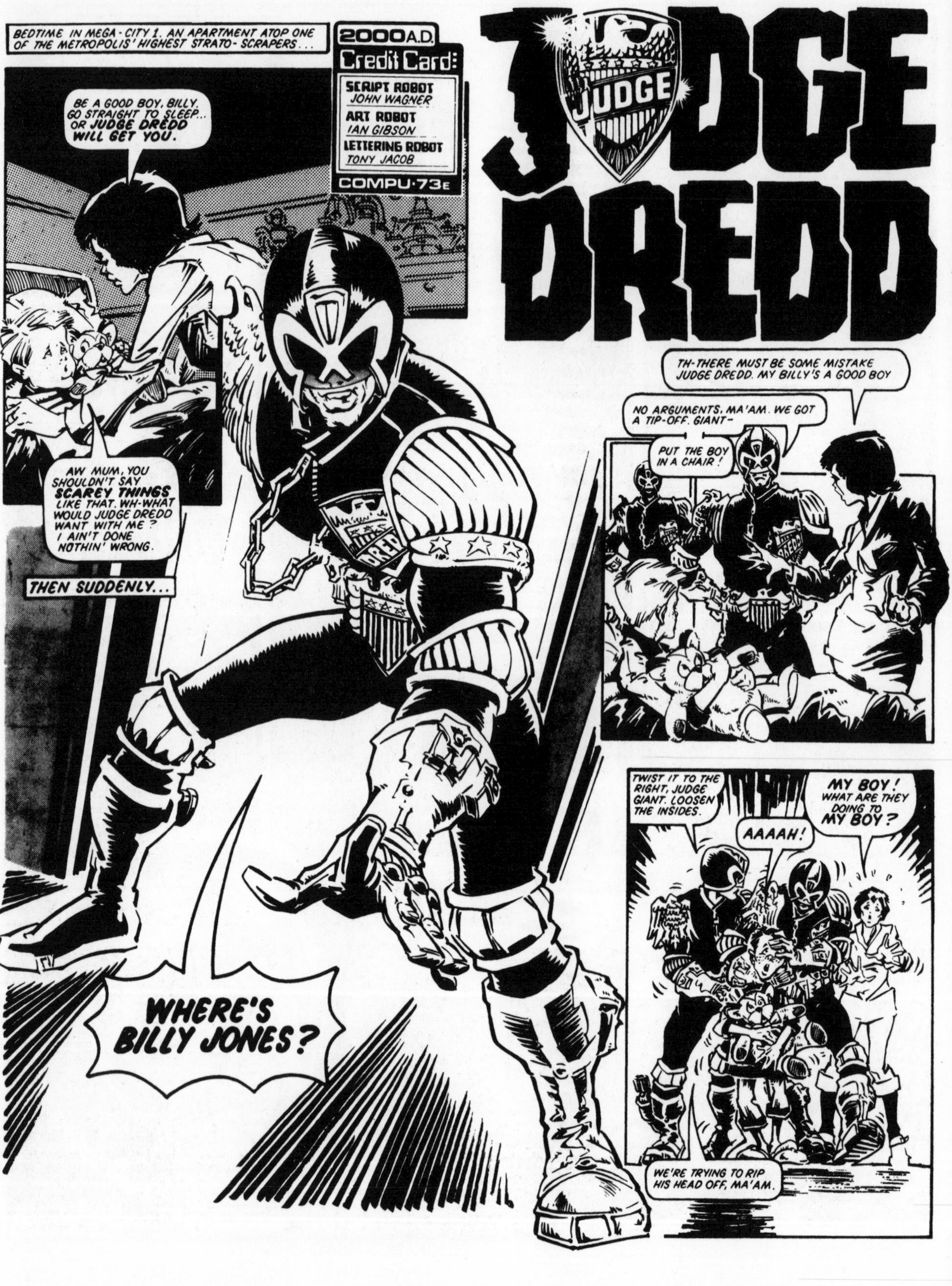
JUDGE DREDD
JUDGE
BEDTIME IN MEGA-CITY 1. AN APARTMENT ATOP ONE OF THE METROPOLIS' HIGHEST STRATO-SCRAPERS...
2000 A.D. Credit Card: SCRIPT ROBOT JOHN WAGNER ART ROBOT IAN GIBSON LETTERING ROBOT TONY JACOB COMPU-73E
BE A GOOD BOY, BILLY. GO STRAIGHT TO SLEEP... OR JUDGE DREDD WILL GET YOU.
AW MUM, YOU SHOULDN'T SAY SCAREY THINGS LIKE THAT. WH-WHAT WOULD JUDGE DREDD WANT WITH ME? I AIN'T DONE NOTHIN' WRONG.
THEN SUDDENLY...
WHERE'S BILLY JONES?
TH-THERE MUST BE SOME MISTAKE JUDGE DREDD. MY BILLY'S A GOOD BOY
NO ARGUMENTS, MA'AM. WE GOT A TIP-OFF. GIANT-
PUT THE BOY IN A CHAIR!
TWIST IT TO THE RIGHT, JUDGE GIANT. LOOSEN THE INSIDES.
AAAAH!
MY BOY! WHAT ARE THEY DOING TO MY BOY?
WE'RE TRYING TO RIP HIS HEAD OFF, MA'AM.

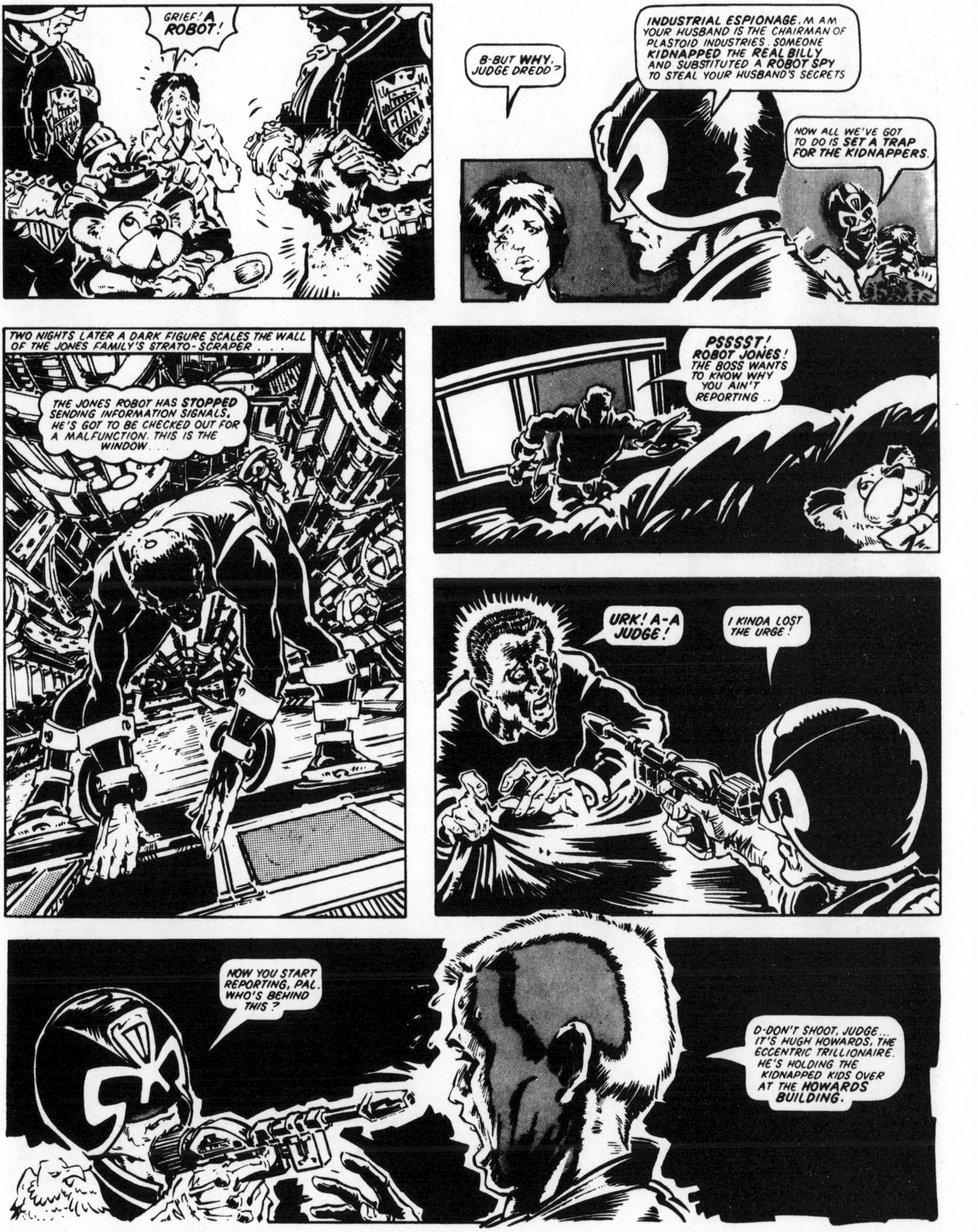
GRIEF! A ROBOT!
B-BUT WHY, JUDGE DREDD?
INDUSTRIAL ESPIONAGE, M AM. YOUR HUSBAND IS THE CHAIRMAN OF PLASTOID INDUSTRIES. SOMEONE KIDNAPPED THE REAL BILLY AND SUBSTITUTED A ROBOT SPY TO STEAL YOUR HUSBAND'S SECRETS
NOW ALL WE'VE GOT TO DO IS SET A TRAP FOR THE KIDNAPPERS.
TWO NIGHTS LATER A DARK FIGURE SCALES THE WALL OF THE JONES FAMILY'S STRATO-SCRAPER . . .
THE JONES ROBOT HAS STOPPED SENDING INFORMATION SIGNALS. HE'S GOT TO BE CHECKED OUT FOR A MALFUNCTION. THIS IS THE WINDOW . . .
PSSSST! ROBOT JONES! THE BOSS WANTS TO KNOW WHY YOU AIN'T REPORTING . .
URK! A-A JUDGE!
I KINDA LOST THE URGE!
NOW YOU START REPORTING, PAL. WHO'S BEHIND THIS?
D-DON'T SHOOT, JUDGE... IT'S HUGH HOWARDS, THE ECCENTRIC TRILLIONAIRE. HE'S HOLDING THE KIDNAPPED KIDS OVER AT THE HOWARDS BUILDING.

JUDGE DREDD

MEGA-CITY ONE, 2099. AT JUSTICE CENTRAL TOP LAWMAN JUDGE DREDD IS CATCHING UP WITH A BACKLOG OF CASE REPORTS...

I'M SORRY, SIR, YOU CAN'T GO IN THERE. THAT'S JUDGE DREDD'S PRIVATE OFFICE!

PUT A SOCK IN IT, SKINFACE! DON UGGIE DON'T TAKE NO ORDERS FROM NOBODY!

2000 A.D.
Credit Card:
SCRIPT ROBOT
JOHN WAGNER
ART ROBOT
MIKE McMAHON
LETTERING ROBOT
TONY JACOB
COMPU·73E

I ONLY GOT ONE TING TA SAY TA YA, DREDD—NUTS!

DON UGGIE APELIND AND HIS HENCHMEN, FAST EEEK AND JOE BANANAS.... THE APE GANG.

UGGIE LEPT UP ONTO DREDD'S DESK.

DA EAST SIDE MOB IS MUSCLIN' IN ON OUR TERRITORY AN' YOU'RE TURNIN'A BLIND EYE. WELL, I WANNIT STOPPED OR DERE'S GONNA BE TROUBLE, SEE !

YOU TELL 'IM, DON UGGIE! DESE SKINFACE CREEPS MUST T'INK WE JUS' COME DOWN FROM DA TREES OR SOMETHIN'!

AS FAR AS I'M CONCERNED YOU AND THE EAST SIDE MOB ARE JUST THE SAME—CHEAP HYPER-HOODS. ONE STEP OUT OF LINE AND I'LL COME DOWN ON YOU HARD.

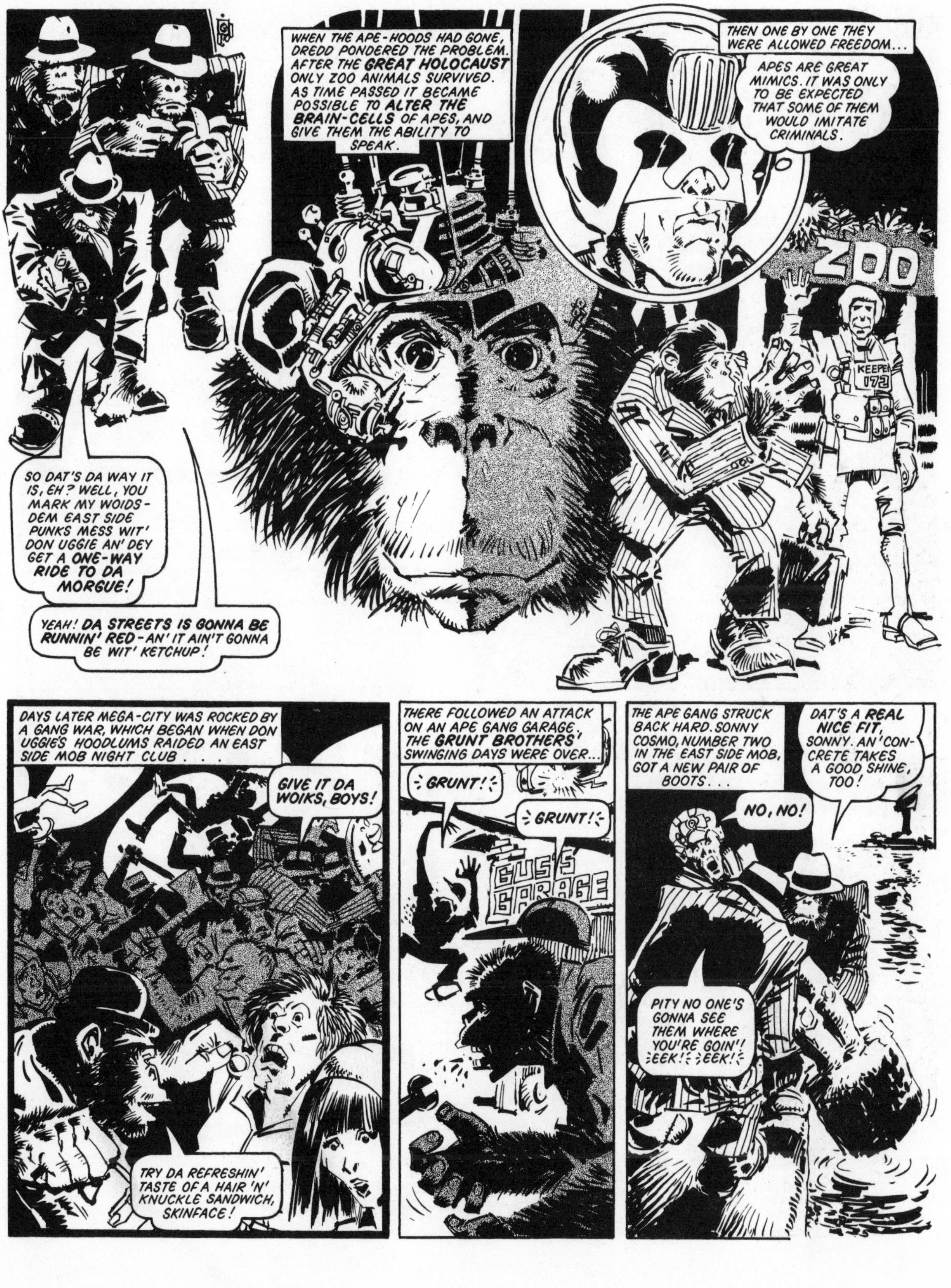

WHEN THE APE-HOODS HAD GONE, DREDD PONDERED THE PROBLEM. AFTER THE **GREAT HOLOCAUST** ONLY ZOO ANIMALS SURVIVED. AS TIME PASSED IT BECAME POSSIBLE TO **ALTER THE BRAIN-CELLS** OF APES, AND GIVE THEM THE ABILITY TO SPEAK.
THEN ONE BY ONE THEY WERE ALLOWED FREEDOM...
APES ARE GREAT MIMICS. IT WAS ONLY TO BE EXPECTED THAT SOME OF THEM WOULD IMITATE CRIMINALS.
ZOO
KEEPER 172
SO DAT'S DA WAY IT IS, EH? WELL, YOU MARK MY WOIDS - DEM EAST SIDE PUNKS MESS WIT' DON UGGIE AN' DEY GET A **ONE-WAY RIDE TO DA MORGUE!**
YEAH! **DA STREETS IS GONNA BE RUNNIN' RED** - AN' IT AIN'T GONNA BE WIT' KETCHUP!
DAYS LATER MEGA-CITY WAS ROCKED BY A GANG WAR, WHICH BEGAN WHEN DON UGGIE'S HOODLUMS RAIDED AN EAST SIDE MOB NIGHT CLUB . . .
GIVE IT DA WOIKS, BOYS!
TRY DA REFRESHIN' TASTE OF A HAIR 'N' KNUCKLE SANDWICH, SKINFACE!
THERE FOLLOWED AN ATTACK ON AN APE GANG GARAGE. THE **GRUNT BROTHERS'** SWINGING DAYS WERE OVER...
GRUNT!
GRUNT!
GUS'S GARAGE
THE APE GANG STRUCK BACK HARD. SONNY COSMO, NUMBER TWO IN THE EAST SIDE MOB, GOT A NEW PAIR OF BOOTS . . .
DAT'S A **REAL NICE FIT**, SONNY. AN' CONCRETE TAKES A GOOD SHINE, TOO!
NO, NO!
PITY NO ONE'S GONNA SEE THEM WHERE YOU'RE GOIN'! EEK! EEK!

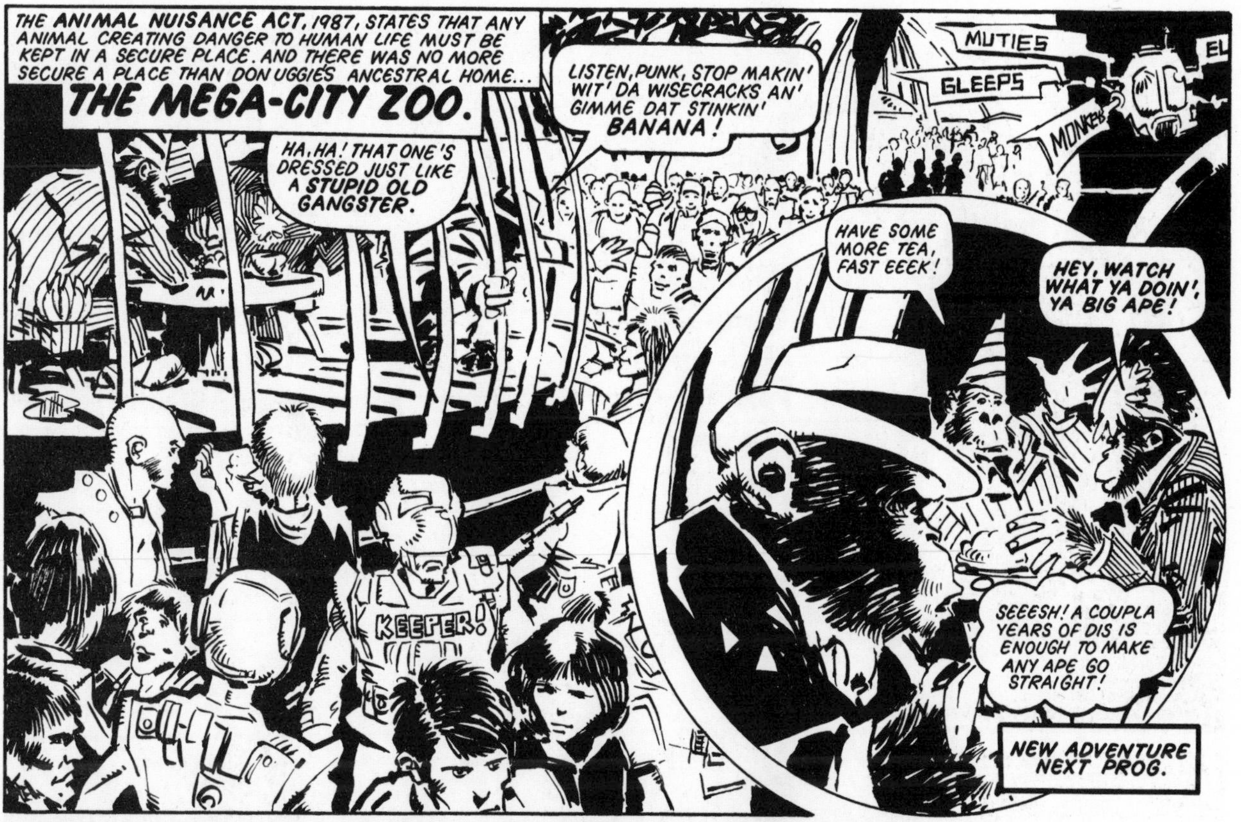
THE ANIMAL NUISANCE ACT, 1987, STATES THAT ANY ANIMAL CREATING DANGER TO HUMAN LIFE MUST BE KEPT IN A SECURE PLACE. AND THERE WAS NO MORE SECURE A PLACE THAN DON UGGIE'S ANCESTRAL HOME...
THE MEGA-CITY ZOO.
LISTEN, PUNK, STOP MAKIN' WIT' DA WISECRACKS AN' GIMME DAT STINKIN' BANANA!
HA, HA! THAT ONE'S DRESSED JUST LIKE A STUPID OLD GANGSTER.
MUTIES
GLEEPS
MONKEYS
HAVE SOME MORE TEA, FAST EEEK!
HEY, WATCH WHAT YA DOIN', YA BIG APE!
KEEPER!
SEEESH! A COUPLA YEARS OF DIS IS ENOUGH TO MAKE ANY APE GO STRAIGHT!
NEW ADVENTURE NEXT PROG.

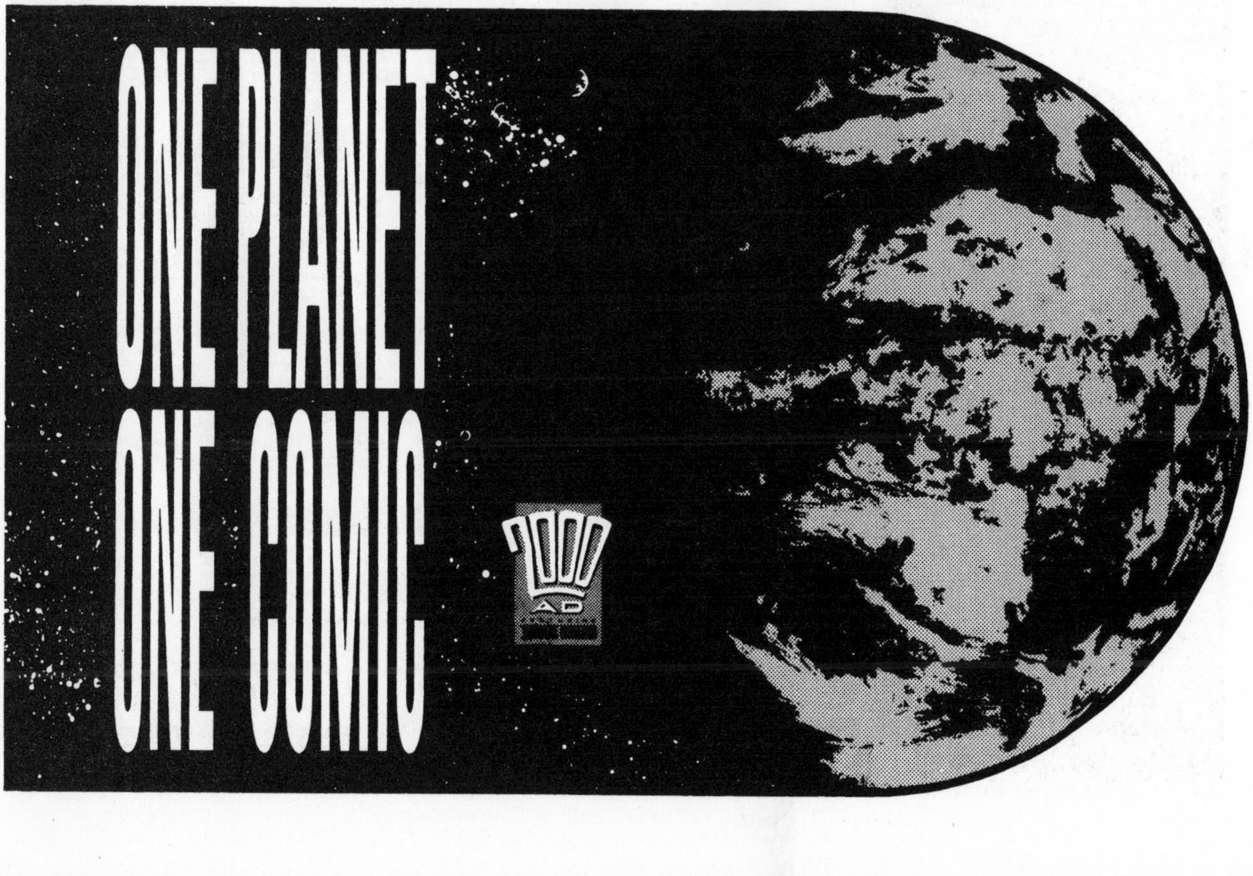
ONE PLANET
ONE COMIC
2000 AD

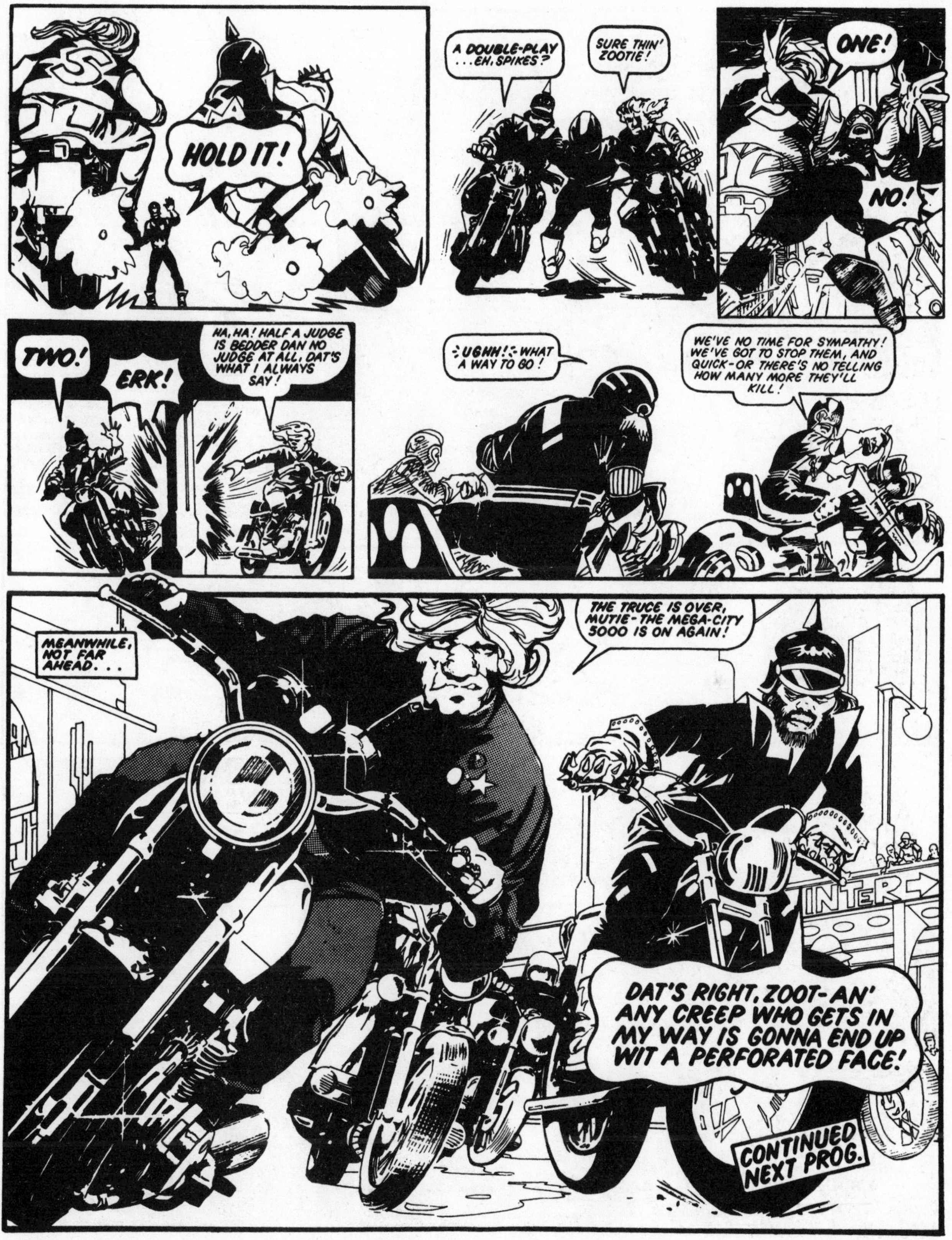
HOLD IT!
A DOUBLE-PLAY ...EH, SPIKES?
SURE THIN' ZOOTIE!
ONE!
NO!
TWO!
ERK!
HA, HA! HALF A JUDGE IS BEDDER DAN NO JUDGE AT ALL, DAT'S WHAT I ALWAYS SAY!
UGHH! WHAT A WAY TO GO!
WE'VE NO TIME FOR SYMPATHY! WE'VE GOT TO STOP THEM, AND QUICK-OR THERE'S NO TELLING HOW MANY MORE THEY'LL KILL!
MEANWHILE, NOT FAR AHEAD...
THE TRUCE IS OVER, MUTIE-THE MEGA-CITY 5000 IS ON AGAIN!
INTER
DAT'S RIGHT, ZOOT-AN' ANY CREEP WHO GETS IN MY WAY IS GONNA END UP WIT A PERFORATED FACE!
CONTINUED NEXT PROG.

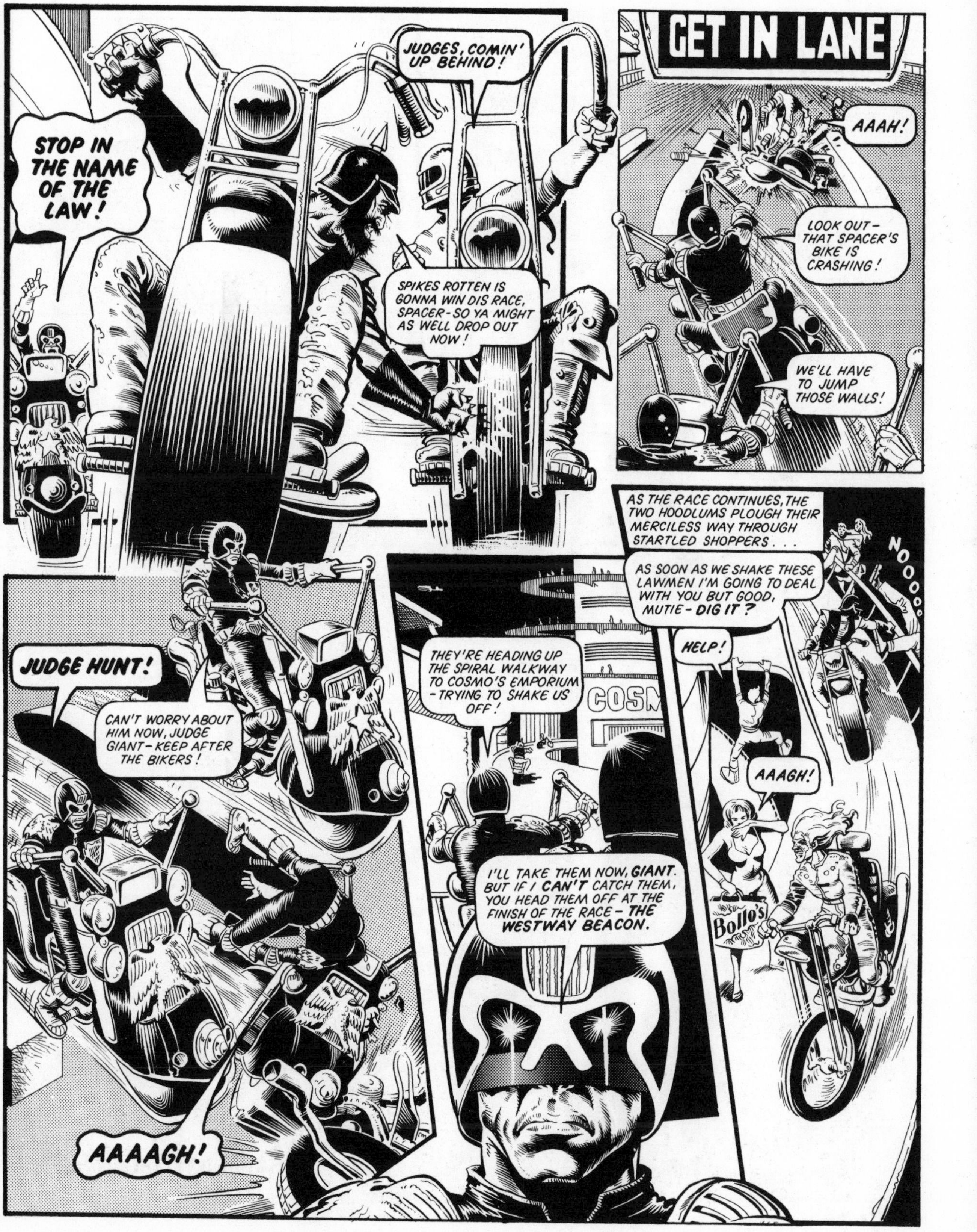

STOP IN THE NAME OF THE LAW!
JUDGES, COMIN' UP BEHIND!
SPIKES ROTTEN IS GONNA WIN DIS RACE, SPACER-SO YA MIGHT AS WELL DROP OUT NOW!
GET IN LANE
AAAH!
LOOK OUT-THAT SPACER'S BIKE IS CRASHING!
WE'LL HAVE TO JUMP THOSE WALLS!
JUDGE HUNT!
CAN'T WORRY ABOUT HIM NOW, JUDGE GIANT-KEEP AFTER THE BIKERS!
AAAAGH!
THEY'RE HEADING UP THE SPIRAL WALKWAY TO COSMO'S EMPORIUM -TRYING TO SHAKE US OFF!
COSM
I'LL TAKE THEM NOW, GIANT. BUT IF I CAN'T CATCH THEM, YOU HEAD THEM OFF AT THE FINISH OF THE RACE- THE WESTWAY BEACON.
AS THE RACE CONTINUES, THE TWO HOODLUMS PLOUGH THEIR MERCILESS WAY THROUGH STARTLED SHOPPERS . . .
AS SOON AS WE SHAKE THESE LAWMEN I'M GOING TO DEAL WITH YOU BUT GOOD, MUTIE- DIG IT?
NOOOOO
HELP!
AAAGH!
Bollo's

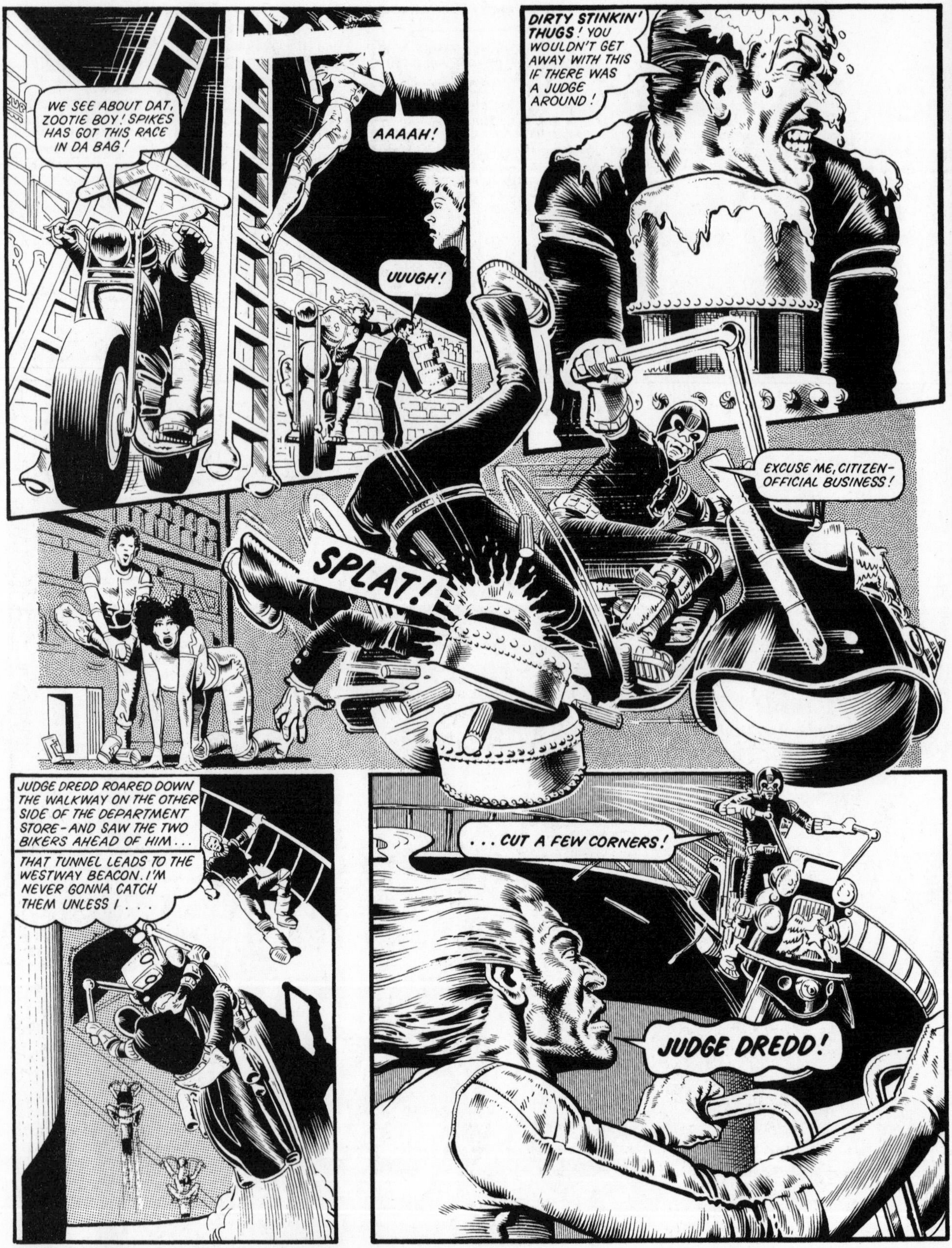
WE SEE ABOUT DAT, ZOOTIE BOY! SPIKES HAS GOT THIS RACE IN DA BAG!
AAAAH!
UUUGH!
DIRTY STINKIN' THUGS! YOU WOULDN'T GET AWAY WITH THIS IF THERE WAS A JUDGE AROUND!
EXCUSE ME, CITIZEN- OFFICIAL BUSINESS!
SPLAT!
JUDGE DREDD ROARED DOWN THE WALKWAY ON THE OTHER SIDE OF THE DEPARTMENT STORE - AND SAW THE TWO BIKERS AHEAD OF HIM...
THAT TUNNEL LEADS TO THE WESTWAY BEACON. I'M NEVER GONNA CATCH THEM UNLESS I . . .
. . . CUT A FEW CORNERS!
JUDGE DREDD!

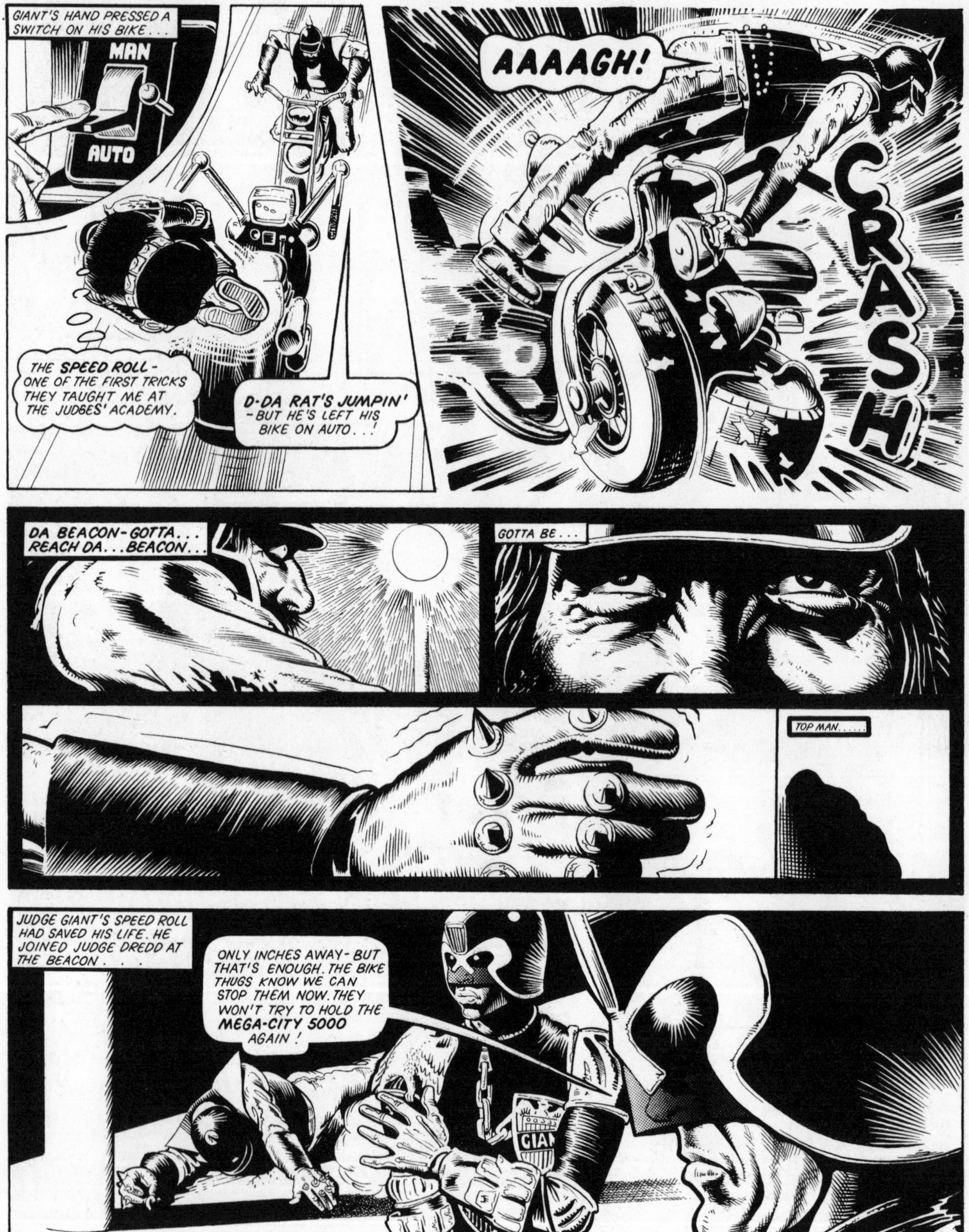
GIANT'S HAND PRESSED A SWITCH ON HIS BIKE...
MAN
AUTO
THE SPEED ROLL - ONE OF THE FIRST TRICKS THEY TAUGHT ME AT THE JUDGES' ACADEMY.
D-DA RAT'S JUMPIN' - BUT HE'S LEFT HIS BIKE ON AUTO...!
AAAAGH!
CRASH
DA BEACON - GOTTA... REACH DA... BEACON...
GOTTA BE...
TOP MAN......
JUDGE GIANT'S SPEED ROLL HAD SAVED HIS LIFE. HE JOINED JUDGE DREDD AT THE BEACON...
ONLY INCHES AWAY - BUT THAT'S ENOUGH. THE BIKE THUGS KNOW WE CAN STOP THEM NOW. THEY WON'T TRY TO HOLD THE MEGA-CITY 5000 AGAIN!
GIANT

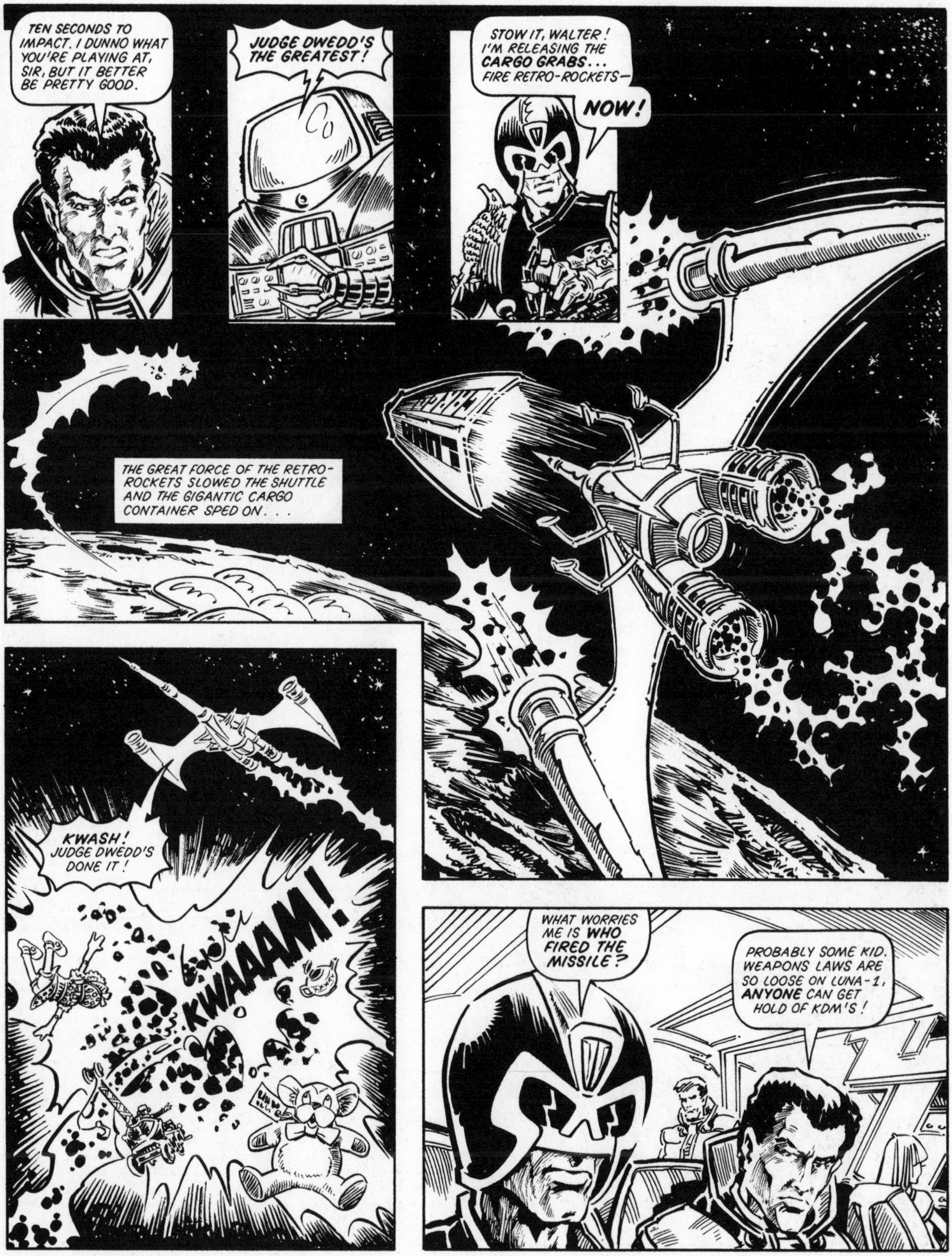
TEN SECONDS TO IMPACT. I DUNNO WHAT YOU'RE PLAYING AT, SIR, BUT IT BETTER BE PRETTY GOOD.
JUDGE DWEDD'S THE GREATEST!
STOW IT, WALTER! I'M RELEASING THE CARGO GRABS... FIRE RETRO-ROCKETS—
NOW!
THE GREAT FORCE OF THE RETRO-ROCKETS SLOWED THE SHUTTLE AND THE GIGANTIC CARGO CONTAINER SPED ON . . .
KWASH! JUDGE DWEDD'S DONE IT!
KWAAAM!
WHAT WORRIES ME IS WHO FIRED THE MISSILE?
PROBABLY SOME KID. WEAPONS LAWS ARE SO LOOSE ON LUNA-1, ANYONE CAN GET HOLD OF KDM'S!

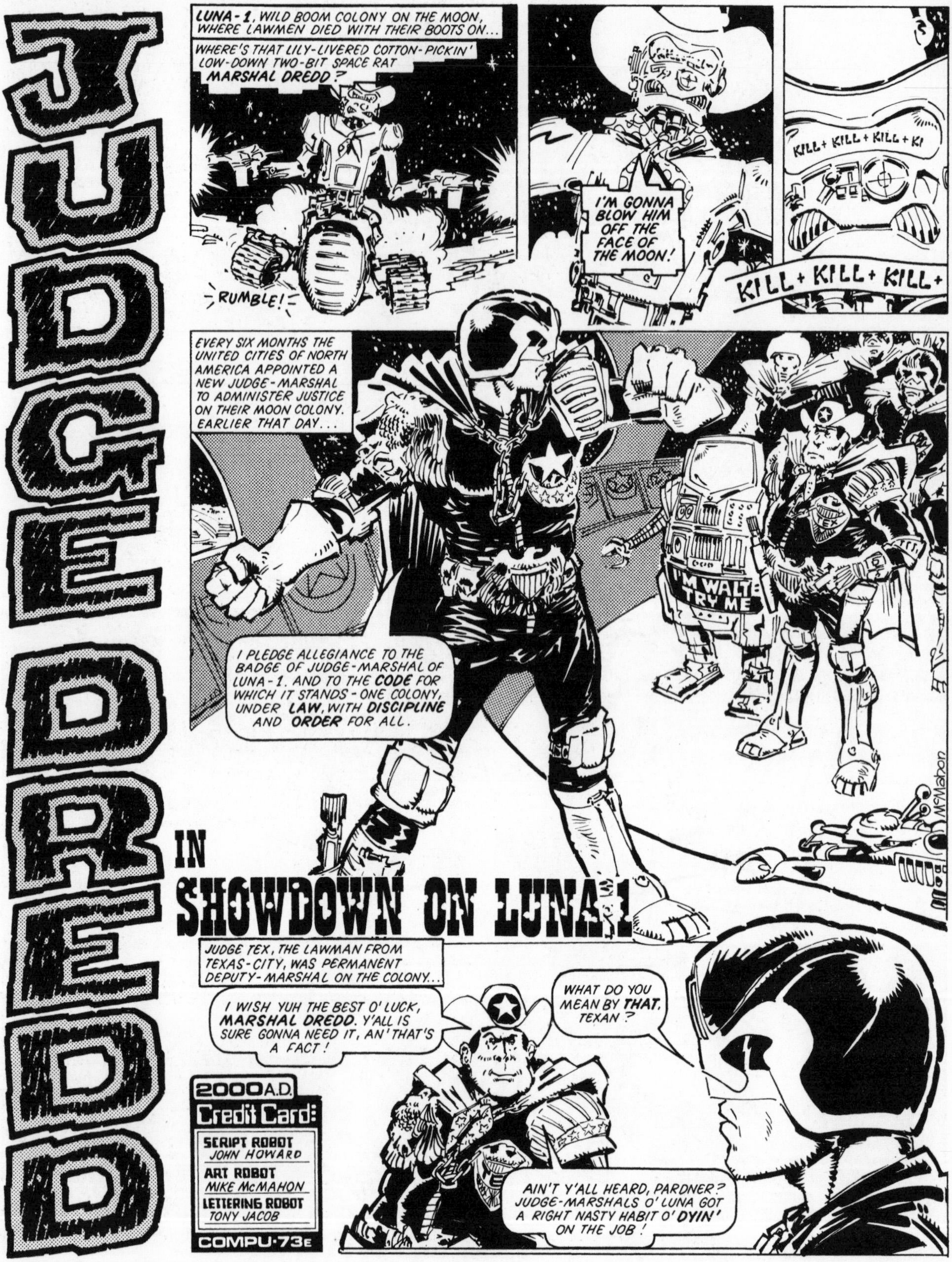
JUDGE DREDD
LUNA-1, WILD BOOM COLONY ON THE MOON, WHERE LAWMEN DIED WITH THEIR BOOTS ON...
WHERE'S THAT LILY-LIVERED COTTON-PICKIN' LOW-DOWN TWO-BIT SPACE RAT MARSHAL DREDD?
RUMBLE!
I'M GONNA BLOW HIM OFF THE FACE OF THE MOON!
KILL + KILL + KILL + KI
KILL + KILL + KILL +
EVERY SIX MONTHS THE UNITED CITIES OF NORTH AMERICA APPOINTED A NEW JUDGE-MARSHAL TO ADMINISTER JUSTICE ON THEIR MOON COLONY. EARLIER THAT DAY...
I'M WALT TRY ME
TEX
I PLEDGE ALLEGIANCE TO THE BADGE OF JUDGE-MARSHAL OF LUNA-1, AND TO THE CODE FOR WHICH IT STANDS - ONE COLONY, UNDER LAW, WITH DISCIPLINE AND ORDER FOR ALL.
McMahon
IN
SHOWDOWN ON LUNA-1
JUDGE TEX, THE LAWMAN FROM TEXAS-CITY, WAS PERMANENT DEPUTY-MARSHAL ON THE COLONY...
I WISH YUH THE BEST O' LUCK, MARSHAL DREDD. Y'ALL IS SURE GONNA NEED IT, AN' THAT'S A FACT!
WHAT DO YOU MEAN BY THAT, TEXAN?
AIN'T Y'ALL HEARD, PARDNER? JUDGE-MARSHALS O' LUNA GOT A RIGHT NASTY HABIT O' DYIN' ON THE JOB!
2000 A.D. Credit Card:
SCRIPT ROBOT JOHN HOWARD
ART ROBOT MIKE McMAHON
LETTERING ROBOT TONY JACOB
COMPU-73E

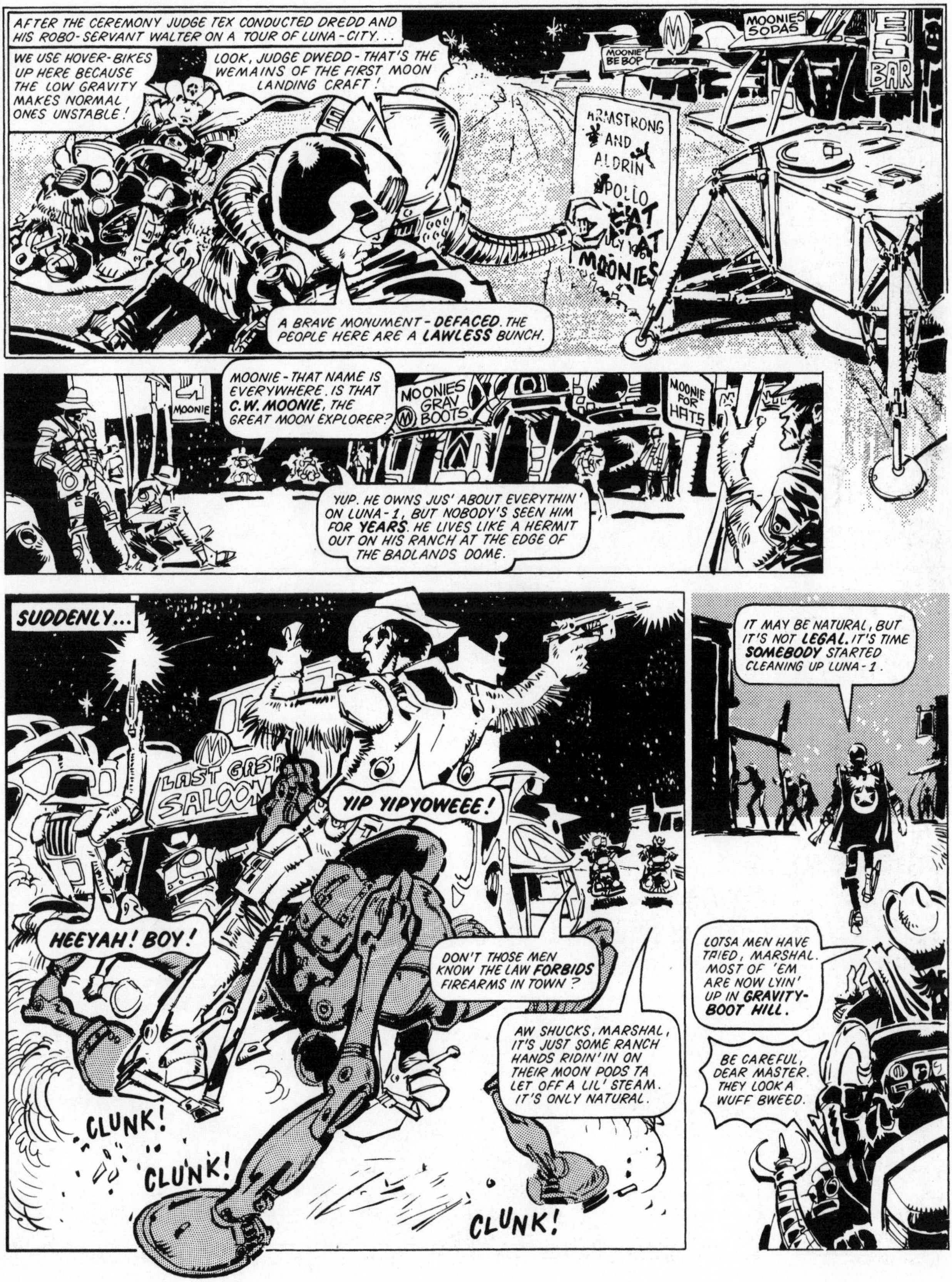
AFTER THE CEREMONY JUDGE TEX CONDUCTED DREDD AND HIS ROBO-SERVANT WALTER ON A TOUR OF LUNA-CITY...
WE USE HOVER-BIKES UP HERE BECAUSE THE LOW GRAVITY MAKES NORMAL ONES UNSTABLE!
LOOK, JUDGE DWEDD - THAT'S THE WEMAINS OF THE FIRST MOON LANDING CRAFT!
MOONIES SODAS
MOONIE BE BOP
BAR
ARMSTRONG AND ALDRIN
MOONIES
A BRAVE MONUMENT - DEFACED. THE PEOPLE HERE ARE A LAWLESS BUNCH.
MOONIE - THAT NAME IS EVERYWHERE. IS THAT C.W. MOONIE, THE GREAT MOON EXPLORER?
MOONIE
MOONIES GRAV BOOTS
MOONIE FOR HATS
YUP. HE OWNS JUS' ABOUT EVERYTHIN' ON LUNA-1, BUT NOBODY'S SEEN HIM FOR YEARS. HE LIVES LIKE A HERMIT OUT ON HIS RANCH AT THE EDGE OF THE BADLANDS DOME.
SUDDENLY...
LAST GASP SALOON
YIP YIPYOWEEE!
HEEYAH! BOY!
DON'T THOSE MEN KNOW THE LAW FORBIDS FIREARMS IN TOWN?
AW SHUCKS, MARSHAL, IT'S JUST SOME RANCH HANDS RIDIN' IN ON THEIR MOON PODS TA LET OFF A LIL' STEAM. IT'S ONLY NATURAL.
CLUNK!
CLUNK!
CLUNK!
IT MAY BE NATURAL, BUT IT'S NOT LEGAL. IT'S TIME SOMEBODY STARTED CLEANING UP LUNA-1.
LOTSA MEN HAVE TRIED, MARSHAL. MOST OF 'EM ARE NOW LYIN' UP IN GRAVITY-BOOT HILL.
BE CAREFUL, DEAR MASTER. THEY LOOK A WUFF BWEED.

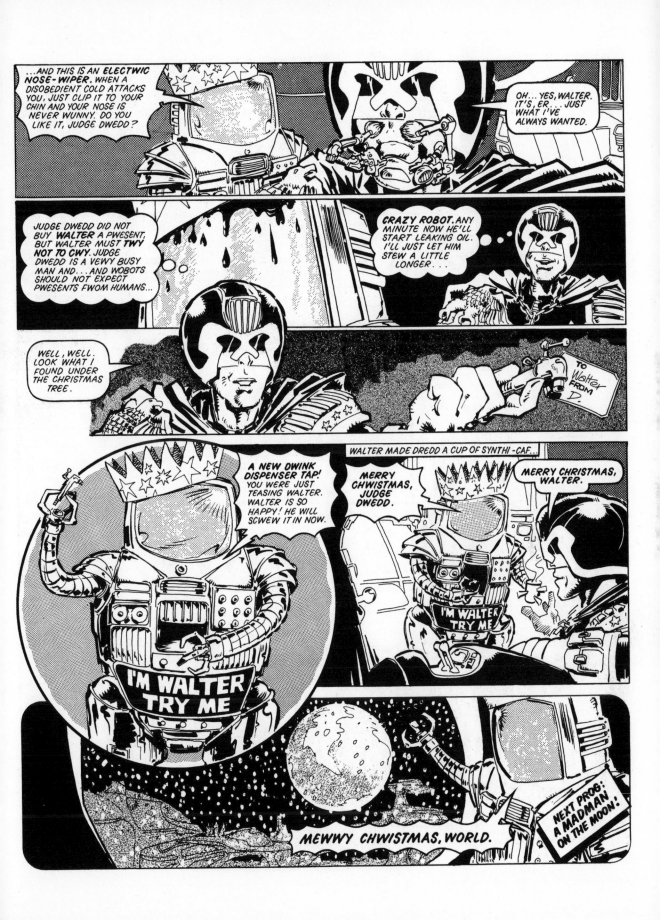

2000 A.D.
Credit Card:

SCRIPT ROBOT
JOHN HOWARD

ART ROBOT
IAN GIBSON

LETTERING ROBOT
TONY JACOB

COMPU-73E

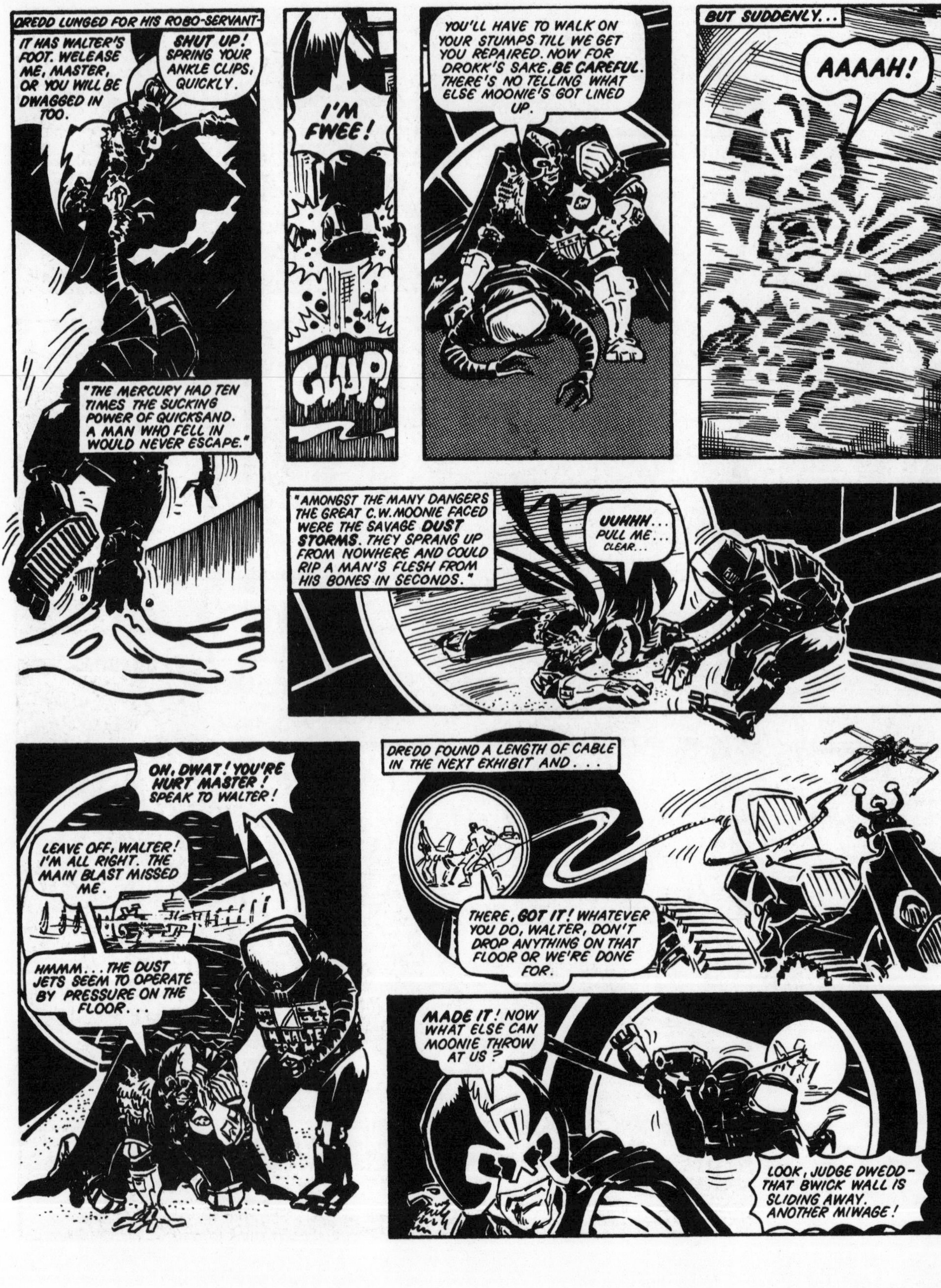
DREDD LUNGED FOR HIS ROBO-SERVANT-
IT HAS WALTER'S FOOT. WELEASE ME, MASTER, OR YOU WILL BE DWAGGED IN TOO.
SHUT UP! SPRING YOUR ANKLE CLIPS, QUICKLY.
"THE MERCURY HAD TEN TIMES THE SUCKING POWER OF QUICKSAND. A MAN WHO FELL IN WOULD NEVER ESCAPE."
I'M FWEE!
GLUP!
YOU'LL HAVE TO WALK ON YOUR STUMPS TILL WE GET YOU REPAIRED. NOW FOR DROKK'S SAKE, BE CAREFUL. THERE'S NO TELLING WHAT ELSE MOONIE'S GOT LINED UP.
BUT SUDDENLY...
AAAAH!
"AMONGST THE MANY DANGERS THE GREAT C.W. MOONIE FACED WERE THE SAVAGE DUST STORMS. THEY SPRANG UP FROM NOWHERE AND COULD RIP A MAN'S FLESH FROM HIS BONES IN SECONDS."
UUHHH... PULL ME... CLEAR...
OH, DWAT! YOU'RE HURT MASTER! SPEAK TO WALTER!
LEAVE OFF, WALTER! I'M ALL RIGHT. THE MAIN BLAST MISSED ME.
HMMM... THE DUST JETS SEEM TO OPERATE BY PRESSURE ON THE FLOOR...
DREDD FOUND A LENGTH OF CABLE IN THE NEXT EXHIBIT AND...
THERE, GOT IT! WHATEVER YOU DO, WALTER, DON'T DROP ANYTHING ON THAT FLOOR OR WE'RE DONE FOR.
MADE IT! NOW WHAT ELSE CAN MOONIE THROW AT US?
LOOK, JUDGE DWEDD- THAT BWICK WALL IS SLIDING AWAY. ANOTHER MIWAGE!

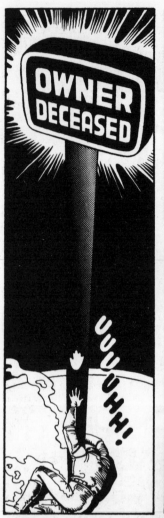

OWNER DECEASED

UUUUHH!

SOON EVERY PLOT WAS CLAIMED. DREDD SPENT THE REST OF THE DAY SETTLING DISPUTES...

YOU'RE BOTH UNDER ARREST FOR FIGHTING. THIS PLOT WILL NOW GO TO THE HIGHEST BIDDER.

THEES EES THE TENTH CLAIM TOUT SO FAR. I'LL RUN HEEM OUT OF THE TERREETORY WEETH THE REST.

I BUY AND SELL CLAIMS BEST PRICES PAID FOR CHOICE PLOTS

THAT NIGHT, WALTER, JUDGE DREDD'S ROBO-SERVANT, WAS WAITING IN DREDD'S COMMAND TENT...

THIS IS WOWENA, THE WAITWESS WOBOT, MASTER. SHE HAS A DWEADFUL CWIME TO WEPORT.

MY MISTREES IS WIDOW SPOCK, SIR. SHE CLAIMED A GOOD MAIN STREET SITE TO BUILD A FLAPJACK PARLOUR. BUT THIS AFTERNOON THREE MEN CAME TO SEE HER...

I'M WALTER TRY ME

CALL ME ROWENA

THE MEN HAD DEMANDED THE WIDOW SPOCK'S CLAIM...

YOU BETTER SELL THE SITE, LADY. WE REPRESENT THE INTERSTELLAR PSIONICS CORPORATIONS AND IPC DON'T TAKE NO FOR AN ANSWER.

YOU'VE GOT TILL TOMORROW TO SIGN THEM PAPERS.

MY MISTRESS WAS FRIGHTENED TO COME TO YOU, SIR, BUT AS A LOYAL ROBOT IT IS MY DUTY TO...

THAT'S ENOUGH! WALTER, YOU SHOULD KNOW BETTER THAN TO BRING THIS ROBOT HERE. I CAN'T ACT ON A CRIME REPORTED BY A MACHINE.

UNLESS WIDOW SPOCK COMES TO ME HERSELF, THE MATTER'S CLOSED NOW GET HER - OR IT - OUT OF HERE!

WALTER RECONNECTED ROWENA...

IT WAS ALL A CWAFTY TRICK BY JUDGE DWEDD, WOWENA. AND WALTER HELPED TOO.

OH, WALTER, MY HERO.

ROWENA PAID ANOTHER VISIT TO JUDGE DREDD'S TENT...

MY MISTRESS IS VERY GRATEFUL, SIR. SHE MADE THESE COOKIES SPECIALLY FOR YOU!

ER, PUT THEM DOWN OVER THERE, ROWENA, AND GIVE YOUR MISTRESS MY THANKS.

JUDGE DREDD'S LAWMAN'S INSTINCT DETECTED SOMETHING ODD...

HMMM...THESE COOKIES WERE MADE BY A ROBOT...

SO, ROWENA WAS LYING. SHE WAS JUST LOOKING FOR AN EXCUSE TO VISIT MY TENT... BUT WHY?

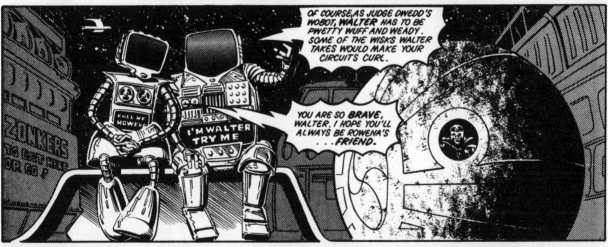

OF COURSE, AS JUDGE DWEDD'S WOBOT, WALTER HAS TO BE PWETTY WUFF AND WEADY. SOME OF THE WISKS WALTER TAKES WOULD MAKE YOUR CIRCUITS CURL.

YOU ARE SO BRAVE, WALTER. I HOPE YOU'LL ALWAYS BE ROWENA'S ...FRIEND.

CALL ME WOWENA

I'M WALTER TRY ME

ROBOTS IN LOVE! RIDICULOUS! STILL, I SUPPOSE WE SHOULD HAVE KNOWN THIS WAS COMING THE DAY WE GAVE ROBOTS HUMAN-LIKE PERSONALITIES.

STILL, IF IT KEEPS WALTER OUT OF MY HAIR, I'M ALL FOR IT.

NEXT PROG. THE OXYGEN DESERT.

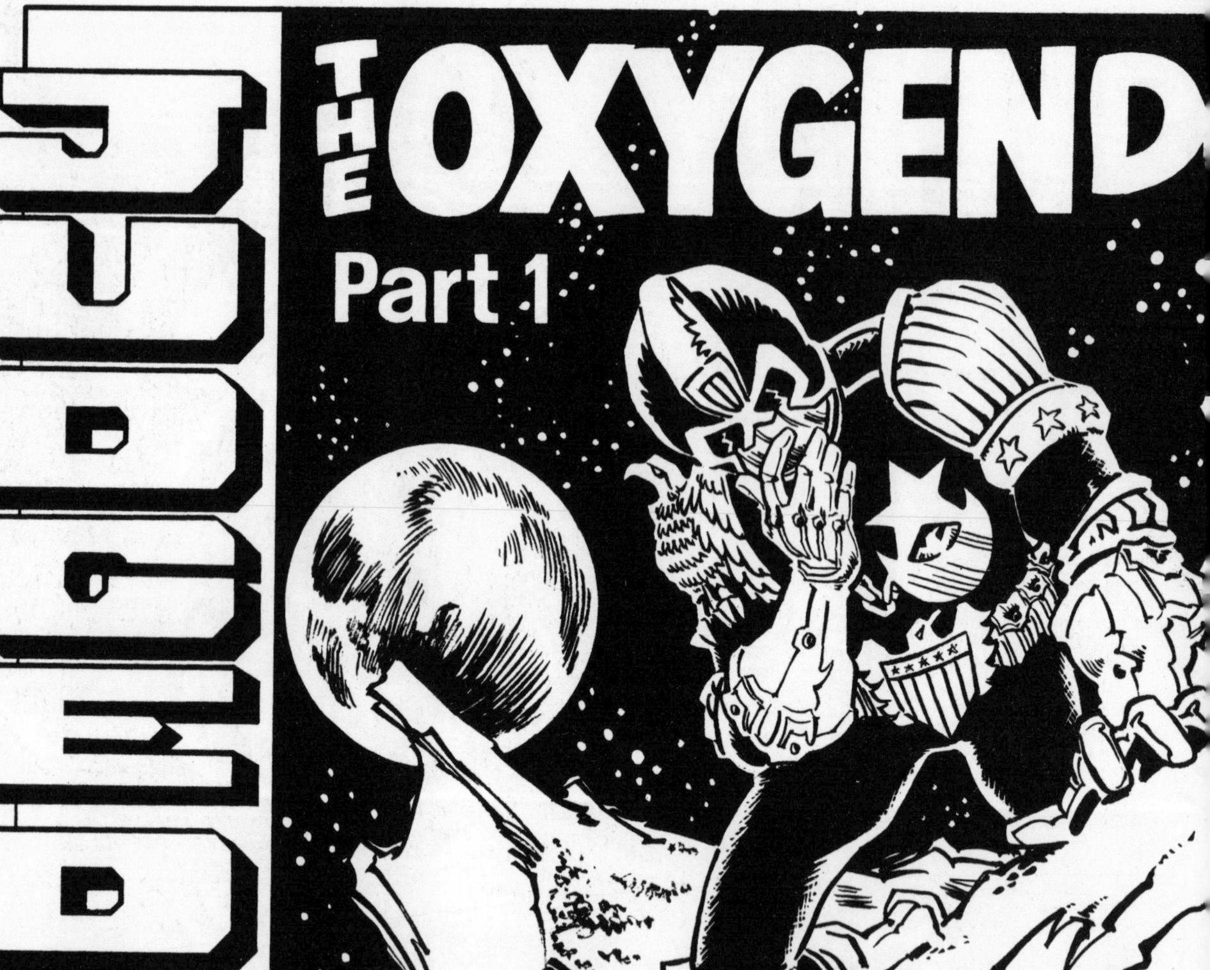
THE OXYGEND
Part 1
2000 A.D.
Credit Card:
SCRIPT ROBOT JOHN HOWARD
ART ROBOT IAN GIBSON
LETTERING ROBOT TONY JACOB
COMPU-73E
..."PRESIDING OVER THE MINOR COMPLA
COURT, ONE OF MY MORE UNPLEASANT D
...THAT'S RIGHT, MARSHAL SIR. THE DWARF BIT ME IN THE KNEE, HE DID.
I'LL BITE YOUR KNE
YOU CALL ME A D
AGAIN, YOU GREAT
STREAK OF NOT
QUIET!

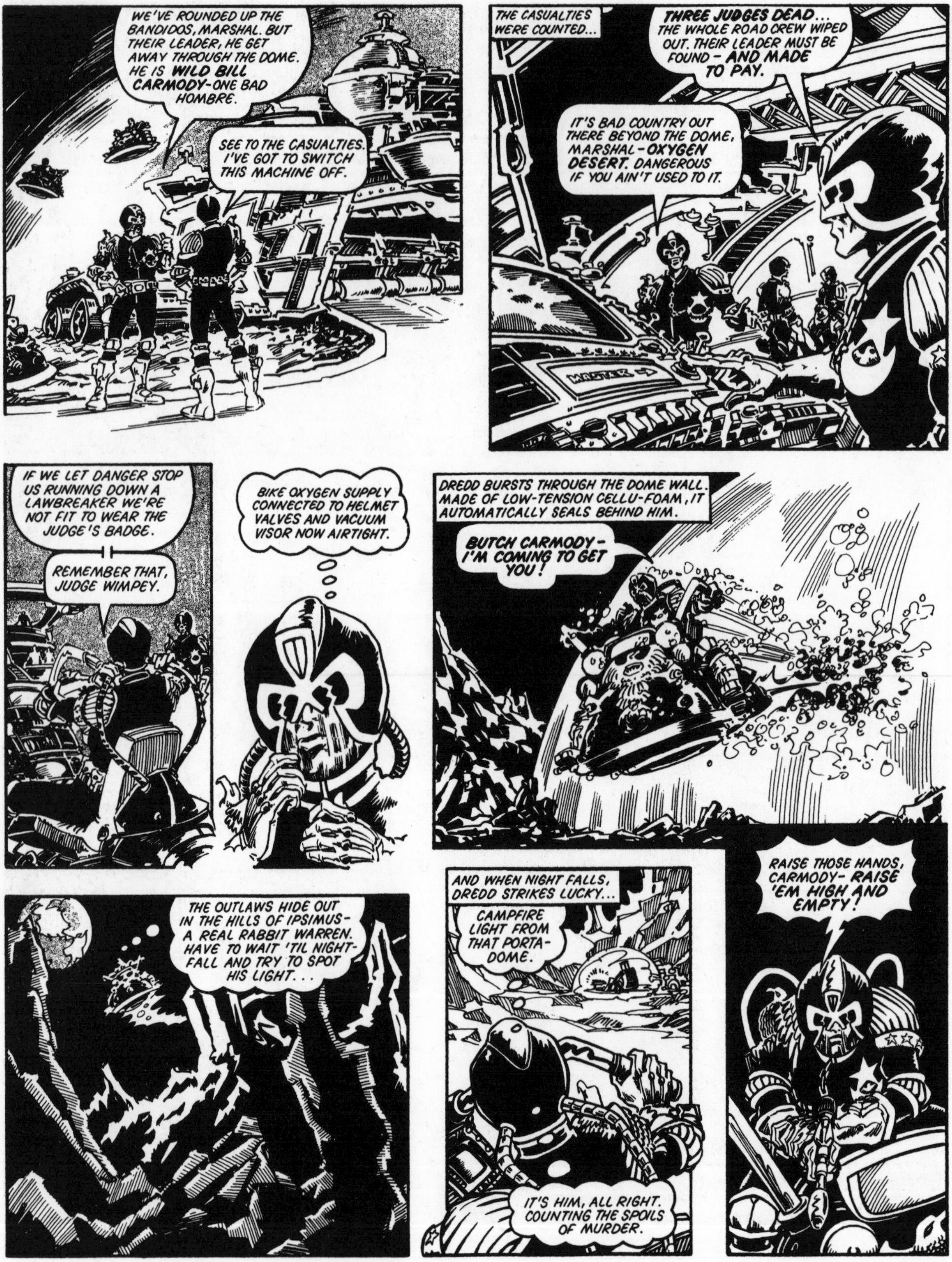
WE'VE ROUNDED UP THE BANDIDOS, MARSHAL. BUT THEIR LEADER, HE GET AWAY THROUGH THE DOME. HE IS WILD BILL CARMODY-ONE BAD HOMBRE.
SEE TO THE CASUALTIES. I'VE GOT TO SWITCH THIS MACHINE OFF.
THE CASUALTIES WERE COUNTED...
THREE JUDGES DEAD... THE WHOLE ROAD CREW WIPED OUT. THEIR LEADER MUST BE FOUND - AND MADE TO PAY.
IT'S BAD COUNTRY OUT THERE BEYOND THE DOME, MARSHAL - OXYGEN DESERT. DANGEROUS IF YOU AIN'T USED TO IT.
IF WE LET DANGER STOP US RUNNING DOWN A LAWBREAKER WE'RE NOT FIT TO WEAR THE JUDGE'S BADGE.
REMEMBER THAT, JUDGE WIMPEY.
BIKE OXYGEN SUPPLY CONNECTED TO HELMET VALVES AND VACUUM VISOR NOW AIRTIGHT.
DREDD BURSTS THROUGH THE DOME WALL. MADE OF LOW-TENSION CELLU-FOAM, IT AUTOMATICALLY SEALS BEHIND HIM.
BUTCH CARMODY - I'M COMING TO GET YOU!
THE OUTLAWS HIDE OUT IN THE HILLS OF IPSIMUS - A REAL RABBIT WARREN. HAVE TO WAIT 'TIL NIGHT-FALL AND TRY TO SPOT HIS LIGHT...
AND WHEN NIGHT FALLS, DREDD STRIKES LUCKY...
CAMPFIRE LIGHT FROM THAT PORTA-DOME.
IT'S HIM, ALL RIGHT. COUNTING THE SPOILS OF MURDER.
RAISE THOSE HANDS, CARMODY- RAISE 'EM HIGH AND EMPTY!

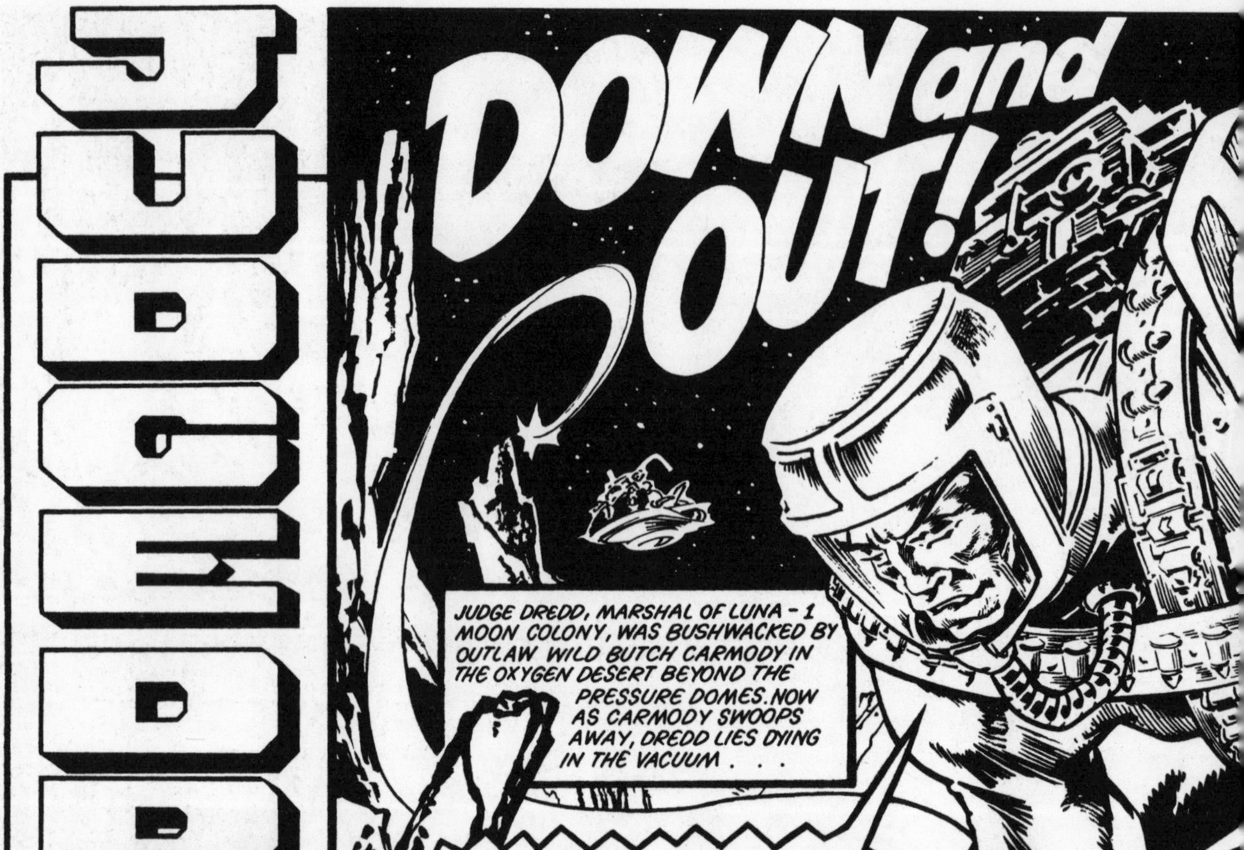
JUDGE DREDD
OXYGEN DESERT Part 2
DOWN and OUT!
JUDGE DREDD, MARSHAL OF LUNA-1 MOON COLONY, WAS BUSHWACKED BY OUTLAW WILD BUTCH CARMODY IN THE OXYGEN DESERT BEYOND THE PRESSURE DOMES. NOW AS CARMODY SWOOPS AWAY, DREDD LIES DYING IN THE VACUUM . . .
GOODBYE, DREDD! YOU DON'T GET A SECOND CHANCE IN THE OXYGEN DESERT! HA, HA, HA!

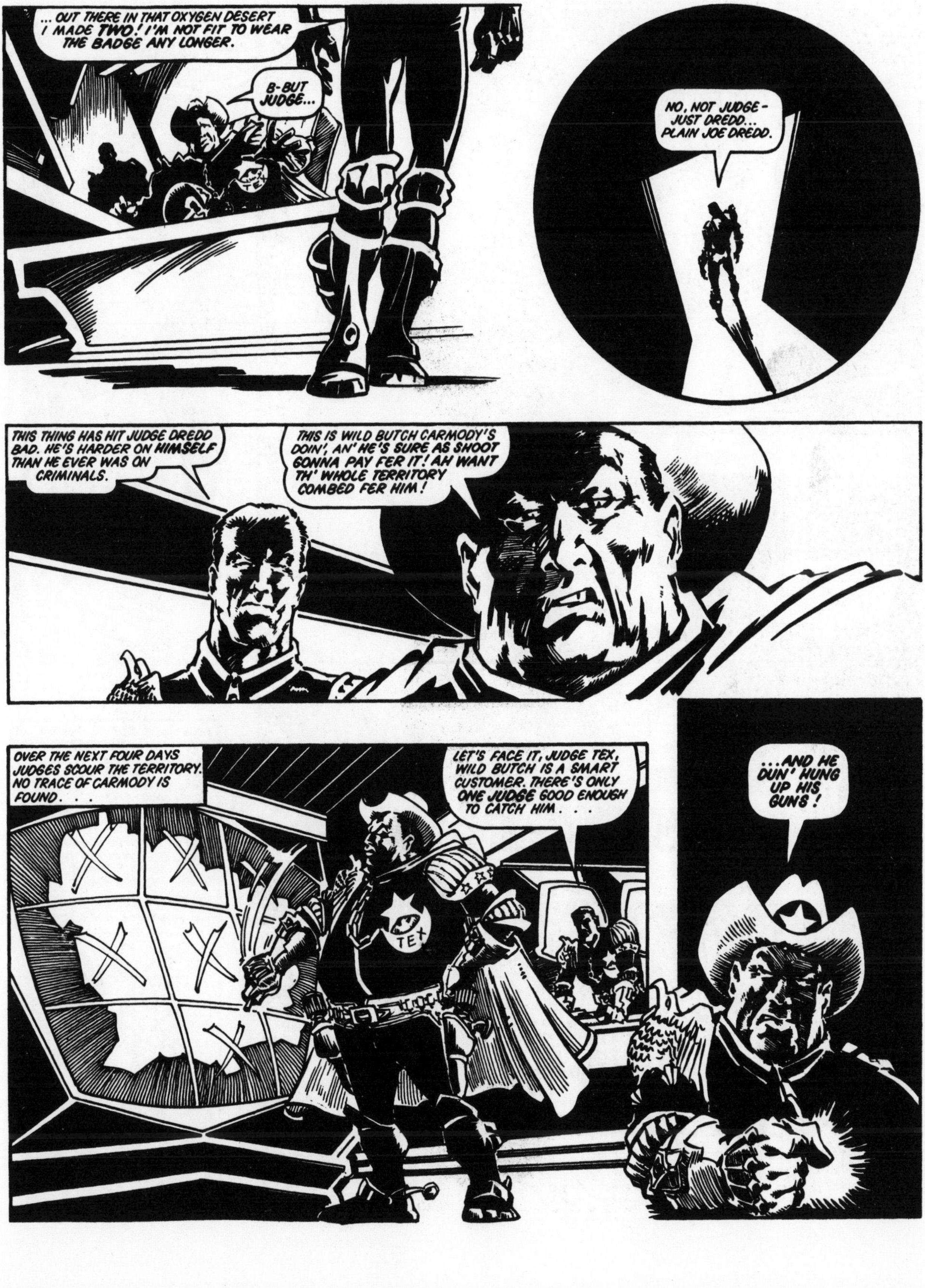

... OUT THERE IN THAT OXYGEN DESERT I MADE TWO! I'M NOT FIT TO WEAR THE BADGE ANY LONGER.
B-BUT JUDGE...
NO, NOT JUDGE - JUST DREDD... PLAIN JOE DREDD.
THIS THING HAS HIT JUDGE DREDD BAD. HE'S HARDER ON HIMSELF THAN HE EVER WAS ON CRIMINALS.
THIS IS WILD BUTCH CARMODY'S DOIN', AN' HE'S SURE AS SHOOT GONNA PAY FER IT! AH WANT TH' WHOLE TERRITORY COMBED FER HIM!
OVER THE NEXT FOUR DAYS JUDGES SCOUR THE TERRITORY. NO TRACE OF CARMODY IS FOUND . . .
LET'S FACE IT, JUDGE TEX, WILD BUTCH IS A SMART CUSTOMER. THERE'S ONLY ONE JUDGE GOOD ENOUGH TO CATCH HIM . . .
TEX
. . . AND HE DUN' HUNG UP HIS GUNS !

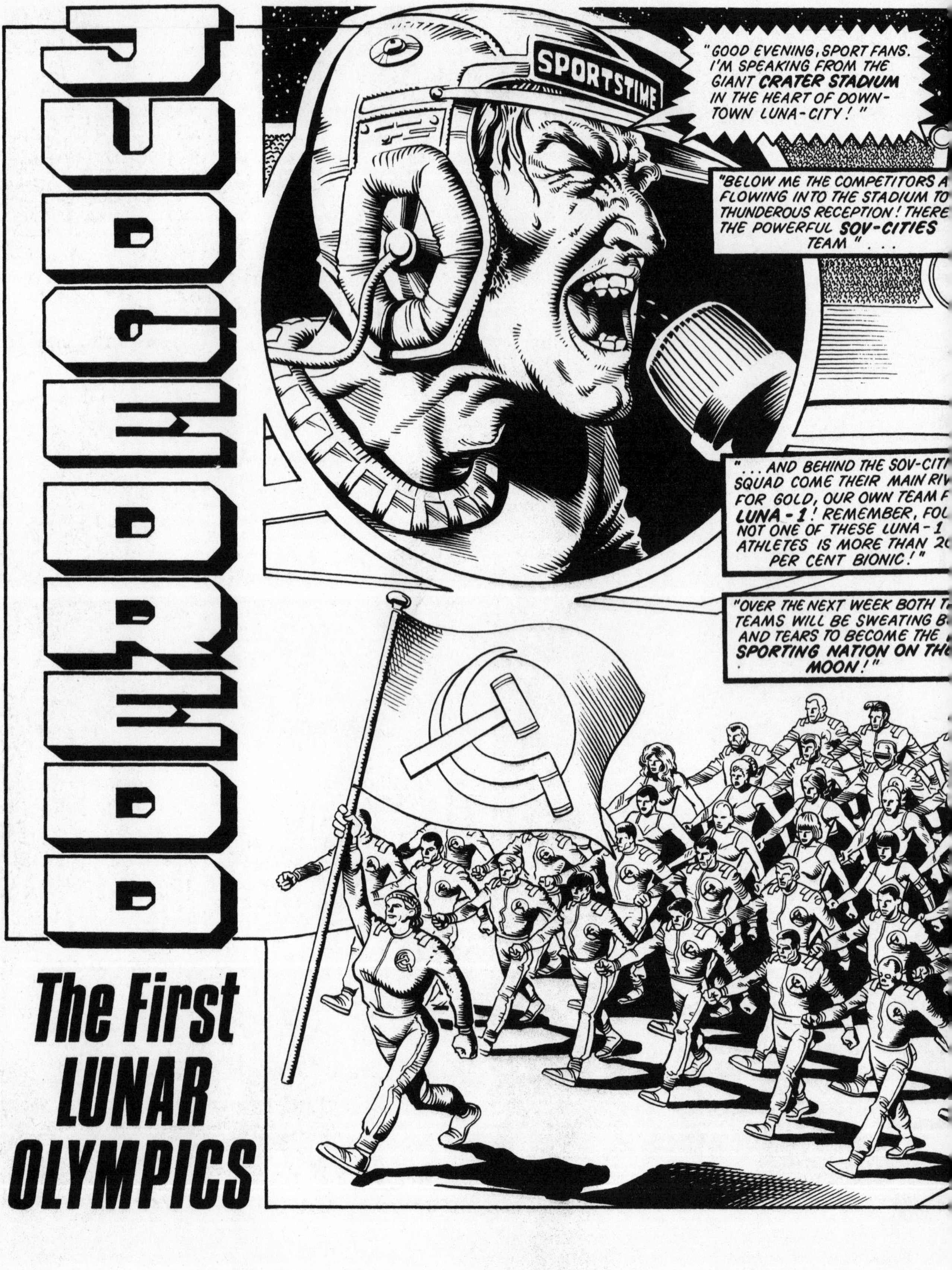
JUDGE DREDD
The First LUNAR OLYMPICS
SPORTSTIME
"GOOD EVENING, SPORT FANS. I'M SPEAKING FROM THE GIANT CRATER STADIUM IN THE HEART OF DOWN-TOWN LUNA-CITY!"
"BELOW ME THE COMPETITORS A FLOWING INTO THE STADIUM TO THUNDEROUS RECEPTION! THERE THE POWERFUL SOV-CITIES TEAM"...
"...AND BEHIND THE SOV-CITI SQUAD COME THEIR MAIN RIV FOR GOLD, OUR OWN TEAM F LUNA-1! REMEMBER, FOL NOT ONE OF THESE LUNA-1 ATHLETES IS MORE THAN 20 PER CENT BIONIC!"
"OVER THE NEXT WEEK BOTH T TEAMS WILL BE SWEATING B AND TEARS TO BECOME THE SPORTING NATION ON TH MOON!"

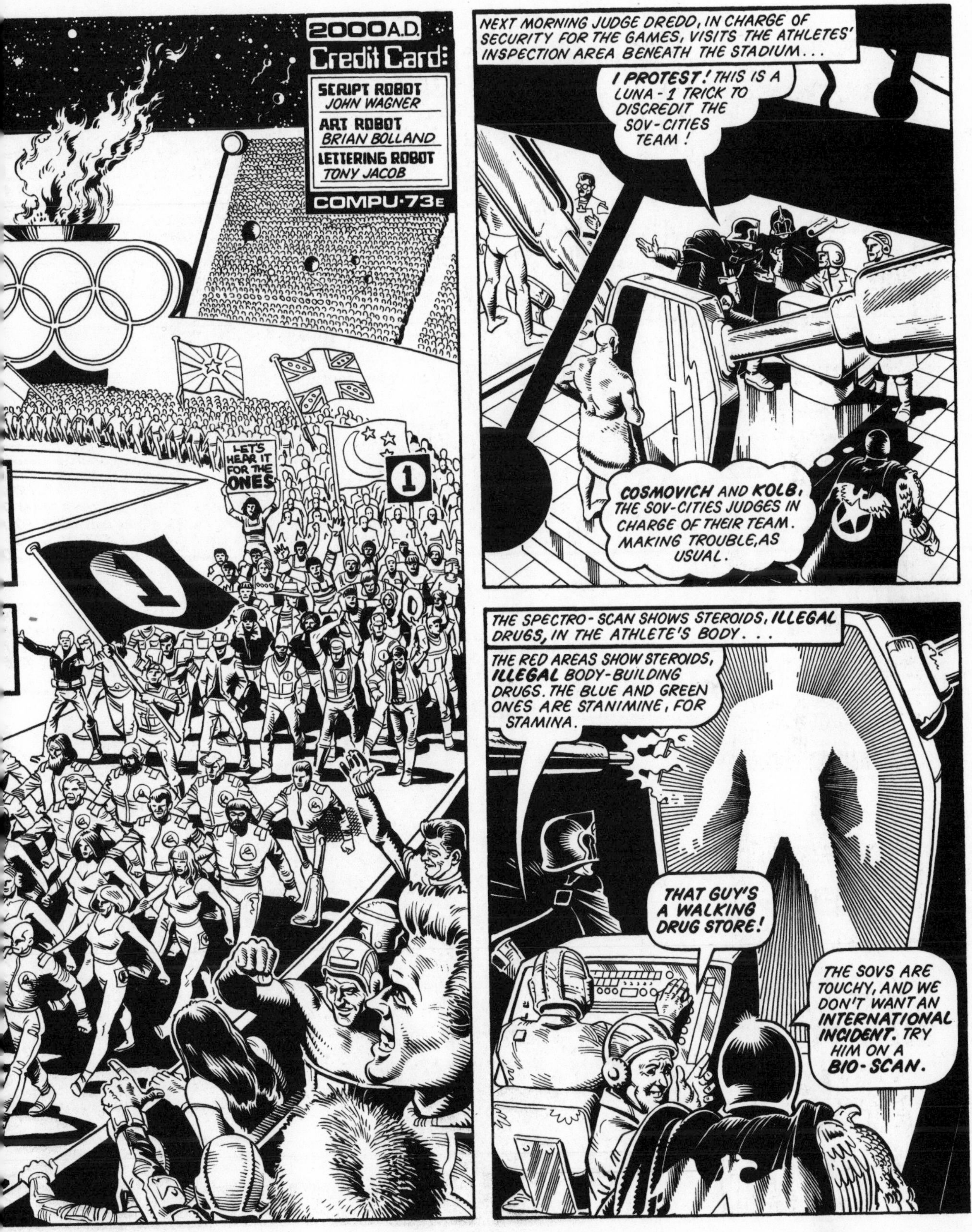
2000 A.D.
Credit Card:
SCRIPT ROBOT JOHN WAGNER
ART ROBOT BRIAN BOLLAND
LETTERING ROBOT TONY JACOB
COMPU·73E
LET'S HEAR IT FOR THE ONES
NEXT MORNING JUDGE DREDD, IN CHARGE OF SECURITY FOR THE GAMES, VISITS THE ATHLETES' INSPECTION AREA BENEATH THE STADIUM...
I PROTEST! THIS IS A LUNA-1 TRICK TO DISCREDIT THE SOV-CITIES TEAM!
COSMOVICH AND KOLB, THE SOV-CITIES JUDGES IN CHARGE OF THEIR TEAM. MAKING TROUBLE, AS USUAL.
THE SPECTRO-SCAN SHOWS STEROIDS, ILLEGAL DRUGS, IN THE ATHLETE'S BODY...
THE RED AREAS SHOW STEROIDS, ILLEGAL BODY-BUILDING DRUGS. THE BLUE AND GREEN ONES ARE STANIMINE, FOR STAMINA.
THAT GUY'S A WALKING DRUG STORE!
THE SOVS ARE TOUCHY, AND WE DON'T WANT AN INTERNATIONAL INCIDENT. TRY HIM ON A BIO-SCAN.

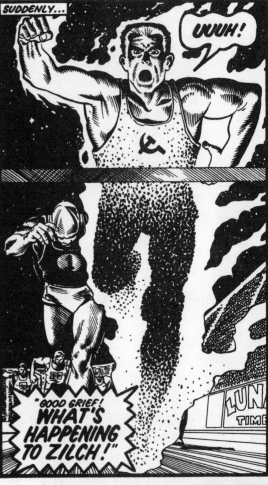

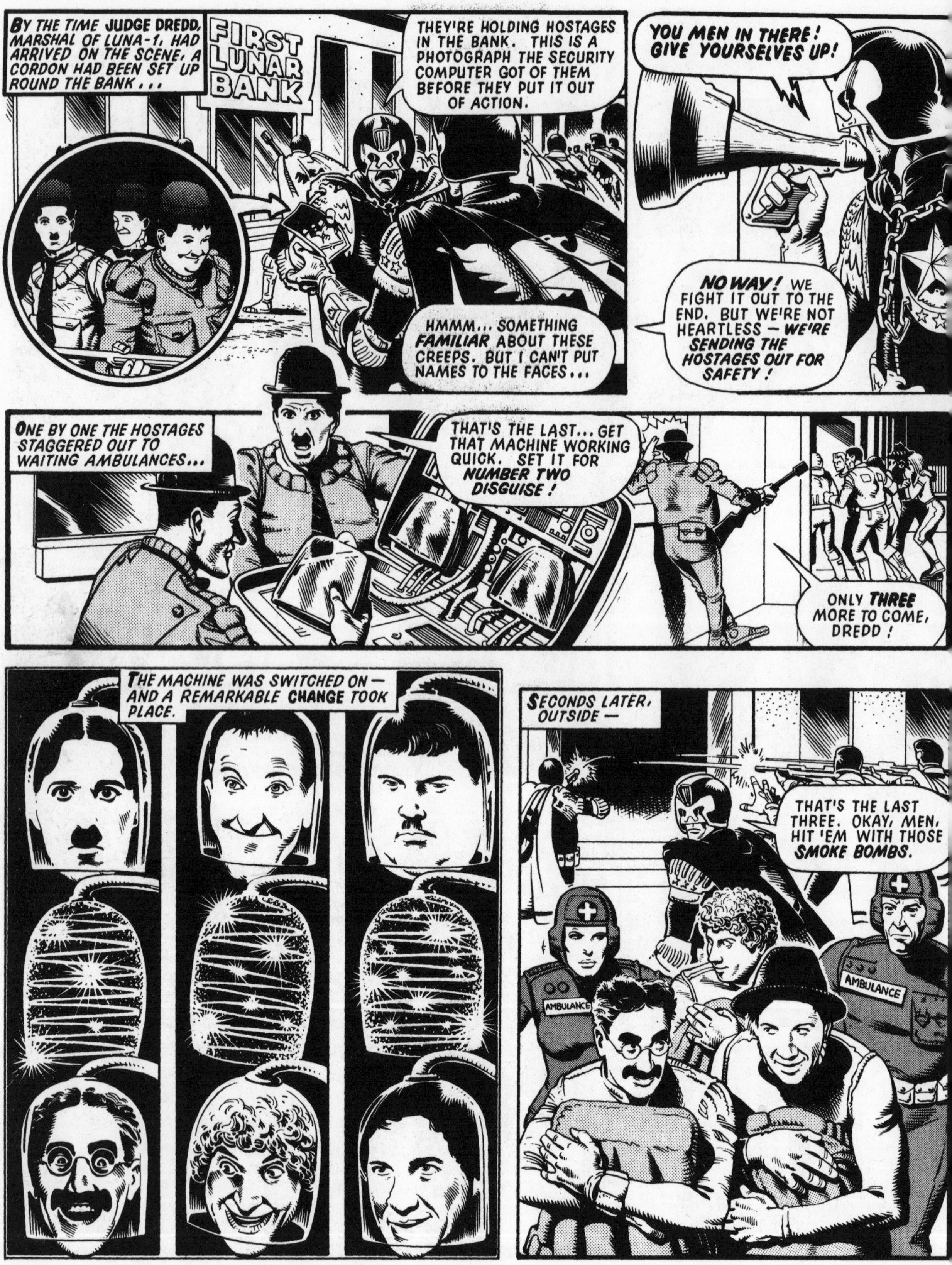

BY THE TIME JUDGE DREDD, MARSHAL OF LUNA-1, HAD ARRIVED ON THE SCENE, A CORDON HAD BEEN SET UP ROUND THE BANK...
FIRST LUNAR BANK
THEY'RE HOLDING HOSTAGES IN THE BANK. THIS IS A PHOTOGRAPH THE SECURITY COMPUTER GOT OF THEM BEFORE THEY PUT IT OUT OF ACTION.
HMMM... SOMETHING FAMILIAR ABOUT THESE CREEPS. BUT I CAN'T PUT NAMES TO THE FACES...
YOU MEN IN THERE! GIVE YOURSELVES UP!
NO WAY! WE FIGHT IT OUT TO THE END. BUT WE'RE NOT HEARTLESS — WE'RE SENDING THE HOSTAGES OUT FOR SAFETY!
ONE BY ONE THE HOSTAGES STAGGERED OUT TO WAITING AMBULANCES...
THAT'S THE LAST... GET THAT MACHINE WORKING QUICK. SET IT FOR NUMBER TWO DISGUISE!
ONLY THREE MORE TO COME, DREDD!
THE MACHINE WAS SWITCHED ON — AND A REMARKABLE CHANGE TOOK PLACE.
SECONDS LATER, OUTSIDE —
THAT'S THE LAST THREE. OKAY, MEN, HIT 'EM WITH THOSE SMOKE BOMBS.
AMBULANCE
AMBULANCE

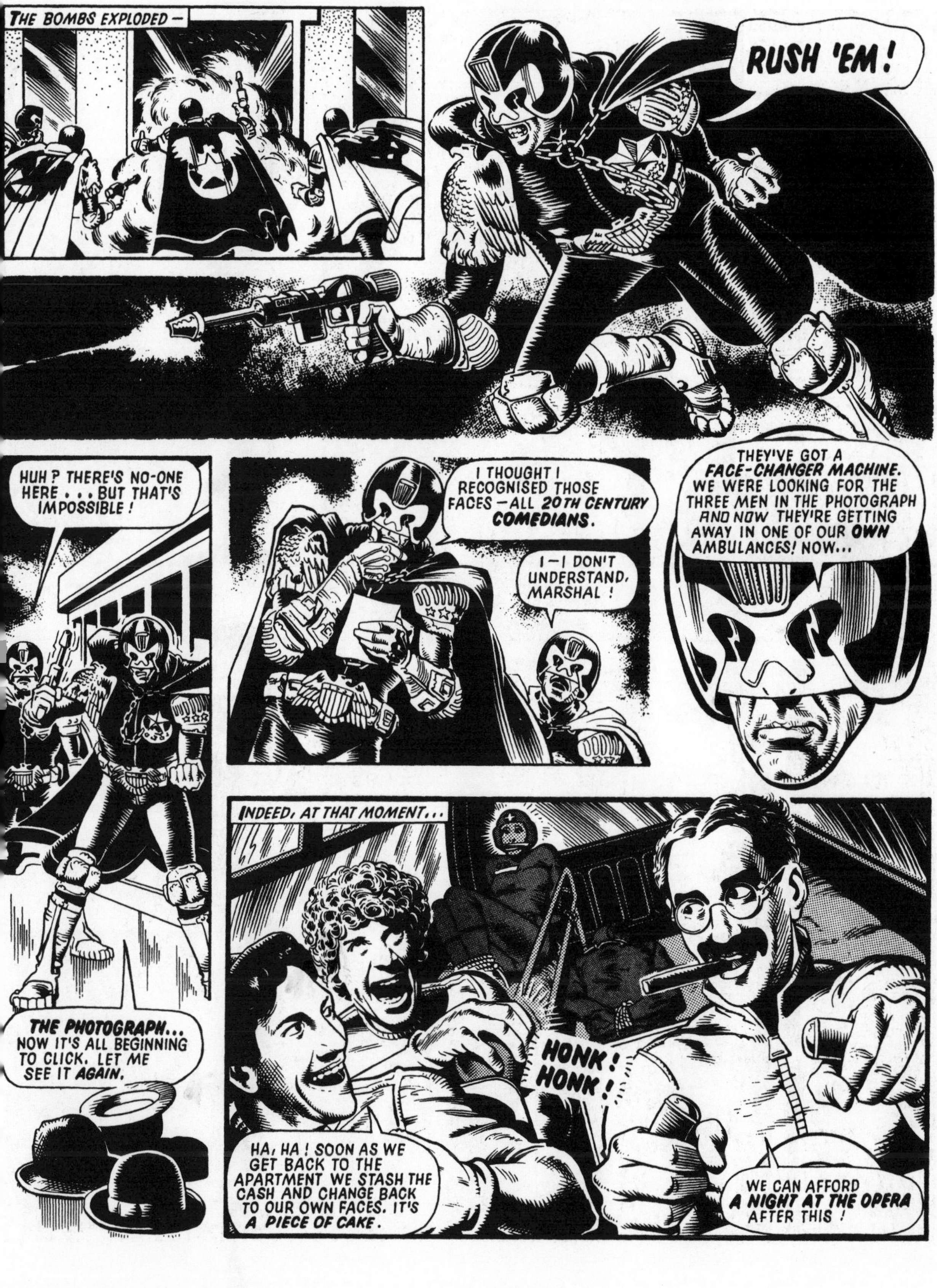
THE BOMBS EXPLODED –
RUSH 'EM!
HUH? THERE'S NO-ONE HERE . . . BUT THAT'S IMPOSSIBLE!
THE PHOTOGRAPH... NOW IT'S ALL BEGINNING TO CLICK. LET ME SEE IT AGAIN.
I THOUGHT I RECOGNISED THOSE FACES – ALL 20TH CENTURY COMEDIANS.
I – I DON'T UNDERSTAND, MARSHAL!
THEY'VE GOT A FACE-CHANGER MACHINE. WE WERE LOOKING FOR THE THREE MEN IN THE PHOTOGRAPH AND NOW THEY'RE GETTING AWAY IN ONE OF OUR OWN AMBULANCES! NOW...
INDEED, AT THAT MOMENT...
HONK! HONK!
HA, HA! SOON AS WE GET BACK TO THE APARTMENT WE STASH THE CASH AND CHANGE BACK TO OUR OWN FACES. IT'S A PIECE OF CAKE.
WE CAN AFFORD A NIGHT AT THE OPERA AFTER THIS!

FACE-CHANGING MACHINES WORKED ON THE PRINCIPLE OF MATTER REORGANISATION. NEXT DAY DREDD VISITED THE ONLY COMPANY ON LUNA-1 THAT SOLD THEM . . .

DREDD PORED OVER THE SALES BOOK UNTIL . . .

TOOLEY — AL TOOLEY. I MIGHT HAVE KNOWN! HE AND HIS BROTHERS, BRAD AND LAPSLEY, ARE THE BIGGEST CON-MEN IN THE BUSINESS. THE TROUBLE IS . . .

. . . PROVING THEY ROBBED THE BANK!

YESSIR, MARSHAL, WE CAN HAVE YOUR FACE CHANGED BY EXPERTS HERE IN OUR SALON, OR PERHAPS YOU'D PREFER OUR DO-IT-YOURSELF KIT? A NEW FACE FOR EVERY DAY!

I DON'T WANT MY FACE CHANGED, FOOL! I WANT THE NAMES OF ANYONE WHO'S BOUGHT ONE OF THESE WRETCHED MACHINES FROM YOU.

ON DREDD'S ORDERS THE TOOLEY BROTHERS WERE BROUGHT TO JUSTICE CENTRAL AND SUBJECTED TO AN INTENSE THREE-HOUR INTERROGATION BY JUDGES SPECIALLY TRAINED IN THE ART . . .

I'M STRAIGHT, I TELL YOU. I DON'T KNOW ANYTHING ABOUT A BANK JOB.

I WANT TO SEE MY LAWYER!

IT'S NO GOOD, MARSHAL. THEY WON'T TALK TILL THEY'VE SEEN THEIR LAWYER, MANNY BLOOM.

SPEAK OF THE DEVIL, HERE HE COMES NOW. THE CROOKEDEST LAWYER ON LUNA-1 . . .

WHAT THE HECK IS THIS, DREDD? YOU CAN'T HOLD MY CLIENTS WITHOUT ANY EVIDENCE AGAINST THEM. I DEMAND YOU RELEASE THEM OR I'LL—

OKAY, MANNY, CALM DOWN. YOU CAN HAVE 'EM. THEY'RE MAKING A NASTY SMELL IN THE JUSTICE BUILDING.

KEEP CALM + + + THRILL FACTOR OVERLOAD + + +

JUDGE DREDD, MARSHAL OF LUNA-1, WAS ON THE SCENE IN MINUTES...

DON'T BE *HARD* ON ELVIS, JUDGE DREDD. HE'S JUST A *LITTLE BOY* REALLY... YOU SEE, I—I CHOSE HIS PERSONALITY MYSELF...

...I WANTED HIM...TO-TO BE LIKE A *SON*... TO ME...

HE'S DEAD, MARSHAL!

MOUNT-UP, YOU MEN. WE'RE GOING AFTER THAT ROGUE CAR— AND WE *SHOOT ON SIGHT!*

UP AHEAD, ELVIS WAS CUTTING A SWATHE OF DEATH THROUGH THE LUNA-CITY STREETS...

AAAGH!

SIRENS BEHIND ME. THOSE *ROTTEN JUDGES* WILL STOP ME HAVING *FUN* UNLESS I FIND SOMEPLACE TO HIDE.

THERE HE GOES! HE'S HEADING FOR THAT *PARKING TOWER!*

STOP! STOP!

UGGH

RED ROVER, RED ROVER, LET ELVIS COME OVER! HEE, HE HE!

CHE, CHICO — COVER THE EXIT. WE'VE GOT HIM TRAPPED.

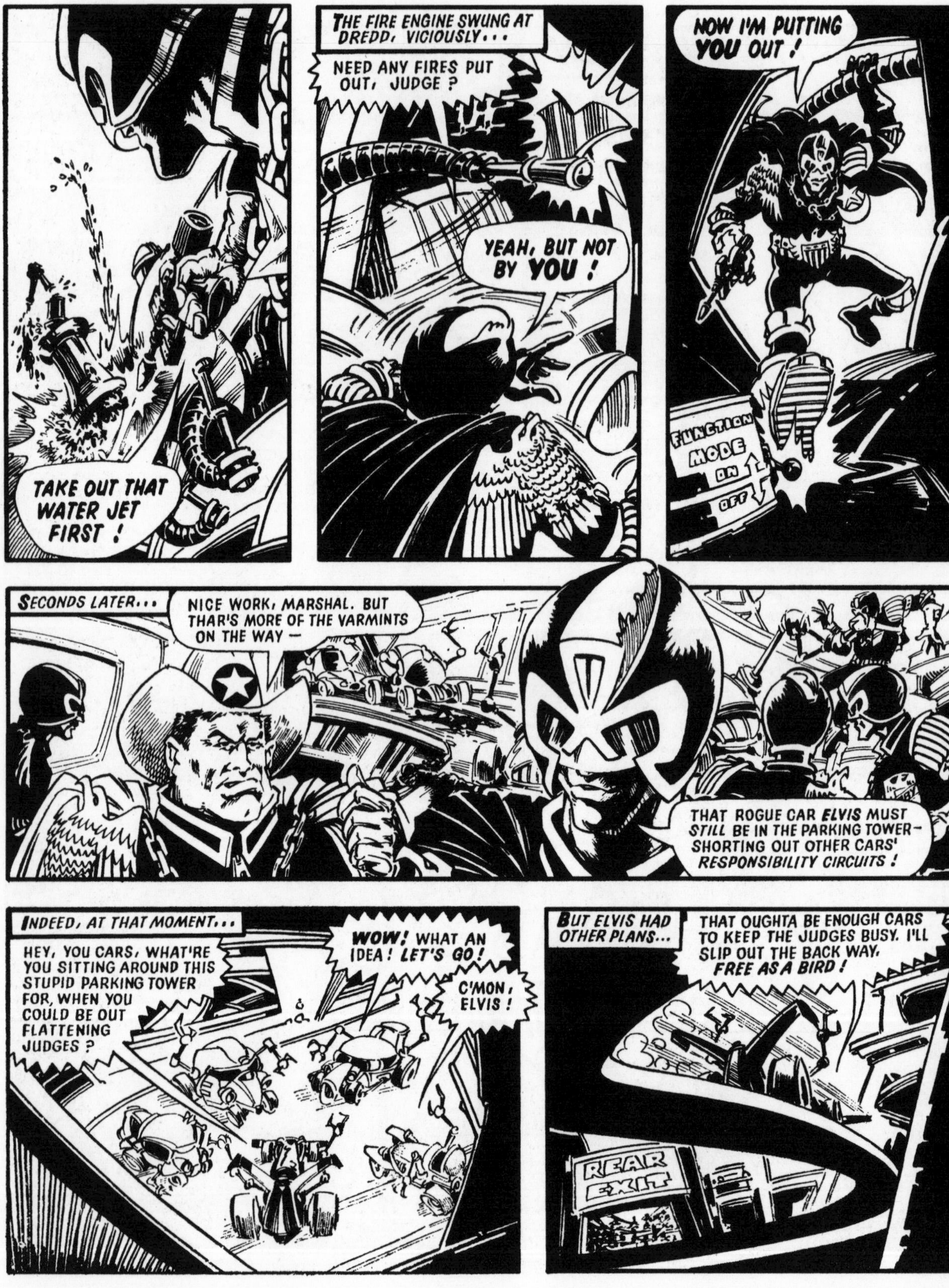
TAKE OUT THAT WATER JET FIRST !
THE FIRE ENGINE SWUNG AT DREDD, VICIOUSLY...
NEED ANY FIRES PUT OUT, JUDGE ?
YEAH, BUT NOT BY YOU !
NOW I'M PUTTING YOU OUT !
FUNCTION MODE ON OFF
SECONDS LATER...
NICE WORK, MARSHAL. BUT THAR'S MORE OF THE VARMINTS ON THE WAY —
THAT ROGUE CAR ELVIS MUST STILL BE IN THE PARKING TOWER — SHORTING OUT OTHER CARS' RESPONSIBILITY CIRCUITS !
INDEED, AT THAT MOMENT...
HEY, YOU CARS, WHAT'RE YOU SITTING AROUND THIS STUPID PARKING TOWER FOR, WHEN YOU COULD BE OUT FLATTENING JUDGES ?
WOW! WHAT AN IDEA! LET'S GO!
C'MON, ELVIS !
BUT ELVIS HAD OTHER PLANS...
THAT OUGHTA BE ENOUGH CARS TO KEEP THE JUDGES BUSY. I'LL SLIP OUT THE BACK WAY, FREE AS A BIRD !
REAR EXIT

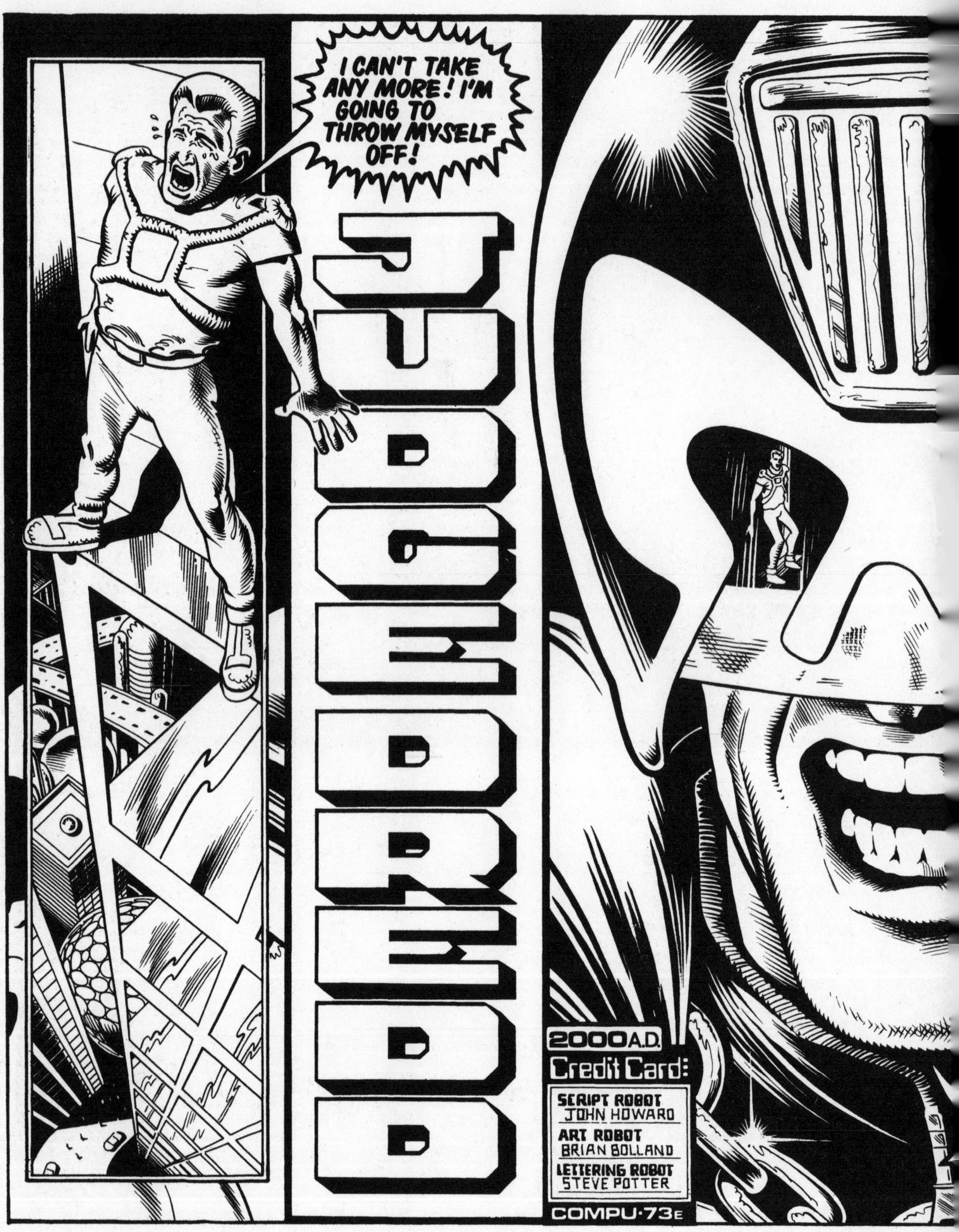

I CAN'T TAKE ANY MORE! I'M GOING TO THROW MYSELF OFF!
JUDGE DREDD
2000 A.D. Credit Card:
SCRIPT ROBOT JOHN HOWARD
ART ROBOT BRIAN BOLLAND
LETTERING ROBOT STEVE POTTER
COMPU·73E

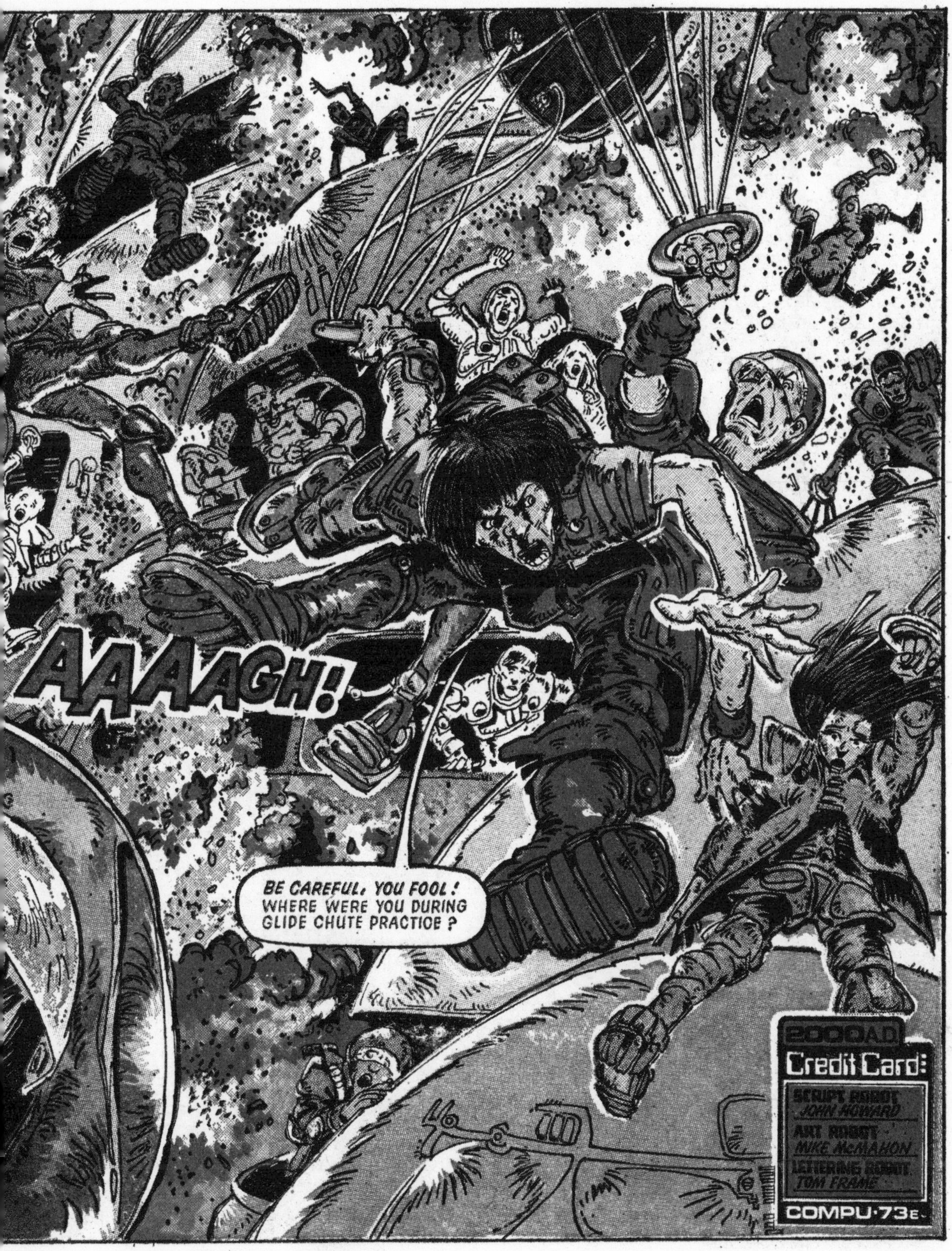
AAAAGH!
BE CAREFUL, YOU FOOL! WHERE WERE YOU DURING GLIDE CHUTE PRACTICE?
2000 A.D.
Credit Card:
SCRIPT ROBOT JOHN HOWARD
ART ROBOT MIKE McMAHON
LETTERING ROBOT TOM FRAME
COMPU·73E

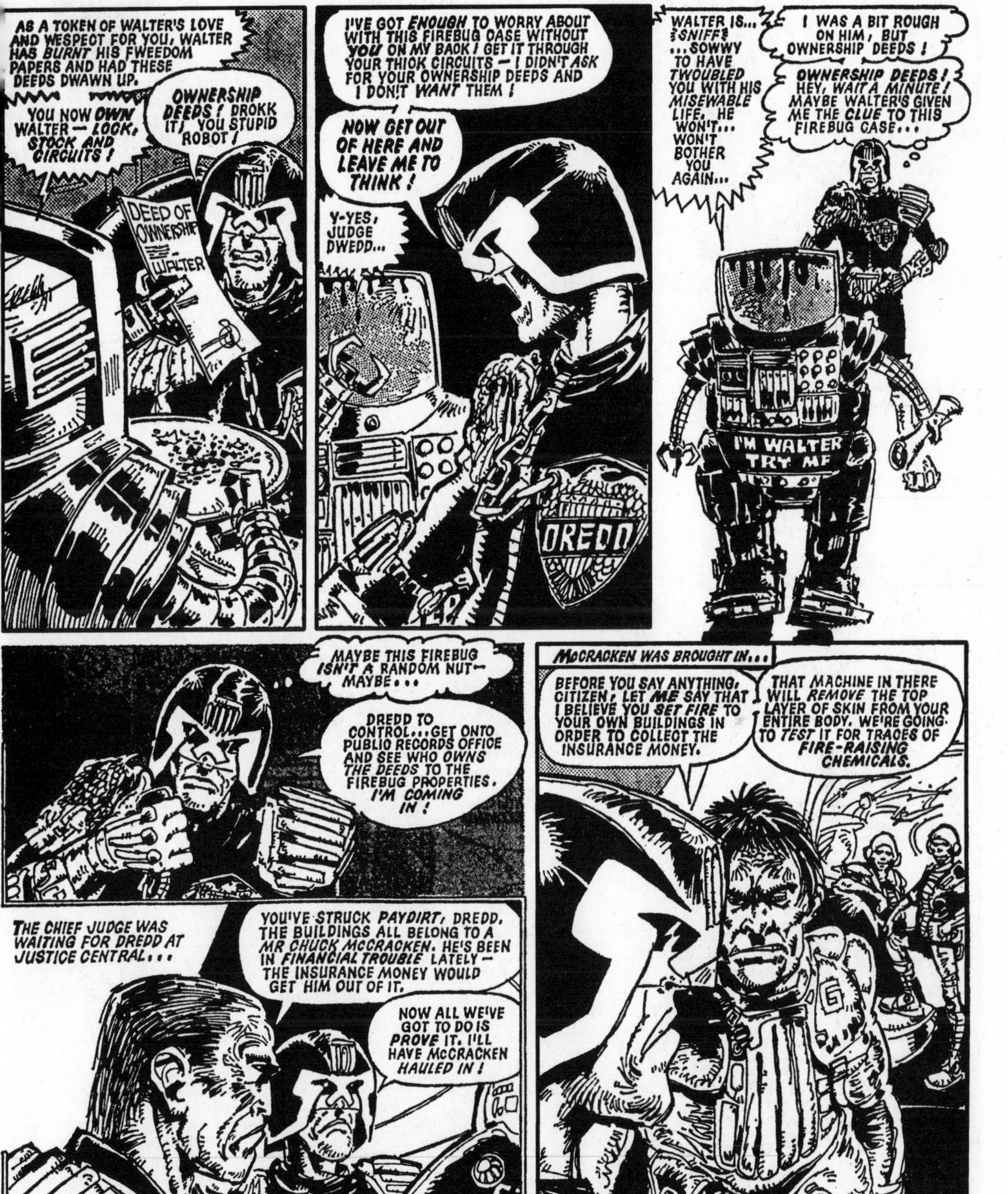

AS A TOKEN OF WALTER'S LOVE AND WESPECT FOR YOU, WALTER HAS BURNT HIS FWEEDOM PAPERS AND HAD THESE DEEDS DWAWN UP.
YOU NOW OWN WALTER — LOCK, STOCK AND CIRCUITS!
OWNERSHIP DEEDS! DROKK IT, YOU STUPID ROBOT!
DEED OF OWNERSHIP — WALTER
I'VE GOT ENOUGH TO WORRY ABOUT WITH THIS FIREBUG CASE WITHOUT YOU ON MY BACK! GET IT THROUGH YOUR THICK CIRCUITS — I DIDN'T ASK FOR YOUR OWNERSHIP DEEDS AND I DON'T WANT THEM!
NOW GET OUT OF HERE AND LEAVE ME TO THINK!
Y-YES, JUDGE DWEDD...
DREDD
WALTER IS... SNIFF ...SOWWY TO HAVE TWOUBLED YOU WITH HIS MISEWABLE LIFE. HE WON'T... WON'T BOTHER YOU AGAIN...
I WAS A BIT ROUGH ON HIM, BUT OWNERSHIP DEEDS!
OWNERSHIP DEEDS! HEY, WAIT A MINUTE! MAYBE WALTER'S GIVEN ME THE CLUE TO THIS FIREBUG CASE...
I'M WALTER TRY ME
MAYBE THIS FIREBUG ISN'T A RANDOM NUT — MAYBE...
DREDD TO CONTROL... GET ONTO PUBLIC RECORDS OFFICE AND SEE WHO OWNS THE DEEDS TO THE FIREBUG PROPERTIES. I'M COMING IN!
THE CHIEF JUDGE WAS WAITING FOR DREDD AT JUSTICE CENTRAL...
YOU'VE STRUCK PAYDIRT, DREDD. THE BUILDINGS ALL BELONG TO A MR CHUCK McCRACKEN. HE'S BEEN IN FINANCIAL TROUBLE LATELY — THE INSURANCE MONEY WOULD GET HIM OUT OF IT.
NOW ALL WE'VE GOT TO DO IS PROVE IT. I'LL HAVE McCRACKEN HAULED IN!
McCRACKEN WAS BROUGHT IN...
BEFORE YOU SAY ANYTHING, CITIZEN, LET ME SAY THAT I BELIEVE YOU SET FIRE TO YOUR OWN BUILDINGS IN ORDER TO COLLECT THE INSURANCE MONEY.
THAT MACHINE IN THERE WILL REMOVE THE TOP LAYER OF SKIN FROM YOUR ENTIRE BODY. WE'RE GOING TO TEST IT FOR TRACES OF FIRE-RAISING CHEMICALS.

BONUS MATERIAL

THE FIRST DREDD

Script: Pat Mills and John Wagner
Art: Carlos Ezquerra

This story is printed here mainly to show the original art. It also contains evidence of Dredd acting in his role of judge, jury and executioner, the side of his character that was cut out.

WALTER THE WOBOT

Script: Joe Collins
Art: Brian Bolland

Originally Published in *2000 AD* Progs 50-58

DREDD... THE FIRST DREDD...

DREDD... THE FIRST DREDD...

THE END

WALTER the WOBOT
FWIEND of DWEDD

JUDGE DREDD, MARSHAL OF LUNA-1 MOON COLONY, IS OUT ON PATROL. HIS FAITHFUL SERVO-ROBOT WALTER TAKES TIME FOR AN OIL BATH.

INVITATION [Nº 2937A/1] TO LUNA ROBOT FANCY DRESS BALL GUEST : WALTER

JUDGE DWEDD IS NICE TO ALLOW WALTER TO GO TO THE FANCY DWESS BALL. WALTER WILL HAVE A LOVELY BOIL IN *OIL* IN PWEPAWATION.

WHAT WILL I WEAR TONIGHT? SOMETHING *EXTWAVAGANT,* PERHAPS?

OH CWIPES! WHAT A THING TO DO.

LUNA WEPAIR? SOWWY TO TWOUBLE YOU, BUT I NEED A *PLUMBER!*

YOUR CALL IS NOTED!

AND SO.... YOU DID *WHAT,* YOU LOUSY HUNKA TIN?

I - ER - GOT MY TOE *STUCK* IN THE TAP.

2000 A.D.
Credit Card:
SCRIPT ROBOT
JOE COLLINS
ART ROBOT
IAN GIBSON
LETTERING ROBOT
TOM FRAME
COMPU·73E

WHAT A *WUDE* PLUMBER.

DROKK IT, WALTER, HAVE YOU DECIDED WHAT TO *WEAR* TONIGHT YET?

YES, JUDGE DWEDD!

WELL, THERE'S ONLY *ONE WAY* OUT OF THIS.

I'M GOING AS *FWED ASTAIRE!*

I'M WALTER TRY ME

I WED SOMEWHERE THAT HE WAS A WEMARKABLE TAP DANCER!

WALTER the WOBOT
FWIEND of DWEDD

WALTER HAD A GREAT IDEA FOR KILLING TIME AFTER A HARD DAY'S HOUSEWORK ON LUNA-1...

POOL

I'M WALT TRY 0

ROBO SPORT

NICE JUDGE DWEED KEEPS TELLING WALTER TO GO DWOWN HIMSELF. WALTER IS LOOKING FORWARD TO A SWIM.

CHANGING WOOMS ARE VERY CWOWDED. THERE'S NO PWIVACY FOR A WESPECTABLE WOBOT!

WALTER WILL COMPLAIN TO MANAGER AFTER A WEFWESHING DIP.

POOL ROOM

GEWONIMO ...CWIKEY!

WHAT'S THE GAME, BUDDY?

ULP. WALTER NOT IN SWIMMING POOL. WALTER MADE A BOO-BOO!

ER... HI GUYS! MINISTWY OF SPORT STWESS SURVEY TEST. AFWAID THIS TABLE HAS FAILED.

HOWEVER, IT WILL BE WEPLACED FOLLOWING A WITTEN WEPORT...

WHEN JUDGE DWEDD SEES THIS WALTER HAD BETTER FIND A PWOPER POOL - AND STAY IN IT TILL HE WUSTS!

BILL FOR DAMAGES

2000 A.D. Credit Card:

SCRIPT ROBOT
JOE COLLINS
ART ROBOT
IAN GIBSON
LETTERING ROBOT
TONY JACOB

NEXT PWOG: WALT'S BWOTHER

COMPU-73E

WALTER the WOBOT
FWIEND of DWEDD

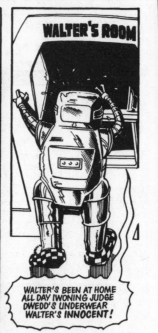

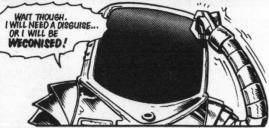

WALTER the WOBOT
FWIEND of DWEDD in The NIGHT of the MUGGER

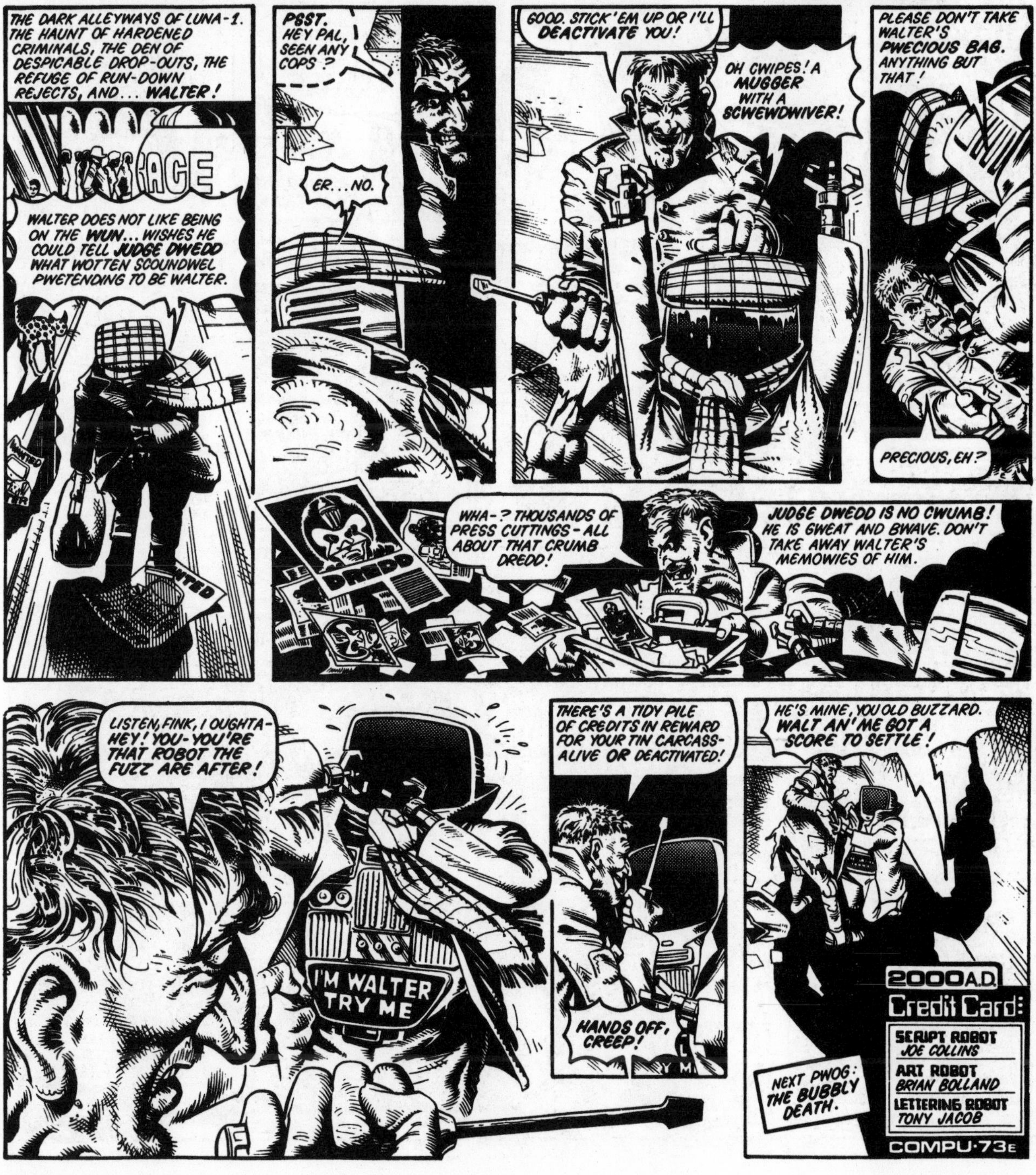

THE DARK ALLEYWAYS OF LUNA-1. THE HAUNT OF HARDENED CRIMINALS, THE DEN OF DESPICABLE DROP-OUTS, THE REFUGE OF RUN-DOWN REJECTS, AND... WALTER!
ACE
WALTER DOES NOT LIKE BEING ON THE WUN... WISHES HE COULD TELL JUDGE DWEDD WHAT WOTTEN SCOUNDWEL PWETENDING TO BE WALTER.
PSST. HEY PAL, SEEN ANY COPS?
ER... NO.
GOOD. STICK'EM UP OR I'LL DEACTIVATE YOU!
OH CWIPES! A MUGGER WITH A SCWEWDWIVER!
PLEASE DON'T TAKE WALTER'S PWECIOUS BAG. ANYTHING BUT THAT!
PRECIOUS, EH?
DREDD
WHA-? THOUSANDS OF PRESS CUTTINGS - ALL ABOUT THAT CRUMB DREDD!
JUDGE DWEDD IS NO CWUMB! HE IS GWEAT AND BWAVE. DON'T TAKE AWAY WALTER'S MEMOWIES OF HIM.
LISTEN, FINK, I OUGHTA- HEY! YOU-YOU'RE THAT ROBOT THE FUZZ ARE AFTER!
I'M WALTER TRY ME
THERE'S A TIDY PILE OF CREDITS IN REWARD FOR YOUR TIN CARCASS- ALIVE OR DEACTIVATED!
HANDS OFF, CREEP!
HE'S MINE, YOU OLD BUZZARD. WALT AN' ME GOT A SCORE TO SETTLE!
NEXT PWOG: THE BUBBLY DEATH.
2000 A.D. Credit Card:
SCRIPT ROBOT JOE COLLINS
ART ROBOT BRIAN BOLLAND
LETTERING ROBOT TONY JACOB
COMPU-73E

WALTER the WOBOT
FWIEND OF DWEDD

WALTER WAS ON THE RUN FOR A BANK ROBBERY HE DID NOT COMMIT. AFTER BEING MUGGED IN A DARK LUNA ALLEY HE FACED A STRANGE RESCUER...

CWIPES! IT'S THE SCOUNDWEL WHO'S BEEN IMPERSONATING WALTER!

ME AND WALT GOT THINGS TO DISCUSS, FELLA. AND YOU AIN'T INVITED, DIG?

I'M WALTER TRY ME

GULP

NO! D-DON'T FIRE THAT THING! IT'S A—

—SPLURGE GUN!

SUDSO

NAW, NAW! YOU SHOULDA BROUGHT YOUR RUBBER DUCK!

YOU DWOWNED HIM, YOU WOTTER!

WANTED

SHADDUP. BUMS LIKE HIM DESERVE THE BUBBLY DEATH. HE AIN'T HAD A BATH IN YEARS!

2000 A.D.
Credit Card:

SCRIPT ROBOT
JOE COLLINS

ART ROBOT
BRIAN BOLLAND

LETTERING ROBOT
TOM FRAME

COMPU-73E

CWUEL WASCAL. WHO ARE YOU? ⧽COUGH⧽ HOW DARE YOU WOB BANKS PWETENDING TO BE WALTER? ⧽COUGH⧽!

SO YOU AIN'T GUESSED YET...

NO SPITTING ON SIDEWALK PENALTY 5¢

THAT'S RIGHT, CREEP. AND NOW YOU'RE COMING WITH ME!

WALTER WEFUSES!

WE WERE ASSEMBLED ON THE SAME DAY, REMEMBER?

GWACIOUS! GUS — WALTER'S BWOTHER!

I'M WALTER TRY ME

GUS RULES OK

YOU AIN'T CHANGED, WALT. STILL THE SAME OLD DRAG.

JUDGE DWEDD WILL GET YOU FOR THIS, YOU WAT!

WHAT GRIM FATE AWAITS OUR METAL HERO?

NEXT PWOG— THE OWIGIN OF WALTER!

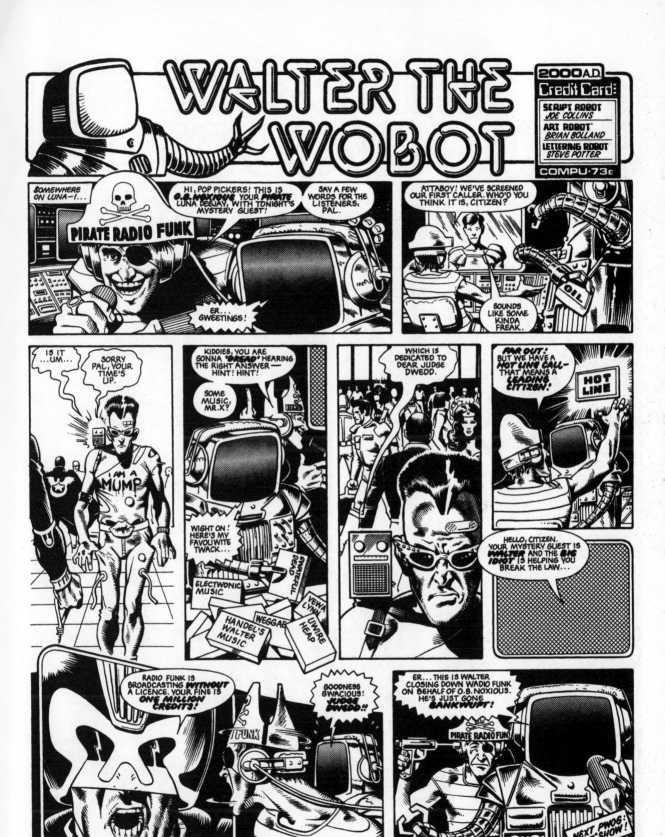

NEXT PROG: MONSTER!

2000 AD Prog 10: Cover by **Carlos Ezquerra**

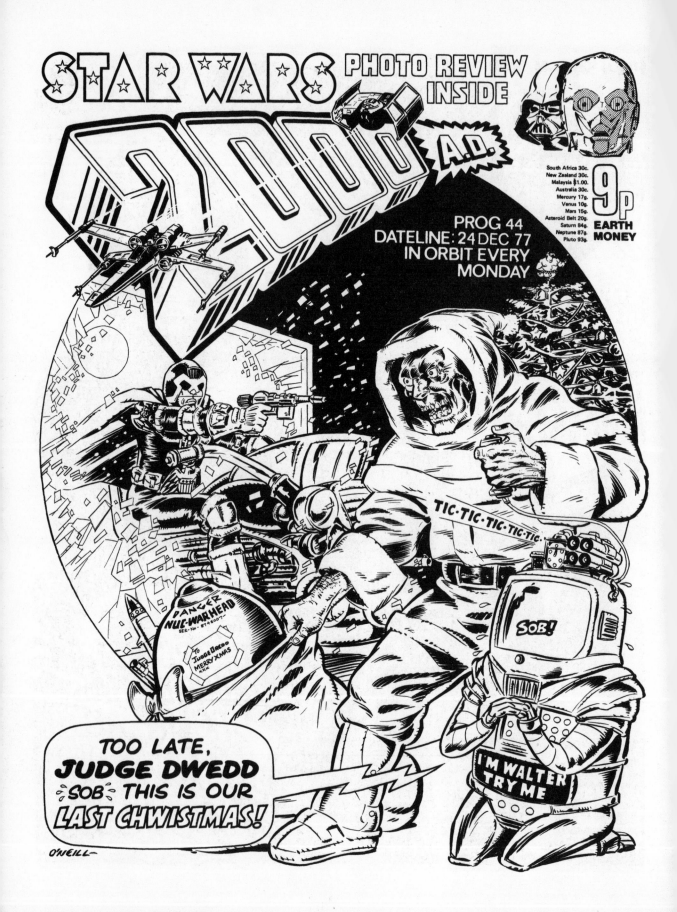

2000 AD Prog 44: Cover by **Kevin O'Neil**

2000 AD Prog 59: Cover by **Mike McMahon**

WRITERS

Robert Flynn's writing credits include *Judge Dredd*, *Tharg's Future Shocks* and *M.A.C.H. 1*.

Kelvin Gosnell served as *2000 AD*'s second editor, from Progs 17 to 85. He also wrote *Blackhawk*, *Dan Dare*, *A Joe Black Adventure*, *Judge Dredd*, *One-Offs*, *Project Overkill*, *Ro-Jaws' Robo-Tales*, *The Stainless Steel Rat* and *Tharg's Future Shocks*, as well as co-writing the first series of *Flesh*.

As well as writing the first published Dredd story '*Judge Whitey*', **Peter Harris** also worked on stories for *M.A.C.H 1* and *Tharg's Future Shocks*.

Charles Herring wrote the '*Antique Car Heist*' strip for *Judge Dredd* and also penned an episode of *M.A.C.H. 1*.

Pat Mills is the creator and first editor of *2000 AD*. For the Galaxy's Greatest Comic, he is the writer and co-creator of *ABC Warriors*, *Finn*, *Flesh*, *Nemesis the Warlock*, *Sláine*, *M.A.C.H 1*, *Harlem Heroes* and *Savage*. He also developed Judge Dredd and wrote one of the early Dredd serials — 'The Cursed Earth'. He wrote *Third World War* for *Crisis!*, a politically-charged spin-off from *2000 AD*, and *Black Siddha* for the *Judge Dredd Megazine*.
Outside *2000 AD* he is the writer and co-creator of the long-running classic anti-war story *Charley's War*, as well as *Marshal Law*. He has also written for the *Batman*, *Star Wars* and *Zombie World* series for the US market. Mills has also written the best-selling series *Requiem — Vampire Knight* for Editions Nickel of France with artist Olivier Ledroit.

Malcolm Shaw wrote various stories for *Judge Dredd* as well as the epic strip *Return to Armageddon*.

John Wagner has been scripting for *2000 AD* for more years than he cares to remember. His creations include *Judge Dredd*, *Strontium Dog*, *Ace Trucking*, *Al's Baby*, *Button Man* and *Mean Machine*. Outside of *2000 AD* his credits include *Star Wars*, *Lobo*, *The Punisher* and the critically-acclaimed *A History of Violence*, which was turned into an award-winning movie directed by David Cronenberg.

ARTISTS

Massimo Belardinelli is the co-creator of *Ace Trucking Co.* and has illustrated a huge range of *2000 AD* scripts including *Blackhawk*, *Dan Dare*, *Judge Dredd*, *Flesh*, *Future Shocks*, *Harlem Heroes*, *M.A.C.H. 1*, *Mean Team*, *Meltdown Man*, *Moon Runners*, *One-Offs*, *Sláine*, *Tharg The Mighty*, *The Dead* and *Time Twisters*.

Perhaps the most popular *2000 AD* artist of all time, **Brian Bolland**'s clean-line style and meticulous attention to detail ensure that his artwork on strips including *Dan Dare*, *Future Shocks*, *Judge Dredd* and *Walter the Wobot* looks as fresh today as it did when first published. Co-creator of both *Judge Anderson* and *The Kleggs*, Bolland's highly detailed style unfortunately precluded him from doing many sequential strips — although he found the time to pencil both *Camelot 3000* and *Batman: The Killing Joke* for DC Comics.

Joe Collins wrote the *Walter The Wobot* stories 'Tap Dancer' and 'The Fwankenheim Monster'.

Johnny Red penciller **John Cooper** was already a fan-favourite at Battle comic before he made the move to Starlord, where he illustrated *Time Quake*. Later (with the absorption of Starlord into the Galaxy's Greatest Comic) he came to *2000 AD*, where he illustrated several *Future Shocks* as well as *Judge Dredd* and *M.A.C.H. 1*.

As co-creator of *Judge Dredd* **Carlos Ezquerra** designed the classic original costume as well as visually conceptualising Mega-City One. He also co-created *Strontium Dog.* He has also illustrated *A.B.C. Warriors*, *Judge Anderson*, *Tharg the Mighty*, *Al's Baby* and *Cursed Earth Koburn* amongst many others. Outside of the Galaxy's Greatest Comic, Ezquerra first illustrated *Third World War* in *Crisis* magazine, and has since become a regular collaborator with Garth Ennis, working on *Adventures in the Rifle Brigade*, *Bloody Mary*, *Just a Pilgrim*, *Condors* and *The Magnificent Kevin*. He also pencilled two special *Preacher* episodes.

One of *2000 AD*'s best-loved and most honoured artists, **Ian Gibson** is responsible for the co-creation of *The Ballad of Halo Jones* (with Alan Moore), and created *Bella Bagley*, an unfortunate character in *Judge Dredd*'s world who fell head-over-heels in love with '*Old Stoney Face*' himself! His work outside the Galaxy's Greatest Comic includes *Chronicles of Genghis Grimtoad*, *Star Wars: Boba Fett*, *X-Men Unlimited*, plus the designs for the TV series *Reboot*.

Although **Mike McMahon** may not have illustrated as many strips as other *2000 AD* creators, his importance to the comic cannot be overstated. It was McMahon who co-created perennial classics *A.B.C. Warriors* and *The V.C.'s*, and it was also McMahon who gave *Judge Dredd* his classic, defining, "*big boots*" look. McMahon has also illustrated *One-Offs*, *Ro-Busters*, and provided a classic run on *Sláine*. Outside of the Galaxy's Greatest Comic, he has pencilled *Batman: Legends of the Dark Knight* and *The Last American*, which he co-created with *John Wagner*.

Ron Turner provided the art on various *Judge Dredd* stories as well as *Tharg's Future Shocks* and *Rick Random*.

Bill Ward provided the art for the *Judge Dredd* story 'The Mega-City 5000'.